One Fo

D0525914

Anecdotes from a Life in the Slow Lane

by

Alan Mawson

Windsor and Maidenhead

95800000201892

Copyright © 2016 Alan Mawson

All rights reserved, including the right to reproduce this book, or portions thereof in any form. No part of this text may be reproduced, transmitted, downloaded, decompiled, reverse engineered, or stored, in any form or introduced into any information storage and retrieval system, in any form or by any means, whether electronic or mechanical without the express written permission of the author.

ISBN: 978-1-326-63795-8

PublishNation
www.publishnation.co.uk

"All for one and one for all." The motto of the Three Musketeers.

After working at the Butlins Holiday camp in Clacton, during the glorious summer of 1959, bright as a button Mitch went back to his old job. Working in the Matador coffee bar wasn't the occupation that he relished or particularly wanted, but he reasoned that it would do until he found something better.

The large coffee bar had lost much of its former glamour as the décor had begun to look worn and tired and the customer base had deteriorated since its early days and Mitch's enthusiasm for the place had dipped with it. Although it was still owned by suave Cato and cleaver Anton, their attention was now firmly on the night club scene and their three coffee bars were of secondary importance. But for all its faults, the Matador was still a Birmingham hot spot and magnet for pretty girls looking for a good time and was a place to meet interesting and odd characters. Zac, the fearsome Greek Cypriot was still managing the place and welcomed Mitch back with open arms.

"So, you're looking for work after your long holiday?" Zac said with a grin as he greeted Mitch cheerfully.

"Just a few hours until I can find a proper job." Mitch replied smiling.

"You can have Jojo's shift." Zac said firmly.

"Won't he mind?" Mitch queried.

"Who cares, he's a lazy bastard, I only use him when I've got no one else." Zac said with a shrug, "So start tonight, about six."

"Thanks Zac, you're an officer and a gentleman." Mitch said while shaking Zac's hand.

"And you're a big liar," Zac said with a laugh, "Only one condition, no shagging the customers during work time."

It was as simple as that and it was as though he'd never been away. That evening he was back chatting with old friends and making new ones, especially among the girls, just as before. As for me and Billy, after returning from our summer adventure, we were now employed as van drivers, Billy had gone back to his old job at Wrensons grocery supplies and me, at a small bakery in Harborne and after our marvellous time working at Butlins, none of our jobs filled us with ecstatic pleasure.

"Mitch!" Agitated Brendan whispered urgently as his wild eyes scanned the almost deserted coffee bar, "Do us a favour and look after this!"

Mitch reached out and automatically took hold of the small canvas holdall bag that Brendan was offering him and said questioningly, "What is it?"

"I'll explain later," Brendan answered quickly, beads of sweat visible upon his worried face, "Just hide it! I'll see you tomorrow!" and with that he made a quick exit back into the street and disappeared into the darkness of the night.

With the small holdall in his hand, Mitch stepped behind the serving bar and lifted the bag up and down while testing its weight and wondered what the hell he'd been lumbered with. As there were still a couple of customers in the coffee bar and two part time girl helpers, he decided to shove the bag beneath the counter and investigate later.

Being a Tuesday night, it was a quiet night and Zac had gone out with his friends and wouldn't be back until the early hours of the morning. He'd left Mitch in charge and it was while Mitch was preparing to close up for the night that wild eyed Brendan had appeared and forced the mysterious bag onto him and as soon as the last customers and the two part time girls had departed, Mitch locked the front door, switched off the remaining lights, extracted the mysterious bag from its hiding place and carried it into the brightly lit kitchen. He placed the bag on the metal topped kitchen table for inspection and pulled back the bags long zip fastener. It contained an old towel that had been rolled up into a bundle and which was evidently rapped around something that was heavy.

"I touched the bundle and I tell you Jaco, I nearly shit myself."

"Why? What was it?" I asked.

"A bloody gun! A sawn off shot gun! As soon as I touched and felt the bundle I could tell straight away what it was."

"Bloody hell! What did you do with it?"

"Well I took the bundle out of the bag and unfolded it just to make sure that it wasn't some sort of practical joke and there it was, a bloody sawn off shot gun."

"Was it loaded?"

"I don't know, I didn't look. I just wrapped the bloody thing up again in the towel and put it back into the bag and then I thought, where the hell am I going to hide the bleeding thing?"

"Bloody hell Mitch, you do get yourself involved don't you?"

"Look, it wornt my fault was it, I didn't ask the daft bastard to give me the bag did I?"

"So where did you put the bag?" I asked fully intrigued.

"In one of the cupboards, I just shoved it behind the saucepans. They never get used do they? So I thought it'ud be safe there till the next day anyway. Oh, and I wiped the bleeding handles on the bag just to make sure my prints wornt on it."

"So then what happened?"

"Well the next day I heard that the bouncer at the Celtic club had been shot in the legs and I thought straight away, I bet I know who did that and bloody muggings here is holding the fucking evidence."

"Did Brendan come back for the gun?"

"Did he bollocks, the next thing I knew, he's skipped town. They recon he's gone back to Ireland."

"So what have you done with the bloody gun?"

"Dumped it in the cut and that's where it's staying. If he comes back for it he can bloodywell swim for it."

Brendan never did return and reclaim his property and as far as we know, the sawn off shot gun is still at the bottom of the black waters of the Grand Union Canal.

After his enjoyable Butlins adventure, Mitch came to the conclusion that he needed to find a new form of employment, one that offered a more fruitful career. There were two things that had brought him to this sober state of mind, firstly there was the undeniable fact that the Matador and all the other coffee bars for that matter, were gradually turning into tired and jaded establishments. The night clubs that were now beginning to pop up were gradually taking away the better cliental. The coffee bars had shown that the young were looking for places other than old pubs in which to meet and spend their money and night clubs was the obvious answer in the changing entertainment evolution and a few sharp and shady entrepreneurs such as Eddie Rogers, were only too willing to open them up.

The other reason that he felt uncomfortable with the status quo was that the last young woman, with whom he'd had a passionate affair with at Butlins, had informed him that she was pregnant. He could not be sure if this was true; as she'd only mentioned it to him two days before he was too due to leave and move back to Brum. She also revealed, which made him highly suspicious, that she was not only going to leave Clacton and move back to London, but that she had a plan of how they could set up home together and live happily ever after.

The sobering news of pregnancy and her well thought out domestic arrangements were the last thing that Mitch wanted to hear and he automatically made up several reasons why he would have to visit Brum before he could even think of setting up home in London with her. The reasons he put forward not only included a need to visit his parents, but he had to collect a large sum of money that was owed to him which would help them to buy a property in London. He could not be sure if she could remember the name of the coffee bar that he'd been working in before going off to Butlins, but he realised that with so few coffee bars in the centre of town, it would not be difficult for her to track him down while he worked there if she had a mind to.

Eventually he found a full time position at a department store that was situated in the city centre and once settled; he only worked part time at the coffee bar and kept a sharp eye on who was entering the front door while he did so. His Clacton lover never did turn up, so he concluded that her claim of being pregnant was nothing more than a canny way of enticing him to her London home.

The department store was an old established business that was known as Greys and when another vacancy became available, he immediately made contact with me and within a few weeks we were working side by side in the despatch and distribution department. The store was situated on Bull Street which was close to Snow Hill station and seemed to have been part of Brum for as long as anyone could remember and was certainly there when the roads were lit by gas lamps and full of costermongers and horse manure. On the opposite side of the busy road was the side entrance to Lewis's, a larger and more modern department store and was well known across the Midlands.

Greys, the business and the building was literally stuck in a pre-war time warp and some of the older staff who'd joined the company as young sales assistants, were now heads of departments and knew no other life. The fixtures and fittings throughout the store were made up of a mixture of highly polished dark wood counters, brass fittings and ornamental wrought iron rails and grills. The decorative handrails that lined the stairs and the whole ambience of the store were a reminder of another age, an age when class was much more pronounced and many of its loyal customers who arrived with walking sticks and in wheel chairs looked back on those times as a golden age. They openly moaned about the attitude of today's brash young serving staff and sneered at anything that was remotely modern and only brightened up when they remembered and reminisced about the good old days when everyone knew their place and when good manners and forelock tugging subservience was not only considered the norm, but essential to good customer relations.

As is the nature of large department stores, most of the management posts were held by people that were heading for retirement and most of the serving staff were much younger. A large proportion of the staff were female and was one of the reasons why Mitch and I enjoyed working there. It wasn't quite the same as working at the Butlins holiday camp, but was a good runner up and would certainly do for us until something better turned up.

"So what exactly is the job then?" I'd asked, when Mitch had informed me that there was a vacancy at the department store.

"It's in the despatch and distribution department. It's a bit like the department that Billy used to work in at Larkins."

"Bloody hell Mitch, that place was like the black hole of Calcutta! I'm not going to pack up my van driving job just to work in a pit like that!"

"No. I mean the job is similar. You know, dealing with parcels coming in and going out. But the place is much better than Larkins. You'll love it, it's free and easy."

"Well, I suppose it can't be any worse than driving all the way to Wolverhampton at the crack of dawn each morning." I said as I allowed myself to be persuaded. Rising from a warm bed long before the sun rose on a winter's morning was a routine to be avoided if at all possible.

"It's much better than that mate and besides, the place is full of crumpet, it's nearly as good as Butlins."

"Is that all you ever think about?"

"No it's not, sometimes I'm asleep. But anyway, you've got to admit, it's a bonus aint it? I bet you don't meet many girls while you're driving to Wolverhampton first thing in the bloody morning do you?"

"No I don't, the only people I see are bleary eyed milkmen." I replied and with that sobering thought in mind I was easily persuaded to join Mitch at the Greys department store.

We took up our duties together in the despatch and distribution department which was a large well lit room that was divided into two sections, wide packing benches on one side of the room for wrapping the purchased goods that were destined for home delivery and a large open area for unpacking the new stock which continually arrived by the ton into the room on a daily basis. The three packers who dealt with the continual flow of purchased goods were elderly men, two of whom had served in the First World War and the odd thing about these two was that the oldest, was actually the most active. He was as bright as a guardsman's button and had a tendency to hurry even when there was no reason to do so. He would run upstairs instead of walking even though he was constantly being told to slow down.

On the goods inward side of the room there were five employees who unpacked and distributed the goods to the stores various departments. So beside Mitch and myself, there was Trevor, who was also twenty years old and two middle aged men one of whom was named Ben and who was obviously a sandwich short of a picnic. The whole department was run by an ex-soldier named Ted, who evidently had complicated domestic problems and was in the process of solving them by chasing after a young woman that worked in the children's clothes department. This of course meant that his main focus was upon his girlfriend's voluptuous body instead of his

6

managerial duties and it allowed Mitch and I the freedom to organise ourselves and meander around the department store at will.

Each day, after opening the numerous parcels, we would load the various goods into large wicker basket trolleys and dressed in brown cow gowns, deliver them to the appropriate departments and bring back any goods that were destined for despatch. The monotonous jobs we left for Ben, who having very little mind to occupy, did not seem to mind occupying it with endless monotonous work. The whole despatch and packing department had an easy-going atmosphere about it and although we were of differing ages, we got on quite well with each other.

The management of the department store had put into place the commendable policy of employing a number of disabled personnel, some of whom were physically disabled, while others were just plain barmy. Harold, who was employed as the goods lift driver, unfortunately came into both categories as he was four foot six inches high and had a head that was the size of a large beach ball. There is no doubt that these were unfortunate physical deficiencies, but what made his situation even worse was that he had an in built aggressive curmudgeonly nasty attitude that could turn good beer flat at twenty paces. Amazingly, Harold not only had no friends, but went out of his way to make sure that he never acquired any.

I was entering the store early one morning along with the other backroom staff, when Harold, scowling as usual, arrived for work. Several of the staff members wished him a good morning and as usual he ignored them and because of this snub, one of the lift drivers made a comment concerning Harold's small stature. As Harold walked past, he gave him a piece of advice, "Harold," he said, "if I were you mate, I'd see about suing the council. It looks to me as though they have gone out of their way to build the pavements to near your arse."

On hearing comments like this, I being new to the place, instantly felt sorry for poor old Harold, after all he couldn't help having the disabilities that he'd been born with, but when I became aquatinted with his vicious and vindictive attitude to all the people who worked in the store, all sympathetic thoughts evaporated. He worked all day standing inside the dimly lit goods lift as he directed it up and down the building and would constantly chastise people for ringing the lift bell, but as everyone who needed the goods lift to move goods from one floor to another were obliged to ring the bell when they required the lift, this seemed to be a futile request. Never the less, he persisted with his obnoxious and loud protestations and had evidently done so for many years and as a consequence he'd terrified many of the female staff, so much so that many would not use the lift unless they had no option.

"Can you hear him again?" Mitch asked one morning as we sorted through the mass of parcels and placed them into appropriate piles. Mitch's question had come after hearing Harold's high pitched voice cascading down the goods lift shaft, as he screeched and balled out some unfortunate young girl on one of the upper floors. Mitch then declared. "You know, it's about time we taught that foul mouthed little goblin a lesson he won't forget."

And so Mitch began his campaign of annoying Harold whenever he could and much like the Chinese water torture, he did it by constantly ringing the lift bell no matter which floor he was on and when Harold arrived at the appropriate floor and furiously wrenched the sliding lift gates open and demand to know who was persistently ringing the bell. Mitch would casually say, "What do you want Harold?"

Harold, his huge head flushed with anger would shout, "Somebody on this floor rang the bell! And they keep on ringing it!"

Mitch would then answer him in a calm and unconcerned way and just say something along the lines of, "Harold. No one on this floor rang the bell you silly old bugger, it must be another floor." He would then add, "You must be hearing things or perhaps you're going round the twist."

Harold, still fuming would repeat," Somebody rang the bell on this floor!"

"Harold," Mitch would then say with a note of boredom in his voice, "Go away, I'm busy."

Harold would then storm off up the building in his gloomily lit lift and the whole process with different variations would start all over again. Of course there were many times when Mitch did require the goods lift to do his job and when Harold arrived on those occasions Mitch would give him a bollocking for being so slow. After a few weeks, Harold began to shout less and less and replaced it with almost inaudible insulting mutterings, which the girls did not like, but found preferable to his histrionic tantrums.

"Here," Mitch said one day, while he and I were waiting with an empty wicker basket skip for the goods lift to come to the top floor so that we could take it back to the despatch department, "I'll hide in the wicker basket and you get Harold to drop it off at our floor."

With that Mitch jumped inside the wicker basket skip, crouched down and covered himself with a few sheets of crumpled packing paper that had been left lying in the bottom of the skip. I pressed the lift bell and when Harold arrived I rolled the skip onto the lift and told him that Ted, the despatch department's boss, wanted him to drop the skip off at the despatch department. Reluctantly, he took charge of the supposedly empty skip and proceeded to take the lift back down the building. After a while, Mitch began to make strange and weird haunting noises. Harold eventually brought the lift down to the despatch department, wrenched the lift doors open with a clatter, jumped out of the lift and with unrestrained agitation, screamed, "Get that thing off my lift!"

Shaking with fright and dancing on the spot, he cried, "Get it off!"

"What's up then Harold?" I asked innocently as I had raced down the stairs so as to be there when the lift arrived in the department.

"Get that thing off my lift," He screamed as he stood well away from the skip and trembled, his face marked with genuine terror, "I'm not taking that skip anywhere and I'm not having it on my lift."

Eventually, after I'd told him to calm down and to stop acting like a stupid child, I rolled the skip off the lift while he nervously stood to one side and showed little desire to see what was inside. Once it was off his lift, he nervously stepped back into the lift and travelled back up the building without a shred of aggression left in his body. His days of bullying the staff from morning till night were well and truly over.

As happens in other department stores, as Christmas drew near, a Christmas grotto was erected in the children's toy department and a jolly, friendly old man that was blessed with red rosy cheeks was employed to play the part of Father Christmas. Of course during the day this man had to have breaks from his duties for calls of nature and for his lunch time sustenance. The calls of nature breaks were not much of a problem as it was easy enough to close the grotto for five minutes at a time, but a lunch time break required someone else to be there to fill the role of the cheerful Father Christmas for at least half an hour. The powers that be decided that that someone should be Horace, one of the old packers from the despatch department. Now this decision somewhat puzzled the rest of us, as Horace was without doubt, the most miserable old goat on the face of the earth and was the last bloke anyone would associate with, "Oh, Oh, Oh, and a very merry Christmas to one and all."

He could easily have got away with playing the part of the miserable old Ebenezer Scrooge, but the roll of a merry Father Christmas was way beyond his limited acting capabilities. At about ten minutes to one each day the telephone would ring in Ted's office and a member of the Christmas grotto staff would request Horace's assistance. Ted would then shout from his glass windowed office which was situated in one corner of the large room, "Horace! You're wanted in the Christmas grotto; the little kiddiewinks are waiting to see your smiling face."

With a face full of gloom and with the world and all its worries upon his round shoulders, Horace would reluctantly shuffle over to the goods lift, mutter something along the lines of "Bleeding snotty nosed kids" and "Not my bleeding job" and ring the goods lift bell. Harold, the bad tempered lift driver, would come to the department, open the lift doors and scowl and Horace would step inside the lift, and standing side by side, the two miserable sods, one much taller than the other, but just as dour, would disappear from view as the lift doors were closed and they travelled up the building together to the toy department.

Later, they would reappear looking as glum as when they'd departed and if anyone ventured to enquire as to how Horace had got on during his stint in the Christmas grotto, they would inevitably be subjected to a burst of vitriolic abuse. Many were to wonder just what effect Horace had on the children that he was forced to entertain during his stint as Father Christmas and if they would be psychologically scarred for life, but of course it was impossible to calculate.

We were to discover that Ted had put Horace's name forward for the role of Father Christmas's stand-in at a meeting of department managers, as a humorous joke, but the other managers, not knowing who Horace was or his dour demeanour and not wanting to lose one of their own staff during the busy Christmas period, much to Ted's surprise, had accepted the suggestion with open arms and for several years, miserable Horace was called upon to stand in for jolly Father Christmas and his yearly comment on the matter was a lot more profane than Scrooge's, "Humbug. Bah!"

The stores bailing machine was situated in the dark and dank bowels of the building and its purpose in life was to compress and bail up all the waste paper and discarded cardboard that was collected each day from the various departments, into large square bundles ready for the waste collecting company to take away. The man who operated this machine was a little Irishman named Chris, who was pleasant, fun loving and a compulsive drunk and whose wife had left him a number of years earlier claiming that he was, "Bloody hopeless" and "married to the bludy pub, so's he is and o'im just the ijiot that's expected to look arter 'im!"

Now directly opposite the department store, stood The Beehive, an old city centre pub and this pub acted as a magnet to Chris's alcoholic cravings and just like the ancient sirens of old, each morning at opening time, it called alluringly to him from across the street. Although Chris worked all alone down in the dismal paint peeling bailing room, and for most of the time, no one in the building knew whether he was there or not, he still had the problem of not only crossing busy Bull Street to reach the pub, but to do it without being seen by his pay masters. And the man that was most likely to see him taking an informal break and shop him, was the Commissionaire doorman, Big Bill Morrison, who was an ex Sergeant from the Coldstream Guards.

Big Bill was a large barrel chested man with a very stern disposition and just the kind of bloke that you would want standing next to you on the battlefield when the Zulu's charged at your precarious position, but he was not the kind of man that you would wish to keep an eye on you when you wanted to break a company rule and as far as Chris was concerned, Big Bill was an unwanted nemesis.

Attired in his smart black uniform which was adorned with gleaming brass buttons, gold braided epaulets, a shining leather chest belt and a white topped military peaked cap, Big Bill spent his day parading around the stores main entrance, welcoming customers and deterring with his formidable presence, any vagabonds that dared to dawdle near the department stores gleaming frontage. He had already caught Chris visiting the Beehive when he should have been working on his bailing machine on a number of occasions and although Chris, like many Irishmen, had the gift of the gab and had talked himself out of trouble on those occasions, he knew that he could not get away with it on a regular basis and after some thought, he requested the assistance of a willing and wily accomplice and the person he chose to help him solve his problem was Mr Personality himself, Mitch Bryson.

And so it came to pass that Mitch occasionally helped Chris to reach his desired watering hole by simply distracting Big Bill in a light conversation, while Chris, at exactly half past eleven, with eyes and ears twitching like a huntsman's quarry, shot across the busy road at the speed of light into the pub. Chris would return to his bailing duties at two o'clock, full of the joys of spring and merrily drunk.

This simple ploy worked on many occasions, but, for numerous reasons there were days when it was impossible to set the scam up, Mitch could be busy at that time of the day or Big Bill could be standing in a completely different position. What was needed Chris reasoned in one of his rare moments of lucidity, was a fool proof-plan, one that would work every day no matter where Big Bill was standing.

Now in the back street that lay beyond the pub, there was an old Victorian warehouse that belonged to the department store and where large amounts of every day stock was stored and this stock was systematically shuttled across to the store when needed by men

pushing large wicker basket skips. These men tended to be mentally handicapped, but as the job only require them to push and pull skips and deliver the goods to the right department in the store, they were more than capable. Chris reasoned that these wicker basket skips would be full of goods when they entered the store by way of the goods entrance which was at one side of the imposing ornate building, but they would be empty when on their way out of the store when the men took them back to the warehouse and that a small agile, desperately thirsty man, could easily fit inside one of these skips and could be transported across the busy road without Big Bill noticing.

For several weeks his plan worked perfectly, but one day the man he chose to transport him across the busy road while hidden in the skip, was Bobby. Bobby was a strong, but slow moving young man who wasn't just a sandwich short of a picnic, but the whole bloody hamper.

Bobby, who as usual, was not fully alive to the situation around him, pushed his skip with thirsty Chris hidden inside, into the busy road just as the traffic lights at the corner of the street changed to green, and as the heavy traffic began to roll forward, a passing lorry gave the skip a glancing blow and Bobby, being startled by this unforeseen turn of events, let go of the skip and off it went rolling down the road with the rest of the moving traffic. Because the road had a gentle slope, the skip, picked up speed and rolled to the corner of the street and there it proceeded to cross the traffic light junction and make its way over to the corner of Snow Hill, while cars swerved, buses stopped and startled shoppers looked on in disbelief. The driverless speeding skip eventually hit the curb of the pavement right in front of Harrison's the opticians on the other side of the road with a hefty bump and immediately tipped over, spilling a terrified Chris out in a tangled heap.

Outside the department store, Bobby, who'd stood statuesque and dumb struck throughout the whole episode, looked upon the scene in mesmerised wonderment and Big Bill, curious to see what all the fuss was about, walked determinedly towards the incident.

Chris, after crossing himself and murmuring several religious thank you's to the Virgin Mary and several saints, quickly righted the skip and ran it back through the busy traffic towards the store where breathlessly he explained to Big Bill what had happened.

"I was just d'ere," he said, gasping for breath and pointing at the pavement where Bobby was still standing, "Helping young Bobby to push d'e skip across the road so's I was, when dat great big lorry hit the skip and I fell inside and the next t'ing I knows, I'm on me way to Tipperary so's I am."

As no one, except Bobby could disprove Chris's version of events and as Bobby was so confused as to be useless as a witness, Big Bill had no option but to accept Chris's cock and bull story, but when Chris suggested that after receiving such a traumatic shock, a small brandy at the Beehive was called for, Big Bill put his foot down and sent Chris back to the baling room. This traumatic incident gave Chris cause to think seriously about his drinking addiction as it had shook him to the core, but the following day, the sweet alluring sirens called once more and the whole cat and mouse game between began all over again.

Eddie was one of the stores uniformed lift drivers, he was a bright and cheerful middle aged man who was extremely good at his job as he could rattle off the floor information to his passengers with machine gun speed, "First floor, ladies wear, coats, dresses, lingerie, knitwear and shoes, second floor, children's wear, coats, dresses, trousers, shirts and shoes," and he was always extremely helpful to the customers.

He was a cheeky chappie that was always good for a laugh and an ever ready source of tittle-tattle gossip and with such an abundance of staff working at the store, there was plenty of gossip to be had. As he drove his lift up and down the building he amused himself by soaking up and redistributing, with suitable embellishments, stories of ongoing feuds, elicit liaisons and any secrets that happened to cross his path.

"Did you know that old man Baxter is chatting up Joan Evans in stationary.'

"She's married aint she?"

"So's he! The randy old bugger. Oh, and did you know Peter Bright's wife has just left him."

"Who? That tall gorky bloke in the men's department?"

"That's him, they recon she's run off with the insurance man."

The reason for Eddie being employed as a lowly lift driver, which for such a bright and lively individual could have been seen as a waste of talent, was that he only possessed one leg and was unable to take on a more physically demanding job. He'd lost his right leg in a terrible road accident and although he'd been fitted with an artificial leg which allowed him a reasonable amount of mobility; it did force him to walk with a pronounced squeaky limp.

One day, at approximately ten in the morning, the store and surrounding area, was hit by a power cut which not only knocked out all the lights in the store, but automatically grounded all the lifts. Eddie, like the other three lift drivers that the store employed, welcomed the break from the daily routine and stood by his lift, which was some distance from the three main central lifts and was encased by a wire cage and a wide staircase for those that wished to walk from floor to floor and it climbed around the lift shaft from the basement to the highest floor.

Eddie stood chatting to anyone who came near and as Mitch and I were passing, we stopped and had a friendly chat with him.

"Here lads! Did you hear this one," Eddie beamed as he got our attention, "How can you tell which is the blind man on a nudist beach?"

"Go on, I'll buy it." Mitch replied while making a conscious decision not to laugh at the joke so as to wind Eddie up a little.

"Well, it aint hard!" Eddie replied as he burst into mock laughter and lightly pushed Mitch on the shoulder, "Get it? It aint hard! His dick aint hard."

"Eddie," Mitch said shaking his head in false exasperation, "If you have to explain a joke, it just aint funny."

"Oh, you two aint got no sense of humour that's all."

Secretly we both thought that the play on words was quite good and would use the joke ourselves when we had an opportunity to do so.

After approximately ten minutes, power was suddenly restored to the area and the whole store burst back to life, lights on all floors came back on and all the lifts became active once more. To our combined surprise as we were still discussing the merits of the Aston Villa team and their chances of beating Arsenal, the sliding doors on Eddies lift closed and off it went up the building to where someone had pressed the call button, leaving Eddie, standing helpless on the ground floor. He'd left the lift in automatic mode and forgotten all about it. The consequence of this error was that his lift was now operating completely independent of him and which was a sack-able offence as it contravened safety regulations.

As the lift travelled up the building, Eddie sprang into action and attempted to catch the runaway lift by running up the stairs that enclosed the wire caged lift shaft. He ran up to the first floor, but when he got there, the lift had moved on to the second. Now, running up flights of stairs at any time of the day is an exhausting activity, but for a man who was fitted with an artificial leg, it was bloody murder. Up he went, as fast as he could, his artificial leg swinging out at the side like Old Father Times scythe cutting corn.

On reaching the fourth floor he was gasping for breath and was about ready to collapse and to his dismay, he saw through the wire cage, that his lift was now on the way down and passing him by. Taking a deep breath, he turned and descended the stairs as fast as his artificial leg would allow and gradually he built up a good rhythm and reasonable speed and on reaching the second floor he collided with Trevor who happened to be crossing in front of the lift doors while carrying an armful of parcels. They ended up on the floor in a tangled heap and Eddie was now ready to call it a day and face the inevitable consequences. While, Trevor' who was now lying flat on his back and looking at the decorative ceiling was wondering "What the bleeding hell hit me?"

While the pair awkwardly picked themselves up, Eddies lift suddenly stopped at their floor and out popped Mitch who called out brightly, "Anybody here want to buy a lift?" Eddie scrambled into the lift, wheezing, spluttering, choking and gasping for breath, but very, very relieved and for the rest of the week, he became the stores topic of tittle-tattle gossip and knowing winks.

Trevor, who worked alongside us was the same age as Mitch and I, but whereas we were into the latest Italian style clothes and the coffee bar culture, Trevor was still entrenched in Teddy Boy gear and his local pub, so when not at work, we never socialised, but the one thing that Trevor and I had in common at the time was that we had a regular girlfriend and just like young men the world over, we were obsessed by how to acquire some form of sexual favour from them and were curious to know how to perform the sex act properly so that we could not only satisfy ourselves, but also our partners. To be thought a great lover was a goal that we all aspired to, so any knowledge concerning the sexual act and how to perform it safely was welcome as none of us wanted to be trapped into an early marriage. The essential information of safe sex that we sort was not as readily available as it was to become in later years and to make matters even more confusing, many myths and old wives tales were constantly being bandied about. For example, there was the ridicules belief that, "If you do it standing up, a girl can't become pregnant."

At the end of one Saturday lunch break, Trevor, while combing his head of thick greasy black hair and grinning like a Cheshire cat, came strolling into the despatch department and quite unable to hide his obvious excitement he gleefully showed Mitch and me a packet of small tablets that he'd just purchased from a city centre chemist and said, "So, what do you think of them then?"

"What are they?" I asked as I didn't recognise the name on the packet and was sure that I'd never seen them before.

"They're to stop a bird from getting pregnant." Trevor answered with an air of superiority as he realised that we were completely ignorant of the liberating power that the tablets had.

"So how do they work then?" Mitch asked as he was just as intrigued as I was.

"Well you take one of these pessaries'," Trevor replied as he grinned knowingly, "then you push it into the girl's vagina, then wait a few minutes for it to dissolve and then you can bang away without a care in the world and it stops the girl from becoming pregnant."

To Mitch and I, who were still as green as grass when it came to contraceptive knowledge, it sounded to be a much better option than using the traditional "French Letters" which seemed to be universally disliked by most young men, as to put one on during a heavy petting session, inevitably caused problems. For the unmarried, it meant that the passionate mood that had been created with gentle foreplay had to be put on hold while the fitting of the condom took place and worryingly for the young man, it gave the girl plenty of time to change her mind. And as condoms were not on display or as readily available as they eventually became, most men were far too embarrassed to even purchase them openly. Packets of condoms tended to be hidden away in chemist shops and in barbers cupboards and barbers would offer them to customers wrapped in small innocuous brown paper bags, with the words, "Anything for the weekend sir?" And because of the embarrassing atmosphere that surrounded the purchase and use of them, they were rarely seen and never mentioned in every day conversation between friends or husband and wife. The only time we ever heard of them being mentioned openly up until the mid-sixties, was in the telling of a "dirty" joke.

Trevor was on a high and looking forward to his Sunday evening sex session with his girlfriend and as we left work that night, Mitch and I wished him well by calling out, "Give it some bloody wellie, Trev."

On the following Monday morning, Trevor came into work with a condemned man's tread, a face as long as Livery Street and a complexion as pale as watered milk.

"What the bloody hell's up with you?" Mitch asked a little concerned, "you look bloody awful. Got yourself a hangover have you?"

"It's them bleeding tablets," Trevor answered mournfully, his head bowed in defeat, "That's what's up with me. They were no bleeding good; they don't bloody work do they."

"Why? What happened then?" Mitch asked as he and I stopped what we were doing and waited for a detailed explanation.

"Well, last night," Trevor sighed, "Me and Jean waited till her Mom and Dad went off to the Merryvale pub like they usually do on a Sunday night and then we went upstairs to her bedroom for a bit of hokey pokey. Anyway I put one of them bleeding tablets up her "minge" see, like it said on the packet, and we waited for ages to let it dissolve. Anyway when we thought it was time, we started shagging and it was great."

"So what happened?" Mitch asked.

"Well," Trevor said as he shrugged his shoulders forlornly and continued with his tale of woe, "When we'd finished, I rolled off her see and there lying on the bleeding bed sheet was the bleeding tablet. Completely untouched. The bleeding thing hadn't dissolved."

The next few weeks hung heavy on poor Trevor, but at last the good news that he had been praying for arrived, his girlfriend Jean had her next monthly period bang on time.

Whether this good fortune made the two lovers a little careless with their lovemaking I know not, but four months later Jean declared that she was well and truly up the duff and Trevor, full of the world's worries once more, was making plans for their forthcoming and hastily arranged marriage. His only cheerful comment being, "Well, at least I won't have to put up with knee tremblers in that draughty bloody alleyway anymore."

When seeing George for the first time, one would be forgiven for thinking that he'd been designed by a Walt Disney cartoonist as he was short and stocky in stature and had a head that was not only large, but perfectly round. And permanently set upon the front of this pumpkin shaped head, was a wonderful man in the moon face that constantly sported an innocent baby like smile. Looking at George, it would be hard to imagine that a more inoffensive man had ever been born anywhere on the planet.

His function at the department store was to help unload delivery vans that arrived and unloaded in busy Bull Street and then to wheel the numerous crates, boxes and parcels by means of a large railway porters trolley, up the sloping driveway that ran along one side of the building and to place them in an enclosed goods inwards yard where they were checked and recorded before being passed onto the despatch and distribution department.

Just like the other manual workers, George was supplied with a brown cow gown to protect his personal clothing from the workaday grime. Now George was very broad across the chest and the cow gown that he'd been supplied with fitted him perfectly around the shoulders, but having very short legs, it almost reached his shoes which gave him a comical dwarf like image and as if that wasn't enough to make most people smile, he also wore a very large flat pancake cap on top of his big round head, which not only kept his head dry in inclement weather, but most of his shoulders as well.

The stores staff looked upon George as if he were a cuddly pet and although they would pull his leg at times; it was all done with good humour and without any malice whatsoever. With the exception of one obnoxious individual, everyone who worked at Greys liked George, as just looking at him cheered them up.

The trouble was that the one obnoxious person who tormented him on a daily basis was his boss. Albert was in his late fifties and was in charge of the goods inwards yard and was a miserable old bugger on the best of days. He constantly criticised others when they were not in his vicinity and seemed to be an expert on other people's occupations. Although he'd worked at the store for many years, he'd only risen to the rank of goods inwards clerk who was in charge of a staff of one, the ever smiling George. Whether his grumpy disposition had been caused by an unhappy marriage, lack of promotion or some other disappointment in life no one knew, but Mitch and I came to dislike him intensely.

Time and again we witnessed Albert's poor treatment of the ever smiling George and occasionally we caught him treating him no better than a rabid dog. When he thought that no one was around, he would shout at George and call him demeaning nick-names and play practical jokes on him which were often sadistic and cruel. George was never seen to complain, he seemed to think that it was normal to be bullied by his boss. We came to suspect that George's mother was so frightened of him losing his job that she had drummed it into him that he must never upset his boss by answering back.

We decided that something should be done about it. We should have compiled a dossier of factual evidence and presented it to senior management and left them to do deal with the matter, but we never even thought of using these channels of communication. Workers back then did not enjoy the protective rules that they were later afforded and as we were still young, we not only had little patience, but had a distrust of formal avenues of whistle blowing and we wanted to see an appropriate punishment meted out to Albert there and then.

For several days we mulled over many ideas for bringing about Albert's comeuppance, we thought of putting salt in his sugar, a kipper behind his electric fire and we even contemplated pissing into his teapot, but all our ideas seemed to be juvenile and silly. What we needed was something that would hurt Albert for a long time, preferably something that would put him in a bad light with the management.

Days rolled into weeks and the bullying continued and neither one of us could think of a way of teaching the obnoxious Albert a lesson that would stop him bullying George forever. Then, out of the blue Mitch said, "Why don't we just hide one of his parcels. Then when the department complains that they haven't received it, he'll get into trouble."

"That's no good," I said, as I thought it through, "He'll just blame someone else for stealing it and don't forget, he'll already have it booked into his goods inwards book, so he'll have proof that as far as he's concerned, he's already dealt with it and passed it on."

"I've got it!" cried Mitch with uncontained excitement, "Let's combine the two."

I didn't know exactly what he meant, but was a little surprised to find that he'd even come up with an idea that exited him, as from past experience his thoughts very rarely went past which girl to chat up next.

"Look," He explained excitedly, "We steal a parcel right or better still several, and then we steal the goods inwards book as well. That way, he can't prove that he's booked the parcels in and past them on and with the book missing, it'll look as though he's covering something up."

Suddenly the large boring goods inward ledger that Albert religiously kept up to date each day looked to be the most important book in the world. This ledger lay solidly on top of Albert's high office desk and all we had to do was to find a way of removing it while he was not looking, which was a lot easier said than done.

In those days, all movement of goods up and down the country, in and out of factories, warehouses, shops and stores were recorded in hand-written ledgers, it was many years down the line before computers came along and did the same function in a fraction of the time. These imposing hard backed ledgers were kept with pride by the clerks who looked after them and who wrote in them each day with neat copper plate hand writing, an art that has now died out among the general public.

And so, a plan was finally hatched and we set about executing it on a warm sunny Friday lunchtime. Albert was eating his lunch in the staff canteen and moaning to anyone who had the patience to listen to him. Chris, who always walked through the goods yard and down the drive to reach the Beehive, was already in the pub and sinking his third pint and the ever smiling George was relaxing in the far corner of the goods inwards yard and so the scene was set for our furtive commando raid.

The wide driveway that led up to the goods inwards enclosed yard and Albert's office, was a hundred yards long and ran up from the street between the department store on one side and the plain brick wall of a tobacconist shop on the other. Albert's office was nothing more than a small wooden lean-to that had been attached to the side wall. When in residence Albert had a good view of anyone coming up the driveway, but had a restricted view of the goods inwards yard behind him. The structure had two windows, one at the front and one at the side next to the door, which was locked when he was not in residence. The window at the front had a long narrow ventilation window at the top and during warm weather; he always left it open.

We crept up the drive to the front of the small office, which was in deep shadow and looked around to make sure that the coast was clear. The object of our furtive raid, the large goods inwards ledger, from which protruded several delivery notes, lay on top of the schoolteacher desk and George, who was never allowed to use the office when Albert was absent, was sitting snugly in the far corner of the goods inwards yard. It was a spot that Albert placed him when he was away from the yard and referred to it sneeringly as the dunce's corner. The dunces corner was well away from the office and did not afford a view of the driveway that led to the street, but from where he sat George could keep an eye on all the parcels that had been booked in and were ready to be sent up in the goods lift to the distribution department.

Standing in front of the lean-to office, I cupped my hands together, Mitch placed his right foot into them and with a heave, I helped to lift him up onto the narrow window ledge to where he could easily open the long narrow ventilation window. Mitch was then able to wriggle his slim body through the gap, stretch down and, using a see-saw motion, he was able to grab and retrieved the large ledger from off the high office desk and he was able to extract himself from the tight window space and pass the heavy ledger down to me.

With the ledger firmly secreted beneath my jacket, I made my way back down the driveway and away from the goods inwards yard and into the busy street with Mitch close behind. We re-entered the store by way of the front entrance and made our way through the store and down to the basement and the bailing machine where we had earlier hidden three medium sized parcels which we'd removed from the goods inwards yard. Once there we put the whole kit and caboodle into the bailing machine and covered it over with several layers of crumpled cardboard. We reasoned that after lunch, Chris, who would be well and truly tanked up, would finish off the bale that was in the machine and then fall asleep as usual in his old battered arm chair that he kept out of view in what he perceived to be his secret hidey hole and sleep away the afternoon oblivious to what was hidden in the bale of waste cardboard. The whole escapade took approximately ten minutes to complete and we were able to mix with other members of the stores staff in the Beehive without anyone suspecting a thing.

On opening his office door, Albert discovered that his treasured ledger was missing and raised a hue and cry and was consumed with anger and bewildered worry. He was angry because someone had stolen his goods inwards ledger, but he was also worried, as a nagging doubt had crept into his mind and he wondered if he'd moved the book before going off to lunch and had forgotten that he had. And the reason why this nagging doubt troubled him so much was because everyone that he spoke to about the missing ledger inevitably asked him the same questions, "Was the door locked?" "Who had the key?" "Why would anyone want to steal a goods inward ledger?" "Where was George?" and "Did George see anyone go into the office?"

During the following two week period, heads of three departments came looking for their missing parcels and Albert of course could not say where they were or even whether they had been delivered or not as he had no record of them. The girls in the accounts department complained that they could not tie up the relevant paper work concerning the three missing parcels and the chief accountant decided to change the booking in system and instead of using an impressive ledger, Albert was obliged to use a daily sheet which he was to hand over each day to the accounts department.

Whenever the incident came up in conversation, in the staff canteen or in the Beehive, Mitch and I mudded the water by spreading the rumour that Albert had got rid of the goods inwards ledger to cover up the fact that he had stolen the goods that were missing. No one really believed that he'd stolen the parcels, but as they did not like him either, they were more than happy to spread the rumour themselves.

Albert did not get the sack, after all he hadn't actually done anything wrong, but he was reprimanded by the management and received a black mark against his name as he had no rational explanation for the mystery, which is exactly the result that we were looking for. This in turn made him a lot more wary of how he treated the ever smiling George, as at his age and looking towards retirement, he could ill afford to have any more black marks put against his name.

The staff canteen was situated on the top floor of the building and there the staff could purchase cooked food at a reasonable price and most used it on a regular basis. It was very basic and designed for easy cleaning and during the busy lunch period it was filled with a background noise of clattering plates and cutlery, chattering conversation, clouds of steam and tobacco smoke and during the morning, a faint aroma of disinfectant permeated the area after it had been swept and moped.

Although the Formica topped tables and tubular framed chairs were identical, over many years a seating plan had evolved where senior staff sat together at certain tables and the lower orders at others. And even amongst the lower orders, a pecking order had evolved by where all the youngsters inevitably sat together. The youngsters didn't mind this class discrimination of course as it suited them to sit together and talk about the latest music, films, fashions and which dances and football matches they were interested in and of course, who fancied whom. And when these teenagers became too excited and boisterous, they were subjected to grave looks and tut-tuts from the old cronies, but as none of the youngsters saw themselves staying long-term at the department store, they took little notice of these snide snubs.

Mitch was always in the thick of the girls during his lunchtime visits to the canteen and was to be seen regularly, laughing, joking, flirting, scheming and looking for any chance that might come his way and one that did come his way was a pretty little plump girl named Carol. For a while, he regularly met Carol during the afternoon tea break in one of the store rooms that was adjacent to the canteen and housed piles of display stands, damaged manikins and advertising boards and there they indulged in a bit of slap and tickle. What promises he made to young Carol during these short, but evidently passionate afternoon sessions, I never discovered, but I could see that she was well and truly smitten and so much so, that she could hardly take her eyes of him.

Then one day, the management decided to reorganise the display storeroom that had acted as Mitch's secret afternoon love nest and the job was scheduled to take several weeks, which put a temporary halt to his regular afternoon hanky-panky sessions with love struck Carol.

After a few days of scratching his head and looking for a new venue, he decided that the only safe place left in the whole building for his liaisons with cuddly young Carol was Chris's grubby bailing room which was situated in the dank basement. And so one afternoon he took Carol down into this area of the basement, a place that she, like most others, had never visited before, to meet Chris and supposedly, to show her the bailing machine in action and after introducing her to Chris, who'd been in the middle of his afternoon nap and was not at all pleased at being rudely woken, Mitch set about manoeuvring young Carol into a corner of the grubby bailing room and began kissing and cuddling her.

Chris, although a habitual drunk, was a man with morals and on seeing this attempted fornication taking place within his private domain became extremely agitated. His eyes widened with disbelief as he looked on and he not only became very worried, but extremely animated and cried out, "Bejabers Mitch! What da hell do you tink you're a doing? You can't be doing dat sort of ting down here so's you can't!"

"Just look the other way or go for a walk," Mitch replied as he ignored Chris's protestations and became more and more passionate and tried to manoeuvre reluctant Carol into an even darker and secluded corner of the shabby bailing room.

"You can't be doing dat down here!" Chris screamed as he began to run around in little tight circles, while trying to decide what to do for the best. The question of, "should I go or should I stay?" ringing in his fuddled mind, "We'll all be sacked! Oh Jasus! If Big Bill cumes down here right now, we'll all be sacked so's we will! Oh Jasus, Mary muther of God, will ya stop ya shernanikins right now!"

Chris continued to run around and up and down the limited space the crowded grubby room afforded him, while shaking his hands, crossing himself and uttering prayers to every Saint that he could think of as he could see that Mitch now had young Carol trapped in a corner of the grubby room and was trying to roll up her tight mini skirt with his free hand. Now young Carol may have been madly in love with Mitch and far from being as pure as the driven snow, but even she wasn't going to succumb to Mitch's advances in these grubby and chaotic conditions while in the background Chris was jumping about like a bouncing ball and the whole business became farcical and eventually she broke away and ran quickly up the cast iron spiral staircase and into the safety of the main store.

Chris, who was emotionally exhausted, collapsed into his old armchair muttering, "Jasus, Mary, muther of God, I'm near to having me a heart attack."

And as for Mitch, he wondered what all the fuss was about and freely cursed Chris for ruining his afternoon's bit of slap and tickle and decried Carol for being such a, "bleeding prude." This was yet another example of how he looked upon the world and its odd morality. From his point of view, a bit of lovemaking fun was as normal as breathing, no matter where it took place and he could never understand why other people did not see it in exactly the same way that he did.

Chas was one of the general storeman and for a few weeks during the busy Christmas period he was seconded to the despatch and distribution department to work alongside the rest of us and in that short period Mitch and I got know him as well as anyone at Greys, which wasn't at all well as he was a man that hid his true feelings and past history behind a prolific outpouring of humorous antics. All we knew for certain was that he was in his forties, footloose and fancy-free and had travelled the country while engaged in numerous labouring jobs. He was an itinerant that was incapable of settling down in one place. This fact alone would have set him apart from most, but the oddity that made him really unique was his outrageous manic sense of humour.

His humorous outlook was not only decidedly odd, but outrageously shocking as there was not a single taboo that he would not challenge, which left the other workers either rolled up with painful belly laughter, or cringing with extreme embarrassment. Not until I came across the written works of Spike Milligan, did I realise that there was anyone else in the world that was remotely like Chas. (To get around the British Army's restriction on keeping a pig on an army base, Spike pretended that the pig was a dog and called it Rover.)

Chas would walk up to a counter in the department store, pick up a pair of fluorescent yellow socks and with a face as serious as a hanging judge, ask the girl behind the counter if she had the same thing, but in a brighter colour and the more the puzzled girl pointed out that it was impossible to obtain anything brighter than the fluorescent colours that were on display, the more he would insist that he required something much brighter. He would end the conversation by explaining to the confused girl that the bright socks were not for himself but for his old Granny who was ninety-two and had trouble finding her feet.

While walking around the store he would stop and make "coochy coo" baby noises to a toddler sitting in a push chair and then attempt to teach it to say, "Say bollocks to your daddy."

Handwritten advertisements began to appear on the staff notice board, "Three legged dog named Lucky for sale" "Nuns needed with dirty habits. Signed, A. Monk," "Old bike wanted. Must be rich." Who wrote these messages no one knew for sure, but Mitch and I had a pretty good idea who it was.

Chas would step into the goods lift and politely ask grumpy Harold to take him to the tenth floor and with a face bursting with frustration, Harold, in no uncertain terms, would point out that there was no such thing as a tenth floor in the building.

"No tenth floor!" Chas would reply in surprise, "So what have you done with it?"

And before Harold could reply Chas would add, "I'm sorry Harold, but if you've lost the tenth floor I'm going to have to report you for negligence," and with that he would hurry off leaving Harold steaming, spluttering and jumping up and down in his goods lift.

While talking to an Indian gentleman in the Beehive one evening Chas was heard to say, "My sisters married to one of your lot. They've got a place of their own in Small Heath. Well they're not exactly on their own, they share it with ten others, but she can always tell which ones her husband because he always wears brown boots."

On another occasion he sat next to an elderly couple and told them that he was celebrating. When, with congratulating pleasant smiles they asked him what it was that he was celebrating, he brightly informed them that he'd just been released from prison where he'd spent the last fifteen years for murdering someone. As they looked at him, wide eyed and speechless, he then added that it had all been a ghastly mistake, "I killed and chopped up the wrong person see." With faces drained of colour, the elderly couple hurriedly left the pub.

He would often butt into other people's conversations and say outrageous and contradictory things which would often trigger a heated argument and then walk off, leaving the protagonists angrily arguing among themselves and totally confused. As a defence for starting these confusing arguments, he would claim that because he'd served his King and country during the war years and had almost captured three mile of barbed wire, he had every right to say what he liked.

On a crowded bus trip from Birmingham to West Bromwich one Wednesday lunchtime, it being half day closing, Mitch and I sat on the upper deck at the rear of the bus, while Chas sat near the front and when the bus conductor came along and asked him for his fare, he held out several coins and replied solemnly, "One to West Brom and one for the monkey."

The bus conductor looking puzzled asked, "What monkey?"

Chas looked around and then excitedly exclaimed, "Oh bloody hell! I've lost my monkey!" He jumped up and began to look wildly around and in a voice full of panic, cried out, "Oh no! Where is he?"

The bus conductor, who was at a loss as to what was happening replied with an annoyed scowl, "I don't know? I haven't seen any blooming monkey."

"But I had it with me when I got on the bus, so you must have seen it." Chas stated in an accusing tone.

"Look mate!" The bus conductor replied defensively while shaking his head to show that he was not going to take responsibility for Chas's problem, "Your monkey's got nothing to do with me, if you had a monkey when you got on this bus, I didn't see it and I can't see it now either."

"But I had it when I got on, so it must be here somewhere," explained Chas worriedly, his eyes darting wildly around the crowded bus. He then turned to address the bemused passengers, who were looking on with wide eyed interest and in a firm voice stated, "Everybody up, come on, look under your seats, see if you can see my monkey, come on."

And then pointing at a rotund woman who was sitting with a large shopping bag perched upon her ample lap and who'd glanced around, but had not seen any necessity to rise, he said, "And you missis, he might be under your seat. But if he is, don't touch him because he bites and his bites can be very nasty."

29

At this news pandemonium broke out among the passengers and many began to vacate their seats and scramble down the stairs to the lower deck. Meanwhile the bus conductor, who did not relish being bitten by a bad tempered monkey any more than anyone else, decided that he needed assistance and rang the emergency bell to stop the bus. As the bus came to a halt, many, including the large worried woman with the shopping bag scrambled down the stairs, jumped off the bus and stood looking up at the upper deck from the safety of the pavement, while the bus driver joined the conductor and helped in the search for the missing monkey. By this time all normal English reserve had vanished and the people from the upper deck were only to keen to explain to the people on the lower deck, with animated outrage, just what had taken place during their journey. People who would not normally speak to each other got quite worked up while discussing the unusual situation and they all agreed that, "It just isn't right that innocent people who are minding their own business, should be bitten by blooming monkeys" and "They should not be brought onto corporation buses in the first place" and "Something ought to be done about it."

Eventually the bus was searched from top to bottom, but as no monkey was found, it was decided that the journey should continue, but without Chas and he was ordered off the bus by the driver and the harassed conductor. It was a decision that was greeted with unanimous approval by everyone that was travelling on the bus including Mitch and me as we pretended to be just as outraged as the others.

And as the bus pulled away and continued its journey, the relieved passengers looked out of the side windows as one and saw Chas standing on the pavement wildly gesticulating and shouting threats about how he was going to report the bus crew for their unprofessional behaviour and how he was going to sue the corporation and, "If anyone finds the monkey, hand it in at the nearest police station."

As the bus continued its journey, everyone chattered away to their immediate neighbour about the rights and wrongs of carrying dangerous monkeys on buses, but we couldn't help but notice that for the rest of the journey, no one was fully relaxed and many continually gave the spaces under the seats sly nervous looks.

Chas got on the next bus that came along and arrived at the pub that we'd arranged to visit about ten minutes later. The pub was quite crowded, but Mitch and I had managed to find a small space at the far end of the bar. Chas entered the pub and commenced to make his way through the crowded pub while exaggerating a limp and acting as though he was fitted with an artificial leg.

"Excuse me, sorry, coming through," He said loudly as he swung his stiff limb in a semicircle and cleared a pathway through sympathetic crowd. A man who was sitting on a stool and blocking his path stood up and apologetically said, "Sorry mate" and moved the stool to one side to let Chas pass. Chas stopped, looked at the man with the stool, smacked the side of his supposed artificial leg and said, "Got it at Casino."

The man with the stool and those around him nodded their heads with sympathetic understanding, as they were all aware that the battle at Monte Casino in Italy had been one of the bloodiest in the Italian campaign and that many men had been injured while fighting there.

It was then that Chas, with a puzzled look on his face said, "Not the battle you silly buggers, the Casino club down the Soho Road. I fell down the front steps when I was pissed."

The crowd around him burst out laughing and as the joke was passed on around the pub the laughter followed it.

After a few weeks, we found that Chas's relentless jokes, both verbal and practical, had a draining effect and we became exhausted and when he disclosed that he was leaving Brum and moving in with a pal that lived in Luton, we were both sad and relieved. We'd discovered that although Chas was a tonic to know and even on a dismal day was capable of putting a smile on most faces, it was wise to take his unique form of humour in small doses.

Because the ancestors of every family that live in Birmingham originally came from some other village, town or city, it is not unusual for families to have connections with relatives who live in far off places. Mine were originally from hard-nosed Yorkshire,

Billy's lot came from Devon and Mitch was obliged to visit his mother's relatives, who lived in Northern Ireland. It was a duty that had been pressed upon him and one which he was reluctant to fulfil and consequently, for several weeks he begged both Billy and me to accompany him.

Billy adamantly refused the request as he had plans of his own that summer; he was hoping to accompany his latest girlfriend and her three mates on a caravan holiday in Barmouth. His wild sexy day dreams ran along the lines of becoming an Arabian Sultan with his own harem for a week. It was an opportunity that he felt only came along once in a lifetime and that it was a bit of luck that was just too good to turn down. But I, who'd recently been given the elbow by my latest girlfriend was not only at a loose end, but intrigued with the idea of spending a couple of weeks in Ireland, a place that I knew little about and after my visit was over, I came to realise that I'd actually known nothing at all about the place except where it was on a map.

The small sleepy village that we stayed in was eight miles from Omagh and like most of Ireland, it had to many churches and not enough factories. Everywhere we went during our two week visit; we saw groups of unemployed men standing on street corners idling the day away, which is a recipe for trouble if ever there was one.

Mitch's relatives went out of their way to make us welcome and the food they served was plain, but plentiful. At dinner, a large bowl of potatoes, cooked in their jackets, was placed in the centre of the table and everyone helped themselves to as many as they wanted. Mitch, having been brought up with this custom by his Irish mother, saw nothing unusual in this practice, whereas I thought that it was a wonderful idea as it meant that no one in the family had the boring job of peeling and preparing all the potatoes before they were cooked. The custom struck me as a triumph of logic and I wondered why all big families didn't do the same.

I thoroughly enjoyed every minute of my Irish holiday as I found it both tranquil and fascinating, the people we met were extremely friendly and unhurried and the whole place had a laid back atmosphere. Living in a big city, I was used to hustle and bustle as people rushed with urgency from one place to another; Mitch on the other hand hated every minute of this laidback backwater life and couldn't wait to get back to the bright lights and the dynamism of the big city.

As the two weeks progressed, we came to realise that the village was a place where time was irrelevant, we noticed that the postman knocked on every door that he was delivering to and personally handed the letters to the occupant and would chat awhile before moving on to his next drop, all of which made his working day last twice as long. The pubs shut their front doors at night in line with the law of the land, but kept the back door open for anyone who wanted to carry on drinking. The local bus, while on its way to Omagh, would stop at a pub, which was about halfway along its route, while the driver, the conductor and any of the passengers that felt like it, went in for a quick refreshing drink. Meanwhile the rest of the passengers, who were mostly women with shopping baskets balanced upon their laps, sat happily chatting among themselves. No one was in a hurry to get anywhere.

When all the seats at the small cinema were filled, the manager placed free standing chairs into the centre isle until everyone who wanted to see the film had a seat, which of course contravened all fire regulations and not until everyone was settled did the film show start, no matter what the advertised time for the programme stated. When the board outside that particular cinema stated, "House Full" it really meant it.

After a few days, we decide to hire a car from a local garage, a Hillman Husky and in it we travelled around seeking out places of interest such as the incredible Giants Causeway, Londonderry, Enniskillen, Loch Neagh, the mountains of Mourne and the sleepy village pubs, where to visit the back yard lavatory, one was obliged to walk through the landlords cramped living quarters. On the open road we met, gypsy caravans moving slowly from place to place, chickens and geese running free, cows being moved from one field to another, horses munching at hedgerows, flocks of docile sheep and even six pigs that seemed to belong to no one in particular that were out enjoying a country walk. For city raised lads, the sight of half a dozen pigs meandering about the middle of a quiet country road was quite a shock, especially as we had been travelling at fifty miles an hour at the time and to avoid them we almost ended in the ditch.

One evening we went along to a local dance, which was being held in a community hall which seemed to have been built in the middle of nowhere as it looked to be deep in the countryside and there didn't seem to be another building anywhere near it. It was set back from the road which allowed two or three cars and an abundance of bicycles to be parked in front of it. The hall was a simple structure made almost entirely from corrugated metal sheets and as if to give it status, a Union Jack flag was flying limply from a flag pole that was attached to the front of the building. Once inside the hall, which was sparsely furnished, having nothing more than a small raised stage and a few long wooden benches which had been pushed against the walls, we found that we had entered a time warp in music, fashion and customs.

Much of the music that was played that evening was the bouncy Showband, Jimmy Shand, fiddle-e-diddle type of music, where the dancers were encouraged to clatter around the hall jigging and jumping as if treading on hot coals. One of the young men that we'd met earlier that day was there dressed exactly as he'd been all day and the previous week, which included his hobnailed black boots. His only concession to dressing up for the evening was a gaudy silk neck tie that his older brother had sent him from America.

That evening I also learned the significance of displaying a pair of bicycle clips as a fashion accessory. I'd noticed that several young men in the hall had bicycle clips protruding from their jacket breast pocket and after inquiring as to what the significance of this strange custom was Mitch informed me that it was to show the young ladies with whom they danced, that they had a bicycle outside and would be willing to give a young lady a lift home on the cross bar. Mitch found this and many more of the other simple Irish customs embarrassing as he felt that because he was slightly related to a backward Irish family, it tarnished his modern man about town image, but I took a different view and found many of these simple customs a revelation in plain common sense.

After the dance was over we jumped into the hired car and proceeded to make our way back to our own village along the dark narrow country lanes and were suddenly confronted by the dark side of Irish politics. A group of policemen who were wearing black waterproof capes and flat topped military style caps and carrying rifles at the ready, stopped us in the dark country lane with the aid of a couple of bright beamed lights and asked us to explain where we were going at such an hour. Mitch, who had heard his mother talk about such things, was well aware of what they were and what they wanted and it was he who explained who we were, where we had been and where we were going, but for me, who knew nothing of Irish politics, it was heck of a shock.

"What the bloody hell was that all about?" I exclaimed in amazement as we slowly drove off and continued our journey along the dark country road.

"Oh, them's the "B" specials," Mitch answered totally unconcerned, "They're out looking for the IRA."

Up until that moment, I'd always thought of the IRA as something that had to do with a time before the Second World War. To me, it was something to do with the nineteen twenties, a time before I was even born. I had no idea that not only was the IRA still in existence, but was still bloody active and extremely dangerous.

"Why the hell didn't you say something about it before we came over here?" I demanded, my mind full of images of being caught in a cross fire of the local Hill Billie's taking pot shots at each other.

"Well if I had, you wouldn't have come over with me would you?"

"I might have done."

"No you wouldn't."

"Well at least I could have brought my old helmet with me."

With that, we both laughed, which helped to cover my nervousness.

But the fact which brought me up to date with what was often referred to as, "The Troubles," was the situation that one of Mitch's uncles was in. He lived in a small simple cottage at one end of the village and his lover of many years, lived with her elderly mother, in a house at the other end of the village. Every day, this woman walked through the centre of the village to his home, washed and ironed his clothes, built up the peat fire, cooked his dinner and in the evening, as she had done for fourteen years, walked back to her mother's house where she spent the night and slept in her own bed. The reason for this odd behaviour was that she belonged to a Catholic family and he was a Protestant.

When I asked questions about this situation, which I found utterly ridicules; I was assured that as long as they did not marry, everyone would turn a blind eye to the situation, but if the lovers of many years decided to marry, all hell would break loose, as one of them would have to betray their church. The fact that the pair had a healthy thirteen-year-old illegitimate son, who lived with his mother and his Grandma, running around the village, didn't seem to bother anyone. Religion may be good for the sole, but it sure as hell knows how to mess up society

It was virtually impossible for Mitch to go for two whole weeks without chatting up a girl and trying his luck, but in a village that was in the back of beyond, the pickings were slim. However, being the randy bugger that he was did his best and eventually managed to pair us up with a date. Secretly we met the two girls, who were obviously wearing some of their mother's clothing and makeup on a warm summer evening at one end of the village and walked with them across the local fields, while chatting about the usual teenage nonsense and on reaching a small copse at one end of a field, we pared off and began kissing and cuddling our respective partners and both hoped that our date for the evening would turn out to be daring good time girls.

I pressed my girl up against a large tree and kissed her continuously, to which she readily responded and after a while I began to fumble among the many layers of her mother's clothes which I eventually found included a full length silk slip. I tried to put a hand upon a breast, which she weakly rejected and all the while I asked myself the question that plagues every inexperienced young man in this position, was I going to fast or to slow? We'd been in the small wood kissing and canoodling for about fifteen minutes, and I had even managed to manoeuvre my right hand through the complicated layers of clothing and slide it onto one of her small breasts, when a young boys high pitched voice was heard to shout,

"You's come out of there our Kathy or I'll tell me father what you's is up to so's I will!"

I then heard the girl that Mitch was with shout back, "You be off with you our Wesley and mind your business or I'll punch your face."

It turned out that Kathy's younger brother had followed us and had been spying on us and just as Mitch was getting to the interesting part of his conquest, the young brother had intervened with his verbal warning. Mitch was furious and threatened to kill the little bleeder, his girl Kathy was also outraged and threatened to get her own back on little Wesley and the girl that I was with was now worried that her mother would find out what she had been up to and quickly broke away and I was left standing alone beside the large tree as frustrated as ever.

I enjoyed my Irish holiday; I'd found it relaxing and full of surprises, in every pub we visited there had been someone who was willing to tell a far-fetched story that was full of graphic descriptions and which I found to be great entertainment. Mitch on the other hand hated every minute of his stay in sleepy Ireland and couldn't wait to get back the hectic life and the many girls that he was sure were waiting for him back home in Brum.

And as for Billy's eagerly awaited caravan holiday, not only did he have the misfortune of being ditched by his girlfriend, but he also spent a night in hospital. After being caught red handed snogging his girlfriend's best mate, who Billy had discovered was quite willing to indulge in an extremely passionate embrace, Billy's furious girlfriend had attacked him with the only weapon that she could lay her hands on, which happened to be one of her sharp heeled shoes and which not only put a dent in Billy's head, but also a gash down one side of his face.

Billy, as philosophical as ever, just said of the incident, "I'm just glad she wasn't wearing bloody football boots, otherwise I'd still be in the bleeding hospital."

Dad took Mom and my younger brother Steve on a week's holiday in an old Ford van to a caravan site that was near Weston-Super-Mare and as soon as they arrived and had unpacked the van, he lifted the bonnet and with the aid of the many tools that he'd brought along with him, he began striping the engine down in earnest.

After inspecting the caravan, Mom put the kettle on and proceeded to put a few of their belongings into the cupboards, then realising that Dad was missing, she went to see where he'd got to

"I went to the door," She said when telling me about the incident, "And there he was taking the engine out of the old van." And I thought, "How the hell, are we supposed to get back home?"

But by Monday lunchtime the engine was as good as new, in fact many parts of it were new, and for the rest of the week they were able to explore the surrounding countryside and all with total confidence. His first car had been an old nineteen thirties model that had its spare wheel strapped to the back, his second a black sit up and beg nineteen forties Ford Prefect and the third, a small five hundredweight ex-Wrenson's grocery delivery van. Although the company's name on the side of the van had been painted over it had not been rubbed down thoroughly and was still visible, but as the vehicles purpose was to get the family from A to B, no one cared what the van looked like. There were no windows in the body of the van and it only possessed two seats, one for the driver and one for a passenger. To rectify this lack of seating capacity, he purchased a couple of old car seats from a scrap yard and bolted them to the floor in the back of the small van. With the seats securely fitted he was now able to carry two more passengers, but they were obliged to sit with their knees tucked up near their ears and had a limited view the road ahead.

Most of the vehicles were very basic and were not automatically fitted with heaters and this vehicle was no exception. Actually until reliable indicators became standard, there was little point in having a heater as drivers were often obliged to drive with the window open so that they could use hand signals. Dad decided that this old delivery van required heating and being a heating engineer, he set about the problem with a heating engineer's logic. He connected a copper pipe to the radiator, ran it under the dash board, put a number of heating gills onto the pipe and ran it back to the radiator system. He fitted a stopcock so that it could be turned off during the summer months and as far as is know, this was the first and only hot water radiator centrally heated vehicle on the road and the system worked perfectly, on a long drive in the cold winter months the van became as warm as a bakers oven.

His passion for repairing objects never diminished throughout his life and he purposely went out of his way to build and make things that other people automatically purchased. He built his own garden shed, a greenhouse, a garden bench, a potting shed extension, fitted new windows and doors and installed his own central heating system. But even after he had built his own garden shed which was to house his abundance of useful items, such as bits of string, bent nails, rusty hinges, an extraordinary array of tools and used paint brushes that spent their life soaking in tins and jars filled with turpentine, the house, much to Mom's dismay was never free of tools of one sort or another as they were constantly being used for mending or making objects. She would find tools at the side of the settee, on the sideboard, in the kitchen cupboards, in the bathroom and even under the bed. He not only knew how to take a watch or clock to pieces and put them back together again, but regularly cleaned the inside of his radio and the television set.

One day Mom came home from a local shopping trip and looked through the kitchen window where she expected to see Dad pottering about in the garden, but he was nowhere to be seen. She then went to the bottom of the stairs and called his name.

"I heard a feint reply, but it was not coming from the bedrooms" she said when telling the story and shaking her head in disbelief, "Do you know where I eventually found the daft bugger? In the front room, under the floorboards, he'd decided to rewire the room." Dad was eighty-six years old at the time.

Mom always said of him, "If he'd been dropped in the middle of Alaska and had to fend for himself, he'd have been the happiest man in the world," but as there was never a more contented man, one can only assume that he must have been doing something right for all those years anyway.

His ability to cultivate flowers was something that he'd inherited from his mother as she was a remarkable green fingered gardener and every year, just like other passionate gardeners, she brought to bloom, an abundance of flowers. This feat was quite remarkable when one considers the fact that throughout the whole of her married life she never possessed a garden as she lived in a back-to-back house, which had no garden. Her solution to this minor horticultural problem was to fill every receptacle that she could lay her hands on, old buckets, saucepans, metal bowls, baking trays and paint tins with soil and seeds, then place them, stack them and hang them all around the blue brick yard.

In nineteen forty six, when the Second World War was well and truly over, she even took to planting seeds on and about the bombed building sites in her locality and ended up being featured in the local newspaper. She was pictured standing among hundreds of marigolds on one of the derelict sites that she had cultivated.

Through no fault of her own, Mom had been obliged to move from one school to another when growing up and as a consequence, had received a very basic education. Her childhood had been stable and enjoyable until her father had died when she was nine years old, then everything changed. Her mother married again in what can only be described as a ridicules romantic whirl, but this romantic lover turned out to be a lazy work-shy drunken brute and so from a comfortable family existence, the family quickly descended into abject poverty. Over the next few years they were kicked out of every house that they lived in for none payment of rent and black listed by many shopkeepers. Things came to a head one day when Mom, who was thirteen years old, found her bullying drunken stepfather beating the living daylights out of her mother.

"In a panic," She said as she re-lived the incident, "I opened the cutlery draw and grabbed what I thought was the bone handled carving knife and I stabbed him in the back with it, but providence was with us both that day, otherwise I am sure that I'd have killed him. I'd inadvertently picked up the two pronged meat fork which had an identical bone handle, but still, he carried that scar on his back for the rest of his life.

We were living in a mining community in Huntingdon and I finally decided to leave the happy home and I went to live with my Gran back in Brum. I got a job at the BSA factory assembling bicycle chains. My God! It was like a prison sentence. I didn't stay

40

there very long and I eventually got a job in a factory nearer home which was much better because there were a lot of young girls working there and I could make friends and have a bit of fun at last.

When Mom and my stepfather and the rest of the family eventually came back to Brum, I moved back in with them for a while and then I faced a new problem. I found that I didn't need a wardrobe to keep my clothes in, as all my best clothes were put into the bloody pawn shop every Monday morning by my mother and retrieved every Saturday."

Her lack of education never got the better of her natural strong personality and for the whole of her life, she was never out of touch with what was going on in the wide world and was never short of an opinion or a back handed compliment.

Later in life she looked after her grandchildren with the devotion of a mother hen, she minded them at a moment's notice, took and collected them from school, accompanied them on job interviews, gave them money whenever they were in need and allowed them to use her home as their own and one suspects that her own traumatic upbringing had something to do with her lenient attitude towards them.

Like most people, whether educated or not, she was superstitious and would attempt to read my future by swilling the last dregs of tea around a tea cup and finding an image in the tea leaves. It was a harmless pastime that the introduction of tea bags eliminated. She was wary of courting bad luck by avoiding the number thirteen, the playing with knifes on the table, opening umbrellas in the house, walking under ladders, putting new shoes on the table and many, many more nonsensical prohibitions and one day, when she was in her eighties, she unexpectedly told the following story.

"Way back in the nineteen forties; a ghost once tripped me up while I was climbing the staircase in the little house that we lived in when me and Dad first got married. You had to open a door in the little living room to go up the stairs to the bedrooms and during the day the stairs were only lit by whatever daylight came out of the bedroom doorways at the top of the stairs. But even so, I was young and fit and had no trouble at all in running up them, but several times I'd noticed that I'd had a slight trip. It was just as though something

41

had touched my right foot and had tried to trip me up. Then one day, I opened the door, looked up the stairs and there on the landing, I saw the figure of a little girl in a pretty summer dress. I was startled, because I knew that there was no one else in the house. Dad was at work and Jaco was in the back yard playing with his two friends, Mitch and Billy. Anyway, when I looked up the stairs again, the little girl had disappeared.

A few days later, a woman that I'd never seen before knocked on the back door and she said that she was looking for an old woman named Mrs Raffety that had lived in the house next door a number of years earlier. I told her that Mrs Raffety had died several years ago and that another family was now living in the house. She then told me, that she'd once lived in this house that we were in and then she told me that her little daughter had died tragically in this very house and that's why she and her family had left and gone to live elsewhere. She said that her little girl had been four years old at the time of the accident and had died before the ambulance had arrived. The woman went away and I never saw her again and I never saw the ghost of the little girl again or got tripped up on the stairs again either, I think the little girl had been waiting for her mother and went with her that day."

When asked why she'd never mentioned this story before and why she had kept it a secret for sixty years, she just shrugged her shoulders and said, "Well no one would have believed me would they?"

The only strange phenomena I've ever seen was, "Is it a bird? Is it a plane? No, it's Superman!"

One dark winters evening, while walking through a large darkened open plan office that was situated on the twenty-seventh floor of a tall office block in the centre of the city, I paused for a few minutes to gaze out of one of the large wide widows at the city and at the thousands of tiny lights that peppered the scene before me and casually I began to identify several landmarks within the panoramic view. Suddenly out of the corner of my eye, my peripheral vision picked up the dark shape of Superman and his flapping cape as he flew past the tall building. The apparition was approximately a hundred yards away and about twenty-feet below the window that I was looking out of. Startled from my daydream, I stepped closer to the window for a better view of the caped crusader and what I saw as my eyes focused in on the flying spectacle turned out to be five Canada geese flying in formation past the building while on their way to the Edgbaston reservoir.

Mom never tired of socialising, which for the working class usually meant frequenting pubs or social clubs. She wasn't a regular drinker, though she did enjoy the occasional tipple, so as she grew into middle age, she tended to join social and church groups, not for their religious views which she often disagreed with, but for the company of others.

Dad, who'd given up the demon drink when he was in his late twenties for reasons of his own, was not keen on socialising in pubs either and as they grew older, they solved this problem by taking up ballroom dancing as a regular pastime. Because of her love of company, Mom joined any club that was nearby and was always the first to put her name down for a coach trip no matter where it was going. At one time, she must have held the world record for visiting Weston-Super-Mare as all social groups that she joined inevitably had a trip to Weston on its itinerary. Her take on the town was, "It's full of old buggers with Zimmer frames and wheel chairs." none of which ever stopped her from going time and again.

While attending one of these social clubs she heard the sad news that Ada Bishop, an elderly neighbour, had suddenly died. On hearing this, she suggested that as a mark of respect, the assembled women should sing Ada's favourite hymn. This they did and gave Ada a rousing farewell. She then suggested that they all sign a card of condolence for Ada's family and that she would personally drop it through Ada's letterbox on her way home. This was also done and all the club members went home that day feeling a little sad, but satisfied that they had shown a little respect at poor Ada's sudden demise.

Ten minutes after dropping the card through Ada's letter box, Mom's friend Pansy, agitated and out of breath arrived and gasped, "I've just found out that Ada Bishop is not dead after all, it was Ada Milton what died. Her what lives in Maryvale Road and she hasn't been near the social club for months."

43

"Are you sure?" was Mom's immediate reply as to her it seemed that she had just shed a fair bit of sympathy in the last half hour and she didn't want it to go to waste.

"Of course I'm sure," Pansy replied, "Ada's just telephoned me and asked me to put her name down for the Blackpool illuminations trip."

Mom and Pansy rushed up the street to where Ada lived and rang her door bell and as the door opened Mom dropped a silk scarf onto the condolence card that she had posted a few minutes earlier and as she whisked it away she replaced it with an advertising flyer while Pansy kept Ada's attention by talking to her about the Blackpool trip.

She was to say later, "We had the poor old bugger dead and buried and had sung her favourite hymn and all the time she was sitting at home enjoying a box of Cadbury's chocolate and watching a John Wayne cowboy film on the tele."

A few weeks later Ada Bishop was to cause another little problem for the residents of the street. Going into her back yard to hang out some washing, she smelt a strong whiff of coal gas so she phoned the gas company and informed them that there was a gas leak in the street. Two gas engineers arrived and spent the next hour knocking on neighbour's doors and searching several back yards while seeking out the reported gas leak and they were not at all amused when they found that the smell that Ada had reported, turned out to be Dad's garden fence, which he'd earlier painted with creosote.

Up at the church social club, Mom and her friends all had a good laugh when discussing these and other similar incidents and were even more amused when one day Pansy declared, "I never seem to have the same luck as other people. Just look at old Mrs Frier, her numbers went and won ten pound on the lottery, even after she was dead."

Mom herself was not immune to causing the odd spark of humour and once, when she and Dad had become affluent enough to acquire a telephone, was asked what her telephone number was, she replied, "I have no idea, I never need to ring myself."

During one conversation, I asked her what my grandfather on my father side had been like as he'd died long before I'd had a chance to get to know him. "I didn't particularly like him," She said and

44

thoughtfully added, "He was a man who could talk without using a single word which wasn't very nice."

Puzzled, I asked, "How do you mean?"

"One look at the grumpy old bugger's face and you knew exactly what he was thinking and what he would have said if he'd bothered to say it."

Mitch and I enjoyed working at the department store, but the wages we received did not compare with what many of our contemporaries were picking up who were employed in the manufacturing industries and although we realised that factory work would be dirty and monotonous, we believed that this was a small price to pay for having our pockets bulging with cash when we hit the town at the weekend. Being able to buy new clothes and still have enough money to go out and have a good time was about as far as our thoughts on the subject ever went and it was all part of the illusion of making ourselves feel good and looking a lot more successful than we actually were.

We were now in our early twenties, had no savings or even a bank account, no long term prospects and no clear future planned and yet we seemed to be surrounded on all sides by successful acquaintances who were no better educated or brighter than we were and so we felt that it was time to do something about balancing the books. We were given numerous snippets of advice on where the best paid jobs were by several of our factory fodder acquaintances who frequented the town haunts at night. We learned that there were vacancies at such places as Cadbury's, where men were employed to work on the night shift or at Fisher and Ludlow and the Dunlop which were part of the car industry, but we chose The Birmingham Battery. We were still reliant on buses to get about each day, so it was a convenient place to get to.

To our combined dismay, our short experience of working in the factory turned out to be no better than a boring prison sentence. We clocked in and out of the factory at set times and soon discovered that the time we spent inside the factory was unimaginably mind numbingly boring. The large workshops were not only filled with noisy clattering machines, but oil scented dusty air that penetrated the lungs and clung to our clothes and the clatter of the machine noise made normal conversation impossible.

The job that I was allocated in the great scheme of things, which was typical of most of the jobs that were on offer throughout the factory, was the simple task of sharpening the teeth on huge circular saw blades. One blade every hour, eight blades per day and to do this, all I had to do, was to bolt the five foot high circular saw blade onto a machine and re-set the sharpening grinding wheel every fifteen minutes and I soon realised that it was a task that a chimpanzee could have tackled with confidence. The simple task of re-setting the grinding wheel took all of sixty seconds, which left me with nothing more to do, but stand and stare at the revolving saw blade and the spinning grinding wheel for the next fourteen long, never ending minutes. To counteract the problem of staring at this automatic process, I began to take newspapers, Readers Digest magazines and books to work, wedge them against the machine and read them on and off all day to occupy my mind and to stop myself from turning into a mindless simpleton. A few feet away from where I stood, there was a small man with a pale prison complexion, attired in faded blue overalls and was fifty years old, but looked older. His name was Gilbert Cummins and to my horror, I discovered that he'd been doing the same job for an unimaginable twenty-three years and had become a mindless automaton. He rose at the same time each morning, caught the same bus, purchased the same newspaper from the same shop, ate the same food during breaks, did the same boring job every day, watched the same television programmes every evening, went to bed at the same time and even went to the same boarding house at the same seaside resort every year for his holidays.

Poor Gilbert had been doing the same job for so long that he no longer needed to look at a clock to know what the time was and as I looked at him I decided that no matter how good the wages were, automaton factory life wasn't for me and I began to scan the newspaper situations vacant columns in earnest. Mitch, who was working in another part of the factory, had come to the same conclusion when he witnessed the fractured metal teeth of a circular saw blade zipping through the work shop like machine gun bullets because someone had set a cutting machine at the wrong speed.

The Birmingham Battery factory was ancient in form and outlook and could have stood as a metaphor for much of Britain's industrial decline at the time. The factory buildings were old and dilapidated and much of the machinery was still belt driven. That is to say that a powered shaft ran through the workshops and the leather belts that ran off it, powered the machines below. Many of the machines had been salvaged and purchased at a very reasonable price from bombed and devastated German factories at the end of the war and reassembled back in Britain. At the time this would have been seen as a slick piece of business, but the buyers failed to see that the devastated German factories would eventually be rebuilt and equipped with new, efficient machinery. Machines that were capable of outstripping their British counterparts in production and quality and after just a few years, West Germany became a modern industrial power base while Britain, through lack of investment and foresight, still lingered in the past.

Although we'd worked full time at the department store and for a short time in a factory, we still frequented the Matador in the evenings and would often help out when the place was busy. Zac still ruled the roost along with his clan of Greek Cypriot mates and although the place was not as prestigious as it had been in its early life, it was still one of the most interesting places in town to visit as it attracted a wide variety of girls and many odd and unusual characters, many of whom were undoubtedly destined for Her Majesties houses of correction.

The one big change that had taken place in the last few months was that my beautiful ex-girlfriend Helen had now become the girlfriend of Anton, a move that made both Mitch and I highly suspicious, as Anton was a very reserved character and was not a bit like high flying Cato. It seemed to us that having seen that Cato needed a change and was not yet ready to settle down; she'd simply changed horses to stay within the affluent group.

As the two business partners Cato and Anton had now turned their efforts into running a night club which they named the Mayfair, their interest in the Matador had waned. Both were excited by their new venture and taking a lesson from the past, they were determined to keep the night club free of many of the dregs that had infiltrated the coffee bars. As a consequence, the lovely looking Helen was now rarely seen at the Matador although Anton made regular visits and Cato still retained a flat alongside Zac's above the premises for when he was in town.

The Mayfair, with its restricted membership, was far more to Helen's taste, as there, among the many well-heeled young men that frequented the place, she could parade and flirt to her hearts content and was free of the knowing looks of Zac, Mitch and me who were well aware of her past history and knew her conniving personality better than most.

"Don't be fooled by that beautiful smile and sylph like body, my boy. She's a very shrewd gold digger." Was Zac's simple opinion, when he was once asked what he thought of her and added, "And I suspect she might also be a sociopath, a person who has little or no conscience."

"What makes you say that?" Mitch had asked, as, although he agreed with Helen being a crafty gold digger, he found the accusation that she was devoid of any conscience, a bit strong.

As usual, Zac's reply was simple and to the point and with a broad grin on his well lived in face, he simply said, "It takes one to know one."

A few hundred yards from the Matador coffee bar, there was a popular pub that was situated half way up Holloway Head, which was known as The Greyhound. It was a pub that sold cheap cider and was therefore very popular with many students and those on a tight budget. I had a fondness for the pub as it had a distinct Bohemian atmosphere. It was a place where conversations concerning who would be the next Derby winner ran quite easily alongside discussions on the merits of the American constitution or the intricacies of Shakespeare's use of iambic pentameter. Mitch on the other hand detested the place for it lacked the fashionable good looking, good time girls that he was interested in. The type of girl that used the Greyhound tended to wear sloppy jumpers, zodiac charms; sandals made from car tyres and were obsessed with women's rights. Some even smoked clay pipes ostentatiously to show that they were completely independent.

Throughout his life, Mitch retained a suspicious dislike for women who he thought hid their natural femininity behind a facade of pseudo intellectual protestations or odd religious customs that he believed belonged back in the middle ages "They're so busy fighting non-existent windmills that they end up becoming bitter and twisted and looking about as sexy as a bloody bull-dog chewing a wasp."

Now one of the drinkers that frequented the Greyhound on a regular basis was Owen, a muscular man that was in his mid-twenties and as fit as a butcher's dog. He had lived in the area all his life and used the pub because of the cheap cider that was sold there. Having been involved in many fights, he had a well-earned reputation as a very hard man, a fact that all that knew him would agree with, but he liked to believe that he was the hardest man in Brum, which, with Zac now installed in the Matador coffee bar and which was within spitting distance of Owen's territory, was now in question. The situation was reminiscent of a Hollywood western where two gunfighters of the mythical Wild West were brought together to decide who was the fastest on the draw and who were egged on for a showdown by their sycophantic friends.

Now Zac, who had spent time in prison, was not the sort of man that went looking for unnecessary fights as he had more than enough to deal with in the normal day to day running of the Matador and so if Owen had stayed in the Greyhound, nothing more would have happened, but of course, that is not what Owen's friends, who walked tall in his formidable shadow, wanted. All those that knew of Owen's and Zac's street fighting reputation surmised that one day the clash of the titans might come about, but of course no one could predict when and where it would happen and as luck would have it, Mitch and I were there when the confrontation took place.

Late one quiet Thursday night and a little before the coffee bar was due to close, Owen and three of his mates entered the Matador and there Owen openly challenged Zac to a bear knuckle fight in the back yard to decide once and for all, who was the hardest man in Brum. Zac, who was a proud man and not one to back down from such a challenge, agreed to the fight and they both retired to the back yard with their seconds. Realising what was about to take place Mitch and I quickly shot up the stairs which led to the Matador's office and living quarters and there we quietly opened a window and furtively peered down upon the ill lit back yard which was the chosen site for the forthcoming gladiatorial confrontation. The blue brick back yard which contained a lavatory block and a lean-to store room was the perfect spot for a private battle of brute strength and cunning guile.

As it was late at night, there were few customers in the coffee bar at the time and those that were there, were kept well away by Zac's Greek friends and so there were very few who entered the back yard to witness the savage event. Without a word being spoken, the two protagonists shed their shirts and squared up to each other and with Owen seeming to have all the advantages, as he was younger, fitter and larger than Zac, his three mates must have thought that he would soon make mincemeat of Zac. Mitch and I, who had seen Zac in action on many occasions, had other ideas and although we realised that Owen was ready for Zac's usual onslaught, we had little doubt that Zac would, against all the odds, eventually triumph.

Owen, with body crouched, threw straight lefts to begin with as he sized up his light footed opponent and then when ready, he launched a double fisted fusillade at the dodging Zac and many of his punches caught Zac on the upper arms and chest, as Zac tried to dance out of harm's way. Owen was a fit man and he dictated the pace of the fight from the beginning and it was obvious from the start that his intention was to not allow Zac, the older man, any time to rest and retain any reserves of energy that he might have and he attacked time and time again. Although the spectators from both sides, which, including Mitch and me, were only nine in number, we could all see that Zac was receiving twice as many punches as Owen, but we could also see that Zac was also landing some very sharp jabs which caused signs of pain to register on Owen's face.

The two combatants had been fighting for something like four or five minutes and Zac was taking most of the punishment, when Owen suddenly changed tactics and ignoring Zac's punches, he dashed in and managed to grab Zac around the waist and with his immense strength, he lifted Zac up off his feet and began to squeeze the life out of him. Zac, the ultimate street fighter retaliated by pushing a thumb into one of Owen's eyes and as Owen's powerful grip relaxed, Zac head butted him in the face.

Although almost blind, and his nose now pouring blood, Owen fought on bravely as Zac now threw short sharp punches and kicks from every angle and like a machine that could not be switched off; he showed no sign of stopping the onslaught. Owen staggered from one side of the yard to the other, throwing wild punches and seeking, but not finding respite and eventually he went down on one knee, his strong arms held up in front of his bloody face and his heaving chest gasping for breath, but there was no let up and Zac's punches rained about his head until he sank to the floor and there he received several sharp kicks to the body. It was only then that Zac stepped back and gulping and gasping for air, his taught body covered in sweat and blood, he surveyed his prone opponent and decided that it was over.

Mitch and I had always believed that Zac would ultimately triumph, and so it had proved. The fight had lasted less than ten minutes all told, but it had been sickeningly vicious. Zac staggered but stayed erect while Owen lay sprawled out on the blue brick back yard. Both fighters were covered in their own and each other's blood and were gasping for air and although Zac had won the fight, he was seen to be staggering badly and only his determined will power kept him upright and on his feet. There was no doubt that Owen had proved to be a worthy opponent and he had taken Zac to his limit and all the watchers realised that in a few years' time, Zac would not be capable of producing a similar performance again. The king was not yet dead, but the signs of eventual defeat were there for all to see. At the end of the terrible and bloody conflict, Mitch and I, who were still peering in mesmerised fascination upon the scene below, found that we were also gasping for air and with our body's full of racing adrenalin, we felt both exited and sickened at what we had just witnessed.

Three days later, Owen, his face smashed and badly bruised, returned to the Matador and warmly shook Zac's hand and from that day on, they became firm friends. Owen still frequented the Greyhound, where he once more reigned over his minions, but he would not hear a bad word said against Zac from anyone.

"Zac won the fight fair and square," he declared to anyone who ventured to find an excuse for his failure and that, as far as he was concerned, was that.

Because of the volatile environment that he lived in, Zac had many more confrontations at the coffee bar, but I was not there to see them as I was now seriously in love with a girl named Pamela and my visits to the Matador became less frequent. I realised that the Matador was no longer a suitable place to take a girl that one dreamt of marrying, but as Mitch still frequented the town's hot spots on a regular basis, I was able to keep abreast of what went on in Zac's turbulent world.

Zac was not like anyone else that we'd ever met before or were ever likely to meet in the future. He was a complex character that defied any quick and easy analysis. At times he could be seen as nothing more than a simple sadistic thug, at others, a subtle and crafty manipulator and sometimes, a wise old owl and although he was undoubtedly a natural leader, intelligent and street wise, he often seemed to be unhappy and discontented with his lot in life.

In a past age he would probably have become a chieftain or a war lord and in certain circumstances would have led hordes of wild aggressive warriors on a spree of raping pillaging conquest, but at the time that we knew him, he was no more than the leader of a loose nit gang of petty criminals and prostitutes and although he was King of all he surveyed, we eventually came to the conclusion that what he actually surveyed in the great scheme of things wasn't really much to shout about or to envy.

The nineteen sixties, which eventually became described as the swinging sixties, began with Lonnie Donegan singing, "My Old Man's a Dustman." Many swingers were to say later, when referring to their controversial habit of experimenting with hallucinogenic drugs, "If you remember the sixties, you weren't there." It was probably the song, "My Old Man's a Dustman" that they were trying to forget.

Floyd Patterson was the heavyweight champion of the world, Real Madrid the best football team and the hit films were Hitchcock's, "Psycho," and the kitchen sink drama, "Saturday Night and Sunday Morning." Chubbie Checker introduced, "The Twist" and the book "Lady Chatterley's Lover," which describes a novel form of flower arranging, went on trial for indecency and along came the classic television comedies of, "Steptoe and Son," "Till Death Us Do Part," "Dads Army," "Monty Python" and "Morecambe and Wise."

And at the same time that all this was happening, the National Service conscripted army was finally phased out and what had been known as the "call up" came to an end. During the forties, fifties and even into the early sixties, the "call up," dominated the thinking of most young men as those that were fit were expected to spend a compulsory two years in the British armed forces and this fact hung over them like the sword of Damocles as they made their way through their precarious teenage years. Young men, whether working or at university, knew that whatever they were doing would be interrupted while they completed their two years National Service.

There is no doubt that the armed forces, with its regimes of physical training and strict discipline was the making of many a young man that went through the process, giving them a confidence that they were totally unaware that they had, but to others, it did little to help them and was considered to be a complete waste of time. In many families, uncles, cousins and older brothers had all done their time and the up and coming lads were in turn expected to do theirs. "Get your knees brown," was the macho maxim of the day.

So, when the "call up" came to an end, thousands of young men felt a sense of relief because they'd been spared what they saw as an unnecessary upheaval in their lives, but paradoxically, there was a sense of disappointment. The previous generation had been tried and tested and now they never would be and many often wondered just how well they would have fared under strict military discipline.

Danny Page, my mate in Leicester, was one of the last of the young men to be called up and unexpectedly, he thoroughly enjoyed the experience although he had two of the worst postings possible, the bleak windswept Mountains of Mourne in Northern Ireland, where one night while on guard duty, he accidentally set off the alarm and put most of the British army in Northern Ireland on Red Alert and the Oman desert, where he shared his tent with large camel spiders and his meals with millions of hungry flies. "Whenever we had custard, it was a race to see how much you could eat before the dish became covered in the bloody things." Was one of his grin and bear it observations.

Masochistically, Danny enjoyed his National Service experience, but, being an ardent angler who was used to going out in all weathers and putting up with discomfort on a regular basis; he was probably half trained to be a soldier before he was called up, so his view on the subject could be seen as a little suspect.

When Danny was called up, he was posted to the Glen Parva barracks, the home of the Leicester "Tigers" Infantry regiment and while on guard duty at the main gate, a cocky young nine year old kid gave him a rough time by swearing and insulting him while he stood there guarding the front gate. Danny, seeing that there was no one around, retaliated by threatening the little brat with a little physical violence, namely a clip around the ear and a kick up the arse to go with it. Taken aback by this unexpected response, the little monster quickly cleared off, but ten minutes later he was back again with his irate father in tow who threatened to punch Danny's head for threatening his innocent little son. The sergeant of the guard eventually intervened and a blazing row took place outside the barrack gates.

"Each day we were taken out into the fields and the woods at the back of the barracks and trained to kill a well-armed enemy," Danny was to say, "But when it came to dealing with stroppy foulmouthed kids and their stupid bombastic fathers, we were absolutely bolloxed."

Every man who was called up for National Service had a story to tell about their experiences whilst serving their time and one tale concerned a smart young man that found himself based in West Germany. He was an enthusiastic photographer and while there, he purchased on the black market an expensive Leitz camera at a very reasonable price. His problem was how to get it back home without paying tax on it. A friend suggested that he dismantle the camera and send it home in the post in sections and this is exactly what he did. When he eventually got home on leave, he reassembled the camera and to his great delight, the camera was as good as new.

After his leave was over, he re-joined his regiment back in Germany and a few days later he received a parcel from his mother, which contained his Leitz camera. The accompanying letter from her read, "I noticed when tidying your room, that you'd left your new camera behind and knowing how much you loved it, I thought I'd send it to you in the post."

On leaving school Mitch, Billy and I, just like the rest of our friends, were resigned to the fact that we would eventually be called up for National Service and we looked upon it with mixed feelings. Feelings of nervous trepidation, but also an air of excitement as, although we knew that it would be a tough time and physically demanding, it would also take us to foreign parts where we could enjoy untold experiences. For years we had been told by our elders of adventures in Germany, Cyprus, Malaya, Gibraltar, Hong Kong and many other exotic places where the British armed forces had been based. But we also knew that after two years, when we were finally discharged, we could look upon ourselves as men that had been tried and tested, but as conscription had now been abandoned it was never to be. So, when an elder work colleague suggested that I might like to join the Territorial Army in Thorpe Street and volunteer for the SAS training course I gave it some serious thought and after a while, I agreed to join up and give it a go, as this would be a chance of testing myself and hopefully put me on a par with my elders. The beauty of this type of service, as opposed to National Service, was that if I found that it wasn't the life for me and that I'd made a mistake, I could drop out of it whenever I wanted as there was no compulsory two year stint involved.

If asked at the time why I'd joined up I would have answered with the usual clichés of, "It's a bit of a laugh," "The extra money's always useful," "Be useful to know what to do if it all kicks off," but what I would not have disclosed was that I felt a need to test myself to the full so that I could stand among other men as an equal. I was well aware that I wasn't the strongest, the toughest or the most aggressive of men, but during my rough and tumble games with the schools rugby team back in Leicester I'd discovered that I possessed a hidden aggression and a determination that I'd not been aware of before and now I was ready to test it at a higher level. There was also

55

the glamorous daydream of one day going off to war and firing a lethal weapon at a hated enemy. I was probably still under the influence of the many war films that I'd seen, but it seems that most young men have similar feelings and possess a warmongering aggressive trait in their psyche. I once read that a mother made a conscious effort to ban her young son from playing with toy guns and was astonished to find him one day playing in the garden with a bent stick and pretending that it was a hand gun. He was just four years old, it seems that where there's a will, there's a way.

As I grew older I was to learn all about the stupidity of war, the conniving politicians, the ranting megalomaniac dictators and the religious fanatics who infuse young men with righteous indignation and encourage them to lay down their lives in senseless bloody conflicts. I read about the blundering generals who used men as though they were pawns on a chess board, but paradoxically I also felt a touch of military pride whenever I attended a poppy day parade or saw the Union Jack flapping in the wind and knew that for all the logical arguments against going war, I would never be a pacifist. If ever the chips were down, I knew that I would be there with the other fools ready to go over the top.

In the early nineteen sixties, when I volunteered to go on the SAS training course, the regiment was not as famous or as glamorous as it became in later years, all that came about in 1980 after the successful attack by an elite group of SAS troopers who raised the siege of the Iranian Embassy in London and which was shown live on television. Before that, many had never heard of the Special Air Service and if they had, they'd have probably thought that it was some sort of exclusive holiday airline.

It was a British Army officer named Captain David Sterling while serving in the North African campaign in the early days of the Second World War, came up with the idea of parachuting a special commando force behind enemy lines to cause chaos and that's why the group was mundanely named the Special Air Service and not something more glamorous.

After a few false starts, the SAS eventually became a very effective fighting force in the desert war and actually destroyed more enemy aircraft in North Africa than the RAF. They did this by abandoning the parachute drops which were hard to keep secret and switching to the tactic of travelling many miles behind enemy lines in adapted trucks and attacking the loosely guarded aeroplanes that were neatly lined up on airfields. The troopers would then disappear back into the wide desolate desert where it was almost impossible to find them. It was a hit and run campaign that did an enormous amount of damage in comparison to the small number of men that were involved. They went on to operate in Sicily and Italy and it was during this period that Colonel Paddy Mayne, a one man army became a legend and when the Second World War was over, as there did not seem to be a specific role for such a cavalier and undisciplined force, there was a move by the powers that be, to disband the Regiment, but when the Malayan Emergency broke out, which is an odd name to describe a war, it was quickly realised that the only way to win it, was by taking the war to the enemy who were well entrenched in the vast areas of steamy jungle and it was decided that the SAS troopers, who were not only used to fighting in small tight knit groups, but already had the experience of operating behind enemy lines could be quickly trained to fight this kind of war.

Although the SAS had been born in the vast uncompromising North African desert, it was in the steamy jungles of Malaya where the Regiment eventually evolved into the shadowy fighting force that it later became. The hide and seek jungle war was a completely new experience and many lessons in tracking, navigation, staying hidden for weeks at a time and the logistics of acquiring supplies and basic survival skills were learned there.

After passing the medical, which was the most thorough medical examination that I've ever had, the first thing that I was told to do, along with the other new naïve recruits, was to sit at a desk and not only sign the Official Secrets Act, but also, to our astonishment, our resignation form. The only item missing was the date.

"Don't forget lads," Our training officers would constantly remind us, with a cheery smile, "You can pack up at any time that you like and nothing will be said."

Our in house training took place in the Thorpe Street Army Barracks and mainly consisted of map reading, striping and re-building the SLR rifle and a little in self-defence techniques, such as hitting the enemy with any object that was available. The training sergeant's advice on the subject of self-defence went as follows, "Judo and karate techniques can be very useful in disarming an enemy, but given a choice, I'd choose a heavy spade any day."

After a few weeks of in house training, we, the new recruits were taken out in army lorries with our training officers for map reading exercises in remote areas of wet, wild and windy Wales. Once there, the Territorial soldiers were mixed in with a number of full time regular soldiers, who were all from different regiments and who had all volunteered for the SAS training course and there the fun and frolics really began.

It became obvious from our first day out on the desolate wind swept Welsh hills, that the purpose of the training course wasn't to make us into SAS troopers at all, but was designed to force us to give up and go back to our warm comfortable homes or in the case of the regular soldiers, back to their regiments. When the weather got worse and things got tougher, the officers would remind us that we could pack up at any time and that there would be no recriminations and so, for those that were stubborn enough, a battle of wills began.

The officers exhausted us with continual forced marches across rough terrain from early morning till late at night and just as we were about to camp down and grab some much needed sustenance from our forty eight hour food packs and a relaxing sleep, they would get us up for another cross country trek, but this time, during the hours of darkness.

After spending most of the day climbing up and down wet and windy mountains with legs aching, gasping for breath, rucksack straps cutting into the shoulders and an army lorry parked in the valley below, the temptation to give in was hard to resist and after a number of such gruelling exercises, many volunteers thought that the whole thing was a nonsense and they ceased to resist. Now it could be construed that bringing all these willing young volunteers together and discarding them by the dozen without a second thought was a waste of time, money and effort, but I eventually worked out that what the officers really wanted and were constantly on the lookout for, was the one in a thousand that not only did not give in, but actually enjoyed the gruelling experience. When they found the crazy oddball that they were looking for, he was whisked off and encouraged to join the regular SAS for in depth training.

On one of our first outings into wild Welsh countryside, we were taken up Penny-Fan, a mountain that dominates the skyline near Brecon. When near the top, we found that climbing the final stretch was similar to climbing a steep ladder with a bag of bricks strapped to our backs and many were almost ready to call it a day. Somehow we finally reached the top after scrambling up on hands and knees and while gasping for breath, we crawled to a safe spot and collapsed. To our amazement, just fifty yards away, was a family of four sitting around a chequered tablecloth while enjoying a picnic. Stunned and confused our combined thoughts were, "How the bloody hell did they get up here?" On looking down the other side of Penny-Fan the answer was obvious, it was a gentle slope all the way down to the valley below.

We were now referred to as troopers and began our gruelling cross-country treks and map reading training exercises in groups of six. As we became more competent, we were reduced to four, then three, then two and finally, when the officers were sure that we could hold a map and a compass the right way up we were sent out on our "tod."

On these gruelling cross country hikes, we were constantly given useful tips on how to make our lives a little easier, "don't eat a large meal before setting out on a strenuous cross-country journey, as you will inevitably bring it all back up" which by then, I and several others had already discovered. "Stick to tea and boiled sweets throughout the day," which surprisingly worked well. "When walking in hilly country, try and stay on the ridges as this helps to conserve energy," which often meant that the shortest route on a map may have looked to be the quickest but wasn't always the wisest as it could be exhausting. "When travelling in a large group, spread out as this makes it harder for the enemy to see you and get an accurate count. If you are lost on a mountain in a thick cold mist that muffles all sound, remember that although running water will inevitably show you the way down, it will also find the quickest route, which can lead you into danger."

We were told stories of men that had got lost on dank misty mountains and had ignored this advice and had been badly injured by accidentally falling down a hidden ravine and none of us fancied that and so slowly the initial cockiness of the recruits disappeared and the hard sobering lessons were duly learned. Ignoring the training officer's advice that trying to keep dry during manoeuvres was a complete waste of time and effort, one young trainee attempted to jump across a small stream instead of wading through it. His feet hit the far bank, but the weight of his back pack began to pull him backwards and although he waved his arms about like the sails on a demented windmill, he finally succumbed to the law of gravity and fell flat on his back into the ice cold stream with a mighty splash. He was quickly rescued by his laughing comrades, but his back pack now weighed twice as much as it had previously done and far from being as dry as a bone, he was now soaked from head to foot. On witnessing this hilarious incident it occurred to the rest of us that perhaps the training officers knew what they were talking about after all.

Many regular soldiers must have experienced similar training exercises that we were engaged in and physically, they would have been quite capable of doing exactly the same, but the big difference between a regular soldier and an SAS trooper is that the trooper has to become a Robinson Crusoe who can survive on his own without any help or company for as long as it takes and it was this simple fact that made many volunteers drop out. Most people can confidently tackle a problem when they're part of a team where they have moral support, but when out on their own it becomes an entirely different matter.

The SAS trooper is expected to sink or swim by his own decisions and it was when we were put into circumstances where we had to think and act for ourselves that many felt vulnerable and began to lose confidence. When completely lost in a cold mountain mist or stumbling around a dank boggy moor on a very dark moonless night, a man's confidence can be sorely tested and many, including me, found that our imaginations began to run riot. Making your way through a large unfamiliar dark forest on a moonless night without any form of light to show the way, is not only physically demanding, but mentally draining as it is hard to keep your imagination under control and not to succumb to thinking about the numerous horror stories that are tucked away in the subconscious mind, but until we had stumbled through rough terrain in the dark on our own, none of us knew for certain whether we were capable of doing it or not.

The cross country training was quite simple in concept, we were given a rendezvous point on a map (an R.V.) and with the aid of a compass and our newly learned skills of how to read contour lines on an ordinance survey map, we set out to find the reverence point. On a bright sunny day this was relatively easy as all the relevant hills and streams could be easily identified and cross referenced on the map, in pouring rain it became a little more difficult, but in a thick swirling mist or on a dark moonless night, it became much harder and it was extremely easy to get disorientated and lost.

During one dark night, I, along with a Marine and a lad from the Royal Artillery were trying to find our way to our allocated R.V. and we lost our way while trying to cut through a relatively young pine forest. Being man made and grown for commercial purposes, the pine forests that litter the Welsh countryside can change shape or even disappear over several years and are not always as they appear on the map and things began to get a little hairy when in the centre of the man-made forest we came up against a plantation of young trees whose whiplash branches were at head height. As we groped and blundered through the maze of young trees, we were constantly hit around the head by the young springy sapling branches. After about ten minutes of this torment the lad from the artillery suddenly lost his nerve and literally went berserk.

A little earlier he had shown signs of extreme nervousness when while stumbling across rough moor land in the dark, we'd surprised a few sheep. The frightened sheep suddenly jumped out of a small hidden dell right in front of us and run off among the tuffs of wild grass and disappeared into the dark night. The sudden incident had made all three of us jump with fright, but once the Marine and I had realised that it was only a bunch of frightened sheep; we were able to see the funny side of the incident. The effect on the other lad had been quite different and he became even more nervous and from then on he continually scanned the area for any more unwelcome surprises.

When he finally lost his nerve in the middle of the pine forest, he began to scream and shout obscenities and wildly threw his equipment about the dark forest. The Marine quickly took charge of the situation and on his instructions, we both grabbed hold of the ranting young man and held him down on the ground until he was completely exhausted and calmed down sufficiently to become reasonably rational again. We decided to abandon the night trek to our given R.V, which was still several miles away and make for the nearest road instead, which was much nearer and once there, await a patrolling officer.

I found the whole experience bizarre and frightening and came to wonder what would have happened if the lad, who'd suddenly gone berserk, had been carrying a loaded rifle or a Stirling sub machine gun. In the state the he was in, he could quite easily have tried to take out half the forest and probably me and the Marine with it. I suddenly realised that in such circumstances, it wasn't just the enemy that one had to worry about.

At approximately five in the morning, a Land Rover containing two officers found the three of us resting at the roadside forlorn and tired and after we had explained what had happened, they took the Artillery lad away with them without any recriminations. But before they drove off, the Marine enquired as to the possibility of us cadging a lift back to base with them and was told, "Get stuffed trooper, start walking!"

On another occasion while trekking across the hills, I developed a blister on my right foot which eventually burst and began to bleed. My foot felt sore and I was convinced that my boot was filling with blood. As I limped into the objective R.V. which was nothing more than a sergeant and an officer waiting for us at a small stone bridge that spanned a trickling stream in a valley that was surrounded by wind swept hills. I over emphasised my limp to gain a little sympathy and hopefully gain a much needed lift back to the base camp.

"What's wrong with your foot trooper?" the sergeant asked as I approached.

With a stoic grimace I replied, "It's a burst blister sir and it's bleeding."

"So how's the other foot?" the sergeant enquired.

"Oh that one's fine," I answered cheerfully, "Nothing wrong with that one sir."

"Well bleedingwell walk on that one then!" the sergeant snapped and then the officer, who was standing by, proceeded to give me my next R.V. map reference and off I went feeling disgruntled, but now knowing that even if I'd been crawling on hands and knees, I wasn't going to receive any sympathy or help from them.

We were told that trying to stay dry was a complete waste of time and effort, and so it proved. There was a very old saying that said, "If you can see the mountains in Wales, it's going to rain. If you can't see them, it is bloody raining." But it wasn't just rain that wet us, it was also wading through knee deep streams, tramping over water logged bogy ground and the constant flow of perspiration that we expelled. As we were not supplied with tents to sleep in at night, we were given the useful tip of, "Keep your map and you're sleeping bag dry," so these, along with a spare pair of socks, we kept wrapped in plastic bags and we were so knackered at the end of a long exhausting day that although we slept out in the open in our sleeping bags with a waterproof poncho wrapped around for cover, we slept sound for a few hours even when it poured with rain, we awoke cold, cramped and miserable and it took a great deal of effort to face another gruelling day and carry on. We eventually learned that if we got our hip bone comfortable in dip in the ground, we could often sleep like a log.

On the rifle range, which most of the volunteers looked forward to with Wild West cowboy zeal, we were taught how to fire the SLR rifle, which was an accurate weapon and well worth carrying, but it was the Stirling sub machine gun, which was light in weight, could fold up and was far easier to carry, that was everyone's favourite. The Bren gun on the other hand, which although deadly accurate, was cumbersome to carry and the Browning 9mm pistol turned out to be extremely disappointing. It was as heavy as a pint bottle of milk and only accurate at touching distance. The officer in charge, would bring the new troopers forward one by one, stand them in front of the target and show them how to fire the cumbersome pistol. "Hold with both hands. One below the other. Bend the knees slightly. Take aim. Now gently pull the trigger."

The gun would go off with a loud report, jump violently in the hand and the bullet would as often as not, miss the target completely and hit the sand bank behind. We soon came to the conclusion that if the enemy were more than ten feet away, we would be better off throwing the bloody pistol at them and the experience brought home to us just how much artistic licence was used in the Hollywood films when such guns were seen to be used with cavalier nonchalance and could hit a target a hundred yards with uncanny accuracy.

Because so many young men dropped out during the intensive training courses and the fact that each of us were constantly being moved from one group to another, it was virtually impossible to strike up any long-term friendships with the other volunteers and this was also part of the overall plan, as it was isolationists that could blend into any group that the men behind the training scheme were seeking.

I realised quite early that it was not fun loving Butlin Red Coats that they were looking for, but stoic men who could live for days on end without the company of others. During my time with the TA SAS, especially when out on exercises in Wales, I met many full time SAS regulars and none of them looked remotely like James Bond or Superman. They were a strikingly ordinary bunch of blokes and had come from all walks of life, some were big, others were small, some were short and some were tall and in civilian clothes it would have been difficult to guess just what their occupation was, but all of them were extremely fit and were willing and able to operate alone.

After completing certain sections of the training course, we were told that although we were not regular SAS and most of us had no intention of ever becoming regulars, there was however a roll for us to play if it all kicked off and the formidable Russkies invaded the West.

It was assumed that in the event of war, the Soviet Russian Army would invade West Germany and in that event, we would be parachuted into Poland to protect, for as long as possible, wireless operators who would be passing valuable military information back to base. This was sobering news and to most of us sounded very much like a one way ticket and not the kind of holiday one tends to get too excited about, but after all, this is what joining the army was all about and after the training that we had gone through we were under no illusions that there was a very serious side to all of this.

Halfway through one of my three month training courses I had the misfortune to sprain my right ankle and I was unable to complete that particular part of the training course and was told that I would have to start again from the beginning. This brought to a head what I'd been contemplating for some time. It was time to call it a day. I'd never had any intention of becoming a regular soldier, never mind a reclusive SAS trooper, I'd enjoyed the experience, pushed myself to the limit and learned a great deal, but enough was enough and I duly resigned. The irony of the situation was that I'd not sprained my ankle during parachute training, or by stepping on slippery stones while trying to cross a fast running stream or climbing a Welsh mountain all of which had happened to others, but by simply stepping off a wooden box whilst at work.

When I saw that the war in Vietnam was becoming serious, I realised that I'd never been officially notified as to whether or not I was still on the armies reserve list and I wondered whether or not that the forced holiday in the pine forests of Poland that I had been trained for was still on the cards. It was a thought that made me seriously wonder whether the whole experience had been worth it after all, for I was no longer the gung ho cowboy that I'd once been and no longer relished the thought of going off to war at a moment's notice.

"What time do you call this?" I called out sternly, as I caught sight of Starlin sneaking into the general store by way of the back door. It was a wide double door which opened out onto the back yard of the premises and where an open backed van was in the process of being loaded with some of that day's deliveries, "Your half an hour late!"

"Sorry mate," Starlin replied as he straitened up and gave up on his idea of slipping around the storage racks and pretending that he'd been on the premises and at work for some considerable time and then rubbing a hand over his stomach he moaned, "I feel really rough this morning mate, I'll have to go to the bloody quacks tonight."

"You always feel bleeding rough on a Monday morning," Billy said as he struggled past Starlin while carrying a couple of heavily laden bags down the store room. They were filled with metal pipe fittings and he was about to load them onto his lorry which was parked in the street, "It's the booze; you've drunk too much again."

"It aint that," Starlin snapped back, his face creased with pain, caused by a thumping headache and a churning stomach, "I can hold my booze mate don't you worry about that."

It was a familiar act that all who worked at the builders merchants were used to, Starlin was a young impulsive lad who regularly spent his weekends in a pub where he consumed more beer than was good for him. Although this was a known fact, he vehemently denied it whenever the subject was broached as he saw any criticism concerning his drinking habit as an open attack upon his masculinity.

Although he was young, headstrong and well on the way to being a drunkard, it was generally acknowledged that when on form he was an extremely good storeman. For most of the time he got on well with the rest of the staff and the trade counter customers and had a comprehensive knowledge of the stock, but it was also acknowledged that his weekend boozing bouts did cause him and others problems.

His first problem was that every pint he consumed had the effect of making him think that he was larger and stronger than he was and by the end of the evening, he was usually ten feet tall and ready to fight anyone, no matter how big they were and because of this regular delusion, he suffered many a black eye and split lip as a consequence.

"Every Monday morning you crawl in here looking like death warmed up and every time you claim that you are dying of some dreaded disease that no one's ever heard of," I said to him sarcastically, my hands firmly fixed upon my hips and in a voice that was loud enough for all the storemen and drivers that were in the vicinity to hear, "Don't you think that it could have something to do with how much you've been drinking?"

After many months of being in charge of the stores, I'd had to stamp my authority upon various members of the staff from time to time and I preferred to reprimand any wayward staff with sarcastic humour and in front of the others as I believed that they would see that although I was new to the job, I was no pushover and that I was being fair to all.

"It aint the beer mate," Starlin wined as he sat and slumped heavily onto a wooden box that was used as a seat during tea breaks and was situated near the long work bench that the storemen used for packing the various goods, "I recon it's a gastric ulcer or summat."

"And what do you think has caused you to develop a gastric ulcer you dopey bugger? Too much booze and not enough to eat, that's what." I replied taking on the mantle of a qualified doctor and then added; "Now are you going to start work or are you expecting the rest of us to do your work for you?"

"Give us a minute mate, I'll soon catch up. I'll get a drink of water first," and off he slumped towards the cramped toilet block where there was a sink and for a dying storeman, a much needed cold water tap.

Although I could not admit it there and then, I knew that what he'd said was true, by the afternoon he would be completing picking lists faster than any of the other storemen and that's why I put up with his histrionics. All the storemen under my supervision had problems of one sort or another, but at least Starlin wore his on his sleeve for all to see.

After listening to my chastisements, the storemen got back to work and Starlin eventually returned from the toilet block, seeking as much sympathy as he could elicit from his workmates. Groaning once more, he said, to no one in particular, "God, I feel like I'm bleeding dying."

"Well don't do it here mate," Billy said while smiling, "We've only just swept the floor."

The other storemen laughed and Starlin, realising that sympathy was in short supply as usual and that he would have to get on and do something before I returned and began goading him once more, picked up a picking list and once more slopped of to the toilet area and drank and splashed his face with cold water and swore that he would never drink again as long as he lived just as he did on most Monday mornings after waking with a thumping hangover and a badly bruised face.

"Right, I'm ready to go," said Mitch as he walked back into the stores while rubbing dust from his hands and expecting to see me at the work bench he said to Billy, "Where's Jaco? I'm loaded up and ready to go." Mitch had been in the back yard tying several lengths of steel tube onto the gantry of the open backed van in which he would deliver that days orders and had been absent during Starlin's usual Monday morning reprimand and was now anxious to be off on his round.

"He's up in the office," Billy informed him and looking at his wrist watch added, "I should buzz off if I were you before one of them dopey buggers up there finds you some more urgent deliveries."

As vacancies had occurred in the company, I'd brought Mitch and Billy into the fold by giving them both glowing references and by persuading Mr Frank, the boss of that particular branch of the company, that they were by far the best drivers that had applied for the job and they were now both employed as delivery drivers, Mitch on one of the company's two pickup vans and Billy on the larger seven ton lorry.

The area that this branch of the company covered, obliged Mitch and Billy to deliver daily in Birmingham and the Black Country and twice a week they had to spread their wings and deliver to customers that were situated in either the Coventry or the Telford area and, just as I had done, they'd learned that delivering in the Black Country wasn't as hard as it first appeared as many of the areas, although having different names, were next to each other and often on the same page of the A to Z map book. Once a driver had learned the layout of the many Black Country back street short cuts, he could cut down on his delivery time in the area considerably.

By this time Mitch was well ingrained into the company's daily routine, but his first day had almost been his and my last. I'd informed him that he'd be working in the store for the first week to become familiar with the staff, the stock and the company's paperwork system and as lunch time approached, I'd suggested that we walk up the road and have a pint and a cheese sandwich at the local pub.

"I've got my car outside," He'd declared, referring to an old beat up Austin Somerset that he'd recently purchased from a dodgy acquaintance, "We can go up in that."

And so Mitch, me and a young office lad named Scotty, piled into the old car and Mitch, with a roar, pulled away and shot off towards the tee junction at the end of the street in a boisterous confident manner and there we met the main road and its busy passing traffic and instead of stopping at the junction, Mitch turned the car sharply at the corner and, accompanied by blaring car horns and a screech of tyres, shot into the stream of the fast moving traffic.

"What the bloody hell....!" I screamed, my face contorted in shocked surprise and my tense feet pushing so hard against the floor of the car that they were in danger of going straight through the metal.

"Sorry about that," Mitch replied as he sat hunched over the old cars steering wheel and pushed the accelerator to gain more speed, "I forgot. The brakes don't work very well. I'll have to get them fixed."

Since leaving the factory in Selly Oak, Mitch had become a full time delivery driver and to his surprise, he found that he liked the work. Once loaded and out on the road, he was his own boss and could complete his days' work as fast or as slow as he wished. He could, as many other drivers did, spend long spells in greasy spoon cafes sharing gossip and eating bacon sandwiches or miss breaks altogether and have the afternoon to himself and after a just a few months he could find the quickest way in and out of most local areas without having to refer to a map. Although he wasn't meeting as many girls as he would have liked during the day, he was still free to patrol the city centre hot spots at night and had money in his pocket to do it with.

Like many delivery drivers, he'd found that there was a ready market for many of the commodities that he delivered and having the gift of the gab and many acquaintances; which included my, never miss a trick cousin, Charlie, who was willing to trade with anything Mitch could supply, it was not long before he had a regular list of customers who were willing to purchase his supply of black market goods.

Billy also enjoyed being a delivery driver, but unlike Mitch he never rushed about trying to finish early and he never went looking for customers to buy the pilfered goods that he could lay his hands on. Billy was quite content to wait for them to come to him. He had no scruples about selling stolen goods, but he was far more cautious than Mitch, who he thought was bound to get caught eventually.

As for me, my morals were no better than theirs, but now that I'd been promoted to stores foreman, a position of responsibility, I found that I had to be far more careful and make sure that no blame came my way for items that went missing. When discussing the subject of pilfered goods over a few pints all three of us would defend our criminal behaviour by claiming that as businesses were owned by faceless banks and greedy shareholders who had the power to interfere with our livelihoods by proxy, businesses were legitimate targets. In our carefree discussions we would point out to each other that, even the boss of a company fiddled his expenses and everyone took home office stationary and anything else that they considered useful and that this was no different from us occasionally selling a few lengths of copper pipe, a central heating pump or a bag of cement, but of course we knew that it wasn't the same, but as we were surrounded by people who had the same view, we rarely let thoughts of our dishonesty worry us.

After leaving the hellhole factory, I'd obtained employment at a builder's merchants as a storeman. The company not only supplied sand, cement and bricks to builders, but also a wide range of plumbing and heating fittings to heating and maintenance engineering companies and for a while, I saw a lot less of Mitch and Billy and my flashy "Jack the lad" acquaintances that still roamed the city centre hot spots while they continually sort their own particular brand of fame and fortune.

I'd come to realise that I needed a lot more stability in my life than I'd so far acquired and my continual hopping from one job to another, although surprisingly educational, was actually getting me nowhere on the ladder of financial success. I was not well educated or trained for anything useful and by now I knew that if I didn't do something about it, I'd end up engaged in low paid employment for the rest of my life.

I was aware that because of my lack of education and the fact that I was slightly dyslectic and had cacographic problems, many career opportunities were closed to me, but I reasoned that if I could find the right spot, which I knew by now was not serving cups of coffee in a coffee bar or drinks in a night club, I could, being ever the optimist, bluff my way to a better position and probably make a go of it. Part of my mature thinking on the subject of my future had come about because I'd found my true love. I was madly in love with a girl named and all previous love affairs paled into insignificance. I'd been seeing her for many months and with eyes wide open, I knew that I was heading towards marriage and the responsibility that went with it. I was truly smitten and saw a rosy future ahead.

I'd become acquainted with Pamela while working as a waiter in the Thrussells restaurant where she'd been employed as the receptionist, but at that time she was in a relationship and my clumsy efforts at attracting her attention had no effect whatsoever, but several years later we'd bumped into each other and things had turned out quite differently.

"Hi Pam," I'd said and for once in her presence I'd found that I was totally relaxed, "What brings you to a place like this?"

We were in the stationary department of Lewis's department store. I'd been taking a short cut and just passing through and she was standing in front of one of the glass topped counters while perusing a display of fountain and ball point pens.

"Oh. Hello Jaco. I was looking to buy a pen for my father's birthday," she said while smiling and looking at me with genuine warmth, "But I'm not sure what colour to get."

"Definitely not pink." I joked and to my delight she laughed and without thinking I added, "Do you fancy a coffee in the cafeteria?"

Happily she said, "Yes" and it all began from there. Over coffee I learned that she had split up with her long standing boyfriend some time back and was now working in a city centre shop and before we parted I arranged to meet her later that evening. I behaved admirably throughout the evening, escorted her back home and was rewarded with a warm kiss and the promise of another date which pleased me no end.

For the next few months I was on my best behaviour and the perfect gentleman, but as time went on and we got to know each other a little better, my true personality came to the fore and as usual I became as lackadaisical as any other young man who has to juggle his life around his girlfriend's likes and dislikes, his mates tempting adventures and working for a living.

"Hello Pam," I said smiling as I strolled up to meet her, who, having just finished work for the day was waiting patiently for me on the corner of Temple Street and holding her handbag defensively in front of her in the manner of a Scotsman's sporran, "Been waiting long?"

"I thought you said you'd be here at six." Pam stated a little annoyance evident in her voice. She'd not enjoyed hanging about on the busy street corner for the past fifteen minutes, where she assured me that several randy young men had given her the once over and made rude assumptions about her as they'd passed.

"Sorry about that, but the bloody bus broke down." I lied while continuing to smile as I certainly didn't want to get off on the wrong foot and sour our evening before it had even begun, "We all had to get off the bus and wait for the next one. "

"Well next time let's meet somewhere else. It's much too busy here." Pam replied, though failing to suggest where would be a better place and conveniently forgetting that it was her idea to meet on this street corner because it was close to the shop where she worked.

Ignoring her slight reprimand, as I was determined to avoid any form of disagreement between us and to keep her in a pleasant mood for the evening; I clapped my hands and just said, "Right then, where do you fancy going tonight then?"

"I thought you said we were going to the pictures." Pam replied a little surprised.

"I did, but I thought you might have changed your mind.'

"No, I haven't changed my mind." Pam said shaking her head, "So where do you want to go instead then?"

"Nowhere in particular," I lied once more while looking unconcerned, "I just thought you might fancy going for a drink somewhere or to the Tower Ballroom or something like that."

The reason for my two faced intrigue was twofold, firstly I was not at all keen on seeing the romantic film that we had agreed to see, action films were my first choice, and secondly, although we'd been seeing each other for many months, I was still no nearer having a full sexual relationship with her and thought that the liberal use of alcohol was still my best way of breaking down this last tantalising barrier.

Over the past few months we'd intimately touched and fumbled in cinemas, shop doorways and at the side of her parents' house when I had taken her home, but up to now, she'd not dropped her defences and allowed me to go all the way and although I told her that I didn't mind and that I respected her for it, I never stopped trying to conquer her stubborn reluctance. I realised that I loved Pam far more than I'd loved any other girl that I'd dated in the past, she was attractive and pleasant and I was quite certain that this was true love as I was insanely jealous of any young man that paid her what I considered undue attention.

As the months rolled by and we got to know each other better, we discovered that we had seen many of the same films, liked and listened to the same sort of music, had visited the same dances on occasions and gradually, after seeing each other on a regular basis, we became closer and more intimate and got to know each other's friends and acquaintances. Like many youngsters, we met and mixed with friends and indulge in many of the activities and interests that the young are attracted to, but we were not yet mature enough to realise that many of these group activities tend to disguise true personalities.

I met Pam's family and she met mine and I was quite aware that this steady courtship would eventually lead to marriage, which although I wasn't in any particular hurry to arrive at, I had no firm reasons to be against, as I was convinced that I'd found my true love and the thought of sharing a bed with Pam night after night not only titillated my senses, but filled me with a warm comforting glow. Even the warning that Trapper had mentioned one evening in the

Sailors men only bar, failed to dampen my optimistic spirits as at Pam and I loved each other and like lovers the world over, we firmly believed that love would conquer all.

"I was walking up the isle in the church," Trapper had said wearily, "and I thought to myself, how the bleeding hell did I get here? And when I thought about it, it was just as though I'd stepped onto a conveyer belt somewhere in the past and it had just slowly brought me to this point in time without me realising it. I mean, me and Irean, well, we just got together by accident really. You know how it is; we got chatting one day at work and one thing just led to another. It was off to the pictures or the pub together and then it was round to her house for Sunday tea and then it was sitting with her Mom and Dad in the Bulls Head on a Saturday night at the free and easy and then sometimes we'd stop in with them during the week and watched a bit of telly and then after they'd buggered off to bed, a bit of slap and tickle on the settee and the next thing I know, she's in the pudding club and we're all making plans for a bloody wedding. I mean, don't get me wrong mate, I like Irean a lot, and I get on well with her Mom and Dad, but we don't really know much about one another, do you know what I mean? I mean, I didn't even know that she couldn't cook properly until we'd got married, turns out, her mother used to do all the bloody cooking."

This conversation with Trapper had not worried me or made me question my own motives for courting Pam as I was quite confident that our love was much stronger than Trapper's seemed to be. I'd found Pam attractive from the very first moment I'd laid eyes on her and each morning when I'd seen her at the reception desk at Thrussells restaurant I'd felt a surge of lust and dreamed of cuddling her shapely body and although she wore very little make up, her face had a quiet natural beauty that I found most apealing.

After many months of courting I realised that she could be a little dull and somewhat unadventurous at times, but that didn't bother me as I didn't expect her to be the life and sole of the party all the time. While courting we spent many evenings with our boisterous friends where analysis of each other's personalities was never high on the agenda and none of the group that we knocked about with really knew each other very well as we continually hid behind a facade of acting the part of young carefree, exuberant fun loving ambitious people.

Pam was good company for most of the time and I was always proud to show her off to my friends, but there were times when she admitted that she would have preferred to stay at home and read a book rather than spend the evening in the company of our rowdy friends which irritated me at times, but I wasn't unduly worried as from my perspective I could see that all my acquaintances had similar disagreements with their partners at one time or another.

In my sunny day dreams, I saw us setting up home together in a swanky penthouse flat that had expensive contemporary furnishings, oil paintings on the walls and rows of books by famous authors lined up on pine bookshelves. I thought that these books would impress our numerous visitors and would identify me as a well read and educated man. In the back of my mind I was still smarting from my commercial art studio days when I'd been forced to admit just how ignorant I was. I still carried a fear of being seen as an uneducated plebe.

I saw us inviting friends around for small intimate parties where Pam would prepare delicious dishes of foreign food from recipes that she'd found in the women's glossy magazines and I would serve wine and everyone would be smiling happily as we chatted away in sophisticated manner. In these fanciful dreams I always saw myself as a successful business man, though in what business I was never quite clear, but I always saw Pam fashionably dressed and smiling happily as she stood beside me.

Unknown to me, Pam had a completely different view of what our marriage would be like and the thought of hosting a string of intimate tête-à-tête parties for my friends was not on her list at all. She thought that many of my mates were too boisterous and vulgar and the less she saw of them, the better. Her dream of the future was filled with images of white wedding, grand shiny prams, pretty baby clothes, a bay windowed semi-detached house with flower filled garden and visits to her nice smiling parents on sunny Sunday afternoons with her two well behaved and well-dressed loving children.

But as neither of us were employed in well paid occupations and had no savings whatsoever, both of our fanciful dreams had little chance of coming to fruition in the immediate future and in that we were no different from most of the friends that we knocked about with. We were more like leaves in the wind than a couple with a long term strategic plan and then I finally got my wish and persuaded Pam to go all the way with our love making and after a few months of enjoying each other intimately, Pam became pregnant.

A few months later, after embarrassingly informing our friends and family, we were married and living together in her parents' home, but things did not go well. Unfortunately Pam suffered a miscarriage. She was devastated and so was our respective parents and to a certain extent, so was I, but I also felt a niggling selfish glow of satisfaction which I felt ashamed of and could not quite understand. What I did not want to admit to was that I was relieved that we were not starting a family after all, as I truly believed that we could not afford it.

My thinking was totally concentrated upon our material existence and to me, a baby was still an abstract concept and not a tangible reality, I carried this shameful guilty secret for many years and at times I genuinely thought that there might be something radically wrong with me, but years later when my first son was born and he grabbed my finger, an unbreakable bond was formed between us and all my former worries of material wealth, which had seemed so important, completely disappeared.

It was eighteen months before Pam and I had enough money to put a deposit on a place of our own, but it was not the modern penthouse flat that I'd dreamed of, but a small dilapidated terraced house and after Pam had insisted that it should be decorated throughout with cream gloss paint and traditional flower patterned wallpaper, to me the property looked similar to my parents' home and as far from my modern penthouse dream as it could possibly be.

Because of Pam's pregnant condition, our wedding and the congratulatory reception get together afterwards had been a very low key affair and it was there that Annette, who was dressed in a bright red rig-out for the occasion, pulled me to one side and in her usual no nonsense way prophetically predicted trouble ahead.

"You know Jaco, if I didn't know that she was five months up the stick, I'd think your missis was a bloody nun." She'd said.

"Just because she doesn't like your filthy jokes doesn't mean that there is anything wrong with her." I'd snapped back in Pam's defence.

"Look Jaco," Annette had replied, who was always crude but direct with her remarks and tended to be shrewd with her observations, "I wish the pair of you all the best, but a lot of girls turn out to be just like their mothers and that stuck up old cow over there in the big hat 'as been looking at me and your mates as though there's a bad smell in the room, so be warned."

Briggs Building Supplies was a nationwide organisation and the Birmingham depot, was just one of its many outposts, but as it was situated in the West Midlands and surrounded on all sides by industry, it was a very busy branch. The premises that the business was housed in had once been an old corner pub and had been converted into a building for commercial use. The ground floor and the former low ceiling beer cellar had been turned into a store rooms and what had once been the publicans living quarters were now a series of offices.

At the rear of the premises there was a fair sized lock up back yard that was partly covered by a Gerry built corrugated iron roof and was big enough to park three delivery vehicles, a stock of different sized bricks, paving slabs, sand, cement and steel tubes. As to why British Steel made their tubes twenty-one-foot long, while the rest of the world made theirs in six metre lengths was simply because that was the length of the original railway bogy carriages. I learnt this oddity when the company acquired an order to export a quantity of steel tube to a foreign country. It caused no end of problems as Johnny foreigner had no idea what twenty-one-foot was and when converted into metres, it looked to be an exceedingly odd measurement.

Each storeroom was fitted out with numerous rough wooden storage racks, which were then filled with various building and pipe fittings, numerous types of valves, clips and brackets. With these wooden storage structures in place, the store rooms had become a maze of narrow corridors and what no one seemed to notice was that in the event of a fire, the whole place was a potential death trap. The heaviest items, steel flanges, welding bends and the like, were kept in the cramped low ceiling cellar, which was, because of the weight that was stored above, re-enforced and braced with several steel girders. At some time or another, everyone who ever worked at that particular branch of the company, cracked their heads upon these overhead steel girders and it became an initiation trademark and quickly taught those who ventured into the cramped cellar on a regular basis, to walk around the area with the long armed stoop of a chimpanzee.

I'd joined the company as a storeman, but as I held a driving licence, I was used as a spare driver for emergency deliveries and whenever one of the regular drivers went on holiday. The foreman was a bright and breezy character named Brett. He hailed from Brighton and although he was very knowledgeable about everything connected with the building, plumbing and heating trade, he was also an irritating pain in the arse. This was because he was under the impression that he was a funny comedian and each week he would try out and practice a number of new found infantile jokes upon the staff. Unfortunately for us, we were a captive audience and had no way of avoiding this particular form of torture. Come the weekend, he would use the same jokes on another captive audience at his local working man's club, where he acted as the jolly, laugh a minute compe're.

Although I found Brett to be an irritating pain with his constant flow of Christmas cracker jokes, he did manage, in just six months, to teach me an awful lot about the items we stocked, which became the foundation of my new career and the reason that this education only lasted six months, was because he suddenly disappeared.

One Monday morning comedian Brett never turned up for work and when Mr Frank, the depots bewildered boss enquired as to his whereabouts at the address that he lived at, which was a rented apartment, he was informed that Brett had simply disappeared, owing the landlord several weeks rent. Enquiries at the working man's club where Brett performed his showbiz act also drew a blank and no one seemed to have a clue as to his whereabouts. Eventually puzzled Mr Frank, who had by now become highly concerned at the disappearance of his foreman, contacted the police and the mystery was finally solved. Mr Frank was informed that they were also looking for the missing Brett, as they had him on their wanted list, and wished to interview him concerning two cases of bigamy. It transpired that laugh a minute Brett, had two families in the south of England and was now running around the country with his third wife. So the question on everyone's lips at the company for the next few months was, "was Brett a comedian, an illusionist or just bloody barmy?"

Sid, an elderly storeman who had been at the company for the longest period of time, was now promoted by Mr Frank, to the position of stores foreman in place of the missing comedian. It was a position of responsibility that Sid did not ask for or relish and he soon found that he could not handle it and after many months of worrying it made him physically and mentally ill. Just like many quick fixes by incompetent management, the solution to Brett's disappearance had not been thought through properly and was destined for disaster.

At the same time as Brett's vanishing act had taken place and although I had only been with the company for six months, I was seen by Mr Frank as being the solution to another of his problems and I was given a promotion of sorts. The company had come up with an idea that they hoped would improve sales and they wished to try out a pilot scheme in the Birmingham area and I was chosen as the man to carry it out for them. The idea involved fitting out a large ten-ton van with storage bins and using it as a mobile store and I was to be the driver salesman. Before lunchtime each day, I had to drive the large cumbersome van to all the major building and heating engineer's yards in the area, pick up orders and complete them there and then from the back of the van. The experiment turned out to be something of a semi success, the van was old and had seen better days and had a tendency to break down and although it was a large and roomy van, it was impossible to carry every item that was required. During the experiment, which lasted for just over twelve months, I was to learn a great deal about the art of selling, the handling of the builders and heating engineers and also, how to drive a pig of a large cumbersome van in all weathers, which included the terrible winter of sixty-three.

The large van had a cab that was big enough to stand up in, and in the middle of the cab there was a metal cowling that covered the engine and which, as the day progressed became noticeably warmer and by the end of a long day it was hot enough to fry eggs on. This of course was welcome during the winter months, but was a bloody nuisance during the summer as it tended to roast my left leg. The large diesel engine that the metal cowling covered made a noise that was on a par with a Lancaster Bomber, which meant that conversing with a passenger whilst driving was impossible. All communication in the cab had to be conducted through sign language or by shouting at each other like a pair of town criers. The indicators had given up the ghost and so I was obliged to use hand signals, but even at full stretch only a small part of my hand became visible to the following traffic. The steering wheel was as wide as dustbin lid and in its centre there was a large round Bakelite cap. Without exception, everyone who sat in the driver's seat unconsciously fiddled with this cap and eventually prized it off and hidden inside the cap cavity was a round piece of cardboard with the message "Nosey Bastard!" written upon it

The winter of 62/63 was one of the worst on record and the huge snowfalls hung around for weeks. So much so that by the time that it did decide to melt and disappear from the streets, the regular drivers around the country had become quite expert at driving on ice.

The hairiest experience that I had whilst driving throughout that particular winter was when I hit a patch of ice at the top of the Suffolk Street hill, a city centre street that had not as yet been treated with tarmac and was still paved with smooth Victorian cobble stones. There was a row of parked cars on the left hand side of the road and oncoming traffic coming up the hill on the right as I, and the fully loaded ten-ton cumbersome van, slid down the entire length of the hill. White knuckled and in a cold sweat, I fought for control of the huge sliding vehicle and prayed like I'd never prayed before and miraculously; I reached the bottom of the hill without touching a single vehicle, pedestrian or lamp post. Sterling Moss could not have handled it better.

In the spring of 63, old Sid, the foreman, had a nervous breakdown and left the company never to return. It had been obvious to all the staff that Sid, who had originally been a bricklayer and then a storeman, was not cut out to be a manager of any sort as he was a natural worrier and should never have been made up to foreman in the first place. The responsibility that he took on and the daily pressure put upon him proved to be too much. To solve the crisis, I was taken off the road and brought back into the stores and made up to stores foreman and I found, much to my surprise, that I actually enjoyed it.

It turned out that I had a natural flair for organising men and inanimate objects and was articulate enough to handle the histrionics of the office staff when they bullied and blamed stores staff for late deliveries and the other numerous mishaps that happen in the course of a trading day. I actually enjoyed the arguments that ensued and the move turned out to be the beginning of my new career in middle management.

Although my problems with spelling and mental numeration were still there and were never to go away no matter how much I read or how many mathematical exercises I did, I managed to keep them well hidden and relied upon articulate conversation and a small graph that I kept in my wallet. It had all the times tables written on it and in an emergency I could use it to keep me out of trouble. For spelling problems I used a pocket sized thesaurus as I found it to be far more useful than a dictionary as to look up a word in a dictionary you have to know how to spell it, but with a thesaurus, you only need to know the meaning.

Organising stock and implementing work procedures was the easiest part of the job and was nothing more than applying common sense to basic problems, what for instance were the fastest moving products and where was the best place to stock them and what size storage bins were required, whereas the handling of staff and dealing with their varied temperaments was not only the trickiest part of the job, but fraught with many unforeseen pitfalls. The staff were complex and contradictory, prone to unpredictable mood swings, had ingrained prejudices and were just as deceitful as I was. I also learned that it was impossible to be a good manager and everyone's best friend at the same time, for any sign of weakness was instantly exploited. Managing directors would always stress the need to encourage a culture of good teamwork, but I was soon to find that the most ambitious only paid lip service to this admirable concept and beneath their sycophantic smiles they were only interested in their own advancement.

When I made a mistake, which being new to the position was inevitable, I soon discovered that there were many who were only too willing to broadcast my misjudgement, but I was now in my early twenties and far from the shrinking violet that I'd once been and I was more than willing to give back as much as I took. I was well aware that I wasn't the most intelligent or best educated man in the company, but I was now wise enough to recognise the lean and hungry look of ambition and worldly enough to steer clear of being manipulated by those that clearly had self-promotion in mind. My earlier experiences while growing up with wily cousin Charlie had been a worthwhile education after all.

The depots manager, Mr Frank, was a cheerful and courteous West Country man, who was in his mid-forties and whose favourite saying was, "When I finds that I 'ave a bad apple in my barrel, I hast to get rid of it." It was a cliché' phrase that obviously came from a very mild mannered man and it failed to put much fear into any of his conniving street wise staff. Second in command was the office manager, a thirty six year old man named John who was well educated and intelligent, but was also a hopeless alcoholic and whose purpose in life seemed to be how quickly he could break up his unhappy marriage and drink himself to death. Everyone else that worked at the branch, office staff, storemen and drivers, were all younger than the two managers and because of this, the establishment possessed a vibrant, lively atmosphere and a sense of anarchy prevailed. To the casual observer and even under the occasional inspections that took place from a head office lackey, it seemed that the day to day running of the branch ran along well organised lines and was as efficient as any other, but there was an un-written code of conduct among the staff which put simply meant, "what management doesn't know about, won't hurt them."

Now although I and my two mates, Mitch and Billy were not averse to occasionally pilfering company goods and selling them on for extra cash, when it came to blatant stealing, all three of us were amateurs compared to the antics that Scotty, the young office clerk got up to.

Scotty was a very intelligent lad and had joined the company's office staff straight from school and found that the clerical work that he was given was easy, unchallenging and extremely boring. He had always been a handful for his staid and steady parents and to them; he seemed to be possessed by an unruly impish gene. Throughout his lively childhood he'd always been in trouble of one sort or another and whenever a neighbour found that their bottles of milk, clothes line, dustbin or wheelbarrow was missing, they looked no further than Scotty and nine times out of ten, they would be proved right and as he grew up into a smart young man he found that the simple act of stealing added a necessary excitement to his life.

By the time he joined the company he was a fully-fledged thief, but oddly he rarely stole for his own profit and saw the act of stealing as no more than an exciting game and a challenge to his well-adapted sleight of hand skills. Being extremely articulate, having a good looking open face, above average intelligence and the cheek of the devil, he was well equipped to get away with anything that he chose to do. He completed any task that he was given in record time and found time to play practical jokes, flirt with the office girls and to cover his desk with acquired souvenirs. His first weeks collection included an ash tray and a pint glass from the local pub, a cruet set and an ornamental vase from a nearby restaurant, an Oxford dictionary and a no smoking sign from the library, a transistor radio and a model of a spitfire from Woolworths and a large glass jar of Everton mints from a sweet shop. His collection of miscellaneous souvenirs changed constantly, as each week he acquired more and gave away those that were wanted by the other staff. Small pocket radios, pop records, bottles of after shave and perfume being their favourite commodities.

"Morning Maggie," I said brightly as I opened up the premises for that day's trading, "You're looking gorgeous again this morning."

"You must be joking, I'm still half asleep." Maggie managed to reply as she hugged herself tightly to protect herself from the cold morning chill and as she tip toed through the open doorway on her high heeled shoes she added, "God knows why I agreed to get up at this unearthly hour and sort out the post, I must have been bleeding barmy."

A similar conversation took place most mornings as I opened up the premises as Maggie had, for a little extra money, agreed to come into the office early in the morning to open the post which one of the drivers collected from the local Royal Mail sorting office on his way into work. The store men and drivers started work at eight in the morning whereas most of the office staff were not due in until eight-forty five.

After opening the door, I let Maggie and two of the storemen into the trade counter shop and from there they disappeared among the maze of storage racks as they made their way through the general stores. Just then I became aware that Scotty had just turned the corner of the street and was making his way towards me. This was no real surprise as Scotty always arrived early, but what did surprise me was that he was carrying a heavy wooden crate filled with bottles of beer.

"Give us a hand Jaco, this is bleeding heavy." Scotty called as he got nearer.

"What the hell have you got there?" I asked as I stepped forward to help him with his heavy load.

"Oh I just found it around the corner." Scotty replied casually as he let me take hold of one end of the heavy wooden crate.

"Found it?" I queried as we carried the crate into the stores, "Scotty, you don't just find crates of beer at this time of the morning."

"Well actually, it was on the back of a lorry."

"What lorry? Where?"

"It's parked outside the café just around the corner."

"Where's the driver and his mate!"

"Having their breakfast in the cafe I suppose."

"Did anyone see you?"

"Do me a favour," Scotty replied dismissively, "Anyway, don't worry, I'll put the crate back tomorrow when we've drunk the beer."

After hiding the crate of beer at the far end of the stores, Scotty then bolted up the stairs and into the office and there he smacked Maggie on her well-shaped bottom as she stood sleepily sipping a cup of sweet tea before starting work on her mundane chores.

At school, far from being a blessing, Scotty had found that his quick thinking mind and his natural intelligence had been more of a hindrance than a help, as he always seemed to be ahead of the rest of the class in their studies and had an inordinate amount of spare time on his hands, which, having the personality of a barrow load of monkeys, he inevitably filled with mischievous pranks. But not all of his pranks worked as well as he hoped, one day he decided to take a day off from school and when his mother tried to raise him from his bed, he complained that he was suffering from a sharp pain in his stomach and was too ill to stand. His acting was so good that his mother sent for the doctor and after examining him, the doctor declared that Scotty was suffering from an acute appendicitis and he was whisked smartly off to hospital in an ambulance, where his healthy appendices were swiftly removed.

Although this turn of events was not at all what he had expected, it did give him the bonus of having several days off from attending his catholic school and sowed the seed for a similar scam. A few weeks later he forged an absence note in the style of his mother's neat copperplate handwriting and got a school pal to deliver it to the school for him. The note declared that, "Scotty has broken his leg whilst playing football in the nearby park and is now unfortunately residing in St. Chads Hospital and will be away from school for at least two weeks."

The school sent a priest to comfort Scotty in his unfortunate distressful condition and although the old priest searched the hospital thoroughly, he found no trace of Scotty or his broken leg. When Scotty was brought to book before the schools head, the disgraceful incident was added to his long record of previous wilful behaviour and he was expelled, but it did little to change his behaviour or surprisingly, his education, as when he finally left school, he left with flying colours and had more passes than anyone else.

"Good morning, you bunch of skiving morons!" Tuby Riggs called loudly as he confidently strolled through the general stores and made his way towards the stairs that led the office where he was employed as a telephone salesman. The three storemen who he'd addressed so rudely were busy completing picking lists and were used to this type of greeting and expected nothing less from him. Most of the office staff, who were considered to be nothing more than pansy pen pushers by the stores staff, entered the building through the front door, but not Tuby. In the manner of an eighteenth century landowner striding across his vast estate, he always entered the premises by way of the general stores.

"Bollocks, you stuck up prat." Was Starlin's reply to Tuby's greeting. He then stopped counting the copper fittings that he was dropping into a small plastic bag and added, "Get up them bloody stairs before I ram a u-bend up your fat arse!"

"You and who's bleeding army?" Tuby replied, then faltering in his stride and taking a serious tone he asked, "Is Jaco about?"

"What can I do for you Tuby?" I asked as I made my way towards the trade counter to complete a customer's order.

"Ah! Jaco! There you are old boy. Can you make sure that Wiggins get their bags of cement delivered this morning. Otherwise old man Wiggins will have my guts for garters."

"They're already on their way. Billy's got them on his lorry." I informed him as I disappeared into the trade counter, a satisfied smile on my face as it was another problem solved.

"Thank God for that." Tuby said with a sigh, "Old man Wiggins must have rung at least six times yesterday chasing his bleeding order."

"They was on the lorry before you got out of your stinking pit this morning." Starlin stated smugly.

"Well it's nice to hear that you've got something right for once." Tuby then replied, and then quickly dodged out of the way of a copper fitting that Starlin threw at him and bounded up the creaking wooden stairs and disappeared into the office with Starlin's words, "I'll get you later Fatso!" ringing in his ears.

Tuby was an unusual character, he was a thick set lad and grammar school educated. He played right back for a local football team with the ferocity of Attila the Hun, scything down any swift and skilful winger that dared to come near him with a heavy well aimed right leg. Not being the fastest player on the pitch and unable to out run a fleet footed winger, there was little subtlety to Tuby's game and he declared, "I can't spend my time running up and down the pitch chasing a Will-o-the-wisp can I? So I just set out to frighten the bloody life out of them and then they don't come back for more if they know what's good for them."

Unlike many of the other office staff, who could be quite snobbish because they'd received a grammar school education, Tuby mixed quite easily with the stores staff and traded jokes and insults on a daily basis. He was a forceful and ambitious young man who had a secret goal in life that at the time, no one knew of or even suspected. All the other young men in the company were into anything that was modern and trendy, especially in clothes and music, but Tuby hankered after an image that was associated with a bygone age. From an arrogant back street lad, he changed himself into a confident bombastic middle class pipe smoking English country gentleman.

With the aid of tweed jackets, corduroy trousers, stout leather shoes and the mannerisms of a village pub bore, he became a character that Miss Marples would have recognised immediately as a typical country squire, as British as the Union Jack, as traditional as roast beef and Yorkshire pudding and as sturdy as an oak tree. And although he eventually became a justice of the peace and socialised quite easily in the middle class society in which he integrated, he never lost his link with his working class friends or his self-depreciating humour.

Tuby stayed in the building supplies trade for a number of years, but eventually his longing for a middle class persona grata, forced him to change course. His first step was to become an air steward for British Airways and to his surprise; he found that he was one of the few that wasn't homosexual. By taking up this career, he travelled the world, widened his knowledge of people, places, foreign foods and good wines, all of which helped him to become more rounded as he slowly and methodically changed his image.

An odd claim to fame while on his worldwide travels was that he sold pre-packed packets of bacon in Israel. He purchased the packs in England and at Tel Aviv, he would sell them to the first taxi driver he met. He also claimed to have helped Aston Villa win the league cup by putting a written prayer into the Holy Wall while sightseeing.

Now although Tuby had always enjoyed playing football, his overriding passion was cricket and everything that went with it. Cricket completely dominated his life and village cricket and the codes of conduct that went with it, was his ultimate dream. Any girl that was foolish enough to become his companion, would have to accept that cricket would always come first. This passion was so strong that all that knew him reasoned that the odds of him ever getting married were zero.

"Who the hell is going to put up with a bloke that lives and breathes bloody cricket ? He even spends his holidays at test matches?" Mitch was to say when we were discussing Tuby's obsession with the game.

"He told me that his ultimate dream is to sit on the hill at Sydney and watch a test match between England and Australia." Billy added while shaking his head in disbelief, "If I ever get as far as Australia, it will be Bondi Beach that I'll be heading for. Just think of all them big breasted bronzed Aussie birds walking about in skimpy Bikini's."

"Now that sounds like a good healthy obsession to me Billy." Mitch replied as he laughed and pictured the pleasant scene that Billy had painted, "Count me in, because it certainly beats watching some prat knocking a bloody cricket ball about all day."

Although Tuby's obsession with cricket could be seen as eccentric, he wasn't against indulging in relationships with big breasted Aussie birds or any other good looking girls either; it was just that he realised that when it came to a long term relationship, his obsession would have to be taken into account. He courted many girls, but none of them, although sexy, attractive, well-educated and pleasant had the slightest interest in the game of cricket. After many years of globetrotting he eventually moved back to Brum, purchased a semidetached house in the tree lined suburbs and there as a testament to his cricket obsession; he fixed a souvenir cricket bat to his lounge wall as the room's main ornament.

Then one day, he happened to meet a good looking young woman while visiting his local library. He was instantly attracted to her and not one to let an opportunity pass, he engaged her in pleasant small talk and discovered that she was a Scottish lass from Inverness and who'd come to Birmingham to take up a position as a librarian and as he chatted to her in his usual charming manner, while hoping for a date, he casually mentioned that he was interested in the game of cricket.

"So am I." She replied smiling brightly, "My father's the captain of a cricket team. He taught me to spin bowl at a very early age."

Unbelievably, after travelling the world Tuby's dream came true right on his doorstep and he found that he and the Scottish lass were literally made for each other and were married within the year.

When he eventually retired from British Airways, he and wife sold up and purchased a shop in a small country town and turned it into a respected art and antique emporium and there among the fox hunting green wellie brigade, Tuby polished up his phoney upper crust image and his lifelong dream of becoming a country gentleman became a reality.

Scotty joined Briggs at the age of seventeen and for his age he had quite a lot going for him, he was extremely lively and intelligent and possessed natural initiative. He was also an outstanding athlete and showed it most of all upon the football field where he was considered to be a brilliant player, but what truly set Scotty apart from the rest was that he was even more unpredictable than the British weather. No one, including himself, could, with any certainty, predict what mischief he would become embroiled in next. Even on the simplest journey he would find something that would trigger his impish behaviour. He'd think nothing of moving a neighbours delivered milk onto another's door step, putt a traffic cone on top of a parked car, rearrange the magazines in a newsagents, mix the books up in the library or steal anything that happened to take his fancy.

He would usually start work at eight thirty in the morning and by eleven he'd have finished his main clerical tasks and from then on he would be looking for some entertainment to while away his time until more boring paperwork arrived on his desk in the afternoon. These entertainments usually took the form of chasing and touching up the young office girls, kicking a football about in the back yard, playing on the slot machines in the nearby café or going on a walkabout to the nearby shops and picking up and stealing anything that he came across.

Oddly, he gave away almost everything that he acquired and saw the act of stealing as an exciting game of "catch me if you can." There was no hare-brained scheme that he would not attempt and because he was so cool, calm and collected while being so brazen, he got away with it. Even people who saw him take things, could not believe that he was actually stealing and imagined that there must be some logical explanation for the act that they had witnessed. He would do anything for a laugh. One of his favourite pranks was to put a pebble into the hub cap of a parked car. The driver would hear the odd tinkling noise whilst driving, but when stationary, nothing could be heard. It often took several days of searching before they found out what was causing the noise, but even that little trick was preferable to him hiding a kipper in the engine, for as the kipper slowly cooked next to the hot engine the smell would gradually pervade the car and would linger for weeks.

"Right, I think I've got the round right," said Tuby cheerfully as he placed the metal tray which was loaded with an assortment of drinks onto the pub table and began to distribute them, "Gin and tonic for you Mary and a sweet cider for Pam. That'll put hairs on your chest Pam." He added winking and smiling at her slight embarrassment.

As he handed the girls their drinks, we, the young men at the table helped ourselves to the pints of beer and began to drink heartily.

"Took your time getting the drinks didn't you?" Mitch joked, "I thought I'd die of thirst waiting for you to get the round in."

"Cobblers! It's like a rugby scrum up at the bar. Let's see if you can do any better when it's your turn." Tuby replied as he sat down and lifted his pint to his lips and then added, "Cheers everyone!"

It was Saturday night and a group of us from Briggs had gathered in a lively local free and easy pub and we were intent on having a good time after a week of hard work. The group consisted of Starlin, Tuby, Scotty, Mitch and I, along with my wife Pam and Mitch's latest girlfriend Mary.

We drank, talked, joked and occasionally listened to the volunteer singers who got up to sing along with the resident three piece band. The pubs large lounge room in which we sat was a popular venue in the district as with live music and a continual stream of volunteer singers it was the ideal place for a man to take his wife too on a Saturday night.

"So, are we all coming round to your house for a night cap after this then Tuby?" Mitch asked, half joking as closing time loomed and everyone around the table had grown more relaxed and had slipped into a party mood. Tuby's house was the nearest to the pub and if we were going to carry on enjoying ourselves, his home was the obvious place to do it in. Although he still lived with his parents, they would not object to him bringing a few friends around to party till the early hours as they themselves would have spent the evening in the local working men's club and would still be in a merry mood.

Tuby's reaction to the request was too simply to say, "I don't mind, but I've not got much booze and I can't afford to buy any more either."

On hearing this Scotty jumped up and said quite cheerily, "Leave it to me. I'll see what I can do." He then picked up a round tray and proceeded to visit every table in the large place and asked the patrons to, "Dig deep, show your appreciation for the band; you know they're worth a bob or two."

Now the band was actually paid for by the gaffer of the pub and it didn't rely on tips from the audience and most of the people in the room knew this and yet after hearing Scotty's hearty request, they still put money onto the tray and as we watched this open display of fraud we wondered just how long it would be before the gaffer noticed what was going on and threw Scotty out on his ear, but much to our surprise, nothing of the sort happened. After saying, "I'll see you all at Tuby's house," Scotty walked out of the pub with a pocket full of cash and went to a nearby off licence. There he purchased a quantity of drinks and met us later at Tuby's house. There was more than enough for everyone and the party went on well into the night.

Much to his mother's consternation, Scotty had always had this unpredictable devilish impulse. She and her husband were a hard working, moral and law-abiding couple and were devout Roman Catholics. His mother was an intelligent woman and worked in the accounts department of a large organisation and just like her husband, had never had a day off work unless it was absolutely necessary and so the reason for Scotty's persistent devilish behaviour was just as mystifying and foreign to her as anyone else.

He had an older sister who was studious, conservative and even a little dull when compared with him, so whatever it was that made him the way he was, it certainly wasn't anything to do with his upbringing. Where his impish gene had come from was anybody's guess, but it had been there from birth for he'd been into mischief from the day he could walk and by the time he was ten, he was known to most of his neighbours as public enemy number one.

"I hear Manfred Man is coming to the Odeon" Starlin said as Scotty passed through the general stores while on his way to kick a ball about in the company's back yard.

"Yes I know." Scotty answered, "I saw it advertised in the paper."

"Are you going to see them then?"

"Yeah, as soon as the tickets go on sale, I'll be there."

The reason behind Starlin's enquiry was that Paul Jones, who was the lead singer in the popular Manfred Mann group, was the spitting image of Scotty, or to put it another way, Scotty looked very much like Paul Jones. They were as alike as identical twins and being aware of this, Scotty took full advantage of it and on many occasions he'd pretended to be the pop singer and as he looked the same and dressed in the same fashionable clothes, he found it quite easy to get away with the deception. On the day of the ticket sale, Scotty, along with a couple of his mates casually approached the long queue of teenagers that had formed outside the Odeon cinema in New Street where the Manfred Mann pop group were to appear and within seconds the whole area was thrown into confusion. The queue of teenagers, which had been exited, but orderly, was thrown into utter chaos by Scotty's casual approach as many mistook him for Paul

Jones and when he began to sign any piece of paper that was put in front of him with an imitation of Paul Jones's signature, the queue completely disintegrated and the police had to intervene to bring back a semblance of order.

A local reporter eventually brought Paul Jones and Scotty together and a photograph of them smiling happily and standing together appeared in the Birmingham Evening Mail. What Paul Jones thought about this brazen act of imitation was never recorded, but as Scotty never received a Christmas card from him, everyone assumed that he was not at all pleased about it.

As for Scotty, he took full advantage of the situation as usual and just carried on fooling the numerous woolly-brained teenage girls that wanted to believe that he was the famous pop star. How many of these girls actually carried on believing that they had slept with the singer Paul Jones will never be known, but it seems likely that many did, as Scotty was more than happy to spin a convincing tale to a love struck mesmerised teenage pop fan to obtain a bit of carnal lusting.

"I hope you've remembered that it's Mom's birthday in two days' time." Scotty's sister reminded him and indicated that he would be expected to present his mother with a suitable birthday present.

This unexpected news posed a problem for him, as he was stony broke. But he remedied this oversight of bad financial management by stealing an expensive boxed set of cutlery from a reputable city centre store. On receiving this grand present his mother, was highly suspicious and thought that it might have been stolen, but of course she could not prove it and had to compromise. She put the cutlery set on top of her wardrobe and because of her suspicions, vowed never to use it.

Two years later Scotty's sister brought home for Sunday tea her new boyfriend and for the special occasion laid out on the front room table was a crisp new tablecloth, a large fruitcake, a delicious looking bowl of trifle, a large plate of triangular cut salmon sandwiches, delicate china cups and saucers and much to Scotty's amusement, the expensive cutlery that had been lying in its box on top of the wardrobe.

On another occasion, he took a day off from his mundane office activities and spent the day helping a friend to deliver bread, cakes and pastries to a number of shops in Birmingham. After completing the deliveries, Scotty's friend, informed him that he was going to stop off at the Lewis's department store in the city centre where he had a bank account and where he wished to make a withdrawal.

They parked in busy Bull Street and casually entered the large store wearing brown cow gowns, which was the usual attire for bakers delivery men and the storemen who worked at the department store and before they had reached the bank, they were stopped twice by members of the public and asked for directions to different departments.

"Take the lift to the fourth floor and walk across to the other side of the building." Scotty confidently informed one flustered middle aged woman who was asking for directions to the shoe department.

"How do you know where the shoe department is?" His friend asked as the grateful woman toddled off towards the lifts.

"I don't," Was Scotty's reply, "But it must be up there somewhere."

"She'll have your guts for garters if she sees you again." His friend warned shaking his head in disbelief.

"No she won't," Scotty replied confidently, "She'll just assume that she hadn't been listening properly and got mixed up."

At the bank there was a long queue waiting to be served and Scotty, as impatient as ever, wondered off to explore the stores numerous departments while his friend waited patiently in the long queue.

Scotty eventually found himself in the ladies lingerie department and there he spied and instantly decided to pick up a ladies mannequin, that was on a display stand along with two others and was prettily adorned with a black bra and matching frilly knickers. He lifted the mannequin off the display stand, put it across his shoulder and promptly carried it through the department and down the wide staircase to the ground floor. He manoeuvred it through the large plate glass doors and into the busy street and stood the scantily clad mannequin up in the middle of the pavement and walked calmly back into the store and once more disappeared among the shoppers.

Many people had seen him carry out this act, but because of his cow gown and open approach, assumed that he must be one of Lewis's storemen and was working under orders.

When his friend had finished his business with the bank, he skipped lightly back down the stairs and stepped out into the busy street where he saw surprised pedestrians sniggering and skirting around the scantily clad mannequin that was standing on the pavement and he knew immediately who was responsible. He raced over to his parked van, saw that Scotty was already sitting in it and immediately drove away from the store as quickly as possible. As soon they were at safe distance from the store, he rounded on Scotty and said sharply, "You daft bugger, you could have got us both arrested, prating about like that!"

Relaxing in the passenger seat, his left elbow resting on the open window and with a satisfied grin on his face Scotty just said, "You wait till you see record player that I've got for you in the back of the van. It's one of the best."

There were three drivers employed at Briggs when I joined the company and one was a big barrel chested young man named Tony. He participated in weight lifting exercises in his spare time and his large muscular body gave him a formidable presence and just like all muscular body builders he looked very impressive when posing in swimming trunks, but bulky and awkward when dressed in a suit. With a body like his he had no trouble in acquiring a part time job as a doorman at the Rum Runner, a recently opened city centre night club and as he was employed there for several years it turned out to be handy for me and my mates when we visited the place on a Friday night as we gained entrance without paying. He was an easy going young man and his pride and joy was his Ford Zephyr two-tone car, which he religiously cleaned and polished almost every day of the week. It was an activity that completely puzzled me. Even when I eventually owned a car I never washed it more than four times a year, if that.

He seemed to be a level-headed sort of a chap and because of his muscular body, I assumed that he would be assertive and confident as well as being useful in a fight, so I was quite surprised when one day after having a few beers in a local pub, we walked into the gents toilets and he disappeared into a cubical to urinate while I used the urinal as usual. After seeing my surprise at this unexpected behaviour, he explained that for some psychological reason, he could not urinate whilst standing next to another man even though he knew them and that he was very self-conscious concerning many things and that is why he'd taken up body building. He thought that having a body that others admired, he would not only attain respect, but the self-esteem and the confidence that he sorely lacked, but so far it hadn't completely worked.

He was probably suffering from shy bladder syndrome and which is quite treatable, but I could never imagine big muscular Tony ever going anywhere near a doctor and explaining his embarrassing symptoms. After learning of this hidden secret, I retained a suspicion of all body builders and forever wondered just what psychological weakness they were hiding just as I do when I see men sporting an abundance of tattoos and swaggering along the street with ferocious dogs.

When Tony left the company for a long distance driving job, I was quick to put Billy's name forward as a replacement and within a few days, Billy became the new delivery driver for the seven ton lorry. He still lived in the back street terraced house along with his sister and her family as for now it suited him. Having a pack of sandwiches ready for him when he went to work in the morning and a hot meal when he arrived home in the evening was much to his liking. His clothes were regularly washed and ironed and the weekly rent was a reasonable sum to pay for such a service. Having been brought up in the midst of a large poor family where everything, food, clothes and space had been constantly shared, this was just what he wanted. He was in no particular hurry to get hitched and consequently he never went out of his way to seek a wife and for some considerable time it looked as though he would remain an easy going amiable bachelor.

Good natured Billy became a creature of habit and most evenings he could be found in the Sailors men only bar, drinking mild beer and playing dominoes and to all intent and purpose, well on the way to becoming an old man before his time. His one variation from his humdrum life was that on Wednesday night, he donned his well-worn Teddy Boy suit and visited the Tower Ballroom.

Wednesday night at the Tower was known throughout the Birmingham area as "Grab a Granny Night" as many of the women who attended the dance were married and looking for a good time. What seems to have passed unnoticed when applying this derogatory term, was that many of the men were also married and looking for fun, but what was not in dispute, was that everyone had a good time there. In a philosophically frame of mind, Mitch once stated that, "The Tower Ballroom does so much good for the community in matching up people from broken marriages, that it should be supported by government taxes," It was a sentiment that, over the years, the many who found new partners while attending the dance hall would have readily agreed with.

Billy wasn't particularly handsome or debonair, but he did have a warm personality, a twinkle in the eye and most importantly of all, he wasn't a bit fussy with whom he liaised with. As far as he was concerned, when it came to getting his end away, it was any port in a storm, and that included a fifty-year-old grandmother from Northfield who had two grandchildren and who he often took home.

His transport for these romantic occasions was the seven ton lorry that he drove during the day. He would request the use of the lorry for his Wednesday night out and I would collude with him and let him take it home under the pretext of him having to make an early delivery the following morning and although this practice continued for a long time, Mr Frank, the depots manager, never became aware of it. Like many of the unusual practices that went on at Briggs, it was generally felt by all the staff that it was best if Mr Frank was left unaware of things that might upset him and it was found that as long as the work got done and the business ticked over nicely, he didn't bother delving to deeply into the oddities that he did occasionally come across.

"Oh, by the way Jaco, on my way in this morning, I saw our seven ton lorry going up the Dudley Road carrying a load of furniture. Do you know why that should be?"

"Oh that's just Billy. He's just helping his sister to move a few bits of furniture into her new house."

"I thought his sister lived on the other side of town?"

"That one does. This is his other sister, but he's promised to work over until all his work is done, so we won't fall behind with our deliveries."

"Oh I see." Said bewildered Mr Frank, who didn't see at all and was completely unaware that this was in fact the fifth cash in hand house move that Billy had done during works time.

Next to Billy's sister's house there was an elderly couple on one side and a young couple named Victor and Jean, who had two small children, on the other. Besides the weather, Billy would discuss with them such things as pop songs, the latest films, the fortunes of the local football teams and how the kids were doing whenever he saw them.

Victor, who was a slim anaemic looking young man, who worked in a local factory and liked nothing better than to sit comfortably in front of the television, with his evening meal on his lap and then smoke a few Woodbine fags until it was time for bed. After five years of marriage, Jean had begun to feel that life was passing her by and she yearned for something that would stimulate her mind and body and make her feel happy and vibrant once more. She wasn't at all sure what she should do about it, but she knew instinctively that any change would be better than the hum drum daily ritual of housework and looking after the kids.

Niggardly augments had begun to be commonplace in Victor and Jeans home and Victor to his credit, realised that he would have to do something about it, but oddly, instead of purchasing theatre tickets, reserving a table at a restaurant, booking a holiday or even taking Jean to the local pub on a Saturday night, he turned to Billy for help.

"Here, Billy. Have you got a minute?" Vic asked as he intercepted Billy's usual evening stroll to the Sailors.

Although quite unconcerned about what the time was, Billy automatically glanced at his wrist watch and said while smiling pleasantly, "Yes mate, what can I do for you?"

"Well it's a bit awkward and I know it's a bit of a cheek," Vic said as he subconsciously rubbed his hands together as though washing them with soap and water and nervously shifted his weight from one foot to the other, "but I wonder if you could do me a big favour?"

"Yes mate, course I will, if I can." Billy answered brightly while wondering what mundane time consuming activity he was going to be asked to commit to. Although Billy was an easy going affable young man, he did like having a steady structure to his life and often found forced change irritating. Even when delivering each day, he stuck to the same routes and routine, as opposed to Mitch who would often mix his routine up to give his day variety.

"Well you know how you go to the Tower ballroom every Wednesday?" Vic said.

"Yeah?" Billy replied cautiously while being surprised and intrigued at this unforeseen statement.

"Well Jean's been a bit under the weather lately, you know a bit titsy, what with the kids and one thing and another and I was wondering if you could take her with you to the Tower one of the nights to cheer her up."

"To the Tower?"

"Yeah. Jean loves dancing and I think it would do her the world of good." Vic explained to Billy enthusiastically.

Billy was somewhat surprised at this unusual request and found it hard to digest and find a valid reason for why he should not get involved.

"I'm no good at dancing Billy," Vic continued and who was now putting all his energy into his pitch, "so it's no good me taking her is it and besides, someone has to stop in and look after the kids don't they and I know it's a bit of a cheek, but I think she'd really love it and I trust you and I know that you would look after her." And before Billy could say a word, Vic added, "I'll pay for her ticket and her drinks Billy, I wouldn't expect you to be out of pocket mate, so what do you say?"

After her initial coyness, Jean was more than willing to accompany Billy to the dance and the following Wednesday, off the pair went in the seven ton lorry, Billy in his well-worn Teddy Boy suit and Jean in her very best print frock, her hair freshly styled and her face immaculately made up.

For Jean, who had not been to a dance for many a year, her night at the Tower Ballroom was a tremendous success, she was thrilled to bits with the whole experience as it had made her feel young and vibrant once more and as for Billy, he enjoyed the evening drinking and dancing with Jean, but it did rather cramp his style. There was little point in him chatting up any other woman that evening and offering to take them home while he was lumbered with his neighbour's wife, but, as it was a one off experience, there was little point in worrying about it and there was always next week to look forward to.

But on the following Saturday afternoon, just as he was making his way back home after his usual lunch time drink, Vic stopped Billy in the street once more.

"Hello there Billy," Vic said smiling brightly, as he collared Billy at the corner of the street.

"Oh, hi Vic, everything all right mate?" Billy replied, a little startled to be suddenly confronted by Vic like this, "What can I do for you mate?"

"I just wanted to tell you that Jean really enjoyed the dance the other night Billy," Vic said excitedly, and although his face was a picture of pleasure, Billy noticed that there was also a sign of worry in his eyes, "And she'd love to go again if you can manage it, but if you can't do it next week, don't worry about it, any time will do."

Billy knew that he'd been checkmated and thought, "How the hell do I answer that without hurting his or her feelings."

So that was it, Vic not only wanted Billy to take Jean dancing again, but to make it a permanent Wednesday night fixture. Billy tried to resist and to think of a good excuse for not being able to carry out this unusual request, but being a big softy at heart; he caved in and eventually he agreed to give it a go, "Just for the next few weeks then Vic, okay?"

And so it came about that almost every Wednesday night for the next twelve months, Billy took his neighbours wife Jean, to the Tower Ballroom and on the way home, Billy shagged Jean in the cab of the seven ton lorry with her willing consent. Whether Vic suspected that anything intimate was going on between them was never established, but although it could be said that Vic was as dull as dishwater, he certainly wasn't daft and he probably looked upon it as something he'd rather not know about. Whatever his thoughts on the subject were, he kept them to himself and never openly broached the subject with either his wife or Billy and he seemed to be quite happy to let sleeping dogs lie and just enjoy his wife's new found pleasant mood.

This triangular relationship would have probably carried on for much longer had it not been for Billy meeting another married woman while delivering goods to a factory in Oldbury. It was a regular drop of his and over many weeks he'd got to know the young woman quite well as she was in charge of the goods stores and it was her job to check Billy's deliveries. She and Billy hit it off at once and were able to laugh and joke with each other with ease, which by then Billy had come to realised was always a good sign for a lustful liaison. She disclosed that her husband was a selfish, arrogant bully and that her marriage was on its last legs and by this time Billy was beginning to tire of the predictable Wednesday night arrangement with Jean and welcomed a change.

"It's getting to be as though I'm the one who's married to Jean instead of Vic," Billy explained forlornly to us during a tea break one day, "It's the same bloody thing every Wednesday night. It's got so predictable; I could set my watch by it."

"Blimey Billy! What do you mean, predictable?" Mitch said while shaking his head in disbelief, "You're the most predictable bloke I know. Everything you do is done to a bloody time table."

"Not when it comes to shagging it aint, I like a bit of variety when it comes to getting my leg over. For your information, I'm gradually working my way through the Karma Sutra."

"You mean to say that you'd willingly give up an important domino match for a bit of nooky?" I teased as I winked at Mitch who smiled knowingly.

"Well I wouldn't go as far as that," Billy replied while laughing, "But I might put it off for ten minutes."

"Oh, it takes you as long as that now does it? You must be getting old." Mitch joked and moved away before Billy could give him a playful punch.

Billy and the new woman in his life began to meet each other at weekends and gradually grew closer, but Billy was still taking Jean to the Tower Ballroom on a Wednesday night and he knew that if his new love found out about this strange arrangement, he would have some very weird explaining to do and probably find himself in a load of trouble that he could well do without. Eventually he plucked up courage and brought things to a head and explained to Jean that he'd met another woman that he liked very much and that he could no longer carry on taking her out every Wednesday night and that their dancing and lustful arrangement would have to come to an end.

He confessed to us that giving up the sex had been the hardest part, "I wasn't much bothered about giving up dancing with her," he said thoughtfully, "there's plenty of birds who want to dance at the Tower, but a regular shag on the way home was a nice little bonus and I must admit, it was bloody hard to give up, but I knew that if I didn't, something was bound to go wrong."

Jean did not give up easily; she'd thoroughly enjoyed her regular night out and she was reluctant to give it up without a fight and she began to pester Billy at every opportunity, even as far as pleading with him through a hole in the wall when he was sitting on the adjoining outside lavatory.

"There's a hole high up in the lavatory wall where a pipe goes through," Billy explained, "And when I'm sitting on the lav, she climbs onto the lavatory seat next door and starts talking to me through it. The first time she did it, it frightened the bleeding life out of me. I nearly shit myself."

"Why don't you just bung up the hole with a bit of old rag?" Mitch asked who was nowhere near as sensitive or caring as Billy.

"I can't do that can I? I can't hurt her feelings any more than I already have, I wouldn't feel right."

"Well you can hardly say that talking to you through a bloody hole in a lavatory wall while you're having a crap is very romantic can you Billy." I pointed out.

"Oh I don't know," Mitch quipped, "it's the most romantic thing that I've heard of since Bobby Parsons fell in love with his aunt Nelly and wanted her to run off with him to Blackpool."

This tangled web of intrigue that Billy had got himself involved in seemed to be on the point of blowing up and causing everyone involved some sort of pain, when out of the blue Vic and Jean received a letter from the council offering to re-house them. The house that they had been offered was on a new council estate and they jumped at the chance of moving there. Jean was openly exited by the news and suddenly became full of plans for the new house. She talked of having new furniture, how they should decorate it and what plants they could put in the garden and she even spoke of taking on a part time job to pay for it all and much to Billy's relief, Jean's hole in the lavatory wall pleadings finally came to an end.

"At last, I can have a crap in peace." Billy exclaimed with genuine relief, "For the last few weeks, I've been creeping out to the bog on bloody tip toe and yet she's still been able to catch me out there. It's like she' got bleeding radar fitted in there or something."

By the time that Victor and Jean moved to their new house, Jeans feelings for Billy had diminished a little and they eventually parted the best of friends and promised to see each other in the future, which of course they knew would never happen and it never did.

Once settled into the new house, Jean organised a regular Saturday night baby sitter and made Vic take her to the local pub and it being a new pub, it was big enough to put on regular live music and entertainment, and much to his surprise, Vic actually enjoyed the experience of becoming a regular and even began to make new friends there. As for Billy, he continued to meet his new love, but after a while, he realised that she had a secret agenda.

"I she not only wanted me to get shut of her useless husband," he explained to Mitch and me one evening after he and his girl had split up, "but she evidently had it in her head that I would be just the kind of bloke that would take on her kids and become their new father."

"How many kids has she got then?" Mitch queried, as we were unaware that there were any children involved in Billy's romance.

"It turns out that she's got three small lads and I only found out a couple of weeks ago." Billy replied while shaking his head.

"You'd probably make a very good father Billy," I joked, "don't you fancy being called "Daddykins" and pushing a pram around the park every Sunday morning then?"

"These aint just kids Jaco, they're little brats. By all accounts, they're as mad as their father. They're always in trouble with the neighbours." Billy whined unhappily, "A bloke what lives by 'em, told me that the police call around every other day to keep an eye on them."

Billy took a deep swig of his beer sat back and added, "If we'd met a few years back it might have been a different story, but I'll be buggered if I'm taking on somebody else's nutty kids and all their bloody problems."

As Mitch and I sat and imagined ourselves entrapped in a similar situation, we could only agree with Billy's analysis and we both nodded in agreement. All three of us were quite capable of getting into trouble without any help whatsoever and the last thing that any of us needed was to become embroiled in someone else's complicated marital problems, but as we got older we were to learn that it is not always possible to avoid such scenarios.

In one of Bob Dillon's songs, he prophetically states that, "The world is a changing" and that sentiment fitted the nineteen sixties to a tee. After forty years, Children's Hour was no longer on the radio as television had taken over as the most popular form of home entertainment. George Formby passed on to play his ukulele in the sky, Yuri Gagarin became the first man in space and the charismatic John F Kennedy became president of the USA.

It has often been claimed by those that took drugs on a regular basis that if you remember the sixties you were not there, but the truth was, most teenagers did not indulge in the drug culture at all and were really into fashion and music. Experiments with fashion and pop music continued unabated throughout the sixties and the fashions and fads changed so often that by the end of the decade a person could walk down Oxford Street in London dressed in a psychedelic plastic bag and wearing a dustbin lid on their head and no one would have batted an eye lid. And although rock bands were everywhere, the Beatles and the Stones stood out from the rest.

As stores foreman, I'd moved several slow selling items to the back of the store and brought forward more of the fast moving ones,

I was organising the drivers daily delivery runs with confidence, standing up for the store men when they were being chastised by self-important office staff and the overall business was doing so well that Mr Frank had even agreed to let us have a box van for special and urgent deliveries and I took it home each night and used it for my own use.

Mitch settled into his role as a delivery driver and surprisingly, he also settled down for a while with an attractive young woman named Shirley. This sudden slide into domesticity surprised us all and it came about accidentally. Eighteen months previously, attractive Shirley had married her handsome and flashy lover while living in a romantic cloud of self-deception and had naively imagined that they would live happily ever after. But, as predicted by most of her family and friends, the marriage had not worked out and had slowly become acrimonious. Shirley's flashy young Adonis had not found the constraints of domestic bliss to his liking and he ran off with a cotton brained, ripe breasted young shop girl that he had recently conquered with his exhibitionist charm. The fallout from his untimely desertion was that, Shirley, to her utter dismay, suddenly found herself all alone with her former romantic dreams in shreds and with a number of outstanding bills to be settled.

After the fairy tale marriage had taken place, which had cost her parents a fair whack of their savings, Shirley and her prince charming had set up home in a small rented terraced house and she'd diligently decorated it in a modern contemporary style that consisted of bold patterned wallpaper, multi-coloured carpet and spindly legged cheap furniture and when Mitch had escorted her home one night after dancing with her at the Cedar night club and discovered that she lived alone in her own house, it seemed to him that his dreams had come true. He not only stopped the night, but within a week he'd moved in and began to live with her on a permanent basis.

"It's great!" He said as he explained his new situation, "A bit of nooky whenever I want it and freedom at last from our Mom and Dad's constant nagging. You should try it Billy, it's about time you settled down, there must be an honest woman out there that's dying to give you a house full of kids."

Although Billy was probably more domesticated than Mitch, he was in no hurry to get married as he didn't feel confident enough to take on such a life changing scenario. He'd never been as flexible or as spontaneous in his decisions as Mitch and he felt that this was not the time to start experimenting.

"So, are you and this Shirley getting married then?" I asked.

"Do me a favour." Mitch replied while frowning and shaking his head dismissively, "Besides, technically, she's still married aint she. I couldn't marry her even if I wanted to. It's the perfect situation."

"What happens if her husband comes back?"

"That could be cosy." Billy said while smiling at the prospect, "You could iron his shirts while he goes to the pub and you and Shirley stay in and watch the tele."

"You've got a very weird sense of humour you have Billy. Anyway, there's no chance of that. Shirley recons he owes too much money around here and he's buggered off down to London with a young dolly bird. Even his own mother doesn't know where he is."

"But what if he did come back? Would she have him back? You know what women are like."

"Look if it happens, it happens. You know I don't think that far ahead. It'll be a case of, veni, vidi, vici and then, on me bike."

"What the hell does that mean?"

"It means Billy, that it's your round and tell the barmaid to fill the glass to the top because mi dad's out of work."

And so, uncharacteristically, Mitch tried his hand at becoming an ideal domestic partner. He stayed in at night with his new love and watched television, dug the back garden over and planted rows of potatoes, carrots and lettuce, fixed the broken fence, decorated the back bedroom and dutifully took Shirley out at the weekends to pubs that put on regular live entertainment and for a short while, it looked as though the leopard had finally changed its spots.

"Jaco, I've been talking to a bloke that works for British Rail," Mitch said conspiratorially, as he leaned forward across the table in the crowded pub and divulged his interesting new found nugget of information, "And he reckons that up at the Tyseley railway station, there is an enormous mountain of parcels to be delivered and they have to use outside contractors to do it for them because they haven't got enough vehicles or drivers of their own."

"So what?" I replied suspiciously as I sipped my beer. I knew immediately from Mitch's manner that I was being soft soaped for a sting and knew instinctively that I would have to tread carefully before he talked me into doing something that I would later regret. Being the foreman at the place where we both worked, I was in charge of Mitch's behaviour while we were there and I'd found myself constantly covering up his misdemeanours. The latest being a dent on the wing of his van. He'd popped into a bookies to place a bet and, being in a hurry, had left the hand break off when he'd parked the van and the bloody thing had rolled down the hill and hit a lamppost. There wasn't much damage, but it still had to be reported to Mr Frank and I had to convince him with feigned annoyance that a customer had backed into the van while it had been parked outside the premises and that they had driven off without reporting it.

"So, here's a chance of setting up our own business, that's what." Mitch answered while smiling confidently at me. "We could set up a transport company and deliver some of their parcels for them. This bloke reckons that there are thousands of parcels up there, enough work for the next twelve months without any more being added to the pile."

"Hang on, hang on." I said while holding my hands up and shaking my head from side to side. "Don't get too excited. If it was that easy, other established transport companies would be doing it wouldn't they?"

"That's just the point! They have!" Mitch responded brightly, playing his trump card, "But they can't cope. Look, you know Elvin's transport in Watery Lane?"

"Yes."

"Well, he sends a van up to the station most days, but he can't do it every day because he's got other contracts to see to and his other vehicles are all open backed lorries which are no good for this type of work and it's the same with the other companies, they are all too big to handle this kind of work. British Rail need small and medium sized vans, not big lorries and there aint enough of them around in this area. Its house to house deliveries see, not long distance."

"Who is this bloke who told you all this?" I then asked suspiciously as I felt sure that somewhere there must be a flaw in this scheme and I needed to find it quickly. There must be some missing information I thought, as the way Mitch was describing the situation seemed too good to be true.

"I told you, he's a bloke that works for British Rail."

"Yes but who is he Mitch? What does he do? What's he like? Is he reliable?"

"Look," Mitch said, sitting back with a sigh and realising that he would have to disclose his weakest card, "He's a little Irishman that works up at the Tyseley station and he helps to load the parcels onto the vans every day and he knows first-hand what goes on there."

"So he's not one of the gaffers then?" I replied with an air of triumph, pleased that I had extracted this tit bit of information out of him. I knew from past experience that he would have been quite willing to let me believe that his informant was someone from British Rails executive team, a man who had influence on company decisions.

"No he's not one of the gaffers or a foreman, but he aint daft either, in fact he's a very clever and well-read bloke, he knows all about James Joyce and Oscar Wild and things like that, he's read the lot."

"That doesn't mean that he knows anything about business, does it?"

"No, but it shows he aint just a thick labourer either. Look around you. How many blokes in this pub have ever read or know anything about Oscar Wild or his plays?"

"Look, I'm not saying he's thick," I replied as I realised that I'd never read or seen any of Oscar Wilds plays and therefore fell into the same category as the people that Mitch was referring to. Since my revelation in the Wilson Art Studio, when I'd discovered that my education was sorely lacking, I'd done a pretty good job of covering up my woeful ignorance and although I'd ploughed through many of the so called classics, which I found hard going, as yet I had not got around to Wild, Joyce or Shaw, "But where did you meet him?"

"He uses the Falcon down the road and he's in their domino team and I just happened to get talking to him one night and we hit it off.

You know how it is, we just got talking about this and that and the conversation got around to books and he seemed to have read everything that I'd ever read and a lot more. Anyway I was having a chat with him last night and he told me all about the situation up at the station. He reckons its absolute chaos there and the management haven't got a bloody clue how to handle it. He said that there are parcels in the middle of the pile that have been there for months and each day a new load arrives."

"So, we come down to the sixty four dollar question Mitch."

"Which is?"

"Why doesn't he set up his own business and do it himself?"

"Because he aint got the resources for one thing and to be quite honest, he's a bit of an introvert. You know what I mean, he's not a go getter, he's not ambitious like us, he likes the quiet life," and then laughing loudly he added, "He's not a bit like you."

"What do you mean by that?"

"He don't like ordering people about."

I couldn't help but laugh as I could clearly see the irony behind it, although I could organize most things with confidence, Mitch was the one person that I'd never been able to order about with any success. We knew each other far too well for either of us to adopt a completely subservient roll with each other. Although we had differing personalities we were intellectually on a par and having shared so many experiences, we could anticipate each other's thoughts and actions in any situation.

"Look, it might be a good idea and everything that the little Irishman has told you might be true," I pointed out, "But, there's one big, enormous flaw to your ambitious plan."

"And what's that then?"

"This mate of yours says that he doesn't want to get involved because he hasn't got the resources to do anything about it. Well Mitch, me old fruit! Neither have we! We haven't got any capital either. To put it bluntly, we've no van and no way of getting enough money to even buy a bloody butchers bike never mind start a transport business!"

"No van? Ah! Now that's where you're wrong. We have got a van." Mitch beamed, delighted to have got me interested enough in his idea to be thinking about it, "I've been thinking it over and I know where we can get a van."

"What are you on about? What van?"

"We can use the company's van, the one that you ride about in to and from work."

"What!"

"Look, I've been thinking about it all day." Mitch explained as he leaned forward once more and made his pitch, "Most days I do the deliveries on the south side of Birmingham, right?" and as I nodded in agreement he continued, "Well if you keep me on that delivery run each day in the box van, I could pick up some of the parcels from the Tyseley Station and deliver them at the same time as I'm delivering the goods that I've already got on board for Briggs's customers. They'd all be in the same area see, the company's deliveries and the railways house to house parcels."

"You're raving mad!" I gasped as I let this outrageous idea swirl around my head, "It would never work, something's bound to go wrong. You can't use another company's van to run your own business."

But, that is exactly what we did. The very next morning, I, who'd been thinking about Mitch's idea all night, rang British Rail from Mr Franks office before he arrived and asked the woman who answered my call, if there was any delivery work available for a medium sized van with driver at the Tyseley Railway Station and after a short conversation, she wrote down the details of my fictitious transport company and she not only said, "Yes," but unexpectedly added, "could you have your van there at eight o' clock in the morning?" and when I automatically replied, "Oh yes, of course we could," she said, "thank you, that will be splendid," and added, "Please send your written details to this office and your invoice at the end of each month," and put the phone down.

I slowly walked back down the creaking wooden stairs to the stores below in a confused but excited daze. I was fully aware that I was putting into motion an act that was wrong and that I should put a stop to the mad caper, but the sheer excitement of the challenge drove me on. In the back of my mind I felt sure that something was bound to go wrong and that I would find myself on Mr Frank's carpet groping for a feasible explanation and would be lucky to survive with my new career intact, but having gone this far I was determined to see where this silly prank would lead. I felt just as I had when my mates and I had attempted to extract a few bottles of pop from the backyard of the local newsagents in Leicester. It wasn't the prize that was important, but the excitement of taking part in the adventure, of doing something that was a little out of the ordinary and if Mitch and I made a little money out of the silly scheme, so much the better.

I was convinced that British Rail would soon catch on and realise that Mitch and I were not the owners of the transport company that we purported to be, but with a bit of luck, that could be several days away and by which time we would be owed a small amount of money. So as long as Mr Frank did not inadvertently stumble onto our crazy scheme and was kept well and truly in the dark, we might get away with it for a short while.

"How did you get on?" Mitch asked as he stood in the middle of the main store room while holding his delivery notes for the day which he had been putting into order of delivery, his face a picture of expectancy, "Was I right? Do they need any extra vans?"

"You were bang on." I confessed while unable to keep a wide grin off my face, "Not only do they want a van, but they want it there first thing in the morning."

"They want us to start in the morning?" Mitch exclaimed, as he had expected me to say that we would have to apply for an application form and have to wait a couple of weeks before it was approved and then added, "Bloody hell! What do you think to that then?"

Early the following morning, Mitch and I sorted out that day's deliveries for the south side of Birmingham and with the help of Billy and Starlin, we loaded the box van. Most of the deliveries were small items, a few bags of plaster, some small bags of pipe fittings, boxes of radiator valves and electrical control units and after covering the whole lot with a canvas sheet we could all see that there was plenty of room in the van for the parcels that Mitch was due to pick up from the railway station. Mitch and I had realised right from the start of our jolly caper that we could not keep it a secret from the stores staff and with that in mind we actively encouraged them to join in the fun, which to our combined relief, they readily did. The storemen not only rallied round, but enthusiastically encouraged Mitch in his adventure and wished him the best of luck as he drove off to pick up his second load of the morning.

For the rest of the day, I carried on performing my usual duties, the organising of the picking lists, the stores staff, the serving of trade counter customers, the general movement of goods in and out of the premises and waited nervously for news of Mitch's progress. I put on a brave face, especially while visiting the upstairs office when delivering or collecting the days relevant paperwork, while all the time I was stealing myself for the worst possible outcome, which would be someone from British Rail phoning Mr Frank and demanding to know why a Briggs van was delivering catalogue ordered goods to houses in the leafy suburbs of South Birmingham, or the police reporting a road accident and enquiring as to why the van was carrying domestic parcels.

"How did you get on?" I cried unable to keep the relief I felt out of my voice as I saw Mitch stroll confidently through the stores open back doorway. It was five o' clock, Mitch's usual time for returning back to base and to all intent and purpose; his return to the company looked no different to that of any other day.

"Piece of piss!" He exclaimed, a Cheshire cat grin lighting up his face "Couldn't have gone better. Picked up the parcels with no trouble at all and delivered them dead easy. The bloke at the station just said, "get a signature for each parcel" then winked and added, "if there's no one in, just leave it on the door step and sign it yourself," so it was just the same as what we do when we deliver goods on a building site when there's no bugger about, so everything was fine."

"Was there any problems at all?" I asked.

"None whatsoever and they want us back tomorrow and every day for the foreseeable future. The van from Elvin's was there and I got talking to the driver and he told me that he wouldn't be there for the rest of the week because they were too busy with other jobs. He said this one doesn't pay as well as their other contracts, so they only do the Tyseley station when they haven't got anything else on."

"Did you see your mate Oscar Wild or whatever his name is?"

"Yes he was there; he helped me to load up. Sorted out all the parcels for the same district, which was a great help. I'll buy him a drink next time I'm in the Falcon."

And so the new daily ritual began, each morning I would sort out the delivery notes for the south side of Birmingham, Mitch would load the van and off he would go, spending the day delivering both the goods for Briggs and British Rail.

Eventually Tuby and Scotty were brought into the conspiracy and while they were in the office they listened out for any sign of disclosure, but to my delighted surprise, there was none. All the company's orders were being delivered on time and Mr Frank was none the wiser and at the end of the month Mitch and I sent in our invoice under the grand title of Adam's Transport Company.

"Where the bleeding hell did that name come from?" Mitch asked as we sat together and compiled the invoice which I had type faced with the aid of a child's John Bull rubber lettered printing set.

"Well when she asked me on the phone what the name of the company was, it was the first thing that came into my head and we can't change it now."

"No," Mitch replied shaking his head apologetically, "It's okay with me, I like it. I just wondered where the name had come from, that's all."

"It came straight from the Garden of Eden mate; I just hope there isn't a bleeding serpent hiding in the long grass that's all."

"You worry too much, its going like a dream."

"And that's exactly what worries me, it's to bloody easy."

I had expected the scam to last for a day or two, a week at the most and I still saw the whole thing as a bit of a lark, but Mitch, quite illogically it seemed to me, felt convinced from the outset that this could be his chance of becoming self-employed and the longer the scam lasted, the more convinced he was that this dream would become a reality. As the weeks rolled into months, my worries increased and Mitch's dreams of becoming self-employed and independent solidified, he saw the whole thing as a natural form of evolution and as far as he was concerned, there was no way back.

"Look Mitch, we can't carry on like this," I pointed out worriedly as we sat and had one of our casual boardroom meetings across a pub table in the crowded men only bar with Billy sitting beside us, "It's obvious that eventually Mr Frank is going to find out about what's going on. Somebody's bound to tell him. When Douglas the sales rep saw you delivering to that house in Damson Lane the other day, I had to make out you were doing me a favour and you were delivering a parcel for my mother, well I won't be able to get away with that again will I? If Douglas sees you around there in the company van again, he'll know something's up and then he's bound to mention it to Mr Frank."

"So what do you want us to do? We can't pack it up now can we?"

"There is only one thing we can do. We've got to buy our own van. It's the only way."

"But we still aint got enough money to buy a decent van and pay my wages have we? Although British Rail owes us money, we will still have to wait weeks before we get it."

"I know that, but we haven't got much choice have we, we've got to get our own van otherwise we will have to pack it in. We've been lucky up till now, but that won't last, someone's bound to drop us in it. It's the law of nature, as soon as you think everything's hunky-dory, along comes someone and bangs you over the bleeding head with a shoe, isn't that right Billy?"

Of course Mitch knew that I was right and he had been thinking along the same lines for some time, but he'd hoped that we could have carried on as we were until a little more of the money that we were owed had rolled in and we could become independent. When we'd started the scam, neither of us had realised that we would have to wait three months for payment and that this was the reason why so many small businesses went out of business. We'd since learned that a full order book in any business was meaningless without a healthy cash flow.

"So, where do we get a van that costs next to nothing, but is good enough to do the job day in and day out?" Mitch asked forlornly.

"Have a word with Charlie," Suggested Billy as he supped his beer, "I'll bet he knows where to get a bargain."

Mitch and I looked at Billy and realised that he'd hit the nail on the head. If there was anyone who could get us a van at a rock bottom price, it was Charlie, but we also realised that dealing with Charlie was often fraught with complications and could stir up unknown trouble. Asking Charlie for help could have perils all of its own, but as beggars can't be choosers, there seemed to be no option for us, but to sit down and sup with the devil.

"He's not becoming a partner!" Mitch stated forcibly as he tried to think of what Charlie's terms were likely to be for helping us.

"To right." I replied forcefully, "I've already told him to mind his own business when he started asking me the what we were up to."

"How much does he know about the business then?" Mitch asked, surprised that Charlie was even aware that we were trying to run a transport business, "Have you told him all about it?"

"No I bloody well haven't!" I replied, angry at such a suggestion, "I've just told you. I told him to bugger off and mind his own bloody business."

"What does it matter?" Billy added calmly, "You'll have to tell him what you want the van for won't you? Otherwise he won't help you. You know what he's like, he'll want to know all the details and knowing Charlie, he'll be more interested in what's in them parcels that you're delivering, than running your business for you."

"Your bloody right Billy, we know what he's like and that's what worries me." I sighed, "We'll just have to make sure that he doesn't bugger it up for us," but even as I said it I knew that we had no choice. We needed help and Charlie was undoubtedly the man for the job. With his numerous wheeler-dealer contacts, there didn't seem to be a thing on the planet that Charlie could not acquire cheaper than anyone else.

"Look, stop worrying." Mitch said confidently, "You just leave Charlie to me. I know things about him that he doesn't know that I know."

"Well just make sure he doesn't talk you into him being a silent partner or something like that, that's all." I warned.

"There is nothing silent about Charlie," Billy stated smiling at his own joke, "If he ever becomes your partner, you'll know about it alright and so will everyone else."

"So, how much money have we got?" Mitch asked, "How much do I tell him we've got to play with?"

"Not enough that's for sure," I replied worriedly, "I recon we've got about two weeks wages at the moment and there won't be any more for another month, not until the next invoice is paid."

"Is it all worth it?" Billy asked seriously, "All this bloody worry and having money owed to you all the time and scrapping about for money to keep it going, it don't seem worth the bother to me."

"Of course it's worth it!" Mitch snapped with sincerity as he was determined to find a way to make this opportunity work, "Once we've got properly established and we've caught up with this three month bill lark, we'll be rolling in it."

"Well until then, and before you give Charlie all that you've got," Billy said holding up his empty pint beer glass, "how about getting your round in? I'm as dry as nun's crotch."

"And you'd be the one to know all about a nun's crotch wouldn't you." Mitch answered while laughing. He then grabbed Billy's empty glass from his outstretched hand and made his way up to the bar.

When Mitch returned with the three pints he then said, "Oh, and by the way Jaco you'd better put your artistic skills to good use and make us a tax disk for this van."

"A tax disk?"

"Yes, a bloody tax disk." Mitch stated, "Well it's either that or a label off a Guinness beer bottle stuck in the windscreen, because we can't afford to invest in a real one can we?"

On leaving school Charlie had found employment in the hotel trade, but his career had been interrupted by having to complete his National Service obligation which he found tiresome, boring and a complete waste of time. The army's regime of obey without question was totally alien to Charlie's maverick nature and it brought him into conflict with his superiors time and again. But Charlie was adaptable and within a few months he'd wangled himself, through bribery and corruption, into the camp stores and had made the rest of his time in the army bearable by trading goods out of the back door.

After his frustrating stint in the armed forces, he swapped his kaki army uniform for a black waiters outfit and spent a short time working in the city centre hotels once more, but tiring of that he moved on to delivery driving where he continually made himself extra money on the side by stealing and selling whatever he could lay his hands on. He had worked for several companies and at each he had found something that could be sold on the black market, copper pipe at one, cold meats at another and now he was delivering children's toys for a toy manufacturer, which for a man like Charlie, who was quite capable of selling snow to an Eskimo, was like manna from heaven.

"He's got more bloody toys in his house than the Lewis's toy department." One of Charlie's associates was heard to say in the Sailors one evening, "I went in just a few days ago to get the kids something for Christmas and you couldn't see the bloody furniture for toys. Boxes everywhere, they were even stacked all the way up the stairs" and as a testament to Charlie's well known character, no one in the pub thought for a second that it was an exaggerated claim.

One weekend while on leave from the army and dressed in his smartly pressed uniform, Charlie met a very obliging young girl at a local dance and they became well acquainted. She took a liking to his cheeky attitude and the carefree way that he spent his money and after numerous passionate meetings, he accidentally got her into the family way and as was the custom back then, they married and within a couple of years Charlie was the proud father of two boisterous little boys. It could be said that Charlie was not a particularly good father as, depending on his mood, he tended to be either very strict or as soft as pudding, but actually he was no worse than most men when it came to raising kids. The reason for his temperamental mood swings was that although he was very good at acquiring money, he was an abysmal failure at hanging on to it as he was a compulsive gambler and would literally bet on anything that moved, including rain drops running down a wet window pane and so his life, although full of exciting incidents, became a continual roller coaster ride of never ending highs and lows.

When he was on a winning streak, he would kit himself out with expensive clothes and would buy his wife and kids anything they desired, but when he was broke, he was often forced to scrounge bread for the table and money for the rent and although he was fully aware that his haphazard way of life was stupid, he didn't seem to have any way of stopping the endless cycle. Charlie's view of economics was based upon the belief that his treasure ship was just over the horizon and he never allowed cold logic to cloud that dream no matter how many times he hit rock bottom. His natural egotistical optimism would eventually override any caution that he had and he would once more grab at any opportunity that presented itself, whether it be legal or not.

"I know just the bloke," Charlie said brightly when Mitch explained that he required a cheap, but reliable van so that he could continue the parcel delivery business, "He's got a scrap yard down in Landor Street and he often comes across old wrecks that are worth doing up."

Mitch, a little worried at Charlie's easy going and offhand attitude said, "It's got to be reliable Charlie, I don't want to be pushing the bleeding thing through the streets of Solihull every day otherwise I might as well get a horse and cart."

"Solihull hey? There are some very posh shops in Solihull Mitch." Charlie stated, his eyes twinkling and his interest growing by the minute, "So if you come across any quality gear in them parcels that you're delivering our kid, you let me know, I'll soon shift it for you and by the sound of it, you could do with a bit of spare cash for the fuel that you'll be using."

"Never mind all that now Charlie, just make sure that the van is alright and not liable to break down every five minutes. If this doesn't go right, I'm finished and there won't be any juicy parcels for anybody. I haven't got any more money and I won't have for another month."

"Look, stop worrying. I'll see you alright. All I'm saying is, you'll still need money for fuel to run this van won't you? And if you pass me the odd parcel, now and again, I'll see that you get it."

"And how the bloody hell do I know what's in the parcels Charlie? It don't say what's in them on the delivery note you know, it only gives the address it's going to. It could be full of cheap tea towels or tablecloths for all I know."

"Look, if it's going to a posh shop its worth having a look and all you have to do is rip one corner of the parcel and you'll have a good idea of what's in it. Do you want me to come and show you how to do it?"

"No I bloody well don't!" Mitch cried with alarm, "You just concentrate on getting me a van; I'll sort out the parcels when they need sorting."

Unbeknown to Charlie, Mitch had already spirited away several parcels from the railway depot while he'd been loading up, but it had been a case of hurriedly snatching a parcel and throwing it onto the van while no one was looking and trusting to chance what the contents were.

On one occasion he had struck lucky and had acquired an electric drill, which he would have loved to have kept for his own use, but needs must and he'd sold it for less than half its retail value. But on another occasion he'd not been so lucky and had disappointingly found himself in possession a size sixteen flower patterned dress and three cushion covers which Shirley had took one look at and declared, "they're old fashioned enough to give my grandma" and she had done just that and although her grandma was very pleased, Mitch certainly wasn't. Billy and I were well aware of Mitch's occasional pilfering and we'd warned him to be careful, but with funds so tight we knew that in the same position, we'd have done the same.

Within two day's Charlie had acquired an old battered van that had been hand painted with black paint to cover up its many grazes and rust spots and we immediately christened it, "The Black Maria," a name that it retained even after I'd painted a wide pale blue stripe along each side of the van to give it a bit of status and colour. Then with the help of Briggs facilities, the old van was cleaned up and fitted with two new tyres, topped up with fresh oil, greased where needed and filled up with a tank of diesel fuel that we siphoned out of Billy's lorry and by Monday morning, it was ready to roll and fit for business.

For the next four weeks, I fooled Mr Frank into believing that Mitch was laid up with a bad back which he'd strained while unloading on a building site. "There was no one there to help him and so he had to either bring the delivery back here or unload it by himself."

And after that period was over, Mitch took the holiday entitlement that he was due and by that means, he was able to pick up loads from the railway station each day in the Black Maria and get paid by British Rail and by Briggs. During this period I still had to retain the companies good delivery record and I accomplished this by getting Mitch to pick up and deliver in the Black Maria, a few of the company's deliveries and used a storeman as a spare driver for the rest, but after six weeks, we realised that we'd gone as far as we could with the scam and decided that Mitch would have to give a weeks' notice and from then on, he would have to go it alone.

When Mitch finally cut his ties with Briggs, it was as though a great weight had been lifted off my shoulders and with a replacement van driver, I was able to organise the company's deliveries far more sensibly and as for Mitch, he was over the moon. He felt that being self-employed would bring him the wealth that he'd dreamed of and with this in mind he set about working his socks off. During the next few months he delivered twice as many parcels as anyone else and became highly regarded by all the staff at Tyseley station.

Then one day, I received a message from Mitch saying that he needed to see me urgently and so while on my way home, I stopped off at the small terraced house that he and Shirley shared. This wasn't the first time that I'd called around to his residence while on the way home, I'd dropped off cans of diesel in the past, but it wasn't something that I particularly enjoyed as Shirley was not house proud and I felt embarrassed whenever I entered the house and saw the untidy domestic conditions that Mitch was now living in.

Although the rooms had been decorated and the furniture was new and modern, nothing in daily use ever seemed to get put away or tided up. There was dust on shelves, newspapers and books scattered about the floor, ironing piled up on chairs, stockings and underwear drying on a wooden frame and the kitchen sink never seemed to be empty of soiled crockery and cooking utensils. This would be my sixth visit to the house and not once had I ever been offered a cup of tea by Shirley, which in most working class homes was usually the first question one was ever asked after crossing the threshold.

Mitch met me on the doorstep and invited me in and as we entered the small untidy living room, Shirley, adorned in a new dress and wearing full make up asked Mitch what he would like for his dinner.

"Oh, anything." He replied unenthusiastically, "I'm not fussy."

"I'll pop down the road and get some fish and chips then." Shirley replied chirpily and smiling as she squeezed past us added, "See you in two ticks." She then trotted off down the street to the chip shop. From past conversations, I'd become aware that Shirley never cooked anything other than light snacks and the only proper diners that Mitch ate now was when he visited either his or her mother at the weekend.

"So what did you want to see me about?" I asked now that we were alone in the house.

"Well, do you remember when we first talked about setting up this transport business and you said that there must be a flaw to it somewhere?" Mitch said ruefully as he handed me an official brown envelope which contained a letter that he'd received in the mornings post and was addressed to Adam's Transport, "Well here it is in black and white. We're supposed to have something called a 'B' licence and we're not supposed to operate without one."

Frowning with dreaded anticipation, I took the letter from Mitch's hand and after quickly scanning it, I said, "I've never heard of a 'B' licence, what the bloody hell is it and where the bloody hell do we get it from?" While hoping that Mitch would simply say, "The Post Office" but knowing full well by the exasperated look on his face, that that wasn't going to be the answer.

"It seems we have to attend a tribunal." He said with a weary sigh.

"A tribunal?"

"Yeah. At the transport department at Five Ways House. Evidently, I'm told, it's like an open court and we have to plead our case and if we can't get the licence we can't operate. Legally that is."

"How the bloody hell did this all come about? Who told them that we hadn't got a "B" licence in the first place? No one at British Rail has ever asked to see one."

"Elvin's Transport, that's who, the bastard has stitched us up."

"I thought you said he only sent his van up there occasionally and he wasn't really interested in the business."

121

"He does, but the bastard doesn't want any competition whatsoever does he?"

"Competition? We've only got one van and that's on its last legs."

"Yes but he don't see it like that does he? He wants to control all private deliveries in this area and he probably thinks that with the money that's going into our bank account we will soon be able to buy a better van, one that doesn't need its battery terminals bashing with a bleeding spanner every time you want to start the bloody thing." This small technical hitch had become the bane of Mitch's working day and he cursed Charlie every time he had to go through the procedure to get the engine to start.

Half joking, I replied, "Perhaps we ought to show him our bank account, that'd give him a bloody good laugh."

"The bastard just wants us out of the way."

"So what happens now?" I asked with a resigned shrug, "Do we pack it in and put it down to experience or fight on?"

"I'm not packing it in!" Mitch stated with genuine passion, "There must be a way to get that 'B' licence. It can't be that hard can it? I mean, how did bleeding Elvin's Transport get one in the first place? Have you ever met George Elvin? He aint no bleeding brain of Britain I can tell you, he's as thick as a builder's brick."

"Perhaps there was no such thing as a 'B' licence when he started up. Perhaps it's a new thing that they've just brought out. I've certainly never heard of one before."

After a pause, I looked once more at the letter and said, "You know, what we need is someone from British Rail to help us."

"What do you mean?" Mitch queried, "Who from British Rail?"

"Look, you recon that there's a mountain of parcels up at that station right?"

"Yes, that's right, there's thousands of parcels there. There's probably more there now than when we started."

"Well what we need is someone from British Rail to put that information down on official paperwork and say that there's plenty of work there for both companies."

"And how will that help?"

122

"Well, it would prove that there is plenty of work for both companies and so there is no competition between us and we could say, "We don't mind Elvin's transport being there every day as there is far too much work for us to handle on our own. We can't be fairer than that can we?"

And so it proved, when I nervously stood up at the licensing hearing, Mitch having made sure that he arrived too late to take part in the proceedings, and pleaded our case, British Rail not only backed us up with an official letter, but also supplied a spokesman who said exactly what I'd said, "There is more than enough work for both companies and at the moment we at British Rail would be happy for both companies to supply as many vehicles as they can."

"Where the bloody hell, have you been?" I snapped at Mitch as I tried to retain an air of annoyance, "I had to stand up there on my bloody own and answer their bloody questions. Where were you?"

"Sorry about that mate, I got stuck in traffic."

Although I knew it was an excuse, I was so thrilled that we'd acquired the 'B' licence that I couldn't keep a straight face for long and began to beam with pleasure.

Seeing this, Mitch asked, "Did we get it?" and automatically assumed that the news would be good.

"Yes, **we** did." I answered sarcastically, but using sarcasm on Mitch was about as hurtful as pouring water onto a ducks back.

"You beauty!" Mitch cried, "Well done, I knew we could beat that bastard George Elvin."

"Actually, I've just met him as we were walking out of the hearing and do you know what he said?"

"No, what?"

"The cheeky bastard said, "No hard feelings mate, but you have to try don't you?"

I just put the remark and Elvin's contradictory attitude down to one of life's odd experiences, but Mitch took a more serious view of it and it made him realise that to stay and succeed in this business, he would have to be just as hard and as uncompromising as George Elvin was. He realised that although George Elvin might be as thick as a plank, he was no pushover when it came to applying the simple rules of survival and would do whatever it took to safeguard his business and Mitch became resolved to do exactly the same. Working for himself had given him a taste of what it was like to be in charge of his own destiny and he was determined not give it up lightly.

It was three o' clock on a busy Thursday afternoon when I took the unexpected phone call.

"Hello" I said lightly, as, having been told by the company's receptionist that there was a young woman on the phone that wished to speak to me. I'd expected it to be my wife Pam on the other end calling to say that there'd been a change of plan for the evening and that she was going out somewhere and that I'd find my dinner in the oven, but to my utter astonishment, it wasn't Pam on the line, but Helen, who I hadn't seen for at least two years and then only fleetingly as we'd both been in the same crowded and noisy night club.

"Hello Jaco, it's me, Helen,"

"Helen? … From the Matador?"

"Well I'm not there at the moment, but yes, that's the one."

"Well I'll be blowed! How are you?"

"Not to good actually Jaco, that's really why I'm ringing. I hope you don't mind."

"No, not at all. It's good to hear from you. So, how can I help?"

My mind raced, just what the bloody hell was this all about? Helen, ringing me up out of the blue after we had not seen each other for at least two years and even then she hardly acknowledging my existence. This was truly odd, I was fully aware that Helen never did anything without a good reason and that reason was always a selfish one and I was quite sure that whatever it was she wanted, it certainly wouldn't have anything to do with my well-being. But as soon as I heard her voice, I knew that I would be putty in her hands and that I would be unable to resist her request.

"I'm in a spot of bother Jaco. Can you help me, only I don't know who else to turn to? And you're so logical and understanding."

Where the hell was this coming from I thought. Logical and understanding? As far as I was aware I'd never been any of these things when we'd been together or when apart. So was this just a cunning soft soap attempt to talk me into doing something that I would regret later. I certainly thought so, but I answered, "Of course I'll help. Just what is it you want me to do?"

"I can't talk on the telephone Jaco. I need to see you. To explain properly. Could you meet me somewhere? "

"Well yes, of course I could. When?"

"Tonight. Tonight if possible. I wouldn't ask, but it is urgent.'

Tonight I thought. What about Pam? What could I tell her? I'd just have to think of something, but not now, later. I'd think of something later when my mind was clear.

"Yes, I could meet you tonight. Where? Where do you want to meet and what time? How about the Matador?"

"No, not the Matador, there's too many that know me in there, I'm bound to be spotted and that wouldn't help. Let's make it the Australian bar, you know, on the corner of Hurst Street. It's always quiet in there."

"Okay by me, what time?"

"How about eight? Would that be alright Jaco?"

My god, she has changed I thought, she was actually asking me if the time is alright. It used to be a command. A Royal bloody command at that. Something must have really upset her for her to come begging for my help.

"Eight o' clock is fine by me. I'll see you later then."

"I'm sorry about getting you involved in this Jaco, but I really do need to talk to someone, someone who can advise me and you're the only one that I can think of that fits the bill. Sorry, I'm rambling aren't I? I'll explain it all later."

"Okay, see you at eight then. I'll be the one wearing the red carnation." Even as I said it, I knew that the joke wouldn't go down to well, but I felt that I had to lighten the mood somehow and also show her that I was my own man and no longer the simple pushover that I'd been.

After I had put the telephone down, I thought long and hard to see if I could put a handle on this unexpected turn of events. "What on earth did she mean by inferring that I'm logical? What kind of a problem could she possibly have that would need my logic? After all, she is probably the most cold and logical person that I'd ever met.

No, it must be a sprat to catch a mackerel, she's just baiting the hook to reel me in, she's going to ask me to do something that I'm going to regret and I won't know what the hell it is until I'm well and truly in the bloody trap." I shrugged my shoulders and resigned myself to the fact that until I met her later that evening, I would never know the answer to these tantalising questions and I fully expected to be lured into a trap, but, being curious, intrigued and full of male pride, I just couldn't resist her invitation.

Half an hour later, when my mind had cleared, I remembered that I would have to invent a story that would allow me time to see Helen and as I had promised to be there by eight, I reasoned that I would have to be out of the house by half seven and that a work related excuse would be best, for if I said that I was meeting either Mitch or Billy, Pam might play her face. In fact I knew that there would be no might about it, she would definitely be displeased. By now I was fully aware that she did not trust Mitch at all and to a lesser extent she did not trust Billy either and the less she knew about what they got up to so much the better. I was finding it increasingly annoying to be constantly blamed for what my two pals got up to, so much so that I'd stopped telling Pam anything at all about their romantic adventures, or to be more precise, their lustful escapades.

When I got home that evening I told Pam that the boss had asked me to do him a special favour and deliver a steam reducing valve that was urgently required at a refinery in Wolverhampton and that it needed to be there for when the night shift came on. To my surprise, she accepted my explanation without question and annoyingly, she seemed quite content that I was going out and suddenly I wished that I had said that I was meeting Billy and then I could have made a night of it. But with Helen and her tantalising problem occupying my mind, I had no time to analyse Pam's unconcerned attitude and I just put it down to her being tired.

I'd been standing on the pavement outside the pub that housed the Australian Bar for no more than three minutes when a black taxi cab pulled up and out stepped Helen.

"Hello Jaco, you're looking well." Helen said smiling, as she walked up to me at the entrance to the Australian Bar and to my delight, she looked like a model that had just stepped out of the pages of the Vogue magazine and I instantly wished that all the blokes at work could see me now, wouldn't they be surprised I thought happily.

"So do you." I automatically answered while smiling broadly and although she did look stunning; I couldn't help but notice that there was a tired look about her eyes, it was a look that I'd never seen before on her beautiful face.

We entered the Australian bar and as expected, it was almost empty. There was a young couple sitting at a table at one end of the long narrow room and a middle aged man perched upon a high bar stool who was busy chatting to the barmaid. The three customers and the barmaid gave us a cursory glance as we entered the room, but quickly carried on with their own conversations as we settled at one of the round glass topped tables. The Australian Bar had been designed to resemble an American cocktail bar and although the shape and most of the décor was technically right, the lighting was far too bright. The room was clean and functional, but lacked warmth and because of this it failed to become the romantic setting that those with the original concept had strived for. It was a place where loving couples talked in whispers and often held hands, but never became fully relaxed.

After acquiring our drinks, a small beer for me and a Bacardi and coke for Helen, which was a drink that I'd not come across before and when I realised how much it had cost, I was thankful that I hadn't, I sat down next to Helen at the round table, which was well away from the others in the room and said, "So, what seems to be the trouble?"

Helen pored some of the coke into the Bacardi, took a sip and replied with a sigh, "Where to begin?"

Hearing this sigh, I instinctively realised that I would need to be patient and that whatever her problem was, she was finding it a heavy load to carry.

"When did we last see each other?" She asked as she tried to find a relevant time to where her explanation could begin.

"I can't quite remember whether it was in the Matador or the Mayfair night club." I answered while lying through my teeth, "But it was at least two years ago."

"Ah, yes. It was just before Anton and Cato opened up their new night club, the San Tropez. I remember now. I expected you and Mitch to be at the opening, but only Mitch turned up."

I noticed and thought it odd that she had put Anton's name first when mentioning the two young entrepreneurs which I found unusual, as they were always referred to as Cato and Anton by most who knew them, just as though they were a showbiz double act, but I just said, "Well I don't get into town that much these days. I wasn't about at the time, but I've been in there since."

"Well as you know, at that time I was still seeing Cato on a regular basis. We weren't engaged or anything like that, neither of us wanted to get into anything as heavy as that, so the situation suited us both. Cato is a great guy and a lot of fun, but he's far too unpredictable. Anyway, my mind was on other things, I was managing a shop in Solihull, but I was desperate to open my own shop and I needed good financial advice and backing. Well as you probably know, Cato is the last person to ask for serious business advice, he can't sit still long enough to concentrate, he gets irritable and his mind is always on his next adventure or the next dolly bird that he intends to bed and so naturally, I turned to Anton and he was only too willing to help."

I was impressed by how accurate Helen's analysis of Cato and Anton was and I nodded in agreement, but then again I thought, I suppose I've always known how shrewd she was.

"Well," She continued, "I don't know whether you know this, but at the time, Anton, well he had a bit of a crush on me."

"So did everyone else." I pointed out without thinking.

Helen smiled and continued, "Well, of course I knew that Anton felt that way. The way he kept looking at me when he thought that no one could see him, it was obvious, but I was Cato's girl and I knew that he would never make his feelings known, as long as he thought that I was attached to Cato. But I needed my own shop Jaco, I needed my independence. Running around with men like Cato can be great fun and I have to admit that I enjoy it, but to own your own business is something special and in its way, it's far better than running around with egotistical men. It's hard to explain, but I suppose it's a bit like having a child, once born it's yours and you can shape and nurture it to the way you want it to be, which of course is the best that it can possibly be.

Anyway, I got talking to Anton about it and explained what I required while pretending to be a bit silly and naïve and claiming that I didn't know anything about setting up a business and he couldn't have been more helpful. He took care of setting up all the financial side of things, you know, bank loans and the right amount of credit, the accounts and all that sort of thing and all went well. The shop was a complete success, which I knew it would be and I was the happiest girl in the world. I was there from first thing in the morning to last thing at night, it became my obsession, I couldn't get enough of it, it was mine and I just loved it.

After a while Cato got a bit browned off with me spending all this time at the shop, I don't blame him, but I wasn't going to give it up now not for him or anyone else. So, you know how it is, we had a few arguments and in the end I told him to bugger off and find himself another tart, which of course he did. You know Cato, he didn't need telling twice. Actually I suspect he already had one lined up anyway, he usually has you know. I wasn't bothered though; I'd got what I'd wanted, my own business.

So that was that, I was free to put all my efforts into the business and by this time I was already thinking of opening another shop and to do that I needed Anton's help again. He was there on hand anyway, he was always popping into the shop, you know, looking at the accounts and checking that the suppliers weren't ripping me off. I mean, unbeknown to him, I'd already done all that, believe me, nobody rips me off, but I didn't mind him keeping an eagle eye on the business, I knew sooner or later that I would need his help again when I decided to open another shop."

She picked up her glass, drank from it and then refreshed it with the coke and with a faraway look said, "And that's when things started to become complicated."

I went to take a swig from my glass and realised that I'd almost emptied it so I put the glass down as I didn't want to interrupt her story and disrupt the flow.

"So there we were, Cato running around with a blond tart from Sutton, me running the shop from morning till night and Anton

129

waiting in the wings. Well, with me and Anton seeing more and more of each other, going over the books, checking receipts and accounts and looking for suitable premises for a new shop we became a loose knit couple. We were having the odd lunch and dinner together and well, one thing led to another and one night we finished up in bed. Quite honestly, it didn't mean a thing to me, it was just one of those things that happen after a good night out."

"It never happened to me." I thought wistfully, but sensibly I decided to keep my mouth shut and keep the silly accusation to myself.

"Well from then on I was never free of him and I realised that I'd made a terrible mistake, I mean he'd been around almost every day up until then, but now he was there all the time. I never had a minute to myself, even when he went away on a business trip, he phoned every day. Don't get me wrong, I really do like Anton, I always have and it was flattering to have bunches of roses and boxes of chocolates delivered when I wasn't expecting them, but I was never at any time in love with him and this is what, because we had been to bed together, he would never accept. He'd become infatuated and I couldn't do a thing to stop it without hurting him badly and I didn't want to do that, first of all as I said, I like him very much, but secondly I needed him. Anton may not be the most charismatic character around, but when it comes to business law and controlling finances, he's a bloody genius."

"I see," I said thoughtfully, "And did you tell him that you weren't in love with him?"

"Oh yes, several times, but he just laughed it off. I just found it a bloody nuisance, you know, it was like having a big eyed puppy following me around everywhere I went. But then two weeks ago, quite by accident, things got really serious. Cato turned up at the shop one day, I hadn't seen him for months, he turned on his usual charm, you know what he's like, said he was sorry about what he'd said in the past and all that sort of thing. Quite honestly I couldn't actually remember what he'd said in the past and it didn't matter anyway. Anyway we went out for dinner that evening, visited a couple of night clubs and ended up back at his flat above the Matador and I stopped the night. I mean, I'm a single woman, a successful business woman at that, I'm allowed to do what I want. Surely you can see that?"

"Of course." I agreed, but wondered why I was being asked.

"Well Anton didn't see it that way at all. He went absolutely berserk. Screaming and shouting at me in the shop in front of customers and staff and then he was on the telephone every five minutes, calling me a whore, a Jezebel and whatever else he could think of. It was awful."

"So what was he actually objecting to?" I asked, a little puzzled, as I knew that all the townies were quite liberal with their love lives and that Anton was a part of that culture just as much as Cato was.

"He claimed that I'd deceived him. Led him on. Made a fool of him. Ruined his bloody life. I mean, ruined *his* life? What about *my* bloody life? "

"So what's happened since? Has he calmed down? Has Cato had a word with him?"

"Cato's no bloody use, he just laughs, says I'm over reacting. He says, give it time and Anton will eventually calm down and come to his senses and that his threats are meaningless. Just hot air."

"Threats? What threats?"

"He's threatened to kill us both, me especially."

"Kill you!" I gasped and then after a moment's thought I shook my head from side to side and said, "That's just something people say in the heat of the moment. When they're het up and in a rage."

"I realise that and that's what I thought at the time. I thought, we'll he's in a rage, but he'll soon calm down and I'll be able to smooth things over and pander to his pride and make it alright again, but he said it again two days ago, when he was stone cold sober and it's scared me. That's why I called you. I just don't know what to do."

"Look, what did he actually say? Perhaps you've misunderstood."

Helen gave me a condescending look and said, "His exact words were, "We were meant for each other, you and I, you belong to me and I won't allow any other man to have you. Not even Cato," and when I protested and said that I was free to do as I bloody well pleased and that what I did had nothing to do with him, he just said, "If I can't have you, then no one will. I'll kill you first," and it was

131

all said as calm and as cold as if he were reading a last will and bloody testament."

Helen paused and then said, "I'm frightened Jaco. I've handled men all my life, idiots, drunks, randy buggers who can't keep their hands to themselves, but this is different. This is cold and calculating, I don't feel as though I'm in control of the situation, I'm looking over my shoulder all the time. That's why I took a taxi tonight, he knows my car you see, in fact he helped me when I bought it, and if he saw it parked outside here, I'm sure he'd be in here right now demanding to know why I'm with you. But I tell you this, I'll be buggered if I'm going to bow down to his requests. He's got no right to say and demand what I can and what I can't do."

"Have you discussed it with Cato, I mean he's his friend, he should know how to talk some sense into him."

"I have, but he's no use, he just thinks it's a joke, a weird one, but still a joke, nothing to get upset about."

"Well he knows him better than me, perhaps he's right."

"No Jaco, I know a joke when I see one and Anton's no joke. He's deep, he's like a bloody iceberg, you only see what he wants you to see. I was a fool to go to bed with him, but I felt sorry for him. Grateful for his help, but sorry for him at the same time, but he sees it as a declaration of love and bloody marriage."

"Well it's bizarre, I must admit, but I still can't believe that he would go through with it. I mean, I can understand him wanting you to marry him, but not killing. What the hell could he gain by that? I think he's bluffing, trying to scare you and by the look of it, it's bloody well working. As you say, he's a deep bugger and so perhaps it takes him a lot longer to calm down than most, I mean, I always found him to be a nice bloke and I think underneath, he still is. For the life of me, I just can't see Anton being violent."

"Well I hope your right, but in the meantime what do you think I should do? How do I calm him down, make him see sense?"

"Hmm, it's hard to say, but the priority is not to enflame the situation any more. Keep well away from Cato for a start. You could go on holiday, get away for a few days and then, when you get back, pretend to be ill for a few more days, which should bring in the sympathy vote and then see what the situation is after that. And then you should make it clear to him that you have no intention of marrying anyone in the foreseeable future and that you want to remain good friends."

"And if that doesn't work?"

"If that doesn't work, you've got no option, you have to go to the police and let them sort it out. And now, do you want another drink, because, after listening to all that, I certainly need one."

All the next day, I thought about what I'd said to Helen and wondered if I should have said more, but what else could I say, I understood rivalry and jealousy as well as the next man; I'd had plenty of that, but nothing on this scale. When pursuing specific girls, I'd felt jealous of other men on many occasions, even when I had first met Pam, I had been jealous of her boyfriend who I'd never even met, but not enough to threaten to kill him and it certainly never entered my head to kill her.

After all Helen had told me, I still couldn't bring myself to believe that Anton really meant what he'd said. It just didn't make sense, Anton was a clever and successful business man, he was riding around in an expensive car, wearing smart suits every day, owned several small businesses and there must have been dozens of attractive women that would be only too willing to marry him. So why had he become so obsessed with Helen, she was stunningly attractive, had an instinctive grace and dress sense it was true, but she was also cold and calculating. Couldn't he see that? If Mitch and I could see it, why the hell couldn't he?

Friday was still my regular boy's night out and so far I hadn't allowed my marriage to interfere with that. Pam didn't particularly like the practice and was always wondering what we got up to, but no matter what she said, I stuck to my guns as I was determined not to give up that little piece of freedom. Generally we met in the Sailors and after a pint, we would move on to other pubs while looking for entertainment and any girls who were up for a laugh and good time and having not found any, we would end up at a night club. As Mitch was once more the proud owner of an old dilapidated car, we usually travelled about in that, but, as he had an annoying habit of forgetting to fill the petrol tank, we often found ourselves pushing the bloody thing to the nearest garage.

Back at work on Saturday morning, nursing a slight hangover from the excesses of the previous night, I received a telephone call from Pam informing me that her mother had been taken ill and that she would be going over there for the rest of the day to sort out the housework and the weekend shopping. Pam's mother had actually been ill for some time, but she had now taken a turn for the worse and had been put to bed by her husband who was a nice willing chap, but useless at organising the household chores. As we talked on the telephone we realised that under the circumstances, Pam would probably have to stop the night to look after her mother and so we decided that it would be best if I joined her there on Sunday morning and we could all have lunch together. I not only agreed to fall in with Pam's plan, but secretly I welcomed the news, but for the life of me, I couldn't think why I felt so relieved.

It was later, when I was having a lunch time pint with my work mates before going home that I realised that it was Helen's problem that was occupying my mind rather than my mother-in-law's illness. Her bouts of illness had been going on for months which made me suspect that there was more than a touch of hypochondria involved. "She looks as fit as a butchers dog when no one's looking." I'd confided with my mates.

With Helen's problem occupying my thoughts, I decided to visit the Matador coffee bar that evening and discus the problem with Zac. Zac was an unpredictable character when angry, but he was extremely wise and canny when analysing the puzzling idiosyncrasies of human nature. I reasoned that if anyone could figure out Anton's motives and his unusual behaviour, Zac could.

It was about eight o' clock when I walked into the Matador and was immediately struck by how tatty and run down the place had become. It had been at least six months since my last visit, but I had been a little drunk and in the company of a group of mates on that occasion and I along with them had been more interested in the girls than the décor, but now I could clearly see signs of wear and tear everywhere I looked. Although the pleasing familiar smell of coffee beans still pervaded the place, I could see that a piece of wallpaper was missing from one wall, a seat cushion was badly torn and needed stitching and a rip in the linoleum had been hastily repaired with a strip of wide tape.

I did not recognise any of the bar staff or any of the customers and could see no sign of Zac and began to wonder if my journey had been in vain. Was Zac still the manager of the place? Surely Mitch would have heard if Zac had moved on and surely he would not have forgotten to mention it to me. I decided to purchase a bottle of cola at the serving bar and then make enquiries. Cola wasn't a drink that I was struck on as I found it far to gassy, but I reasoned that a bottle would be easier to hold and walk around with rather than a cup of coffee or hot chocolate while I found out where Zac was, but before I could pay for the cola, I felt a friendly slap on my back and a voice that I instantly recognised said to the smiling girl who was serving me, "On the house! This is my friend Jaco, give him whatever he wants, even the gig-a-gig. Okay?" She gave me a coy smile, but made no comment about the proposed gig-a-gig.

Turning, I saw Zac beaming at me like a long lost brother, "Where you bin?" Zac accused, a look of mock hurt on his face, "You don't come to see me no more. You think you too good for this lousy place now?"

"I don't get into town much these day's Zac," I answered truthfully, "to busy trying to earn a crust. How are you anyway?"

"Me? I'm fine, plenty of grass and plenty of gig-a-gig, what more do I need? How about you? You got regular gig-a-gig now Jaco?"

I laughed as I assumed that he was referring to my marriage to Pam and guessed that Mitch probably kept him up to date with details of my mundane domestic circumstances.

"I know why you stay away," Zac said laughing, a mischievous twinkle in his eyes, "You don't want randy Zac or sweet talking townies chatting up your lovely wife right?"

"You don't miss much do you?" I replied while nodding my head in agreement and added, "And that's partly why I came to see you."

Zac, now realising that I was about to talk seriously and probably ask him for a favour, led me away from the serving bar and over to a quieter corner of the room.

"So, what does my long lost friend want me to do?" Zac said mockingly, "If it is within my power, you shall have it. You want some smart arse put in their place?"

"Oh, it's nothing important Zac, I just wanted a piece of advice."

"Fire away."

"Well, have you heard about Helen and Anton?"

Zac looked puzzled, "Of course," He said nodding his head, "The police were here earlier. They searched the flats upstairs." It was now my turn to look puzzled, "What for?" I asked, completely thrown by Zac's statement, "Why would they be looking for Helen and Anton?"

"They weren't," Zac said and then, with a questioning look in his eyes, added, "You haven't heard then?"

"Heard what?"

"Helen and Anton are dead. They were found this morning at Anton's flat."

"Dead! … What? Both of them?"

"Yes. I thought you knew. I thought that's what you were talking about."

"Bloody hell Zac, I didn't know anything about this. I can't believe it. Are you sure? Blimey, that's a shock," and looking at the bottle of coke in my hand I weakly said while trying to joke, "Bloody hell Zac, that's took my breath away and I don't mean this bloody stuff either."

"Let's go over the road to the pub, I'll buy you a proper drink. In fact, I'll buy you two; you look as though you need it my friend."

In the pub that was directly opposite the Matador, Zac and I sat side by side on a bench seat that was well away from the bar and there we sipped the double whiskies that Zac had purchased and I explained how Helen had rung me at work during the week and how I'd met her in the Australian Bar and what she had said about Anton's threats.

"I came around tonight to ask you what you thought she should do about it and whether you thought Anton was serious." I explained shaking my head in disbelief.

"Oh, he was serious alright," Zac replied philosophically, "It seems that he strangled her and then took an overdose." And before I could ask, he added, "One of the policemen told me the details this morning when they came to look around the flats. I told them that she hadn't been in Cato's flat for at least two weeks, but they said they still wanted to look around. I think they were looking to see if there was a letter or something like that, but I don't know if they found one."

"Where is Cato? I bet he's a bit cut up about it isn't he?"

"Oh he'll be alright. He's like me Jaco, he's too selfish to let it worry him for too long. He'll soon bounce back. How about you? Are you alright? You still look a bit shaky."

"I'll be fine. It's been a bit of a shock that's all. I just can't believe that I was talking with her on Thursday night and now she's dead."

"Well you know what she was like, it was all or nothing with her. I suppose she told Anton to piss off, he saw red, lost his temper and that was that."

"I told her to cool it. Stay calm. Not to enrage the situation."

"Jaco, she may have asked for your advice, but she was always going to do her own thing wasn't she? She was her own master and she was never going to let anyone else master her and that is what Anton could never see. He wanted to own her, possess her and wrap her up in cotton wool. He wanted to own her and keep her like a bloody oil painting and she was never going to allow that to happen was she?"

Later that week, when Pam's mother had recovered from her setback and Pam was less worried, I told her what had happened to Helen and said that I'd met her by accident on the Thursday evening when I'd popped into the Australian bar while on the way home and I told her what had been said and to my surprise, unlike Zac and Mitch, she wanted me to go straight to the police and tell them what I knew.

"What good will that do?" I asked while frowning, as I was totally amazed at her request, "I only had a conversation with her. I don't know anything about what happened on Friday night."

"Well you've got nothing to hide then have you?"

"What do you mean by that? Of course I've got nothing to hide. I've just explained what was said. That's all there is to it. I told her to go on holiday, not to go and meet bloody Anton and get herself strangled."

"Well I think that you should go to the police and tell them that. If they eventually find out that you were with her on Thursday, they will probably want to know why you didn't tell them earlier."

"No way." I said quietly and shook my head. The thought of getting involved and being questioned by the police was something that I could well do without and I could not see what good it would do anyway except to complicate matters. They might think that I knew more than I did; that I was her secret lover, after all, it was a thought that I had fantasized over and as if to confirm my thoughts, Pam then asked, "Why won't you go to them? Was there more to it than your admitting? Were you seeing her regularly?"

That's what this is all about, I thought, she thinks I've been having an affair and that's why she's pushing me towards the police, but how can I convince her that there was nothing going on.

When I told Mitch and Billy what Pam had said, they both agreed that she was just trying to pump me to see if there was more to my relationship with Helen than I'd admitted and that I should forget it and keep well away from the police.

"There's nothing you can tell them that they don't already know." Billy stated, "Helen went to meet that nut case of her own free will. End of story."

"I know that," I sighed, "But why did she go? I told her to keep away from the bloody idiot for a couple of weeks. Now I keep wondering if I said the wrong thing."

"Such as?" Mitch asked surprised.

"Well not so much said the wrong thing, but should I have said more. You know, should I have taken it more seriously and seen what was coming?"

"Look," Mitch said, taking on the role of a Hollywood lawyer summing up an important case, "She asked you for advice. You gave her the best advice that you could give with the evidence that she presented you with, she ignored your advice. You've got nothing to blame yourself for. You couldn't have done anymore and neither could anyone else. Something similar was bound to happen eventually, she was to pig headed for her own good that was her trouble."

Mitch had never had any sympathy for Helen when she was alive and now that she was dead he had even less and as for Billy, he'd never liked her. But deep down I knew that what was really troubling me was that at the end of Helen's explanation in the Australian Bar that evening, the only thing that had been on my mind was whether I could take advantage of the situation and become the secret lover that Pam somehow suspected that I already was and had hinted at.

For some unknown reason, Helen had visited Anton in his Edgbaston flat on Friday evening and there she'd been strangled by Anton with her own silk scarf. They'd been discovered by Anton's regular morning cleaner. After picking up a note that had been left in the centre of the hallway carpet informing her to expect a shock and to ring the police immediately, she'd found Helen lying on the settee in the living room, the scarf still wrapped tightly around her neck and the ever thoughtful Anton, lying dead in the bath. He'd taken an overdose of pills and washed them down with a bottle of vodka and just to make sure, he'd cut both wrists to the bone. Whether Helen had been summoned by a telephone call or whether she had gone to Anton's flat of her own accord was never established, but all those that had known her knew that she would have eventually confronted Anton and demanded her freedom anyway and so most assumed that that is what had happened that evening and that the outcome was inevitable.

"If it hadn't happened then, then it would have happened a day or two later." Was Zac's view and this was the accepted view by all who knew of the circumstances surrounding the relationship between Helen and Anton, but never the less, I retained a niggling doubt that maybe I could have done more and I carried a tinge of guilt for a long time.

Pam and I carried on as before, but the relationship was never quite the same again. The Helen affair had caused a fracture in Pam's trust in me and as the years slipped by, the fissure grew ever wider. I began to notice irritating habits that I'd not noticed before and she became more offhand and irritable with me and I began to suspect

139

that she'd begun to dream of renewing her relationship with her former boyfriend who I knew still occasionally called in on her mother and was noticeably still single.

Mitch rose groggily from his bed as his befuddled brain forced him to realise that he was dying for a piss. It was late Sunday morning. He had a splitting headache, an obvious lack of balance and after visiting the bathroom and regaining a semblance of consciousness he looked around for his clothes. From his bedroom he found a trail of clothes that led, down the stairs, through the living room into the hall and up to the front door which was wide open and which allowed a blinding beam of sunlight to stream into the house and hurt his eyes.

The evidence clearly showed that he'd discarded his clothing whilst on his way to bed in the early hours of the morning and that he'd obviously been in a drunken stupor as he had no memory of doing so. He found that not only was his old car poorly parked, but two of its doors were wide open. He said that he could not remember driving home at all or even recall with any certainty where he'd been after leaving the Sailors at about ten forty five the previous evening and he concluded that somewhere along the way, he had lost thirteen hours of his life.

"I haven't got a bleeding clue where I was all night or who I've been with and by the look of how the car was parked, I must have driven home on automatic pilot." He wearily confessed.

During this period he'd picked up with two regular drinking companions, both of whom worked in butcher's shops. Jock was a young Scotsman who when drunk, which was quite often, became a kleptomaniac. After consuming a skin full, he woke up in the morning with salt cellars, ash trays, bottles of sauce or other odd nick-knacks in his pockets and had no idea where they'd come from and began to believe that some ghostly apparition was filling his pockets with these oddments. But when asked to explain why a ghost should do this to him he was lost for a logical explanation, but quite reasonably pointed out that as there were no logical explanations for ghostly apparitions anyway, he shouldn't be the one that was expected to find one.

Mitch's other regular drinking partner was Stumpy, a one legged butcher who limped about on an artificial leg. Not only was he a competent butcher, but an enthusiastic part time drummer. He'd lost his leg in a motor bike accident when he was seventeen, but so strong was his personality, that instead of feeling sorry for himself, he set about proving that he was as good as any man that had two legs and in many cases he proved that he was even better as he could out dance and out fight most men. One night, when the three drinking companions were denied admission into the Monte Carlo nightclub, he stepped forward and flattened both of the clubs muscular bouncers outside on the pavement before Mitch and Jock had a chance to get involved.

He was possessed by an impish humour and a fiery, unpredictable temper; he would turn up with un-matching shoes on his feet and explain that the shoe on his good foot was very comfortable, but that he just couldn't be bothered to change the one on his artificial leg. He had many fights, but as he was built and fought like Rocky Marciano, they were usually over very quickly. Once, he stepped out of his car in a busy London street and flattened an impatient taxi driver in full view of everyone around.

"Well, I was lost in them busy streets around Soho and I'd pulled up to read the street sign and this prat behind me kept pressing his horn."

"As it was a taxi driver, why didn't you just ask him for directions?"

"Do you know, I never thought of that?"

The three pals met regularly throughout the week and their regular pitch became The Phoenix, an isolated pub that was surrounded by large grubby factories and it was here that Stumpy accompanied a pianist on the drums at the weekends and where most of the regulars stopped for afters. At times The Phoenix was more like a nightclub than a pub and was packed with drinkers every weekend up until the early hours of the morning and the clientele often included several police officers who, as there was no one living within two hundred yards of the place, turned a blind eye to the irregular drinking hours.

Mitch was blessed with a very strong voice and if he could have remembered the words, which after drinking heavily, often eluded him; he could easily have made a living as a cabaret singer. As it was, because he sang with genuine passion, he was always being asked to sing and very often he had to make up his own words to fit the tune. Even if he hadn't completely forgotten the words, he would inevitably have forgotten in which order they should be sung. Over the years, in many venues, Mitch sang "If I Were a Rich Man" but not many ever heard him sing it the same way twice, but in spite of that, by the time he'd finished, the audience would be singing along with him, clapping in time and begging for more. There was no one better at rousing an audience and at the end of his performance; the audience were ready to follow him to hell and back.

The reason for Mitch's wild behaviour during this period was simply that he and Shirley had split up and not only was he a free agent once more, but had his own house. His former lover Shirley had gone back to live with her mother and had left him living in the small rented terraced house and as long as he paid the rent on time, the landlord was quite happy to let him live there. His experiment with domesticity had eventually failed as Billy and I had sadly predicted and he and Shirley had found themselves arguing more and more about less and less. She refused to do any housework that wasn't essential and he inevitably began to stay out more and chase after other girls.

There's no specific age when a man is supposed to reach maturity and at that time Mitch was a long way from it. He liked the idea of settling down, creating a home with a loving wife and even raising a couple of kids, but in reality, his restless personality would not allow such a scenario to develop. Only age and a lack of energy could cure Mitch of his roving eye and that for the time being seemed to be a long way off.

Mitch and his friend Jock awoke one bright Sunday morning and became aware that they were surrounded by the sounds of bird's song, children playing and lawn mowers. This puzzled them a little as the sounds seemed to be very close.

Eventually they became aware that they were not at home and in their beds, but were lying in Mitch's old car. Mitch in the front with his feet protruding through an open window and Jock, curled up on the back seat. After struggling to right themselves, they looked about through bleary eyes at the scene before them and were surprised to find that they were parked on an unfamiliar road in an unfamiliar housing estate. It was eleven thirty on a beautiful summer Sunday morning and many people were out and about, walking dogs, gardening or cleaning cars. Feeling like death warmed up Mitch croaked "Have you any idea where we are Jock?"

"Not a bloody clue mate." Jock replied, his face a dull mask that showed no significant sign of life.

"How did we end up here then?" Mitch uttered more to himself than to Jock, who had just found an ash tray in one pocket and a crumpled black Sobrani cigarette in another. Looking at the Russian cigarette he croaked, "Must have been somewhere posh" but he really didn't have any idea why they were where they were and had very little memory of the previous night.

Mitch pulled himself together and started the engine and after negotiating a few twisting roads, each one looking identical to the last, he eventually found a way out of the housing estate. Once on the main road, he eventually got his bearings and headed for the Phoenix for Sunday lunch which on that particular morning consisted of a pint of beer and a several aspirin tablets. Mitch and Jock never did find out why they'd ended up on that housing estate and after discussing it for a while they just assumed that they'd dropped off a couple of girls, but who the girls were remained an unanswered mystery.

This incident, especially the lack of memory, had the effect of frightening Mitch somewhat and it pulled him up short. After months of burning the candle at both ends he realised that he was on a slippery slope to oblivion and had to do something about putting a stop to his decadent behaviour, or at least slow it down a little. This was no dazzling bright light revelation on the road to Damascus. Mitch, for all his wild ways, was an intelligent young man and he knew long before this incident that he could not continue with this life style without there being consequences, but this particular loss of memory brought it to a head. He cut back on his heavy drinking bouts and his visits to nightclubs and spent more time in the Sailors where he played dominoes or cards with his mates. Of course at the weekend, along with Stumpy and Jock, he'd occasionally let rip, but at least during the week he was now getting to bed at a respectable hour while only mildly intoxicated.

Stumpy was the first to brake their inevitable cycle of self-destruction. After a whirlwind romance, he married an intelligent and forceful young woman who realised that although Stumpy was a rough diamond, he did have an amiable disposition and she led him away from the butcher's trade and into the lucrative business of running a popular pub. Her instincts proved right for within a few years, Stumpy and his forceful wife were running a large and popular pub in the Black Country and were adorned with gold necklaces, chains and wrist bands which at the time were the accepted signs of success among publicans.

Stumpy and his pushy business brained wife were the perfect pair to run a pub, she had a very in your face and outgoing personality and Stumpy was not only hardworking and affable, but capable of handling any trouble that occasionally occurred. Once, during their apprenticeship days, they ran a pub that had more than its fair share of petty villains and to guard the back yard, they acquired a vicious Rottweiler. Stumpy stepped into the yard one morning with the intention of tidying up a number of beer crates and the dog went for him. It bit him on the forearm and fetched blood. Instead of retreating, as any normal man would have done, he rolled up his shirtsleeves, stood toe to toe with the vicious brute and punched it into submission. He was badly bitten on his arms and legs but he came out of the fight triumphant and the dog eventually accepted that Stumpy was his master. It was an indefensible way to train a dog, even a vicious one, but Stumpy always saw the solution to any problem in simple terms and to him there was no difference between a vicious dog and a raging drunk.

Although similar to thousands of other pubs across the country in size and shape, the Sailors Arms had one unique feature, it contained a "Men Only" bar and in this small, but exclusive barroom, men could drink, sing, play cards, dominoes, belch, fart, swear and say whatever they liked whenever they liked and no one gave a monkey's cuss. Because they lived near the pub, Mitch and Billy used the bar on a regular basis for many years and on most Friday evenings, I would meet them there. The club atmosphere of the bar eventually left us with many wonderful memories of male camaraderie and examples of down to earth belly aching humour. It may not have been politically correct to allow such an institution to exist, but there are times when all the sexes, whatever their bent, need a little space and privacy to let their hair down among their own and in its defence the men only bar did that admirably. Many of the regulars were married to sharp as sciatica shrews, who would constantly snap at them when they showed any sign of independence at home, but in the men only bar these very same men were free to express themselves in any way they wished.

There was a hard core of regulars who were to be found there on most evenings. Among these was Billy's older brother Trapper who'd decided not to go to Canada and become a fur trapper after all and instead, became a fruit and veg market trader, there was a gritty elderly man named Darky Price, who because of ill health, had not worked for many a year, but who's mind was still razor sharp and who enjoyed the lucrative hobby of buying and selling any stolen goods that happened to come his way. There was Big Sid, a jovial seventeen stone drayman who had worked at the brewery since leaving school and would sink a pint of beer in five seconds flat and bang his empty glass down upon the counter before the barman had finished pulling his next pint. Wingy was a dapper well-dressed man who had lost an arm during the invasion of France in the Second World War and used his remaining hand with the dexterity of a first class seamstress. Another was Westy, whose passion was Frank Sinatra's songs and who made those that wished to sing on a Friday night, sing in controlled harmony and another character that occasionally used the place was Charlie Horne, of whom it was said, was the bastard child of a passing First World War GI soldier. The circumstances of his conception, his birth and his upbringing were shrouded in myth, but what was not in doubt was that he was a vile foul-mouthed grumpy bugger who hated the whole world and everyone in it. One crafty bugger who popped in occasionally when off duty was Webber, a young copper who, being very keen,

145

ambitious and looking for promotion, was always seeking inside information concerning any criminal activity that was going on in the area, but as everyone knew he was a copper he acquired very little.

There was also a middle aged man named Ernie Nichols. Ernie had two hobbies, one was racing pigeons and the other, playing dominoes and as long as his daily timetable wasn't interrupted, the two activities complemented each other admirably. Ernie lived in a small terraced house that had a long narrow back garden at the end of which he built a large pigeon loft and each evening he would visit his beloved pigeons and let them out for their much needed exercise. After an hour or so, depending on the weather and his mood, Ernie's voice could be heard floating softly across the back gardens calling his much loved pigeons back home as he shook his tin of bird seed rhythmically.

"Come on mi babies, come on mi babies, come to Daddy" he would fondly call, but if Ernie was running late and there was a chance that he would miss an important domino match, his mood became agitated and his language would change accordingly. "Come on you fucking bastards, I'm late! If you don't come in now I'll ring your bleeding necks!" It was a command that could not only be heard by the pigeons circling above the grey slate rooftops, but by many that lived several streets away.

Of course many of these men and others that used the men only bar also visited other pubs in the district, especially when they took their wife's out on a Saturday night, but at some time during the week they would find time to drop in for their much-needed "Men Only" therapy session.

Mitch was to become such a regular that he was still using the pub long after the men only bar had disappeared and had been consigned to history after the pub had been renovated by the brewery to make it look and feel no different to thousands of others. Annette was also there before and after the transition, she had started as a young barmaid and she was still working there when she eventually popped her clogs. As a young girl she often served in the men only bar and when it came to swearing or the telling of dirty jokes she gave as good as she got. She became such a popular barmaid and such an integral part of the place that when a new manager took over the pub one day and threatened to get rid of her and her foul mouth, the pubs regular clientele told him quite clearly that if she went, so would they.

A couple of years after the pub had been renovated, Mitch popped into the pubs lounge early one evening for a quick pint before setting off to see a midweek football match and to his surprise he found the room was not only empty of customers, but also bar staff. On hearing feminine cries of distress and the unmistakable sound of a scuffle emanating from the passageway that led to the toilets, he opened the door to investigate. There he found an angry young man in the process of strangling one of the pubs barmaids who was gurgling and rapidly turning blue. After quickly intervening and saving the young barmaids life, he demanded an explanation with the words, "What the fucks going on!"

He was informed that the barmaid was the young man's wife and while the young man had been away working on a North Sea oil rig she'd been flying her kite with several young men that were willing to show her a good time. Mitch, acting as a marriage guidance mediator finally calmed the young man down by explaining that his violent actions would only lead to a prison sentence and he would be better of serving his time on an oil rig where he would be paid good money for it.

"Then, while the daft bugger was contemplating his options," Mitch explained, "his flighty young wife, while holding her badly bruised neck, stupidly croaked, "You stupid big bastard, you nearly killed me!" To which he said, as he was fired up once more, "Don't you worry about that you bitch, there's still time" and with that, he went for her again."

While shaking his head in disbelief, Mitch said, "A whole bloody hour I was there trying to stop the dopey prat from murdering his missis, I was late for the match and I never did get the pint that I went in there for."

Eighteen months after its conception, Adams Transport continued to do well and several of the Briggs staff members were only too willing to help out on occasions. Scotty took a day off from his boring clerical duties and rode shotgun with Mitch for the day and

Billy even drove the old van for a whole week while Mitch went on holiday with his latest girlfriend. Scotty of course found no trouble at all in stealing a parcel from the Tyseley Railway Station while he was helping out on the van. The parcel he acquired was addressed to a reputable tailor's shop and on ripping open the corner of the parcel he could see that it contained many pairs of good quality cavalry twill trousers.

He offered the parcel of trousers to Darky Price who held office in the men only bar and was well known for buying and selling stolen goods. Darky declared that he was interested in purchasing the trousers and told Scotty to take the parcel round to his house and hide it in his garden shed where he'd examine them later.

The following day Scotty approached Darky for his expected payment and said quietly, "Did you get to open the parcel then Darky?"

"I did indeed and I must say Scotty, I was most intrigued." Darky replied, his crinkled well-worn face showing no noticeable expression, which was not unusual as in Darky's chosen profession a straight face was essential when negotiating a price that suited both parties.

"And are they good quality like I told you?" Scotty asked while nodding and smiling confidently at Darky.

"The quality of the material is excellent Scotty," Darky replied, then after sipping his half pint of ale he added, "There's only one problem."

"What's that then?" Asked Scotty beginning to frown as he suspected that Darky was about to try and swindle him out of his rightful payment.

"Well Scotty, although the goods are of excellent quality, I'm afraid that they are not what they seem. You see, they are not men's trousers at all," Darky explained, "they are in fact, girls riding britches and the only bleeding horse in this neck of the woods is the gypsy's cart horse that's tethered on the waste land in Landor Street."

"Girls riding britches!" Scotty exclaimed incredulously.

"That's right. So, who do you suggest I sell them to, the Woman's Institute or the Girl Guides bleeding Land Army?" Darky asked.

But as all good things come to an end, so eventually did the parcel mountain at the Tysely Railway Station and Mitch found that he was only required to be there for two or three days a week and so, with very little income coming in and certainly not enough to cover both Mitch's usual weekly wage and the expense of the fuel and the maintenance of the van, I dropped all claim to the operation and left Mitch to scrape a living out of it as best he could.

It had come to a point where I was doing very little for the business anyway and as I was still the foreman at Briggs, I felt that I was not in a position to take any more risks. A steady job looked a lot more attractive to me than a leap into the uncertainties of the cutthroat world of the transport business. From then on Mitch scouted around the West Midlands and took on all sorts of odd delivery jobs with his old van; for he was still determined to stick with his dream of independence and after six months he began once more to acquire a few lucrative jobs, enough to survive on anyway. For the next few years Mitch's business fortunes went up and down as though it were a demented yo-yo, but eventually he reached a point of safety where he was working almost every day.

Charlie was having a lean time of things and was well and truly on his uppers. As forecast, he'd lost the lucrative driving job at the toy factory after being caught taking a risk to many and by placing his ill-gotten gains on many racing certainties, he'd frittered away all the money that he'd acquired from the stolen toys. He eventually found himself a lowly storeman's job at a warehouse which was just three mile from his home and to travel there as cheaply as possible and if the weather wasn't too inclement, he borrowed a friend's old bicycle. He kept this mode of transport a secret from his wife as she allowed him a set sum of money each day for his bus fare and the old bike saved him the indignity of walking home after he'd lost the paltry sum of money at the bookies.

One grey morning while peddling away on the old bone shaker and deep in thought he was cut up by an aggressive driver in a large car and had to swerve wildly into the gutter to avoid being knocked for six. Now wide awake and a little aggrieved he peddled like fury after the large car and caught up with it at the traffic lights. Pulling up alongside the car he banged his fist on the driver's window and gave the driver a good piece of his mind. The driver, who was a large, well dressed middle aged man, wound his window down and as Charlie bent down to remonstrate through the open window, the man punched Charlie on the side of his head and sent him sprawling. The traffic lights changed to green, the car with the laughing driver moved off and dazed Charlie and his old bike was left lying in the middle of the road in a tangled heap while the busy morning traffic passed by on either side.

The following morning Charlie, who had spent the last twenty four hours thinking about the incident, was waiting by the same traffic lights at exactly the same time, hoping to catch sight of the driver in the large car. He did this for three consecutive mornings and was finally rewarded with a sight of his enemy. The large car pulled up in the stream of traffic at the traffic lights and Charlie ran towards it. The lights changed and the traffic began to move slowly forward, but Charlie was in a determined mood and ignoring the danger, he dived among the moving cars and reached his target. There, armed with an open tin of industrial grease in one hand and an old oily rag in the other, he quickly smeared the windscreen of the large car with a thick layer of grease. Unable to see, the shocked driver stopped the car immediately. Charlie then smeared the driver's window, the door handle and all the other windows before making his escape and disappearing around the corner where he'd left the trusty old bike. He rode off through the back streets laughing all the way. Although he considered others property fair game, he had a strong sense of moral indignation if ever he was crossed and he firmly believed in an eye for an eye and he was a very happy man when he arrived at work that day.

Charlie was constantly on the lookout for lucrative money making schemes and when his pockets were empty, he looked a damn sight harder and one evening, just before closing time, he hid himself in a large shop so that he could burgle it after it had closed for the day.

"When everyone had buggered off, I got out of my hiding place which was a little space behind a load of suit cases and had a good scout around." Charlie said when telling his mates the story of his desperate adventure, "Anyway I realised that I couldn't carry too much, so I grabs a holdall bag off the shelf and goes around the shop picking out small saleable items and when I'd filled the bag, I went to the back of the shop. The back door was locked of course, but I'd hoped that a key would be hanging up on a nail somewhere, but if it was, I couldn't find the bloody thing, so now I'm stuck aint I, I can't get out of the front door and now I can't get out of the back door either and there's iron bars on the bloody back window. Anyway the room that I'm in at the back of the old shop, is one of them old kitchens, so I gets a chair and some wooden boxes that were nearby and I stands on them and I cut a hole in the plaster ceiling with a knife that I'd found, then I got a broom and smashed a few roof slates out of the way and made a hole big enough for me to get through and hoped that no one had heard the noise of the broken slates as they slid off the roof and into the back yard. I threw the bag out, squeezed out the hole, climbed over the back yard gate and ran like hell."

"Charlie," Billy asked when he'd heard Charlie relate the story," Did you know that you're bleeding barmy?"

"Look mate," Charlie answered with a shrug, "Desperate times require desperate measures. I hadn't paid the bloody rent for two months and my missis was ready to kill me. So what choice did I have? It was either chancing a prison sentence or being battered to death by the missis."

Nigel was considered by all the staff at Briggs to be an oddity and in that particular environment; he truly was a fish out of water. All the workers at the branch, the drivers, the storemen, the office staff and even the boss, came from working class stock, Nigel was the exception.

Nigel had had the good sense to be born to a doting couple who were decidedly upper middle class and it not only showed in every word that he uttered, but in every action he performed. All the staff, with the exception of Nigel, had been educated at either a Secondary or Grammar school, whereas Nigel had attended a private public school and consequently he'd been brainwashed into believing that he was an officer, a gentleman and a natural born leader.

He'd gone into the school a nervous child and after years of specialised tuition and indoctrination, he'd emerged believing that he was a strong confident man that was born to rule, but unfortunately, he was as thick as two short planks and within a few weeks of joining the company, everyone realised it. All that is, except Nigel himself, for he'd been trained to accept all criticism as a sure sign of lower class envy and to deflect any adverse comments with no more than a shrug. It was as though he'd been coated with an invisible enamel shield that prevented any remarks from the lower orders, no matter how insulting or hurtful, from penetrating his beaming self-confidence.

All agreed that he would have made a first class First World War "Rupert" army officer and would have undoubtedly gone over the top leading his troops in the certain knowledge that he was immune from machine gun bullets, but as luck would have it, there was no First World War at the time and instead of leading his men to glory as he'd been trained to do, he found himself stuck at an office desk employed as a humble sales clerk and consequently he became the butt of many verbal and practical jokes. Within weeks of arriving at the company and taking up his duties as a telephone salesman, it became obvious that Nigel was supremely incompetent and a natural born fool.

Within minutes of sitting at his desk each morning he would become confused and disorientated and as a consequence he messed up customer's telephone orders, ordered the wrong materials from suppliers and constantly sent goods to the wrong address, but oddly, none of his numerous mistakes ever concerned or worried him as he was totally immune to all forms of criticism.

During breaks, he was invited to join in games of three-card brag where, unsurprisingly, he never won a hand. Whenever he was dealt a good hand his face lit up like a Belisha beacon and everyone, with the precision of well-rehearsed synchronised swimmers immediately packed their cards. His doting mother made him packs of delicate triangular sandwiches for his lunch each day and during the morning Scotty and Starlin would freely help themselves to them and by lunchtime Nigel would find that there was almost nothing left for him to eat, but although he constantly complained, he never had the wit to find a way of stopping them from distracting him and stealing his delicious sandwiches.

Whenever he walked into the local pub with his work colleagues he found that it was always his turn to buy the first round of drinks, and if he pointed out that he didn't have the necessary funds, some kind person would always lend him the appropriate amount of money until pay day. When a Centurion Tank that was being transported on the back of an Army low loader was seen from the office window trundling past the premises one day, everyone immediately accused him of ordering the wrong type of water tank.

He was fit and well-built and often played Rugby Union at the weekends with his ex-school chums or as he would say, "Played a spot of rugger at the weekend, don't you know."

After each game, as was the custom, he, along with his upper class chums would indulge in a pint or two at the Rugby Club and sing the odd filthy ditty to show that they were men of the world and knew all about the hairs on a dicky-dy-dow and on Monday morning he would enter the office and attempt, with beaming enthusiasm to include his riveting weekend experience into the general office conversation, but with little success as none of the staff were interested in what he'd got up to at the weekend. Monday morning conversations, in the office and in the stores, were dominated by the well-worn subjects of how the local football or cricket teams had fared, the drinking sessions that they had been involved in and the carnal lusting exploits that they had had or almost had and so "Rugger," politics and "hoo-ray" Nigel's childish antics with his school chums never got much of a look in.

One evening after working late, he managed to get himself locked into the first floor office after everyone had gone home. In his infinite wisdom he'd decided to go to the toilet at the last minute without informing anyone, including me, who was in the process of locking up the building for the night. The office was on the first floor and as the premises had been an old pub in its former life, the windows were just ordinary four paned bedroom windows, locked with a simple catch. It would have been quite easy to open a window, climb out onto the roof of the storeroom below, drop into the back yard and climb over the gate into the street. But instead of doing that and discreetly saying nothing to anyone the next day, Nigel telephoned Mr Frank at his home which was twelve mile away and begged him to come back and rescue him. Mr Frank had no option but to drive all the way back to the premises and release the unfortunate distressed prisoner. The following morning, after Nigel had unwisely recounted the incident to the office staff, Scotty and Starlin were unmerciful in their criticism and laid into him with unremitting vindictive glee.

"You bloody great sissy," sneered Starlin while standing in the centre of the office and pointing his finger at the scene that was visible from the back window, "Do you mean to tell me that you couldn't climb down there? A sloppy fat tart could have done that with her eyes closed."

"I don't believe it, a big strapping rugby player and he can't find a way out of this place" taunted Scotty and all the other staff enthusiastically joined in the bear baiting. The sarcastic and barbed taunts lasted all day, but they did not affect or ruffle Nigel's stoic demeanour one jot, where another young man would have considered running off to hide in the jungles of darkest Africa, Nigel sailed on through the spiteful calumny as unconcerned as ever. But one Monday morning, he inadvertently overstepped the mark as he unwisely claimed to have drunk seventeen pints of best bitter beer in the course of one day's jollifications with his boisterous upper crust "Ruger" chums. John, the office manager and the company's resident alcoholic pounced upon this boastful statement and not only challenged him to a drinking contest, but announced that all the staff were invited to attend and that they would all make a night of it.

At six o' clock on the following Friday, we all met in the local pub. It was a very ordinary back street corner pub that relied heavily upon local trade. The only time a stranger ever ventured into the place was if they were either lost or belonged to a visiting domino team. There were two rooms, the saloon bar and the so-called lounge. Both rooms were as drab and dreary as a grey day in Siberia and had the ambience of a Victorian workhouse. Sixteen staff members turned up at the pub at the start of the evening and we all crammed into the small lounge bar and during the evening plates of sandwiches were supplied by the pubs happy gaffer who looked forward to a good night's takings and to make the night go with a swing, he laid on the services of a ham fisted pub pianist for the evening. Billy and I sat together throughout the evening and matched each other pint for pint. We drank mild ale, which was a popular drink back then and which thankfully was not the strongest of drinks, but even so, after downing many pints we could not clearly remember leaving the pub, but we did remember waking the next morning and thinking, "Where the bloody hell am I?" and prophetically stating, "I'll never drink another drop as long as I live."

Billy and I were not the only ones to uttered those sentiments; as all who had taken part in the drinking competition suffered in much the same way and we all spent the rest of the weekend trying to regain some sort of normality as we were chastised by either wives or mothers for being so bloody stupid.

As for Nigel, the catalyst for all these hangovers, he'd actually flaked out after just six pints. He'd been violently sick in the back yard of the pub and had been driven home quite early in the evening by Tuby and Scotty. They propped him up against his front door and rang the doorbell and he fell headfirst into the hallway when the door was opened. His mother, doing a fair impression of Queen Victoria, was not at all amused. Again, the humiliation heaped upon Nigel's head for only managing to down six pints in the drinking competition after his earlier claims, would have undoubtedly disturbed a normal man's pride, but it never scratched his enamelled confidence. He just said in his plumy upper class voice, "Oh, I would have done rather better had I not been suffering from an awful cold, but I decided to soldier on, mustn't let the side down must one."

He eventually left Briggs and became a representative for a worldwide organisation and we never saw him again, but to be fair, we never exactly went looking for him. We didn't particularly dislike Nigel; it was just that we were from different worlds. As Mitch said, "He's a character from a bygone age, he reminds me of a stiff upper lipped hero that used to be in boys own books" and for his part, Nigel probably saw us as a bunch of rebellious peasants who occasionally got above their station.

Tuby was still living with his parents in their small terraced house in what he always referred to as "The centre of the universe" and it was here that he held his twenty first birthday party. Pride of place in the dowdy front room along with an old three-piece suit was Tuby's motor bike, with many of its worn parts soaking in buckets and bowls of oil. For this reason the party was held in the back room and the adjoining small kitchen and when Pam and I arrived, the atmosphere in the place was still a little muted. We were casual acquaintances that just happened to be working at the same company and we knew little about each other, our likes, dislikes or social life. All that was to change the minute Mitch, Billy, Stumpy and kleptomaniac Jock arrived. They'd already had a few early drinks at a nearby pub and were well into the party mood when they noisily tumbled into the house and within a short while they made sure that everyone else was in a mood to party.

Throughout the evening and well into the night, Tuby played pop records on his portable record player, which included the first Beatles LP that had recently been released and had been liberated from a local shop by Scotty. Tuby's elderly father constantly filled everyone's glass with beer and tried unsuccessfully to engage his guests in small talk, but being a manual foundry worker it was clear that he felt out of touch with his sons young brash confident friends and didn't feel comfortable until he himself had reached a state of inebriation whereupon he gave up on talking and just beamed benignly at everyone. Meanwhile Tuby's mother, who was slightly embarrassed at having a house full of strangers, passed around plates of thickly cut cheese and tomato sandwiches and slices of pork pie to keep busy and to show everyone that she was more than glad that they had come.

The everlasting memory for all of us that night was the uninhibited antics of Mitch and Stumpy. The highlight being, as the party got louder and wilder, the sight of Stumpy playing his drumsticks to a syncopating rhythm upon his outstretched artificial leg as Mitch sang and imitated the voice and sexy hip gyrations of Elvis Presley. From that night on, this group of young men from the Birmingham branch of Briggs became a band of brothers and although we had different aspirations, we were to share many more celebrations and adventures over the coming years.

One of the directors at the Briggs Building Supplies headquarters, which was based in Leicester, was keen to promote closer ties and establish friendly relationships between the staff who worked at the far-flung depots around the country and to bring this about he occasionally organised friendly sporting events where any employee could participate, or attend as a spectator and we from the Brummagem branch of the company, decided to join in two of these events. The first being a twenty mile marathon run through the beautiful Leicestershire countryside to raise money for a local charity and the second, a friendly football match between a team from Brum and a team from the head office at Leicester. When we examined our numerous bruises on the day after the match, the term, friendly, struck us as being a misleading title, but never the less, we all remembered the experience with affection.

In the marathon race I managed to finish in sixth place and as I was one of the first ten to reach the finishing line, I received an engraved stainless steel tankard for my efforts. The finishing line for the race was situated in the grounds of a mansion and in the house hot showers and refreshments were provided before the grand congratulating speeches were inflicted upon the assembled audience of exhausted runners and by now, totally bored spectators. Proudly clutching my well-earned trophy, I climbed into the company's box van which we were using for our transport that day and collapsed onto the blanket covered floor. The uncomfortable company van was not fitted seats for passengers and so we were obliged to relax upon the floor of the van as best we could.

Although exhausted, I was feeling rather proud as no one from our branch had beaten me to the finishing line. A few miles down the road however, much to my astonishment, Scotty and Tuby who were sitting opposite on the floor of the van, produced from their coat pockets, two identical engraved tankards to the one that I'd been presented with and grinning with pleasure, they held them up to the light to examine them.

"Where the bloody hell did you get those from!" I exclaimed as I knew that neither of them had covered more than ten miles before falling out of the long exhausting race.

"Oh," Scotty said casually, "There was a cupboard along one of the passages in that big house and it was full of the buggers."

Scotty's mother proudly displayed Scotty's "Winning" tankard in a prominent position in her living room and made sure that any visitor to the house not only saw the trophy, but had a full explanation of how young Scotty had run Twenty-six mile to win it. She even told me twice and I was sorely tempted to tell her the truth of how Scotty had procured his trophy, but she was so proud of his noble achievement that I just didn't have the heart to spoil it for her. As for Tuby, he sold his winning tankard to Darky Price for the price of a pint of beer.

A few weeks after the marathon trophy incident, we once more made the uncomfortable journey to Leicester in the box van to participate in a friendly football match. With pitch, goal nets, referee, football shirts and afternoon tea all supplied by the company, the whole day was a great success from beginning to end. After the match, which, because we had the services of the super striker Scotty, we won by five goals to one, we were treated to a substantial buffet in the club house and the usual hand shaking congratulations that are part and parcel of these events. Eventually, after many inane jokes and friendly back slapping, we said our goodbyes, promised a return match in the future and drove off crammed once more into the box van which was driven by Billy who was the dedicated driver for the day.

Before hitting the road for home, I took the victorious team to meet Danny Page over in Aylestone and we all ended up celebrating our win in the Black Horse pub until closing time. Danny, who'd been overjoyed at seeing us, waved us off to a cacophony of ribald friendly remarks and we merrily headed for home. After travelling a few miles Scotty then revealed that the blanket covered box that he'd been sitting on was if fact a crate of beer which he'd liberated from the back of the club house where we had played the football match and he'd stealthily concealed it in the van while we were happily indulging in the celebratory buffet.

The road back to Brum was along dark unlit winding country roads which snaked through sleepy villages and there was a distinct absence of any toilet facilities as the garages along the route were all closed for the night and with bellies and bladders full of the beer, it wasn't long before the cry of, "Pull over driver, I'm dying for a piss" was heard.

Billy parked the van by a wide grass verge in the middle of nowhere and we tumbled out into the dark night. Eagerly we stumbled over to the wild hedgerow that ran along the side of a field and there we lined up against it and began to relieve ourselves with gasps of, "Oh, that's better" and "Bloody hell, I needed that."

As we stood there, lined up in a long line and urinating freely into the wild hedgerow, the headlights of the occasional passing car illuminated our efforts for few seconds and which all but one of our number, totally ignored. The lad who did not wish to be seen, was a smart young office clerk and he made his way along the hedgerow until he came to a low wall, which was about waist high and jumped over it to find himself a little privacy. What he actually found was a six-foot drop on the other side of the wall. Pleasantly urinating into the hedgerow, we heard a dull thud as the unfortunate lad landed and an accompanying scream of pain.

As it was pitch black on the other side of the low wall, it was some time before we located the unfortunate young man who was lying flat on his back and moaning in agony. He'd sprained his ankle and was unable to walk properly and had to be supported by two unsympathetic lads who could not stop laughing but who eventually found a gateway and got him back to the van. Three miles down the road the van had to stop again, in all the commotion of injuring himself, the unfortunate young man had forgotten to relieve himself. This time however he wasn't the least bit shy of being seen by the passing traffic and he urinated quite freely up against the vans back wheel while balancing precariously on one leg.

In 1962 the Beatles released their first single "Love Me Do", the James Bond Film "Dr, No" hit the cinemas and there was the little mater of the Cuban missile crisis to be sorted out.

It had come to the notice of the Americans that Soviet Russia had been helping to construct secret missile sites on the island of Cuba and had not only supplied Cuba with several missiles, but intended to deliver many more. On learning of this audacious plan, the charismatic President Kennedy stepped up to the plate and gave both Cuba and Soviet Russia an ultimatum, which was roughly translated as, "Get those missiles out of our back yard and don't deliver anymore or we will blow you bastards to kingdom come."

The crises reached its peak when it was discovered that several Soviet Russian ships were in the middle of the Atlantic Ocean and on their way to Cuba loaded with more missiles. As they got closer to Cuba the whole world held its breath as the United States Navy swung into action and straddled the sea lanes and prepared to stop the soviet ships from reaching Cuba. The B-47s and B-52 of Strategic Air Command were put on full alert and all the US missile silos across the world were made ready. The world was on the verge of a nuclear war. A war that would destroy the structure of the civilised world, Armageddon was at hand.

While this was taking place, life at Briggs went on as normal, the staff turned up for work on time, telephone orders were taken, orders for building materials and plumbing fittings were picked out and got ready for next day delivery. Drivers continued to deliver the goods across the Midlands and from the old radio set that was sitting on a shelf in the general stores the latest pop songs were broadcast as usual and calm BBC news bulletins were issued which informed us of the current state of play in the coming conflict. Outside, pedestrians, cars and lorries passed by as normal and at the local shopping centre, housewives did their daily shopping and stopped to swap the latest gossip with friends and neighbours. From Wigan to Walla Walla, from Tashkent to Tahiti, life went on as normal and one wonders what else they could have done?

It was reminiscent of something that had happened in Germany during the final days of The Second World War. Although many German cities were being bombed on a daily basis and much of the infrastructure was nothing more than a mass of tangled rubble, the inhabitants of those battered cities still went off to work as normal and did so right up until the allied tanks rolled up the street and

160

stopped them. It would seem that people do not run around like headless chickens in a blind panic as the Hollywood filmmakers like to portray in their disaster movies.

Thankfully, the Russian ships, turned around and went back home, which was rather good news for all and right across the world Mr and Mr's Ordinary carried on as normal and continued to worry about how to pay their latest utility bill and what the state of the weather would be like at the coming weekend.

Later it was disclosed that a complication in the crisis was caused by Nikita Khrushchev's answers to questions. Being of peasant stock his speech was littered with obscenities and this anomaly caused no end of problems for the interpreters. Time and again the exasperated Americans had to decide, "Is he actually threatening to press the goddamn button or not?"

Maggie was employed as a typist, but as typing did not completely fill her working day she helped out where she could and became a general all round office dog's body. She was not exceptionally intelligent, but was reliable and competent. She was always good for a laugh and although she did not possess the stunning good looks of a film star, she did have a curvaceous figure that stopped men in their tracks and filled their minds with lustful thoughts.

Mother Nature, in her infinite wisdom, had given Maggie a body that in a tight dress absolutely radiated sex appeal. When she walked around the office, her hips naturally swaying from side to side, all the young men would gaze longingly at her voluptuous peachy rear and whenever she tottered through the general stores, she was immediately greeted with a fusillade of wolf whistles and cat calls of, "Get 'em off Maggie," and if Scotty or Starlin were around at the time, a hand fumbling grope.

William, who sat at a desk in the office taking telephone orders and enquires for most of the day, was also captivated by Maggie's voluptuous figure and he could not take his eyes off her firm round buttocks and ample breasts and he dreamed of spending long lustful nights with her. Every day as she did her various duties and passed

161

near his desk, he looked at her inviting sexy body and all thoughts of selling building materials vanished from his mind.

He was a well-built, well-educated, good-looking young man who was always well groomed and smartly dressed. He was a bit of an all-round sports enthusiast who played football, cricket and tennis and being articulate he was confident and was quite capable of turning on the charm and when Maggie gave him the opportunity, he did just that. Over several weeks he was able to cultivate a close friendly relationship with her and managed to throw in many sexual innuendoes into their conversations. A love affair between the two seemed to be inevitable, but there was a fly in the ointment, Maggie, although still very young, was married and the proud mother of an eighteen-month-old daughter.

Maggie and her dreary semiliterate husband had been raised on the same council estate and had known each other since their early school days. They'd hung about in the local streets with the same group of mates and over a period of time the members of the group had gradually paired off into courting couples. There'd been no strong romance involved in Maggie and her boyfriend's eventual bonding and what they occasionally referred to as being in love, was probably no more than normal physical animal attraction and a curiosity concerning sex. There was certainly no coming together of like minds or shared interests involved in their bonding and without much knowledge of contraception their inevitable rough and ready experiments with the sexual act had eventually got Maggie pregnant and they, like many youngsters in a similar situation, had got married not because that they thought that they could not bear to be apart from each other, but because it seemed to be the right and proper thing to do and if asked, Maggie would have undoubtedly have said, "For the sake of the kid and all that."

After a rushed wedding, Maggie and her immature husband moved in with his parents in their small council house which was just a stone's throw from where she'd been raised. Sharing a small house with a moaning mother-in-law and a henpecked father-in-law afforded her little privacy, but at that time she had no option but to grin and bear it.

Maggie was attracted to William's good looks and his charming manner, as many a girl had been before and as he wooed her constantly, she fell romantically in love with him. As for William, at no stage in their relationship was he ever in love with her, for him the whole affair was simply a case of sexual lust, but it was a lust that was strong enough to drive him to lie until he possessed her. Maggie's voluptuous body became Williams's blind obsession and his ultimate goal.

Living with her in-laws, Maggie had little time for herself and her weekly timetable was tediously predictable. Her ever moaning mother-in-law looked after her young daughter while she was at work during the day and Maggie looked after her daughter at night. Her unromantic husband worked in a nearby factory all-day and visited the local pub three times a week where he was a member of their darts team and if they ever went out together, it was usually to the local cinema or to the working men's club along with the in-laws on a Saturday night while leaving her daughter with a baby sitter. The fact that at no time during the week did Maggie ever go out on her own in the evening was the stumbling block to Williams's lustful ambitions and seemed to be an un-solvable problem. At work the sight of her body and the daily sexual innuendoes that they regularly exchanged only served to fuel Williams growing frustration and he desperately sort a solution to his problem.

One evening while having a few beers in the Phoenix while listening to Stumpy and his piano playing partner knock out a few lively numbers, I introduced William to Mitch, "Mitch, this is William. William this is Mitch," I said and nodding towards Mitch I added with a satirical wink, "He's one of the filthy rich, he works for himself."

"Oh, you've got your own business?" William exclaimed a little surprised.

"Oh I just drive a van and deliver goods up and down the country, that's all." Mitch replied shaking his head dismissively, "and not every day either."

"But it is your own van?" William asked.

"Oh yeah, it may be a wreck and on its last legs, but it's all mine."

William had seen Mitch when he'd called around to the company when visiting either me or Billy, but up until that evening he knew very little about how Mitch earned his living or his personal circumstances. During the evening William was to discover that Mitch not only worked for himself and travelled around the country delivering goods, but had inherited a small rented terraced house after his girlfriend Shirley had gone back to live with her mother.

A few days later and one suspects having given it a great deal of thought, William realised that while Mitch was out at work driving his van, which could be two days at a time if he was on a long distance trip, the small rented house was empty all day and that it would make a perfect lovers retreat. After Mitch had listened to Williams's audacious plan, which was to borrow his house for an hour at lunch time, Mitch shrugged his shoulders and said that he had no objection and agreed to let William have the spare key to his house whenever he needed it. All William had to do was to persuade Maggie to join in with his audacious plan and all his lustful dreams would come true and after an Oscar winning performance of relentless persuasive banter, he finally persuaded Maggie to visit Mitch's house with him during one of their lunch breaks.

The first time that the secret lovers used Mitch's little terraced house, for their illicit shenanigans was during a mid-week lunch hour. Maggie told the other office girls, that she had a special errand to see to and off she went and William picked her up around the corner in the box van which he had persuaded me to let him have the use of. The two lovers arrived back at work on time for the afternoons session looking a little flushed, but smilingly happily and it seemed to those of us that were aware of their lunch time lovemaking adventure that it had been a complete success and we could not but feel a slight twinge of jealousy. The ravishing of Maggie's curvaceous sexy body was considered to be as good as winning first prize in any competition and now the lucky bugger William had just claimed it.

Over the next few weeks the lovers were to repeat the same procedure many times, but because of the time restrictions that they had, it was inevitably a hurried performance and because of this, William was still not quite satisfied. So, with Mitch's ever-ready permission, they decided to take over the little house for a whole working day, from nine till five. To accomplish this they both had to ring in sick and take the day off work and luckily for them, the company had a policy of paying wages to people who were sick so long as they did not abuse the privilege.

Their day of unbridled passion was a complete success and three weeks later they repeated the experiment again. After the fifth time, alarm bells began to ring in a certain part of Briggs's office, the part where the wages, overtime and absenteeism were collated and sent to head office in Leicester. The woman who'd noticed these absent days knew nothing of William and Maggie's love affair and just reported the absentee figures to Mr Frank as a matter of course. Maggie and William were both warned separately by Mr Frank that in future they would not be paid for any time that they took off work and if he did have any suspicion of why they were both absent on the same dates he never showed it. Although Mr Frank was averse to having bad apples in his barrel, there were many times when he preferred to look the other way when he found them.

So that seemed to be that, Maggie could ill afford to take home a slim wage packet on a Friday night even if William, a carefree bachelor, could. After discussing the matter, the two lovers reverted back to the occasional lunch time quickie, but gradually the frustration of the situation began to tell. William wanted more passionate sex sessions and by this time Maggie desperately wanted William to declare his undying love for her and was waiting for him to ask her to run off with him. In her romantic dreams she could see herself and her young daughter living happily with William in a sunlit world where blue birds sang and sweet scented flowers grew in abundance. Maggie was now hopelessly in love and her dreams of living a better life with William lifted her way over the rainbow.

When Maggie realised that she was pregnant and was convinced that it was William's child that she was carrying, their torrid love affair suddenly turned from romantic dreams to reality. The sobering news hit William with the force of a ten ton truck. Devastated, he became sick with worry and begged Maggie to give him time to sort things out and for the first time in his life, he prayed hard and earnestly to all the God's that he could think of. On hearing of his troubles, Tuby, with a whimsical twinkle in his eye, informed William that, "I've heard that there's a creepy herbalist up in Bearwood that sells a potion that does the trick and would get rid of Maggie's unwanted sprog," but when William broached the subject with Maggie she would have none of it, she was determined to have William's child no matter what the future held for her.

Now unbeknown to William, who was wracked with worry, a few miles away a solution to his problem was already unfolding and ironically it turned out that Maggie's boring, but ever reliable husband was to become his saviour. The company that he worked for was in the process of moving its main manufacturing base to the new town of Telford and being pleased with his work record; the company had offered him a better position at their Telford New Town works. Maggie's husband was delighted with the news for it meant that he would have a new job, an increase in income and he and Maggie would also have their own house in a new town. As far as he was concerned it was an ideal situation, he and Maggie would now be able to settle down properly in their own little house and raise their family. He truly believed that this was not only his dream, but also Maggie's and he would have been amazed to learn that it was anything but. He also believed that in a new house and with a couple of kids to look after, Maggie would be less testy and would be happy and contented at last. What he didn't know was that the next member of his happy family was already on the way.

William was sick with worry, he was afraid that Maggie might take it into her head to leave her husband and end up on his doorstep which would completely ruin his carefree man about town life. The last thing he wanted was to be lumbered with another man's wife and child, a child that would not only be a complete stranger to him, but would bring along all the domestic responsibilities that went with it.

When he heard the news that Maggie's husband had been offered a job in Telford, he knew that his prayers had been answered. From that moment on, he ducked and dived and came up with numerous excuses as to why he and Maggie could not be together at that particular time and that it would be better if she stayed with her husband for the time being and moved to Telford with him. He confessed that he was no good for her and that he was the type of man that would always let her down as he could not accept domestic responsibility and he broke her heart.

Maggie eventually accepted that she would have to move to Telford and that William, for all his promises for the future, would never send for her. Deep down, she'd always been aware that her love affair with him was a fanciful dream and that it was bound to end this way. For William the liaison had been a lustful conquest, but for Maggie, it had been the one and only truly romantic episode in her young life and she would treasure the memory forever. She was a practical working class woman and had no burning ambition or aspirations other than to live in a "nice" house with a "nice" garden. And so she accepted her fate and went off with her hum drum, but reliable husband, to raise her children as best she could and accepted life and all its troubles philosophically. She'd had the good fortune to be born with an optimistic personality and she did not become depressed or bitter in spite of Williams hurtful rejection and for the most part, she enjoyed her new life in Telford.

As for William, he never did see his love child and he did his level best to forget that there was one, but every now and then, a guilty thought would creep into his mind and spoil his good humour. It especially affected him after he'd married and saw his own legitimate children growing up and he occasionally wondered what his secret love child had turned out like. He'd purposely refrained from making any enquiries as to what had happened to Maggie and was completely ignorant of whether their child was a boy or a girl and whether it resemble himself. What tormented him at times was whether the child was better behaved than the two selfish brats that he was now raising and one evening, with the aid of a liberal dose of alcohol, he confessed that he sometimes felt like Scrooge waiting for Marley's ghost to turn up out of the blue.

William's Achilles heel was his obsession with image. From an early age he'd wanted to stand out from the crowd and he believed that portraying the right image was the way to achieve it. His hair had to be just so, his aftershave expensive and his cloths trendy; he did not feel at all comfortable unless he was wearing the correct clothes whether it was for business or pleasure. He purchased flash cars to impress his associates and felt on top of the world when he parked in front of his golf club. He worked hard at gaining the visible trappings of success which included a detached house in a well-heeled district, a perfectly charming wife and two children who he put through university.

When the flexible credit card was introduced into the consumer society, William was the perfect recipient and he used it to the full and he was one of the first to cry foul when it all went horribly wrong and he found himself saddled with debts that he could not settle and a wife that was not only willing to label him a failure, but was quick to desert him in his hour of need.

For a short while a young attractive girl named Ann was the telephone receptionist at Briggs and as she possessed a natural warm friendly personality, she was well liked by everyone in the company. Although it soon became well known that she had a boyfriend and had been linked with him for some considerable time, it did little to stop the young bucks in the company from seeking her favours and Starlin in particular was at the forefront of those that wished to know Ann a little more intimately. He tried hard to be amusing and charming in a bid to win her affection, but she would have none of it and eventually she turned to me, who was technically in charge of Starlin during working hours, for protection when he became too boisterous with his playground antics.

I willingly obliged and after several weeks of supplying a loose form of protection which took the form of finding Starlin something to do when I caught him pestering her, Ann and I got to know each other a little better and eventually I asked her out for a date and she agreed to meet me one evening on the condition that it should be on a Wednesday evening. The reason for this condition was that her boyfriend, who by all accounts was a dour bad tempered young man, attended a night school class on a Wednesday evening and afterwards went to a pub with his mates so it was the one evening when she was free to do whatever she liked.

Her motive for going out with me was not because she thought that it would lead to a long term relationship, but simply because she was completely fed up with her sourpuss boyfriend's attitude towards her. He'd become so used to their relationship that he no longer paid any attention to her wishes and she had to endure many evenings sitting on her own in pubs while he laughed and joked with his mates up at the bar. Even though they were not married, their life together had already become tedious and stale and their conversations nothing more than predictable clichés.

And so began this strange Wednesday evening arrangement between Ann and myself. I would tell Pam that I was meeting a few work mates for the evening and then nip round to my parents' house and borrow Dad's car as I did not want to be seen driving Ann about in the company van. I would pick her up near her home and then drive out to a quite pub near Bromsgrove and there we would have a couple of drinks, a friendly chat where I would listen attentively to whatever she wished to talk about and on the way back, we'd stop for a kiss and a passionate cuddle in a secluded lay-by. This arrangement went on for a number of weeks until we realised that as we were not in love, the affair was going nowhere and we decided to end the situation and remain good friends.

When William, the good looking office salesman heard on the ever open grape vine that Ann and I were no longer seeing each other on a Wednesday evening and that our short affair was well and truly over, he made a bee line for Ann who he'd fancied for some time and he asked her out and Ann, who it turned out, had fancied him for some time, readily accepted.

The following Wednesday evening, they met and went out in William's newly acquired second hand car and later, William dropped her off at exactly the same spot and at exactly the same time as I had previously done, but this time there was a slight difference to the procedure, for out of the dark shadows stepped Ann's miserable boyfriend and what's more, he was carrying a short steel bar in his hand and murderous black anger in his heart. He dashed over to the car with the steel bar above his head and before William could react, he proceeded to whack seven bells out of the cars bonnet and as he did so, he swore loudly and declared that Ann was, "a two timing filthy bitch."

William, who, for a few seconds sat in the car watching this act of vandalism in a state off utter shock, suddenly realised what was going on and seething with rage at seeing his beloved car being systematically demolished, jumped out of the car and ran towards the steel bar wheeling maniac with the intention of ripping his head off his shoulders. On seeing this unexpected turn of events, the boyfriend, who evidently was no hero even with a belly full of beer and a steel bar in his hand, turned tail and fled as fast as he could and was never seen again by either William or Ann.

The following day, William, who understandably was a little peeved and upset at what had happened to his beloved car, confronted me in the general store and cried out in frustration, "You bastard! It was you he was after, not me! You've been taking her out for bloody weeks. I take her out once, just once, and I get my car smashed up!"

"What the hell are you ranting on about, you dopy sod!" I cried as I had no knowledge of what had happened on the previous evening and was unaware that William's car had been attacked.

"Last night! That's what I'm on about. Ann's stupid boyfriend attacked my bloody car! The bastard smashed it up with an iron bar!"

"So what the hell has that got to do with me?" I asked as I was still puzzled and still did not understand what had happened, "You don't think I told him to do it do you?"

"No you prat," William replied with exasperation, "He thought it was you! The daft bastard thought it was your car! You've been taking her out every Wednesday and somebody must have told him. I take her out just once and he thinks I'm you and he's smashed my car up."

Now that I had the facts I could now visualize the scenario at last and unlike William, I could also see the funny side of what had happened and couldn't help but retaliate with a smile and a touch of wicked humour, "Well that just shows you what a prat he really is," I quipped, "you look nothing like me. I'm much better looking than you."

"Somebody must have told the little runt that you'd been seeing her every Wednesday night and he was waiting in the bushes for you to turn up." William finally said as his frustration and angry mood gradually subsided. And as the day wore on his angry mood was to be replaced by the depressing thought of, "Why the bloody hell do these catastrophes always happen to me?"

Of course all the staff had a good laugh about the incident, but it was a long time before William was able to see the funny side of the episode.

Many of the regulars that frequented the Sailors men only bar were followers of the sport of kings, which is a fancy way of saying that they were addicted to the precarious art of working out which horse, would positively win a specific race and then place a bet on it doing so. These men would spend an inordinate amount of time working out why one particular horse would win a race and spend the rest of the day analysing the numerous reasons why it had not done so. Mitch was also a member of these horse racing experts who sort the magic formula that would lead to instant wealth and it was he, who suggested that it might be worthwhile organising a coach trip to the Glorious Goodwood race meeting that takes place in August and as Goodwood was near Brighton, they could make a weekend of it and within no time at all, forty men had signed up for the "Men only" weekend trip.

Come August, forty men from the Sailors travelled down to Brighton in a hired coach on the Friday morning, stayed in a hotel and attended the Goodwood races on the Saturday. Friday and Saturday nights were spent trawling the pubs of Brighton looking for good time girls. Sunday morning was reserved for a relaxing stroll along the sea front promenade and through the Lanes looking at the pricey antiques while they recharged their batteries and at opening time, they all meet at a designated sing-a-long pub and had a bloody good booze up and a community singing session. Actually there were no sing-a-long pubs in the centre of Brighton, but when forty ardent beer drinking men walked into a pub and began to sing, that's what the pub inevitably became and as they were such good singers, individually and collectively and could sing in harmony, the gaffer of the chosen pub and the regular customers welcomed the event.

After the lunch time booze up, they staggered back to the hotel, collected their belongings, boarded the coach and settled down for the long haul back home and face the reality of going back to work, which for many was a noisy factory or a hell hole foundry.

It was agreed by all that there was no better way for a man to spend a weekend and well worth the effort. For three days these hard working men from the industrial Midlands, who clocked in and out of work for most of their lives, tasted a special form of freedom and they revelled in it as children do on a school trip and so much so that the Brighton trip became a regular annual outing for many years and because forty men had taken part in the original trip; it became known as the Forty-Club trip irrespective of how many went.

Over the years and for many reasons, the membership of the Forty-Club changed, but a hard core of original members remained constant and Mitch, the founder member, was one of them. Billy and I went along on many of the trips and we all witnessed many amusing and often hilarious incidents and occasionally, ones that were hard to categorise.

One in particular was to stand out as it was one of the most unbelievable experiences that any of us were ever to witness and afterwards it left us with the distinct feeling of having been involved in a very bizarre dream. There were six of us, me, Mitch, Billy, Trapper and two others, Wingy the one armed ex-soldier and a head strong young man named Bronco and we were making our way back to our small hotel after having spent the evening on a pub crawl around the centre of Brighton. It was a fine Friday night and we were all in good spirits and were now looking forward to a late night tipple in the hotel's bar, before getting a little sleep as in the morning, we were off to the Goodwood races and to court Lady Luck.

We slowly walked away from well-lit the sea front and up the side street in which our hotel was situated. It was a street that had a slight incline and had a number of parked cars in it and at the top, a group of boisterous young men appeared and for no apparent reason, began shouting abuse at us and challenging us to a fight. We were a little puzzled by this as we'd never seen them before and assumed that we'd been mistaken for some other group of men. The obnoxious bunch of louts, nine in all, spread out across the road and as they got closer, they began taunting as they endeavoured to dominate us.

"Bloody hell!" Mitch exclaimed as we slowly walked forward, "It's like the bloody gunfight at the OK Corral."

It was an off the cuff remark that not only broke the nervous tension that had been building up within us, but had the effect of making us all laugh as we recognise the surreal absurdity of the situation. One minute we'd been strolling along happy and contented and the next, we were in a scene that was reminiscent of a showdown in a Wild West movie. It was as though we'd passed through a time warp along with Jimmy and his magic patch and we were now heading for the last showdown in a windswept clapperboard frontier town. This was hardly the time for laughter and levity, but somehow, along with the beer in our bellies, Mitch's remark helped us to relax as we took in the bizarre situation that was confronting us. We were about thirty yards away from the ranting yobs when, without a word passing between us, we automatically spread out across the street to take them on and for once in my life I did not feel paralysed with fear. I'd had a few drinks and had Dutch courage, but I also realised that the five friends walking beside me, were all capable fighters. Despite having only one arm, Wingy was more than a match for most men as he'd served as a commando during the war years and in one raid had actually killed two Nazi guards, so he was not only no stranger to physical violence, but had actually done what most men could only dream of.

Although outnumbered, I realised that we were not going to be the easy push over that these braying louts thought we were and with this in mind, we all seemed to draw strength from each other. We got to within a few yards of them and fists clenched we were ready for the fray. I could now see my immediate opponent quite clearly and was confident that I could give him as good as I got, when suddenly, and as if by some form of supernatural magic, the whole street, from one end to the other, became inundated with police. Uniformed police and their vehicles were suddenly everywhere. There were police men and woman, some had helmets, others caps, some on foot, others in vans and on motorbikes and they even had an ambulance in attendance. None of us had ever seen so many police personnel assembled together in one spot before other than at a football match.

On seeing this, we six instantly walked away from our intended pugilistic engagement and shuffled over to the side of the street

173

where our hotel was and looked on the scene before us in mesmerised astonishment and as we did so we were amazed to see the police move in swiftly and arrest the wild bunch of yobs that a moment ago had been taunting us with threats of annihilation.

We were to discover that this bunch of loudmouthed louts, who hailed from Liverpool, had already attacked several other groups of holidaymakers in the adjoining streets as they'd been peacefully making their way back to their hotels and the police were already hot on their heels when the louts had turned in the street that we were in. What the wild bunch had not known was that all police leave had been cancelled in Brighton on that particular weekend as they'd been informed that a notorious criminal, who'd escaped from prison some days earlier, was hiding in Brighton. They'd been systematically searching the nearby hotels when the call had come through informing them of the trouble that the wild bunch were causing and that was the reason why so many turned up.

And really, that should have been the end of the bizarre incident. Although the street was now full of people who had spilled out of the various hotels to see what all the fuss was about, the police had the whole situation under control. But one person in the street that night was not quite ready to retire for the night and that was Bronco. Bronco was a well-built young man who was as fit as a fiddle and full of volcanic energy, but as well as having these admirable traits he also possessed a very volatile personality and even on the very best of days, he could be wildly unpredictable and a law unto himself.

He left us standing on the pavement at the side of the street and strode boldly through the milling policemen while saying politely to each that he passed, "Excuse me" and finally he came face to face with the lout who'd sarcastically taunted him a few minutes earlier and he hit him. He punched him full in the face with a punch that was as straight as an arrow and as hard as a pile driver and would have floored any man no matter how big he was.

The loud mouthed lout was unconscious from the instant the punch landed, as he went down backwards without his body or legs bending. He fell just as a pine tree would fall when felled with an axe. The stiff as a board, pole axed lout hit the floor and all the startled onlookers heard his head crack loudly against the hard unyielding tarmacadam road and all except Bronco shuddered in apprehension and my mates and I instantly thought, "Oh my God! Bronco's killed him."

On witnessing what had happened, two hefty policemen jumped on Bronco, handcuffed him and threw him roughly into a police van which instantly whisked him off to the lock up and where we thought that he would be charged with manslaughter and become front-page news in the tabloids.

The following day, we attended the Goodwood races as planed and later, we had our carefree night out on the town, while head strong Bronco remained locked up in a police cell. The general feeling was that we would not see him for a number of years as not even a silver tongued lawyer could save him from a prison sentence, but much to our astonishment we were all proven wrong. Luckily, for impulsive Bronco and the Liverpool loud mouth, the thick sculled lout had miraculously recovered and because of this and one suspects a feeling among the police officers that the lout had deserved a bloody good hiding, Bronco faced a lesser charge and was even on the Forty-Club coach when it left Brighton late on the Sunday afternoon.

The first time Bronco went on a Forty-Club trip, almost every other member, especially Mitch, Billy and I tried our level best to avoid him when we went out on the town on the Friday evening. The reason for this boycott wasn't that any of us disliked Bronco, but we all felt that he would cramp our style. We were all well aware that Bronco could be loud at times, but the reason for our combined reluctance to associate with him that evening was there for all to see.

Back in Brum, he had taken on the role of master of ceremonies at a pub that put on regular entertainment at the weekend and he now believed that he was a wonderful effervescent entertainer and hilarious comedian and to help him in his act he had a bright red blazer which he'd adorned with dozens of beer mats that advertised numerous drinks.

He believed that this jacket not only made everyone who saw it laugh, but gave him the right to organise everyone he met into an audience for his side-splitting comical stage performance. His slap stick routine worked well for the inebriated regulars who frequented the Red Lion back in Brum on a Saturday night, but it did little to impress me and my mates when we wished to attract the attention of the elegant good time girls that frequented the hot spots of Brighton. The last thing that we required when walking into one of Brighton's many sophisticated pubs was to be accompanied by Coco the bloody Clown.

On the Friday night we three mates dodged around Brighton from one pub to another, often avoiding Bronco's shocking appearance by seconds as he tried in vain to track us down and make our night, a night to remember with his party act. His piece de resistance was actually very funny, it was an imitation of a chicken squawking and strutting around a farmyard, which we had all enjoyed seeing, but after seeing it repeated twenty odd times and each performance becoming noticeably longer, for most of us, the novelty of the act had worn off a little. The last time that we'd witnessed Bronco's chicken strutting performance, he was up to ten minutes with the chicken impression and had added pigs, sheep, ducks and an elephant into his vociferous gesticulating farmyard act.

On the following morning, Mitch, who could be quite diplomatic when he put his mind to it, pulled Bronco to one side and had a quiet word with him about the ridicules situation and pointed out that the "Hilarious" beer mat coat would not go down to well at the Goodwood races especially among the height of fashion, London set and it would be best if he put the coat away for the rest of the weekend. After some strong protestations, he eventually relented and the "Hilarious" coat of many colours was never seen again in Brighton, though he did continue to use it back in Brum when he performed his pub entertainment show.

Even without his startling coat, Bronco could be as mad as a March hare and many of the Forty-Club members avoided his company, but at least without the clowns outfit, we found that we could handle him a little easier. But if he did happen to blow his top, as his volcanic nature was likely to do, we found it best to walk away and leave him to it as we were all aware of his unpredictable and volatile reputation.

While working as a barman at the Kings Head pub, he once took on several members of a local ruby team when a private function went disastrously awry. The fallout from this little altercation was that he was given the sack by the pubs manager for fighting with the customers, but unexpectedly he was invited to join the rugby team by the team's captain who thought that Bronco's mad aggressive attitude was just what was missing from his team.

Most men, no matter how articulate, tend to use profanities at one time or another and the less articulate tend swear much more frequent than others and Bronco certainly came into this category, but what set him apart from those that swore in every sentence was that he swore in the middle of words as well. He would quite naturally say, abso-fucking-lutely, or dia-fucking-bolical, or even fan-fucking-tastic.

By the time he'd reached his twenties his habit of habitual swearing had become part and parcel of his normal speech and although his friends, work associates and his long suffering wife, continually tried to help him curb the habit, he never did get rid of it completely and many years later during a conversation concerning foreign holidays he was heard to say, that while travelling around India he'd visited the, "Taj-Ma-fucking-hal." It was a term that slightly sullied the romantic image of Shah Jehan's white mausoleum.

But for all his faults there were the two things that he possessed in abundance, he had boundless enthusiasm for a project and a phenomenal supply of physical energy and much to the astonishment of most of the Forty-Club members, those two attributes were to serve him exceedingly well in later life.

Even though I was young and carefree, I could not take to gambling and tended to be very careful in the way that I wasted my money. After a couple of disastrous attempts at courting Lady Luck, I knew that I would never be a gambler. Unlike my mates, I saw quite clearly how much I was liable to lose rather than how much I was bound to win. It not only grieved me to loose even a modest amount of money on a simple bet, but the memory of the foolish act stayed with me long after the event and left me feeling stupid for some considerable time, but in spite of this oddity, I absolutely adored the Glorious Goodwood Races. The event was filled with colour, beauty, expectation, excitement and fascinating characters all rolled up in a wonderful vibrant atmosphere. I enjoyed everything about the experience. There were the fascinating sights of elegant frisky race horses, the little wizened jockeys in their bright coloured silks, the well-dressed pompous owners and their earnest trainers who nodded at each other knowingly, the sharp eyed bookies and their runners communicating in their white gloved secret arm waving language and the numerous punters.

Punters came in all shapes and sizes and from all walks of life, but what united them was the belief that at the beginning of each race, they possessed the winning formula. Many studiously studied newspapers for the horses form and an analysis of the going with the concentration of a crime scene detective. Was it heavy or was it firm? Will it suit this or that horse? And for those who had no time for science and the mathematics of form books, there was the time honoured tradition of using one's own brand of superstition. Some had lucky numbers or favourite colours while others were attracted to the names of the horses and took them to be a sign from the gods, "I must back Mary Rose, it's my mother's name you know." Why the name of a horse should have any bearing on why it should win a race defies all logic, but when it comes to courting Lady Luck, logic is superfluous.

Among this horde of wishful thinkers there were a few gamblers who were hardnosed and would have no truck with superstitious nonsense and would watch the bookies like hawks, which was probably the wisest technique of all as it was obvious that the bookie was not there to give money away and if he thought that a certain horse had a good chance of winning, he would inevitably shorten the odds to balance his book and after following this technique for many years, Mitch gradually became one of the shrewdest punters around and at the end of the meeting he came out of the with more money than he had gone in with.

Most of the people that attended the Goodwood races went there with the sole intention of winning money, but not all, many of the stunningly good looking young women went with the sole purpose of being seen and admired and they spent their time parading elegantly around Tattersall's dressed in the latest London and Paris fashions and to someone like me, who was not particularly interested in the gambling side of the meeting, watching these delicious long legged young women continually parade around the place was just as fascinating and as entertaining as watching the thoroughbred horses.

Like many other members of the Forty-Club, Mitch enjoyed participating in games of cards and dominoes and often joined in any game that was going, but unlike the horses, he found this form of gambling far less predictable. On one memorable occasion he lost all his weekend spending money while playing cards on the coach while we were travelling down to Brighton on the Friday morning. On hearing of his self-inflicted plight, I lent him some money so that he could hold his head high and buy his round of drinks on the Friday night, but Mitch was desperate to find a decent stake for the visit to the Goodwood races on the following day, for this after all was the whole point of why he was there. The amount he needed was far in access of what Billy or I could provide him with and so on this occasion, other than buying his drinks, we were of little use to him.

After spending Friday evening out on the town, we drifted back to our hotel and there we carried on drinking in the hotels bar and for some it was yet another chance to gamble on another few hands of cards before retiring to bed. It was rare for anyone to go to bed before two in the morning on any of the Forty-Club trips and it was during this gathering of the clan that Mitch had his brainwave for raising enough money for a decent bet at following day's races. He asked everyone in the room including a number of total strangers who were also staying at the hotel, if they would bet against him doing a naked streak along the, far from deserted, Brighton promenade. As everyone there was up for a laugh they all agreed and when fifty-pound was raised and placed upon a table, Mitch simply stripped off all his clothes and ran naked out of the hotels front door and into the street, which was well lit and filled with people casually strolling along the sea front promenade. Many cars and taxis were still passing by at the time and their surprised drivers and passengers did a double take at the unusual sight that flashed by them. Certain lampposts along the front had been designated as the required markers of the course that Mitch had to take and a rule had been laid down that he had to run round each one to complete the bet.

Naked streaking was quite a new phenomenon and there was a large proportion of the population who'd never even heard of the practice, so to many of the onlookers that night it was quite a shock to see a virile young man running around the promenade completely naked with his tea and two sugars bouncing about for all to see. Mitch returned to the hotel bar puffing and panting as though he were a four-minute miler and was greeted by a huge ovation and after slipping his trousers back on, he picked up his well-earned winnings and the next day, with his newly acquired stake money, he went on to win over two hundred-pound at the Goodwood races.

Although seventy years old and considered by many to be past it, Aka was a regular on the Forty-Club trips. As luck would have it, Aka was not only elderly but had the misfortune of being born with a humped back and on reaching old age, he'd become a dead ringer for old man Steptoe of television fame, but these slight drawbacks did not stop him from enjoying himself. He and his drinking partner, a little Irish man named Tommy, sat together on the coach all the way to Brighton and all the way back and they rarely left each other's side all weekend. If you saw one, then you knew that the other was not far behind. Aka's claim to fame was that he played the accordion in a local pub at the weekends, his other claim to fame was that very few of the patrons could recognise any of the tunes that he played. Someone once asked him to play the Sinatra hit song, "Something Stupid" and, having no idea what it was, he played "I've got a lovely bunch of coconuts" instead, reasoning that that particular song came into the same category.

No matter what the season or the temperature, Aka always wore an old fashioned double breasted two piece suit which had wide lapels on the jacket and wide bottoms on high waist trousers. He wore elasticised braces to hold the trousers up and whenever he sat down, his high waist trousers tended to stay where they were, but because of his humped back and sunken chest Aka sank within them. One Sunday lunchtime, we were sitting in a pub with our first pint of the day and feeling somewhat delicate from the previous night's debauchery, Trapper looked across the room at Aka who was also drinking his first pint and said quite solemnly, "I hear that Aka's taking that suit back to the tailors first thing on Monday morning."

We all looked lazily across the room to where sour faced Aka was sitting, his high waist trousers covering most of his chest and after a short pause Billy asked, "Why's that then?"

"Because," Trapper replied, his face showing no sign of emotion, "The top of his trousers are rubbing his arm pits something rotten."

When the coach left Brighton on the Sunday afternoon, it usually contained between thirty five to forty men, men who had just consumed large quantities of beer during the lunch time session and so inevitably a few miles out of Brighton the cries of, "Driver, pull over, I'm dying for a piss" would begin.

One year the driver pulled over next to a substantial wooded area and all the men tumbled out of the coach and disappeared into the wood and proceeded to relieve themselves against the trees and the wild bushes that were growing there. After relieving themselves, one by one, they boarded the coach to continue their long journey and Trapper took it upon himself to count them back on board to make sure that no one was left behind. As Aka approached the coach he smiled at Trapper, held out his open hand to show the blackberries that he'd just picked and was hurriedly eating.

"Look Trapper," He said in his squeaky high-pitched voice, "These blackberries are gorgeous. Lovely and juicy."

"They should be," Trapper replied, a dead pan look upon his craggy face, "I've just pissed all over them."

A small group of us were sprawled out and relaxing on Brighton's pebble beach one sunny Sunday morning. We were as usual, a little jaded after our fun packed Saturday shenanigans and were waiting for our tired bodies to recuperate and for the pubs to open at twelve o'clock.

Earlier we had breakfasted at our hotel, strolled slowly along the front and filled our lungs with exhilarating sea air, explored the Brighton Lanes, gazed at the overpriced antiques and now, in a melancholy mood, we were relaxing on the pebble beach. We could see a couple of speedboats bumping and bouncing across the blue shimmering bright water and as one came closer we could see that it was towing a water skier behind it at high speed. On seeing this, Mitch suddenly sat up, put a hand up to shield his eyes from the dazzling sun and cried out, "Good god! That's Aka and his hump out there water skiing!"

The absurd thought that the athletic water skier skimming across the sea might have been Aka, made us all laugh until our bellies ached and was the perfect pick me up tonic for our previous lethargic mood.

This sort of wicked de-bagging humour was continually used by all the members of the Forty-Club. At some time or another during the weekend we would all be made fun of, but none of us ever took offence as it was all part and parcel of our weekend's fun.

During one of the earlier trips, the coach, that had definitely seen better days and was probably why we'd got it so cheaply, broke down and we did not arrive at the small hotel in Brighton until well after midnight. The hotels night porter, who wasn't in the best of moods at having to deal with this invasion of boisterous men entering the hotel at this late hour and the extra work load that it put upon him, booked us in and distributed the room keys. We carried our belongings up to our allotted rooms, then, much to the night porters surprise, came back down again and gathered at the hotels small bar.

"What do you lot want?" The bemused night porter asked frowning with annoyance.

"Thirty five pints of beer for a start." Stone faced Trapper replied.

"You're not going to start drinking now are you?" The night porter asked questioningly, a look of incredulity upon his old face.

"No, of course not," Trapper explained, while shaking his large head of blond hair from side to side, "We started drinking in Brum this morning. This is where we intend to finish."

Realising that it would be somewhat foolish to stand up to thirty five men, some of whom, such as Bronco, were quite capable of ripping the protective grill off the bar, the night porter reluctantly opened the bar up for service. It was probably the hardest night's work that he'd ever done while working in the hotel trade, but even he mellowed when he realised that these men, although rough and ready, were gracious with their tips. Mitch and I shared a bedroom on the second floor which contained two single beds and two bedside cupboards and when I awoke the following morning the first thing that I noticed was a full pint of flat beer standing on my bedside cupboard. Evidently I'd, though I had no recollection of doing so, carried a pint of beer up two flights of stairs when I'd retired for the night. Presumably it had been meant as a night cap, but I was astonished to find that I hadn't spilt a drop, it was a feat of balancing that I knew I would have had a great deal of difficulty in accomplishing had I been stone cold sober.

I awoke from my drunken stupor on the Sunday morning to find that Mitch was sharing his bed with a young woman that I'd never seen before. Late on Saturday night, after visiting several pubs, Mitch and I had gone our separate ways and he'd met this young woman in a night-club and had smuggled her back into the hotel and into our shared bedroom while I was fast asleep. What this young woman's view of this unusual cosy liaison was, I was never to find out, as she quickly departed from the hotel soon after waking and Mitch's shrugged explanation for her hurried departure was simply, "Oh, she's married; she had to get off back home or she'd be in trouble."

The men who went on the Forty-Club trips were mostly married men and they roughly fell into three categories, there was the odd one or two who went on the trip and specifically looked for an extra marital relationship. On the Friday night they would put on their best bib and tucker and make for the pubs, dance halls and nightclubs that good time girls frequented and seek out a likely target. Having found one, they would then spend the whole of Saturday, wining, dining, strolling, canoodling and generally buttering them up for a hopeful romp in bed on the Saturday night. To most of the men, this plan of seduction seemed to be an awful lot of effort for a very unpredictable outcome and not worth the bother. Over the years there were some notable successes of course, but there were far more failures. Not all the good time girls were as naive as these men hoped they'd be.

The second category were the ones who didn't exactly set out to find a willing good time girl, but would certainly not turn the offer down if the opportunity came their way and Mitch was a good example and did at times have the good fortune to strike lucky, but the vast majority of the men were simply there to booze, gamble, sing their hearts out and have a good cheerful time while laughing and joshing each other at every opportunity and a good example of this type was the Big Bopper.

The Big Bopper was a fine example of a young man that had devoted his social life to the act of consuming as much beer that he could manage while avoiding as much physical exercise as possible. Although still a relatively young bachelor, he'd acquired the physique of a large pear and the mind set of an old man. Even in his early teens when he was just a little Bopper, he would never have been mistaken for a ladies man, but now with a bald head, an African elephant's arse and a barrage balloon belly, he had even less physical attraction than he'd ever had. And it was because of this that Alfie, who was a carefree Jack the lad sort of a bloke, one Friday evening picked on the Big Bopper for a bit of bear baiting fun. We were assembled in the hotels bar and indulging in a quick drink before deciding where to go for our evening's entertainment and Alfie turned to the Big Bopper and, already knowing what the answer would be, asked in a loud voice so that all those around could hear, "Are you coming out on the town with us then Bop?"

"No," replied Bopper while shaking his shiny bald head, "I'm staying in here for a while, then I might wonder up to the Royal George later, they do a bostin pint up there."

"Why don't you come with us and pick up a bit of crumpet for the night." Alfie joked.

"You can keep your bleeding crumpet," Bopper replied dismissively, "I'm quite happy with a good pint of beer in my mit. Women want too much looking after and they tend to complicate things, you can have the lot for all I care Alfie."

"I bet you've never had a woman in your life have you Bop?" Alfie asked smiling artfully.

"Oh, I've had my moments Alfie. You'd be surprised." The Big Bopper replied as he laughed humorously, and as Alfie and his mates disappeared out of the front door of the hotel, the Big Bopper turned to the remaining audience who were finishing off their drinks and said, "He don't know it, but Alfie's missis was the first bird that I ever shagged." He took a swig of his beer, wiped his mouth with the back of his hand and explained, "When she lived in Tilton Road, long before Alfie married her, we all used to have a knock at her in old man Fletchers air raid shelter. She had very loose knicker elastic back then and I wouldn't mind betting, she still has."

Charlie, who'd hit a lucky streak of late and had enough money to make a splash at the Goodwood races had decided to grace us with his presence. As it turned out he had a lucky weekend in more ways than one as he not only won a substantial amount of money at the races, but he and Steak met two girls on the Friday night at a disco dance and had a date all lined up for Saturday night. His partner in crime was a young man who, because his name was Kidney, had become known as Steak. Although Steak was not as quick on his feet as Charlie, he was no slouch when it came to chatting up young women who dreamed of romantic scenarios with a Prince Charming and he was quite adapt at filling their heads with honeyed promises.

What tall tales Charlie and Steak told the girls that night no one but themselves ever knew, but they must have been extremely good, because the two girls willingly cavorted with them in their beds on the Saturday night. After a bracing walk along the sea front on the Sunday morning, the two starry eyed girls accompanied Charlie and Steak to the Forty-Clubs traditional drink and sing-song session at the pub that had been designated for the event and they sat staring moon struck at Charlie and Steak throughout the session.

When we boarded the coach for the long journey home the two dewy eyed girls stood together on the pavement, waving and blowing kisses to Charlie and Steak who while kneeling on the back seat of the coach waved back and promised to keep in touch. And as the coach slowly pulled away from the hotel, the two girls clutched each other and burst into uncontrollable sobs. We onlookers sat in our seats and watched this heart wrenching romantic scene draw to a close and couldn't help but wonder if the girl's reaction would have been the same had they known that Charlie was a married man with two kids and Steak was being sued for maintenance by his former wife and now had two kids in another relationship. As Shakespeare said, "All the worlds a stage.... and one man in his time plays many

parts," and Charlie and Steak acted their socks off that weekend and could have given Laurence Olivier a run for his money
.

On the 22nd of November 1963 a failed loner shot President John F. Kennedy dead during his visit to Dallas, Texas, USA. The news of the assassination stunned the world just as the sinking of Titanic had done in 1912.

1963 was the year Tottenham Hotspur F.C. became the first British side to win the European Cup-Winners' Cup, the film "Lawrence of Arabia" won seven Oscars and Henry Cooper put Cassius Clay on his arse with the sweetest left hook ever thrown in a boxing ring. No one at the time was more amazed than loud mouth Clay, who later became Mohamed Ali and no one was more elated than Starlin, when Cassius Clay went on to win the fight.

Starlin was Cassius Clay's biggest fan and had been right from the beginning of his professional career. He continually sang the praises of the new boxer on the block to anyone that would listen, but to most of us, Clay was just a loud mouthed braggart and we were very reluctant to accept that he was anything special. Clay had burst upon the British scene as a big headed, loud-mouthed American show off and we were looking forward to seeing him get his big head knocked off his shoulders and when Henry Cooper put him down on the canvas, for one delicious moment, we thought that our dream had come true, but as luck would have it, the knock down came at the end of the round and Clay survived.

Twice Clay fought Sonny Liston, the heavyweight champion of the world. The first time was in 1964 and the fight lasted eight rounds. The second fight, in 1965 seemed to be nothing more than a money making farce. The infamous fight with the mean, man mountain, Sonny Liston was televised and transmitted over to Britain in the early hours of the morning and many of us rose from our warm beds in the middle of the night, to watch the fight. We switched the tele on, made a cup of tea and found that the fight was already over and we had to watch the re-runs to find out what had happened.

The American commentators reported that Clay had landed a "phantom" punch; a boxing term that none of us had ever heard of and none of us believed for a second. Whether Liston took a dive, for money or out of fear no one will ever know for sure. And so, although he'd won, we were far from convinced that the loud-mouthed Clay was a worthy world champion and preferred to believe that he was part of a Mafia engineered fraud. The Humphrey Bogart film "The Harder They Fall," had shown us how match fixing was possible. But a couple of fights later, we reluctantly realised that this good looking athletic boxer, who became known as Ali, was something outstandingly special and an absolute treat to watch. Never in the history of boxing had such a big man been so light on his feet or shown such quick reactions. He was able to flick his head away from thrown punches with the agility of a mongoose and to top it all, he proved that he was a strategic genius.

Eventually he revealed that his early loud mouth bragging antics had been a deliberate ploy to get him noticed by the media and to put bums on seats and make him more money. It was an idea that he copied from an exuberant American Show Time wrestler that he'd seen perform. As for Starlin, not only was he proved to be right in his assessment of Ali's boxing skills, but he even persuaded me to paint him a picture of his hero to put on his bedroom wall.

During the summer of 1965, Starlin who was naturally pale faced, went on holiday to Rimini in Italy with three of his mates and there, he fell madly in love with a girl that was staying at the same hotel, While they were there he was able to see her every day, but when he discovered that she lived in Nottingham, he foresaw a problem, Nottingham was over sixty miles from where he lived and there was no way he could travel that distance on a regular basis.

When he arrived back at work after his holiday he was just as pale as before he'd gone, but full of excitement and romantic plans. He was determined to keep in touch with his new love by sending her regular love letters. Full of romantic intent he attempted to write the most beautiful love letter that the world had ever seen, but not being a natural romantic and rather inarticulate to boot, the task proved to be a lot harder than he'd anticipated.

Totally demoralised by his puny attempts at composing a heartfelt message; he turned to Mitch and begged him to help. Mitch, who'd always loved poetry and sweet verse, had a flare for romantic prose and consequently he wrote a draft letter that Romeo himself would have been proud of. Starlin hurriedly copied the affectionate letter word for word and sent it off to his true love and for a whole week he walked on air while awaiting a reply. When the letter from his sweetheart arrived, he was starry eyed and begged Mitch to compile a second love letter for him. Mitch told him to piss off as he could see that this love by proxy could go on forever and although he'd found it fun to compile the original letter, he realised that it was time to bring some reality to the situation. When confronted with this snub, Starlin became extremely angry and although inarticulate, he still managed to find some very descriptive words to describe what he thought of Mitch and his despicable selfish behaviour.

A few weeks later, Mitch bumped into Starlin in a pub and slapped him on the back, asked him how he was and bought him a pint and all was forgiven. By then Starlin had tired of his long distance love affair and his interest in the girl had waned considerably and sadly the love story of the century withered and died a natural death. Although distance can make the heart grow fonder, without some form of regular communication, true love will surely suffer and Starlin eventually met and married a girl that resided in a house that was just a couple of hundred yards from where he lived and she was never to receive a single love letter composed by either him or Mitch.

As Jack Rushton was tall, broad chested, had a face chiselled from granite and possessed a commanding voice, he was not easily missed. He was a confirmed bachelor and almost sixty years old when he joined the company as a goods inwards clerk and as the rest of the stores staff were all much younger; he stood out like the proverbial sore thumb.

Mr Frank, the branch manager, had interviewed Jack for the vacancy that had recently occurred and had been suitably impressed by his previous employment record and had decided to take him on. To begin with, I, who was still in my early twenties, felt quite uncomfortable about giving Jack, an older and probably wiser man, daily instructions, but I needn't have worried as within a few weeks, he'd totally reorganised the goods inwards department and didn't need me, or anyone else, to give him any advice on how to run his department.

He spoke without any noticeable accent and unlike me, he had a phenomenal memory for figures. He could remember what items had been allocated to particular order numbers and which customer they were for. He had a mental filing system all of his own and all agreed that he was extremely efficient and that the goods inwards department had never been run better, but for all that, the other workers found him a bit strange as he frowned upon their juvenile antics and did not seem to be bothered about forming any close friendships and so they tended to keep their distance. And so, because of his age, his size, a slight limp which prevented him from joining in with the kick about football games in the back yard and his stern demeanour, he was looked upon as a typical, grumpy old bugger, but as he was never late and did his job efficiently, there was nothing that he could be openly criticized for.

He lived alone in a small terraced house and had applied for this job as it was nearer his home, but that was about as much as anyone knew or wanted to know about him for some considerable time. Then one day when the stores staff were sitting about on various wooden benches and upturned boxes during a tea break, Mitch, who was a regular visitor when he had no work for his fledgling transport business, started spouting off about his latest discovery, which in this instance was Persian poetry, or to be more precise, "The Rubaiyat of Omar Khayyam."

Mitch stood in front of the open mouthed and mystified storemen as they sat with their mugs of tea in one hand and sandwich in the other and with the grand gestures of a Victorian stage actor, he proceeded to recite the lines, "The moving finger writes; and having writ, moves on: nor all the piety nor wit shall lure it back to cancel half a line, nor all thy tears wash out a word of it."

Jack, put down his newspaper and walked towards Mitch and the other storemen and said, in an equally powerful voice, "And all that inverted bowl we call the sky, where under crawling coop't live and die, lift not thy hands to it for help, for it rolls impotently on as thou or I."

Mitch and the storemen were gobsmacked and were in danger of dropping their mugs of tea. He then went on to quote several other verses from the ancient poem and then stumbling on one line he apologised and went on to explain that it was many years since he'd last read the "Rubiaiyat" and that there were several interpretations of the ancient poem. He went on to explain the full history of Edward Fitzgerald's life and how he became involved in the translations and Mitch was so overwhelmed by Jack's phenomenal knowledge of the "Rubaiyat," that he hungrily begged him to tell him more about the subject and continued to asked him questions for the rest of the day.

It became apparent that this old Persian poem was not the only subject that Jack could discuss in depth, as he seemed to be an expert on anything that was mentioned and he was soon being called upon to answer questions on numerous subjects and just like the others, I became fascinated with his phenomenal encyclopaedic knowledge. What impressed most of all was not just his undoubted knowledge, but his deep analysis of the subject in question. He wasn't just a facts and figures memory man that could tell you the names of the horses that had won the Grand National for the past twenty years or who had scored the winning goal in the nineteen forty seven cup final, but a man that not only queried so called facts, but had the ability and the desire to analyse them and hold them up to scrutiny. He took nothing at face value and questioned everything and gradually, over many months, he encouraged those of us who were interested, to look beyond the simple platitudes that appear in the media and seek out the truth behind them.

In one discussion, for that's what many a tea break now became, he pointed out that one of the most important events in modern history was the fall of Constantinople in 1453. As none of us knew what the hell he was referring to, we demanded an explanation. He pointed out that when Constantinople fell and became part of the Ottoman Empire, all trade routes to India and China for the emerging Western economies, England, Holland, France, Spain, Portugal, and Italy were disrupted and this became the spur for exploring seamen to find new ways to reach the Indies and the Orient. Columbus, Magellan, Vasco De Gama and Drake all went looking for new routes to reach the promised wealth that they all dreamed of. These brave acts of seamanship in tiny ships, eventually led the way for the Western kingdoms to dominate the Seven Seas and consequently, most of the world. It was a direct result of this mania for exploring the unknown seas that eventually led to the emergence of the Americas and the land that was to become the United States. We sat and listened to every word that he spoke on the subject and were astonished by his simple analysis and explanations for what we had previously thought to be a boring part of historical knowledge. We'd recently completed our ten years compulsory education and although we had heard of some of the seamen that he mentioned, we knew next to nothing of the consequences of their epic voyages.

As the weeks rolled by, Jack was called upon to talk about such things as Isaac Newton's experiments with gravity, which lead to a better understanding of the solar system and became the bedrock of space travel, how the science of geology was born and how it led to the finding and understanding the age of the dinosaurs and the intricacies of evolution. He told us things about the English civil war that we'd never heard of before, such as the fact that the first open violence had actually occurred in Scotland. He exploded the romantic myth of Bonnie Prince Charlie by informing us that more Scots were against Charlie than for him. He explained how Nelson won the Battle of Trafalgar and was then pickled in a barrel of brandy, why many odd social customs came about, where many of our everyday sayings came from and numerous other oddities such as who was the first moving nude at the Follies Begere and that the Arab explorer Ibn Batuta had travelled further than Marco Polo and that the insulting word meddler originally meant dogs arse. In fact any subject that came up in the daily chit-chat that went on in the stores, Jack would supply a detailed history if requested and it had to be requested as he would never force his views upon anyone who didn't want to hear them. He taught us to look at some of the headline stories and try to discover what motive and prejudice the writer had and said, "You cannot know anyone well, unless you know what their prejudices are."

He believed that good manners and the basic rules of law were the essential building blocks to a civilised society and because of this, he was often intolerant towards the stroppy teenagers and their couldn't care less attitudes and now and then there was an inevitable clash of personalities. On one occasion, reminiscent of a large angry ogre, he marched through the stores, up the creaking wooden stairs, burst into the office and there he confronted Nigel, the confident ex-public school boy with a delivery note. He waved the delivery note menacingly in front of poor Nigel's terrified face and in a loud threatening voice he asked, "Young man, did you order this cast iron boiler? A boiler that because of its size and weight is by necessity delivered in large individual sections and did you instruct the company that you ordered it from, to deliver it to these premises where you know that there is no lifting apparatus capable of lifting it off the lorry, instead of informing them to deliver it direct to its ultimate destination?"

Nigel, looking sheepish and not fully understanding just what he'd done wrong examined the delivery note and replied meekly, "Yes, I must admit, it does look very much like something that I ordered."

"Then perhaps you can show me how to unload it."

With that, he marched Nigel out of the office, down the creaking wooden stairs, through the general stores and out into the small back yard where the delivery lorry with its heavy load was parked and once there he left Nigel confronting the agitated delivery driver and of course the problem of how to unload the cast iron boiler. Nigel, as usual, had no idea of what to say or do, so he ran hot foot back up the stairs and immediately handed the problem over to higher management. Eventually the irritated delivery driver was redirected with the aid of a substantial tip for his trouble, to the building site that the boiler should have gone to in the first place and where they did have lifting equipment and after that incident every young man in the office showed extra care when quoting delivery addresses to suppliers.

On occasions, Jack turned up for work on a Friday with a small brown leather suitcase and took it with him when he left the premises at the close of play. Curiosity getting the better of me, I asked what the small suitcase was for and I was surprised to learn that he was off to Chester for the weekend.

"Do you have relatives there then?" I asked which seemed to be the logical reason for going there.

"Oh no," He replied, "I have very few relatives who are still alive and they all live locally. No, I'm just going off to explore the town."

Puzzled by this reply I said, "I don't quite follow. What do you mean by, explore the town? Which town?"

"Well this weekend it will be Chester, but another time it could be Bath, Bristol or Brighton."

He then went on to explain that every six weeks or so, he hopped on a train or a bus on a Friday evening and travelled to another town, booked into a bed and breakfast and spent the weekend exploring the place, its museums, library, historical sites, places of interest and on Saturday night, he would find himself a comfortable pub and mix with some of the locals. It turned out that he'd been doing this for many years and as a consequence, had acquired an intimate expert knowledge of most of the towns and cities in Britain. When visiting long distance places, such as Stirling, Inverness, Belfast and Dublin, he usually added a couple of day's holiday to his weekend.

Another oddity was that although his political leanings were left wing, though not fanatically so, he always purchased a blatantly right wing newspaper. When asked about this, he just smiled and said, "Know thine enemy," and went on to explain that, "If you look around, you will find that the newspapers that are designed for the working classes are nothing more than comics. It used to be said that religion was the opium for the people, the substance that stopped them thinking. Well now its mundane television programmes and newspaper comics."

Much like George Orwell, Jack distrusted ardent socialists as much as he disliked fanatical right wingers and so he never joined either camp. By discussing many things with him, several of us began to expand our interests and began to read works that we'd never looked at before. There was Shaw's play, "St. Joan," Huxley's "Brave New World" Tolstoy's "War and Peace" Graves "I Claudius" and the delightfully funny short stories of W.W. Jacob. He also got us interested in reading The Sunday Observer and listening to Alistair Cooke's "Letter from America" which was a regular item on radio four.

As time went on, the staff started to take Jack and his phenomenal knowledge for granted and bothered him less and less with their questions. Then one day Mr Frank had one of his better ideas and took on board a young student to help out during the summer months while each storemen took their annual holidays. I escorted him into the general stores to meet his fellow workers of whom he was very nervous of meeting, suspecting that being an intelligent student; he would become an object of derision. His name was Peter and when I asked him what he was studying, he reluctantly disclosed that it was Greek history and Greek mythology. I explained to him that for the next two weeks he would be working alongside Jack in the goods inwards department and left them to it.

I'd just washed my hands ready for my lunch break, when Peter stopped me in the corridor and with a look of wide eyed amazement he said, "Excuse me for asking, but who the hell *is* that man that I'm working with?"

"Who? Do you mean Jack?" I replied.

"He's incredible!" Peter said, utterly astonished, "He knows more about Greek history and Greek mythology than the tutors at the university!"

"Ah, yes," I replied, nodding with understanding, "I'm not surprised, I thought you two would hit it off." And with a smile, I went off to enjoy my lunch knowing that this young lad had just learned a lesson in humility and would now probably look upon the stores staff in a different light.

Although Peter undoubtedly gained a lot of knowledge by working alongside Jack, his help to me in the general stores as the utility storeman was negligible, as I could never prize him away from Jack in the goods inwards department for very long and I was sure that when he eventually returned to his university studies he would be well ahead of his class mates as he now knew as much about ancient Greeks, Spartans, Greek mythology, Plato, Socrates and Minoan civilization as anyone.

The small yard at the rear of the premises had never been large enough for the work load that it was expected to cope with. Under a make shift corrugated sheet metal roof, long lengths of steel tube, various sized bricks, paving slabs, bunkers containing sand and bags of cement were stored, delivery lorries and vans were expected to load and unload in the limited space, wooden crates opened and unpacked and what little space was left was filled with empty bag's, boxes and crates that had contained goods that had been previously delivered. And next to all this there was an old oil drum that had been converted with the aid of a few holes punched into its side into an incinerator for burning the constant flow of unwanted packaging. As a consequence, there was little room for manoeuvre in the back yard and items were constantly being moved around for one reason or another.

During the summer months the wide double doors of the general stores, which opened up onto the back yard, were often left open to let whatever fresh air there was to circulate around the stores, but during the winter months, when ferocious cold winds blew along the cavernous side streets, there were constant cries from the storemen of, "Shut that bleeding door," if and when they were considered to be opened up for more time than was necessary.

Being in charge of the goods inwards, Jack's desk come work bench was by necessity situated next to the back doors and midway through one cold winter morning, Jack became aware of a mild tapping on the back doors and he called out, "Come in," but no one answered his call. There then came a second series of taps on the doors, but this time they were a little louder. "Come in!" Jack bellowed once more and this time the door opened slightly and a little meek man's face appeared and said apologetically, "Er, Sorry to bother you, but did you know that you have a bit of a fire out here in your back yard?"

Starlin, who'd heard what the meek man had said, shouted back down the stores in his usual diplomatic manner, "Course we know there's a fire, that's where we burn the bleeding rubbish."

"Er, no," The little meek man said, stuttering to explain, "I mean, you've got a fire in your wooden crates and boxes."

On hearing this news all the storemen dashed out into the back yard and in doing so, inadvertently pushed the little man, who was in the middle of muttering something about, "I thought I ought to let you know," to one side.

Out in the back yard, the storemen were confronted by a huge wall of flame. Evidently sparks from the oil drum incinerator had blown among the numerous boxes and packing crates that had been stacked against the back wall of the yard and had caused them to ignite and now the whole lot was merrily blazing away. Jack calmly returned to the stores, picked up a large red fire extinguisher and marched back out into the back yard and in a firm commanding voice said, "Stand back" a command that the storemen instantly obeyed. He ripped off the safety clip, banged the black button as per instructions, pointed the nozzle at the fire and bugger all happened. He tried again and still nothing happened. It seems that the lack of maintenance can thwart even the most knowledgeable of men.

Realising that this particular fire dowsing method was not going to do the trick, all the storemen now began to run around each other in the manner of Keystone Cops, and all with different ideas of how to put the fire out. Starlin picked up a metal bucket and ran towards the toilet block to fill it with cold water, but realised before he got there that there were several holes in the bucket and discarded it with disgust and a fusillade of ripe swear words. Two other storemen picked up large hessian sacks and began to beat the flames with them, which for a short while looked to be quite successful, but then the sacks themselves caught fire and just added to the blaze. I ran for another fire extinguisher which turned out to be just as faulty as the first. I then filled a small bowl with water and threw it onto the huge fire and saw that it had no effect whatsoever on the ferocious blaze. Eventually we pulled a few of the burning wooden boxes away from the back door with help of a long handled broom, then stood back forlornly and just let the whole lot burn it's self out and Starlin commented philosophically, "Do you know, this is the warmest I've been all bloody winter."

Jack was a sensible and pragmatic man and not only had he ideas for what he would do when he finally retired, but plans to fund them as well. He paid into a private pension fund, had a number of company shares and purchased among other things, first edition stamps. Someone once asked him if he would move out of the city and into the idyllic countryside that so many seem to favour when they retire and to their surprise his answer was an emphatic, "No!"

Seeing that his audience were surprised by this firm answer he proceeded to explain why he would stay in the city rather than move to an idyllic picture postcard country village. "Look, at the moment, I live in a small house that suits my needs and economical to run, I have gas and electricity, hot and cold water, a bathroom and WC, a pavement and street lighting outside the front door. I'm a short walk from various shops, pubs, cinema, library, swimming baths, park, the doctors and the hospital. I'm just a short bus ride away from the city centre where there are theatres, art gallery, museum, coach station, railway station and transport to the airport. Why would I, as I get older, more decrepit and forgetful, want to live in an isolated spot in the back of beyond that has few of these amenities?"

We realised that he had probably overstated the case for staying in the city as there were many quiet rural towns to choose from, but we could also see what he was driving at, and that was simply that when approaching retirement many people tend to see that the grass is greener and the sun is warmer elsewhere and completely overlook what that they already have. Jack had been born and bred in a bustling town environment and although he accepted that the countryside was a wonderful place to visit during the glorious summer months, it was not in his opinion a place to be stuck in when he became old and frail and to rubber stamp his opinion he added, "And besides, if I moved into the country, I'd be living among the obnoxious, self-opinionated fox hunting clique and who in their right mind would want to put up with that lot."

One day I was informed by Mr Frank, that he had recruited a new driver who's was name was Mike Smith. On the following Monday morning I showed him the box van that he would be driving for the day, checked the oil and petrol for him, gave him a few local deliveries to deliver, an A to Z road map and an emergency telephone number in case he broke down and at approximately eight thirty, I waved him on his way and I never saw him again.

The police eventually found the missing van in the seaside resort of Great Yarmouth with the deliveries still inside it. It was eventually established that the driver's name was not Mike Smith after all and that his real name was Rodney, Mike Smith's younger brother and he'd used his brother's driving licence to acquire the position of driver. It became clear that he'd not wanted the driving job at all; he just wanted the use of the vehicle so that he could take his mates to the seaside.

A few months later, Rodney and one of his mates, who must have been as daft as he was, broke into the Briggs company office one night and stole the office safe. They lifted the small, but heavy safe, out of one of the office windows and carried it across the roof of the general stores and dropped it over the back wall onto a patch of wasteland. It was noted by some that this was the escape route that young Nigel, the strapping young ruby player had failed to find when he'd got himself locked in the premises. The small heavy safe was found the next morning a hundred yards from the premises, still locked and its contents still intact. The futility of the exhausting exercise was brought home when it was realised that there was no money in the safe and that there never had been. The cash that was kept on the premises was in a tin box, which was kept in the secretary's desk, which the enterprising cat burglars had failed to find. During his job interview, Rodney had spied the small safe in the corner of Mr Frank's office and had assumed that it contained a vast amount of money.

Eventually this arch criminal went on to try his hand at a much bigger job and one night; he hijacked a lorry and its ten-ton load from a cake manufacture. He was arrested the next day and it was then that he confessed to being the mastermind behind the safe burglary, but the question everyone asked was, "How did he expect to sell ten-ton of almond nuts?"

With such a disastrous criminal record at such an early age, it was suggested that this particular incompetent crook could have done with far more advice and guidance with his chosen profession and that his careers teacher had let him down badly.

My shaky marriage to Pam finally came to an end in the spring of sixty five. The doubts and fissures in our relationship had been there for some time, but for some illogical reason we'd both tried to ignore them hoping that time would eventually put things right, but eventually we realised that it never would. There had been an uneasy feeling between us ever since I'd told Pam about my unusual meeting with Helen just before she'd been murdered and although Pam eventually declared that she accepted my explanation of how I'd met Helen that evening, she could never quite bring herself to believe that I'd told her the full extent of my involvement in Helen's life. Having never met her, Pam judged the situation by what she would have done in similar circumstances and could not bring herself to believe that Helen could have been as strong willed and as manipulative as I continually claimed and forever after that incident she held a nagging suspicion that I was holding something back from her.

Of course, this wasn't the only bone of contention between us, but it certainly didn't help matters and it tended to crop up whenever we had a row, but the real problem between us wasn't anything to do with Helen or the fact that we had married in haste or that Pam had had a miscarriage, the truth was, we were simply incompatible. There were just too many differences in our basic personalities to overcome and it was these differences that eventually destroyed our relationship.

With the benefit of hindsight I eventually saw that when we'd first started seeing each other on a regular basis, we'd often been accompanied by our friends and work associates, we had constantly been surrounded by people who were of a similar age and as a group we'd listened to the same sort of music, gone to see the same films, visited the same cafes, pubs and dances and we all believed that we liked and were interested in the same sort of things, but when Pam and I left the group culture behind us and had got to know each other a little better, it became obvious that we actually liked very different things from our associates and each other The real mystery was why it took us so long to admit the fact to each other when it became so obvious.

After months of courting we'd finally got around to indulging in sexual activity, but it had always been awkward and rushed and Pam, for some unknown reason, had developed a strong sense of guilt about it and even when we were married, she was never fully relaxed about indulging in sex or of being seen naked. She saw the act of sexual intercourse as a duty rather than a pleasure and inevitably neither one of us was completely satisfied with the situation. As our differences became apparent we automatically began to put up barriers and found ourselves censoring what we said to each other as each knew how easy it was to upset the other. Frustratingly, I'd begun to notice that I was often being blamed for not only what I did, but what my mates got up to. If I happened to mention the details of one of my mate's romantic dalliances, Pam would immediately round on me and viciously say something along the lines of, "Typical! You men are all the same. You're all bloody selfish" and I would find myself quickly changing the subject to keep the peace.

The final row that broke the camel's back came about when I informed her that I'd put my name down for the Forty-Club trip to Brighton. It was a concept that she just could not and would not understand. Why I would want to spend an August weekend with a group of beer drinking drunks instead of with her was beyond her comprehension and as she did not trust Mitch as far as she could throw him and who she knew was the main force behind organising the trip, she suspected that there was a lot more to it than she was being told. When I pointed out that even if I stayed at home on that particular weekend we'd do nothing more than visit her mother just as we always did, she of course accused me of hating her parents and told me to get out of her life. But every cloud has a silver lining and after we finally separated, Pam very quickly found that her former boyfriend was ready, willing and waiting in the wings and wished to continue with their former romance and as for me, right out of the blue, I was offered a job with a rival company and I jumped at it, reasoning that a fresh start all round would be a good thing at this moment in my life.

Immediately after our marriage had broken up, I went through the usual macho emotions of anger and jealousy as I pondered on all the things that had gone wrong with my relationship with Pam and I tended to blame her for most of it, but as time passed, these juvenile emotions gradually subsided and to my surprise they were eventually replaced by a feeling of relief and I gradually began to realise that Pam and I had never been right for each other and if we had stayed together, we would have undoubtedly made each other miserable for the rest of our lives. I came to realise that we both had another chance and I began to see more and more that Pam was not to blame for what had gone wrong with our relationship and I genuinely wished her well in her new life and surprisingly, Annette kept her big gob shut did not say, "I told you so."

Even though I was now employed by a rival company, I still kept in touch with Jack and my other mates who still worked at Briggs and occasionally we would meet up for a beer and a friendly chat. During these evenings we would discuss any topic that came to mind from football to world affairs and often end up having a curry. We had a good laugh about one thing or another and inevitably during our informal discussions we all picked up knowledge, information and understanding from each other's arguments and differing points of view.

Although I'd left school without any qualifications and a certain amount of blinkered vision, I now saw that the acquisition of knowledge was limitless and that each piece of information fitted into a huge gigantic jig-saw puzzle and through Jack, I'd acquired an abundance of new pieces and although many seemed to be disconnected, they eventually fitted into the overall picture. As the years passed I saw that finding and filling in the missing pieces of the picture was the perfect hobby, as it has no end. During one of these casual informative nights out, Jack supplied us with another piece of knowledge when he explained how the Americans had not only helped Britain to win the Second World War with troops, Sherman tanks and Mustang aeroplanes, but also after the war was over; how they had helped to rebuild devastated and bankrupt Europe. He informed us that the policy for rebuilding Europe, which became known as the Marshal plan, was all down to a man named Dean Acheson, a man that we had never heard of.

"You would think that there would be a statue or even a commemorative day set aside for the saviour of Europe wouldn't you," Jack said philosophically, "but there is absolutely nothing. He's been completely ignored and forgotten. There is more interest in what happened to the band leader Glenn Miller than Dean Acheson."

Then one day while busy at work, I received a message from Billy who was still driving for Briggs that informed me that Jack had been taken into Dudley Road Hospital and was undergoing a series of tests. I visited Jack that afternoon and found him in a cheerful mood, but looking pale and drawn around the gills. We chatted for about half an hour and Jack hid the four cans of Guinness that I had brought along for him and I promised to drop by in a couple of days' time. It was only when I'd got outside the hospital that I realised that I still did not know exactly what he was in there for as he had been very vague about what was wrong with him and had just said that he was in there for a series of tests.

I re-visited the hospital three days later with another four cans of Guinness. I walked into the ward and found that he was not there. On asking the ward sister where he'd been moved to, I was informed that Jack had died the previous day. I don't recall walking out of the hospital or what happened to the bag containing the four cans of stout and I found that I was walking around in a daze for several days afterwards.

No matter how much knowledge you acquire during your life, you are not immune from cancer; for that's what killed Jack just before he was due to retire. Neither I nor any of my mates had any idea of how long he'd known about his terminal condition or if he was in much pain, as he told no one anything about it, which was typical of him as he was a very proud and private man and would not have made a fuss.

My mates and I came across the Beatles when we accidentally saw them on an early evening television programme and just like thousands of others up and down the country, we were struck immediately by their natural raw vibrancy. The song that they sang was simple, but the delivery was dynamic and the group made an instant impact on us.

We eventually got to know the Beatles through listening to their early records, "Please Please Me" and "She Loves You," and by occasionally seeing them on television and we came to realise that the Beatles were simply the boys from next door and almost a mirror image of ourselves. At the time you could have walked into any coffee bar or night club in the land and met numerous young men who dressed, walked and talked in exactly the same way as the four Beatles. And it was this down to earth appearance and their cheeky attitude that we identified with. To us, the Beatles were refreshingly different from the glitzy show biz smooth talking sycophantic pop singers that we were used to seeing and who had dominated the world of pop music for many years.

At the time Elvis was considered to be the king and had a huge following and his style influenced the performance of many up and coming stars. Even Cliff Richard imitated him for a while and because the Beatles had a new raw style all of their own and songs that were different from Elvis's there was an obstinate reluctance by some of the young to acknowledge that the Beatles were anything special. But as time went by, more and more people, even those that had accused them of causing the end of civilisation with Beatlemania, were won over and found themselves inadvertently singing and whistling their songs. It would be hard to find anyone in the world now who did not recognise and wasn't able to hum a Beatle song.

It was eventually revealed that John Lennon had had a very odd upbringing, evidently his father had deserted him and his weak willed mother when he was very young and he'd been raised by a severe single minded aunt and because of this, John had always been plagued with insecurity and it is now believed that the fans subconsciously picked up on this when they heard him speak in his early interviews. His answers to questions, although often witty, had a touch of defensive aggression within them and often seemed to echo the thoughts and feelings of all teenagers.

Although Mitch pursued several girls after his domestic liaison with Shirley had come to an end, he was often so drunk that by the end of the night, he couldn't remember who they were or where they lived and he lurched from one, hazy one night stand to another. There were even times when he found himself chatting up a girl in a night club who he'd chatted up the previous week and had no recollection of having done so until she embarrassingly reminded him. All this came to an end when he met Verity.

Verity was an attractive school teacher and having been born and bred in Edinburgh she was quite new to the Midlands at the time. She was, in every sense of the word, a lady and had a presence that could stop a drunken man stop swearing in her company. Now Mitch's attraction for Verity wasn't just physical, though that played its part, but for all his rough behaviour at times, he was in fact a romantic at heart and he and Verity shared kindred interests in poetry, music and a love of nature.

The first time that I'd become fully aware of Mitch's interest in his fascination for the clever use of words and ultimately the wit and the poetry that they could produce, was when we'd started the Adam's Transport business together. While collecting the parcels from the Tyseley Railway Station, Mitch had gradually got to know the little Irishman who worked there and whose interests included the works of Oscar Wild and Mitch had been bowled over by what he'd learned from him. He began to read everything that Oscar Wild had ever written and he encouraged me to do the same. He then talked me into accompanying him to the Alexander Theatre to see a one-man show by Michael McLamore on the works of Oscar Wild. From that moment on Mitch retained an ever growing interest in what he considered to be good literature and poetry.

Mitch and Verity set up home together in a small comfortable flat in Sutton and together they were to visit museums, art galleries, and theatres and often went on weekend country rambles. They went to Ireland for a Gypsy caravan holiday and for a while; everything in their garden seemed to be coming up roses, but during their holiday, an incident occurred that saw Mitch reverting to type and Verity was to see that Mitch was not the sophisticated gentleman that she thought he was and that he possessed an unpredictable wild streak. They were unceremoniously ejected from a folk club one evening after he had drunkenly stood up and attempted to sing "Land of Hope and Glory."

"Well, they kept on singing those bloody rebel songs, you know, the ones that run down the English and have about a hundred and twenty bloody verses in them." He explained ruefully to Billy and me as he re-lived the incident.

It was during this relatively tranquil period in Mitch's life that I, who was still living with my wife Pam and employed at Briggs, received an unusual telephone call from him while I was busy at work.

"Jaco, I've been stopped by the police in Redditch," He said apprehensively down the line, "and I desperately need your help mate."

"My help?" I replied with some surprise as I immediately wondered how the hell I could help him as I wasn't anywhere near Redditch and didn't have a clue as to why the police had stopped him.

"Well I've done something that's a little bit stupid." He said apologetically.

"What are you talking about? Have you had an accident?" I queried, "Look, just start from the beginning will you."

"It's not an accident or anything like that, nobody's been hurt."

"Oh good," I replied sarcastically, "It's not a blood transfusion that you want then?"

Ignoring this comment he continued, "When I was out delivering today, I was stopped by the police and they went all over the van and found all sorts of things wrong with it."

"Well that is a surprise!" I replied sarcastically as I wasn't at all surprised at this news as I already knew that he was driving around in a vehicle that not only should have been on a scrap heap, but had actually been retrieved from one before he'd purchased it.

"So, as I've already got points on my driving licence and I knew that your driving licence, you being such a good and careful driver, was clean."

"Never mind the soft soap Mitch, what happened?"

"Well I gave them your name instead of mine."

"What! ... You did what?"

"Hang on, I haven't finished yet, that aint all of it."

"What do you mean that aint all of it? Aint that enough? I don't believe this, have I got this right? You've given the police my name for a traffic offence and you want me to pay the bloody fine and have my licence endorsed for it?"

"Actually Jaco, there's a bit more to it than that...mate."

"What! I can't believe what I'm hearing. So go on then, *mate*, what else is there that's going to make my day?"

"Well I did say that I'd been a bit stupid didn't I."

"You're not bloody kidding, so what more is there for God's sake? I'm not up for smuggling heroin and a bank robbery as well am I?"

"Well, they wanted to know all about the van and the business and I told them that Mitch Bryson was the owner of the company and as I'd already told them that I was you, I said that I was just driving the van for him and thought that would be that. You know, they'd just send a fine through the post, that sort of thing."

"So? Go on. What do they want to do?"

"Well it turns out that one of the coppers lives in Erdington and he's coming round to my flat tonight to have a word with Mitch Bryson about the state of the van and I've already told him that I'm you, so Jaco … you'll have come round to my place tonight and pretend that you're me."

Having already telephoned and made the appointment with Verity, the traffic policeman was due to arrive at their flat at eight o' clock that evening, so I, reluctant but resigned, got there at seven thirty, slipped off my jacket and shoes, put on the carpet slippers that Verity made Mitch wear whilst in the home and sat in Mitch's armchair. I then proceeded to nervously sip a mug of hot tea and pretend to be the tight fisted boss of the fledgling Adam's Transport Company. Mitch meanwhile, still dressed in his working attire pretended to be the ill put-upon van driver.

Verity, who'd been put into the picture, nervously answered the door when the policeman arrived and escorted him into the comfortable living room and for the next half an hour all four of us went through the appropriate motions. The policeman told me, who he still believed was the owner of the van, what was lawful and what was not while I sat uncomfortably in the armchair and ate humble pie by the spoonful and promised to put everything right immediately. Mitch subserviently promised never to drive a vehicle that wasn't roadworthy again and poor petrified Verity said as little as possible and looked a little like a Victorian heroine who was on the verge of swooning.

When the policeman had completed his stern lecture and finally departed, Verity and I took Mitch to task for putting us through this half-hour of mental torture and we swore that we would never help him out again under any circumstances.

"Not even for a justifiable cause." I assured him with a parting shot.

Later I was surprised to find that I got over the nerve-racking experience quite quickly and I even began to feel a strange sense of elation. Being involved in something that was daring, illegal and completely out of the ordinary had had the effect of bucking me up and for several days I walked about with a strange smile on my face. It had been a crazy experience and certainly not one that I'd wanted to get involved in and yet I felt strangely exhilarated by what had happened.

Verity on the other hand was, as the odd saying goes, beside herself with worry. She'd already seen on other occasions the, devil may care side of Mitch's personality and this was yet more proof that he was not all that he had seemed to be when they'd first met and for a variety of reasons, his gambling, unpaid debts, heavy drinking sessions and his occasional dalliance with other young women, Mitch and Verity went their separate ways. And once again Mitch became footloose and fancy free, but unfortunately for him, his business was not doing so good and he was still struggling to make ends meet and so he couldn't make the most of his new found freedom.

About six months after that unusual incident, he was in trouble once more and asked for help. His latest dilapidated vehicle had broken down on the Meriden bypass while on the way back from Coventry late on a Saturday afternoon. He explained that he'd left it in a lay-by and he wanted me to help him to tow it back to Brum the following morning and after the usual bout of chastisements and sarcastic comments, I, as usual, agreed to help him.

Very early on the Sunday morning, I picked Mitch up in the box van and we drove off to where his stricken vehicle had given up the ghost and come to rest. It was a bright and beautiful summer's morning and there was not a cloud in the clear blue sky and being very early there was very little traffic to be seen in the city or on the bypass. I'd not seen this vehicle before and I was not only shocked to see that it was a small open backed lorry, but that it had what can only be described as a homemade garden fence erected around the bed of the lorry. His explanation for this unusual fence was that the original panels had rotted and fallen off and he'd replaced them with the only thing available which was a higgledy-piggledy homemade wooden fence. He'd painted the rough wood with black gloss paint with the aim of giving it a conservative commercial look, but as no undercoat had been used, the effect was shabby and makeshift and my first words on seeing this dilapidated monstrosity, which looked as though it had been abandoned by Irish tinkers, were "Bloody hell Mitch, how do you manage to drive this about without being stopped by the police?"

"I do get stopped," Mitch replied with a shrug of acceptance, "but so far, I've always manage to talk them round with a sob story about having to make a living."

After walking around the monstrosity a few times we decided to pull the old lorry down the duel carriageway with a towrope, pick up a little speed, slam it into gear and see if the engine would once more start up. This we did and low and behold after two hundred yards the old lorry's engine burst into life with an almighty roar and as it did so it began to belch out a continuous cloud of thick black smoke which built up and gradually covered the duel carriageway from one side to the other. The black cloud was so dense that passing vehicles began to switch on their headlights as they passed through it and because there was not a breath of wind to blow it away, the black cloud was very reluctant to disperse. Not wanting the engine to give up the ghost, Mitch continued to rev the old engine, which added even more black smoke to the low lying black cloud while I, who expected a police car to appear at any second, hurriedly untied the oily towrope.

Once free of the rope and belching black smoke all the way, Mitch headed towards Brum in the dilapidated lorry while I followed on close behind in the company van and anticipated the disaster of another breakdown happening at any moment. As we travelled down the duel carriageway, I continually glanced into my rear view mirror to see if the police had been alerted and were hot on our trail and even after travelling half a mile I could still see car headlights appearing through the remnants of the black cloud which was still hanging about.

As we entered the suburbs of Brum we came to traffic lights which annoyingly changed to red and I noticed that as Mitch pulled up, the small lorry swerved to one side. When I asked him about this, he, with his usual unconcerned shrug informed me that the brakes were not working properly, but as yet, he'd not had the money to put them right. He then had the audacity to ask me if I knew of anyone who would drive the lorry for him while he went on holiday with his latest girlfriend. Much to his surprise I rudely informed him while shaking my head in disbelief, "Drive that bleeding thing? Mitch, there aint no bugger in the whole wide world, who would want to drive that bloody death trap no matter how much you paid them!"

"Yeah, you're probably right," He conceded then added with a rueful smile, "Well at least it won't get stolen while I'm away will it?"

Over the years Mitch was to use many clapped out old vehicles while keeping his fragile transport business ticking over, there was even one that had no gear stick as it had snapped off and he'd replaced it with a six inch screw driver. Every time he changed gear he was obliged to duck down to one side and to oncoming traffic, it looked as though there was no driver in the cab, but that little black beauty, with the dilapidated garden fence was by far, the worst of the bunch.

On another occasion he broke down on a city centre traffic Island at the beginning of the evening's rush hour and on receiving the inevitable call for help, I sent Billy in his lorry to help tow him to a safer spot. They used the old towrope that Mitch carried for these occasions as breakdowns were a regular feature of his travels, and they managed to not only to pull the large van off the traffic island, but to bring the engine back to life. Mitch desperately revved the engine to keep it going and Billy struggled to untie the frayed oily tow rope. Exasperated with his efforts, Billy declared that it was impossible to undo the knots on the rope. With no knife handy, Mitch came up with the instruction, "Use your cigarette lighter, burn the bugger in half!"

Billy took out his cigarette lighter and lit it under the old oily towrope and soon it was blazing merrily. When it had burnt through, the two ends fell and continued to blaze, but the part that was attached to Mitch's van swung under the engine and two minutes later they were calling for the fire brigade, as the van was now on fire.

Mitch was to own many different vehicles as he carried a vast variety of goods for different companies up and down the country. He broke down on numerous occasions, slept in the cab on long hauls, and at times patched up his old clapped out vehicles with pieces of wood, canvas sheeting, bits of string; rope and wire and at times, he had even resorted to using papier Mache and chewing gum to fill holes in the metal panelling.

During one lean spell, he advertised as, a very reasonably priced, cash in hand, furniture remover and picked up quite a few local orders. As furniture moving required two pairs of hands he employed the out of work dour Steak and Kidney as a cash-in-hand helpmate and together they tackled any job that came their way, no matter what or where it was and gradually they learned the art of furniture removing. Over many months, Mitch and Steak lost count of just how many pieces of furniture they accidentally damaged with their ham fisted efforts, but they soon became experts at hiding broken mirrors and ornaments with sheets of newspaper, blankets and bed sheets.

At one particular job, the owner of the furniture that was to be moved was taking no chances with very reasonable priced ham fisted removal men and he himself carried out of the house his prized possession, which was a large antique grandfather clock. He stood it safely on the paving slabs in front of the bay windowed house and gave firm instructions that Mitch and Steak were not to go anywhere near the tall clock as he intended to transport the it to its new home on top of his large Volvo estate car. As Mitch and Steak were struggling to load a heavy sideboard into the van, they heard the unmistakable sound of a grandfather clock crashing onto paving slabs and on looking back towards the house they saw that a gust of wind had blown the tall clock over and it had landed upon its ornamental face. The owner, distraught with grief was holding his head in his hands and dancing around as though he were stepping on hot coals. On witnessing the tragic scene, Steak said in his usual matter of fact way, "Silly prat, if he'd left it to us; we could have smashed that bleeding clock an hour ago."

Eventually, after many years of struggling, Mitch finally got a lucky break and acquired a regular delivery contract with a reputable company and from then on, he never looked back and he built himself a profitable transport business. The practice of using clapped out commercial vehicles to ply his trade was forced upon him because of the dire lack of funds, but even when he became more prosperous, he was reluctant to invest in a decent reliable vehicle. This self-inflicted meanness also affected his choice of cars and many years were to pass before he purchased a car that was reasonably reliable. Having a lift with Mitch tended to be a bit of a lottery, he either ran out of petrol, "Oh, I meant to buy some earlier," had a puncture, "The tyres are a bit bald," or the engine conked out, "For some reason it keeps doing that, but I haven't figured out why yet."

On many a Friday night Billy and I found ourselves being asked to push one of his clapped out bargain buy's to the nearest garage. When I eventually acquired the use of a company car, I took over the driving whenever we went out together. I took the philosophic view that it was better to risk a drink-driving ban rather than a hernia while pushing one of Mitch's old bangers.

One day, whilst driving a clapped out Vauxhall Vectra through the suburbs of Wolverhampton, Mitch broke down and having no luck after tinkering with it, he eventually left the car with a back street mechanic with the intention of picking it up later in the week. As his finances and his prospects at that time were extremely poor, when the call came through that the car was ready for collection, he was unable to raise enough money to pay the bill and retrieve the car. Weeks rolled by and his financial situation did not improve and eventually he decided, as the car was not worth a great deal, to leave it where it was and let the mechanic in Wolverhampton do what he liked with it.

Twelve years later, the police telephoned him to inform him that a car that had been registered in his name had been found in a lock up garage in Bilston and would he please remove it as soon as possible as the row of small garages were due to be demolished. A little bemused by this information and having no idea what it was all about, he went over to Bilston and found that the car in question was the black Vectra, which he'd completely forgotten existed. Although covered in a liberal coat of dust, the old car started first time and by the end of the week, he'd sold it to a motor enthusiast for more than he'd originally paid for it.

"Aint it bloody marvellous," He said ruefully, "When I hadn't got two pennies to rub together there was no sign of Lady Luck and now that I'm financially sound, along she comes smiling at me like a Parisian tart."

During the sixties, the controversial charismatic politician and outstanding war time leader, Sir Winston Churchill past away, the USA became embroiled in a messy war in Vietnam that was to drag on for a decade. I left Briggs and went to work for Turners, a rival company and Ian Brady and Myra Hindley were found guilty of murder.

Mitch's Sister Ann had two little daughters at the time of the Moors Murders and because of this Mitch readily identified with the victim's parents and felt very close to the case. He could see that these arbitrary murders could just as easily have happened to his sister's children and the despicable disclosures affected him on a personal level. He tried to understand why this pair had murdered these children and why they had gloated and taken photographs of each other standing on or near the children's makeshift graves, but like most, he could find no understanding whatsoever and was left with a seething anger. It was suggested by an expert that the answer to their crimes lay in the fact that they were inconsequential nobody's and just like Oswald, they'd sort some form of warped recognition. Mitch just thought they were contemptible scum and should have been executed just as many Nazi war criminals had.

Many years later, when the do-gooders popped up and tried to obtain an early release for Myra Hindley, Mitch's anger returned and he said. "These self-righteous people seem to miss the point that these murders were done for the fun. Brady and Hindley went out and kidnapped, degraded and murdered youngsters as a weekend hobby. That's not just murder, that's diabolic. So how can anyone forgive that?" It was a question that none of us could ever answer.

During the sixties Uncle Jed sold his small Morris eight car and purchased a second hand mini bus. The mini bus was fitted with long continuous plastic covered bench seats that ran down each side of the bus from front to back and as a consequence, passengers found themselves sliding up and down the bus as it stopped and started, which was bloody exhausting. Jed's reason for purchasing the mini bus was not only to carry him and his family about, but to earn a little extra money by running small local groups to and from various venues. He reasoned that there were numerous darts and domino teams in the area that needed to be transported to different pubs for their regular competitions, fishermen to be taken to distant rivers on a Sunday morning and old aged pensioners wanting to visit such beauty spots as Warwick and Stratford upon Avon.

During normal working hours Jed worked in a factory turning out hundreds of accurately machined parts, but during his own time, evenings and weekends, he did his best to mix a little business with pleasure and the mini bus became his latest money making venture. By running these local groups around to darts and domino matches he could enjoy a drink or two with them and get paid for the privilege, which suited him fine. These local trips were a huge success, but on long distance runs Jed had the annoying habit of getting lost and it sometimes required all his diplomatic skills to quell the riot that often broke out in the back of the bus by those that objected to arriving late or not at all at their required destinations.

The most famous incident, which entered local folk law and was the topic of conversation in many a pub for some considerable time, was when he took a party of exited dolled up women to the Royal Ascot races for Ladies Day. All the ladies, including the very vocal wife of the local bookie, were dressed up to the nines and each had purchased a new wide brimmed hat for the occasion. In fine spirits and long before the sun had risen over the yardarm they set off and it must be said, that by taking the mysterious route that Jed took, they saw some wonderful country scenery, but, arriving just in time for the last three races put a bit of a damper on the whole proceedings and Jed came very close to being hung, drawn and quartered and suffered from severe ear ache for several days after.

After a number of these unplanned mystery tour disasters had taken place, several of the regular groups began to cancel their forward bookings and looked elsewhere for reliable transport to take them to their destinations. It was then that Jed's wife Dolly with the fortitude of a dedicated suffragette stepped into the breach and became Jed's no nonsense navigator. From then on Dolly accompanied Jed on every trip. She would sit directly behind him with a map on her lap and a very wary eye on the road ahead and whenever they came to a traffic island or unfamiliar crossroads, Dolly, in a loud clear voice would give precise instructions directly into Jed's ear, such as, "Left! Left! Left! Turn left!" and just to make sure that he'd got the message loud and clear, she would poke him in the back with a solid forefinger.

On several bank holidays, my extended family, hired Jed and his mini bus to take us to such places as Warwick Castle, Worcester Races, Cheddar Gorge and Weston Super Mare. They were fun packed days with lively irreverent banter thrown about all day, a drink at lunchtime while on our way to our destination and several drinks and a singsong on the way back. One picturesque pub that we stopped at was situated alongside a canal and when Jed parked the mini bus and jumped out, we, who were still sitting in the back almost ended up in the canal. Jed had parked on a gentle grass slope and had forgotten to put the hand brake on. As Dolly and several other passengers began to scream, Roy who luckily was an agile young man dived forward into the driver's seat and saved the day by turning the steering wheel sharply with one hand, which threw the terrified passenger into a heap and pulling on the hand brake with the other. Poor Jed, who was most apologetic, received several solid fore finger pokes in his chest from Dolly as well as on his bruised back that day.

The mini bus had been far from new when Jed had purchased it and as it began to clock up more miles, regular breakdowns arose to thwart the long distance journeys. They, along with a badly bruised back, now became the bane of Jed's life. Time and time again, Jed and Dolly, found themselves stuck in the middle of nowhere with a mini bus full of irate passengers and no garage in sight. Jed, who was a born optimist and always looked on the bright side, would head off to find the nearest pub and seek help. He was a firm believer in the maxim of, "I know a bloke what knows a bloke" and over many years he'd found that a pub was the best place to start looking for a bloke what knew a bloke and to give Jed his due, this theory of his worked well. While the stranded passengers walked from the clapped out bus and refreshed themselves in the pub, a bloke what knew a bloke, what was a bit of a motor mechanic, would be found and soon the bus would be temporally fixed and once more they would continue with their eventful journey.

As the bus got older and Jed's reputation for either getting lost or breaking down became even more well known in the area, bookings eventually dried up and when Dolly caught him using their young son Joey to control the faulty carburettor with a long piece of wire, Jed was forced to sell the old bus and look for a new commercial venture.

His new venture was selling and fitting, chiming doorbells and to help him, he enlisted the help of super salesman Charlie. All went well for about six months, then one day Jed decided that it was time for a stock check and to his dismay he found that what they had in stock did not tally with what they had sold. It turned out that for the last few months Charlie had been using much of the money that they had earned to keep the local bookie from going out of business and the successful doorbell partnership ended with a few acrimonious words right there and then. Jed continued to dabble in numerous small business ventures to earn a little extra money, but he steered clear of anything to do with transport and wisely never ever contemplated forging a partnership with any member of the family again.

A few weeks before I left Briggs, a friendly football match was arranged between the staff at Briggs and the staff at Turners, the rival company that I was to eventually work for and it was all done without the management of either company's knowledge. Tuby who'd recently moved from Briggs to Turners and still had a foot in both camps thought that it would be a good idea to introduce the staff of both companies to each other. His commendable idea was that the two groups of young men would play a game of football in a local park and when the match was over, we would all have a friendly drink together and become lifelong friends.

To make the match a fair competition, Tuby insisted that Scotty, who was the best player and was capable of winning the match on his own, should play in goal. I played in the centre half position and my task was to mark out of the game the opposition's stocky bulldog centre forward whose was known to one and all as "Butch."

Turners won the toss and they elected to kick off and I just had time to see the ball being passed over to their right winger when I suddenly found myself lying flat on my back and severely winded. Butch, the bulldog centre forward, had just run straight through and over me and was now twenty yards away and grinning like a Cheshire cat, and so the tone was set for one of the most bruising bloody "friendly" football match's ever to be played in the history of the game. The gladiators of ancient Rome would have been proud of the players who took part in the game that day. Throughout the match we barged, kicked, gouged, punched and elbowed each other until we were covered in bruises. Long before half time there were split lips, bruised ribs, grazed limbs and even a nosebleed.

The climax of my game came about when Turners team won a corner kick and Butch, who I was closely marking, deliberately jumped on top of Scotty who was our goalkeeper. I saw quite clearly that Butch had ignored the ball and had deliberately flattened Scotty. Incensed at witnessing this blatant crunching foul and with adrenalin pumping through my body, I jumped on Butch and we both ended up in the back of the gaol net punching seven bells out of each other and had to be wrenched apart by the other players.

The bizarre goal that finally won the match for the Briggs team and surprisingly ended the game was scored by Mitch, who although no longer working for the company, was playing as a guest player. He was standing in the centre of the pitch when the ball bounced right in front of him and he kicked it hard and high into the air in the manner of a competent rugby player playing an up and under. All the players on the pitch stopped running and looked on as the ball arched its way towards Turners goal.

It would have been a simple catch for any goalkeeper in any league, but Tuby, feeling confident that his team would dominate the match, had chosen to put his poorest player in goal and as the ball came out of the clouds, Tuby's voice was heard booming down the pitch, "Watch the bounce! Watch the bounce!" but to no avail, the ball hit the rock hard sparsely grassed pitch and bounced over the poor goalkeeper's head and into the empty net.

At seeing this unusual goal, the players from Briggs were jubilant and danced with joy, but the players from Turners, who were not at all pleased with their goalkeeper's puny effort, went off down the pitch with the sole intent of tearing him limb from limb. Tuby and Butch were seen to be at the forefront of the chase to catch the miserable goalkeeper and as they all disappeared into the distance at the far end of the park the lads from Briggs knew for certain that the friendly football match was well and truly over.

The following day, two young men from Briggs and one from Turners did not make it into work and had to have several days off with their injuries while the other survivors of the battle, limped around and compared bruises. Consequently Mr Frank banned all future friendly football matches between the two companies. Not only was he averse to "bad apples" in his barrel, but he made it known that he had an aversion to badly bruised ones as well, especially those that didn't turn up for work because they had taken part in, "a stupid bloody football match."

It was Tuby who encouraged me to apply for the vacancy that had occurred at Turners. The position offered me a higher income and rosier prospects, but there was just one little niggling worry that I had to face if I accepted the job and that was that I would be working in the general stores alongside my football rival, the fire eating bulldog Butch. My job interview was a success and so I accepted the position and gave notice at Briggs.

Apprehensively, I walked into the Turners main storeroom on my first day, not knowing what kind of reception I'd receive and to my delighted surprise I was greeted with a hearty slap on the back and a, "How ya doing mate" welcome from smiling Butch and from that day on, we became the best of friends and on occasions we even played football, but this time, much to my relief, we were on the same side.

Although Turners sold exactly the same products as Briggs and had the same customer base, the make-up of the staff and the working atmosphere in the company was completely different. Briggs had a rigid paperwork system where nothing moved in or out of the stores without the right paperwork and the appropriate order number, whereas at Turners, it was often a case of, "Deliver the goods now and we'll sort the paperwork out later" and by encouraging this cavalier attitude to business, the company had built itself a reputation for speedy delivery which helped to bring in more orders. The staff at Briggs had been overloaded with youthful employees, which made for a carefree and sometimes anarchic workforce, but at Turners there was a complete mixture of ages and a more conservative mood prevailed throughout the company which took me some considerable time to adjust to.

The boss, Mr Cain not only took a hand's on approach to the running the company, but was a chronic workaholic which was a condition that I'd never encountered before. He was a self-made man who hated Sundays because they interfered with his busy working week and never completed a full week's holiday as he always found an excuse to cut it short. He refused to venture abroad among; "those bloody foreigners" preferring to be within easy reach of home. Summer or winter he would be one of the first to arrive at the company in the early hours and would set about opening the mornings post. This habit of arriving early also included Saturday morning, when there was only a skeleton staff on the premises and very little for him to do. He was a passionate fan of the West Bromwich Albion Football Club, and he supported the "Baggies" throughout his life religiously purchasing two season tickets every year, but now that he was in his twilight years, he no longer attended any of the games due to doctor's orders. Evidently, while watching a match, he was prone to become far too excited for his own good and his doctor had informed him that he could easily bring on a heart attack. It was a sentiment that many of the Aston Villa fans could not comprehend and were often heard to say behind his back, "I can't imagine the Albion ever being that bloody exciting."

He was also cricket fanatic, but being a workaholic, he never found time to actually attend any of the matches and listened to the commentaries on the radio or watched them on television. Because of this monistic dedication to work he eventually became very wealthy and could quite easily have attended every test match as he had a full set of competent managers who could run the company, but he would have none of it; he saw himself as an indispensable.

As you can imagine, this dogged attitude put a tremendous strain upon his marriage and eventually he and his wife came to live separate lives while still sharing the same large house. They had their own living quarters and rarely saw each other from one week to another. This inside information came by way of Bert, their gardener, who was supposedly a stores foreman, but although that was his title, I'd been at the company for six weeks before I even set eyes on him and that was only for a fleeting moment before he went back to tend Mr Cain's substantial garden's. As for all the money that Mr Cain accrued during a lifetime of hard unstinting dedicated work which he never had much use for, when he finally had the fatal heart attack that his doctor had predicted, his two children, who inherited it, had no trouble at all in spending it.

Although Mr Cain was a good natured boss, he did possess a quick temper and was liable to flare up when he was tired or frustrated and when in this mood he was liable to sack someone on the spot for making a stupid mistake, but the next day, full of genuine remorse, he would as often as not, reinstate the offender. Over a period of time, this peculiar habit of his happened quite often and there was hardly a man that worked at Turners that hadn't been sacked and reinstated at one time or another. Butch and I were eventually sacked and reinstated twice during our time under Mr Cain's reign, but every day, he would mix freely with his work force joking, handing out cigarettes and enquiring about the health and wellbeing of their families. His words of encouragement and concern were not just empty gestures either, on many occasions he gave out interest free loans to workers who wanted to purchase consumer goods and who were strapped for cash, but being as British as the

Union Jack he was very reluctant to introduce foreign goods into his business and for many years he would not allow the company to purchase foreign cars for either its representatives or its directors much to the chagrin of the young fliers in the company who could see that many of the foreign cars were far superior to the British ones.

Eventually, during the seventies, due to business pressure from his competitors, he was forced to give way and introduce a range of Japanese fittings and Italian valves into the stock and although he personally stuck with a British made car for the rest of his life, he did eventually allow his directors to purchase foreign ones. The item that upset him the most was the Japanese goods, "They are very cruel people," he stated while examining the fittings and shaking his head in disappointment. "They did some terrible things to our poor soldiers you know, but they say we have to forgive and forget, but I don't know, I really don't know if I ever will."

I came to admire Mr Cain an awful lot, but not enough to make him my role model. "If it takes as much dedication and effort as that to become wealthy, you can count me out" I thought. I wasn't against the principal of becoming overtly rich, but I was buggered if I was going to devote the whole of my life to the pursuit of the mighty dollar.

It was Saturday lunchtime and I was standing by the entrance to the general stores and gazing idly across the wide yard that separated the main store from the company's office block while waiting for a delivery lorry to return so that I could lock up the yard gate and go home. There was a staff rota for Saturday morning and I was on duty and had to stay until the delivery driver returned. I could clearly see the blurred figure of Mr Cain through the frosted glass of his office window as he moved about and I wondered once more why the old bugger hadn't gone home as there was no more work to be done now that the company was closed for the day. Then I not only saw the blurred figure of Mr Cain, but also the figure of his secretary and unmistakably, they were both in the process of undressing and once undressed they both came together into a lovers clinch and slowly disappeared from my view as they sank to the carpeted office floor. Smiling, I thought, "So the old workaholic is human after all" and all my pent-up frustration at having to wait for the lorry driver disappeared completely.

Although Mr Cain's secretary was younger than him, she was much older than me, so I could never quite see what the physical attraction was that he obviously saw. In fact I felt a little uncomfortable with the thought of them having regular bouts of passionate sex as to me it felt a bit like accidentally catching grandparents having a bit of slap and tickle. I was aware that elderly people might indulge in sexual activity from time to time, but I certainly didn't want to witness it. Eventually I learned that Joan, his secretary, had fallen in love with him when they'd first worked together and she'd followed him like a subservient slave ever since, hoping that one-day he would divorce his wife. But it was never to be, whether he loved her or not know one knew, but everyone was aware that he was a man with strong principles and it is doubtful that he ever considered divorce, even though his marriage was a blatant sham.

Joan, having been involved in the business from its conception, had become a director and had taken it upon herself to hire and fire all the female staff. This power inevitably created a false picture of what the female staff thought of her. They were very pleasant to her face, but behind her back most secretly despised her and the aggressive attitude that she sometimes showed did little to dissuade them that she was anything more than a bitter and twisted spinster. Not having married, she still lived with her elderly mother and one day she purchased a very expensive pearl necklace for her mother's eighty third birthday.

She brought it into work before presenting it to her mother and with great pride; she showed it to the office staff. All the girls "Ooh'ed" and "Aah'ed" and commented on what a wonderful thoughtful daughter she was and how they would love to own such a treasure. She then said, showing her true colours with a Freudian slip, "Of course when mother dies, I shall inherit the necklace along with all her other jewellery."

During my first week at Turners, I became aware of an oddity that occurred every morning while the delivery lorries were being loaded and the storemen were completing urgent orders and it simply defied explanation. Being new to the company I didn't know anything about any of the storemen or the delivery drivers and for a while I tended to stand back and watch when they all laughed and joked with each other and in that way I gradually picked up a picture of each ones personality and more importantly, what the pecking order was among them. I'd already realised that Butch, although one of the youngest storemen, was respected for his strength and his willingness to settle any argument with a hard punch, but the strange oddity that I'd noticed and only I seemed to be aware of, truly bamboozled me.

One of the delivery drivers was a small elderly man that was skinny and small in stature, but very vociferous with his comments while he was loading his small open backed lorry with his day's deliveries. He would constantly moan about the size of his daily workload and how much he was being put upon and how much he was expected to do and unbelievably, he was blatantly offensive to any members of the management that came within his sight. Every time he saw a manager or director, he would sound off with a tirade of abuse and shout such things as, "I've had enough of this bleeding nonsense! I'm not putting up with it! I'm packing the job in here and now! You can deliver your own bleeding stuff for all I care, I'm off!"

Time and time again he would dramatically throw his delivery notes onto the floor while declaring that he was refusing to deliver any goods that day and then angrily storm off down the general stores to the toilet block. But to my utter amazement, no one, not Mr Cain, the company directors, the managers, the other drivers or the storemen took the slightest bit of notice of him or his extraordinary manic outbursts.

After witnessing this bizarre pantomime for several days and expecting the old man to be given his marching orders, I could not contain myself any longer and pulling Butch to one side, I asked him for an explanation.

"Oh you mean Jack Cotton," Butch said nonchalantly as he gave the impression that he'd had to think hard as to whom I was referring to, "Take no notice of him, he was a prisoner of war and was locked up in Changi jail by the Japs."

And that was the simple explanation for this man's strange behaviour, Jack Cotton who'd been a soldier in the far east at the beginning of the Second World War, had been captured, tortured and almost starved to death by the Japanese Imperial Army and as a consequence, he was no longer the full ticket and evidently a mere shadow of the man that he'd once been and much to my surprise, he was a lot younger than I'd previously imagined him to be.

The soldiers who'd come back from the Japanese prisoner of war camps were unfortunate in that although the general public sympathised with their obvious distress as most of them resembled walking skeletons, there was a slight stigma attached to them. Although the army that had been pushed out of France and Belgium at the beginning of the war had technically been defeated, the fact that many of them had been unexpectedly rescued off the Dunkirk beaches had in the minds of the general public turned them into heroes. The evacuation from the Dunkirk beaches had been portrayed and held up as an example of British grit and determination. It was an event that declared to the world that, "We may be down, but we are not defeated and we'll be back."

The soldiers in the Far East were less fortunate, there was no Armada of small boats to rescue them and being trapped in such places as Malaya there was nowhere to escape to. What was hard for the general public to understand was how a race of little slant eyed men, about whom it had been widely rumoured before the hostilities broke out, could not see very clearly in the dark, could conceivably conquer a regular British Army and big strapping bronzed Australians in such a short space of time.

The reason for the unexpected defeat was simply that the British government and the military hierarchy had completely misjudged the situation in the Far East and the defeat had little to do with the soldier's ability or courage at all. Singapore had fifteen-inch guns that could blow any ship in the world out of the water, but they faced the sea and were incapable of being turned around to defend a land attack, which of course was the way the Japanese army came.

Out patrolling the Java Sea, there were two of the biggest warships that Britain possessed, ships that had enormous firepower and were a match for any other warship, but astonishingly, they were sailing without air cover. The Japanese simply attacked them with aircraft and both ships were lost. It would be fair to say that the British were caught out because those in power were still thinking about how to fight the First World War and had not had the foresight to prepare for the Second. The result was that thousands of British, Australian and Indian soldiers had to surrender without firing a shot, but far from being cowards, they showed an enormous amount of grit even as they were systematically tortured, butchered and starved to death. They also showed that they had not lost hope or will power for in Changi jail they organised debating societies, literary circles, stamp collecting clubs and even, unbelievably, a dry land yacht club.

The extent of the torture and butchery that was perpetrated upon the prisoners was truly horrific and was fully exposed after the war was over. During one period of Jack Cotton's incarceration he was kept on starvation rations for several months and was barely alive when he was finally admitted into a P.O.W. hospital where after several weeks of eating rice husks and grass soup for much needed vitamins, he began to slowly recover. The starvation diet that he'd been surviving on for months, had addled his brain so much that he could no longer read properly and, just like a child, he had to learn to read all over again and it was because all the staff in the company, with the exception of me, were well aware of this background knowledge, that Jack Cotton's tantrums were tolerated and ignored and after a few weeks, even I no longer noticed them.

There was a driver who came into Turners yard on a regular basis to collect building materials for his company and he had the annoying habit of creeping up behind young storemen and enveloping them in a debilitating bear hug. He was a fat slob, who weighed about eighteen stone and when he squeezed his chosen victim, it was obvious that he did it to cause maximum pain and to show others just how strong he was. Laughing like a drain, he thought it was great fun and no matter how many times the storemen complained that he was going too far, he invariably ignored their aggrieved protestations and carried on seeking his sadistic pleasure. Butch and I, who were just as sick and tired of this hurtful and debilitating habit as the other storemen, got together one morning and decided to do something about it. We caught the big fat slob getting out of the cab of his lorry and jokingly we began to bait and spar with him as one would do when pretending to shadow box.

In his youth, he'd probably been quite fit and athletic, but over the years he'd gone to seed and was now cumbersome and slothful, but for all that, we realised that he was still strong and dangerous. Butch and I were fully aware that if he managed to grab hold of one of us, we would be in dire trouble, but we also saw that he was middle aged and slow, whereas we were young and could move much faster than he could.

As the big lumbering bully made to grab one of us, the other punched him hard in his side and took the wind out of his sails. Butch and I danced about, smiled and pulled his leg about being too slow to catch us, but every punch we threw, we put in with force and meaning. We ducked, dived, jabbed and feinted like two bantamweight boxers bouncing around a sumo wrestler and very soon the fat bully was not only gasping for breath, but begging for mercy. When we thought that he'd had enough, we went through the act of pretending to be his mate, but the lesson had been learned and he never touched either one of us again and if we were around, he never bothered the other storemen either. There are times when it's necessary to fight fire with fire and from our point of view, it was a most satisfying and rewarding workout.

Although he was in his twenties and had been working since he was fifteen, Robert still possessed the looks of a naïve schoolboy and strangely, he was completely obsessed with the subject of war. He read books; magazines and comics that dealt with war and went to see every war film. But most bizarrely, he made, in the privacy of his bedroom, tape recordings of bloody battles by using his own voice for the sound effects. As proud as Punch, he brought a couple of these tapes to work one day and played them to Butch and me during a lunch break.

"This is D Day" he said excitedly as wide eyed Butch and I listened to the noises of, "Voom, rata tat rata tat, nearrrrrrr....boom, boom."

After listening to these tapes I was convinced that young Robert was yampy and needed the help of a psychiatrist, but Butch, who had known him for many years, just shrugged his broad shoulders and said, "He's always been like that. When we were at school he was just the same. He was always copping out of the teachers for day dreaming in class. It's nothing new; he's always been a bit barmy, but he's harmless."

As well as being obsessed with war, young Robert also suffered with an odd sort of depression. He believed that any good luck that came his way would be counter balanced by an equal amount of bad luck. This meant that he could never achieve any long-lasting happiness as he knew that as soon as anything good happened, something bad would come along and spoil it and so he spent most his days in a kind of limbo while awaiting bad news.

One morning he came into work with a face as long as Livery Street and I automatically asked him what the trouble was and expected him to say that a close relative or at least a favourite pet had passed away, but instead, he informed me that as he'd stepped off the bus that morning, he'd found a quantity of small change in the gutter and had picked it up. Completely puzzled by this explanation, I asked, "So what?"

"Well it's obvious isn't it," He stated as he shook his head in disbelief and looked at me as though I was an Idiot, "Something bad is bound to happen to me now isn't it?"

"Robert," I replied, while trying to impart some sort of logic into the conversation, "What you've just found in the gutter doesn't even add up to a pound, how much bad luck can that possibly be worth?"

"Oh you don't know how these things work," He replied sadly while shaking his head once more, "You just see, something will happen. Something will probably fall on my head before the day is out."

Butch, who had been standing nearby and had overheard every word of this bizarre conversation, crept up behind young Robert and with a firm hand, smacked him sharply on the back of his head and declared, "There's your fucking bad luck bang on the head for today, so now you can think no more about it."

When young Robert was really depressed, his concentration suffered badly and his work rate slowed considerably, then one day, just by chance I discovered a cure for his debilitating melancholy moods. He was in the process of putting into the wooden stock bins a large quantity of different sized fittings, which was a boring job at the best of times and it was obvious that Robert was not enjoying the task at all. If he'd gone any slower, he'd have probably stopped altogether. So, just as a joke I said, "Are those hand grenades that you're throwing?" Then, pointing at the storage bins that he was throwing them into, I added, "And are they the Nazi bunkers that you're blowing up?"

Instantly, he began to throw the "hand grenades" into the bins with exaggerated zest. After a while he got right into the mood and added the appropriate booming sound effects to go with his expressive wartime game as he accurately lobbed the fittings into the appropriate bins. After that Butch and I got him to do many boring jobs by simply making out that they were secret wartime commando raids that he'd been chosen to carry out.

He eventually married his childhood sweetheart and on the face of it, he should have lived happily ever after, but Robert was having none of that nonsense as he was still convinced that happiness was for others. It soon became apparent that he was even more miserable than before he'd married. When Butch and I tackled him about this strange turn of events, he explained with a shrug that, "She's stopped me making my war tapes in the bedroom."

It transpired that his new wife had put her foot down and she'd stopped him from playing his soldier games in the bedroom. She evidently thought, much to Robert's surprise, that the bedroom was the ideal place for other physical activities. For a while, the pair toyed with the idea of emigrating to the warm and sunny climes of Australia and for a short time Robert was quite buoyant, but inevitably his black dog cloud descended once more and totally changed his mood.

"It would be just my luck to step off the boat and be called up by the Australian army and be sent to Vietnam to fight," he moaned and no amount of argument would convince him that this just would not happen. For a young man who'd spent most of his life pretending to be a soldier, this sudden anti-war attitude seemed somewhat contradictory, but it was obvious that Robert's wartime exploits were mere fits of childhood fancy and nothing to do with reality.

He eventually left Turners and became a dour, "You never know what's around the corner" insurance salesman and we lost touch with him for a short while, but when he did eventually turn up again, he'd given up his wartime fantasies and had turned to religion. He'd become a Jehovah's Witness and was out and about every weekend trying to convert the sinners of the world to take the path of righteousness. Evidently he was quite good at delivering the message of impending doom that was to befall all none believing sinners and was highly regarded by his new Bible thumping companions and so, by believing that in the next life there would be a comfortable armchair waiting for him, he acquired a happiness that he'd never had before.

His pretty wife meanwhile was having the time of her life with a close companion of Robert's who was also an insurance salesman, but who's philosophy was to cherish what was on offer now rather than wait for his rewards in the next life.

At first sight, Boris could easily have been mistaken for "The Wild Man of Borneo," as he looked like a curiosity that had escaped from a travelling circus sideshow. He had a mop of uncontrollable black hair and a wild bushy beard to match, both of which went some way to hiding a blotchy pitted face and a pair of permanently bloodshot eyes. It was widely believed that his constant consumption of alcohol had something to do with his poor complexion and his dishevelled appearance. He was not a pretty sight even on the best of days and looked to be one step away from becoming a meth's drinking tramp. His demeanour was on a par with his wild appearance and the consensus of opinion was that he was best left alone, just as one would avoid disturbing a wasp's nest. He was not a man for idle chatter and he tended to speak, if at all, in short sharp word bites as though he were being prodded with electrodes and he hid his private and personal thoughts in much the same way as Fort Knox hides the American gold reserves.

Everyone's perception of Boris was that he was a scruffy bad tempered boozer and this, because of his ferocious independence, is how he chose to be seen by the rest of the world. But underneath this shaggy bad tempered facade, there lurked another much more interesting man, a man who over many years had acquired an enormous amount of technical information and knowledge.

His hobby and only interest in life, was anything and everything to do with aeroplanes and after buttering him up and plying him with many searching questions I eventually learnt that there wasn't a single thing that he did not know about aircraft. For many years he'd read and consumed vast amounts of information from almost every publication that had ever been published on the subject of aeroplanes. He could supply without any trouble at all, the details of any aeroplane that had ever been produced anywhere in the world, the size, wingspan, engine capacity, when it was introduced, when it was modified, its pluses, its minuses and even at times, the test pilots name. He knew where all the museums and private collections in the world were and what models they kept. In short, if he did not know about a specific detail concerning an aeroplane, you could bet your bottom dollar that that particular detail had not yet been released for publication. Even his holidays were taken to coincide with the air shows that take place up and down the country and he attended almost every one.

He was a confirmed bachelor and taking into consideration his general aggressive manner, his shabby appearance and his drinking habits no one thought that that situation would ever change. Then one day, for some reason that was never explained he splashed out and bought himself an old "banger" car, cut down on his beer consumption and even made a conscious effort to smarten up his appearance. He had his hair cut short; his wild beard trimmed, polished his boots and even took to wearing a clean shirt occasionally.

"You mark my words, there's a wench behind this." Was Butch's opinion when he saw the dramatic change in Boris's appearance, but so little was known about his private life that no one had a clue who it could be. After some discreet enquiries by one of the storemen that lived in the same area as Boris, the reason for his transformation became apparent and just as Butch had suspected, it turned out to be a buxom divorcee who was working as a barmaid at the Queens Head pub.

During the next few weeks Boris's anti-social demeanour lifted somewhat and on occasions I was able to engage him in light conversation and I eventually learned that his obsession with aeroplanes had begun during the Second World War when his grandfather had blatantly refused to cower in any of the air raid shelters during the bombing raids and would, along with little Boris at his side, stand in his back garden and swear and wave his fist at the German bombers as they passed overhead. When I enquired as to what his mother thought about this highly dangerous habit, he just said, "Oh, she'd buggered off long before that and me dad was away in the army, so there was only me and me granddad and I loved watching the planes going over."

He'd been driving his old car to and from work and to different air shows around the country for about ten months, when one evening whilst travelling through the busy city centre, it broke down. It was now that his bloody-minded independent nature came to the fore once more, instead of contacting a garage or asking a friend to tow him, he pushed the old car back home. The distance he covered was over a mile and after all that effort, which would have made a cart horse sweat; he abandoned it outside his house and after six months he let a local scrap dealer take it away for nothing. He never replaced the old car and gradually he reverted back to his former shabby self and even resumed his former heavy drinking habit. Then one day during a general conversation concerning the idiosyncrasies and foibles of women in general, he just said when asked about what had happened to the buxom barmaid, "Oh, she buggered off with another bloke, just like my bastard mother did. You can't trust any of the buggers can you?"

Three of the delivery drivers were considered to be part of the back bone of the company. There was Vern, a dour boring pedantic man who drove one of the large lorries. Each morning he would place every item that he was delivering systematically onto the back of his lorry with the precision of a laboratory assistant, a ritual that to most seemed to be a complete waste of time and effort. He was married to a straight-laced house-proud woman and between them they had produced a son who had the misfortune to resemble his father in looks and personality. Vern's normal recreation was playing dominoes at his local pub, but his secret vice was buying sexy girlie magazines which after scrutinizing with infinite care, he passed on to the storemen as he was afraid that if his wife found him with them, he would be in deep trouble, which was a good indication of what his sex life at home was like.

Benny was also the driver of a ten-ton lorry and he also played dominoes at his local and considered to be a bit of a fool, but he was always happy and helpful. He'd been born and raised in Ireland and although he'd lived in Brum for most of his life, he never lost his accent or the natural cheeky fun loving twinkle in his eye. He was married, but separated, they'd had three kids and being a born romantic, he and his wife had spent their honeymoon at a Saturday afternoon football match. What she thought of this short, but memorable honeymoon is not known, but we all had a pretty good idea.

He was never violent when inebriated, but he did have a habit of bumping into and falling over immovable objects, movable objects and invisible objects. He'd always been a heavy boozer and after his marriage had broken down, he was still a boozer, but oddly, the booze never seemed to hinder him as he suffered no hangover, no upset stomach and was as bright as a blackbird at dawn. Although he had a number of bizarre driving accidents in his career, none of them could be directly put down to the amount of alcohol that he'd consumed, but many years later it was discovered that he'd never actually taken a driving test, which may have had some bearing on his accident record. It seems that in Ireland when he was a youngster and learning to drive, all one was required to do was to go to the local village post office for a driving licence and no formal test was required.

While involved in an important domino tournament at his local pub one night, a couple of drinking pals asked if they could borrow his lorry for half an hour to move some furniture. Benny, being good natured readily agreed and handed them the keys to his lorry. An hour and a half later they gratefully handed the keys back and bought him a pint to thank him. Later that night the police arrested him. It turned out that his lorry had been used during a break in on a factory estate and had been spotted by a security guard. Benny spent the night in the cells and Mr Cain had to bail him out. Eventually the real culprits were caught and Benny was subsequently cleared of the crime, but he still remained a soft touch.

The third driver was Sam Bane who much to my surprise turned out to be the young soldier that had taken a beating from Zac outside the El Tonto coffee bar. I was not aware of this when I first met him at the company, but as we both lived in the same area, I occasionally scrounged a lift with him in his old car and over a period of time I got to know Sam and his unconventional personality quite well.

On the face of it Sam was a virulent right winger, he was anti-union and believed that all the layabout youth of the day should be put into the army for at least five years and all violent criminals should be hung drawn and quartered. He believed that all Labour and Liberal politicians were namby pamby do gooders and cared more about "the wogs" and "bloody foreigners" than "us, the proper English."

But on the other hand he was equally scathing about the, "greedy lying Tory politicians and the money grabbing bosses who spent their lives lining their own pockets and screwing the working man."

He had no inclination to join any group, whether it be a union, a working man's club, a golf club, the conservative party or even the flat earth society. He strongly objected to people ripping off workers to become stinking rich, but he had no objection to becoming rich himself. Although listening to these contradictory opinions was frustrating at times, they were all part and parcel of his strange personality and nothing anyone said was ever going to change that.

With fingers like Cumberland sausages, Sam was never ever going to be much good at needlework or origami, but give him a bag of heavy tools and he was quite capable of building a working replica of the Flying Scotsman steam engine and was never happier than when he was covered in oil and grease.

These three drivers, Vern, Benny and Sam, were looked upon as loyal workers and a benchmark for other staff to aspire to, so it was quite a shock when I discovered that all three were up to their necks in a systematic theft from the company, a theft that had been going on for many months.

One evening, after accepting a lift home in Sam's car, I noticed that he seemed to be unusually agitated and I was somewhat taken aback when he suddenly said, "This traffics terrible tonight, I need a cup of tea" and turned into a back street and pulled up outside a corner café. As I was a passenger, I had little option but to join him in the café and wondered if I'd have been better off travelling home by bus. As we sat in the steam filled café sipping hot tea, I noticed that he not only looked ill, but that his strong workman's hands were actually shaking. Worried by this observation I asked him what the problem was and bit by bit he began to unburden his conscience and to explain what had brought him to this nervous state. He explained that he was an accomplice of the storeman who, a week earlier had been arrested by the police for the theft of a huge amount of building materials. The storeman's cousin, who worked for a local building company had been a constant visitor to the Turners general store as he regularly picked up orders that had been phoned through on the previous day and when collecting these orders, he would produce another list of materials that he needed to pick up at the same time and his cousin would serve him to these extra items.

Then one day, while the police were investigating a stolen car crime, they chanced upon a lock up garage that was full of building materials and as many of the bags and boxes had Turners labels attached to them, it was obvious where the materials had come from. The subsequent investigation led the police to the two cousins and both were hauled off to the nick and charged with theft. The building materials and pipe fittings from the lock up garage were loaded onto a ten-ton lorry and brought back to Turners and Mr Cain gave me the job of cataloguing them and putting them back into stock. There were so many odds and sods, that it took me four solid working days to complete the task.

Sam, over what was now a cup of lukewarm tea, explained that the reason why the haul in the lock up garage had been so large was that he and the other two drivers, Vern and Benny, had been helping the two cousins by delivering the odd bag of cement, paving slabs and plumbing fittings to the lock up garage during the day while they were out on their delivery rounds. All three were now convinced that the two cousins would tell the police of their part in the illegal scam and that they would lose their jobs and probably go to prison.

For some unknown reason, perhaps sometimes there is honour among thieves, the two cousins said nothing to the police about the help that they'd received from the three drivers and they took the rap themselves. The three drivers carried on working at Turners for many more years and Sam was eventually promoted to a position in the office and he became Mr Cain's chauffeur and as he needed his chauffeur to be near at all times, he helped Sam, with a substantial interest free loan, to purchase a delightful cottage in the countryside that was just a mile from where he lived.

A few weeks after this confessional chat in the steamy café, I was astonished to hear Sam saying that in his opinion, "criminals got off far too lightly and should be sent to somewhere like Devil's Island and left there to rot," but I came to realise that that was just how controversial Sam could be and that he was just as likely to say the opposite the following week.

Mr Gatlin, the company's sales director was a small middle aged man who at times of stress was apt to lose the plot and become very excitable. He was totally unpredictable and could turn either aggressive or forlorn in an instant. Once, when he was informed that an important contract had gone terribly wrong, he became so agitated that he slammed his telephone down, picked up all the paperwork that covered his desk and threw the whole lot into the air. Those that witnessed the bizarre scene said that, "His office resembled a New York ticker tape parade and as the sheets of paper fluttered back to earth, he slumped down onto his leather chair, put his head in his hands and moaned forlornly, "Why do these things always happen to me?"

While the transport manager was away on a fortnight's holiday, Mr Gatlin covered his duties for him. He arrived early on the Monday morning and keenly set about sorting the delivery notes into appropriate areas and divided each pile equally among the various drivers. As each driver arrived, he gleefully handed him his delivery notes for the day and offered a few words of encouragement just as he did when sending company representatives out on the road.

By eight forty five, most of the drivers were on their way and there was only one pile of delivery notes left on the storeroom work bench and he began to pace nervously up and down while constantly looking out of the open doorway for the missing driver's arrival. Meanwhile, we storemen who had been busy picking out orders couldn't help but notice that he was beginning to show signs of nervousness as he paced up and down by the open entrance to the store, but of course we had no idea why he was becoming so agitated. Suddenly he stopped pacing, looked at his wristwatch and seeing that it was almost nine o' clock, said to no one in particular, "This is just not good enough, Sam Bane is extremely late this morning, I'll have to have words with him."

Butch, who'd been walking nearby and had overheard Mr Gatlin's exasperated outburst stopped in his tracks and queried, "Did you say Sam Bane?"

"Yes" Mr Gatlin, said shaking his head from side to side and looking at Butch with obvious distaste. He then tapped his wrist watch with his fore finger and added as though addressing a three-year old child, "Sam Bane is late for work - not here yet - not yet visible to the naked eye."

"No and he won't be either," Butch replied, eager to bring this pompous fool down to size, "Because for your information, he's away on holiday."

We could see that Mr Gatlin was visibly shaken by this startling news, but for some reason he was reluctant to accept that this could be true.

"On holiday! He is not on holiday, he's got a full day's work waiting for him here!" he stated emphatically, as he pointed to the pile of delivery notes that he'd carefully put aside on the work bench for Sam.

"Oh yes he is," Butch replied with a self-satisfied smirk on his broad face, "and right now, I'll bet he's sitting in a deck chair on the beach, reading his morning paper and smoking a fag."

As the reality of the situation sank in, Mr Gatlin became visibly shaken and his proud shoulders drooped in defeat, but suddenly he straightened up again and said, "He can't be!" and then wailing without much conviction, he added, "No one informed me that he was on holiday."

"Well, I can assure you that he is," Butch stated with glee and walked off whistling the tune "Colonel Boggy" as he was feeling very pleased with himself for having trumped Mr Gatlin's supercilious slight.

Five minutes later Mr Gatlin was still pacing up and down the stores oblivious of everyone around him and wailing, "He can't be. No one told me he was on holiday. He'll be here in a minute, I know he will," and then as his mood changed yet again he began saying, "He's let me down, that's what he's done." and after a final frustrated outburst, he slapped his outer thighs in exasperation and with his head bowed, he slowly slumped off across the wide yard and disappeared into the office.

Early the following morning, Mr Cain came across to the general stores and efficiently sorted that day's delivery runs for the drivers and Sam Bane's name or the fact that he had had the audacity to take his holiday while Mr Gatlin was organising the Monday deliveries, was not mentioned by anyone.

An electrical engineer had been called in to fix a new fire alarm bell to the outside wall of the single storey office block and Mr Gatlin, in his usual mother hen roll, was overseeing the operation. The large bright shiny red alarm bell had been fixed to the outer office wall directly outside the office where the fire alarm control box was situated and as the engineer switched the alarm on to test it, Mr Gatlin stood outside in the wide yard looking at the engineer through the glass window. The alarm went off and not only did it work efficiently, but could be clearly heard for up to half a mile away and as it loudly clanged away, Mr Gatlin stood with his hands cupped around his mouth and began shouting a message to the engineer through the glass window.

"What?" the engineer called back while frowning.

Mr Gatlin, his hands still cupped around his mouth shouted once more, but because the loud noise that the alarm bell was making, the engineer was unable to hear what Mr Gatlin's message was, so he opened the window that separated them and called out, "What did you say?" his face screwed up in pain because of the high decibel noise that was now ringing in his ears. He then switched the alarm off and in the deadly silence that followed Mr Gatlin bellowed, "I said, it's working."

The engineer nodded his head in agreement, closed the window, turned to those that were sitting at their desks and said, "Is he bleeding barmy or what? There's only a pane of glass between us. Of course I know it's working. Everyone this side of the black stump must know it's bleeding working by now."

In 1966, England's football team, led by its charismatic Captain Bobby More and managed by the reserved Alf Ramsey, did the unthinkable and won the World Cup. The goalkeeper Gordon Banks, arguably the best that England has ever produced was once asked to name his dream team and predictably his choice included Bobby Charlton, Georgie Best and Bobby Moore, but he then added, "And my manager for such a team would be Alf Ramsey, there was no one better."

The main part of Turners premises had once been a dairy and its long low shed like buildings surrounded a large concrete yard, but as the business had grown, Mr Cain had purchased several of the adjoining buildings in the street to house the ever growing stock and office staff. One of these buildings was a large house which he converted into offices and another was a chapel which had originally been the meeting place for an obscure religious sect, in this he housed radiators and plumbing equipment. Because these buildings were independent of each other, the stock and the office staff were to be found all over the place.

The personnel that worked in these scattered offices were a mixed and varied bunch, the majority being middle aged women and from a young man's perspective, these matronly figured women had no physical attraction whatsoever, but thankfully, there were several young girls around with which the young men could flirt with. I eventually got to know all these women and I became quite familiar with all their differing personalities, but as I was now seeing a girlfriend on a regular basis I wasn't particularly interested in cultivating any long term friendship with any of them.

There was Joan, a pleasant easy going woman whose passion was opera, an art form that the rest of the staff knew nothing about and consequently were constantly amazed by her in depth knowledge of the subject. In the same office was Flo, a small middle aged formidable workaholic who chain-smoked all day and who knew everything that there was to know about the business. In another office there was Sandra, a young attractive blond girl who Butch took a fancy to and as a consequence spent as much time as possible in her company. His rugged persistence and his open personality eventually paid off and a few years later the pair tied the knot which delighted everyone in the company.

Vera, another young office girl, shared the same office as Sandra and although middle class and well educated, was totally off her trolley. She constantly surprised everyone around her with outrageous right wing opinions and stupid comments. She once claimed that she not only had a guardian angel looking after her, but that it sat beside her in the office each day and constantly informed her of who to trust and who not to trust. I was informed that I was on the not to be trusted list, even though I'd never showed the slightest interest in her. Helen on the other hand, a young Irish girl, was an uncomplicated soul, but had the ability to complicate even the simplest of things. When asked what the time was, she looked at her watch and said, "Its two minutes to five to twelve"

She once claimed that due to a strike, the ITV television channel had been off the air for three solid hours. When asked why she had not turned over and watched what was on another channel instead of looking at a blank screen for three hours, she said with genuine surprise, "But we always watch ITV."

There were many more women in the various departments, but the one that stood out from all the rest was Jenny, the youngest of them all. She was a slim young girl with long flowing hair, attractive legs and had a mesmerising elegant walk. She'd recently left school and was still comparatively naive to the conniving ways of smiling sweet talking men and the pitfalls of the wicked world, but she was no fool and had the good sense to tread carefully. She'd previously worked part time at the Woolworth's store in New Street on a Saturday, but her position as "The general office dog's body," as she was apt to describe her job was her first full time position.

I was ten years her senior and on the face of it, we had little in common as we moved in completely different social circles. Being so young, Jenny's friends were scatty teenagers who seemed to giggle and screech at all or nothing, were mad about pop music and various naive boyfriends and my friends were mostly beer drinking blokes who reluctantly took their wives out on a Saturday night and moaned about the trials and tribulations of their work colleagues, their marriages and the numerous bills that they had to pay. But for some odd reason, Jenny and I not only got on well together, but actually found that we were on the same scatty wavelength. Although still very young and naive about many things, Jenny had a quick and agile mind and was a very fast learner, but most surprisingly, she had a unique sense of humour, it was amazingly quick and sharp. I'd never met a woman who possessed this unique ability before and to find it in a girl who was straight from the confines of a school classroom was a wonderful surprise.

Whenever we happened to meet during the course of the working day and had a chance to chat, we inevitably found that we laughed at the same things and gradually we became more and more comfortable in each other's company. We built up a repertoire of in-jokes concerning other members of the staff and by this means we were able to keep ourselves amused during the boring routine rituals of our daily slog.

Because the various offices were in need of brightening up, Mr Cain asked Butch and me if we would decorate the offices for him by painting all the walls with cream coloured emulsion paint. The job was to be done in the early hours of the morning and on Saturday when there were very few members of staff in the offices so that there would be no disruption to the normal days trading and as we were keen to earn extra money, we readily agreed.

Jenny, who helped to sort the morning post, was one of the few who came into the office early in the morning and while Butch and I were painting the office walls and ceiling, Jenny and I sang songs from the show, "The Sound of Music" much to Butch's disgust. It transpired that we both loved musicals and now had yet another topic to add to our ever growing catalogue of interesting conversations.

Over the next few years this easy going camaraderie between Jenny and I grew stronger and I began to realise that she was the only real female friend that I'd ever had. As a child I had been very close to my cousin Annette, but that relationship had been on a par with what most brothers and sisters experienced and as we'd matured we had grown apart and although I'd experienced a close relationship with several girlfriends, I had not felt as comfortable in conversation with any of them as I did with Jenny. At times I flirted with her just as I did with one or two of the other young girls that worked at Turners and come Christmas, I always made a bee line for her with a sprig of mistletoe for a kiss, but as I was ten years her senior and seriously involved with another girl, that's as far as our romantic leanings ever went and the thought of asking her out for a date never ever crossed my mind.

Jenny, who was as bright as a Guardsman's button, mastered routine office work with ease and gradually she earned promotion and was eventually, moved from the general dog's body duties of filing and overseeing the daily post and was put onto the reception desk which included controlling the company's telephone switchboard. While answering the telephone switchboard, which was the old plug in, plug out type, she invariably picked up snippets of interesting information some of which concerned the running of the business and some, the staff's personal problems and she often shared these little titillating secrets with me and it was through this channel of inside information that I discovered that the company was in the process of purchasing a large warehouse in Smethwick to house its ever-increasing steel tube stock.

I immediately realised that this warehouse would require a manager to run it and when the time was ripe, I put myself forward for the position before anyone else in the company had even had time to think about it. My eager application was successful and I was appointed manager of the newly purchased tube store along with a rise in salary and the use of a company car, a beat up second hand Mini, but from my point of view, it was a luxury that was well worth having. I'd recently purchased an old car and now that I had the use of a company car, I was able to sell the old hand painted banger and put the cash back in my pocket.

After I'd taken up my position at the tube warehouse in Smethwick, I still spoke to Jenny on the telephone each day when for various reasons I had to contact head office and I often saw her during the working week while I was delivering paperwork and our easy going friendship continued as before. But eventually, for reasons of her own, she decided to leave Turners and began working for another company. She then married her longstanding boyfriend, set up home with him and disappeared from my life and to my surprise; her departure left me feeling depressed. It wasn't until she'd gone out of my life that I realised just how deep our friendship had been. For several years we'd shared light hearted gossip and numerous jokes on a daily basis and now that easy going relationship had disappeared completely.

I became aware that I had lost something special, but at that precise moment I still wasn't quite sure what it was. What probably confused me was the fact that because I was in a relationship with a married, but separated young woman, my thoughts were constantly on her unpredictable moods rather than on Jenny and of course there was the ten year difference in our ages which meant that we still moved in different social circles. During the time that we'd known each other we had often swapped stories concerning our various friends, but we'd never met any of them. I'd not even met her boyfriend who had now become her husband. Sadly, I now realised what was meant by the saying, "You never know what you've got until you've lost it."

In 1967, Celtic FC the well-known Glasgow football club raised a team that defiantly beat Inter Milan 2-1 and became the first British team to win the European Champions Cup. This was a great achievement, but what was even more remarkable was that every Celtic player in the team came from within thirty miles of the ground. Today, with teams made up of mercenaries from all over the world, whose only allegiance to the club depends upon the size of the pay cheque, this feat would now be impossible to achieve.

What was just as remarkable was that Jock, Mitch's long lost kleptomaniac friend, turned up with two tickets for the match and Mitch was in the stadium to witness the event.

"I was proud to be Scottish that day." He declared.

"You're not Scottish, you lying bugger!" Billy stated while shaking his head in amused disbelief.

"I was that day Billy." Mitch replied, "I was there with a tam-o'-shanter on my head and just like Rob Roy, ready to pick up my claymore and take on all boarders."

As Cyril had not yet reached the age of twenty, technically he was a teenager, but Cyril was a phenomenon and had never been a teenager in the recognised sense of the word. He was extremely uptight and formal and gave one the impression that he not only went to bed in double breasted pyjamas, but probably had them starched.

With his stiff attitude and formal mannerisms, he put one in mind of a Victorian Major General that had served in some far flung part of the British Empire. He spoke in a stilted plumy voice that lacked warmth, treated women with formal respect and addressed every man as "Sir." He was visibly ill at ease when conversing with rough storemen and seemed to believe that they should be treated with a certain amount of distain. He was so formal that he could have bored Nelsons Column death.

Why he was like this, no one really knew, or cared, but because of his peculiar reserved personality and his stilted old-fashioned mode of speech, he found it difficult to make any headway with members of the opposite sex, especially the younger ones whose conversations tended to be somewhat lightweight and frothy, but it wasn't through want of trying. Things really came to a head when he received an invitation to attend a dinner and dance at his old school. Formal eveningwear was the order of the day and chaps were expected to bring along wives or fiancés. He confessed to one of the girls that to turn up at the school reunion unaccompanied was frowned upon and was considered to be bad form. "Smacks of pansyfication, don't you know."

The problem was plain to see, not only was Cyril short of a fiancés, but he had little chance of persuading a girl to tolerate him for more than five minutes, never mind a whole evening. But undaunted, he systematically propositioned almost every female that was employed at Turners, the married, the single, the old and the young and he even offered bribes in the form of expensive presents while trying to persuade them to accompany him to his old schools dinner and dance.

It was to no avail until he lighted upon young Vera, the middle class, well-educated fruit cake. Coming from a similar background to Cyril, she was quite used to formal dinner and dance events and not only possessed an evening gown, but had a collection of matching jewellery and so all was settled. Snobby Vera would accompany ramrod Cyril to his old schools dinner and dance and all would be well in the world.

Two days later we were surprised to hear Cyril announce that he and snobby Vera were about to be engaged to be married and he took great pleasure in showing several of the office workers a very expensive engagement ring that he'd purchased to celebrate the occasion. The following day, all hell broke loose as it turned out that Vera knew nothing about this proposed engagement and took great offence at being told the good news by Edna, the foul mouthed office cleaner who was at the centre of most of the salacious gossip that circulated around the company. Evidently Edna had enquired as to whether the reason for the forthcoming marriage was because Vera was "up the duff."

"Pardon?" Was Vera's eye popping puzzled reply.

"You know dear, a bun in the oven. Pregnant! Is there any urgency for you to get married?" and to make matters worse she added, "Is Cyril actually the father, only looking at him, I wouldn't have thought he'd know what to do in the bedroom department."

It seems that when Vera had accepted Cyril's invitation to accompany him to the dinner and dance, Cyril was so happy and excited that he went on to say, "Not only am I pleased that you have accepted my invitation, but I would be glad to have you accompany me throughout life" and Vera, not fully understanding what he was talking about, had smiled and said, "Oh, I don't mind accompanying you" and Cyril had taken this to mean that she was willing to accept him as her beau and lifelong partner.

When Vera heard about the proposed engagement, she was not at all pleased and when she realised that many in the company believed that she was "up the duff" as foul mouthed Edna had assumed and was desperate for a husband, she became most indignant and not only did she reject the idea of marrying Cyril, but rejected his formal dinner and dance invitation and poor Cyril found himself back at square one, only this time he had a redundant engagement ring in his pocket.

So, as far as we were concerned, that was the end of that, for all his efforts, Cyril would not be attending his school reunion after all, but ever determined, he fooled us all. He contacted an escort agency and hired a young lady for the evening and took her along to the dinner and dance as his female companion.

Several years later, Mitch, Billy and I were drinking in The George, a popular city centre pub that was Mitch's latest hot spot. The pub had a large lounge, live music and was frequented by many young women who were there to be admired and chatted up before they moved onto the vibrant night clubs. One of the young women we knew from our happy days in the coffee bars, and after reminiscing about the good old days, she casually enquired as to where I now worked. I told her the name of the company and fully expected her to say that she'd never heard of the place, but to my surprise, she not only began to tell me what items Turners sold, but even more surprisingly, she even mentioned the names of one or two of the people that worked there.

"Do you work for a building company then?" I asked, convinced that this was the only explanation for her in depth knowledge of Turners and its staff.

"Oh no," she replied shaking her head dismissively, "I once went out with a bloke that worked there and he told me all about the place. In fact, it was the longest day of my bleeding life and I was only with him for one evening."

She then told us how she had once worked for an escort agency to earn extra money and went on to explain how most of the men, who were usually middle aged men from out of town, were very polite, but invariably wanted to get their leg over before the night was over, but this one she explained was completely different to any that she'd ever met before, "He never stopped talking all night, though half of what he said was above my head and never registered," she said in exasperation as she re-lived the mind numbing experience, "I've never been so bored in all my life and he never flirted at all. It was really weird; he kept calling me "My dear" all night. It was, "Would you like a drink my dear?" and "Would you care to dance my dear?" and "Is the meal to your liking my dear?"

Her date for that evening, as I suspected, turned out to be none other than ramrod Cyril. Her parting shot as she prepared to move off with her friends was, "After that night, I took a fortnight off from the escort agency, I was mentally drained and almost ready for the loony bin."

A few years after the dinner and dance saga, Cyril purchased a small boat that was moored on the river Severn at Stourport and there he spent his weekends sailing up and down the river and reliving the exploits of his hero, Horatio Hornblower. To compliment his image of a competent sea captain, he rigged himself out with a navy blue blazer, white flannels and a captain's cap complete with an intricate gold braid badge. Sam Bane, who was also interested in messing about in boats, went along with him on several occasions and between them they eventually came up with the ambitious plan of taking the boat down to the south coast and spending their two weeks annual holiday sailing it upon the open sea. To do this they needed a boat trailer and rather than buy or hire one, they decided to build their own.

At the side of the newly purchased tube store that I was now in charge of, there was a fenced off piece of waste land that was an ideal spot on which to build the trailer and Sam was the ideal man to build it. Cyril and Sam spent numerous hours of their spare time building the trailer and when completed, it was second to none. It sported three sets of wheels, an efficient braking system, and a full set of lights and was sturdy enough to carry a boat twice the weight of the one that it was built for.

On the Friday evening that they broke up for their two weeks holiday, Cyril and Sam arrived at the tube store and hooked the trailer onto the back of Sam's old Land Rover and off they went. I locked up the tube store for the night and went home, but when I arrived the following morning, there was the mighty boat trailer, but ominously there was no sign of a boat. A short while later Sam turned up and towed the trailer back onto the patch of waste land and explained what had happened.

"We towed the trailer down to Stourport as planned," he said with a dispirited shrug of his shoulders, "backed it down the jetty, the crane picked up the boat from the river and lifted it onto the trailer and then we discovered that it didn't fit. Cyril had measured the boat while it was still in the water and had got the dimensions completely wrong and our planed two-week escapade to the south coast had to be cancelled, so the boat was put back into the river and I bought the trailer back here."

"So what are you going to do now?" I asked.

"Me? I'm off potholing with my brother-in-law."

"No, I mean about the trailer."

"Bugger all. It belongs to Cyril, not me. He can do whatever he likes with it, but count me out I'm of to Derbyshire. See you in a fortnight." And with that, off he went. The boat trailer was abandoned and over the next few years, the tyres lost their air, the paint peeled off the sturdy metal frame and rust began to form all over. Wild grass gradually enveloped the whole contraption and Cyril's boat never did reach the open sea.

Cyril was thirty when he finally married, and the woman that he married was not only twice his age, but had a daughter that was slightly older than him. A psychiatrist would have probably put forward some Freudian mother fixation theory for this liaison, but to us, it seemed to be an act of extreme desperation. He'd met his future wife while attending dancing classes at his local night school, he'd tried almost everything that the night school had to offer, art classes, photography and woodwork and had no luck at all in meeting the girl of his dreams in any of them, but ballroom dancing was by its very nature a place where man meets women. Cyril took to it with the enthusiasm of an excited child and was soon partnered by an elderly widow who was slightly deaf and didn't seem to mind his boring ways. She saw him as a perfect gentleman and together they went on to obtain, their bronze, silver and gold medals and finally they married.

Many, many years later, while being dragged around one of the events that they have at Cannon Hill Park by my two sons, I happened to meet Cyril and his elderly wife. Cyril, as stiff and as formal as ever, was slowly pushing his wife around the park in a wheel chair and after a friendly chat with them, I came to the conclusion that they were happy and contented with their lot in life. Although quite reserved, they radiated an amiable devotion that after many years of marriage, most couples would have envied and it struck me that boring ramrod Cyril had indeed found the female company and the elusive happiness that he'd sort after all.

Although Mitch was living with a young woman once more, it made little difference to his predatory womanising. His passion for chasing after women was an intrinsic part of his nature and he could no more change that urge than a leopard can change its spots. Billy and I knew nothing about psychology, but we were fully aware that one woman, however good, would never be enough for Mitch's psychological needs. It wasn't that he was deliberately disrespectful of his partners or thought any the less of them, but he seemed to need and thrive on the fun of the chase and there was no doubt that his constant cat and mouse pursuits kept him in sparkling ruddy good health.

Most of the married men that we knew at the time would have welcomed a sexual dalliance with another woman if the opportunity had presented itself and from my limited experience I had little doubt that there were quite a few married women who felt the same, but courtship rituals take time and time is the one commodity that most of those that are married or in close relationships, don't have. And because of this lack of time they tend to build up a relationship with someone that they fancy quite slowly and it takes many weeks or even months before they become anywhere near being intimate and unfaithful.

Although not married, Mitch was living in a close relationship and he too was restricted by the amount of time that he had for his leisure pursuits. He could no longer go out every night chasing women as he had when he was single and he had to make the most of the two or three evenings a week that he was let off the leash and this

247

he did quite successfully. Once he saw a girl that he fancied in a pub or a night club, and it didn't matter if she was with another man or not, he would strike up eye to eye contact with her and converse across the crowded room and if she responded, he would intercept her and quickly arrange a date. Most men wait for an accidental meeting to occur before they do anything about starting a relationship, but Mitch made the meeting happen right there and then.

When out on the town, Mitch had always made a point of keeping himself well-groomed and smartly dressed and even though he was now living in a state of marriage, he still kept to that rule.

"Putting on a suit and a clean shirt once a week would be a dead give-away." He said when explaining his philosophy, "So I tend to dress smart all the time, even when I'm just going to the corner pub."

One woman that he had cultivated for extra marital nooky took him out to a country pub one evening in a car that her wealthy husband had just purchased for her birthday and on the way back they pulled over onto a grass verge in a quiet country lane and there they indulged in a bout of exhausting passionate lovemaking. When they had re-dressed they found to their dismay that the wheels of the car had sunk into the soft earth and they were well and truly stuck.

"I pushed and shoved that bleeding car for twenty minutes before I finally got the bugger out of the mud and onto the road." Mitch said with genuine feeling as he re-lived the exhausting episode, "I was completely knackered and covered in bleeding mud and wondering how I was going to explain the state of my clothes to the Missis. Anyway, I got back into the car looking like I'd just been playing rugby with the "All Blacks" and all this dopey bird can say is, "What am I going to say to my husband, there's mud all over my new car."

"And just what did you say to your Missis?" Billy asked somewhat intrigued and amused.

"Pretty much the truth," Mitch said as he recalled the conversation, "I told her that an old lady had lost control of her car and me and Brian Cox had helped to push it out of some mud. I said that the car had spun off the road after being cut up by a road hog."

"And you reckon that explanation was near the truth?" Billy asked while grinning at him.

"It's as near the truth as I'm going to go with my Missis." He answered with a knowing wink.

Benny the lorry driver, had been separated from his wife for quite a while and rather than spend a week on his own whilst taking his holiday entitlement, he preferred to book himself onto weekend coach trips and when he heard that I was off to Brighton with the Forty Club and would be visiting the Glorious Goodwood races, he booked himself a place on the trip. The itinerary for the weekend trip was ideal for him as he was able to drink and play dominoes all the way to Brighton, visit the races on the Saturday and in the evening, he could meander around the Brighton pubs with some of the other men.

On the Friday afternoon, we booked into our hotel, which on this occasion was situated on the sea front and overlooked the promenade, the pebble beach and the shimmering sea. We collected our room keys from reception, found our rooms, washed, shaved and after a drink in the hotel bar, we split up into small groups and full of excited anticipation, we hit the town. It was a usual practice to break off into small groups and make our way slowly through the town, wondering in and out of various pubs that took our fancy and that evening Benny just tagged onto one of the small groups and explored the town with them.

Somewhere along the way, Benny accidentally parted company with his fellow drinkers and after many more drinks, he happily staggered back to the hotel on his own. He had one more drink in the hotel bar, "just for luck," collected his room key from the night porter and staggered up the stairs to his bedroom, fell on the bed and slept like a log all night.

The following morning he washed his forlorn face in the wash basin and as he was still fully dressed he made his way to the restaurant where a young waiter was in the process of serving a couple of early risers to breakfast. After managing to down a cup of tea and a slice of toast, he decided to go out onto the front for some exhilarating fresh air before returning to his room to shave and get himself ready for the coming day. It was while standing there on the hotel steps that he discovered that he had spent the night in the wrong hotel, the one that he should have been in was right next door.

"I wondered why I hadn't seen any of you lot in the bar last night." He said as he tried to piece together what had happened to him, "And this morning I thought, that's funny they're all missing breakfast."

On the Saturday night after winning a fair amount at the races, Mitch was in fine form, full of jokes and laughter, flirting with every pretty woman that he saw and ready to sing the night away. He joined in the communal singing and being quick of mind he would often make up words to fit the song as he went along. But there was one particular song that he knew very well and he had been trying to drop from his limited repertoire for quite some time, but his boozy mates would not allow him to do so. Repeatedly, they begged him to sing the song time and time again.

The song was entitled, "Just Because" and when he came to the penultimate line in the song which ran, "Just because my teeth are pearly," he would extract from the front of his mouth a small denture that he had acquired in his teenage years after being involved in a motor bike accident and toss it into the air and with his arms held wide he would catch the denture in his mouth and carry on singing. Whenever he performed this singing, juggling act, he brought the house down.

The drawback was that it suited some venues much better than others and when he was chatting up a good looking woman and pretending to be a suave and sophisticated young business man, the last thing he wanted to do was to show her that he not only had a small front denture, but was willing to throw it around a rowdy pub and here he was in the ever popular Sussex pub on such an occasion. He was chatting to a well-spoken, good looking woman while Trapper was doing his best to entertain her friend when the Forty Club singers demanded that he should perform his party piece.

After much protest, as it was the last thing that he wanted to do, he finally relented and began to sing the song. His deep rich voice filled the room and talking from one end of the pub to the other ceased and a space miraculously appeared around him as he sang and gesticulated his way through the words of the song, "Just because my hair is curly, Just because my teeth are pearly, Just because I, always wear a smile, I like get my gear, in all the latest style."

It was one of the finest renditions of the song that he'd ever performed and on the second verse out came the small denture and as usual, up in the air it went leaving him with a comical gap toothed grin on his face. Whether it was the poor light or just that he was a little inebriated, he was never quite sure of, but when the denture came down, he missed catching it in his open mouth and the denture bounced around the room with Mitch jumping after it. After finding the denture upon the carpet among the audience's feet, he picked it up and without a moment's hesitation he sterilised the denture by dipping it into the nearest glass of alcohol and which happened to be a gin and tonic that was sitting upon the bar before popping it back into his mouth and attempting to perform the trick again.

This time he was far more successful and the flying denture fell back accurately into place and on seeing this, it brought the house down. Everyone in the pub was clapping their hands and calling for more, all that is except the woman that Mitch had been chatting to, she, looking as though someone had just pissed in the porridge, was collecting her things and was on her way out of the pub and dragging her bemused friend behind her. It seems that it was her gin and tonic that Mitch had inadvertently used to sterilise his denture and being a well brought up young lady, she was not only disgusted by this barbaric act, but highly embarrassed and extremely upset at the thought that she was the butt of a vulgar joke.

"Now look what you bastards have done." Mitch called out loudly in mock anger at his amused companions, "She's buggered off just as I was about to invite her over to my yacht for a night cap."

Quick as a flash Billy replied, "Your best out of it Mitch, I met her earlier in the bog, she's really a bloke dressed up as a woman."

Billy's joke went down well in the pub that night, but like all good jokes, it was born out of a serious subject. These rough and ready working men from the Midlands had been visiting Brighton for many years and knew many of the pubs and the type of clientele that frequented them, there were pubs that catered for the youngsters and there were those that were cosy and intimate and designed for the more mature drinker, but now a new type of pub had appeared, a pub that was dominated by homosexuals. Many of the Forty Club members were not at all comfortable with this new trend and back home they decided that they should try other venues for their annual weekend trip. Such places as Weston, Margate and Blackpool were considered and eventually all these towns were eventually visited by the Forty Club. These venues were not as sophisticated as Brighton and unfortunately they did not include a trip to the Goodwood races, but they still managed to spawn an amusing tale or two.

On one of our last trips to Brighton, the vote for Goodwood still being strong among the Forty Club racing fraternity; Mitch the ever-romantic dreamer was at last to meet his true love. It was reminiscent of a Hollywood film script where lover's eyes meet across a crowded room and all previous troubles suddenly disappear and butterflies, blue birds and romantic sweet music fill the air.

He was out on the town with a group of his Forty Club mates and looking for a good time and she, along with her mother, was sitting in the corner of the crowded pub while enjoying a quiet drink and it was love at first sight. He introduced himself and immediately bought this vision of beauty and her mother a drink and with the help of the Forty Clubs singers he entertained them for the rest of the evening. He discovered that they were German and had been living in Brighton for some considerable time and at that precise moment, they were actually looking forward to starting a new life as it transpired that the young woman, whose name was Heidi, had recently separated from her husband.

Heidi was elegantly good looking, sophisticated in manner, always well dressed and undoubtedly middle class. She had a confident personality and was charmingly pleasant to all, but she was no soft touch and had a steely resolve. When confronted with a problem she dealt with it with the confidence and bearing of an aristocrat. She belonged to wealthy family and as a teenager she'd met and married a British Army officer while he was stationed in Germany. They'd moved to Brighton when he'd returned to civilian life and taken up a position in his father's business. Her widowed mother had been an opera singer before the Second World War and had recently joined Heidi and now that Heidi's marriage had irretrievably failed, they were deciding what to do next. Should they stay in Brighton or to move back to Germany where family members could help them settle into a new life? None of these details were known to Mitch at the time, but after one glance across that crowded room, he was totally convinced that Heidi was the woman for him.

To his delight, Heidi was immediately attracted to him and as he sang to her and made her the centre of attention, she felt better than she'd felt for a long while. She knew nothing about Mitch, but did not care, as he was tall, good looking, suave and extremely entertaining and most of all, he seemed to be more interested in her, than any other man had ever been. It was a match made in heaven and they both allowed the romantic situation that they had created to envelope them.

Mitch accompanied Heidi and her mother home that night singing, dancing and swinging on lampposts in the best Hollywood tradition and agreed to call on them the following morning. As planned, on the Sunday morning, the three of them happily strolled along the bright sunny Brighton front and took in the invigorating sea the air and gradually through chit-chat conversation they got to know each other a little better. At mid-day he took them to lunch and afterwards, he escorted them to the pub where the Forty Club members were drinking and there he gaily entertained them once more.

As the Forty Club members boarded the coach outside the hotel, he said his fond farewell to Heidi and kissed her passionately and to all of us that witnessed the romantic scene through the windows of the coach, it looked as though the new lovers had been acquainted for many a year. He promised to keep in touch during the following week and as the coach headed for the Midlands; he sat back in his seat and blissfully dreamed and planned for a life of marital bliss.

During the journey back home, a minor altercation broke out between Alfie and Stan and for a short while, it spoilt Mitch's romantic mood. Sometime that morning, Alfie had taken a young women back to the hotel room that he'd shared with Stan and there he and the girl had indulged in a full passionate sexual session and on finding that his own belongings were already packed, he'd used

Stan's towel to clean up with. All except Stan, who was fuming, thought that this revelation was highly amusing.

A week later, Mitch, who was truly smitten, was back in Brighton and once more sweeping Heidi off her feet while making plans for their future and a week after that he brought her and her mother up to the Midlands where he installed them into an idyllic rented country cottage that was just outside Brum and there they set up home together.

Their romantic honeymoon lasted all of six months. Mitch's transport business wasn't doing as well as he'd made out when tempting Heidi to leave Brighton and live with him and due to lack of funds, he was forced to give up renting the expensive country cottage and he moved his new charges into a small terraced house that was one of many in a very ordinary Birmingham back street. It was now that the Forty Club members were to see the real metal that Heidi possessed, for far from being depressed or downhearted about this forced downturn in her financial and social circumstances, Heidi accepted the situation with resolve and showed that she was determined to make the best of it.

Within a matter of weeks she had transformed the little shabby terraced house into a showpiece home. She decorated it tastefully, filled it with fine furniture and ornaments and the little house became a small middle class oasis in the middle of a working class desert and was the envy of all who entered it.

Part of Heidi's family owned a brewery back in Germany and they sent her a small monthly allowance, but she was never too proud to mix with her neighbours and went out of her way to be friendly and helpful to them. She would talk quite easily with the people that she met in the local shops and with strangers while sitting in a pub or on a park bench. On discovering that Heidi was middle class and German to boot, many of the wives of Mitch's friends were quite ready and prepared to dislike her, but they found it impossible to do so as she was immune to silly snubs and would greet them with warm enthusiasm. She had a charm that was infectious and could, much to Mitch's relief, make a creditor, a joyless bank manager or a hard faced debt collector do whatever she desired and she even had the knack of making them apologise for upsetting her.

And so this fine lady, who'd been raised to believe in the aspirations and values of the middle class and Mitch, who had the easy going instinct of a wondering gypsy, settled down and attempted to make a go at married life. There were to be many ups and downs in their long relationship and when they did row, which, with their opposing personalities was quite often, Mitch would refer to her as, "a square headed kraut" and she would counter by calling him, "a bullying pig faced Tommy." But although they fell out and rowed acrimoniously on many occasions, Mitch admitted that on the whole, he proffered his married state to any other.

"She's a great cook, keeps a lovely clean and warm home and is willing to have sex at any time and in any position. And although she drives me up the bloody wall, where am I going to find anyone better?"

They lived in the little terraced house for many years and visitors were always made welcome. When Mitch's business eventually became more successful, they purchased a larger house and Heidi produced her magic once more and converted it into a showpiece property, but of course, living with Mitch, life for Heidi was never ever going to be easy or dull.

"I'm in trouble again." Mitch sighed as he began to explain his latest sexual liaison.

"Go on then," Billy said, intrigued as to what this latest tale of woe would reveal, "What the bloody hell have you been up to now."

"Well a few weeks ago." Mitch explained, "I was in the bedroom strumming on my guitar and singing a few simple blues numbers when the front door bell rang. I took no notice and let the Missis answer it. I'd got no work that day and I like to hide away in the bedroom for a bit of peace and quiet and then I hear Heidi calling up the stairs and telling me that I'm wanted. Anyway, when I get to the front door I see that it's our neighbour Phyllis, you know Bert Winslow's Missis, him that thinks he runs the working men's club. They live just a couple of doors away see. So she tells me that her lights have fused and as Bert is at work could I mend the fuse for her.

"Of course he can" my Missis is saying, before I've had chance to say anything and the next thing I know I'm standing on a chair in her hallway and stretching up to find which fuse has blown. Well, while I'm standing on this chair stretching up, this Phyllis is holding the chair with one hand and my leg with the other and while I'm prating about with the fuse she starts rubbing her hand up and down the inside of my leg. I glance down and says, "Phyllis, you'll get me all worked up doing that" and she say's cool as you like, "I don't mind, I'm grateful for your help."

So when I've fixed the bloody fuse I gets down off the chair, pins her against the wall and slips my hand up her skirt and find that she's got no panties on and she's all wet, warm and willing, so its bang, bang, bang and few minutes later I'm playing my guitar and thinking, what the bloody hell was that all about.

Two weeks later she's on the phone asking my Missis if I can fix her back door. The locks come loose and Bert is down at the working men's club as usual. Anyway, I said to the Missis, "Look love, I'm on my way out, I've promised to meet my mates in half an hour, Bert can soon fix that when he gets home." "Don't be so selfish" she says, "it won't take you many minutes" and I'm thinking, "You don't know how right you are."

"Anyway, the same thing happens, I gets round there, there's bugger all wrong with the lock and she's there without any panties on again and grabbing me as soon as I enter the bloody house and just like before, it's all over in a matter of minutes.

"Well this has been going on in one form or another for about three months now, she's either got some fictitious job she needs doing in her house or if I'm not at work and the Missis has gone shopping she's round at the back door like a shot."

"So what are you complaining about," Billy asked a little perplexed, "if your Missis don't know what's going on and Bert's none the wiser, what's to worry about?"

"The truth is mate, I'm not enjoying it."

"What! You aint gone queer have you?"

"No you prat, I mean there's no fun involved. There's no mystery, no chat up, no chase, it's there on a bloody plate, bang, bang and it's all over. For the life of me I can't see what she gets out of it, she could be eating a bloody apple or reading a book at the same time."

"She's pissed off with Bert and looking for a bit of excitement aint she." Billy suggested philosophically, "and quite honestly, I aint surprised, he spends all his time down at the bloody club. The trouble is, he thinks he's indispensable, I'll bet he's more interested in booking the entertainment acts for a Saturday night than he is in his Missis."

"So what do I do?" Mitch asked, and then looking at me he said, "Has anything like this ever happened to you?"

"Me!" I replied genuinely surprised, "I've got more chance of being hit by a bloody bus than being raped by a lonely housewife. You're the bugger with all the luck, not me."

"Well I don't see it as lucky, I'm bloody browned off with it and I have to keep making up excuses of why I can't see her."

Ten months later Mitch's sexual stalking nightmare came to a sudden end. Bert was made redundant and he and Phyllis had a long hard look at their future and decided to sell their home and with proceeds they bought a newsagents shop in Wolverhampton. The shop and the hard work that went with it had the effect of bringing them closer together once more and Bert forgot all about being indispensable at the working man's club and he, Phyllis and Mitch come to that, felt all the better for it.

Scotty and his friend Neil who were on a golfing holiday in Scotland, decided to visit Brian, a friend of theirs who was also on holiday and was renting a secluded cottage near Loch Rannoch. The two young men had already visited some of Scotty's relatives that lived in Stirling and they were now visiting the many golf courses that Scotland had to offer.

On the evening of the visit, the three friends drove up the road to the nearest hotel bar, which was three mile from the secluded cottage and situated near the Rannoch Moor railway station. The road from Pitlochry actually ends at the station; from then on it is open moor land as far as the eye can see, so the hotel and it's bar was only visited by a few locals, dedicated anglers and keen hill walkers complete with sturdy walking boots, rucksacks and ordinance survey maps.

As the three young men entered the hotels small lounge they were greeted by the owner who was standing behind the bar. He was a large Scotsman and wore a kilt and sporran and cheerfully served them to three pints of Guinness and three Talisker malt whiskeys, which he recommended. Brian bought the first round, Scotty bought the second and Neil, who was not a whiskey drinker, went up to the bar for the third.

"Three pints of Guinness, three Talisker whiskeys and a small bottle of Canada Dry" Neil said in all Sassenach innocence.

The large and formidable proprietor rose to his full height and balancing upon his two large fists he leaned across the bar to within an inch of Neil's face and said in a low strong humourless Scottish accent, "Your'r no puttin' Canada Dry inta mar fockin' whiskey."

Scotty shot up to the bar and immediately ordered Neil to sit down. He apologised profusely to the angry proprietor and told him to forget the Canada Dry and after finally being served he then explained to Neil that, "You must never put anything but water into a malt whiskey and you must always sip the drink and not gulp it down" and realising that it had been a close run thing, he reminded Neil that, "and you have to remember that its over twenty bloody miles to the next bar which is back in Pitlochry you prat."

The 1970's brought along decimalization, the Ugandan butcher Idi Armin, the Hollywood murderer Charles Manson, the terrorist attack at the Munich Olympic Games and the catchy, but incomprehensible song "American Pie." The fleet footed footballer Trevor Francis made his debut for the "Blues" at the tender age of sixteen and became known locally as, "The diamond in the dustbin" and the Prime Minister Ted Heath, in his infinite wisdom, introduced the three day week which was very confusing and disruptive for all concerned.

I was now managing Turners tube store which was in the industrial back streets of Smethwick and had the use of a company car which was a second hand Mini Clubman. It had previously been one of Mr Cain's daughter's plaything and it had been well and truly thrashed, but I didn't mind. I felt on top of the world; I was a manager at last and my foot was on the first rung of a career ladder, which was not bad for a back street lad with no academic qualifications. What I didn't realise was that it would be another twenty years before I managed to get my foot onto the next rung. I was to learn that being good at a job does not automatically bring promotion; ironically, in many instances it can actually be detrimental. Directors like to retain stability in their workforce and they often avoid moving good staff from one department to another and seek to strengthen the management structure by upgrading someone who is already in the department or bringing in new blood from outside. Sometimes it works and sometimes it's a disaster.

When filling the vacancy for a Transport manager, they brought into the company a man that had no experience whatsoever and although well educated, he was at a complete loss when it came to organising delivery runs and the bloody minded delivery drivers quickly learned how to run rings around him. If ever there was a case of a square peg being put into a round hole, this was it. After just eighteen months in the hot seat, he had a nervous breakdown and simply refused to leave his home or answer the telephone.

He would probably have been fine had he been employed in a less stressful position, but his incompetence as a transport manager became a company legend. Long before the Severn Bridge that links England to Wales was built, he instructed one of the lorry drivers, who already had a full day's work to do in the Bristol area, to, "Pop over to Cardiff and pick up a number of old cast iron valves from the gas works."

"Pop over to Cardiff?" the astonished driver retorted in disbelief, "That's bloody miles out of my way. There's a bloody great stretch of water between Bristol and Cardiff you know."

On hearing this rebuff, the affable transport manager took out a small pocket diary and pointed to a map of England and Wales that was printed in the back pages and said brightly, "Here you are look; it's not all that far is it?"

The driver shook his head in disbelief and replied, "Not all that far? On a map of that size, from here to bloody Australia would only measure six inches, would you like me to do a few deliveries in Sydney on my way back?"

The man who replaced the incompetent transport manager, had far more knowledge of transport and possessed a more aggressive personality, but in his own way, as he had little grasp of forward planning, he was also liable to make mistakes and so from then on, although over the years the company gradually grew and expanded, the transport department was constantly plagued with problems.

As the company became more successful, it began to expand on all fronts and during this period a small run down building supplies business that was situated in the heart of the Black Country was taken over and the employers at Turners were duly introduced to its resident manager. He was short, thick set, had a beer belly and a bald head and reminded me of Benito Mussolini. He seemed to be an amiable sort of a chap and showed every sign of being pleased to be part of the fold and once more I learned to never judge a book by its cover, as he turned out to be the most obnoxious man that I ever met. His attitude was so hateful that after just a few months, many were circulating the rumour that he'd once been a concentration camp commandant.

During the summer months some of the young men would meet after work at a local park on a Wednesday evening and participate in a football kick-a-bout. It helped to brush up their limited football skills, keep them in reasonably good shape for when the football season began in earnest and sinking a pint in the nearest pub afterwards was a social pleasure. One Wednesday evening, the manager of the new satellite company thought fit to join these young men and take part in the friendly kick-a-bout. Whether he was invited by one of the storemen, no one seemed to know, but he was made welcome and the usual kick-a-bout was duly organised.

Being short in height and having a beer belly that had a tendency to bounce about when he attempted to run this new manager put one in mind of a comical sea side picture post card character and to make matters worse he, walked in the manner of spray footed Charlie Chaplin. These physical characteristics may be well suited to a Penguin who has to walk about on ice flows, but they are of very little use to an athletic football player. Now although he did not see himself as a short fat slob, he was aware that he had limited running abilities and did not consider himself suitable as an outfield player.

He informed Butch that his best position was in goal and so without further ado, he took up his position between the sticks.

There being but ten outfield players that evening, they divided themselves into two teams of five and they all shot at the same goal. After a while it became apparent that this beer bellied goalkeeper was not only slow to move, but had no intention of diving and hopped across the goal mouth on one foot. Although it was only a friendly kick-a-bout, Butch was a good battling centre forward and played for a Sunday team during the winter months, was disgusted with this lack of commitment and let it be known. "What the fuck are you playing at you great lump of lard?" Butch demanded to know as he stood with his hands on his hips and glared disgustedly at the incompetent goalkeeper, "You look like a bleeding overweight ballet dancer hopping about and you ain't stopped one bleeding ball yet."

The following morning, while Butch was describing what had gone on at previous evenings kick-about to several storemen and drivers, he said while trying to get his disgusted point of view across, "...and the little fat bleeder, wouldn't dive for a ball and he hopped about the goal mouth like a bleeding fat penguin." And from that day on, the obnoxious satellite company manager became known as "The Flying Penguin."

The Turners tube store in Smethwick was just a stone's throw from Black Patch Park, the spot where many years before, it is believed Charlie Chaplin was born in a gipsy caravan before being moved to London. The building had once been part of the Tangy Empire, a Victorian company that had specialised in heavy lifting gear and hydraulic pumps. Many of their hydraulic pumps that had been built for extracting water from deep wells were still to be found working away in offbeat places that used to be part the British Empire. Tangy's also had close links with Isambard Kingdom Brunel, the Victorian engineering genius and they helped him to launch his huge ship, The Great Eastern, into the River Thames at the Isle of Dogs in 1858.

Factories around the Black Country supplied the miles of heavy link chain and Tangy's supplied the pump engines with which to pull and push the huge monster into the Thames. It took three months to get the huge ship into the water which was launched sideways into the river. Tangy's, was owned by Quakers and was the first company in the country to introduce the revolutionary idea of letting their employees work for half a day on a Saturday. There was no such thing as a forty-hour week back then and this act of humanitarianism was seen by many Victorian business men as insane and commercial suicide.

When I took over the tube store, those Victorian days were long gone and the original Tangy factory buildings had been broken up and sold off as separate units and were now occupied by numerous companies. The tube store was a large dilapidated warehouse with an office block attached and it covered an area as large as two football pitches. The walls were as thick as a medieval castle and there were four overhead cranes that had been installed in 1900 and these cumbersome cranes ran the full length of the warehouse. The old cranes had driving cabs and were held up in the air on an ornate steel structure that was reminiscent of a Victorian railway station. It was to be a few years down the line before any money could be spared to modernise the premises, so it wasn't exactly a state of the art enterprise that I was taking over when I and my three labourers moved in.

Before opening for business, steel girders were welded together to make strong storage pens for the different sized tubes and once in place, we proceeded to fill the whole warehouse from one end to the other with steel tube. In its heyday, I was ordering up to eight hundred ton of steel tube per month from British Steel in Corby and lorries were coming in and out of the place every hour of the working day. To help me run the tube store, I was obliged to recruit a small group of labourers one of whom was a man named Joey Jones.

Joey was a local man who'd been a labourer all his working life. His one break was when he'd been called up to do his two years National Service in the army. Joey could be as stubborn as a mule and having decided even before he'd been called up that he did not like the army, he tried to work his ticket by claiming that he could not wear a hat of any description without it giving him a headache. This act alone proved that he wasn't exactly the brain of Britain and as the army had had a great deal of experience in matters concerning swinging the lead, it didn't give an inch and far from giving him his ticket home, the army supplied him with a sturdy broom and Joey spent his two year army career, sweeping floors and doing a string of other menial jobs and as a consequence, learned absolutely nothing concerning the defence of the realm.

He was a married man with three sons when he joined Turners. Two of whom had already flown the nest and were standing on their own feet, but unfortunately, the third was a young tearaway who seemed to be either in trouble or doing his level best to find some. For most of the time, Joey was a good honest worker and had a likable nature which was enhanced by a mischievous sense of humour and he was the perfect man for life in a tube store as he was a strong simple grafter who had no ambition whatsoever and as long as he picked up a reasonable wage packet on a Friday, enough to keep the wolf from the door and a pot of jam on the table, Joey was happy with his lot in life.

Teddy, one of the other labourers', was a strong, but overweight young man who was full of bouncy self-confidence and had little respect for anyone but himself. He'd found that he could run rings around his father, who was a weak willed drunk and he was now under the mistaken impression that he could do the same with anyone else, but there was a flaw to his cocky juvenile attitude, he wasn't as smart as he thought he was. All the workers clashed with young Teddy at some time or another and I was constantly reprimanding him for one thing or another. Joey, who worked alongside him, clashed with him almost every day and over a period of time a tit for tat game of practical jokes developed between them as each one tried to get the better of the other.

On one occasion, Joey drenched the inside of Teddy's jacket with cold water and then placed the coat back on the coat hook and Teddy, not being aware of it until he had hurriedly put the jacket on at the end of the working day, was surprised to find that his arms and back were suddenly ringing wet. By the time he'd realised what had happened and who was responsible and had run out of four letter expletives, Joey was already on his way home with a bright smile on his craggy face.

The following day, Teddy let the air out of Joey's bicycle tyres. Joey then retaliated by nailing Teddy's jacket to the mess room wall and so the tit for tat pranks continued. If it looked as if their practical jokes were getting out of hand and were going to interfere with the smooth running of the working procedures, I would intervene, but on the whole they both took their games of revenge in good part.

One day Teddy turned up for work wearing a brand new pair of light brown, calf length ornate cowboy boots of which he was extremely proud and paraded about looking like the king of the Wild West. The boots had cost him quite a chunk of his hard-earned money and as he changed into his old battered working boots in the mess room, he gave Joey a deadly warning.

"Joey!" He stated solemnly as he pointed a warning finger, "You touch them boots and you're a dead man."

"I have no intention of touching your smelly old cowboy boots," Joey replied in all innocence, "They don't interest me one little bit, so stick that in your pipe and smoke it."

At the end of the working day when the storemen were changing out of their overalls and getting ready to go home, to his horror Teddy found that his cowboy boots had a substantial number of damp used tea bags inside them. Every time that Joey had made a cup of tea either for himself or a lorry driver, he'd deposited them into Teddy's cowboy boots. Once again Teddy was forced to use a significant number of Anglo Saxon expletives to vent his pent up anger. Joey just shrugged his shoulders and said dismissively, "You look a right Jessy in them boots anyway you silly big tart."

The following day, when Joey went to mount his bicycle for his short journey home he found that his saddle was missing. At this point, I stepped in and calmed things down and put a stop to their artful pranks for a while, but then one-day an opportunity presented itself that Joey just could not resist. He walked into the mess room during the lunchtime break and found young Teddy, sprawled out and fast asleep on an old dilapidated armchair. Joey carefully tied Teddy's boot laces together, then called in from the street, a group of young office girls who were just passing the premises and on their way back to work, to witness Teddy's rude awakening.

Joey dropped a metal dustbin lid onto the mess room's stone tiled floor and the ear shattering clatter brought Teddy back to life with an almighty start and he leapt out of the old armchair and fell flat onto the hard floor much to the amusement of Joey and the office girls, who, with a screech of excitement turned tail and ran off into the street.

I intervened once more, but to no avail, war between the two combatants had been declared and over the next few days each one tried to out manoeuvre the other. Joey's sandwiches went missing, Teddy's jacket was found hanging from a girder thirty foot in the air and then Joey's bicycle disappeared for three days. Teddy had put it onto the back of an empty delivery lorry while no one was looking and it spent the next few days travelling all over the Midlands before the driver had a chance to bring it back.

Standard steel tube can be purchased in a self-colour condition or coated with black paint and depending on what it's going to be used for the customer will choose which type he requires. If it's for welding the customer would avoid paint covered tube, but if it is to be cut and threaded, painted tube would be preferable to prevent rust. Occasionally, we would run out of black painted tube in one size or another and to put this right, I would organise the painting of a small amount of tube to tide us over until the next delivery arrived. We spread a quantity of the self-colour tubes onto a designated area and paint them with a long handled broom. It was a messy, but to paint the tubes individually would have been far too time consuming.

One glorious summer's day I was outside the store on the piece of waste land that acted as a back yard and general storage area to the building when a worried looking driver came out and anxiously said, "Jaco have you seen what that pair of idiots are doing in there?"

"Well I hope they're painting the bloody tube," I replied, "We need them for tomorrow," but looking at the drivers face I could see that he was referring to something quite different.

"You'd better come and have a look, because I can't believe what I've just seen." The driver said while shaking his head from side to side.

We approached Joey and Teddy who were standing on a platform of freshly painted tube and each held a paint-drenched long handled broom and each one was covered from head to foot in black gloss paint. There was hardly a single part of them that had escaped. While painting the tube they had got into one of their stupid tit for tat arguments and with the paint covered brooms they had systematically covered each other in black paint. When they stripped off their paint covered overalls, it was found that the paint had soaked right through their clothes in many places and their bodies were a patchwork of black stains. When Teddy finally removed his paint sodden trousers, he looked as though he was wearing black tights.

Over the next few days, the pair spent many hours scrubbing themselves down with turpentine and several days passed before they got rid of the dark stains. While smiling inwardly, I gave them both a severe dressing down and threatened each one with instant dismissal if anything like that happened again and after that incident, the pair gave up all physical attacks upon each other for a short while and concentrated instead on childish verbal insults.

After a few years had passed, the company directors decided that the forlorn premises required a few major repairs; this decision wasn't brought about by their concern for the comfort of the staff, but for the wellbeing of the steel tube stock. Rainwater dripping onto a storeman was a nuisance, but rainwater falling onto the steel tube created rust and lessened the value of the stock. So new press button cranes and roller shutter doors were installed and the roof water proofed from one end to the other. The company that won the contract to seal the roof with a coating of thick black bitumen was the one that had put in the lowest bid and unknown to us working below; the roofers were cutting corners by not adhering to their safety procedures.

It was a bright sunny morning and sunlight was streaming into the warehouse through the open doorways and the skylights above and in the third gangway, Joey, Teddy and I were pulling out quantities of tube from the stock bins and creating bundles ready to be lifted by the overhead crane. Other workmen were doing the same in other parts of the large warehouse when suddenly above the background noise of clattering steel, at one end of the long warehouse, an unexpected sound was heard. A loud crack was instantly followed by a crashing sound that continued for several seconds and as luck would have it, I happened to be facing towards the area where the sound was emanating from. I saw the figure of a man crash through the high asbestos roof with two large tins of bitumen and broken portions of asbestos sheeting on either side of him. As the man fell, he hit an electrical conduit tube on the way down, bounced off it and crashed to the ground in a heap, the two large tins and broken portions of the asbestos roof all around him. The roofer had fallen fifty feet and onto a hard unyielding surface and he showed no sign of movement.

Joey and Teddy, who had been facing in the opposite direction, did not actually witness the incident and for a moment they were baffled by where the crashing sound had come from as the noise had echoed around the warehouse and they looked at my shocked reaction to give them a clue as to what had happened. As I automatically ran towards the prone figure lying on the ground, they quickly followed and realised what had happened. A quick examination of the blooded-heaped figure confirmed that the young man was stone dead and that there was absolutely nothing that we could do for him.

I rang the emergency services and instructed Joey to stand by the stores entrance and to let no one into the premises except the ambulance and the police when they arrived. With many thoughts spinning inside my head, I then informed the head office of what had happened and told them not to send any lorries for loading until further notice. All this took but a few minutes and yet the first man to arrive on the scene was a smiling local newspaper reporter. He had been in a car nearby listening to the emergency frequency on his radio. He marched straight into the warehouse and brightly asked me for details of what had happened. I was still in a state of shock, but instinctively I knew that it would be better if I said nothing and so I told him that I'd not witnessed the accident and ushered him back to the open doorway where he stood chatting to Joey.

The police and the ambulance arrived and took over and I never saw the newsman again and thought no more of him, but that evening, the local evening newspaper printed a full report of the tragic accident and not only named Joey as the only eyewitness, but also claimed that Joey had tried to save the man's life and that it was he that had called for the ambulance. I did nothing to counteract the story and let Joey bask in his moment of glory, who, having read the newspaper several times, now believed every word of it and I became even more sceptical of newspaper reports than before.

One dull and dismal morning, Joey and Teddy were together in the mess room, enjoying a well-earned tea break. Other than having a two bar electric fire and a calendar that portrayed a naked woman with an enormous bust, the room was Spartan and devoid of any physical or spiritual warmth. The walls had been painted with pale grey gloss paint and the floor was paved with cold stone tiles. There were two windows, one giving a view into the large warehouse and the rows of steel pens that held the tube stock and the other, a limited view of the cold grey street outside. There was a wash basin and a cold water tap in one corner and the only furniture was a kitchen cupboard, a steel table and an assortment of chairs and as Joey and Teddy sat at each end of the table and chatted about nothing in particular, a fierce thunderstorm that had been threatening for some time, broke out over the area and the mighty sound of thunder rumbled throughout the cavernous brick walled streets. As the storm approached, the street outside became noticeably darker, but undeterred by the lightning flashes and the loud thunder claps, the two storemen continued to eat their sandwiches and drink their tea.

As was the nature of the tube stores business, with lorries arriving at all hours of the day, it was not possible for the men to take their tea breaks together and while Joey and Teddy took their break that stormy morning, the other workers were busy in the warehouse loading lorries.

While the two were eating, the large black Bakelite telephone, that sat on the table between them, began to ring and Teddy grabbed the receiver before Joey had a chance to move and just as quickly, he dropped it as though it was red hot and screaming with pain, he flew backwards across the room and hit the brick wall behind him with a heavy thud. Freakishly, he'd received a sharp electrical shock from the overhead thunderstorm. Unbelievably a shot of electricity had travelled through the telephone wire and ended up in his hand.

As Teddy lay on the floor groaning and holding his burnt hand to his chest, he cried out to Joey with a pain stricken plea, "Joey!, ring nine, nine, nine, call an ambulance. I've been electrocuted."

Joey, who'd witnessed Teddy's sudden unexpected gymnastic leap from the table, was still calmly drinking his tea and eating his sandwich and replied, "You piss off you daft sod, I aint touching that bleeding phone, I might get electrocuted mi-self."

On hearing this, Teddy quickly recovered from his state of near death, sat up straight and with raging anger spat out the words, "You rotten bastard, I could be dying here! I could be having a bleeding heart attack! Ring for a bleeding ambulance you unfeeling git, I need help!"

"Not me mate," Joey replied as he shook his head dismissively, "I'm not touching that phone, it might still be live. If you want an ambulance that bad, you ring for it."

Teddy, who was now fuming with rage, shook his head in temper and pointing a warning finger he said with a snarled grimace, "I'll get you for this Joey Jones, I could be dying here and you, you selfish bastard, won't lift a finger to help me."

Joey stood up, finished what was left of his tea and said, "You ain't dying you idle bleeder, your just trying to get out of loading the next lorry." And with that he walked out of the mess room and left poor Teddy sitting on the cold floor cradling his burnt hand and basking in his misery.

In 1973 Ted Heath's government, because of its intractable argument with the nation's coal miners, introduced the three day rationing of electricity, which became known as the three day week. On the days that there was no electricity, we were obliged to load lorries without the aid of an overhead crane. Some of these lorries were taking out ten ton of tube at a time and every steel tube had to be carried up the long warehouse gangways to the vehicles. It was hard, dirty and exhausting work, especially when handling the larger sized tubes. What made the situation even worse was that without electricity we could not boil a kettle or warm ourselves by the two bar electric fire in the mess room when eating our grub. We solved the first problem by bringing in flasks of hot tea from home and the second by burning scrap wood in a hastily contrived brazier set up by the entrance to the warehouse.

There were times in this period of industrial mayhem, when the power went off in the evening without any warning whatsoever and everyone, no matter where they were, were obliged to scramble for stand by emergency lighting. Mitch and Billy were in the Sailors one evening when the power suddenly went off and the room was pitched into total darkness. A huge roar of light hearted banter and the usual cat call swearing went up from the assembled customers, while the bar staff scrambled for torches and candles which when lit gave the room a Dickensian ambiance. After twenty minutes, the power came back on to be greeted by another surge of light hearted banter and it was then that the pubs manager noticed that several of his brass ornaments, including two replica duelling pistols that had been fixed to the wall, were now missing.

"You rotten bastard's," he shouted loudly while pointing at the bare space on the wall where the brass ornaments had been. Then shaking his head in disbelief and surveying the pubs assorted clientele with anger he demanded to know, "Who did it? Which one of you bastards stole my bleeding ornaments?"

No one owned up to doing the dirty deed because at that moment no one in the pub knew for certain who the culprit was, but they all began to notice that unpredictable Bronco, who had been very vocal before the power cut, was no longer in the room and as if by magic, he seemed to have disappeared.

Such songs as, "My Ding-a-Ling," "My Sweet Lord," "Your so Vain," "Gonna Make you a Star," "When will I see you Again," and the cracking Rolling Stones number "Brown Sugar," were recorded in the early seventies and in 1976 the band, Queen, released the great classic "Bohemian Rhapsody," which appealed to all ages, but it was another song dominated tube store during this period.

Teddy's mother had become involved in an intimate relationship with a man that was known as Uncle Paul. We knew all about this affair and its intimate details because Teddy, in his infinite wisdom, had discussed his mother's passionate goings on with numerous drivers and storemen during their tea breaks.

"Of course he's not my real Uncle," Teddy had disclosed in all innocence, "He's just a friend of the family."

"And does your Dad know this friend of the family?" Joey craftily enquired.

"Well he knows him, they used the same pub at one time," Teddy had answered naively, "but he's more our Mom's friend than our Dad's."

Teddy was apt to sing to himself while working and one of his songs was, "Where's your mother gone, Chirpy, Chirpy, Cheep, Cheep" and every time Joey heard him singing this song, he would call out, "You know where your mothers gone, she gone shagging with Uncle Paul'y."

Teddy did not take too kindly to these crude, but probably accurate remarks and threatened to inflict all manner of horrible and illegal torturers upon Joey's person, but it made little difference, Joey was quite impervious to Teddy's threats and when he saw that his ribbing upset Teddy, he baited him even more, so much so that I was constantly having to part the pair of them and make them work in different parts of the warehouse.

Teddy had two oddities that none of us had ever come across before. He did not drink tea or coffee and preferred cold water. He ate potato crisp sandwiches almost every day and never touched any fruit or green vegetables. The other oddity was that he could, within seconds, fall asleep anywhere at any time. On many occasions he'd have a lift in someone's car, or lorry and before it had travelled more than two hundred yards, he was fast asleep. This also happened when he travelled on buses and many a time he would be found fast asleep when the bus arrived at the terminus.

Although the tube store had a substantial office block, several of the rooms were permanently vacant. So when the company decided to put on a sales presentation of their new range of threading, cutting and welding machines, these unused rooms were seen to be the ideal location for it. Customers from across the Midlands were invited to come along and witness the demonstrations. Knowing full well that many of the customers would expect large amounts of alcoholic drinks, these were brought in and made available by the sales staff.

Unbeknown to me, Joey and Teddy had diverted a full crate of beer into a nearby spare room and all through the afternoon, while the salesmen were busy demonstrating the machines to their prospective customers, they nipped into the spare room and liberally refreshed themselves. By the end of the working day they were found to be grinning stupidly, staggering about and suffering from slurred speech.

Joey managed to stagger off home without too much trouble, but Teddy who was much younger and not used to alcohol, needed to catch two buses to reach home and so, after giving him a rousting; I gave him a lift in my car. I dropped him off a mile from his home, reasoning that a walk would help to sober him up.

Before setting off for home, he decided to relieve his bursting bladder against a brick wall in an alleyway at the rear of some shops and seeing an unoccupied van, he climbed into the back for a rest. When he woke from his drunken slumbers, he found that he was not only locked inside the van, but it was morning and he was in Worcester, twenty mile from where he'd climbed into the van the night before.

He eventually left the tube store to take up the prestigious position of selling burgers from a portable kiosk which was situated in a busy shopping area and my role of diplomatic referee came to an end.

The small council estate, on which Joey lived, had its fair share of layabouts and benefit scroungers and a typical example was the Blob. He lived opposite Joey's humble abode and so, being a close neighbour, Joey was well acquainted with the him and his slothful ways. Being in his mid-thirties, the Blob was still relatively young, but he had the appearance of a much older man. He had a wife and five kids and had convinced himself that he suffered from far more bad luck than anyone else. No one on the estate could remember him ever having completed a full week's work and it would seem that he never intended to do so, as any mention of finding a job brought on instant debilitating back pains

One day the Blob's scruffy overweight and downtrodden subservient wife knocked on Joey's door in earnest and when he answered, she pleaded with him for "a loan of a fag for 'im indoors" which she promised to replace by the end of the week. She then explained, her face a picture of worry, her podgy hands clenched together and resting upon her ample, but sagging bosom, "He's been asleep on the settee see Joey and he's had a terrible nightmare and it's really upset him. He said that in the 'orrible dream he saw one of the babbies fall off a canal bridge and into the "cut" and he said, you go and ask Joey to lend us a fag and after I've smoked it and calmed me nerves down a bit, I'll get back to sleep and find out where this canal bridge is."

Billy, who claimed that he'd tired of driving for Briggs, joined me in the tube store when a vacancy suddenly became available and he was soon helping me to run the place more efficiently. We hadn't seen each other for some time and so I was overjoyed when he'd come along looking for a job and that I was able to help him out. Through conversations with Mitch, I'd been aware that Billy had moved out of his sister's house and had shacked up with a young woman who'd ditched her husband, but I'd never met the woman and knew nothing of his domestic circumstances and his problem. If it had been anyone other than Billy telling me the unlikely tale, I would have dismissed it as pure moonshine, but Billy and I went too far back to even think of kidding each other.

One morning he arrived late for work and I commented upon his tired demeanour and said, "Your eyes look like piss holes in the snow. What's up? Are you ill?"

His forlorn answer was, "I look buggered because I am buggered. I'm living with a bird who's a nymphomaniac and it's bleedin' killing me."

I'd always assumed that there was no such thing as a nymphomaniac and that it was a figment of imagination, a wishful thinking titillating myth that helped to sell soft porn magazines, but Billy assured me that the young woman that he was living with was not only willing, but eager to have sex with him all the time, "night and day and every bloody day!"

"What do you mean by all the time?" I asked intrigued and feeling slightly titillated at the thought of having sex sessions every day.

"Well, she wants sex first thing in the morning when I wake up, then when I get home from work in the evening, when we get back from the pub and sometimes she even wakes me up in the middle of the night playing with my bollocks." He declared sadly as he slumped into the mess room's dilapidated armchair.

The thought instantly crossed my mind that a good many men, including myself, would consider that was a dream come true, but Billy claimed that not only was the situation killing him, but it was also the true reason why he'd just lost his last job.

"Some mornings," he wailed dejectedly as he opened up his heart, "I was just too knackered to get out of bed and go to bloody work."

"Well what about this job?" I asked, "You can't keep coming in late every morning and expect me to keep covering for you." Actually, it was an idle threat as we both knew that I would cover for him as much as possible, but at the same time it needed saying.

"I've already told her that we've got to cut down on all the shagging. I told her that if I don't get enough sleep I'll end up losing this job just like I'd lost the last one."

"And what did she say to that?"

"Oh, she don't like it and she played her face a bit, but tuff. That's how it's got to be, I told her straight, I ain't bloody Superman, little Willie needs a rest."

But for all his brave words, some mornings Billy arrived for work looking like an old Basset hound that had been up all night and I guessed that his energetic temptress had persuaded him to go back on his new resolution. During several conversations, he explained that when he'd first met her, he'd been overjoyed to find that she was sex mad and that she insisted on experimenting and trying out all manner of positions. But over time the novelty had worn off and his stamina had eventually waned and he now felt that this constant supply of insatiable sex was more of a daily chore, than an exciting bonus.

Things came to a head when he found that she'd been having a secret sexual liaison with a middle-aged shopkeeper. On discovering this cuckolding news, Billy became consumed with rage, confronted the shopkeeper and punched him in the face. After his temper had subsided, he became extremely remorseful. "I felt bloody awful and ashamed," he said when explaining what had happened, "The poor prat was lying there on the floor with his lip split and looking terrified and I couldn't help but feel sorry for the old bugger, so I helped him up onto his feet, brushed him down and when he'd calmed down a bit, I took him to the nearest pub and bought him a pint of beer and a whiskey chaser."

"Why?" I asked astonished.

"Well," He explained, with a shrug of his shoulders, "I couldn't really blame him could I? If an attractive bird offers an old bloke like him a shag with no strings attached, he'd be a mug to turn it down wouldn't he?"

"How old is he then A hundred and one?"

"No, nothing like that, he's about forty."

"And you recon that's old?"

"Well it's a lot older than her aint it."

Billy and the nymphomaniac broke up after that acrimonious incident, but surprisingly, that wasn't the end of the unusual tale. The factory buildings that were near the tube store had once been part of the Tangy complex and they had connecting driveways and employees parked their cars along these driveways during the day while they were at work. While travelling along one of these driveways in a ten ton lorry whose large cab window gave a high and wide view, Billy and I happened to spot Billy's ex-girlfriend fully engaged in a steamy sex session with a young man in one of the parked cars.

Billy recognised the car as belonging to a young man that his ex-girlfriend worked with in a nearby office and after making some discreet enquiries with people from the same office; he discovered that she'd been seeing the happily married young man on a regular basis for the last twelve months.

"Well bugger me," Billy exclaimed in amazement on learning this unexpected revelation, "Not only was she having sex with me and the bloody shopkeeper, but she was also shagging that little runt that she works with as well!"

In one of the many conversations, he disclosed that for all the sex that she'd indulged in, she'd always refused to use any form of contraceptive. I thought this odd and I pressed him on this point, but he was quite adamant that she never used any form of contraceptive and that she would not allow him to use any either.

"She said something about it not being necessary and that condoms got in the way." Billy said thoughtfully.

This information seemed to throw a completely new light upon the young woman's exceptional wanton behaviour and I began to wonder if perhaps she wasn't a nymphomaniac in the physical sense at all, but a barren woman with a disturbed psychological problem, who was desperately trying to become pregnant. But shortly after, she took up with another young man and left the district and we never saw her again and so my feeble stab at psychoanalysis was never to be proved one way or the other.

After Billy's energetic sex mad experience was over, he dropped back into his old habits of playing dominoes in the local pub and putting on his glad rags and visiting the Tower Ballroom to try his luck once more. He found himself a new sidekick to accompany him to his "Grab a Granny" nights at the Tower Ballroom. He was a lorry driver named Trevor who'd been involved in many romantic liaisons that had gone belly up and wasn't at all fussy about whom he picked up. The transport that these two young lechers used for their Wednesday night romantic sorties was one of the company's ten-ton lorries, which they brazenly parked in the middle of the ballroom car park, and while dancing and chatting with women of a dubious age, but who were all dressed up and looking for a bit of fun, they would offer them lift home.

"It works every time," Billy said with a gleeful chuckle, "As soon as the women realise that they have to climb up into the lorries high cab, they go into hysterics. None of them have ever been in a lorry before and getting them up into the cab is a right good laugh. You have to push them up by getting your hands and your head under their big fat arses and they have to hitch their skirts up to manage it. But it's all good fun and puts them in the right frame of mind for a bit of slap and tickle on the way home."

"I'll bet you won't find that gem of wisdom in any of the dating manuals," Mitch commented with a chuckle when he heard of Billy's dating practice, "but I suppose the early cave men used similar technique when they dragged their females off into a cave."

Like many others Billy, eventually found his true love at the Tower Ballroom. She was a married woman who had a small child and who was having a much-needed night out with her older sister and after dancing with her, Billy learned that she was trapped in an unhappy marriage. She found Billy and his easy going fun loving manner was just the tonic that she needed and they began to see each other on a regular basis. They were able to keep their clandestine meetings secret for a good six months and then one summer's day, while in a romantic mood, Billy took her and her small son to Barmouth for a day out and there they had the misfortune to meet one of her "goby" neighbours who happened to be on holiday there. Knowing that the cat was now well and truly out of the bag and that their meetings would now become impossible to keep secret, they realised that it was decision time.

With little persuasion, Billy's new love decided to leave her husband and set up home with Billy and this time it really was a case of living happily ever after. She eventually gained a divorce and she and Billy were able to marry and they lived together for the rest of their lives. It was yet another triumph for the Tower Ballrooms ability to bring lonely and unhappy people together and give them a second chance at partnerships.

Over the years the staff that worked at the tube store changed for numerous reasons and as the work required nothing more than brute strength and a lack of ambition, some of the young men that worked there, were little more than Neanderthal in manner and outlook. "And that's putting it mildly." Billy was to comment on several occasions when discussing many of the incidents that he'd witnessed.

Bob was a prime example. He arrived for his interview with his very large and formidable mother. She had arms that were as muscular as any man that I'd ever met and I concluded that she herself would make an excellent tube store labourer. Bob, a large thick set lad, sat on the chair that was offered, lowered his eyes and never uttered a word all through the interview. Every time I asked him a question, such as, "How old are you?" "What school did you attend?" or "Where have you worked before?" He said nothing as he was obviously embarrassed by the whole occasion and his strapping mother rambled on and answered every question for him; it was like interviewing a ventriloquist act.

Bob had been recommended for the job and I'd been assured that he was as strong as an ox. This turned out to be a monumental understatement. He may have been blessed with a feeble mind and little confidence, but he had super human strength and could lift and carry with ease, weights that would have crippled a normal man.

He worked in the tube store for fifteen years and in all that time he hardly said a word to anyone, not to me, his workmates, the lorry drivers or the regular customers, but what was even stranger than this monastic silence, was that no one ever saw him eat anything. When one considered that he lifted and carried heavy steel tube all day, where did he get his enormous reserves of energy from? From eight o'clock in the morning, till five thirty or even later if it was necessary, he never ate a single thing even though his workmates offered to share their biscuits, crisps, cakes, fruit and sandwiches with him.

We concluded that when he arrived home, he sat down to an enormous cow pie complete with protruding horns and as his mother put one in mind of Desperate Dan's daughter, it all made perfect sense.

One of society's misfits that Joey took under his wing was Timothy. He was a short stocky young man who had a large round head and obvious learning difficulties, but as is often the case, he had a big happy as Larry smiling face. Timothy was not only a sandwich short of a picnic, but was liable to have epileptic fits. He was a happy chap for most of the time and he walked about beaming at anyone he met and plaguing them with numerous irritating questions. "What's your name?" Where are you going?" "What are you doing?" "Can I do that?" "Can I have a go?"

He was employed as a labourer come messenger boy at a nearby factory and two or three times a week he would walk past the tube store while engaged on an errand and he would inquisitively peer into the tube store with open mouthed curiosity and Joey struck up a friendly rapport with him, which wasn't hard, as he was quite willing to talk to anyone who would give him the time of day. As time went on he took to entering the tube store and talking to anyone who was in the mess room and his simple conversations would invariably turn to the merits of the West Bromwich Football Club of which he was an ardent supporter and attended every home game. Of course the tube store lads, especially those that were Aston Villa fans, would rib him about his team, but it was all done with harmless humour.

Then one day, quite out of the blue, while visiting the mess room he had an epileptic fit. He fell onto the stone tiled floor and thrashed about until it was over. An ambulance was sent for and his place of work was duly informed. Now because the tube store could be a dangerous place to walk around, what with heavy steel tubes being constantly moved around by crane and by hand, I banned him from entering the building.

Although I did this to save him from having a serious accident, I was looked upon by Timothy and by some of the storemen, as a mean spirited spoilsport. Once again I was to learn that when making and imposing what I thought were logical management decisions, it was impossible to win them all and that at times, managing workers was just as frustrating as raising a house full of kids. So, because of the ban, Timothy went back to his previous routine of passing the time of day and calling out his WBA football clichés, such as "Up the Baggies" from the street whenever he passed.

While clearing out a cupboard at home, Joey came across an old khaki coloured army great coat that had epaulets and two rows of brass buttons and he gave it to Timothy to keep him warm when he attended the football matches on a cold Saturday afternoon. When Timothy put the army great coat on, he glowed with pride and was completely oblivious to the fact that having such short legs, the long coat almost covered his boots. He was so proud of his army great coat that he not only wore it at the football matches as Joey had intended, but every day.

Now, what we were not aware of at the time, and only learned of much later, was that when attending a Saturday afternoon football match, Timothy discarded his grinning idiotic face for a while and one suspects, copying the behaviour of some of the local louts, became a foul mouthed biased football fanatic and went around insulting the visiting supporters. As he wasn't capable of understanding any of the intricate tactics that took place on the football field, this habit of letting off steam with his verbal outbursts was his reason for going to the matches.

Most of the away supporters that he insulted saw him for the harmless idiot that he was and either ignored him, or took the mickey out of him as he ranted at them. But one Saturday afternoon outside the Hawthorns football ground, he ran into a gang of visiting supporters who thought that he needed to be taught a lesson and they decided to hang him up on the spiked railings in Halfords Lane. They took hold of him and lifted him up against the iron railings, and ran two of the railing spikes through the wide collar of his army great coat and left him dangling there.

The weight of his body pressing onto the front of his coat prevented him from undoing the brass buttons and his little legs were too short to reach the pavement and so he was well and truly stuck. He was hanging up by his coat collar, kicking his legs, waving his arms about and hurling insults to the passing crowd for at least five minutes before another group of supporters, although laughing at the unusual sight, took pity on him and lifted him up and extracted the spikes from his coat collar and put him back onto terra firma where he once again carried on abusing all those around him.

Those that saw him stuck on the spiked fence and witnessed his frantic kicking and jerking while trying to free himself, agreed that it was a great shame for him to be put upon like that, but they also agreed that it was one of the funniest sights they'd ever seen. The inevitable joke of, "Timothy, have you been hanging around the football ground again?" went straight over his head, but served to remind others of the incident and set them off laughing time and time again.

Smithy and Steak were so alike that they could easily have been mistaken for brothers. They were both thirty three years old, the same height and build, came from similar backgrounds, had a hang dog attitude to life and were as stubborn as mules. Both believed that it was about to rain on their parade, that their glass was never half full, but always half empty and although they were working as labourers in the tube store, many thought that they would have been better employed as funeral directors. So, having the same dismal downtrodden attitude to life, you naturally assumed that they would have been the best of pals, but they were anything but, and openly showed it.

"How come you never say good morning to me when I come in to work in the morning?" Steak asked Smithy accusingly one grey Monday morning.

"Because you never say good morning to me when I come in." Smithy snapped in reply.

"Well I would if you said it to me." Steak stated firmly.

"Why should I be first to say it?" Smithy answered sharply, "You say it to me and I'll say it back."

"I'm not saying it first," snapped Steak, "You say it first and I'll answer you."

And so it went on, the same sort of trivial argument would ensue concerning whose turn it was to fill the kettle, make the tea, fetch a sandwich from the café or purchase a cheap tabloid newspaper and who should study the big breasted pin-up on page three first. Even when they walked into a pub together they would inevitably buy their own drink and smoke their own cigarettes.

At the time Steak was separated from his wife and child and was living locally with another woman who had had two children by him. He was a fully trained electrician and could have commanded a reasonable salary if he'd stayed in that profession, but because he stubbornly refused to pay any maintenance whatsoever to his legitimate wife; he worked in the tube store and picked up a much lower wage. This way he reasoned, he could legitimately claim that he wasn't earning enough to hand over any money to, "That money grabbing bitch." He was so stubborn and bloody minded about the situation that he had even served time in prison for none payment of maintenance.

One day, a lorry driver after unloading his load of tube, asked if anyone wanted the rough wooden pallets that were left on the back of his lorry as he was taking the lorry into the garage for a service and didn't require them anymore. Smithy jumped at the offer and said that he'd take the lot. On hearing this Steak intervened and demanded that he should have half of the wooden pallets that were on offer.

"Why do you want half?" Smithy challenged, "You don't bloody well need them!"

"Oh yes I do and It's none of your business what I do with them." Steak replied spitefully.

"What do you need them for then?" Smithy demanded.

"Never mind what I need them for; what do you want them for?" Steak shot back.

"To build my garden fence up higher see," said Smithy smirking as he knew that Steak was not expecting him to have a legitimate reason for wanting them.

It transpired that Smithy, who lived in a small corner council house with a wife and two kids, had become very upset by the fact that a gang of teenagers had acquired the annoying habit of hanging around his house in the evening. Evidently, they gathered by the lamppost that was on the corner of the street and while doing so they often leaned against his garden fence as they talked and jostled each other in the way that teenagers do. Although they didn't seem to be doing anything other than fool around with each other, Smithy was determined to build a fence that was high enough to keep these barbarians at bay. When the other workers suggested that he might change tactics and make friends with them so that after a few weeks, he could politely ask them to move on when they became too noisy, Smithy thought the suggestion, "Bloody ridicules" and were raving mad to suggest such a thing.

"Make friends with that lot of yobs!" He spluttered, his face reddening at the very thought, "You must be joking, I wouldn't piss on them if they were on fire!" he snapped, "No, it's either build a big fence or blow their bleeding heads off with a shot gun!"

As far as Smithy was concerned; his problem with his local teenagers had no solution other than all-out war.

Steak eventually relented, as we all knew he would and he let Smithy have the rest of the wooden pallets for his proposed new garden fence and over the next few weeks Smithy collected many more wooden pallets and then got a lorry driver to deliver them to his corner house and he set about building his new anti-yob garden fence.

For the next few days his fellow workers enquired as to how the building of the fence was proceeding, but all they got from Smithy was a disinterested, "Okay," so after a while, they just stopped asking and lost interest. Then one day, while I was at head office, I was asked if I could deliver a steam valve to a factory while driving back to Smethwick which I gladly did. Like most people, I enjoyed any diversion that would help break up the daily routine. The factory was not far from Smithy's home, so being a little curious; I decided to take a look at his new anti yob fence. I pulled up a short distance away from Smithy's corner house and saw his new fence standing in all its glory and I was absolutely stunned.

I'd assumed that Smithy had used the rough wooden planks to replace old and missing ones that had been in the existing fence, but he'd completely dispensed with the original fence and in its place he'd erected the four-foot high wooden pallets in their original state, completely devoid of any paint or preservative and had put a second tier on top of the first. His anti yob fence not only looks hideously amateur, but it was eight foot high. The monstrosity resembled, a rough-hewn Wild West frontier fort that had been built to keep marauding Red Indians at bay, all it needed was the seventh cavalry riding by to complete the picture.

One look at the fence and I could see that there was no way Smithy's neighbours were going to put up with this hideous fence being planted in their midst and in no time at all the council's planning officers were called in. Without even inspecting the rough wooden barricade thoroughly, the planning authorities immediately demanded that the offensive barricade be dismantled at once. Smithy, being as stubborn as a disgruntled mule, was all for putting up a fight, but when his wife and kids threatened to leave home if he didn't take the hideous fence down; he reluctantly conceded defeat and with his teeth firmly gritted, he eventually dismantled the wooden monstrosity and put the original fence back up.

At the tube store, Steak declared that no one would have made him take the fence down, but the other storemen were well aware that Steak was so bone idle around the home, that if it had been left to him, the fence would not have been built in the first place.

Some months later, Steak somehow or other acquired, for he never purchased anything other than cigarettes, beer and the occasional new shirt, a small portable sun lamp. It was designed for people with rheumatic problems and had two settings, one for heating the painful rheumatic joint and the other to lightly tan the skin. With it, there was a pair of small dark goggles to protect the eyes and a pamphlet of instructions. Steak used the lamp a few times, but quickly tired of the contraption when he realised that to acquire a healthy looking sun tan at the two recommended sessions a week, it was going to take a very long time, time that could be much better spent in his local pub where he made a habit of chatting up the buxom barmaid that worked there.

When Smithy first asked Steak if he could borrow the sun lamp so that he could acquire a sun tan, Steak immediately wanted to charge him for the use of it, but after a while he relented and let him borrow the lamp for a couple of weeks free of charge. He also supplied the protective goggles, but for some reason the instruction pamphlet was not in the box when he handed the lamp over to Smithy. After using the lamp a couple of times, Smithy complained that it hadn't made the slightest difference to the pallor of his skin and that he was beginning to think that it was all a waste of time.

"How long were you under it for?" Steak asked sharply.

"Twenty bloody minutes both times." Smithy replied just as prickly.

"Well, what setting have you got it on then?" Snapped Steak.

"What do you mean what setting? I thought there was only one setting?" Smithy said amazed at learning this vital piece of information, then added, "Why the bloody hell didn't you tell me there was more than one setting you daft bat?"

"Because you never asked," sneered Steak maliciously and added for good measure, "Anyone with any sense would have realised that."

The following morning we could see that Smithy had found the correct setting for obtaining a healthy looking sun tan, for his face now resembled a baboon's red arse. The whole of his face was glowing bright red and looked to be very sore to the touch. The workers were soon saying that Smithy's face was so bright that it actually glowed and he could now read a newspaper in the dark.

"What the bleeding hell have you done to your face you daft sod?" Steak asked while desperately trying not to laugh.

Through gritted teeth and bright red face, Smithy answered quietly, "I fell asleep."

This turned out to be the only explanation that we were to receive that morning as Smithy refrained from talking to anyone and he totally ignored the constant snide remarks and raucous laughter that rained down upon him from his work mates, which ignited afresh each time a delivery driver appeared and was informed of what had happened.

It was eventually established that he'd taken a hot bath before using the sun lamp in the bedroom and had fallen asleep while lying under its rays and didn't wake until his wife had returned two hours later from her evening at the local bingo hall. But it wasn't until the following morning, when his face felt extremely hot and he looked into the bathroom mirror that he realised exactly what damage he'd done to himself.

He blamed Steak for not supplying him with the instructions, claiming that if he'd read them, he wouldn't have fallen asleep while under the lamp, but it was seen as a feeble excuse as Smithy had never read an instruction manual in his life and even if he'd read this one, that alone would not have prevented him from falling asleep on the bed that night.

Steak eventually sold the sun lamp to the buxom barmaid that he'd been chatting up and a week later he reported, "You won't believe it, but the daft cow has done exactly the same thing that Smithy did and now the cheeky mare wants her money back."

Smithy's wife's younger sister was a constant visitor to his home and had developed a romantic crush for him and to show just how much she loved him, she persistently slipped secret love letters into his jacket pockets when he wasn't looking. When he first mentioned this odd situation during a tea break in the mess room one day, we were a little sceptical of just how serious this situation could possibly be, but the following day Smithy brought in a couple of the love letters for us to peruse and to prove that his concern about the situation had credence. On examining the love letters, they looked to have been written by a pre-adolescent schoolgirl as they were full of childish phrases, phrases that none of us had seen since our school days. There were such phrases as, "I love you be cus I think you are good lookin and smashin" and although we could now see that Smithy had been telling the truth, we still couldn't quite associate the declared sentiments to him.

"Does your wife know about this?" I asked after reading the two infantile letters.

"Oh bloody hell no!" Smithy replied while shaking his head vigorously, "She'd bloody well kill me if she thought that something was going on, but I'm worried in case she finds one of these bleeding daft letters and thinks there is something going on. You see the silly cow keeps hiding these notes in my coat pockets when I'm not looking."

"Why do you think she's chasing after you?" Steak asked who was genuinely puzzled by this unusual scenario as for the life of him he couldn't see why any woman would be attracted to Smithy and to be fair, it was something that we all wondered at, as we were all well aware that Smithy was not a ladies man and that he was far more interested in getting his head and his hands under the bonnet of a car than under a woman's skirt.

"Has she fell out with her husband ?" Steak added questioningly as he tried to figure out why she should be chasing after Smithy.

"Oh no, she ain't married." Smithy stated dismissively, while shaking his head, "With her looks, no bugger would have her."

"Why, what's wrong with her then?" Steak asked intrigued at this unexpected answer, after all he reasoned, Smithy had married her older sister and so he'd assumed that the younger one would be just as attractive if not more so.

"She's got big ugly buck teeth." Smithy replied with a shrug, "She looks like a bleeding cart horse."

On hearing this revealing news Steak then got straight to the point, "Well why don't you just shag her then and then tell her to piss off." Steak was a man of few words and had very few romantic notions, but he spoke from the heart, for that's exactly what he would have done if he'd found himself in a similar situation. On overhearing this brutal macho conversation, some of us couldn't help but feel sorry for the young lady of letters, as from what Smithy was saying, it began to look as though she'd had a loveless life and was becoming desperate for some form of romantic love and affection. We felt that she had to be pretty desperate to fancy Smithy and although this may have been a whimsical thought, it was an earnest one for all that, for the truth was, Smithy radiated no more romance than a flat iron.

Over the next few weeks, Smithy received several more love letters which he brought to work and openly displayed and discussed the contents with anyone who was interested. He then informed ua that "Miss Buck Teeth" as he referred to her, had invented a new ploy with which to entrap him. She would visit his home three or four times a week and would purposely miss catching the last bus, whereupon Smithy's wife would ask him to run her home in his old car.

Eventually, as everyone expected, lust and opportunity got the better of Smithy's sensitivities and one evening while taking "Miss Buck Teeth" home, he stopped his car in a secluded spot in Park Lane and proceeded to break his marriage vows with his wife's younger sister.

Park Lane, was known locally as Lovers Lane as it was a secluded hedge row lane, that ran between a golf course, a cemetery and a wildlife park and it was a favourite venue for courting couples in the area who wished to get to know each other a little more intimately.

The following day, during the morning tea break, Smithy supplied us with the graphic details of his moment of lust with "Miss Buck Teeth" and I was both appalled and amused by what Smithy had to say.

"I thought bugger it," He said, as he explained his reasons for his ultimate action, "If I've got to keep running her home nearly every bleeding night, I might as well have something for it."

All his work mates who were sitting around drinking their tea and listening intently nodded in agreement and Steak added by way of encouragement, "Well, she'd been asking for it hadn't she? I told you that you should have got stuck in weeks ago."

"Anyway I pulled over onto a grass verge down Park Lane," Smithy continued, "told her to pull her pants off and then I gave her a right good seeing to."

"Did you kiss her?" Steak asked, for he knew how much Smithy hated those buck teeth.

"Did I bollocks!" said Smithy, shaking his head in denial, "I shagged her doggy fashion while we was kneeling on the front seats of the car. I made her stick her head out of the open window and I got up behind her and give it some wellie."

On hearing the details of Smithy's romantic escapade, we were left with the graphic, but comical image of courting couples driving slowly down Park Lane while looking for a suitable spot to spend the evening and seeing a buck toothed woman's head protruding from the open window of a car and rhythmically moving up and down in the manner of an ornamental nodding dog.

Because of his continual maintenance payment problems, there was never any danger of Steak ever becoming a workaholic; in fact he'd gradually acquired what was commonly known among his fellow workers as back trouble, "He has great difficulty in getting it off the bed in the morning." Time and time again he was either late for work or he just didn't turn up. I'd been as lenient as I could, but eventually it came to a point where I had to give Steak his marching orders purely to encourage the others. "I can't pull one man up for bad timekeeping if I'm letting another get away with it, no matter what the circumstances are." I explained. And so, with a shrug of the shoulders, Steak left the tube store and went to work for Mitch as a cash in hand drivers mate when Mitch was busy and when he was not, Steak just stayed in bed and rested his bad back.

Once when transporting a large load of wooden crates across the Yorkshire moors, the waterproof sheet that covered the load became loose during a violent gale and they had to stop and re-tie the sheet before they could continue their journey. "It was just like being on one of them old sailing ships in a storm" was Mitch's description of the episode. Both he and Steak attempted to re-tie the billowing waterproof sheet as the gale force winds billowed the loose sheet and buffeted them against the side of the lorry. Grabbing one of the loose ropes that was whipping around the side of the lorry, Steak hung onto it and attempted to pull it back down into place and tie it off. The strong gale force wind got right under the sheet once more and up in the air went Steak just as though he were a church bell ringer who'd forgotten to let go of the bell rope. Mitch grabbed Steak's legs and for a short while as they battled against the ferocious wind, their flimsy puppet like bodies were flipped up and around the side of the lorry as Mother Nature showed them who was boss. Bruised battered and soaking wet they eventually delivered their load, but on the way back home they broke down and spent several hours dismantling and cleaning parts of the engines fuel system.

During those early days of his business and with the clapped out lorries that he was forced to use, Mitch inadvertently became an expert at breaking down on route and often found the most inhospitable places to do so and so, although Steak was no longer working as a lowly labourer in an often cold and noisy tube store, he wasn't exactly living the life of Riley by riding shotgun with Mitch on the open road. All of which went some way to proving that when Steak was there and something hard and unpleasant had to be done, he got stuck in and did it, but because of his lack of self-motivation, he was very rarely there in the first place.

During a weekend visit to London, Mitch, Billy and I meandered around the area of Leicester Square and Soho before attending a football match and we came across a completely new innovation, a sex shop. We'd read about this new revolutionary innovation in the Sunday newspapers, but had never actually seen one before and so we boldly entered the shop to investigate what was on offer.

We looked at all the weird and bizarre paraphernalia that was on display with open-mouthed astonishment and were soon giggling like three bashful schoolgirls who'd just been confronted with an unexpected male erection. We just couldn't believe that anyone in their wildest dreams would want to use, or needed to use, the many kinky items that were on display when indulging in the sex act. Our feelings were unanimous; just what the hell was wrong with the people that needed such contraptions to do, what to us came quite naturally?

All three of us had experienced several intimate relationships, but not once had any of us had the slightest inclination to use anything like we saw in that shop. We'd never needed the use of drugs to have a good time and we certainly didn't need such things as spanking paddles and leather masks to have a satisfying vigorous sex session. We were all for trying out different positions as described in the Karma Sutra, but what the hell were we supposed to do with a long leather whip, a black head mask and a wide studded belt? It was all completely beyond our comprehension.

Just for the fun of it, Mitch decided to purchase a large pink nine-inch long penis shaped candle and over the next few months, at parties and general get-together's, we enjoyed many a laugh with the outstanding phallic object. In one party game, the blindfolded victim sat upon a chair in the middle of the room and had to guess by touch what the article was that was placed in front of them. It could be, and often was, a mundane object such as a cup or a bottle, but then other objects were added that were a little more unusual and designed to bring on a shocked response, such as a peeled orange or a bowl of cold spaghetti, but the reaction was always shocked horror when the large candle penis was placed in the hand and was made worse by seeing, as the victim snatched off their blindfold, Mitch quickly zipping up his flies.

Over many months the much used the phallic candle became bruised, battered and chipped and it eventually ended up in the tube store mess room where it was to play out its last joke before its eventual demise. Whenever a stranger entered the mess room, Joey would go over to the sink in the corner of the room, turn the cold water tap on fully and hold the large phallic candle in front of him.

Attracted by the noise of gushing water, the stranger would automatically glance over and see what he assumed was an enormous pink penis. Joey would then quickly turn his back on the stranger and pretend to go through the exaggerated motion of putting a very large penis back into his trousers. The look of shocked astonishment on the stranger's face was a picture to behold and the joke worked time and time again.

The nineteen seventies became known for bushy afro hairstyles and flared trousers, which made many of the wedding photographs of the period look like hilarious jokes. TV programmes such as "The Likely Lads," "Porridge," "MASH" and "Faulty Towers" kept audiences laughing and proof of their excellence is that they still do many years later.

Many men came and went in the tube store. Some were ordinary while others were decidedly odd, but all of them in one way or another caused me problems. Many brought their domestic problems with them and expected me to solve them and there were petty squabbles that arose occasionally, which meant that much of my time was taken up with poring oil upon troubled waters. My job was to simply see that the stock went in and out of that store as quickly as possible, but at times, I felt more like a social worker than a manager and no matter how hard I tried to stay aloof from the staffs varied problems, something would crop up that I could not ignore and I would get sucked into the thick of it.

During one period I had to deal with the disruption that a religious fanatic caused among the staff. The religious nut not only thought that the rest of us were all sinners and destined for the fires of hell, but continually told us so, which may have been good advice, but it was hardly conducive to good working relations. During my many employment interviews, I would enquire into the applicant's previous education and work experience and if the interview was going well and I liked the applicant, I would often make some light hearted reference to which football team they supported, but I would never ever mention the tricky subjects of politics or religion and it

291

was because of this lapse in my interviewing technique that this religious fanatic had slipped through the net.

The young man belonged to a family that had joined a Christian splinter group that gathered together in a prefabricated tin hut several times a week and there they loudly decried everything that they believed was wrong with the sinful society. Like all the other religious fanatics no matter what their religion, they truly believed that they alone were the chosen people and that all others were beyond the pale and destined for the blistering fires of hell.

What was particularly suspicious about this particular group of pious people was that they willingly gave ten percent of their earnings to their tin pot church and that the minister in charge of the group purchased a new car every two years with the proceeds. When one of the men pointed out that, "As all the parishioners live locally, the minister could use a bike" he was informed that he was being sinful. When he light heartedly asked the young man to explain the phenomena of burning bushes and the spectacular opening of the Red Sea, the religious fanatic became apoplectic, so he thought it wise not to mention the tricky business of being swallowed by a whale.

Being a fanatical Christian, the young man believed that every word in the bible was the literal truth and he was incapable of seeing that many of the stories were allegorical and had been tailored for an unsophisticated audience. To my relief, he didn't stay long and soon moved on to pastures new and from then on, I became a little more cautious when interviewing new applicants.

There was one youth that possessed a manic passion for driving fast cars, the problem being that the cars that he drove were stolen and one morning I received a message from the police informing me that the youth had been arrested and had put my name forward to stand bail for him, but he'd used up his quota of luck and ended up in prison and that was the last that I ever saw of him.

The young man who took his place turned out to be a slot machine gambling addict and would at times blow the whole of his week's wage in a single day. Because of this stupid behaviour, his mother turned up at the tube store and demanded that I give her his wage packet every Friday. When I pointed out that the young man was nineteen years old and how he chose to spend his money had nothing to do with me or the company and that it was quite illegal for me to give his wage packet to anyone else, I was ferociously chastised and accused of encouraging her son to gamble.

"In your position, you should be more responsible." She declared vehemently, "You know very well how weak willed he is." This claim struck me as quite odd, as I had only known the lad for five weeks and other than his name I knew next to nothing about him.

Then along came Paul, he was a small black African from Nigeria. He was married, had two children and had come to England with the sole purpose of furthering his education. He was an old fashioned Christian who saw all behaviour as either good or evil and he found the Western Europeans relaxed attitude to authority, morality and religion extremely puzzling. As I got to know him, I began to realise why he thought and behaved in the way he did. The Christian religion that Paul had been taught was the good old-fashioned bible thumping missionary fire and brimstone version, where the Devil had to be physically conquered on a daily basis and as if that wasn't enough of a doctrine to cope with, he also had two other codes of strict discipline to abide by. First and foremost there was the role of his father. He had been brought up to believe that his father could not be challenged and secondly, there was a strict tribal law that he was also expected to follow. Add all that to the hell fire religion and you had a man that was as solid as a rock and as unforgiving of sin as a hanging judge.

Although Paul came from what is now known as Nigeria, ethnically he was Ebo, which is a proud and resourceful race, and as such, he not only regarded education as a top priority, but was also determined to obtain a bona fide degree while he resided in England. To do this, he rose early in the morning and studied before setting off for work, he studied during his tea and lunch breaks and after completing a hard day's graft in the tube store, he attended Aston University for his evening classes. He did this, day after day for many months, passed seventeen exams and eventually earned his degree in business studies.

Through talking to him on, I began to learn a little of African attitudes to African politics. I began to see that petty tribal squabbles and racial prejudices played a big part in the continents troubles. I eventually came to the conclusion that most African countries were going through the same growing pains that Britain had gone through during the Middle Ages while on the long road to democracy, but whereas the tribes in Britain had fought each other with pitchforks and swords, Africa was cursed with an abundance of Armalites and Kalashnikovs.

He disliked West Indians because he believed that they lacked moral fibre, were drug addicts and possessed no culture to speak of. He would site the fact that many of them would stand outside his local pub on Sunday morning waiting for the doors to open. The fact that men from all races did the same thing never seemed to occur to him, but the story that he often quoted when on the subject of West Indians and their loose morals was shocking and could not be defended by anyone.

He'd been told that a West Indian shop stocked inexpensive children's clothes, so, having two children to clothe; he went along to see what was on offer. "When I entered the shop," he explained, "there were five people in there and the West Indian shopkeeper was having an argument with his teenage daughter. They were shouting at each other and the father was objecting to his daughter's wayward behaviour. He said that she was getting into bad ways with a group of young men and then unbelievably, the daughter suddenly screamed at him and said, "It's my cunt and I'll do what I like with it."

"I was shocked beyond belief and I left the shop immediately." He said and then added solemnly, "If that had been my daughter, I would have struck her down there and then and killed her on the spot."

And knowing Paul as well as we did, we knew that that is exactly what he would have done. We were all aware that as far as Paul was concerned, there were no grey areas to be found where morals and family respect was concerned. He saw all acts of moral behaviour as either good or evil and if it was evil, it had to be eradicated.

Paul went back to Nigeria armed with his well-earned diploma and he obtained a well paid managerial position with a German soft drinks company in Lagos and there he should have prospered and lived happily ever after, but it was not to be. Circumstances that were way beyond his control just would not allow such a happy ending.

Three years later he was back in England and working in the prison service in London. When I spoke to him on the telephone, he explained what had gone wrong.

"In the large Nigerian towns, such as Lagos," He explained, "corruption and armed criminals are everywhere and it's not a safe place to be. I was robbed three times at gunpoint while driving back home from work and so I decided to go back to England so that my children could obtain a good education while Nigeria sorts out its law and order problems."

The longest serving storeman was a young man named Guy. He was a giant of a lad when he first began working in the tube store and he was even larger, when he finally left the company many years later. Although he was six foot four, he was not lanky as all his limbs were in proportion to his height and, like many rugby players; it was only when he stood next to someone of normal size that his large physique became apparent. Just like Lenny in Steinbeck's story of Mice and Men, Big Guy was never fully aware of his own strength and he was liable to hurt someone without even knowing by simply patting them on the back, but unlike dumb Lenny, Big Guy was not stupid and was soon promoted and relied upon to control the other labourers in the tube store.

Because they spend most of the day on their own, lorry drivers often become very tense and irritable and find themselves wanting to vent their pent up frustrations onto any poor humble storemen that they happen upon, but one look at Big Guy in the tube store and their tune changed dramatically and for most of the time tranquillity reined while Big Guy was around. He looked upon the numerous heavy steel tubes as ideal pieces of keep fit equipment. Rather than use the overhead cranes, he would pick up the lengths of heavy steel tube and carry them up the long bay to the lorry that he was helping to load.

He was a passionate fan of rugby league and was desperate to join a club, but as the Midlands is a rugby union area, rugby league games are hard to find. To help, I hunted around and eventually got him a trial with the West Midlands Police Rugby League Club which was based at the Tally Ho training centre on the Pershore Road and he passed the test with flying colours. Although he was the only man in the team that was not a member of the police, he played for them for several years. His father Ben, who was also a large man, volunteered to carry and administer the cure all pain, bucket of cold water. At every game he gave his son constructive advice from the touchline, "Get stuck in you great lummox!" "Don't hang about you big tart" "Get stuck in you big tit."

I was standing next to Ben one day when Big Guy went down hard under the bodies of two meaty men and looked as though he was hurt.

"Do you think he's hurt Ben?" I asked, while drawing his attention to the fact that Big Guy was getting to his feet rather slowly and looked a bit groggy. Ben looked across the pitch at his son staggering about and said, "He'll be alright. He's just a bit dazed that's all," then added philosophically, "He don't do bugger all around the house anyway."

Twenty years after the release of the Beatles LP "Sergeant Pepper" the pop radio stations paid tribute to this mile stone by playing Beatles records all day and in the tube store, from the radio that was fixed above the mess room, these well know songs boomed out across the large warehouse. Half way through the day, Big Guy who seemed to be a little agitated was heard to object to the format of the programme by saying, "Why are they playing all these old songs all day?"

As a lifelong Beatles fan, I took great exception to this remark and looking up at Big Guy I said with undisguised irritation, "Look, you big lummox! It's the twentieth anniversary of Sergeant Pepper, that's why they're playing all these Beatles records."

Big Guy's flippant reply of, "So what?" annoyed me even more and I realised that I would have to explain. "Look," I said, while trying to control my exasperation, "When the Beatles made Sergeant Pepper, they were so popular that if they'd brought out a blank record, thousands of people would have bought the bloody thing. But," I continued, while doing a reasonable impression of a condescending school master, " they released a completely new experimental record, namely Sergeant Pepper, and it has been a great influence on pop music ever since."

Then after taking a good deep breath, I said, while still feeling a little exasperated, "Why the hell am I telling you all this? A young pop fan like you should know all this."

"What do you mean?" Big Guy replied frowning, "I wornt even born then was I!"

He was right, he was just nineteen years old and to him, the Beatles songs were old hat, a bit like my view of Al Jolson or Bing Crosby, good, but rooted in the past. It was probably the first time that I'd ever become conscious of losing touch with the younger generation and realising that I was growing old. I'd assumed that the general knowledge that I'd acquired over the years, the Second World War, the years of austerity, the beginning of the consumer society, the changing pop and fashion culture and all the details that went with these periods of time, were known by everyone, but I'd been pulled up short and realised that those that had not lived through those periods as I had, knew very little about them and what's more, had very little interest in them either.

It reminded me of when my mates and I were kids and had been influenced by such things as Flash Gordon, the Festival of Britain, the Eagle comic and the miracle of television; it was the future that we'd been interested in back then and not the old fashioned past and Big Guy's generation was no different.

Because of variances in temperature and pressures, plastic tube comes in many grades, sizes and lengths. The type of plastic tube which is used underground for carrying either water or gas was delivered to the tube store in rolled up coils. The coils of small sizes were similar to the size and shape of a formula one racing car tyre, but the largest size coils were six foot high. These large coils were very awkward to handle and they usually required two men to roll them for any distance and to place them in their specific storage pens.

One day I saw Big Guy, who was six foot four tall and Little Willie, who was less than five-foot, rolling a number of these plastic coils into the designated stock pens. I noticed that Big Guy was becoming more and more agitated with the awkwardness of the heavy coils and every now and then, he would put an extra burst of effort into moving them about, while little Willie scurried around him trying to look useful.

One large coil became stuck as the pair manoeuvred it into position in front of the stock pen and Big Guy decided to put all his strength into bowling the coil into the pen. He grabbed the large coil with both hands and with a mighty heave and an angry roar; he rolled the six-foot coil into the storage pen. Unfortunately, one end of the plastic tube got caught under Little Willies overall jacket and being caught like a fish on a barbed hook, he went up and over with the momentum of the rolling coil and ended up headfirst in the storage pen along with the coil.

It was yet another example of Big Guy not fully realising his own strength, but to those of us who witnessed the incident, it was as funny as a slapstick Laurel and Hardy film. Although a little shaken, Little Willie was unhurt and he was full of apology for getting in the way. Big Guy accepted the apology with grace, picked him up with one hand and brushed him down with the other as though he were a jacket that had just fallen onto a dusty floor.

Big Guy had been born and bred in a small terraced house and was as working class as a pair of hob nailed boots, but like many city dwellers, he had a passionate interest in nature. He was especially interested in the habits of birds and wild animals. Many of his type take to keeping pigeons in their back yards, but he went one step further and decided to raise a kestrel. He visited the local library and book shops and devoured every piece of information that he could find on the subject of rearing a kestrel and he became quite an expert on the subject and was often seen in his local park exercising his kestrel.

I called around to his house one day to see the kestrel up close and found that there were two other visitors already in the back yard. A young man and his girlfriend were inquisitively looking into the well-built bird loft that Big Guy had constructed in the small back garden at the steely eyed kestrel. While there, Big Guy proceeded to feed the kestrel with a few dead mice that he regularly purchased from a nearby pet shop. As the kestrel ripped the dead mouse apart with its hooked beak that was perfectly designed for the purpose, the young man's girlfriend, turned to me and with a look of disgust upon her face said simply, "Isn't nature wonderful?" and then added as she glanced at her boyfriend who was still gleefully watching the bird ripping the mouse apart, "He takes me to the most romantic places"

The steel tube that was delivered to the tube store was purchased from British Steel in Corby and was packed into two or four ton bundles. They were delivered by articulated lorries which were hired by British Steel and we got to know many of the drivers quite well. There was the odd one or two that were a little grumpy at times, but on the whole the delivery drivers were quite affable and helpful and many would stop for a chat and a cup of tea. One of the most pleasant and cheerful was a middle aged man named Norman. During one of the tea time chats he disclosed that his hobby was photography and he brought along many examples of his work on his visits. The photographs were mostly black and white studies and were of cold windswept landscapes, still life studies and photographs of people whilst in the process of completing their mundane chores. He attempted to educate some of the lads on the finer points of light and shade and how to compose a good photograph and also the complicated use of filters.

We all liked Norman and so it was quite a shock when we heard that he'd been arrested and charged with sexually molesting several little girls. He was found guilty and sent to prison and we never saw him again. It was very sobering to realise that on such a nice easy-going, ordinary man could not only be harbouring such vile fantasies, but acting upon them. As Smithy, who had never read a book in his life, succinctly put it "Yow can't never tell what's in a book until yov read it."

One morning, during a quiet period of trading, a gleaming new car rolled up to the entrance of the tube store and out stepped fly by night Charlie. He was dressed in a new dark blue suit, a crisp expensive white shirt, a silk tie, a pair of black shoes that shone like polished mirrors and a cat that got the cream grin on his face. I'd not seen Charlie for several months and so I had no idea what he'd been up to, but as he reeked of new found wealth, I guessed that it certainly wasn't anything legal.

We exchanged the usual ribald pleasantries, asked about each other's families, enquired after long lost friends and eventually Charlie got round to why he'd come to see me. Bronco had told him that he knew someone who was willing to buy steel tube at a very reasonable price and as I was now managing a warehouse that was full of the stuff, it seemed logical to Charlie that he should help me to make my fortune by letting him sell a substantial amount of the tube on the black market. I listened to Charlie's get rich quick proposal and with as much grace and good humour that I could muster I told him to piss off.

"Charlie," I said as I tried to explain my position, "I am quite capable of getting into a boat load of trouble all on my own, the last thing I need, is an expert like you to help me get into it."

And I meant every word. I was well aware that Charlie was capable of selling snow to an Eskimo, and given the chance he could have sold every length of tube that was in the tube store, but I was also aware that Charlie was about as reliable and predictable as the British weather and he was the last man that I would want to form a business association with, even if it was legal.

He looked at the numerous pens of steel tube that stretched to the far end of the long warehouse and were full to overflowing and said, "I guessed you'd say that, you're just like your dad you are, to bloody careful for your own good, but I tell you Jaco, if I was in charge of this lot, within six months, I'd have a car as long as New Street and a house as big as Buckingham Palace."

But I was having none of it; the thought of doing a stretch in prison far outweighed the dream of owning a big expensive car, but before he departed, he opened up the boot of his gleaming new car and revealed an Aladdin's cave of marketable items, items which included watches and Stratton cuff links which were in presentation boxes and which he offered to all the workers at a very reasonable price.

Eight weeks later, Charlie rolled up at the tube store again, but this time he looked a shadow of his former self as he was without his gleaming new car or new suit and looked decidedly dejected. He was not only flat broke once, but on the run. His wife had kicked him out of the happy home once more for not paying the rent for several weeks and it had not been an amicable parting. She'd not only broken a broom handle over his back, but she'd broken her wrist whilst punching him. As well as being homeless, Charlie disclosed that there was an added complication to his topsy-turvy life.

"I owe the Rainbow Casino over five thousand pound and they've threatened to put the heavies onto me if I don't pay up pretty soon. So with no money, no home and no bloody job, I'm off to the South coast for the summer season. Just till the dust settles" He said with a shrug.

Experiences of similar scrapes informed him that it would be wise to disappear for a while and wait until the hue and cry had died down before attempting to reason with his unpredictable creditors and his angry wife. Eventually, he got round to why he'd called in at to the tube store that morning, but I'd already anticipated that it was to borrow money to help him on his way. He not only asked for money, but also a lift on one of the lorries that was going south. I supplied him with a small amount of money, a padded car coat to keep him warm and arranged a lift for him and with fingers crossed I waved him on his way and prayed that I wouldn't be bothered by him for some considerable time.

The following day, the lorry driver that had given Charlie a lift, reported that he had dropped him off on the outskirts of Bristol where Charlie intended to hitch a lift down to the south coast. He also informed me that Charlie had tapped him for a fiver and had said, "Our Jaco will pay you back. He meant to give it to me before we set out, but he forgot."

Four months later, Charlie was back in town, brown as a berry and with a wallet bulging with bank notes. He revealed that he'd spent the summer working in a large hotel in Torquay and that he'd been stealing meat from the kitchen fridge and selling it to the owner of a local café. The management at the Rainbow Casino meanwhile had scrubbed Charlie's gambling dept., reasoning that an addicted gambler would not only eventually repay the money that he owed, but eventually lose a lot more if they let him continue to use their facilities. And that little episode just about summed Charlie up, one day he'd be flying high without a care in the world and the next, down in the gutter begging for scraps.

During Charlie's absence that summer, Mitch received a phone call from him asking him if he would be interested in handling a van load of stolen meat. Evidently Charlie had set up a shady deal with a deliveryman and was looking for a suitable customer to purchase a load of stolen meat. Mitch turned the offer down flat, not because he was averse to handling stolen goods, but because the deal posed too many problems. He pointed out that he would need a refrigerated van to keep the meat fresh, a technical point that Charlie hadn't thought important. A few days later, Mitch phoned Charlie at the hotel and disguising his voice, he pretended to be a police officer who was investigating the theft of a quantity of meat. Quick as a flash Charlie responded to the strange voice by saying in a Welsh accent, "I'm afraid you're too late, Charlie's not here see. He checked out yesterday and he left no forwarding address you see."

As soon as Mitch revealed his true identity, Charlie's language became a little colourful, but the humorous exercise revealed just how quick Charlie was when the chips were down.

Fly by night Charlie and unpredictable Bronco were both chirpy Jack the lad characters and were ideal market stall salesmen as they could coax, cajole and charm bargain hunters without any trouble at all, but it takes more than sales to make a business successful and when they teamed up together to sell imported shoes on the local markets, quite a few of their acquaintances thought that the enterprise was doomed to failure. But undeterred by negative comments, the pair set about proving the doubters wrong and purchased a quantity of boxed shoes from a large warehouse and in an old van, they travelled to the local open markets and proceeded to sell their stock. As they were both brimming with confidence and had an ample supply of cheeky chat lines to offer, they had no trouble at all in selling their goods.

"Roll up ladies and gentlemen and get the bargain of a lifetime. Hand crafted shiny leather shoes all the way from the orient. Here you are sir; put a pair of these on your feet and you'll dance like Fred Astaire."

Month after month their cash in hand business grew more successful and each time they visited the warehouse in the city centre, they were able to increase their stock.

"Here you are madam, the latest Italian high heeled fashion as worn by Sophia Loren at a quarter of the price. With these on your feet, you'll have the milkman and his mates chasing you around the block."

Trade was so good, that Bronco said the time had come to rent an old shop and expand the business. He reasoned that from a shop, they could not only sell their shoes, but they could also store their ever increasing stock. Charlie readily agreed to the plan of renting a shop as it would cut down on their constant time consuming trips to the warehouse, but he was less than enamoured with Bronco's next suggestion.

Bronco's idea was to install his younger brother Sam the Man into the shop to look after it while they were at the markets. Now Charlie, just like everyone else in the district knew that Bronco's younger brother was not only as daft as a brush, but totally unpredictable and had a reputation for doing very odd things. When young, he'd perched himself upon the school roof saying that he wanted to see if he could see London and had refused to come down until his angry mother had threatened to tan his arse red raw if he didn't. He'd been known to walk into a pub, stand behind a group of thoughtful domino players and blow a football referee's whistle very loudly and after seeing the dominoes fly through the air as the startled players jumped in fright, walk out of the pub smiling. He'd visited shops and brazenly drunk the contents of several bottles of alcohol based after-shave lotions. He once entered a pub, ordered a pint of beer, drank it in one go and informed the bewildered barman that he had no money to pay for it and many people had witnessed the sight of him staggering home late at night completely oblivious to the swerving cars that constantly skimmed past him as he walked down the centre of the road. There were many other things Sam the

Man was liable to do, but all agreed that becoming a competent shop manager was certainly not one of them, but Bronco took a different view and believed that he was more than capable of keeping his younger brother under control.

Aka the humpback had claimed that he not only knew exactly what was wrong with Sam the Man, but also the cure for his unpredictable behaviour. In the manner of a medical consultant he put forward the theory that Sam's brain occasionally slipped out of place and all that was required was a slap across the back of the head to put it back in place.

"My brother Jacob suffered with the very same condition," Aka declared nodding his head knowledgeably, "and a hefty clip around the head worked every time."

No one believed Aka's medical theory, but Bronco was not averse to giving his younger brother a hearty slap when he thought the occasion warranted it. Charlie was far from convinced that Sam was the ideal candidate for the job, but what finally swayed him, was that Bronco proposed to pay Sam next to nothing for looking after the shop.

"I'll just give him a couple of quid each day and tell him I'm saving the rest for him." Bronco explained and Charlie, seeing the wisdom of this tight-fisted plan, readily agreed to it. And so it came about that the two whiz kid entrepreneurs found themselves an old side street shop which was situated just off the high street and after they had stocked it out with cheap imported shoes they left Sam the Man in charge of it each day, while they went off to the prosperous open markets as usual.

The shop was closed during the lunch period while Sam the Man went to enjoy his break which usually lasted from twelve noon to well after two, so not many shoes were sold during that period. This situation carried on for several weeks, but as there had been no serious mishaps, Charlie and Bronco, who were still doing well on the open markets, were quite happy to let sleeping dogs lie. As long as he sold a few pairs of shoes each week, they were quite happy, as this more than compensated them for what they were paying him. Then one morning, just before setting off for the local market, Bronco took from his pocket a large bundle of bank notes that were secured with a thick rubber band and he put the bundle into an empty shoe box which he then hid underneath the shop counter. The money was needed for the following day as they intended to visit the warehouse to replenish their dwindling stock and wisely, Bronco had decided that it would be foolish to carry such a large amount of money around with him all day or leave it in the parked van. After the money had been safely hidden under the counter, Bronco then told Sam to, "keep a weather eye on that money Sammy and guard it with your life."

The day followed its usual pattern, Charlie and Bronco went off to a local market and at twelve, Sam shut the shop and skipped along the road to the nearest corner pub for his lunch. He was rather late reopening the shop and there was an amiable customer waiting for him. Because Sam was three sheets to the wind the amiable customer had to more or less serve himself to the pair of shoes that he required, but he was quite happy to do so and after paying for them, he left with a smile on his face. After a hard day's trading at the market, Charlie and Bronco arrived back at the shop to find Sam in the back room sprawled out in an armchair and well and truly in the land of nod. They were not at all pleased to find him in this comatose condition, but when Sam informed them that he had just sold a pair of shoes and then showed them the money that he had taken that day, they brightened up a little, but the prevailing mood of good will quickly evaporated, when Bronco discovered that the shoebox that had contained their working capital had disappeared from its hiding place beneath the shop counter.

"Where the fuck has the box with the money gone?" Bronco screamed at Sam as he was in no mood to mince his words, "It was in the shoe box under here you stupid bastard, where's it gone? What have you done with it?"

But Sam, who was still under the influence of his substantial liquid lunch, found it hard to concentrate and just whimpered, "I don't know where the box has gone Bronco," and pointing a finger at the shops counter he added miserably, "I'm sure it was there this morning or was that yesterday?"

For the next fifteen minutes, all three frantically searched the old shop for the shoe box that contained the bundle of bank notes and after dozens of shoes had been tipped out of their boxes and scattered across the floor, there was still no sign of the missing money.

After all the available evidence had been analysed, which because of Sam's sozzled memory was as scant as a striptease artists G-string, it was assumed that the amiable gentleman who'd purchased the pair of shoes that afternoon, had taken the box with the money in it. Whether Sam had given him the box by mistake to put the shoes in, or whether the customer had helped himself to the box, could never be established, but the story was quickly absorbed into the local folk law and those that repeated the story were quick to add that it was probably the cheapest pair of shoes that anyone had ever purchased.

"I've heard of shops giving free gifts with every purchase, but that's bloody ridicules" was Trappers verdict.

Bronco put Sam the Man's brain back into place numerous times that evening and continued to do so for the rest of the week, but as far as anyone could tell, it made little difference as Sam seemed to be as daft as ever. The unfortunate affair putt an end to Charlie and Bronco's cheap shoe market business venture, as without their working capital they could not purchase the stock that they needed and being effervescent salesmen and not hard-nosed business men, they did not have the stomach to start all over again. They remained friends, but Charlie retained a sneaking suspicion that somehow he'd been duped by either Sam or Bronco.

"What if Sam had taken the money for himself and there had never been an unknown customer?" He thought, "Or, what if Bronco had never put the money into the box in the first place and had slipped the bundle of bank notes back into his pocket while I wasn't looking." These nagging doubts continually plagued Charlie's tortured mind and the reason they did, was because if he'd thought of it, that's exactly what he would have done.

Charlie was not only a compulsive gambler, but he was also a serial womaniser and when added together they became a recipe for matrimonial discord and disaster. They caused his marriage to disintegrate into what could be described as a continual Punch and Judy show. The bad-mouthed slanging match's that Charlie and his long suffering wife continually engaged in, occasionally exploded into ferocious punch ups and when Charlie confessed to his exasperated wife that he was unable to pay his way once more, she exploded and slung him out of the happy home and to show him just how serious she was, she took in a lodger. Charlie's attempt to smooth things over by presenting his ill-used wife with a bunch of flowers that he'd picked from the local council park had not worked this time and he realised that he was out for good.

He then shacked up with a young woman who was a modern art enthusiast and a vocal advocate for the benefits of vegetarianism and Charlie, who was always willing to please a young lady when it suited him, went along with it. His new girlfriend did an excellent job of educating him on the reasons why he should become a vegetarian and why we should all refrain from eating meat. She claimed that meat poisoned the body and soon, Charlie was not only a willing convert, but also an enthusiastic preacher for the cause.

While sitting in the Sailors one day, he gave Mitch a lecture on the benefits of a vegetarian life and not only insisted that Mitch should seriously think of becoming one, but as he knew Mitch had read a great many books, he was surprised that he wasn't one already. His coup de grace in his knowledgeable argument was the fact that a gorilla, one of the strongest animals on earth, never ate meat. Mitch, who had never given the matter any serious thought, countered Charlie's argument by pointing out that a lion, another wild animal known for its enormous strength, was a meat eater and Charlie, thinking that Mitch was being contrary, ended the conversation in a huff and buggered off.

A few weeks later, Mitch bumped into Charlie in a local pub one lunch time and was surprised to see him devouring with undisguised relish, a large roast beef and mustard sandwich.

"What happened to the fantastic live forever vegetarian diet?" Mitch asked sarcastically, thinking that he'd caught Charlie out.

"Oh, that bird gave me the push," Charlie explained as he munched hungrily at his beef sandwich, "She said she couldn't afford to keep me any longer and told me to piss off. She's a typical do-gooder; she wants to save the bloody world, but she aint much bothered when it comes to helping individuals like me. So I thought, bugger it then, I might as well go back to eating meat again."

After finishing his beef sandwich, he then looked at Mitch and in all seriousness said, "Besides, for some reason, being a vegetarian don't half make you fart you know. It can be really embarrassing. There were times when I could rival the wind section of a bloody orchestra."

No one would ever have described Charlie as an intellectual, in fact it is doubtful whether he'd ever read a book from cover to cover outside of school lessons, or given any serious thought to anything other than the day's racing results, so when he expressed a profound gem of wisdom, it came as quite a surprise. Charlie and Billy were quietly discussing the trials and tribulations of marriage and Billy asked Charlie if he had an explanation for his broken marriage and his constant philandering.

Charlie thoughtfully shrugged his shoulders and simply said, "Look mate, the pursuit of love and sex has brought Kings off thrones, sent great armies off to war and at times, it has destroyed whole nations. What fucking chance have I got?"

For one reason or another and usually with the management's insistence, Charlie changed jobs frequently. He was employed as a delivery driver on many occasions and while he was travelling up and down the country, he was constantly looking for any lucrative opportunity that would help fill his ever empty coffers. But no matter how fast Charlie filled his pockets with cash, he always managed to find a quicker way of emptying them and so the constant need to find an opportunity that could be turned into hard cash was always there. While working for one company he was obliged to call on several old dilapidated warehouses around Leeds and his keen eye had noticed that several of the buildings had metal framed glass sky lights and from past experience he knew that they were relatively easy to open and once open would allow an agile young man to gain access to the goods that were stored below.

After selecting a suitable target and completing his homework, Charlie took Bronco into his confidence and within a week the pair had borrowed a box van and were on their way to Leeds. The warehouse that they'd chosen had cast iron drain pipes attached to its side and Bronco, who was fearless to the point of stupidity and as agile as Tarzan, had no trouble whatsoever in climbing up the drain pipe and reaching the flat roof. He pulled his tool bag up after him with the aid of a long rope and quickly wrenched the sky light open and within minutes he was opening the sliding wooden doors of the loading bay at the rear of the premises where Charlie was waiting with the box van.

A few days later, the piles of towels, blankets and packs of bed sheets and pillow cases were being sold from market stalls all over the West Midlands and the intrepid pair were on their way back to Leeds to pay a visit to another old warehouse. How many old warehouses they broke into remained a closely guarded secret, but within six months they were rolling in money and riding around in new cars.

A few weeks before Christmas, Bronco was offered a large amount of Christmas wrapping paper. He took delivery of twenty boxes and after stacking them neatly in the front room, he promised his wife who wasn't at all pleased that her best room had just been filled with large cardboard boxes, that she could have her front room back within a week as he would have sold the lot by then. Then, to give his eight year old son something to do and to earn himself some pocket money, he put a number of rolls of Christmas paper into his lad's arms and told him to, "Go and knock on a few doors and see how many you can sell."

Half an hour later, a police woman was at Bronco's front door and asking him the searching question of, "Did you know that your son is knocking on your neighbour's doors down the street and trying to sell rolls of Christmas paper?"

"The little bugger!" Bronco cried out indignantly, "You just wait till I see him. I told him to take those rolls round to his aunty. Thank you for letting me know officer, I'll see to him when he comes home."

That evening Bronco and his wife were watching a television programme that highlighted items of criminal activity that had taken place in the West Midlands and they were surprised to see that the police were looking for a substantial amount of Christmas wrapping paper that had been stolen from a warehouse and would be grateful for any information concerning this theft. Within minutes, Bronco had all the boxes of Christmas wrapping paper out of the house and into the back of a friends van and as he drove off, he could still hear his wife's angry protestations ringing loudly in his ears.

"Here! Would you be interested in buying a diamond ring for your Missis?" Charlie asked Bronco as they settled at a table in a local pub.

"Where's it come from?" Bronco immediately asked, as he knew that it would not be legitimate.

"I don't know do I?" Charlie replied a note of irritation in his voice, "They aint going to tell me details like that are they? All I know is, these two blokes that I know have three diamond rings that they want to sell and if you're interested, I can pick them up and bring them round to your house to show you and your Missis and she can pick one."

"How much do they want for them?" Bronco asked and immediately assumed that Charlie had stolen the rings himself and that the story of the two unknown thieves was a fictitious cover.

"Three grand each" Charlie replied.

"Three grand!" Bronco exclaimed, his eyes bulging out of his head, "Are you bleeding mad? Do you think I'm going to pay out three grand for a bleeding ring for my Missis?"

"Look, it would be a good investment Bronco. They're worth four times that much."

"Who's told you that?"

"They did. The two blokes what's got them. They know how much they were asking at the shop where they stole them from don't they."

"Well I'm not paying out three grand on something I don't know the true value of and anyway, if it's such a good investment, why don't you buy them?"

"I have, my Missis is walking about with one on her finger right now."

This news confirmed Bronco's suspicion that Charlie himself had stolen the rings and that there were no mysterious strangers to negotiate with for he knew that Charlie would never fork out three grand on any bird no matter how willing she was and he knew that he'd only been living with his present partner for a few months.

"Alright," Bronco said brightly, "bring them round to the house tomorrow evening and if my Missis likes one, I might buy one, but I tell you this Charlie; I'm going to have it bloody valued first."

Bronco's wife fell in love with all three rings, but in the end she was forced to choose just one and the next day Bronco took the ring down to the jewellery quarter and had it valued and discovered that the ring was worth much more than three grand, but while he was waiting, the police had been summoned and he found himself under arrest.

Luckily, Charlie had taken the other two rings back home with him so when the police searched Bronco's house they found nothing to link him with the robbery at the jewellers shop and as he did not fit the description of the two thieves that had run out of the jewellers shop with the tray of diamond rings, the police had to accept Bronco's cock and bull story of having found the ring in the street.

"It was in the gutter just outside the hospital in Steelhouse Lane. You ask my mate Joey Flynn, he was with me when I found it, he'll tell ya." Explained Bronco and then, with a look of complete innocence he asked, "By the way, is there a reward for finding it?"

My duties at the tube store were to organise the loading and the unloading of the constant flow of lorries that arrived each day, the hiring and firing of staff, the maintenance of the building and ordering the steel tube from British Steel which had to be ordered three months in advance. To keep all this going, I had to keep all the necessary paperwork up to date and each day, I would take it up to head office, which was three mile away, to be processed. There I would chat with other members of the staff, catch up with the latest gossip and find out if there were any large orders of tube to be catered for. Having to order tube twelve weeks in advance, meant that I had to constantly make a calculated guess as to what we would need in three months' time.

During one particular dull and dreary Monday morning in March, when the weather was still in winter's grip, I drove up to head office and began to distribute my paperwork to the relevant departments.

The head office complex was made up of a higgledy-piggledy assortment of buildings each containing either store rooms or offices. For a new employee, getting to know what was kept in each of the scattered store rooms and which office personal resided in which office was a mind boggling experience and trying to negotiate and remember the layout of the buildings was much the same as visiting the Hampton Court maze. I was half way through my familiar journey around the numerous stores and offices, when I entered the accounts department and there before me stood my long lost friend, Jenny. On seeing her once more, my heart literally skipped a beat and as I took in the pleasant vision of her, her long flowing hair and shapely long legs, I became transfixed.

I was completely puzzled as to why she was in this office talking to a girl named Christina as it was the last thing that I'd expected to see on that dull and dreary morning. She eventually ended her conversation, turned to make her way out of the office and as she saw me standing dumbstruck by the doorway, she smiled radiantly and called across the busy office, "Hello fish face."

In her absence she'd been employed in the office of a large city centre garage, but she'd recently fallen out with the bullying and bombastic manager that ran the place and having heard that there was a vacancy at Turners, she'd applied for the position and been accepted and I, being based in the far off woolly wilds of Smethwick, knew nothing about the arrangement. After recovering from the initial shock, I warmly welcomed her back into the fold and happily chatted with her for several minutes before making my way back to the tube store. During the drive back, I realised that the day was no longer boring and dull and I felt strangely happy and elated.

Jenny was young, slim and had long shapely legs which, as she wore fashionable miniskirts, were always on display and I'd always found her sexually attractive, but that didn't fully explain my deep interest in her. There were other girls in and around the company who were equally attractive and I'd never been particularly interested in any of them. I began to realise that it was Jenny's fun loving bright personality and her unique witty sense of humour that I enjoyed. She was a joy to talk to and it didn't seem to matter what subject we talked about as by the end of most conversations, we were laughing. Even when annoyed, she would find a witty quip that would defuse the situation and put her back on an even keel and I envied her for it. I could hold a grudge for several days, which inevitably made me feel bad and never solved anything.

Within a few weeks, Jenny and I were once more the best of friends and looked forward to being in each other's company. Almost every day, I would seek her out and for a few minutes we would chat and laugh about anything that came to mind, the latest films, the books that we'd recently read, what we'd seen on television and the general office gossip and we found that we were closer than ever. I began to realise that during her long absence, my spirit had been somewhat morose and now it suddenly seemed to be alive again. I began to look forward to my daily encounters with Jenny, much as a drug addict looks forward to a fix.

I'd been seeing a young woman that I'd met at a friend's party two years previously, but through one thing and another, that had died a death and I was now a free agent. But I was well aware that Jenny was married and that being ten years younger, she belonged to a different era from my own, but the more we met, the less these complications seemed to matter. I knew that I had no right to interfere in her domestic life and at that particular moment I had no intention of doing so. In fact I had no long term plan at all and was quite happy to let things stay exactly as they were. I felt better now that she was around and I wanted to spend more time in her company, but I had to be content with what was reasonable and practical, which was easy chats in the office where she worked. There were occasional telephone conversations and then, as the months rolled by, we got to spend the odd lunch hour together where we would do a little shopping in the local shops and share a sandwich or a portion of fish and chips whilst sitting in my car.

The days rolled into weeks, the weeks into months, Christmas came and went and then one warm sunny spring day, I drove her over to the Edgbaston reservoir during our lunch break and there we strolled together for half an hour taking in the tranquil sight of the large glittering lake while enjoying the liberating warm sunshine. The feel good atmosphere of getting away from the day's hectic work routine for a short while was relaxing and we walked side by side as one. There were not many people to be seen around the lake, just a few anglers, surrounded by their fishing paraphernalia. Then, while following a well-worn path that ran through a clump of trees at the edge of the sparkling lake, we stopped walking and I pulled Jenny gently towards me and kissed her passionately on the lips and I was overjoyed to find that she responded with equal passion.

Later I discovered that she'd been hoping that I would take her in my arms and kiss her for some considerable time and had not known how to bring it about without appearing to be fast and loose. Fourteen months had gone by since we had renewed our friendship and during that time we'd become closer than ever and it became blindingly obvious that after that passionate kiss at the lakeside, we were going to have to make a decision that would not only change our lives, but the lives of others. We had to decide whether we were going to live together and take on all the trouble and upheaval that that decision would bring about, or part forever and become the well-worn cliché, ships that pass in the night.

We'd tried hard not to become too involved, but deep down we'd known for some considerable time that we were in love and it had only been the fact that others were involved that had made us deny the fact. At the forefront of my mind was what would her family think of me, as I was ten years her senior, had a broken marriage behind me and was now about to break up hers. But after that fateful trip to the lake, we realised that we had gone past the point of friendship and that we were truly in love and needed to be together. We began to arrange clandestine evening meetings and gradually a future together began to seem possible. Over the next few months, we met when Jenny came out of her pottery night school class, while she was on her way to town on a Saturday morning and occasionally, at the Tower Ballroom.

After many arguments Jenny and her husband finally parted and went their separate ways and we decided to inform our families of our commitment to each other and informed them that we were going to live together no matter what anyone said and as soon as it was legally possible, we would tie the knot forever.

We eventually married and although we experienced many problems, things turned out to be better than we could ever have anticipated. After a while our families came to accept the situation and we settled down in a small terraced house and got on with our new lives. We had two children who grew up to be well-balanced lively individuals that were blessed with inquisitive minds and open personalities.

There were times when we seemed to be telepathically connected and although, like all couples, we faced many problems, we remained the best of friends throughout all the trials and tribulations that came our way and we became as comfortable in each other's company as was humanly possible. As we slowly drifted into old age, we resembled a pair of old slippers, worn out and in need of repair, but retaining an indefinable feeling of comfort.

I put our comfortable marriage down to the fact that Jenny was very open minded and devoid of any strong prejudices. I could express myself in her company quite openly and without ever having to censor a single word, phrase or sentiment. She didn't always agree with my point of view, but she always allowed me to have one and to voice it. I'd never experienced this before and once I'd found it, I realised just how important it was to a relationship. Having to censor your speech in mixed company is a strain at the best of times, but having to do it at home with your partner would always be a recipe for "trouble at mill." Henry the VIII may have had six wives and numerous mistresses, but he was never as lucky or as happy as me that's for sure."

One warm summer Saturday evening, during our early years together, Jenny and I attended a garden barbecue party at Tuby's house. He'd been working for British Airways for a number of years and as a consequence, most of the guests were work colleagues who Jenny and I had not met before and we were not familiar with their work related conversations. In the garden we mingled as best we could while our host, adorned in white apron and chef's hat cooked away on the barbeque and we managed a few stilted conversations, but it was difficult to sustain a meaningful dialogue.

The sun slowly sank behind the trees at the bottom of the garden and while sipping our drinks, we become aware that there was one young stewardess that seemed determined to be the bell of the ball and as time went on and the alcohol took its effect, her behaviour became puerile. Her manner became sillier, her voice and her pantomime laugh louder and her wild statements more aggressive and insulting.

When most of the cooked meats had been consumed and the evening had begun to cool, the guests gradually made their way into the house and Jenny and I looked at each other and without a word being spoken, we decided to slip quietly away. The atmosphere was friendly enough, but like the Bisto kids, we felt we were on the outside looking in.

As we prepared to make our furtive departure, the loud-mouthed bell of the ball was still holding centre stage, much to the annoyance of many of the other guests and when Tuby entered the room carrying two large bottles of Greek wine, she shrieked hysterically with delight and called everyone's attention to the fact that this was her favourite wine. She turned to Jenny and in a condescending manner asked loudly, "Have **you** ever been to Greece dear?"

Without a flicker of annoyance, Jenny smiled and replied, "No, but I've seen the film."

The other guests burst out laughing and the bell of the ball went crimson with embarrassment as she realised that she had been put down in such a simple manner and from that moment on Jenny and I were made most welcome by all the guests who evidently disliked the way their loud mouthed colleague had been behaving. It was minor incident, but it filled me with happiness. My love for my sharp witted partner was to grow and grow and she kept me amused and on my toes for many years.

When Scotty finally left Briggs, he found employment with a small, but successful dental supply company. With his first class brain and enthusiasm, he soon gained promotion and a handsome income. Because of this change in circumstances he tended to hang about with a set of friends who were either involved in their own business or in one of the highly paid professions. So we saw very little of him for quite a while as we were all stuck in mundane jobs and could not afford to drink and dine in the places that he and his affluent set frequented.

He eventually married his long standing girlfriend, purchased a semi-detached house on a new housing estate and became a respectable well set up married man. He then started up his own dental supply business and on the face of it, at the age of twenty-five; he was a very successful young man. He was intelligent, charming, witty and very practical when it came to financial business matters, but unknown to his young wife, his family and many of his friends Scotty had a problem, he was a chronic alcoholic.

Scotty's business premises were not far from where I worked and he invited me to meet him for lunch at a local pub. The place that he favoured was The Woodman which was adjacent to the West Bromwich Albion Football Club. Scotty's idea of lunch was a small amount of food and a large amount of alcohol and I arrived back at work in an advanced state of bow legged inebriation and realised that this habit could get me into serious trouble. I decided there and then, that whenever I met Scotty for lunch, I would stick to lemonade shandies.

Scotty patronised the Woodman because it was near his business premises, but more importantly, it was the pub that many of the WBA football players used after their morning training sessions. Scotty had always been an extremely good football player and under different circumstances he may well have gone on to be a professional player, but because of the business opportunities that had come his way, he'd taken a different path to fame and fortune. Instead of becoming a professional footballer, almost by accident, he'd become a young dynamic businessman who retained a strong interest for the game and by mixing with the professional footballers that frequented the pub, he was able to enjoy and mix in both worlds.

Many of the footballers who used the pub were well known and included the likes of Lennie Cantello, Willie Johnson, Asa Hartford, Cyril Regis and the young Bryan Robson, the player who eventually become known as Captain Marvel and captained England. Scotty became a friend of all these players and he drank and socialised with them on a regular basis. After their morning training sessions, they would often visit the Woodman for a drink and a small lunch and in the afternoon; they would either go off to play golf, snooker or occasionally, visit one of the strip clubs that were situated along the

317

Soho Road. None of this was for me of course, as by the time they were enjoying these activities, I was back at the tube store organising the loading of lorries and humping heavy steel tubes about.

This group also used The Hawthorns pub after Saturday and mid-week games because there was a large room which could be cordoned off from the general public by the pubs manager, who was a small excitable Italian. "Is there any other kind?" Scotty stated when he introduced me to him. The small Italian had a passion for football and being an expert on the subject, he was only too willing to share his opinions on all and sundry. He spoke with a pronounced Italian accent, gesticulated wildly and his favourite word was, "consequently," which he managed to fit it into almost every sentence.

"The blady fools dida not a tackle a properly, so consequently, they losta the blady ball too much, anda consequently, they losta the blady match." He would state with passion and defy anyone to disagree with him. Just like Scotty, he was also an alcoholic and was constantly sneaking drinks when his wife, who he affectionately referred to as, "The Blady Dragon," wasn't looking. He would walk behind the bar with a glass containing a small amount of cola, enquire as to the whereabouts of, "The Blady Dragon," and if all was clear, he would pop the glass under the optics on display and take a sample from each one. "Consequently," by the end of the night, he was often bow-legged and blot'o, much to, "The Blady Dragons," disgust and she would be left with the job of checking the bar tills and locking up the premises.

In this crowded reserved bar one evening, the barmaid, who knew all the football players, picked up the Albion's goalkeepers car keys and called across the crowded room, "John! Here's your keys!" and threw the keys towards him, but they dropped just short of his reach and the inevitable calls of, "Call yourself a goal keeper, you couldn't catch a bleeding cold" rang out.

"Bugger me," He said, while shaking his head in disbelief, "I fall for it every bloody time."

One afternoon, after the pub had been officially closed to the general public, a group of players were drinking with the Italian manager in the lounge bar, while another three players were taking it turns to shag one of the barmaids in the ladies toilet. Unluckily, the three were caught in their energetic recreational act by "The Blady Dragon," and consequently all three were given a severe dressing down and banned from the pub for the rest of the day. "The Blady Dragon" then sacked the obliging barmaid on the spot.

"Personally, I thought it was rather unfair of the Dragon to sack the poor girl," Scotty said when he related the story, "after all, she was keeping the customers happy and by all accounts, she was doing a bloody good job of it."

From the age of sixteen, when the world was at his feet and he was dreaming of a career in football, alcohol was never out of Scotty's system. His drinking eventually had a catastrophic effect on his business and when it finally collapsed, he and his wife were forced to clear their many dept.'s and they sold their house.

He then approached a brewery and became a publican. It was a fatalistic move if ever there was one and it became obvious to his friends that his marriage would never survive the ordeal. The pub that he took on was a small corner pub that was situated in the back streets of Smethwick and with Scotty in charge the old pub quickly gained a reputation for being an open all hour's venue. The pub had one major advantage over its rivals and that was its unique location. As the pub was situated on a corner that overlooked a large traffic island and faced a long factory wall on one side, it was almost isolated from domestic premises. The few terraced houses that were near, were due for demolition and many were empty, so there were few people nearby to complain about hearing any late night noise. It also had adequate parking space as there was a piece of flat waste land nearby and parking alongside the long factory wall disturbed no one.

The pubs most celebrated visitors were Scotty's football friends one of which was Bryan Robson who became the Albion's star player and was on his way to becoming the captain of the England team. To give him his due he'd come a long way in a very short space of time. When Scotty had first met him in the Woodman, Bryan was still the new boy and he was fetching and carrying for all the other players and was having difficulty in finding a regular place in the first team, but his undoubted ability and tenacious willpower prevailed and he became one of the best players Albion ever had.

To liven things up, and to distinguish his pub from any of the others, Scotty organised many weekend fancy dress parties and take away meals were regularly ordered and fetched in late at night and it was often daylight before many of the bleary eyed customers left the pub. As well as domino and darts teams, he also formed a football and cricket team to represent the pub and organised friendly games with other pubs in the district, all of which contributed to a happy and carefree atmosphere. Every weekend some sort event was being celebrated and if there wasn't an official one, he invented one.

On occasions he organised live music entertainment as a special treat. The best of these was Reg Keirl, one of the finest pub piano entertainers in the business, his only rival in the Midlands being his good friend, Tommy Burton, the local jazz celebrity. Reg, just like Tommy, was a Black Country lad through and through and a natural pianist. He spent the winter months playing in and around the Midlands and the summer season in Cornwall. He could play any type of music and would vary his repertoire to suit the venue, but what set him apart, was his unique ability to tell a tall story. When telling even the simplest of jokes, he became an animated actor and played every part. His voice took on any accent or variance that was required to make the story work. Even when he told a story that the audience had heard many times before, he still had the ability to make them laugh until their ribs ached. He showed no sign of show biz glitz whatsoever and when he entered a venue he often looked more like a bloke that had come to unblock the drains than the star entertainer. Just like Tommy Burton, his piano fingers seemed to have a life of their own and would play on even though he would be holding a conversation with someone nearby about the latest football results. He would be half way through a tune and suddenly stop and say something like, "In the Second World War my Dad was a prisoner of war. He was captured by the Japanese at Singapore. Anyway they took him up country and put him to work on the infamous Burma railway where hundreds of prisoners died. When he got back home after the war, I asked him what it was like. He said,

"Son, it was bloody awful; - it pissed down for the first fortnight," he would then continue playing.

"Scotty's Place," for that was what pub was now known as, seemed to be open twenty-four hours a day for when Scotty did force himself to catch up on some sleep; he left the running of the pub in the capable hands of anyone who happened to be around at the time. Billy swore that he'd visited the pub one Monday lunch time and had been served by Bob Smith who hadn't been home since the previous Saturday nights fancy dress party.

"Honestly," Billy said, while shaking his head in wonderment, "When he served me, he was still dressed as Sitting Bull with his Red Indian feathered head dress on his head."

In 1978 the Scottish football team went off to the World Cup competition in Argentina in a blaze of glory and Scotty, having Scottish ancestry greeted the news with fervent enthusiasm. He set up a large television set in the lounge bar and a large crowd of beer swilling football experts were invited to attend every match. As most of the Scottish players played in the English leagues, they were well known and most wished them well. Not enough to actually go on and win the world cup of course, but enough to hope that they could get near the final. Unfortunately "Ally's Army" failed to live up to expectations and, but for a brilliant goal by Archie Gemmel, it was a poor showing and once again British football was taught a lesson.

Scotty was crestfallen and it was the first time that any of his customers had ever seen him in a bad mood and for several days he stopped all stopovers and sent his hard drinking customers home on time, which was not only a shock for them, but for their wife's as well. But with being the type of character that he was, this melancholy mood did not last and a few days later he was as bright as a button and planning his next venture, which turned out to be a Sunday Morning pub crawl which lasted all day. The men who went on these boozy boisterous excursions were overjoyed with the free and easy atmosphere that these Sunday runs attained and got themselves merrily drunk, their wives however took a completely different view of these events and many hit the bloody roof when their sozzled spouses finally staggered home and Scotty was seen by many as a wicked home braking pied piper.

When Jenny's divorce cleared the way for us to wed, Scotty offered to put his pub at our disposal for the wedding reception. It wasn't the most impressive of venues, but as neither of us wanted an extravagant wedding or reception, we readily accepted the offer. With plenty of bottles of Verve De Verna, "It's as good as Champaign, but less than half the price." Tuby assured us, on every table it wasn't long before any snobbery or reserve among the guests disappeared and everyone was having a ball. Although Jenny and I were obliged to leave the wedding party quite early as we had a train to catch for the first leg of our honeymoon, the party we left behind carried on until the early hours of the following morning and was a huge success.

The company car that I was driving at the time was a red Marina and my friend Gibo was most surprised when Jenny and I said our farewells to the assembled well-wishers that were gathered on the pavement outside the pub as he found to his horror that he'd inadvertently trimmed up the wrong car in the traditional, "Just Got Married" livery. He was even more astonished to find that it was his girlfriend's car that he'd plastered with white foam and coloured confetti. It seems he'd had more than his fair share of the Verve De Verna when he'd slipped out of the ongoing party to trim the car up.

Some weeks later, Gibo pointed out that it was my fault that the mix up had occurred. "You always park your car on that patch of waste land on a Friday night, so I thought that it was your car that I was trimming up." he explained quite logically.

"Even though Diane's car only has two doors and his has four and Diane's is a different colour?" Mitch pointed out as he was still a little bemused at how the mistake had occurred.

"Trust you to notice something like that," Gibo replied, "I might be suffering from a little dementia, but I can still remember that it's your turn to get the beer in."

One Saturday night, Mitch, Heidi, Jenny and I, arrived at "Scotty's Place" for a fancy dress party dressed in various disguises and when we entered the pub we found that we were the only ones in fancy dress. Scotty had informed us, but no one else that Saturday night was to be a fancy dress party. Everyone had a good laugh at our expense, but by the end of the night we'd all enjoyed ourselves and my pith helmet, which was part of my Jungle Jim outfit, had been worn by everyone in the place and had ended up on top of a lamppost. As for the leather bullwhip that Mitch had brought along as part of his gaucho outfit, it became a permanent pub fixture and was brought out in the early hours of the morning for macho competitions of, "Who can flick the cigarette packet off the bar at ten paces?"

Mitch, Gibo and I among others, became regular Friday night customers at "Scotty's Place" which had gradually become an open all hour's pub. We would meet together earlier in the evening, drive out to a sing-a-long pub somewhere in the Black Country and after closing time, arrive back at "Scotty's Place" for a nightcap and a friendly chat before going home. No matter what the time, day or night the pub always had plenty of customers, most of whom lived locally and at eleven fifteen on a Friday night, Damon, a genial regular, would take orders from all those that wanted an Indian take-a-way meal. He would then phone the order through to the restaurant, which he claimed was special and situated in the centre of Birmingham and then along with a willing volunteer to help him, drive off to collect the meals. His helpmate on these regular Friday night excursions was a pretty young woman named Joy and was the wife of another pub regular, but unlike Damon, this bloke was a boring young accounts clerk and who by that time of night, was usually bloto.

One Friday night while in conversation with Scotty, I enquired as to why it was necessary for Damon to drive all the way into the centre of Brum to fetch these take-a-way meals, when there were restaurants much closer to the pub that were equally as good.

"He doesn't," Scotty revealed quietly, and then with an artful wink he said, "He only says that he's driving into town so that it gives him more time. You see him and Joy shag the arse off each other every Friday night in the back of his car which is parked just around the corner before he collects the meals from the Indian take away that's just up the road."

Because of Scotty's unpredictable and outrageous behaviour, his wife eventually became a martyr to the cause, though of course that had never been her intention when she'd first met him. When Scotty had courted her in their teenage years, he'd been on his best behaviour and on the way up in the world. He was attractive, athletic, had a pleasant lively personality and good prospects. He was a good catch and she'd been very happy with her beau. She stood by him, moved into the pub and attempted to save their marriage and help him make a financial success of his new venture. With Scotty allowing the pub to be open almost every hour of the day, there was little chance of any time alone with her exuberant care free husband, but her sacrifices were all in vain, abstinence was not part of Scotty's nature and no matter how many times he promised to change his ways, it was obvious that the demon drink would come before everything.

For numerous reasons, the brewery that owned Scotty's pub, decided enough was enough and Scotty lost the tenancy of the pub and his wife and daughter, finding themselves homeless, moved in with her widowed father. Scotty and his long suffering wife never lived together again, but amazingly she still stood by him and remained his closest friend through all the many trials and tribulations that were to follow.

His next business venture was finding return loads for lorries that were travelling around Europe, but to do this, he had to raise a substantial amount of capital and no bank would lend him the money, so he borrowed it off his many friends. There was no doubt in the minds of all of us that lent him money, that the business plan that he'd devised was a good one and in any other hands would have succeeded, but he was now beyond help and much of the money went on drink and none of his trusting friends ever saw a return on their investment and one by one they turned their backs on him as they knew by now that he was a hopeless case.

Many years later, I received an unexpected phone call from Scotty, who, as I hadn't seen him for over fifteen years was now a total stranger. He invited me to attend his fiftieth birthday party which was to be held at a pub that was situated in Langley on a Friday night. He said that it would be a small affair and that I should not expect too much. Not only did I not know what to expect, with

Scotty's unpredictable history, I'd never known what to expect. I seriously contemplated not attending the party, after all, he did still owe me money and after all the years that had passed, I wondered if we still had anything left in common and there was also the thought that I would not know any of his new friends so would I fit in or would it be another Bisto kid experience?

"I'll go and just see what the party's like," I eventually said to Jenny, after much deliberation, "and, if I don't fit in with his new friends and I feel uncomfortable, I can always slip away unnoticed."

As it turned out I was glad that I made the effort because I was one of the very few who actually turned up. When Scotty had informed me that it would be a small affair, I'd expected the party to be held in a private room complete with disco and running buffet. But when I arrived at the pub, this clearly was not the case as there was no sign of boisterous revelry and I actually thought that I was standing outside the wrong pub. Apprehensively, I entered the lounge bar to make enquires and there to my surprise was Scotty sitting alongside his ever-faithful wife and their daughter who was now a fully-grown woman and besides them, there were just two other old friends. I joined the small group in one corner of the lounge and gradually the room filled with regulars who Scotty seemed to know quite well and after a while they all sang "Happy Birthday" to him and several large platters that were laden with bar snacks were passed around.

I thoroughly enjoyed the evening, it was intimate and friendly and it was fun to reminisce with Scotty about old times, but when the evening eventually drew to a close and we all said our fond farewells, I knew that I would never see him again. He was just fifty years old, yet he looked eighty, he'd lost a considerable amount of weight, hair and mobility, he not only shuffled about in carpet slippers, but needed the aid of a walking stick. During the course of the evening I learned that he'd not worked for many years and had lost all his former friends, all that is except for his ever faithful wife who was a sucker for punishment and had never contemplated divorcing him. He was unrecognisable from the young whiz kid that I'd first met in the nineteen sixties at Briggs Building Supplies. Back then he'd been a healthy, vibrant young man, sharp as a razor and mentally equipped for a successful commercial life and yet here he was, thirty-three years later, looking older than my father and living on benefits.

Because of his willingness to self-destruct, Scotty died relatively young and many of his former friends believed that he got what he deserved, but for me the mystery remained as to how this could have come about to such a bright and sparkling intelligent man.

After completing his apprenticeship with Josh White's painting and decorating company in the City of Leicester, Danny Page stayed there for several years, but as it was an ailing business and was continually running short of contracts, he eventually left the ragged trousered philanthropists and went to work alongside his father who was a master builder and was running his own small building company. Alongside his father, Danny not only did the painting and decorating, but he also helped with the other numerous jobs that are done on a building site and gradually he became a very competent odd job man who could tackle any type of household repair with confidence.

When his father past away, Danny just carried on where his father had left off and he became a one man company who became so well known in the district for reliable building repairs that he was never at any time without a full work load. His reputation as a good honest, reliable worker grew with every job and he never had to resort to advertising for business. His regular clients gave him the keys to their homes and premises and just let him get on with the job as it suited him.

During the early nineteen eighties Danny did some work on an old couples home and while he was on the roof replacing several missing slates and pointing the chimney brick work, the old couple asked him to readjust their television aerial that was affixed to the chimney stack as they had never been able to pick up the commercial channel. Danny adjusted the aerial by pulling it this way and that, and each time he called down to the old couple standing in the garden below who looked up at him expectantly and took it in turns to run back into the house to check the television screen.

"Is that any better?"

Over and over again he called, but woefully the negative reply continued to be, "No, it's still the same."

After many frustrating minutes and having by this time put the aerial through three hundred and sixty degrees several times, he climbed down from the high roof to investigate and scratching his head he went into the house to find out just what the problem was. On inspecting the small-screened television set he was amazed to discover that the set was over thirty years old and was actually a left over from the early nineteen fifties and had been produced long before the commercial channel had come into existence.

"This set was never programmed to receive anything but the BBC." He explained.

"We always wondered why we couldn't get ITV." The old couple said in unison, "we always thought that the aerial was facing the wrong way."

"Still" the old man added philosophically, after giving it some thought, "I don't suppose we've missed much, I've heard tell that most of the programmes are bloody rubbish anyway."

For many years, I met Mitch and occasionally Billy; in pubs for a typical boy's night out and there we would drink a few pints, talk about numerous subjects and putt the world to rights. Occasionally we would play snooker, dominoes or cards and sing whenever the opportunity arose. Over the years, many of our numerous mates had accompanied us from time to time, but for one reason or another, they had gone their separate ways and we saw less of them. But we continued to meet each other on most Friday nights. The only time that I showed any reluctance to accompany Mitch on these nights out was when he decided that he wanted to visit a casino or to chase after good time girls in a night club. I had no liking at all for gambling and losing my hard earned cash and the older I got the less I liked the noisy ear bashing atmosphere of night clubs and after I had teamed up with Jenny, I completely lost my appetite for chasing after other women. There was nothing moral about this decision, the fact was, I found it quite a relief as I'd never been very good at chatting up young women in night clubs and now I no longer needed to try.

Then one Friday evening, while enjoying a drink in a pub which was a typical flat cap working man's establishment, we were introduced to a tall handsome young man whose name was Gibo and from then on, Mitch's nights of visiting the noisy night clubs on his own were at an end.

Our first impression of Gibo was not at all complimentary as he struck us as being far too well dressed and lively for the environment that the pub afforded and we suspected that he might be portraying a false persona. The pub was a working man's beer and domino pub and yet here before us stood a man that looked and dressed like a handsome Hollywood film star and conversing with the confidence of a holiday camp entertainer. He was dressed in a navy blue double breasted brass buttoned blazer with a well knotted regimental tie and his white shot shirt cuffs revealed expensive gold cuff links. He stood, all six-foot two of him, ramrod straight and spoke with the confidence of a seasoned politician and had the easy going language of a well-rehearsed stand-up comedian. Much to our surprise, we were to learn that not only was Gibo's immaculately attired appearance and jovial persona quite genuine, but there was also much more to him than met the eye.

He was a master carpenter by trade and an old fashioned tradesman at that, as he was a man who took genuine pride in doing a first class job and would refuse to botch a job up just to save time. "If a jobs worth doing, it's worth doing well" was his motto and he rigidly stuck by it. We eventually learned that he'd served in the Coldstream Guards when younger and had never lost the habit of looking smart while on parade and when he went out for the evening, he was always on parade, but the paradox was that although he always looked like an officer and a gentleman, he had the wily ways of a crafty urbane fox. His father had been a sharp wheeler-dealer market trader for most of his life and although Gibo had trained as a carpenter, to some extent he still followed in his father's footsteps and was always on the lookout for a black market bargain and was always buying and selling goods of one sort or another with no questions asked.

He was a brilliant flamboyant dancer and because of his passion for women, he'd developed an easy-going repertoire of chat up lines that could charm birds out of the trees or a young woman into his well-made bed. We were to learn that although he was very particular about his appearance, he was not as shallow as we'd first thought and anyone who became his friend was a friend for life and there was no favour that he would not do for them.

As time went by, a new pattern began to emerge. I would meet Mitch and Gibo on a Friday evening and we would go out together and if we didn't end up at "Scotty's Place," I would go home and Mitch and Gibo would go on and hit the night club scene. Most Wednesday evenings and the occasional Saturday night, they would visit the Tower Ballroom and as both were tall and good looking and had a natural gift of the gab; they were very successful in their pursuit of women who were looking for a good time. Gibo, who was divorced, had no worries about being caught out by a jealous wife, but for Mitch it was a different matter and he found himself constantly having to invent excuses of where he'd been and why he was so late arriving home and so early on a Friday evening when we met, Mitch would invent a cover story to explain why he was late home so that we would know what to say if asked. It was an excellent plan, but Mitch often forgot what the cover story was and occasionally, we were saying one thing and Mitch quite another which made Heidi, who was no fool, highly suspicious.

As well as a Black Country pub-crawl, which was an area that was littered with sing-a-long venues, one of our favourite weekend drinking areas was the Hagley Road where there were many up market lively bars full of vibrant youngster's intent on enjoying themselves. The Garden House was a particular favourite and after closing time Mitch and Gibo would often visit the Rainbow Casino which was nearby and at times, they would drag me along with them. I was a reluctant gambler and on the roulette wheel, I would spend an inordinate amount of time waiting for a colour sequence to appear before placing a meagre bet. My superstitious theory being that if either red or black came up four times in a row; it would change on the next spin of the wheel. I never ever won much money using this dodgy system; but as I avoided the natural temptation to double up when I did lose, I never lost much either. The most amazing gamblers that we ever saw in the casino were a group of Chinese.

They would rashly place bets all over the roulette table, shovelling their chips on as fast as they could and then become over exited as the small white ball bounced around the roulette wheel and towards a particular number. They put so many chips across the board that some of them even forgot which numbers they were rooting for.

One evening a young man, who was a regular at the Sailors and was known as Carthorse, accompanied us to the Rainbow casino and having never been in such a place before he was somewhat bewildered by all that was going on around him. He stood away from the green baized gambling tables and with his hands firmly wedged in his trouser pockets; he did his best to keep out of the way and just looked on as the others took their chances and courted Lady Luck. After half an hour, Gibo, who had been concentrating hard on the roulette wheel, turned to Carthorse and asked him to order four cups of coffee while he carried on playing. Carthorse looked around the room expecting to see some sort of bar or serving hatch and on finding neither asked Gibo where he was supposed to get the coffees from. Gibo a little irritated at being disturbed while he was playing, said, "Just ask one of those girls over there" and he pointed at two of the casinos pretty female staff members who were standing to one side of the plush room and waiting for orders, "that's what they are there for."

Carthorse duly obliged and eventually four coffees arrived and we stopped gambling on the roulette table while we drank the coffees. While drinking my coffee, I noticed that Carthorse seemed a little agitated as he kept looking across the room at one of the casino girls who was now taking orders for coffee among the many punters.

"What's up?" I queried.

"Oh, I'm just waiting for my change." Carthorse replied.

"What change?" Gibo asked, a puzzled frown upon his face.

"The change from the coffee, I gave that wench a ten pound note." explained Carthorse.

"You prat, the coffee's free," exclaimed Gibo, "She thinks that you've just given her a ten pound tip out of your winnings."

"What winnings? I haven't even had a bleeding bet yet!" Carthorse wailed forlornly.

It turned out to be the most expensive cup of coffee that Carthorse had ever purchased in his life as at that time, ten pound represented a large proportion of his weekly wage. He never had a bet that night or ventured anywhere near the Rainbow Casino again.

Occasionally we would meet up together for a night out with our wives, or in Gibo's case, his latest girlfriend and during these sessions, Mitch's extra-curricular activities were never mentioned, but Heidi who was always suspicious would watch Mitch like a hawk and listen out for any clue to his philandering. Once, when she came across a strong smell of perfume on his jacket while tidying up the bedroom one morning, she did no more than throw all his clothes out of the bedroom window into the front garden below. And that's exactly where Mitch found them when he returned home that evening from his days work.

"It looked like a bleeding hurricane had hit the street." Mitch said wearily as he recounted the event, "and I thought, here we go again, I'm in for a right good bollocking now."

"So what did you say to her about the perfume?" Gibo asked.

"I told her that Sam the Man had sprinkled perfume over everyone in the Sailors for a joke and that I'd forgotten to tell her about it."

"And did she believe you?" Gibo asked.

"Well she might when Jaco here confirms what happened, because I told her that he was there and it went all over him as well."

"Thanks mate." Was my resigned reply as I realised that I'd been check mated and set up once more. For some reason Heidi was more inclined to believe my lies than smooth talking Mitch's.

After that silly slip up Mitch took to avoiding any woman that wore strong smelling perfume and just to be on the safe side he even took to holding his jacket out of the car window when driving home late at night to freshen it up. This airing procedure worked reasonably well until one night his jacket accidentally slipped from his grasp and a following car ran over it.

When looking for good time girls in the bars, clubs and at dances that they frequented, Mitch and Gibo worked well together as they were both tall, handsome, well groomed, charming and attentive when they needed to be. Mitch favoured a romantic approach and would capture their attention with his mesmerising eyes and then go on to converse with a soft seductive voice whereas Gibo used a store of stock jokes to break the ice, one of his favourites being, "You won't believe this, but six months ago I couldn't even talk to a woman."

"Oh, why was that then?"

"Because I was in the nick."

When introducing Mitch to a young woman, Gibo would say, "I bet you don't recognise my friend here do you?"

"No, I don't think so, who is he?"

"He was the lead singer in the Black and White minstrels."

One evening, while drinking in the lounge of a large pub along with Mitch, Gibo and a couple of friends, I witnessed the pair at their best. Although large, the room was full of people and there was little space for anyone to manoeuvre anywhere in comfort and while we were standing near the bar, Mitch and Gibo were constantly weighing up the available and for the moment, the unavailable young women that were in the room. Suddenly on the other side of the crowded room two good looking women entered the pub and seeing that the room was crowded they looked around deciding whether to stay or not. One of them took a packet of cigarettes from her handbag, put a cigarette to her lips, offered her friend one and before she could light them, Gibo was there with his lighter. How he managed to get from one side of that crowded room to the other so quickly, was a mystery that only a scientist studying quantum physics could work out, but after a few minutes of humorous banter, he brought the two women over to where we were standing and half an hour later, he and Mitch were walking out of the pub, arm in arm with them and Gibo's parting wink indicated that it was mission accomplished.

There was a group of young women who used the Tower Ballroom on a regular basis who came all the way from Cradley Heath in the Black Country and although several of them were good looking, they all spoke with the thick Black Country accent which comedians often use when pretending to be Brumies. Under no circumstances can a thick Black Country accent ever be described as sensuous or romantic. When a Black Country wench says, "Yo'm a nice chap an' yo baint 'arf cheeky, but look at the bloody time, me 'usband ul kill we if I baint 'ome soon." the chances of bedding her that night are very slim.

But Mitch and Gibo were no snobs and the thick Black Country accent did not bother them one bit and in due course they bedded several of these delightful young ladies and always referred to them affectionately as "The Cradley chain makers," a reference to the heavy industry that had made Cradley famous in the past. After one night of passionate love making, one of the "Chain Makers" asked Gibo if he'd used a condom, when Gibo replied, "No, I thought you were on the pill." She replied indignantly, "I am, but ar don't even let mi 'usband do it without putting a Johnny on you cheeky bugger."

Mitch and Gibo had many amorous adventures and a friendly rivalry sprang up between them, a rivalry that eventually came to a head on one of the Forty Club weekend coach trips. A large number of the Forty Club members were now very uncomfortable with the way that many of the Brighton pubs had been taken over by the homosexual community who now referred to themselves as Gay's (Good as you) and because of this trend, they voted for new venues for the weekend trip. And as there wasn't as many horse racing fanatics in the group during this period that were desperate to go to the Goodwood races, they won the vote easily and chose, the seaside resort of Weston Super Mare.

The clubs secretary booked reservations at The Webbington Hotel for our weekend trip. It was a large establishment that was situated on the side of a hill deep in the countryside and just a few miles from Weston and was chosen because a regular dance was held there, every Friday and Saturday night. The dance was held in a very spacious dance hall and the Forty Club members had been informed that it was always well attended as the venue was well known in the area. The dance was open to all and the young and not so young, who were looking for a night of fun, came from miles around to attend it. And so, for a crew of beer swilling working class Romeo's from the Midland's, it seemed to be the ideal spot for a weekend base and so it proved.

On the Friday evening, thirty-three members of the Forty Club, with ages ranging from eighteen to seventy, settled down to their evening meal in the hotel's restaurant. The restaurant overlooked a spacious car park and as we ate and joked, we noticed that a number of coaches were arriving at the hotel and all the passengers were female. A group that fancied themselves as suave smooth lady killers called a waiter over and enquired as to the purpose of this unexpected female invasion.

"What's all the crumpet here for then mate?" Trapper asked, his thick blond wavy hair which he had had specially cut for the weekend looking immaculate.

"Oh, they're here for the darts." The smartly dressed young waiter informed them.

"What bleeding darts?" Trapper then asked with a puzzled frown clearly showing upon his rugged face.

"Oh, didn't you know? There's a women's darts competition on this weekend in the ballroom."

And so it proved, dozens of women from Wales and different parts of the South West were booked into the hotel for the weekend and although many of the women were to participate in a woman's darts tournament which was to be held over two days there were many more that were just there to enjoy themselves. As far as the Forty Clubs members were concerned, things couldn't be better and after we'd finished our evening meal, many hurried back to their rooms to splash extra dollops of scented aftershave on their face and chests so that they would be ready for the Friday evening dance.

The Friday and Saturday night dances were a great success and at the end of the dance, many of the women and the Forty Club Romeo's retreated to the hotels bar and a good natured party rumbled on well into the night. Over the weekend several of the blokes reported scoring a home run with the happy-go-lucky darts enthusiasts and Mitch and Gibo were among them. Their partners for the Saturday night shernanakins were two good looking, well dressed women, who were related, one being a forty year old mother and the other, her teenage daughter. They were from Bristol, married and determined to have a good time. And although the daughter was almost twenty and the mother claimed to be just forty, they could easily have passed as older and younger sisters. Whether this was a one off experience or whether they had a fling on a regular basis, it was never established, but they did reveal that they'd been to the hotel before and seemed to be quite at home there.

Forever after that passionate weekend, whenever any rival banter was exchanged between Mitch and Gibo concerning good time women, Gibo would always remind Mitch that it was he that had slept with the daughter and that Mitch had been left with the mother. As both of the women were attractive and desirable, it didn't really matter who had made love with whom, but when telling the story to men who were not at the Webbington that weekend and had not seen the two women, it always sounded as though Gibo had won first prize and Mitch had had to settle for second best.

On the Sunday morning, we made our way into Weston and casually strolled around the town, while waiting for twelve noon when the pubs opened. Wingy was known affectionately as Wingy because he'd lost an arm during the battle for Normandy after the D-Day landings. He was well known for being a competent domino player which was commendable, but he was also known as being tight fisted which was not so endearing and no one had ever managed to manoeuvre him into buying the first round of drinks when entering a pub. It is well known that if four friends drink five pints, the first man ends up buying two rounds. Among friends this is never a problem, as each man will take a turn on being the first to buy a round of drinks, but Wingy would have none of it and he always found a way of avoiding buying the first round. His shoe lace would come undone as he entered the pub, or he was in urgent need of the toilet or he'd dropped his wallet and had to dash back to find it. He was criticized relentlessly, but it made little difference, his miserly instincts were deeply ingrained and were in his DNA.

At exactly twelve noon, Wingy walked into the chosen pub first while the rest of us held back. We pretended to be interested in an article that was in a shop window and after a good three minutes, we walked into what was an almost empty pub. Had Wingy ordered the beer? No he had not; he was sitting all on his own at a long table and greeted us with the words, "I've saved the seats lads."

The pub gradually filled with smiling holidaymakers and the rest of the our clan and a warm friendly atmosphere soon pervaded and after downing a few pints, the Forty Club men began to sing and soon the whole of the pub's clientele joined in. Before pubs across the country were "modernised" and had blaring juke boxes and brightly lit chattering games machines installed, there was no better place to be than in a warm British pub along with good company where one was allowed to sing at will.

The following year we visited the Webbington once more, but although we enjoyed our weekend, there was no woman's darts tournament that year, so many were slightly disappointed. After working in a dirty oil smelling noisy factory all year and re-living their amorous memories among their friends, several of the men had been looking forward to another weekend of slap and tickle with a female darts enthusiast. What they found instead was a Sunday morning antiques fare which was populated with musty experts sporting droopy dickey-bows and corduroy jackets and did their best to impress each other with in depth knowledge of articles that no one in their right minds wanted. The antiques fare was interesting to walk around in a, "I've got nothing better to do" sort of way, but to the working men of the Forty Club, it was certainly no substitute for a room full of fun loving female darts enthusiasts.

The vote then went in favour of Blackpool as it had the advantage of supplying a kiss me quick and fun fair holiday for those that wanted that sort of thing and a trip to the Haydock races on the Saturday for the racing fraternity. There were twenty of us that went to the races with a copy of every newspaper that contained any racing tips or relevant information and was avidly studied by the horse racing enthusiasts. At Haydock, the race card was then studied, other booklets were purchased and more vital information was gathered and exchanged by all the knowledgeable experts, but not being too familiar with the noble sport of kings, I decided to limit myself to just three bets and all of them would be on one well-known jockey. I reasoned that the jockey was likely to have at least one winner that afternoon. My simple theory paid off and after I'd won more money than I'd lain out, I stopped betting and just enjoyed the racing spectacle and the atmosphere of the meeting. There were many good looking girls parading about the race meeting, but Haydock is not Glorious Goodwood and there were not nearly as many fashionable girls as we'd seen at Goodwood, but what Haydock lacked in snobby society debutantes, it more than made up for in the culinary delight of fish and chips.

Heading back to Blackpool, a general autopsy of the days racing was held and it was discovered that I, having cleared twenty five pound in winnings had unexpectedly won more than most. It seems that many of the day's reliable tips and dead cert favourites, had failed ignominiously and my total ignorance of horse racing had for once in my life paid off.

Later that evening, after preening ourselves to look our best, Gibo as usual outshining us all, we went in search of a good time in Blackpool's nightlife scene. We decided to avoid the plastic beer glass bars that were near the sea front as we all knew that if there was going to be any trouble, those were the places where it was most likely to happen. A taxi driver recommended the Flamingo Club, which was a mile from the sea front and we decided to give it a go. The club had seen better days, but we'd all been in much worse places and as it was still quite early in the evening, we decided to have a couple of drinks and see if it improved as the night wore on. As is usual, the men outnumbered the women, but most of the men were not bothered and were just content to drink, swap stories, listen to the music and take in the promised cabaret.

There were five young women sitting at one table and during the evening, all but one, who was a very plain Jane wallflower, were constantly being asked to dance. After watching this process for some time, Mitch, who was one of the best looking men in the room took pity on the forlorn ugly duckling and decided to ask her for a dance. He ambled over to where she'd been left sitting alone once more and he politely asked her if she'd care to dance with him.

"Piss off." she screeched in an unusual high pitched voice, "I ain't dancing with nobody."

It was rare to find Mitch speechless, but that reply did the trick, his genuine act of kindness had been thrown back in his face and he was absolutely gobsmacked.

"I only asked her to dance because I felt sorry for her." He wailed as we all laughed at this unexpected rebuff and we laughed even louder when Gibo promised to go and find her mother for him.

The star turn in the night's cabaret was billed as Mr X. which, in such a seedy club, seemed to be a bit of hype that was way over the top. A quick glance around the cheaply furnished room informed us that no top line star had appeared at this venue for a very long time, if ever, but to our amazement, Mr X turned out to be the old campaigner, Joseph Lock.

Joseph Lock was an Irish singer who'd become famous to a previous generation by singing good strong marching songs such as, "I'll join the Legion, that's what I'll do." But on finding that he owed the taxman an enormous amount tax, he'd fled the country and gone back to Ireland and hidden away in the back of beyond. And here he was, singing in the seedy Flamingo club and flitting back and forth across the Irish Sea to evade the tax man. He wasn't the type of singer that graced Top of the Pops, but the older men who'd seen him before declared that his voice was as good as ever and after he'd raised the roof with his songs, he was off like a shot to another venue.

Three lads from the Forty Club picked up good time girls that night, unpredictable Bronco being one of them. Unfortunately, the young woman had a laugh that sounded similar to a braying mule and as we wearily walked back to our hotel, we could hear her dulcet tones echoing throughout the quiet early morning streets as Bronco guided her towards the beach where he hoped to have his wicked way with her underneath the North pier.

While searching for a newsagents shop early on the Sunday morning, I witnessed several people eating an unusual breakfast. They'd spent the night sleeping in parked cars along the sea front and were now enjoying fish and chips washed down with mugs of hot tea.

When we'd arrived in Blackpool that weekend, there was a young man on the coach who was unusual as he was reluctant to drink beer. He preferred drugs. He claimed that drugs were cheaper and healthier. As he was a leftover from the flower power sixties and had many oddball ideas, most of the drinking men thought that he was just a weird nutcase and took little notice of him or his peculiar ways. It was agreed by all that he'd definitely arrived in Blackpool with us, but when he'd left, no one ever found out as when he finally turned up, he was so stoned that he had no idea where he'd spent the previous three weeks.

The wives and the girl friends of the Forty Club members, could not help but wonder what their men got up to on these weekend trips and conversely, some of the men who knew that their wives were not the type to sit knitting a pair of socks on a Saturday night, also wondered what they got up. James's wife organised women's Saturday night out sorties when the Forty Club went away for the weekend, but not many wives went along on these shindigs. Jenny, attended one, but said that she didn't feel comfortable attending pubs and night clubs without a partner and came home early.

The reason behind these revenge night outs was simply based on the belief that, "If he can go and hang his hat up at the weekend, so can I." But this belief was a misunderstanding of why these men enjoyed these weekend trips so much. Many of the wives were under the impression that their men went on these coach trips with the sole purpose of seeking slap and tickle affairs with dubious women. Now, although there were very few men on these trips that would not have turned such an offer down, the likelihood of it ever happening to most was about as likely as winning the football pools. A middle aged factory worker with a large beer belly and a working class Midland accent doesn't suddenly become Prince Charming overnight, even if he has shaved, splashed on aftershave and is wearing a new shirt purchased from a mail order catalogue.

The real attraction was the complete freedom that they felt once they boarded the coach with their mates and it really didn't matter to most where the coach was going. For a whole weekend they were as free as birds, free of nagging women at home and grumpy bosses at work. They could drink as much as they desired, did not have to worry about what time that they got home, where they'd put the car keys or even where they'd parked the bloody car. They had no worries of driving through traffic at night and avoiding police traps and knew that whatever happened, their mates would look out for them. They could flirt outrageously with women that they would never meet again and sing their hearts out. Once aboard the coach, these rough gritty men were free of the boring conventions that dominated their lives and for a short while they were able to act like a bunch of silly kids on a school trip.

Jenny did go on a weekend trip to a Belgium beer festival once and she and her friends had a wonderful time, but she never felt the need to repeat the experience. Occasionally she'd go to Blackpool for the day with her friends, but they were not heavy drinkers and spent their time wondering around the shops and looking at the spectacular illuminations. So, although the women had the same opportunity to organise an annual, get away from it all coach trip, they never really took to the idea with the same enthusiasm as the men. They simply never really felt the need to be as silly or as childish as their menfolk.

The Forty Club trips had supplied me with many enjoyable memories over the years, but now many of the original members, through age, illness and death, had dropped out of the club and the balance of membership had gradually changed. The old guard had been replaced by a vibrant younger set that had a different concept of what constituted a good weekend coach trip and were much more interested in frequenting disco dances and flirting with like-minded young women, the days of meeting in old fashioned sing along pubs was well and truly over and I stopped going.

When discussing the history of the Forty Club, which had never been a club at all, as it had never had any form of official membership or any rules to abide by and was just a cover name for bunch of working class men to enjoy a weekend trip, I could go on for hours, but there was one incident that typified the sort of things that happened on those weekend trips and at the time, it made me laugh so much that it hurt my ribs.

As soon as we boarded the coach, no matter where we were going, a card school commenced and it continued all the way to our destination. On one such journey, the coach was fitted with strategically placed small television monitors that were high above the passenger's heads. A cheap illegal pornographic movie was being shown in full colour. It contained graphic close ups of wet vaginas and big dicks and most of the men on the coach, who were battle weary, had seen much the same type of film many times before and couldn't be bothered to watch it. The quality of the film was very poor and the coloured images were much darker than they should have been.

Four card players who were concentrating on their game were completely oblivious of the film and when one, who had his back to the television monitor, asked his mate opposite what the film was, his mate glanced quickly at the screen and on seeing a close up of a large red-brown erect penis said in all seriousness, "It's that ET film" and carried on playing his cards.

Mitch's transport business during its early years took him through good times and bad and because of his precarious financial position, he occasionally dabbled in other areas of commerce to fill his empty coffers. On one occasion he dabbled in open market trading, on another he went into partnership with Charlie and helped him to run a corner café for six months and he was one of the first to realise that money could be made out of collecting old clothes and unwanted furniture from households and selling them on for charity. The charity was himself and as he was skint, he claimed that it was a very deserving cause.

But the most interesting venture that he took on during this particular lean period was his promotion of a graphic striptease show. The business concept was quite simple, hire an out of the way venue that had a licence to sell alcohol, show two blue movies, hire a couple of young erotic striptease artists and sell as many tickets to as many randy men as possible. The show took place on a Thursday evening at a small rugby club near Hagley. Billy and I both helped to sell tickets for him among the men that we worked with and so there were a number of men from Turners at the show which included Benny the lorry driver. Now that he was separated from his wife, he was constantly seeking as much slap and tickle as he could get his hands on and he wasn't the type of man that was bothered about where he got it

The venue was a typical wooden ruby clubhouse that was situated at one end of a wild hedge bordered field and which overlooked a couple of rugby pitches and was well away from the main road and prying eyes. The main room contained a small bar and a two foot high triangular shaped stage. The small stage, had no curtains, but was brightly lit by overhead spotlights and the taped music was relayed through two large speakers, which were on either side of the stage. By eight o clock the room was full of exited men who were from a variety of backgrounds and represented all age groups.

At about eight thirty the first young woman stepped onto the stage accompanied by slow dance music and began to perform her well-rehearsed striptease act and was greeted with boisterous hoots and hollers from the assembled beer-swilling men. When she'd finished doing her best to titillate the audience by slowly showing them all that Mother Nature had equipped her with, the second stripper took her place and the whole process began again. The men nearest the stage, who were almost within touching distance of the strippers, sat on stools, while the majority stood banked up behind them and several at the back of the room stood on stools, chairs and tables. Although the women were relatively young, they both had a well-worn look about them. Their faces in particular were already marked with the tell tail signs of excessive drinking, to many cigarettes, numerous late night stands and a lack of natural sunlight.

During the evening the assembled men were predictably childish and crude in their boisterous attempts at humour and used such catcalls to the strippers as, "Get em off" and "Show us your tits." And among their mates, in-jokes abounded, "Bet you ain't seen a muff like that for a long time have you Harry?"

"Not since last week George, and that was your wife's."

The show was predictably crude, lewd and tacky and I for one was surprised to find that it didn't excite me as much as I'd expected. After the girls had performed their striptease, Mitch who acted as compe're for the evening informed the boisterous men that there would be a short interval and that there was more to come later and that the second part of the girls act would include a little audience participation, meanwhile, while they set about refilling their glasses they would be entertained with a blue movie.

342

During the interval, I made my way to the gent's toilet for a run out. There were four men already in the toilet when I entered and as I stepped up to the long urinal that ran along one wall, a man who was already standing there silently mouthed the words, "look at that," and pointed over his shoulder towards the lavatory cubicles that were behind us. Puzzled by this strange request, I glanced back over my shoulder and was shocked to see that one of the stripers was sitting in one of the cubicles, with the door wide open, her panties around her ankles and smoking a small cheroot cigar while conversing with a man who was leaning against the open cubical doorway. Because of the familiarity between them, I assumed that the man, who was quite shabby in appearance, was either, her manager, minder, husband or all three. Up until that point, I'd felt little in the way of erotic excitement from the striptease show and now I had none whatsoever. I'd gone along to the show with a sense of exited curiosity and because it was the macho thing to do and now I was puzzled as to why I wasn't enjoying the experience. I was to learn that several men felt the same, but such is the code of male bravado, none of us would own up to it at the time. But this slight feeling of disgust did not affect all the men and many relished the crude intimacy of the strippers, Benny being one.

In the second half of the show, when many of the men were noticeably more intoxicated, the striptease acts became even tackier than before and Benny was first up onto the stage when they called for a volunteer. The two strippers, amid thunderous applause, much of which was from a sense of relief at not being chosen to be the man on the stage, slowly and systematically stripped Benny of his clothes until he was standing naked and with the help of a large feather duster, in a state of sexual excitement. And after undergoing a number of simulated sexual antics with the two strippers, he was then paraded around the crowded room by one of the girls who'd tied his necktie around his scrotum and was leading him about with short sharp tugs. And such is the law of nature, when she pulled on the necktie; Benny went along with her, much to the delight of the beer swilling raucous audience. After that performance, the girls followed it with a series of physical demonstrations with the aid of ping-pong balls, candles and a beer bottle.

343

This was the only strip show that Mitch organised. A few weeks after, his transport business picked up and he admitted that he'd also found the striptease show, although profitable, sordid and distasteful.

A couple of years later, Mitch, Gibo, Billy and I visited London to see a football match at Wembley and on the Saturday night, we saw a completely different type of strip show. We were booked into a small hotel and after the match; we hit the town and visited several pubs. Looking for something a little more exiting we asked a taxi driver to take us to a lively night club where there were plenty of good time girls. The taxi driver, who probably had an arrangement with the club, took us to what must have been one of the most expensive rip off clubs in Mayfair. The club was large and extremely plush and along one side of the spacious room there was a glittering long bar. The whole room was delicately lit with warm sophisticated subdued lighting and in one corner of the room there was a stage complete with silk curtains and a state of the art sound and lighting system.

After paying our entrance fee, we were shown to a table by a very attractive young woman who, dressed in a tantalising short tight dress walked slowly and provocatively before us and once settled, we were then waited upon by another equally attractive and provocative young woman who wore a low topped dress which amply showed off her large round breasts as she bent forward to place four glasses and a bottle of champagne before us. As expected, the champagne was mediocre and cost a fortune. Sipping our champagne slowly, we took in our surroundings and saw that seated on high bar stools at the long bar were six gorgeous looking young women who had varying shades of skin colour. They were all dressed in expensive figure hugging dresses and were expertly showing every male in the room their long inviting legs. There were many middle aged business men in the room who were being pampered and entertained by similar gorgeous young women. The attractive hostesses laughed at all the customer's inane jokes and encouraged them to order more Champaign and spend their money freely and this they did willingly as much of the nights expenses were being borne by the company's that they worked for.

The nightclub was not at all the type of place that we had hoped for and we sat there a little downhearted and sipped our expensive drinks as slowly as possible while we decided what to do next, but one thing was certain, we would not be purchasing anymore drinks. The music that had been playing in the background changed. The shimmering silk stage curtains opened, revealing a stage set that represented an expensive looking executive office. Sitting at the office desk was a young studious looking secretary dressed in a light grey two piece costume. Her long blond hair was tied into a pony tail and she wore a pair of thick horn rimmed glasses and although attractive, she looked prim and proper and the image of an ideal secretary that one would expect to find in the office of a large corporation. She sat at the large desk writing on a pad while soft music played in the background, then a white telephone began to ring. The attractive secretary answered the telephone in a perfect English accent and with the aid of a gold pen she wrote down a message onto her desk pad, the plush executive illusion was perfect.

Then, with great style, she rose from the red leather swivel chair and walking slowly in her red high-heeled shoes she came round to the front of the desk and with the elegance of a cat walk model, began to parade up and down the stage while she slowly disrobed. She took off her horned rimmed glasses, released her tied back hair and with natural grace she discarded one item of clothing after another. She elegantly paraded around the stage and then slowly discarded her bra, stockings, suspender belt and finally her flimsy panties. Completely naked, she stood posed elegantly on the stage while bathed in the warm glow of stage lighting and it was the sexist performance that we had ever witnessed.

We sat stunned, not one of us had ever witnessed a striptease show performed with such elegance and style and we were completely bowled over with the experience and none of us ever had an urge to attend another tacky strip show as we knew that we would never see a performance better than that.

Once outside, Billy summed up our thoughts when he said, "Well I don't know about you lot, but I'd have preferred a pint of Guinness instead of that bubbly piss, but that striptease was incredible, it's the best thing that I've seen since Betty Brewster dropped her drawers in Bradnocks air raid shelter."

My first family holiday was spent at Ramsgate in Kent, in 1949. My parents and I, along with Aunt Nell, Uncle Frank and their two children travelled there in hired car that was driven by its owner. It was a large black Humber, but even so, along with our luggage it was a tight squeeze. With suitcases strapped to the roof of the car and bulging from the open boot, we could easily have been mistaken for a group of dust bowl Okies looking for a new life in California. The reason for travelling all that way in such cramped conditions was because the boarding house that we stopped at for the week was owned by an old friend of Uncle Franks.

The boarding house at Pegwell Bay, was typical of its type at that time as it had a strict time table for meals and a set of regimental rules. Each day, no matter how inclement the weather, the guests from all the claustrophobic boarding houses commuted into Ramsgate after breakfast, to escape these constricting rules and regulations. Meal times in these strict houses of correction were horrendously formal and while sitting at the white cloth covered tables, we children were expected to be on our best behaviour at all times. There would be a constant stream of sharply whispered instructions issued by nervous and embarrassed parents as the lady of the house walked about and gave everyone in the room either cold smiles or disapproving looks.

"Sit up straight" "Don't play with your knife" "Take your elbows off the table" "Don't talk with your mouth full" "No, I don't know what it is, just eat it." "No, you cannot leave the table until the others have finished." "Walk, don't run, don't make a noise and don't show me up or you'll get a belt!"

Why families paid to stay in these dismal boarding houses and put themselves through this form of mental torture, where for a whole week, they had to pretend to be people that they were obviously not and to obey rules that they hated, is a mystery that has never been fully explained to my satisfaction.

Being young at the time, my memory of this holiday is rather sketchy, but I vividly recall playing on the beach, paddling in the cold sea and having to hang on to my heavy water filled woollen swimming trunks to stop them from falling down around my ankles. Once woollen swimming trunks got wet the crutch simply turned into a heavy water logged sack which was bad enough for us kids, but for men it was even more embarrassing. On emerging from the crashing waves of the cold sea, the men looked as though they had a pair of bollocks that a prize winning bull would have been proud of.

Several years later, we had a holiday on a farm at Hampton Load which is an insignificant spot that's situated on the river Severn and a few years after that, we put up with a cold breezy week at Skegness while residing in an old four-birth caravan that looked to have been abandoned on the edge of a farmer's rough fallow field along with three others. These holidays were not the type that are ever likely to be advertised in a glossy holiday brochure and yet, I was extremely lucky to have experienced them, as the vast majority of working class families did not go away for any sort of holiday. Billy Butlin did his best to change people's perception of a summer holiday by opening his none stop, fun for all, holiday camps, but even so, it was a long time before it became the norm for many families to take a regular holiday away from home.

At junior school a teacher asked, "How many of you have visited the seaside and have seen the sea?" and out of a class of forty kids only three put their hands up. Nobby Clarke was one and his description of the magnificent sight was, "Its ever so big Miss, yow can't even see the other side."

When my mates and I reached maturity, we tended to hire six berth caravans on beach site caravan parks. When the sun shone, we spent the day lazing about on the beach, building sand castles, paddling in the cold sea, reading books and newspapers and doing our best to keep sand out of ice cream and intimate crevices. When it rained, we traipsed dripping wet from one gift shop to another or visited the nearest historical site until it was time to eat. Our chips with everything meals were taken in cramped steamy cafés that were furnished with easy wipe tables where containers were filled with damp sugar that refused to pour, damp salt that refused to sprinkle, and tomato ketchup that had been weakened with vinegar. Most of these cafes served weak tea and had two or more unruly kids running about the place and before sitting down it was often necessary to move the previous customers used dishes to one side and wait for a gormless girl who was laughably called a waitress to wipe the table with a well-worn dishcloth that was liable to be carrying the plague virus. This type of experience seemed to be compulsory and part of the conditions of a British holiday, as they were to be found in every seaside resort up and down the land.

In the evening, we visited the caravan site club for noisy children's games, a bingo session, second rate cabaret and an ear blasting dim the lights disco where everyone could show just how badly they could dance. It was all extremely naff, but everyone loved it. With a couple of drinks under their belts the holiday makers, who came from different parts of the country, would exchange stories, moan about the weather and laugh at anything and everything. The whole experience was a complete break from the normal routine and everyday life and that for most was all that was required.

The holiday resort that we were to return to many times was the higgledy-piggledy town of Tenby and the wild Pembrokeshire coast, which unlike North Wales, was a friendly area. The pubs were warm and comfy, had comprehensive menus and were not a bit like the uninviting cold tiled floor bars that were to be found in other parts of the country. It was Mitch who first suggested, "As we've all got kids, we should look for a family holiday where we can all meet up together and Tenby's the ideal place." And soon a whole gang of friends and family members were booking their annual holidays at the Lydstep Caravan Park which is in a picturesque horseshoe bay and just a couple of miles from Tenby. From the horseshoe bay, the land rose steeply and ran up to the top of a high ridge and a cliff top walk and the whole camp was wonderfully landscaped so that each group of caravans was hidden from the next by areas of wild forest. There were wonderful views of the cliff lined bay and a few miles out at sea sat flat topped Caldy Island, the home of a monastic order that welcomed visitors who were shipped across from Tenby on motor boats each day.

The caravans had improved greatly over the years and were nothing like the four berth dilapidated tin can that Mom and Dad had hired in Skegness when I was thirteen and were no longer referred to

348

as caravans, but mobile homes. They were better planned and had bathroom and toilet facilities, fitted kitchens complete with fridge and in the comfortable living room there was now a "Tele" in the corner.

The holidays were wonderful, carefree and full of fun. There were numerous things to do in and around the Lydstep camp, in Tenby and in the surrounding countryside. There was something to please everyone and to avoid arguments in the group, who often had differing view on what to do and when to do it, a rule was introduced whereby we would do our own thing during the day and meet in the evening for a friendly drink together. We played cricket and football with the kids, occasionally swam in the cold sea to show how brave we were, took long invigorating cliff top walks along the wild wave lashed coast, visited castles that had been knocked about a bit, wildlife and amusement parks and occasionally went horse riding.

After my hair raising childhood experiences with Charlie, I'd developed a belief that horses and I were not meant for each other and after being thrown from the saddle on one ride, I had my fears truly confirmed. Being tall, the girl at the riding school had decided that I needed a big horse with plenty of spirit and while getting comfortable in the saddle I noticed that unlike the others, my feet were in stirrups that were made with a metal bow on one side and a thick rubber band on the other. Being a novice the significance of these odd stirrups completely failed to register. Half way through our pleasant ride across the open downs my spirited horse decided to jump about and rear up. The thick rubber band on the left stirrup flipped open, I lost my balance and with a heavy thud, I landed flat on my back. Fuming with indignation, I jumped back into the saddle and rode the startled beast back to the ridding school with the determination of a Derby winner. It was the last time that I ever rode a horse and several weeks after the holiday was over, I had a Eureka moment and realised what the rubber band stirrups were for.

"Bloody hell!" I suddenly cried, interrupting Billy's boring observations on the inclement weather, "I know what those bloody rubber band stirrups were for."

"What bloody stirrups?" Billy asked as he sipped his pint.

"Do you remember when that bloody horse threw me off its back at Tenby?"

"Do I? I haven't laughed so much for ages."

"Well I've just realised what those rubber bands stirrups were for."

"To keep your feet in position while your ridding aint they?"

"No Billy, just the opposite. When you fall off they let your foot drop out so that you don't get dragged along when the horse bolts. That girl that put me on that bloody horse knew that it was liable to play up and bolt."

"Well it's your own fault for pretending to be an expert rider."

"What are you on about? When did I pretend to be a good rider?"

"When she put you up on that horse, you sat there looking like the Duke of Wellington inspecting his troops."

Annette once took Nan to Devon for a holiday, or to be more precise she got Trapper to run them down in his car and pick them up a week later. She'd decided to take up the offer of using a friend's caravan for a week and as they were getting into Trapper's car and ready for the long journey, Annette suddenly turned to Nan and asked in her usual diplomatic manner, "What the bloody hell have you got in that great big shopping bag?"

"It's some food for the trip."

"Bloody hell Nan, how much have you brought?"

"Well there's some cheese and pickle, some ham and tomato, sliced beef and mustard sandwiches and there's some pig's pudding, a jar of pickled onions, a pork pie and some pork scratchings."

"My God! Were only going for a week Nan, we aint going around the bloody world."

"Look, I've been to Devon before, it's a long way you know."

"Nan, the last time you went to Devon was in the days of stage coaches and bloody highway men, they've got motorways and service stations now."

"Yes, well that's all very well and good, but I bet they don't have black pudding and pickled onions in them places."

Their holiday was a success, but being a mixed bag of unexpected incidents it wasn't exactly what they'd planned when they'd set off.

"When we got there, we couldn't find the bloody caravan, they all look the bloody same don't they?" Annette said when describing the holiday, "Anyway the caravan was at the top of the site, which give us a smashing view, but the beach and the bloody camp shop was at the bottom of the hill which nearly killed us every time we went there. It was like walking up and down to the bloody Bullring market every day. Then we found that the nearest pub was bloody miles away and to get to it we had to walk along a country lane. It wornt so bad going, but coming back in the dark was bloody dangerous what with bloody cars zipping by and no pavement to walk on and when we finally got back to the caravan we found that we'd left all the windows open and it was bloody freezing inside. Anyway the next night I asked this old farmer who was in the pub, if he could give us a lift back to the caravan park in his old Land Rover and from then on he picked us up and brought us back every night and do you know what, by the end of the week, he was asking me to marry him. I said to him, you must be joking Jethro, me live in the country with all them horrible smells and a bleeding dawn chorus waking me up every morning at an unearthly hour, I'd never get any sleep and do you know what the cheeky bugger said, he said, I wasn't thinking about having much sleep myself either. He kept looking me up and down like I was a prize cow and just what he needed for his breeding stock."

Trapper and his wife arrived at the hotel in Eastbourne where they had reservations for the week and parked their small mini car between a large silver Bentley and a black shiny Jaguar in the hotels car park and Trapper looked at the two cars and at the hotel and with a heavy heart as he realised that it was posher than he'd anticipated. He hadn't listened attentively when his wife had informed him that she had booked a holiday in Eastbourne and he'd assumed that they'd be staying in a small side street hotel, the type that the Forty Club stayed in.

Looking at the large hotel he realised that he had a slight problem. Their belongings were not packed in suitcases as was the usual practice for people going on holiday, but in a holdall and two black plastic bags. Only ever having had holidays together in caravans, they'd never needed a suitcase before and clothes in plastic bags were easier to pack into a small car, but now as he looked at the posh hotel before him he realised that it would have been prudent and not especially difficult to have borrowed a suitcase.

While Trapper extracted the holdall and the two large plastic bags from the boot, his wife hurriedly made her way inside the hotel to obtain the key to their room as quickly as possible. Once she'd got the key she reasoned, they could stealthily whisk their plastic bags up to their room without anyone noticing. She also made a mental note that she would force Trapper into purchasing a suitcase before the week was out as she felt decidedly embarrassed about the whole situation.

After waiting a few minutes to give his wife the necessary time to acquire the room key, Trapper, holding his bundles, walked nonchalantly up the three steps that led up to the hotels revolving entrance door.

As he squeezed into one of the four sections of the revolving door with his bulbous luggage, two of the hotels guests who were on their way out, stood back and looked on in puzzled bewilderment. By shuffling his feet and by pushing his bulbous bags against the glass panel in front of him, he was able force the revolving door to move round and he entered the hotels reception area in much the same manner as a cork leaves a bottle of Champaign, but unfortunately, one of his plastic bags split wide open and its contents of shirts, blouses, dresses and various items of his wife's underwear spilled willy-nilly onto the floor.

He frantically scooped the various items of clothing off the floor and pushed them into his remaining plastic bag which now began to resemble a barrage balloon, as several hotel guests and the sniffy reception staff looked on in silent amazement.

"I've never felt such a prat." Trapper was to say time and time again, "and it was three days before my Missis calmed down and spoke to me in a civil manner and she spent the whole week sneaking in and out of the hotel wearing dark sunglasses and a big straw hat."

Towards the end of the seventies one of Billy's lads was playing for a successful football team which was run by a competent manager named Ron Brown. The team, like kids teams the world over, was plagued with the usual petty politics, where parents of competent players wanted to win trophies and the others wanted more democracy, where all the lads, no matter what their ability, were given a fare crack of the whip. It's a debate that goes on behind every amateur team no matter what the sport and it's a problem that all managers have to deal with.

Some of the parents that stand on the touch line at a kid's football match no very little about the game and continually shout ridiculous advice at their offspring and make inane comments about the ref and some know even less and shout even louder.

"It's amazing how many times I find myself standing next to the only bloke in the world who knows what's wrong with the team." Billy declared after one exasperating Sunday morning football match.

"And I suppose you're an expert are you?" Mitch taunted.

"No, not me mate, my Missis is the expert. She doesn't know her offside from her elbow, but she can shout louder than me."

Ron Brown handled his young team and their selfish parents extremely well and he not only got them to win several trophies, but he also gave every lad a chance to shine. With the parent's permission, he entered the team into a football tournament that was held in the Duisberg area of West Germany over the Easter holiday period and Jenny and I went along with them to lend moral support to Billy and his talented lad.

We were pleasantly surprised by the warmth that the Germans showed us and were extremely impressed by the superb sporting facilities where the football matches were played. We were also impressed by the cleanliness of the whole place. "It's just like being back home aint it, not a crisp packet in sight." Billy sarcastically quipped.

This will to keep the area clean and tidy was brought home to us while we were being entertained at one of the sporting clubs. The football competition had just ended, the congratulatory speeches had been given and we were all chatting and relaxing. While we were drinking our coffee, a few small children were running around the room and one of them accidentally bumped into a man who was carrying two cups of coffee. A tiny amount of coffee spilled onto the wooden floor and a German woman who was sitting nearest the tiny spillage took out a paper tissue and without breaking her conversation with the others at her table, slickly wiped the spillage up. The man who'd spilled the coffee and the child who had caused the accident were complete strangers to her and yet she had, without a conscious thought, automatically reacted to clean up the spillage.

On another occasion, we saw four young lads repairing the scuffed area of the running track where the teams had crossed to reach the football pitch and by the time we'd received our cups of coffee in the clubhouse, the running track looked pristine and the whole arena looked as though no one had used it that day. Throughout our stay in Germany, and we returned the following year for yet another tournament, we witnessed many instances of this neat and tidy attitude.

At one event, the sports club members used a local bar as their clubhouse. After the match was over all the players and parents piled into this large bar, listened to the usual thank you speeches from both sides and drank glasses of pop or beer. To obtain a drink one had to attract the barmaid's attention and she brought the required drinks over to the table and marked the customer's beer mat with a pen and then carried on serving the next customer. No one was expected to pay for anything until the session had ended. This sounds all very reasonable and civilised, but as we looked around the room we saw that there were over forty adults in the place and an even larger number of youngsters and we realised that it would have been quite easy for any of them to slip out of the room without paying for anything. We were truly astonished at this trust and we could not imagine the same thing happening anywhere back home. "Can you imagine what Charlie would do under this system?" Billy pondered with a shake of his head.

One evening a group of us visited a local bar for a quiet drink. The bar was far from the tourist haunts and we were the only foreigners in the place. We settled at two tables and kept ourselves to ourselves. The other customers in the bar, who were mostly men, did much the same, but after an hour the barmaid brought over a tray of eight small glasses of applecore schnapps.

"There must be some mistake," Billy said a little puzzled, "We didn't order these drinks."

"No." the barmaid said smiling, "The gentleman at the bar would like to buy you a drink."

We all looked over to the bar and a middle-aged man smiled, waved and said, "Please accept from me. Good health to you all."

This unexpected act of friendship broke whatever conservative feelings there had been in the room as we Brits were only too willing to accept the kind gesture and within half an hour the gentleman from the bar and several of his friends had joined us at our tables and with more beers and backslapping jollity we all became the best of pals. It was one o'clock in the morning when we eventually rolled out of the bar; having sung with our new German friends, every pub song that we could remember, including "We're Going to Hang out the Washing on the Siegfried Line" and surprisingly, the German's not only knew all the songs, but were word perfect.

In 1979 Lord Mountbatten was murdered by a group of cowardly hide and seek members of the IRA. The singer Gracie Field and the Hollywood actor John Wayne passed away and Maggie Thatcher became Prime Minister, but it wasn't all bad news, Trevor Francis, the young skilful football player, became the first British footballer to be sold for one million-pound and Jenny and I decided to holiday in the USA. Although the directors and the invisible shareholders didn't know it, our holiday was actually paid for by the company that I worked for. Charlie wasn't the only one who had friends that were crooked businessmen and were in the market for shady deals.

"How do you manage to do it?" Mitch asked.

"It's surprisingly easy if you're not too greedy," I replied with a knowing smile, "All the directors are on the fiddle, and I've got copies of invoices to prove it, there are loop holes everywhere."

We spent our holiday in the wonderful scenic city of San Francisco and as fully expected, the city was vibrant and full of surprises. We travelled on the cable cars up and down the steep streets, saw dozens of keep fit fanatics jogging around Fisherman's Warf and amazing street entertainers who performed outstanding shows at designated spots. We met tourists from every state in the

USA while visiting Alcatraz penitentiary, art galleries, China Town, Jazz clubs, striptease shows and in the gay area around Cato Street that had gay policemen, which at the time was considered unusual.

The city is never to hot or too cold and as it is overflowing with restaurants, there is an abundance of food and so it's the ideal place for a drop out. These dropouts were rarely hungry and were extremely polite when approaching anyone for loose change.

San Francisco is a booming modern city that was rebuilt after a severe earthquake and like most American cities it is built on a square grid pattern, but because it is situated on a series of hills it has a variety of scenic views and as a consequence it has been used in many Hollywood films such as "Bullet," "Dirty Harry" and "Escape from Alcatraz."

Because of its pleasant climate and liberal views, the city became widely associated with the 1960's Flower Power hippies. Originally known as "Beats" and "Hipsters" they were eventually to become known under the collective title of "Hippies." They may have believed in many things at different times, but the two core beliefs was the liberal use of hallucinogenic drugs and a disdain of established rules.

As this was our first visit to the USA, we were surprised at the huge portions of food that we were served whenever we ordered a meal and we quickly learned to stick to light snacks during the day and eat a main meal at night. We were also caught out by the unusual custom of having our coffee cup continually refilled and of being asked, "How would you like your eggs."

On one of our un-American walkabouts we came across a small restaurant that had tables and chairs outside beneath coloured parasols. I sat at one of the tables while Jenny went inside to order two cold drinks and a cheese and tomato sandwich. By now we knew it was wise to order just one item of food and share it. After a few minutes I became aware of happy chatter filling what I was sure had been an empty restaurant and puzzled by this, I looked into the doorway and saw that Jenny was talking to the staff and the discussion concerned Jenny's pronunciation of the word tom-ar-to as opposed to the American tum-a-to. The three staff insisted that she say it over and over again. When that word was finally put to rest they began to ask her to say other words and catch phrases. It was fifteen minutes before we finally received our cheese and tum-a-to sandwich, which as expected was four inches thick, came with a large side salad and could easily have fed a small family.

Each evening we visited a restaurant that represented a different culture for our evening meal and in this way we were able to sample meals from around the world, our biggest disappointment was the Japanese experience, which we found rather tasteless. The most enjoyable were the Indian, Italian and Mexican meals which were full of spice and flavour. The meals were reasonably priced and so were the motels and we soon learned that with a bit of homework, one could holiday in the USA quite cheaply. Getting about was no problem either, taxis were plentiful and the public transport system, much to our surprise in the land of the flash car, was excellent, but the icing on the cake was the friendliness of the people. Although made up of different creeds, cultures and races we found the Americans to be very open and helpful and the widely used saying, "Have a nice day," may have been as automatic as saying, "Good morning," back in Britain, but it did sound genuine and it did put a smile on the face.

A downside was ice-cold beer. Holding the glass was uncomfortable and taking a satisfying swig was impossible. It also killed the taste and reminded me of the no nonsense detective Andy Dalziels description, "It's so cold it tastes like penguin piss."

One night after spending an enjoyable evening at a jazz club, we walked back to our hotel through the sparsely populated streets and were treated to an unexpected, but enlightening piece of sales technique. Twenty paces in front of us; a young man was propositioned by a very attractive and provocative young lady of the night. She was well-proportioned and dressed in a very short, low slung, tight fitting red dress and as the man approached she minced across the pavement in front of him with an exaggerated sexy swagger, turned a little and lifted the back of her short skirt which revealed her tantalising peachy naked bottom. Provocatively she wiggled her bottom at him and he stopped dead in his tracks. Jenny and I carried on walking by, as the two fell into conversation and presumably negotiated a price. It was undoubtedly the most erotic and blatant piece of salesmanship either of us had ever witnessed.

Being readers of the John Steinbeck novels, we wished to visit Cannery Row and we took a tourist coach trip that not only stopped at Monterey, but took in Carmel and the Salinas Valley. During the trip we saw giant redwood trees, Pacific seal's basking in the sun, sampled and purchased California wine and visited a store that sold the largest samples of fruit that we'd ever seen. The trip included a self-service buffet lunch in Monterey where Jenny and I modestly filled our plates and sat down opposite two American teenage girls whose meals we noticed were three times the size of ours and resembled models of the Egyptian Pyramids. The two friendly teenage girls knocked off their meals without any trouble at all, whereas we struggled to finish ours. "Where the hell do they put it?" Jenny queried, "I'd have to lie down for a couple of days after eating half that amount."

Sharing the sightseeing coach trip with us was a small party of boisterous Italian tourists. What they lacked in numbers they more than made up with noise and chatter and throughout the trip they jumped up and down in their seats, argued and contradicted each other and hardly listened to a word of the drivers interesting running commentary. But the strangest was a woman, who whenever the coach stopped, purchased a souvenir. As there were no shops on or near the beach when we stopped to look at the Pacific seals, she collected a handful of sand and put it into a plastic bag for a keepsake. When we finally arrived back in San Francisco that evening, she'd collected so many bags and boxes that several of her friends had to help her off the coach with them.

"I wonder what her luggage will look like when she eventually returns to Italy." Jenny wondered while shaking her head in bewilderment, "She'll probably have to charter a private plane."

The following year, John Lennon, the ex-rebellious Beatle and man of peace, was shot dead whilst walking out of his New York apartment by yet another misfit who craved notoriety.

During the holidays that we spent in Spain and the Balearic Islands, we became aware of the differences between the Spanish culture and our own. Their offhand attitude to cats and dogs and the process of turning from sleepy easy going pedestrians to formula one racing drivers once behind the wheel of a car, we also noticed that they had little trouble in understanding the various holiday makers no matter where they came from. The young Spaniards seemed to take all the different accents no matter where they came from, in their stride. But there was one occasion where I had to step in and act as interpreter for a young puzzled barman. We were half way through a Jeep safari ride in the mountains and had stopped at a small bar for much needed toilets and refreshments. The young barman was handling the many varied orders with the usual efficiency, when a woman with a strong Geordie accent asked for, "Wa-a."

The puzzled barman repeated the unfamiliar word "Wa-a?"

"Aye," the woman then repeated, "Wa-a! A boo-ul of wa-a."

Seeing that the barman was completely baffled, I said, "Water. A bottle of water."

"Ah!" the barman exclaimed, his face beaming with understanding and in perfect English he said, "Water. You want a bottle of water?"

"Aye, that's wo' o' said mon." the woman confirmed, "Wa-a!"

Holidays are meant to be relaxing, revitalizing and full of fun, but there are times of course when they can be anything but and can turn out to be extremely stressful. Like most people, we had our fair share of minor mishaps, but thankfully nothing that could be called disastrous. We once found ourselves rushing around a hotel bedroom at 7.15 in the morning desperately trying to wash, dress and allow time for a quick breakfast as we were due to catch a tour bus at eight sharp. Halfway through dressing, I checked my wrist watch and suddenly realised that the time was actually 3.35am and not 7.15am. Waking up in the dark bedroom, I'd misread the small travel clock. Jenny's response to the good news is unsuitable for print.

While on a holiday in Sorrento, we met a sweet old couple who, while shaking their heads in unison, admitted that they had a habit of getting lost whilst on holiday. "We listen attentively to every word that the tour guide says, but we don't seem to be able to retain the information." After boarding the wrong bus and ending up at the wrong hotel one evening after a visit to a small theatre, the exasperated tour guide tracked them down and brought them back to the fold. He took the couple to task and asked them to explain how they'd managed to board the wrong bus.

"We just followed the crowd when we came out of the theatre." The elderly gent explained.

"But didn't you realise that you were getting onto a bus with forty people, none of whom you had ever seen before and that you had arrived at the theatre in a small mini bus."

"I'm afraid all buses look alike to us." The old lady replied and then added while smiling pleasantly, "But we don't worry about it as we always get found eventually."

After apologising the old women added light heartedly, "Perhaps we ought end our holiday now and go home in the morning."

The exasperated tour guide replied, "Yes dear, but are you sure that you would ever get there?"

The following morning having recovered from the scare of losing two of his charges, the tour guide admitted that this sought of thing happened on a regular basis and that this particular couple were far from being the worst case that he had had deal with. He revealed that two weeks earlier, he'd lost a couple of middle aged women who'd boarded the wrong tour bus in Naples and had ended up at Monte Casino, forty miles away. They had chatted away to each other throughout the long journey and failed to notice until the coach reached its destination, that they were on a bus full of Germans.

Our tour coach pulled onto the shale covered car park on Mount Vesuvius and there Jenny and I along with the other passengers alighted so as to take in the spectacular view of the Bay of Naples and feel the thrill of walking near the top of the impressive volcano. After being shown around by the tour guide, we, just like the other tourists on the mountain, collected a few small pieces of dark black magna that was lying about for souvenirs and slipped them into our pockets, but one middle aged man was unable to put the piece that he had chosen into his pocket as it was as big as his head and as he struggled to walk under its weight he called to his wife, "Look Alice! See what I've got."

"What on earth are you going to do with that?" Alice asked in shocked amazement, her face clearly showing that she was far from happy with his find.

"I'm taking it home with us" He said. Then, on seeing no enlightened response from her he added as an explanation, "It's from Vesuvius! It's unique!"

"So what?" She asked sharply, but as she turned and walked away we could clearly see that she did not require an answer to her question.

"It's living history!" He called after her, his legs bowed as he struggled to hold the heavy weight, "Nobody back home has got anything like this."

"That's because no one's as daft as you Jeffrey." She called back and with a defeated sigh she carried on walking away while shaking her head in bewilderment.

Mishaps seemed to seek Dee out with the accuracy of guided missiles. As far as he could remember, he'd been accident prone, but when he joined the fire service and became a fully trained fire-fighter, he was delighted to find that many of his colleagues were also accident prone. Although this was a great comfort to him, it was a terrifying prospect for his family and friends who on hearing this news immediately checked their fire insurance policies. The question asked was, was it better to let the house burn down or let the energetic accident prone fire-fighters wreck the place?

"This is the spot where I fell into the canal last week," fire-fighter Brian said, as he and his two friends cycled along the canal towpath, "I hit that bump there and toppled in." And Brian promptly hit the same bump and toppled into the canal once more.

"Is this the Conrad Nursing Home?" The hurrying fire-fighter called out urgently as he dashed into the reception area of the nursing home and saw two startled nurses staring at him.

"No," Said a voice from behind him, "It's next door. This is the Newton nursing home."

It was then that the fire-fighter realised that he was talking to their reflections in a large wall mirror.

Dee and his wife, after deciding to take a well-earned five-day break, hired a narrow boat on a nearby peaceful canal and took their two young lads for ballast and unpaid lock opening duties. They picked up their narrow boat, which was to be their living quarters for the next five days, at the Alvchurch dock, which is just a few miles outside the Birmingham boundary and as is the nature of narrow boat sailing, a couple of days later, they were still only a few miles outside the Birmingham boundary. Halfway through the first day, after hitting the canal bank and a number of bridges several times, they settled down to enjoy their slow peaceful meandering journey through the green and pleasant countryside and it was then that Captain Dee, noticed that his wallet, car and flat keys were missing. A frantic search of his jacket and trouser pockets revealed nothing of importance and neither did his search of their suitcases, which his wife, who was used to these minor catastrophes, pointed out couldn't possibly contain the missing items, as the suitcases hadn't been opened since they had left their flat that morning. Being on a canal boat, one is never far from civilisation and at the next bridge; he clambered over the wall and found a telephone box. He called grandad and gave him instructions to cancel his bank card at his bank and to collect his spare flat keys from his flat. But the bank, quite rightly, refused to cancel the bankcard and informed him that only the owner of the card could cancel it. Undaunted grandad carried on to his next task, which was to retrieve the spare keys from Dee's flat. To enter the flat he was obliged to break a small square pane of window glass which was part of the front door and later that day, to ensure that the flat was secure; he replaced it with a fresh piece of glass.

That evening Dee rang grandad and learned to his dismay that he would have to travel into Cotteridge by bus the following morning to cancel the bankcard himself. While he was there and having forgotten that he'd asked grandad to do it for him, he decided to retrieve his spare keys from his flat. He broke the small pane of window glass that grandad had just replaced and on finding that his spare keys were missing, suddenly remembered that he'd asked grandad to collect them for him. After another apologetic phone call, grandad once more replaced the broken pane of window glass.

Grandad then set about acquiring a set of keys for Dee's car, which was parked at Alvchurch. On phoning the car dealership and explaining the situation, he was told that it would be no trouble at all to replace the car keys, all he had to do was to bring the car in and they would sort it out. When he asked the helpful young lady, how he was supposed to get into the car and drive it from Alvchurch to the city centre without the use of car keys, there was a deathly silence at the end of the line.

Back on board HMS Disaster, Captain Dee was having problems of his own; his favourite red baseball cap had fallen into the canal and it stubbornly refused to move from the middle of the "cut." He decided that if he and the two young lads lobbed small stones into the canal just beyond the floating cap, the rippling waves would eventually bring it ashore. After ten minutes of careful lobbing, the floating cap had not moved one inch nearer the bank and so larger stones were brought into play. Unfortunately one stone scored a direct hit and his favourite red cap disappeared without trace. This disaster upset him more than losing his wallet and the keys, as he'd worn the cap for many years and he felt that it was on a par with a family pet.

Other than the two young lads being almost squashed to death by the narrow boat, falling in the canal, spilling the dinner when the boat hit the canal bank, nothing much happened for the rest of the week and when they returned the boat to its rightful owners, there on the office shelf was a black bum bag which contained the missing wallet and the lost keys. On hearing the good news grandads comment was, "I'm just glad you only went for five days, I dread to think what would have happened if you'd gone for a fortnight."

A man that Danny Page knew took his long suffering wife and their two daughters, on a coastal caravan holiday in the inexpensive, but unpredictable month of April and during their first night, a fierce storm that had been widely predicted to last for at least three-days hit the coast. During the night on the almost deserted caravan site, the strong gale force wind tipped over several caravans, theirs being one of them. The family crawled out of the overturned caravan bruised and shaken and spent most of the following day, which was still very wet and windy, transferring their belongings from the overturned caravan to another that the site manager had allocated to them. Later that day, the storm, which had shown no sign of abating, did no more than tip this caravan over onto its side as well.

"Why didn't you just pack up and come home after the first catastrophe?" Danny asked when he heard the details of the fun packed holiday, "After all, you must have known that the storm was going to last for a few days."

The man looked at Danny with genuine astonishment and replied, "We'd paid for a week! You don't get a refund if you go home early you know?"

For quite a while Jenny and I held out against going to Orlando, for we were seriously opposed to the idea of spending two weeks in a boisterous fun fair. The thought filled us with dread, but our lads were now at the right age to enjoy the experience and so we decided that we should go and get it over and done with. We did our homework and went in October, when it was not to hot and when there would be shorter queues at the park rides. We chose a modestly priced motel that was on International Drive and decided to use the shuttle busses as opposed to a free car that would have cost us well over three hundred-pound in tax and insurance.

The American visitors came from all over the states and some had driven well over a thousand-mile or more to get there. One that we got into conversation with was from Seattle and although he lived in the USA, he'd actually travelled as far as we had to get there.

"It's only when you hear things like that that you begin to realise just how big and wide this country is." Jenny said afterwards, as she pondered the mind numbing thought of driving such a distance, but the Americans thought nothing of driving long distances.

Through trial and error we became aware that the humble meandering European pedestrian is not welcome on or near American roads. To most Americans, it seems that walking even a short distance was a crazy idea when a car was available and so walking and jogging was looked upon as an activity for keep fit fanatics.

The Orlando experience was unlike any holiday that we'd encountered before and if not planned with careful thought, could soon become mentally and physically exhausting. The best advice that we received was to visit a theme park one-day and relax at a water park the following day and visit such places as Church Street Station and Ripley's "Believe It or Not" museum. Sea World was the first theme park that we visited and it turned out to be a wonderfully experience. All day we wondered from one stunning show, featuring dolphins, sea lions and killer whales, to another and as the sun set in the West, we were entertained by dare devil water skiers, huge unbelievable holographs such as a giant Neptune with tripod rising from a boiling sea and a fantastic firework display.

Each theme park was filled with stunning shows, participation rides and wonderful sights. After each show I would say, "Well, they can't top that," but found that the next show was just as good, but in a different way and so much so that it became extremely difficult to compare one show or exhibit with another. I was also impressed by the immaculate organisation of the whole area, the theme parks, the water parks and the establishments on International Drive. The workers, the waitresses, road sweeps, grass cutters, pool attendants, bus drivers, theme park actors and attendants all seemed to be laid back and relaxed and yet everything ran on time and everywhere we looked was spotlessly clean. Every job in the tourist industry had been analysed to find out not only what was the most efficient and economical way of doing it, but what worked best for the customer. Even the queue lines for the rides were organised in such a manner that no one became bored. They either had entertainment in the form of an introductory film or were filled with interesting artefacts. While waiting for the "Jaws" ride, the queue line snaked through a New England fishing museum which was filled with sea and fishing paraphernalia. In the "Back to the Future" queue line a film was shown on overhead monitors which told a story and by the time we reached the actual ride, we were part of the story and had a purpose to be there. At the "ET" ride we walked through a replica of the dark spooky forest that was featured in the film before we mounted a bike that gave us the illusion of flying through the air.

The water parks were landscaped to a specific theme, River Island had a sand beach and a frontier log cabin look about it, Typhoon Lagoon was based on a tropical South Sea island and Blizzard Beach was a snow capped ski resort. All had a huge central pool complete with wave machine and around that there were numerous side pools with a variety of water slides and amusements. Each night with our heads full of fantastic images, we hit our beds with a thud and slept as sound as fallen logs and each morning we were up before the lark and eager to take in more.

There were many food establishments to choose from and all had reasonably priced menus. One in particular charged for the size of the steak that the customer ordered, but the amount of extras that could be obtained from the long buffet bar was unlimited and what was on offer could have fed the whole of Africa for a year. The abundance of food was everywhere and we found it difficult to cope with such enormous amounts. One evening we dined at an Italian restaurant on International Drive and we received so much food that Henry VIII and his court would have struggled to get through it. The child's portions of lasagne would quite comfortably have fed us all as each one was the size of a builder's breezeblock, but the consequences of this gluttony was plain to see, dozens of overweight families padded around in bell tent tee-shirts and elephant arsed shorts and all looked like beached whales when sunning themselves in the water parks.

We were standing in a quiet spot in Disney's Magic Kingdom one day when two bulbous American ladies waddled by, but what made this particular pair memorable was that the music being played at the time was the Elephant Walk from the Jungle Book film and as the buxom babes passed by, their ample posteriors were swaying in perfect time to the music, it was a sight that Walt Disney himself would have enjoyed.

Steve, my younger brother took his family to Orlando on several occasions and once when visiting the Magic Kingdom he chose to wear a red T-shirt for the day. Unbeknown to him, so did several hundred gays who were also visiting the theme park. They were there in force and he was not best pleased when all day long these nice friendly boys continually smiled and waved at him.

"I felt as though I was a bloody raffle prize on show." was his mournful comment.

Charlie, after scooping a considerable amount of money on a roll up bet on the horses, also took his brood to Orlando and he soon discovered that if he rapped one leg in bandages and walked with a pronounced limp, he was supplied with a wheel chair and permission to go to the front of the queue at any of the rides.

The oddest thing we witnessed was a group of Japanese tourists who in the Wet and Wild Water Park were photographing each other. When taking a photograph in and around Orlando there are numerous backdrops to choose from, in the theme parks the favourites were the model of the "Jaws" shark, the Tower of Terror, Epcots futuristic silver ball Spaceship Earth, Cinderella's Castle and Mickey Mouse and his chums. In the water parks there were scenic views, the breaker waves in the large pool or the death defying vertical water slides, but this particular group of happy tourists who were resplendent with cameras slung around their necks chose to ignore all of these backdrops and were taking photographs of each other while standing in front of a plainly painted brick wall.

"If they do that all around the world, can you imagine what their photograph album looks like?" Jenny said as she stared at the exited group in wonderment.

While walking along a Spanish beach, one of our lads, who was ten years old at the time, picked up a piece of driftwood and after throwing it as far as he could, found that he had a large splinter in his hand. I was all for prizing the splinter out with a sharp Bowie knife in the manner of a Rocky Mountain backwoodsman, but for some reason Jenny and our son, who seemed to be a little apprehensive about the process, overruled me. Back at the hotel Jenny asked at reception if they had any tweezers and was informed that they did not, which was a surprise as we had assumed that the hotel would have a comprehensive first aid kit. Back in our room we bathed his hand in TCP and decided to ask the people who occupied the next room, whom we had often heard, but had never met, if they possessed any tweezers. We'd heard chatter and loud laughing through the adjoining wall on several occasions when they'd returned from their late night revelry and we had concluded that they were probably, Spanish.

Jenny knocked on the door and when a small round middle-aged man answered it, she began to explain in slow Pigeon English and with flamboyant gesticulations what she required.

"Have..a..you," she asked while pointing at him with her fore finger, "Gota...tweezers?" and demonstrated this by clicking her finger and thumb together, "for a biga splinter ina little boy's a hand?" And with a look of severe pain upon her face, she pointed at her hand.

The small stocky man turned his head and in a very familiar Black Country accent called to his wife, "Doris, 'ave yo got sum tweezers in ya ond bog for this lady at the doo,er, only I think sumbody's got a splinter in their ond."

The Spanish family had moved out of the room earlier that morning and a family from Walsall had just moved in and because of the slow Pigeon English conversation, they were now under the impression that Jenny was Spanish and they now began to speak to her as though she was a three year old child. After a confused explanation, Jenny eventually sorted things out, acquired the much-needed tweezers and all concerned ended up laughing and conversing in a broad Black Country accent.

The Black Country family consisted of a small round father, a large rosy cheeked mother and two strapping teenaged lads and everywhere they went during their holiday the father was to be seen carrying a very large camcorder camera upon his shoulder and constantly filming the mundane actions of his large wife and his two beefy sons. One evening while drinking a beer at the hotel bar, he confessed that he was fed up to the back teeth with the unfairness of it all by saying, "That bloody camcorder gets 'eavier and 'eavier and when we gets back 'um, I bain't even on the blinkin' film. It's just as though I aint never been nowhere."

No one in the whole world ever fell up and down stairs more than Dee and when he fell up them, he invariably had his hands in his pockets. This sort of behaviour could be seen as an indication that Dee was an idiot, but surprisingly, he was a bright intelligent well-read man who could confidently discus numerous subjects in depth. He was a competent fire-fighter for many years and gradually through hard work; dedication he gained promotion, but beside his many admirable qualities he had the puzzling defect of being accident prone. If anything out of the ordinary was going to happen, such as walking into a cupboard door, dropping a Black Forest Gateau, getting lost just two streets from home or ordering fish and chips and finding that he had no money, you could guarantee it would happen to Dee.

When serving in the army, he was selected to be part of the guard of honour that was to be posted along the Mall and in front of Buckingham Palace for the visit of the King of Portugal. Dee was leading this fine body of men when they marched off Horse Guards Parade and inadvertently, he turned the wrong way and led two hundred soldiers marching off in the wrong direction. While driving along a busy high street in the car that he and his wife shared, he decided that his wife had left the seat to close to the steering wheel so he proceeded to re-adjust it. He pulled on the release handle and pushed the seat back, but instead of moving the required inch or two, it shot back to its full extent and he found that he was sitting in the back of the car and his feet were no longer in contact with the peddles. His wife, who was used to this sort of thing, looked back at him and said with an air of resignation, "Why are you sitting back there, is it something I said?"

Early one winter's morning, while on his way to a three day training course, his car broke down and he found himself stranded on the outskirts of a quiet Cotswold village. It was six in the morning and he decided to walk into the village and seek a garage. As he slowly meandered through the village, a retired colonel, who was a regular early bird, peeped out of his bedroom window and on seeing a strange man creeping through the village decided to call the police. Instead of finding a garage, Dee found himself under arrest and questioned as a suspected burglar.

One evening, he and a work colleague chatted away outside the Cotteridge fire station while waiting for the taxi that they had ordered to pick them up. A big black car pulled onto the wide pavement area and stopped alongside them and while still in deep conversation, Dee and his mate each opened a door and jumped into the car. The woman who was driving the big black car screamed loudly and jumped out of the car with the speed of a scalded cat. She was not a taxi driver after all and had pulled up onto the wide pavement to park while she went to collect her daughter from the nearby Girl Guide group.

While working as a part time security guard at a large city centre office block, Dee decided to spend his fifteen minute break in a designated disabled toilet. "There's more room in them than in an ordinary toilet," he said when explaining his reasons for going in there, "and I wanted to read my book for a few minutes."

Once inside the spacious toilet he locked the door, but found that there was insufficient light with which to read his book in comfort, so he pulled the light cord and, just as many others had done, found that the red cord was attached to an alarm. Before he could make good his escape, helpful do-gooders were banging on the door and loudly asking whether he needed them to break the door down. Now Dee did not want to be found hiding in a disabled toilet as it would be very embarrassing and looked upon as cardinal sin by his employers. So, he cupped his hands around his mouth and in his best nasal imitation of Quasimodo, the hunchback of Notre-Dame he called back through the door, "I'm alright." His would be helpers who were keen to become heroes were not at all reassured and called back, "Are you sure you're alright." Dee then replied in his strangled voice, "Yes I'm sure. I pulled the cord by mistake, I'll be out in a minute." With that, the disappointed rescue party slowly shuffled away muttering something about disabled people being bloody nuisances and after a short while, Dee made his furtive escape.

When he finally got back to the reception area, the other security guard that had been on duty during his absence informed him that, "Some silly old bugger has been and pulled the alarm cord in the disabled toilet by mistake and caused bloody chaos. But the odd thing is," The puzzled guard added as he glanced around the area, "he seems to have vanished into thin air because he hasn't passed me on the way out so I'm buggered if I know where he's got to."

Dee volunteered to act as a uniformed doorman at one of the exclusive corporate tents at the Cheltenham races and was charged with letting know one enter the marquee without having the correct pass. After several hours of standing at the marquee's entrance and checking passes he was relieved of his duties by another guard while he went for a break. After visiting one of the toilets at the race course, Dee along with many other men made his way along the crowded corridor that led to and from the toilet and there he squeezed past men who were going in the opposite direction. The commissionaire's metal badge that adorned his stout leather chest belt inadvertently got caught in a portly gentleman's shirt front as they pushed past each other in the crowded corridor and to the gentleman's surprise, several of his shirt buttons shot off in all directions. With men pushing from behind, Dee had no option but to carry on moving and once out of the crowded corridor he made himself scarce and turned up back at his post twenty minutes early. He spent the rest of the day hoping that the man with the ripped shirt and missing buttons had found a few winners and was able to purchase a new shirt.

Dee arrived home one day to find that he'd inadvertently left, along with his wallet, his house keys on the kitchen table when he'd left home earlier that morning and as his wife was not at home, he could not gain access to the house. He was not a man to give in easily and he decided to see if he could gain entry without the aid of a key and before his wife got home as he knew exactly what her sarcastic comments would be and after a hard day at work he decided that he could forego that pleasure. As he stood on the pavement and studied the problem, his very helpful neighbour, an elderly retired gentleman named Frank, who lived opposite and who had elected himself to be the neighbourhood watch, came bounding across the road to help.

"Oh bloody hell," The intrepid fire-fighter thought as he saw Old Frank approach, "Just what I need, the world's leading expert on every subject under the sun."

Dee knew from passed experience that although wanting to be helpful, Old Frank would probably be of little use and would no doubt get in the way, but he also knew that getting rid of him was impossible and so after explaining his problem, he asked helpful Old

Frank to see if there was anything in his garage that would be of assistance.

"I was thinking along the lines of a box of old keys," Dee said later, "and what did he come back with? A full set of "Do it yourself" books that covered every subject from lighting a fire with a couple of dry sticks to Einstein's theory of relativity."

Undaunted, he made good use of them and stood on them while he tried to open a small ground floor window. Being unsuccessful in this attempt he then hit upon an idea that he'd seen in numerous detective films, namely the access to premises by a stiff plastic card. His own bank card, being in his wallet, which was sitting on the kitchen table, was of no use to him so he asked helpful Old Frank if he could borrow his. Frank gleefully produced his credit card and glowing with pride he handed it over to Dee with the message that, "It's a Gold one. They don't issue those to just anyone you know."

Professionally and with great care Dee inserted the stiff plastic card into the slit of the door where the Yale lock was situated and began to carefully push the card against the locks brass wedge. After five minutes of pushing, pulling, sliding and wiggling nothing had happened and he reluctantly retrieved the card and to his, and helpful Old Frank's dismay, found that the end of the Gold credit card was now tattered and shredded and was of little use as burglar's tool or for withdrawing money from a cash machine.

Plan "B" was now put into action as Dee had noticed that a small bedroom window was slightly ajar and helpful Old Frank had at last remembered that he had a ladder hanging on his garage wall. Dee quickly climbed up to the bedroom window and managed to open the small window to its full extent. He squeezed in and managed to release the catch on the larger window. All he had to do now was to roll headfirst through the open window and onto the bedroom floor, which he managed to do quite easily and only acquired a couple of small bruises in the process. He ran downstairs rubbing his bruised head and shoulder, opened the front door, thanked helpful Old Frank for all his help, apologised again for shredding his Gold credit card and helped him to cross the road with his ladder and on returning, he realised that he'd not only shut the front door behind him when he'd come out of the house, but had also forgotten to pick up the house keys off the kitchen table. And so he and helpful Old Frank, who by now was beginning to tire of being so helpful, had to start all over again.

The tales of Dee's many mishaps, such as driving up one way streets, parking in car parks that closed early, falling off ladders and walking into doors could fill a book, but strangely he was not the only man to find himself plagued with unforeseen problems. A fire-fighter that Dee worked alongside who through having suffered one mishap after another, had acquired the nickname of Lucky Luke and it was a name that fitted him like a glove as he had a history of becoming involved in unusual incidents one of which was getting himself locked inside a toilet in the Barcelona Olympic Stadium. Sweating profusely he was finally released from the hot lavatory cubical and when he finally emerged he was in his own words, "lobster pink and several bloody pounds lighter."

Sitting on the coach that was taking Lucky Luke and his family to the airport at the end of their eventful holiday, he realised that he did not feel at all comfortable. The wide waistband on his brightly coloured designer underpants that his wife had purchased for him to smarten up his manly image in the bedroom was pressing on his stomach and he realised that the long flight home was going to be an uncomfortable nightmare. At the airport, he went to the toilet and took off the offending tight underpants. As he stepped out of the toilet area and back into the crowded concourse he spied a rubbish bin and discretely dropped the offending underpants into it. As he walked the few steps back to where his wife and kids were sitting, a young lad who was in the process of discarding a drinks carton into the waste bin spied the brightly coloured underpants and between finger and thumb he extracted them. He then held the underpants up for all to see and in a loud voice called across to his parents, "Ooow, look what somebody's put in the bin!"

On seeing this, Lucky Luke's youngest son, in a voice that was equally loud, declared to the amusement of all in the vicinity, "Those are your new underpants aren't they Dad?"

There are numerous tales concerning the eccentricities of the fire-fighters, but even they can be considered mild when compared to some of the people that they meet while out on emergency calls.

"I was just cleaning the grease off the kitchen walls with a bit of rag and a bowl of petrol and when I lit a cigarette..." explained the puzzled young man whose shirt front, eyebrows and most of his hair had been burnt away and who's kitchen was now nothing more than a blackened burnt out shell.

The nineteen eighties brought along the Falklands War, the miners' strike, the disaster at Chernobyl and the terrorist bombed plane at Lockerbie. There were riots in Lozells, Birmingham and Argentines Maradona showed the world how to score a goal with the hand of God and a short sighted referee. The eighties also brought along the films "Star Wars," "Raiders of the Lost Ark," "ET" and "Rambo," and the television programmes "The Young Ones," "Eastenders," "Allo, Allo" and "Blackadder." Michael Jackson sang "I'm Bad" and every drunk in the land learned the words to the song, "This is my Life."

Although the residents in Birmingham had no direct link with the coal miners who went on strike in the mid-eighties, they never the less, found themselves sucked into the emotional turmoil that the strike created and inevitably they began to choose sides. There were those that agreed with Maggie Thatcher and felt that it was time to smash, not only the miners and their union, but all the workers unions. On the other side there were those that, although they knew that the miners couldn't possibly win, believed that each day that they held out was a slap in the face for the much disliked Maggie and her bombastic style of government. Money was eventually raised from all quarters for the miners and they held out for a lot longer than anyone expected and by doing so, even earned a grudging respect from the media and the many who disagreed with them.

Feelings and emotions in the country ran high during this period causing families and whole communities to split. The police, who were used by the government on many occasions as a battering ram in the mining communities did their "Hello, hello, British Bobby" image and their reputation for being impartial immense harm and they will never be forgiven by many for what they did at this time. The photograph of a mounted policeman lashing out at a woman demonstrator with a long baton was shown all around the world and it still hangs on many a wall as a reminder of those hateful times. For my friends and I it was the nearest that we had ever come to experiencing what it must feel like to be involved in a dreaded civil war. Many people outside the conflict felt genuinely sorry for the coal miners and their hopeless cause, but their hard line leader was a man that few could take to and most would not have followed him to the corner pub for free drinks, never mind the revolutionary barricades that he seemed to have in mind, but on the other hand, many would not have followed Maggie Thatcher either. When the coal dust finally settled, Maggie was not only looked upon as a figure of fun by many, but hated with a passion that was truly disturbing.

Turners had become so successful that the directors decided to expand the company by acquiring many smaller companies Many of the companies that they acquired were small businesses that had nothing to do with the core trade of building supplies and for a time humble workers such as I had little to do with the new acquisitions or their employees. But eventually a building supplies company was acquired that was situated in the South West of England and as the two companies would be working together, it was thought appropriate for the staff of both companies to meet and become better aquatinted with each other. The venue chosen was an old pub that was half-way between the two companies and had a function room that was furnished with an ancient wooden skittle alley. The workers travelled to the venue by coach while the company directors, to keep the social distance that is required on such occasions, travelled by car. This was a wise move as it is well known that after a few drinks, one or two workers are apt to say things that they are liable to regret in the light of the following morning.

The old pubs long function room was furnished with a small bar, a row of tables and chairs and a well-worn wooden skittle alley. The ancient game of skittles is played in exactly the same way as ten pin bowls, except that someone has to keep putting the wooden skittles back up each time that they are knocked down. In mediaeval times it would have been the village idiot that was talked into doing this monotonous task with the promise of free beer. We persuaded Cyril, our very own aristocrat, to take on this important task, "You're the only one we can trust to do the job without favouring one side or the other," he was informed and as they were the very words that he'd always longed to hear, he set about his task with the seriousness of a cup final referee.

The evening progressed exceptionally well, the directors stayed together near the bar, sipped their drinks and made stilted jolly comments to the various workers as they made their way to the bar to order their pints of free beer. The workers, who were not particularly articulate, grinned sheepishly and agreed with anything that was said and a light hearted ambiance pervaded the room.

Butch and I did our best to cement friendships with the other company's workers and the skittle competition continued throughout the evening. Everyone ate well and drank plenty and towards the end of the evening and after the directors had diplomatically made their escape, the noise in the room became noticeably louder and far more vociferous.

A little later it was noticed that Benny the lorry driver, who'd been drinking heavily all evening, was lying flat on his back in the skittle alley among the wooden skittles and was desperately trying to right himself. He looked as though he was imitating a giant turtle that had found itself upside-down as his arms and legs were flapping about and his puzzled eyes seemed to be trying to work out which was the right way up. A couple of storemen helped him to his feet and propped him up against the bar where he stood in the shape of a letter 'S' and grinned inanely.

When time was called the workers from both companies finished off their beers and said their exaggerated farewells and Butch and I apologised to the pubs gaffer for the numerous broken plates that littered the tables. One silly bugger had thrown a wooden ball and had completely missed the skittle alley and like a cannon ball, it had shot along the table tops. Then in a merry mood, both groups of workers boarded their respective coach's for their trip home. Benny, who'd been half dragged and half carried aboard the coach, collapsed in his seat and disappeared from view and as far we were concerned, that was the last that we would hear from him.

During the journey home we sang the usual pub songs, cracked the usual inane jokes, light heartedly insulted each other and laughed our socks off, then a few miles outside Brum, much to everyone's surprise, Benny reappeared. With his hands on the top of the seat in front of him, he pulled himself up until his head could be seen and with a silly grin upon his sleepy face he asked hopefully, "Has anyone got a drink?"

The first stop that the coach made was at the Black Horse pub on the Bristol Road and was for the sole purpose of dropping Benny off, as he lived but a short distance from it. One of the storemen proceeded to open the coach's sliding door from the inside, but for some unknown reason the door stuck fast and would not open more than a few inches. On seeing this, two more men jumped out of the emergency exit door that was situated behind the driver's seat and attempted to wrench the sliding door open from the outside. Meanwhile Benny, who'd been staggering slowly down the coach and saying his fond farewells reached the front of the coach and on finding that the door was still jammed, did no more than walk straight out of the emergency exit, which was approximately three feet above ground level and he landed in the middle of the Bristol Road. Now that particular thoroughfare is not only busy throughout the day, but also throughout the night and as Benny disappeared from view those of us who were sitting near the emergency door picked up in our peripheral vision the unmistakable sight of several vehicles zipping past the parked coach and for a few seconds, we all stopped breathing as we waited to hear the sickening thud as one of the vehicles ploughed into Benny as he staggered about in the middle of the busy road. But miraculously, he staggering around the coach and seemed none the worse for his fall or his death defying walkabout.

We shouted our goodbyes to Benny who was now standing on the pavement, swaying, waving and unsuccessfully attempting to deliver an articulate sentence as the coach slowly pulled away. The coach driver then pulled off the Bristol Road and made his way to Cotteridge where he dropped several people off and then made his way to Selly Oak where he once more joined the Bristol Road and there, ten minutes after he'd been dropped off two mile away in Northfield, stood Benny. He was standing by the traffic lights and looking dazed and bewildered. The storeman who got off at Selly Oak then took charge of him, called for a taxi and took him home.

The only explanation that we could come up with for Benny's unexpected reappearance two mile from where he'd been dropped off was that he must have stepped onto a night service bus and got off in Selly Oak, but it was all supposition as Benny could not remember anything that had happened after nine o' clock the previous evening.

Having been abandoned by his exasperated wife, Benny now lived alone in a small, but surprisingly clean and tidy council house. He may have been a habitual drunk, but he was surprisingly fastidious in his cleaning habits. Many years earlier, Benny's wife had left him after having decided to live with her attentive lover, but being a staunch catholic she had not seen fit to divorce Benny. She believed that living with someone that she was not married to and sharing his bed was a forgivable sin, but that divorce was not. Such is the power of religious conviction.

Benny spent his leisure time in a working man's club playing dominoes and drinking substantial quantities of beer. The one thing that was missing from Benny's life was regular sexual pleasure and he was apt to fondle a buxom woman's bottom whenever the opportunity presented itself whether the woman required his amorous attention or not. But not far from where he lived, help was at hand in the form of a divorcee who seemed to have a similar problem and after Benny and the divorcee had bumped into each other a few times at the working men's club and had exchanged abbreviated details of their life stories, they became aware that they were in the same boat and could help each other out.

When explaining this situation to his workmates, Benny admitted that the divorcee wasn't the most attractive of women and the fact that she weighed eighteen stone did little to help matters either, but Benny was the first to admit that he was no oil painting either and when their lustful urges were aroused it was irrelevant to either what they looked like. Whether this buxom divorcee was looking for marriage no one knew, but we knew that although he was living the life of a single man, technically, as his wife would never consent to a divorce, he was still married.

The buxom divorcee and Benny began to see each other once a week for a regular night out and Benny, using one of the company's small pickup trucks that he borrowed for the occasion would drive out to a pub near Bromsgrove for a quiet drink and a friendly chat. And on the way back home, when it was nice and dark, he would pull into a lay-by so that they could enjoy a kiss and cuddle and explore each other's intimate parts. During one of these passionate sessions in the cab of the small lorry, they had removed most of their restricting clothing and while they were busy enjoying their sensual groping, a coach containing day trippers who were on their way home, drew up alongside the small lorry and the light emanating from the coach illuminated their contortions. Unsurprisingly, Benny, who had his trousers around his ankles and was in a state of arousal, became quite flustered and in a blind panic and without bothering to dress, he drove off like a bat out of hell while his eighteen stone lover, who filled most of the cab, squealed and scrambled about looking for her clothes to help cover her ample bust and private parts and although she was in a state of shock, she still found time to call Benny a dopey sod for parking in such a busy place. The next day, Benny was heard to say rather indignantly, "Them nosey buggers on the coach was all gorping at us as though we was a bleeding floor show at a night club."

Benny, who was always willing to help anyone who was in trouble, picked up a young Scottish hitchhiker from the slip road of a service station on the M1 motorway one Friday morning. The young man was a little dishevelled and looked as though he had been sleeping rough, but that didn't bother Benny as he himself had been in the same condition on many occasions.

"I'm going as far as Camden Town." Benny said to the Scottish hitchhiker as they drove off down the motorway towards London, "Will that do you?"

"Camden Town?" the dishevelled hitchhiker asked questionably, "Where's that?"

"London." Benny replied rather surprised, "It's in London. This side of the river."

"London!" the hitchhiker yelled and in good Glaswegian added, "I'm no going ti London mon; I'm on ma way ti Glasgee!"

The young man had been to a mid-week football match at Wembley Stadium and after a few drinks to many he'd missed his coach back to Glasgow. He'd hitchhiked north and somehow he'd lost his bearings after using the toilets at a motorway services station and had accidentally crossed the motorway and was now travelling back to London and almost back to where he'd started from.

The Penguin, who was in charge of the Black Country satellite depot, had earned himself the reputation of a man to avoid. He'd upset numerous drivers who delivered goods to his depot and many of the office staff at head office who dealt with him on the telephone. Billy, who had tired of working in the tube store had once more become a lorry driver, had had several run-ins with the Penguin and declared that, "He's a pompous loud mouthed bully, who likes the sound of his own voice."

One way and another, I'd avoided too much contact with the man, but one day, right out of the blue, a row broke out concerning the delivery of a load of goods to a customer and my relationship with the Penguin was to change forever. The Penguin claimed that the wrong sized tube had been delivered to his customer and I claimed that what had been sent was exactly what he had ordered. Eventually the Penguin and I were summoned to head office where the matter was to be investigated by one of the directors. The three of us sat around the large board room table and the Penguin aggressively accused me of being both incompetent and a liar, both of which were true, but on this occasion I knew that I was in the right and I produced a confirmation order which had been sent from the Penguins depot which proved that the goods that had been sent was what had been ordered. On seeing this confirmation order, the Penguin countered with a tirade of fruity bar room language and stated that what he'd ordered on the telephone was not the same as what was printed on the confirmation order. Finding the whole affair irritating and irrelevant as there was nothing that could be done other than send the right goods and pick up that which was wrong, which by that time had already been done, I stated that I thought that the Penguin was just being childish and ought to grow up and by doing so, I inadvertently stumbled upon his Achilles heel.

The Penguin ruled his staff with a rod of iron and he not only expected to be disliked and called insulting names behind his back, but it was confirmation that he was a strong boss. By now he was fully aware that he was known around the company as the Flying Penguin and it did not bother him in the slightest as he fully expected to be feared and called such names, but not to be taken seriously was something that he could not abide and on hearing me dismiss him for being no more than a silly child had the effect of turning him into an inarticulate red faced brat who suddenly found that he couldn't get his own way. On seeing this, the director quickly brought the meeting, which had solved nothing, to a close and without much conviction warned us both to behave ourselves. Although I now knew that I'd made a formidable enemy, I also knew that I'd found the bullies weakness and from that day on, whenever our paths crossed, I made sure that the Penguin was well aware that I was laughing at him.

On the face of it, the Penguin's style of management, which was basically to bawl and shout at his staff as often as possible seemed to work well enough while he was about, but as soon as he disappeared, either into his office or to the local pub, his disgruntled workforce put two fingers up in his direction, took unofficial breaks and their work rate slowed considerably. Because of his constant bullying, numerous drivers and storemen at his depot left the company, but before departing they treated themselves to a little act of revenge. This usually took the form of writing insulting graffiti messages about the stores, stealing something they thought would be useful or direct acts of sabotage. Delivery notes disappeared and bags of fittings had their labels removed so that they could not be delivered until they had been checked.

The Penguin was never bothered by any of these acts of sabotage as he took them to be the normal behaviour of disgruntled staff and it must be admitted that around him, these acts were normal and he would simply order his staff to clear up the mess, employ a new driver or storeman and the whole bullying pantomime would begin all over again.

There were many weird and wonderful agency drivers who were employed by Turners when a regular driver was either on holiday or off sick, but Simon stood out from the rest as he was completely different to any that we had seen before. He was one of the funniest men that we had ever met and brought to mind the film and radio comedian, Kenneth Williams. He was a camp homosexual who had a mincing walk, expressive flapping hands, a voice full of singsong cadence and a face that continually over animated his numerous expressions. For many years, he'd been a coach driver and although he was only with us for two days, we could see that he must have been an excellent one as he was a competent driver and had a lively exuberant personality. He would have made an excellent compe're at a variety club, a member of an airline cabin crew or even a tour guide. What he was not however, was a rough and ready lorry driver who could, and was expected to unload heavy steel tube off the back of a lorry on building sites and at factory maintenance stores in all weather's.

He backed the ten ton lorry into the tube store; introduced himself, handed over his delivery notes for the day and the storemen began loading his lorry with steel tube. As the storemen loaded his lorry, one bundle at a time with the aid of an overhead crane, I chatted to him and discovered a little of his history. It seems that he'd recently fallen out with the boss of the coach company and had left in a bit of a huff and was now doing odd jobs for the agency.

"I told him straight," Simon informed me with a look of "I couldn't care less" on his face, "you can get someone else to blow your trumpet and tinkle your triangle ducky, I'm off to pastures new."

We'd been chatting for some time when suddenly he said with a note of concern in his high pitched voice, "Hold on a minute! How many more of them big heavy pipes are you going to put onto that lorry?"

I, who could see nothing abnormal with what was going on, just replied, "Well, we're about half way through loading. There's about the same amount to go on yet. Why, what's the problem?"

"What's the problem?" He spluttered, his voice rising even higher as he looked at me in wide eyed amazement, "The problem my dear chapie, is that my names Simon not bloody Samson. There is no way I'm going to lift all that lot off on my own."

Trying to placate him, I just said, "Well at some of these places that you're delivering to, you might get a bit of help."

"Might get a bit of help!" He exclaimed, with a look of astonishment on his face as he took in this snippet of information, and then vigorously shaking his head from side to side he stated, "I'd need the help of a brigade of bleeding Guards to get that lot off."

Realising that there was trouble ahead, I swiftly took him into the nearby office and pointing to the telephone I said, "You'd better sort out your problem with the transport manager before we go any further."

Eventually a very irate Simon spoke to the transport manager, the man who in his infinite wisdom had given him such a large and heavy load to deliver and during the ensuing argument Simon said, "Now look love, I'm a driver see, not bloody King Kong. If them steel pipes are heavy enough to be loaded onto the lorry by a bleeding overhead crane, they should be unloaded by a bleeding overhead crane at the point of delivery and not by me on me own."

After more arguing it was eventually agreed that his load for that day should be cut and he eventually left the premises with only half of what he'd originally come for and the next day he came back for the second half of the load. As the storemen loaded his lorry for his second day's delivery run, he told us all about the previous day's experiences and how exhausting he had found the unloading the steel tubes was.

"When I got home last night, I was as limp as a wet lettuce," he stated while imitating a man who'd just crossed the Sahara desert on his hands and knees, "and I hardly had the strength to stir the sugar in my tea. I could hardly pick up the spoon to eat my cock-a-leaky soup and as for my prawn balls, they'll have to wait for another day."

After an exaggerated sigh and putting the back of one hand to his forehead, he said, "I said to mother, mother, a week of this and I'll either look like Mr Bloody Universe or kicking up daisies in the cemetery."

One of the storemen then said, "Don't worry mate, you'll soon get used to it."

"Oh, not me love, I'm off." Simon replied, "I told that pillock of a transport manager, that this is my last day and I'm packing it in after this load is done. I said to him, this aint the life for me chuck, you'll have to get someone else to do it and do you know what the silly sod said? He said, "Nobody told me you were packing up today." So I said to him, I'm a bloody well telling you ain't I? Between you and me love, I don't think he's got a lot upstairs and from what I've heard, what he's got down stairs wouldn't make a Nun blush either. Anyway after that he said, "Well make sure that you fly round and deliver everything today before you finish." So I said to him, look here chuck, I shall do my best like I always do, but I'm just an ordinary run of the mill driver, if you want racing drivers, you'd better get off down to Silverstone and sort some out."

The following week Simon was back driving holiday coaches and entertaining his happy passengers with his endless stock of deadpan double entedre's, "Be careful where you sit love, last week a lady accidentally sat on a cucumber. Oh, it was a terrible shock, but it did put a smile on her face. She said it reminded her of a sailor she once knew" and "Now remember, if you're not back here by eight o' clock sharp, I shall, as the actress said to the Bishop, start without you."

Gibo was out shopping at a busy local shopping centre when a shabbily dressed young woman pushing a pram that contained a small scruffy toddler, ambled by. Suddenly she stopped, pointed an accusing finger at a man on the opposite side of the busy road and in a loud penetrating voice called out, "Arthur Persil! You are the father of my child and I shall see you in court!"

"Bollocks." replied Arthur Persil and he carried on walking.

"In those few words I'd witnessed a whole episode of attraction, love, lust, disappointment, hate and vengeance." Gibo declared.

One evening, Mitch walked into the Sailors and there he joined Billy and his older brother Trapper who were standing at the bar drinking.

"Alright lads," Mitch said warmly as he extracted a ten pound note from his wallet, "How are things with you then Trapper?"

"Oh, not too bad, can't complain. You alright? Business good?"

"Better than it used to be, thank god."

Then catching the barmaids eye Mitch called, "Three pints of larger love, cheers"

"By the way," Mitch then said to his two friends while the barmaid set about pulling the three pints, "any idea who that black taxi cab belongs to that's parked outside?"

"Why?" Trapper asked while smiling, "Going somewhere?"

"Oh no," Mitch replied, "It's just that I've seen it parked out there before. It's just a bit odd that's all, you'd think that it would be out picking up customers at this time of night wouldn't you."

"Perhaps the driver's having a break." Billy suggested while trying to suppress a sly snigger.

"What the bloody hell are you two laughing at?" Mitch asked as he could clearly see that they were trying to stifle silly sniggers.

"That taxi outside," Billy explained, "It's his."

"Whose?"

"Mine." Said Trapper.

"Since when have you been a bloody taxi driver?"

"I'm not; I just bought the cab to get about in, it's the one vehicle that never gets stopped when you've had a drink."

"You're joking!"

"No honest, they never stop a black cab."

"Well don't people try and flag you down?"

"Oh yes and sometimes I pick them up."

"The meter works then does it?"

"Oh no, I just ask them where they want to go and if its local I just say, Well I'm off duty now, but I can give you a lift for a couple of quid and they inevitably say, okay. Well it helps to pay the way don't it."

After surviving many mishaps, Mitch was gradually beginning to establish himself as a successful transport company. One of the reasons for his change in fortunes was that he'd become quite friendly with a transport manager at a large manufacturing facility that was situated in Smethwick and through this friendship; he was able to acquire lucrative delivery jobs that were suitable for a large van. It was also lucrative for the transport manager as he and Mitch had an amicable arrangement that could be best summed up as, "you scratch my back and I'll scratch yours." These jobs were usually urgent deliveries and Mitch found himself travelling all over the country and frequently ended up eating in greasy spoon cafes and back street pubs and after one such long journey, he arrived back in Brum during the lunch period and decided to stop at a back street pub that was just off Spring Hill for some well-earned sustenance. He was not due to do any more deliveries that day and had only to report back to the factories transport manager after his lunch break to see what deliveries there were for the following day. He wasn't sure who used the pub or what there would be in the way of a mid-day menu, but as he was just killing time and needed to relax for a while, he wasn't particularly bothered.

On entering the pub he was shocked to see sitting up at the bar perched upon a bar stool, a young man that he'd been previously informed was dead and had been for over two years.

"Although he had his jacket collar turned up and was wearing sunglasses, there was no mistake," Mitch said as he told Billy and me of the strange meeting, "I could see straight away that it was Joey Steel, the very same Joey Steel that was supposed to have died from a massive heart attack two years ago. Anyway, I sidled up to him slapped him on the back and said, "Hello Joey! What are you doing in this neck of the woods? I thought you were supposed to be dead and buried."

"What did he say to that?" Questioned Billy.

"Well, what with the shock of having his back slapped and seeing me standing there, he choked on his beer and almost had the heart attack he was supposed to have had two years earlier. Anyway, after he'd stopped choking, he splutters, "Shush! Keep your voice down. Someone might hear you." So I say's, So what? What are you on about?"

After taking a swig of his pint, Mitch continued, "Well his explanation boiled down to this. Three years ago, he got into financial difficulties and he borrowed money, one thousand five hundred pound to be precise, from Bomber Banks, that money-lending thug from West Brom and he hadn't realised, that not only did he have to pay back the money that he'd borrowed by a certain time, but also a substantial amount of interest on top. Well when he fell behind with his payments, Bomber increased the interest rate and Joey realised that he would never be able to pay off the debt. Bomber threatened to break his bleeding legs and all that sort of thing and Joey panicked and came up with his master plan. He talked his wife into saying that he'd died of a massive heart attack while he was visiting relatives in London. She was then to claim that these relatives had organised his funeral in London and that he'd been cremated and so there was no grave to visit. Meanwhile, Joey secretly moved out of his own home and moved in with his wife's sister who lives near this pub by Spring Hill and he has been hiding there ever since."

"Hiding?" Billy queried.

"That's exactly what I said," Mitch said as he shook his head in disbelief, "I said to him, what do you mean, you're hiding? You're only two bleeding mile from your own house! It can't be more than six bloody stops on the bus!"

"Well I can't go too far away can I?" He said while looking as though he'd lost a ten pound note, "I have to see the Missis and the kids now and again and I have to draw my dole money from the Labour Exchange don't I? I mean, I haven't told them that I'm dead have I? I'm not that daft."

"Well don't any of your mates recognise you when you're in the Labour Exchange? I asked."

"Well one or two have, but I go in disguise see and if they ask, I tell them that I'm not me, I'm Sid, me younger brother."

It was during this period that Mitch became a semi-professional gambler. He'd been gambling since he'd been a teenager, I think he'd picked the habit up from his old man as his dad was always sending him down to the bookies with his tightly folded bets. Anyway as gamblers go, Mitch had been quite successful up to date as overall he'd always managed to win more than he'd lost and now having a reasonable income coming in from his transport business he was better off than he'd been for years and had more money to throw around. Whether this new wealth clouded his judgement or Lady

387

Luck simply deserted him I don't really know, but after a few months of riding high, he began to lose badly and found himself deep in dept. And as if that wasn't bad enough, it turned out that the money he owed, he owed to Eddie Rogers, the gangland entrepreneur.

We'd first met and got to know Eddie Rogers in the Matador coffee bar when he occasionally popped round to see Cato and Anton and we knew through talking to Zac that he was behind many shady deals that went on in and around the city, though the nearest we ever got to knowing any details of a job was when Max was trying to offload a lorry load of cigarettes. Among the townies it was rumoured that Rogers had bankrolled many hoists and robberies, but wisely, he never took part in any himself.

When the nightclubs began to spring up around the city, he was at the forefront and occasionally we'd see him in one of his clubs and pass the time of day with him and he was one of the first to open a gambling casino and it was in his casino that Mitch had lost his money and had run up his substantial debts. Now a couple of years earlier, when Mitch had been on his uppers, he'd helped Bronco to remove a substantial amount of Aluminium from a large factory. The job had been well set up; the security guard on the gate was in the know and had just waved them through and the scrap yard where they'd delivered it to had a lorry ready and waiting to whisk the illegal load off to another part of the country.

"I was shit scared from the beginning to the end" Mitch later reported to Billy and me, "There was so much weight on the old van, when we were going down the hill in Great Charles Street, the front wheels were hardly touching the road, we were actually doing bleeding wheelies and going round corners was like steering a bloody oil tanker. I kept thinking, if this van breaks down now, we're well and truly stuffed."

Well what Mitch did not know at the time was that the job had been set up by Rogers and now to "Help clear your dept." he wanted Mitch to do another job for him, namely burgle a large house that was full of antiques and that's when Mitch roped me and Billy in to help him. To give Rogers his due, I have to admit that the job was well planned. Bronco turned up with a van that had false number plates and Mitch was supplied with the details of the alarm system and a comprehensive list of all the antiques that were to be removed and which rooms they were in, he also had the combination of the safe. He was under orders to remove all the jewellery from the safe which included a large diamond which Billy and I knew nothing about and while Mitch was doing the safe, Billy and I were to fill our holdall bags with the antiques.

Because the house was secluded and not overlooked by neighbours and the owner was away on holiday with his bimbo girlfriend, who incidentally had supplied all the relevant information to Rogers, it was decided to do the job at three in the afternoon. So as not to draw attention to ourselves, we wore normal clothes with only caps and scarves for disguise, there were to be no comical black and white hooped tops, black masks and swag bags for this job. We'd rehearsed the raid and the whole job went like clockwork, the only note of discord being Billy's enquiry as to whether he could take home some of the old toys that were on display in a glass cabinet for his kids. There were several very old board games such as snakes and ladders and Ludo, wooden jig saw puzzles, a large jar of marbles, clockwork tin toys and a number of wooden toys which included a snapping crocodile on wheels. You'd have been lucky to get fifty quid for the lot.

"Don't be stupid," Mitch snapped his nerves obviously on edge, "Look Billy the antiques are worth thousands, we can't waste time on that old crap, besides kids don't play with that stuff now."

And I had to agree with Mitch, when did you last see any kids playing with a spinning top, marbles or cigarette cards? No, the collection, although interesting, was a trip down memory lane and would not bring a substantial financial reward. It wasn't till we were back in the van and on our way back to town that Mitch informed us that the whole purpose of the robbery was to obtain Big Bertha, a very large diamond and that he'd not found it in the safe where it should have been.

"So what?" Billy said quite logically, "These antiques are worth a bloody fortune, surely that clears your dept. and leaves plenty over."

"I don't know so much Billy." Mitch said a note of trepidation in his voice, "Rogers wanted that diamond more than he wanted my dept. cancelled, these blokes with plenty of money are all the same, its objects like rare paintings and Ming vases that they want more than cash, you see they've all got that, what they need is something to show off, something that nobody else has got."

"Daft I call it" Billy said, quoting our much used line from the Knockout comic.

"You may be right, but I've got a feeling he's going to be a little pissed off." Predicted Mitch depressingly.

And how right he was, a few days later, Rogers thugs caught me outside the Sailors and threw me into the back of a van which sped off into the night and I was systematically beaten up and repeatedly asked to tell them where the diamond was, which obviously I couldn't and which didn't help my cause one bit. I was eventually found lying unconscious, badly bruised and battered near Cannon Hill Park and was whisked off to Selly Oak Hospital. Although hazy for a few days, I had the good sense to keep my gob shut when being questioned by the Police and by Jenny. Later I was told that Rogers had now forgiven me as he now believed that we did not have the diamond after all.

"The way my boys worked him over," He'd said to Mitch, "He'd have told us if you'd pulled a fast one."

Which as you can imagine, was a great comfort to me as I lay in hospital, bruised black and blue from head to toe, but I did notice that he hadn't send me any bloody grapes.

Webber the policeman was the next to turn up. He was now a fully-fledged detective and he still occasionally popped into the Sailors while trying to pick up useful tit-bits of information and because I was a slight acquaintance, he told me that he'd taken it upon himself to get personally involved in the case. I feigned dizziness and loss of memory and let him do most of the talking and I was amazed at just how much he knew and I very soon concluded that he could only have got his inside information through Rogers. Not directly of course, he never worked that way, but he must have told someone to drop us in it as Webber suspected that Mitch and Billy had been involved and that a large diamond was missing. So, did Rogers think that we still had the diamond and was trying to make us panic and force our hand, if so he was barking up the wrong tree, but that didn't get Webber off our backs did it, he was like a bloody dog with a bone, he just wouldn't let go.

It was through Webber that I learned that the house we'd robbed belonged to a crook named Nicos and was a so called friend of Rogers, evidently they'd done some shady drug deals in the past and presumably that's how Rogers knew about the antiques and the diamond. Months past, Nicos claimed the insurance money for the missing antiques and the missing diamond, so there it was, the diamond was definitely missing, so who had it? The only thing I knew for certain was that it wasn't me.

I obtained a small packet of heroin from one of my mates in Leicester where Rogers had no sway or informers as I was determined to keep its source a secret so that it could not be traced back to me. I then dogged Rogers intermittently for several weeks until I found the weak link that I was looking for. I found that when he popped into his many business premises for a short stay, he regularly failed to lock his car, being king of the castle for so long he had the confidence of a dictator and besides, who would be daft enough to steal an Aston Martin that belonged to a ruthless gangster?

It was Friday evening and Rogers had just popped into the hairdressing salon that he owned in Bearwood and I knew that he'd be at least ten minutes or more while he chatted up the three young women who worked there to show them how virile and wealthy he was. I simply opened the passenger door of his car, flipped open the glove compartment and slipped the packet of heroin into it, I then carefully smashed a back light with a hammer wrapped in a woollen sock. A quick walk to the nearest phone box, a call to Webber and the deed was done. As I knew exactly where Rogers next call would be, the police were there waiting for him and because of the broken back light they examined his car and found the packet of heroin which gave them the excuse to search his house and there they found a large stash of drugs as Webber had predicted.

It was during the nineteen eighties that Jenny's mother Betty passed away. She'd been ill for some considerable time so her death was not totally unexpected, but even so, losing a well-loved member

391

of the family was still a traumatic experience for everyone involved. She'd been a hard working woman, had nursed her own mother through old age and had raised three children, two boys and a girl.

I took to Betty from the first day that I met her, even though she could never remember my name with any certainty, but this forgetfulness was not confined to me alone; as she had trouble remembering anyone's name, including her own children. There were times when it got so bad, the family threatened to wear luggage labels around their necks just as the kids had done when being evacuated to the countryside during the war years. Betty was a happy, chatty woman who lived for her family and of course, part of that family was her husband Jim. Jim nursed her through her final weeks and was broken hearted when she eventually passed away, for they'd been a devoted couple.

Jim was small in stature, easy-going and affable for most of the time and he made friends with almost everyone he met, but there were times when he could be stubborn, cantankerous and outspoken. He could be penny pinching mean in one area and philanthropic to a fault in another. When his children were growing up he was often stern in manner and mean with pocket money as his intention was to make them tough, resourceful and independent and yet, as soon as they'd reached adulthood, he was forever forcing money upon them whether they needed it or not. The person he was most hard on was himself.

He'd been born in poverty stricken Glasgow during the nineteen twenties and on becoming an orphan at an early age, he was raised by an Aunt and uncle in a dour tenement block. When he did wrong his uncle would thrash him with a leather strap, which in the environment that they lived was the unusual form of punishment for unruly kids, but even so, it still left its mark. For most of his young life, he was, just like the other kids that lived in the area, perpetually hungry and often very cold. He earned money by doing odd jobs such as selling newspapers to the Celtic supporters outside the football ground and caddying at a local golf club on Sundays, but he never complained about his hard upbringing and always talked about it with a sense of pride and affection and believed that what had been good enough for him, was good enough for anyone. He had no time for self-indulgent behaviour or anything that he considered to be the slightest namby-pamby.

As there was no work to be had in Glasgow, at the age of fourteen, he packed his meagre belongings and moved to London where he found that where there is an abundance of hotels; there are plenty of menial jobs to be had.

On the third of September 1939, the Second World War broke out and although only seventeen, he joined the Cameron Highlanders and soon realised that life in the British army was not dissimilar to the life that he'd been leading while working in the hotels as he was expected to be subservient when taking orders, perform menial tasks at the drop of a hat, be on call at a moment's notice, keep his uniform spick and span and, as he'd been sharing a room with two other men, he found barrack room living no different.

Along with thousands of others, he was given an intensive course of basic training and quickly turned into a fighting machine and when the military authorities judged that the time was right; his regiment was shipped off to Egypt to face the might of Rommel's Afrika Korps.

The Cameron Highlanders were eventually moved up to the front line and there he was to witness the reality of brutal war. The images that he witnessed hit home and were never to be erased from his memory. Young men that he'd lived and laughed with for the past few months were maimed, killed and blown to smithereens. All around him he saw death and destruction and often wondered just how long he would last in this hellish and unpredictable environment.

He was in several battles, but this was at the time when Rommel, The Desert Fox, was in his prime and the allied forces often found themselves in retreat and after one scrappy battle, he was captured and as far as everyone was concerned, Jim's war was over. But having a restless rebellious nature he could not accept life in an Italian POW camp and eventually he escaped.

He and a comrade were on the loose for a whole week before an Italian farmer befriended them and then promptly turned them over to the police. Out of all the farms in the area, Jim and his companion had picked one that housed an ardent black shirt fascist. They were beaten, threatened with a firing squad and eventually sent to a different POW camp. He escaped again and he and another Scotsman, who was also named James, were chased through an area of wooded hillside by Germans on motorbikes. They decided their best chance was to split up and run in opposite directions. While Jim successfully hid in a clump of wild bushes, his friend James was captured and shot dead on the spot. Jim was captured two days later, but luckily, by a different group of soldiers. Once again he was beaten and sent to a third POW camp, one that contained many Americans.

In the middle of 1944 the allied armies took Rome and many of the Italian soldiers, including the guards at Jim's camp, gave up on the war and simply walked away. Many of these soldiers had never been true fascists and hated the Nazis as much as the allies did. Jim saw his chance, although the Italian guards had gone walkabout, he realised that the Germans would soon take over the camp and make escape impossible. So off he went again, this time heading for the mountains and the Italian partisans and leaving behind many allied prisoners including thousands of Americans lazing in the sun.

He was with the partisans for several months and involved in numerous ambushes upon German transport convoys, but because a British serving officer could not verify any of his exploits, these acts did not appear on Jim's service record and later, when he eventually turned up in Rome, this period of his wartime exploits became a bone of contention between him and the might of the British Army.

Because he spoke English, he was given the task of guiding an American pilot who'd been shot down and rescued; to the next link in the chain on his journey back to the allied lines. Although Jim could have accompanied the pilot all the way, he'd decided to stay with the partisans until the allies got closer. When speaking about this over a beer, he hinted that a young woman was involved in his decision to stay, but he never disclosed any details of this liaison to his family.

While walking into the village, Jim and the American, who were dressed as Italian peasants, came face to face with two German officers. Jim had already briefed the pilot not to speak if they met anyone and in a jovial manner, he greeted the Germans in Italian.

"Buon giorno" he called out merrily and then attempted to converse with them in Italian. They indicated that they did not speak Italian very well, so Jim then asked them if they spoke a little English.

"Ja, speak little English." One of them replied and they both smiled and so Jim continued his stilted conversation in broken English, in which they willingly participated.

"It er, a good morning, ja?" said Jim smiling.

The two Germans laughed and replied, "Ja, good morning, guttan tag."

"We, er, international," Jim said pointing his finger at them and himself, "how you say, er... men of world."

The Germans continued to laugh and replied, "Ja, we are all men of the world."

"When the war is er... kaput," Jim continued, "We all become comrades once more, ja?"

"Ja." the Germans agreed, "We all become comrades."

"Chow, aur vedesain, good luck." He then said and continued on his way with the American airman who was visibly quaking by his side.

"Aur vedesain." the Germans replied and returned to their previous conversation. And so the two Italian peasants and the German officers parted the best of friends. The American was eventually put in touch with the right contact in the village and was last seen heading to the safety of the allied lines.

When Jim eventually crossed the allied lines, instead of surrendering to the first British regiment that he came in contact with, which is what the army later said he should have done, he carried on down to Rome. He'd been raised as a Roman Catholic and the chance to see the splendour of the Vatican, was just too good an opportunity for him to miss. After two weeks of sightseeing in Rome, he gave himself up to the British authorities and was promptly put under arrest. He was charged with being absent without leave and sent back to Britain. After many interviews he finally sat before an officer who had a modicum of common sense and who, after listening to Jim's tale of adventure, shook his head and declared, "I advise you to be extremely careful when you go back into civilian life, with your rebellious attitude, you'll either end up as the Prime Minister or at the end of a rope."

Jim did neither, he returned to Glasgow to visit his relatives and friends, but as there was little work to be had in the area he once more hit the open road and headed south. He hitched a ride as far as Birmingham and while resting in a pub he fell into conversation with a group of friendly locals and the following day he found himself a job. Being a keen ballroom dancer, he attended a local dance and there he met his future wife, Betty. Betty and Jim eventually married, settled in Kingstanding, had three kids and raised them to be well balanced responsible citizens.

Jim was a man that lit up a bar room when he walked into a pub and he became known as either "Jim" "Jock" or "Peter." The nickname "Peter" came about through winning a substantial amount of money on a horse that was called "Peters Pride" which he advised many others in his local pub to back and none did and it was a fact that he never tired of reminding them of. As tough as old boots, he was still as aggressively independent in old age, as he'd been when he'd left the mean streets of Glasgow as a young lad many years before. He kept abreast of current affairs and he had an opinion on most things even if they weren't always politically correct. When he died, his family gave him a wonderful send off, which was complemented by a Scottish piper playing Scotland the Brave, for as well as mourning him; they also wished to celebrate the life of this unique gritty individual.

Turners was now growing at phenomenal rate and I, who was still in charge of the tube store, was now ordering eight hundred ton of steel tube per month, but the down side was that the logistics of the business had now become a cause of concern. The tube store where the lorries were obliged to pick up their daily deliveries of tube was based in Smethwick and head office with its adjoining higaldy pigaldy fittings and general stores was still in Lozells, which meant constant journeys from one site to the other. Then in 1985 all hell broke loose in the form of street riots in the Lozells area where the head office and building supplies stores were situated and many nearby business premises were attacked, looted and set on fire and one man died after being trapped inside a burning building.

Head office was quickly closed and all the staff scampered off home, but being three-mile away in Smethwick, this did not affect those of us that worked in the tube store and so we carried on as normal. We unloaded delivery lorries, served several customers and loaded two of the companies lorries with steel tube ready for the next day's deliveries. The driver of one of these lorries was an obnoxious little bloke, who had a chip on his shoulder that must have weighed a ton and he was obliged to stay with us in the tube store to supervise the loading of his lorry. There wasn't a single person on the staff that liked this obnoxious squirt as he was a loud mouthed bigoted racist that claimed to have fought and won numerous fights in pubs, in the street and on the open road when out delivering. He was extremely cocky and the only thing that saved him from being physically attacked by other members of the staff on a regular basis was that he was so small, no one wanted to be accused of bullying the little sod.

This driver found that he had a serious problem to solve and the constant news updates that were being issued by the local radio station were making him very nervous for this man lived in a house that was directly opposite the head office in Lozells and which was right in the middle of the riot zone. As the news issuing from the radio got no better, he begged me to give him a lift home before it got dark, as he was sure that he would be set upon if he walked home alone and knowing how easily he made enemies, I was sure that he was right to think that way.

Reluctantly, I agreed to take him home and we set off at four in the afternoon and as we drove into the riot zone, we saw groups of policemen standing at the major road junctions, but in the side streets where the gangs of black youths gathered, we saw no sign of any police activity at all. As we neared the driver's home the tension mounted as we realised that we were in the only car that was moving through the deserted streets and as we passed the numerous gangs of black youths, we were greeted with suspicious looks. By this time the small loud mouth was a nervous wreck and was crouching low in his seat hoping that he wouldn't to be seen by any of the black lads who watched us pass by. To make him feel even more uncomfortable, I put on a brave face and surprisingly, I found that it helped me to feel better, but beneath the brave façade, I was quacking in my shoes as I constantly wrestled with the frightening conundrum of what I would do if one of the gangs tried to stop us from continuing our journey. Should I run the car into them or surrender? Thankfully, I didn't have to make that decision and we reached our destination. I dropped him off outside his house and without a word of thanks; he shot in doors as fast as he could. I then proceeded to drive slowly out of the eerily quiet and tense district and joined other moving traffic where I was able to let out a sigh of relief and finally relax.

A week later when the riot torn district was getting back to normal, I overheard the obnoxious little runt telling a couple of storemen how he'd confronted a gang of black lads that had gathered outside his house during the riots and had told them all to piss off. No one believed his story, but we often wondered whether he himself came to believe these constant lies as he told them with such conviction.

"I suppose we should feel sorry for him." Billy said while pondering the personality of the little Walter Mitty character who seemed to live in his own world of exiting make-believe.

But Butch's no-nonsense analysis of him was, "I just think the little squirt is a prize prat."

We were overjoyed when he finally left the company and took his bragging lies and irritating personality with him.

Butch was driving to work one morning when he inadvertently became involved in an incident that was worthy of a Hollywood comedy film. He was always one of the first to arrive at work and on this particular winter's morning, it was not only dark, but snowing heavily.

"I could hardly see a bleeding thing," Butch said as he related his tale, "It was snowing so heavily that the windscreen wipers were having a job to move it off the windscreen. But I wasn't much bothered because there wasn't any other traffic about. Anyway, I kept to the middle of the road and crawled along and stared into the blinding snowstorm. When suddenly, out of nowhere a figure, all huddled up in a dark hooded anorak, appeared right in front of me and bang! I hit him full on! I slammed on the brakes and my heart was thumping like a bloody big bass drum and I'm thinking, "Where the bleeding hell did he come from?" So, still shaking, I got out and shuffled to the front of the car to see if this bloke was badly hurt and I looked at the area in front of the car and there was no one there. I looked around, up and down the street and I couldn't see him anywhere. For a second I thought I'd imagined it, but I could see where the snow had been knocked off the bonnet of the car, so I knew that I'd hit something. I looked around the snow-covered street again and I still couldn't see him and then suddenly, a hooded figure, who'd been completely covered over by the snow, sat up right in front of the car. I tell you straight, it made me bleeding jump. I nearly shit myself. It was like a scene from a horror film where a body pops up out of a grave."

"So who the bloody hell was it?" one of the listeners asked.

"It was a little Asian bloke. He'd been walking down the centre of the road with his head bent down against the oncoming snow and had walked straight into the front of the car. He'd bounced off the bonnet, fallen flat on his back and shot along the road and disappeared under the deep snow. Anyway he did no more than pick himself up, shook the snow off his coat, mumbled something that I couldn't understand and carried on shuffling off down the road. I tell you this, it's a bloody good job I worn't going any faster when I hit him, otherwise he'd have shot along the road like a bleeding sledge and ended up in the next street."

While out Christmas shopping in a cold and draughty market, Jenny overheard a conversation between two women, who were evidently mother and daughter. The older woman said, "Are yo' gooing to buy the kid's sum bananas?" The younger woman replied sharply, "Are bloody ain't, the greedy sods always eat em."

As Jenny continued to meander around the market stalls, she became aware that a Father Christmas had left his lucky dip barrel and was heading her way and as he approached, he held out his hands as if to grab her around the waist. On seeing this red and white apparition attacking her, she screamed with fright and began to run.

Father Christmas then chased her around the market stalls. Shoppers and stallholders stood and watched in amazement as the chase continued and when finally caught, Jenny screamed in terror. Father Christmas then whipped off his beard and there before her stood Charlie, as large as life and grinning from ear to ear.

"You silly bugger!" Jenny stammered when she realised who it was, "You could have given me a bloody heart attack."

Ignoring her evident consternation, Charlie's smiling reply was simply, "Do you want to have a go in my lucky dip barrel? It's only 50p."

Unpredictable Charlie was once more back on the scene and for the next few weeks he tagged along with Mitch and I when we met up and did our usual Friday night pub crawl. He informed us that he'd re-married, settled down to a form of domestic bliss and had become a double glazing salesman and being a lover of market trading, he'd set up his lucky dip stunt to cash in on the Christmas spending spree.

By becoming a double glazing salesman, Charlie had accidentally stumbled upon his true vocation. He'd always dabbled in the world of wheeling and dealing, buying and selling anything he could lay his hands on. But other than the time that he'd worked with Bronco on the market stalls selling cheap shoes, his ventures into selling had been small time and inconsistent. He'd never had any sound financial backup behind him, but now he was able to spread his wings and fly as high as he wished, and much to everyone's surprise, he became the top double glazing salesman in the whole of the Midlands.

He explained, with enthusiasm, his simple technique which was the key to his new found financial success. "When I get invited into someone's home I don't even mention double glazing until I'm on first name terms and become their best friend. I ask questions about themselves, their family, their kids or grandkids, their holidays, their friends and I make a big fuss of their pets. A lot of people think more of their bloody animals than they do of their kids. Now, when the husband starts to get a bit restless, I ask him about his car, his favourite football team and even, where he got the lovely wallpaper from that's on his living room wall. You see, unlike the other salesmen, I'm never in a hurry, most of the other salesmen want to get down to the pub for last drinks, but that don't bother me, I'm prepared to stay all night if necessary. Before long, I've become their best friend, I know all about their family, I've seen their holiday snaps and I'm being invited to Sunday lunch. They trust me so much they want me to marry their daughter and they know that I'll get them the best deal I can."

And it was as simple as that; Charlie instinctively knew that a good salesman sells himself first and the product second and as he was as tenacious as a limpet, when it came to selling, he was simply the best.

The Gaiety was a large modern pub that had a spacious car park and had been designed as an entertainment venue. At one end of the large plush lounge there was a stage complete with dressing rooms. Graham, the manager booked guest performers and pop groups on a regular basis, but the most popular nights proved to be those where members of the audience got up on stage and sang. A bright and breezy compere, complete with sparkling jacket and dickey-bow would, with exaggerated enthusiasm, call up the singers and let them sing a couple of songs to the accompaniment of the resident drummer and keyboard player and as he got them off the stage and another one on, he would force the audience to applaud, no matter how poor the performer had been.

Male and female singers of differing ages came along to the Gaiety from all over the West Midlands and all hoped that they would be discovered by a show-biz entrepreneur and whisked off to a life of fame and fortune, but none had the elusive natural charisma that was needed for ultimate stardom. There was one man that had a rich Matt Monroe voice and was a pleasure to listen to, but no matter what he wore, he always looked untidy and on his way home from work.

When there was no entertainment on, the large lounge was often empty and it was Mitch who suggested that it would be a good idea to organise a talent competition for Wednesday evenings. The manager, not only thought that the suggestion was worth a try, but asked Mitch if he'd organise it. And so a mid-week talent competition was organised with Mitch acting as compe're and as the weeks went by its popularity grew. The climax of the competition eventually arrived and the Lord Mayor of Smethwick and his wife were invited to present the prizes. The evening was a great success, even though the Lord Mayor and his po-faced wife looked decidedly uncomfortable when Mitch told a few well-rehearsed bawdy jokes between the acts. The talent competition went on to become a regular item at the Gaiety even after Mitch had given up the roll of compe're, and for a few years, the pub became one of the most successful entertainment venues in the West Midlands.

One of the regular singers was a tall skinny looking chap who was in his thirties and was convinced he was a star, but he wasn't on his own in this delusional belief as there were many that believed that they were stars in the making and would eventually be discovered. But this particular gent did stand out from the rest as week after week he arrived carrying a black leather attaché case containing reams of sheet music.

When called up, he would present his music to the key board player and explain the intricacies of the piece before performing. The compe're endeavoured to put him on early in the evening and after he'd finished his number, whisk him off as fast as possible, but it wasn't easy. Many a time our would be star, would still be folding his sheet music and putting it into his case, when the next singer had already been introduced and started singing their number. No one minded this man's idiosyncrasies, as these early acts were generally the poorest of the night and it all added a bit of humour to the proceedings.

After a few weeks, this poor talentless man added costume to his act. He took to wearing frilly fronted white shirts when singing ballads, bright silk shirts when attempting rock and roll numbers, an American navy top for songs from South Pacific and a cowboy shirt and Stetson for his Oklahoma numbers. But his pie'ce de re'sistance number came one night when, dressed in a loud check cowboy shirt and blue jeans, he stepped onto the stage carrying a large cardboard box from which he produced a flat pack wooden rocking chair and, much to the audience's delight and the compe're's wide eyed astonishment, set about assembling the rocking chair on the stage. Once constructed, he sat in it and while slowly rocking backwards and forwards, he proceeded to sing "Old Shep," the mournful heartrending story of an old faithful dog.

On that particular night, he was the star of the show as he well and truly brought the house down, though it was not in the way that he'd intended. Even after he'd finished singing, the comedy continued, as he now had to dismantle the wooden chair and fit all the pieces back into the cardboard box. All this took place while the next singer was performing and the compe're, consumed with frustration, tried desperately to hurry things along and get him and his clunking bits of wood off the stage.

On another occasion, dressed in his Wild West cowboy outfit, he sang "The Man from Laramie," only this time, he had a toy revolver and a small leather whip which he unsuccessfully attempted to crack. If he'd gone into visual comedy, instead of singing, he'd have made a decent living on the club circuit. As a singer he was a complete failure, but as he had a Buster Keaton expression, as a visual comedian there was no one to touch him.

Mitch was often called up to do a number on these occasions, but with such a small collection of songs in his repertoire, he felt embarrassed at singing the same numbers each week and he often declined, but when he was in the mood and sang the audience's favourite, "If I Was a Rich Man" there was no one better. Over many years Mitch participated in many talent competitions and did very well in all of them, but he knew his limitations. After a few drinks he loved to sing, but to sing for a living, one had to be prepared to sing at various venues night after night while cold sober and he did not have the appetite for such a long haul.

Good pub singers are continually praised by family and friends and are constantly being told that they are not only as good as the professionals, but even better, and this alcoholic induced praise often goes to the singers head as it's exactly what they want to hear and it often distorts their grip on reality.

"Yom better than 'er wat sings on the tele luv. Yo ought to do it for a livin'." one competent singer was constantly being told and after going through a heated divorce, she was only to ready to believe it. She packed up her job, put her house up for sale, told her sisters to sell all her furniture and with her two children in tow, moved to a Spanish holiday resort with the intention of becoming a successful holiday club singer. What she found was that holiday club singers were ten a penny, the wages were poor, the hours of work were long and all decent accommodation was expensive. After three weeks of scratching around and failing to find a permanent singing venue, she ended up trying to sell time-share apartments to hapless holidaymakers and a week later, she was on her way back home. She immediately took the house off the market and much to the astonishment of her sisters; demanded that they retrieve all her furniture that they'd sold.

Looking for an activity where they could enjoy a weekly evening out together, Jenny and her friend decided to try armature dramatics. Although bursting with enthusiasm, the first problem that they came up against was simply acquiring a part, not just a speaking part, any part at all. Having achieved that, the next problem was to acquire a part that was worth acquiring. Most amateur dramatic groups are dominated by a handful of staunch regulars who seem to have been part of the group for ever and are able to claim the lead rolls and as most plays only have four or five rolls worth having; this leaves little scope for newcomers. Jenny and her friend found that if they were lucky, they could be offered the part of a chamber maid, the first murder victim or PC. Plod. If extremely lucky they might have a line or two to say, but as for playing a lead role and showing off their acting talent, there was little chance unless one of the leading actors died or was mysteriously murdered, which in most theatrical groups is a thought that crosses the mind of many at one time or another and has spawned the plot for many a play. The term, "To kill for a part" is no idle threat in the theatrical world.

After towing the line for a couple of years and having played several bit parts, Jenny and her friend, who were forceful women when they needed to be, eventually found a way of altering this tried and trusted formula that had dominated the group since the beginning of time and their idea not only helped the group to stay healthy in numbers, as it stopped frustrated youngsters from leaving after being repeatedly snubbed, but it also made the group financially sound for the first time ever. Their idea was to produce an annual pantomime.

By doing this, those that had never acted before could be found a part as there is no limit to how many village people or spear carriers a panto requires and if any of them were required to speak, no great acting skill is needed as panto acting is by its very nature, over the top.

As Jenny and her friend predicted, the yearly panto was a great success, the group flourished in numbers and the panto became the launch pad for many aspiring actors and helped to fill the empty coffers. The old plays that the group had previously produced rarely brought in a sizeable audience and now with the group becoming financially sound, it allowed them to produce plays that were more up to date. The sliding scale of royalties' forces most amateur groups to produce very old plays where the dialogue is so old fashioned that it's nearer comedy than high drama and before this change; one play had attracted an audience of just eleven people.

To help the panto become a complete success, the young dancers from the Rita Cashmore dance school were used. These versatile children not only brightened up the show with vibrant dance numbers, but they also sold many tickets to their family and friends. Saturday performances, matinee and evening, were regularly sold out, which had never happened before. Rita had been teaching kids to dance for as long as anyone could remember and mothers who'd been taught by her were now taking their own daughters and granddaughters to her classes. She diligently rehearsed the dance numbers until they were perfect and taught by example, demonstrating gracefully and nimbly every step and every move. Even into old age she was as supple as a bamboo shoot and looked younger than she actually was.

Of course not everyone can or even wants to act and I fell into this category. I wasn't afraid of walking onto the stage and giving my all, as I could carry a spear as well as the next man, but I could never reliably remember the lines no matter how many times I rehearsed, but a production needs scenery, props, lights, music, prompt, ticket collectors and tea makers. I found my niche in helping to construct and paint the scenery. I enjoyed the colourful free hand painting that was required for pantomime backdrops, but dreaded any dreary Edwardian drawing rooms that many of the old plays required. Painting dark coloured sets was extremely boring, but it was no use complaining as Jenny would simply say, "Just get on with it, you're not here to enjoy yourself."

During the run up to opening night, dozens of unforeseen problems crop up and each has to be dealt with. A main character is taken ill, part of the set is too large and restricts access to the stage, a curtain jams, the sound system develops gremlins or the lighting begins to play up. Over the years numerous difficulties threatened to stop a show. Back stage crew had accidents, actors arrived late, actors forgot lines, music was played at the wrong time, curtains opened to soon or too late and on one occasion, a young high kicking dancer who when hurriedly changing her costume, forgot to put her knickers on. But for me the most memorable performance was a wonderful giant in a production of "Jack and the Beanstalk."

At the time of this particular pantomime, the group included two gay men. One was very masculine and an exceptionally good and dominant deep voiced actor, but his partner was not only very camp, but an abysmal actor. He had no chameleon skills whatsoever and he not only forgot lines, but delivered them in the same high pitched tone with no variance at all and because of these shortcomings, he'd failed to acquire a part. But he relentlessly pleaded with the producer to find him a part and eventually, worn down by his persistent pleading, she reluctantly caved in and gave him the prestigious part of the fearsome giant.

The producers thinking was not without merit as she realised that the giant did not have any lines to learn. I had genuine sympathy with this poor chap's affliction as I had the same difficulty and was mystified by how actor's memorise page after page of lines and when I learned that Shakespeare's Hamlet is on stage for almost the entire play, I was very impressed. "How the hell does anyone remember all those lines?" I asked Jenny, but she could not see what all the fuss was about as she had no trouble at all in learning a script.

The ferocious giant stood seven foot high as he was decked out in large black riding boots and resting snugly on his shoulders was a large gruesome head made from wire and paper mashie and his padded costume supplied him with a large chest. Everyone agreed that he was a magnificent gruesome giant and with the sound system

406

bellowing out the deep rich words, "Fe, fi, fo, fum, I smell the blood of an Englishman" the threatening image was perfect.

Whilst carrying a paper mashie club, the giant was to enter from the rear of the hall and stomp slowly down the centre isle through the audience towards the stage. He would then clump slowly up four sturdy wooden steps onto the raised stage, turn towards the audience and gesticulate menacingly with his large club. Jack, the panto's hero, who at this point had climbed the beanstalk and was now in the land of the giant, would appear from the wings with sword in hand and a ferocious battle would ensue between the fearsome giant and nimble Jack.

Full dress rehearsal began and out of the loud speakers the deep voice of the giant was heard to boom, "Fi, fi, fo, fum" and the large giant entered the hall and began to make his way towards the stage, but instead of stomping as ordered, he minced down the centre of the hall with his left hand held out as though he were playing a piano and the other holding the large club which drooped impotently towards the floor. When he came to the four wooden steps, much to the producer's horror, instead of manfully stomping up them, he scrambled up on all fours. Once on stage he righted himself and with a limp wrist action he waved his club at the people who were acting the part of an audience to give the performance a little atmosphere. The fight scene ensued and with one hand carelessly flapping the air around him and the other poking the club at Jack, he looked as though he was tentatively poking a hornet's nest with a stick, rather than a ferocious bully trying to destroy his enemy. Jack on the other hand, who was being played by a very agile young girl, looked magnificent as she danced, dived, ducked and handled her sword as well as Errol Flynn had ever done. With the exception of the producer, who was holding her head in her hands and muttering obscenities beneath her breath, all those in the hall, having never witnessed anything funnier, were doubled up with hysterical laughter. The giant's head was then removed and the exasperated producer with a face full of furry, took the mincing giant to task.

"Just what the hell do you think you're doing?" She roared in wild eyed exasperation "You're not walking like a giant! I told you to stomp down the hall menacingly not meander down like a model on a cat walk? And climbing those steps was just awful; I want you to stomp up the steps not scramble up on all fours like a twelve month old toddler. And that fight scene…just what the hell was that all about?" she added, as she flapped a loose hand about in mockery.

The gay actor, his little head partly protruding over the rim of the giant's large padded costume and with hands firmly placed upon his hips, wailed indignantly in his high pitched voice, "With that bloody great head stuck on my shoulders, I can't see where I'm going can I?"

The pantomimes rehearsals continued and although the producer eventually got the giant to hold the club as though he were knocking a nail in instead of poking it aimlessly, she had little luck in ridding him of his mincing walk and his awkward ascent onto the stage. The pantomime was a great success and at every performance each audience roared with laughter at the mincing giant and the producer was forced to pretend that that was how she'd wanted the part to be played all along.

A couple of years later, he turned up on stage as a bandaged mummy in a production of "Aladdin." All he was required to do was stick to a simple routine of creeping up behind the two panto simpletons while all the kids in the audience roared, "It's behind you!" He then had to chase them on and off stage through a series of doorways and he found a new way of performing his role at every performance. When he should have been behind the simpletons, he stood beside them, when he was on stage, he should have been off and when off, he should have been on. The two simpletons became completely confused and disorientated with this ad-lib routine and threatened to go on strike if nothing was done about it and so at the start of the second week's performances, the mincing mummy was replaced. From that moment, the "It's behind you" scene worked perfectly, but as far as I was concerned, it was nowhere near as funny as it had been before the change.

With the help of a wonderful dedicated crew, who came from all walks of life, the group produced an enormous and challenging range of shows which included, Peter Pan, The Wizard of Oz, Noises Off, Abigail's Party, My Fair Lady, and Oliver.

Jenny progressed from the peripheral rolls of chamber maid and murder victim to leading roles such as Buttons in Cinderella and Bev in Abigale's Party. She eventually became the group's main producer and wrote her own pantomime scripts to save paying royalties. So, from looking for an interesting girl's night out many years earlier, she ended up being fully involved in what is undoubtedly a very odd hobby. After weeks of planning and frustrating time-consuming rehearsals, a production is finally produced and once it's over, it's brushed aside never to be seen again. Producing plays in amateur dramatic societies is on a par with building a model aeroplane and then, just when it is perfected, jumping on it and starting all over again with a new one.

In the undertaker's scene in Oliver, a coffin is required on set as the boy Oliver, after running amuck in the funeral parlour, has to be thrown into it and held down while Mr Bumble, the bumptious beagle is sent for. When discussing this scene one member suddenly declared brightly, "No need to make one, I've got one at home, a real one."

Astonished at this unusual news, the inevitable question of, "Why on earth do you have such a thing?" was asked.

"I organised a Halloween dance and a friend gave it to me."

"So where do you keep this little novelty?" one of the stage crew asked, intrigued at the macabre thought of having a coffin in the house.

"Oh it's in the living room," the man answered, "It's covered with a colourful blanket see and the wife has put several cushions on it and we use it as a long window seat."

Being involved with so many productions, many of the lines from the plays and the way characters deliver them tend to find their way into the subconscious and become part of everyday speech and Jenny and I often found ourselves quoting lines from different plays. Whenever the word Spain came up in a conversation, one of us would automatically quote the line from Noises Off, "No, I'm not in Spain dear, I'm in agony." From Oliver we got the pompous "Meat Mam, you've fed the boy on meat?" From My Fair Lady, "I've washed my 'ands and face I 'ave" and from the bard "Out damned spot!" This habit often confused family and friends, but at least they got used to it, but when it happened in the presence of strangers we were looked upon as mental cases.

When walking through a shopping precinct Jenny called to a pantomime colleague, "It's behind you!" On hearing this, an elderly gentleman, who was walking close by, asked what it was that was lost, as he couldn't see a damn thing that was behind them.

Jenny was once asked to write and organise a Christmas pantomime for the company that she worked for, but when she sent a message through the computer system inviting members of staff to attend a first reading of the pantomime, the message brought the whole system to a halt. The pantomime was Dick Whittington and the computer system considered the word Dick to be obscene and it automatically shut itself down. Jenny's comment was, "It's a blooming good job we weren't producing "Fanny by Gaslight" or we'd all be doing time in Winson Green Prison."

Mitch and Heidi finally decided to end their turbulent marriage and go their separate ways. Their relationship had been an emotional roller coaster ride and although Heidi would have probably given it another go, Mitch had had enough. He declared that he was mentally exhausted and punch drunk, "I've reached a point where I need some form of solitude. I know it's selfish, but I feel as though I'm living in a battlefield. If I don't move now, I'll finish up doing something drastic."

He was practical enough to know that everyday life had to go on as before, but he longed for a quite space where he could take time out to read poetry or strum a guitar once in a while. Although Heidi was an intelligent and well educated woman, she had never understood his need for periods of solitude as such a concept was completely alien to her gregarious nature. When Heidi was in the presence of another person, she felt obliged to communicate and in her eyes not to do so was bad manners. To want to spend time alone reading a book, listening to music or sit in a total silence was beyond Heidi's comprehension.

Heidi's strengths were in every day social skills and not in the field of abstract thoughts. When it came to handling people, friend or foe, she was second to none. She could tie people around her little finger and persuade even the most reluctant to do her bidding.

They'd shared many wonderful times together and Heidi had always supported him through good times and bad and had always been good company when socialising. She'd created a clean comfortable home no matter where they'd lived and neither her cooking or sexual appetite could be faulted. But for all that, their differing personalities just would not gel and they inevitably ended up arguing with each other about the most trivial of matters.

During their many fights, Heidi would criticise his bouts of heavy drinking, his constant gambling and his occasional womanising and he became more and more irritated by her constant chattering. There was nothing that got up Mitch's nose more than a woman who twittered on about trivial domestic incidents and unimportant celebrity issues and Heidi was a champion gossip. They were locked in a vicious circle of many disagreements and the only solution was separation and as their son was now old enough to look after himself, Mitch decided that the time had come to do just that.

Strangely, for all his regular womanising, there was no other woman involved in his decision to end his turbulent marriage; he simply and selfishly explained, "I need my own space and I need it now before I get to old to enjoy it and before I go bleeding barmy."

They had once rowed about a rhubarb plant for two whole weeks and at the end of those two weeks, family, friends and neighbours, who had been inadvertently dragged into the disagreement, were all arguing and the scene was set for a civil war. It all started innocently enough as it was just a simple present of a rhubarb plant that Mitch's mother presented to Heidi one day and later, whilst looking into the back garden through the kitchen window, Mitch enquired as to what the new plant was that he could see in the garden.

"It's a rhubarb plant," Heidi replied happily, "Your mother gave it to us."

"It's upside down," Mitch casually commented, without thinking of the consequences of uttering such an inflammatory statement and to make matters worse he added, "you've planted it the wrong way up."

"No I haven't," Heidi retorted indignantly, her hackles well and truly up "I know how to put a plant into a garden."

"And I'm telling you, it'll never grow that way up," Mitch replied, annoyed as usual at being contradicted over such a trivial issue.

"Oh yes it will and I'll see that it does," declared Heidi defiantly.

And so the battle lines were drawn and the argument continued for the rest of that day and as neither one would back down it continued for many days after that. And as each person visited their house, be they family, friend, neighbour, milkman, postman or Jehovah's Witness, they were all asked to give their opinion on whether the plant was upside down or not and depending on their answer depended whether they were to be considered to be friend or foe to either one.

After two weeks there were numbers on either side ready to fight for what they believed was right and before things got completely out of hand, a truce had to be called. Now Mitch's idea of a truce was a house party and by the end of the night everyone had forgotten all about the bloody rhubarb plant and the next morning the troublesome plant had mysteriously disappeared. Heidi never knowingly saw it again, but she was a might suspicious when, while visiting Billy's home one day, she realised that he had a fine patch of rhubarb in one corner his garden which she'd never noticed before.

With Mitch's style of betting, which was usually to wait for a "dead cert," he either lost heavily or won a substantial amount. There was no middle ground when he gambled and he brought the same logic to the card table when he visited a casino. This type of high roll gambling had the effect of frightening me rigid, but Mitch was made of sterner stuff and when sitting in a card school he had a confidence that I'd never had.

Arriving home late one night after attending a very successful night at the casino card table his pockets were stuffed with ten pound notes. Although drunk he had the presence of mind to hide much of his winnings knowing that Heidi would probably search through his pockets the following morning looking for evidence of another woman and would inevitably find the money. In a state of bleary eyed drunkenness, he looked around his lounge for a suitable hiding place before he retired to the bedroom. He knew that if Heidi found his winnings, he would not only be criticised for his gambling, but would be nagged into giving her a substantial amount of the money. His objection to this wasn't because he was particularly mean, the house furnishings and Heidi's wardrobe which was full of good quality clothes was evidence to that, but because he looked upon this particular clutch of money as his stake money. He saw stake money as being an entirely different species to spending money. The money that he earned from working all week was for spending on utility bills, the daily bread and the odd luxury, whereas stake money was a means of acquiring more wealth as it allowed him to sit at the gambling tables with the big boys and once there, he could not only increase his pile but also experience the thrill and excitement of pitting his skill against the other card players.

The following morning, having no deliveries to do that day, he dropped in at the tube store where I was busily working and during a conversation over a cup of tea, he told me about his wonderful win at the card table during the previous evening, but he then went on to say, "Although I'm over the moon with my win, I have a slight problem."

"What's your problem then?" I asked a little puzzled as I assumed that winning a substantial amount of money would have solved most people's problems, especially mine.

"I can't remember where I've hidden the bleeding money." He declared with noticeable exasperation.

"What do you mean?" I naturally asked, "I don't understand?"

"Neither do I." He replied, a distinct look of defeat upon his face. "For the life of me, I can't remember where I hid it."

He then explained that he'd hidden his winnings before retiring to bed whilst in a drunken stupor and on rising that morning, he'd completely forgotten where he'd hidden the money. A quick search of different rooms in the house while Heidi had been busy doing the housework in other parts of the house had revealed absolutely nothing. Mitch and I put our heads together and by visualising the three ground floor rooms in Mitch's home, we proceeded to analytically search them with our minds eye. Mitch made notes of our progress on a piece of scrap paper and by ticking off each of the items that we knew to be in the rooms, we compiled a list of what had been searched and what had not, but to no avail. There wasn't a single place or item that we could think of that he had not already searched.

Three days later while Heidi was out shopping, Mitch once again thoroughly searched the ground floor rooms, but he still failed to find his missing winnings and doubt began to creep into his mind. Had he really won the money, or was it all a dream? Had he dropped the money in the street when getting of his car that night? As he had been blind drunk, he couldn't be totally sure that what little memory he had of the event could be relied upon. The other thought that plagued him was that Heidi may have accidentally found the money and was waiting for him to say something? None of these thoughts were comforting, but try as he might he could not recall where he'd hidden the stash of banknotes.

When, two weeks later, Gibo and I met Mitch in Scotty's pub for our usual Friday night get together and he greeted us with an unusual wide smile and without a word being spoken, we knew that he'd found the missing money.

"Okay," We both said in unison, "Where was it?"

"How do you know that I've found the money?" He said while grinning at us, "I could be smiling about something else. The Missis could have left me and run off with the milkman for all you know."

"You only look that happy when money's involved," Gibo stated, nodding his head sagely.

"Well," Mitch explained, "I came home late last night and I'd had a few and I stood in the living room for a while before going up to bed, just thinking about what I'd got to do in the morning and there in front of me was that picture we have on the wall that Heidi thinks gives the room a touch of class. You know, Constables bloody Haywain. Then it came back to me, that's where I'd put the money. I suddenly remembered that I'd placed the pack of notes behind the picture. I gently pulled the bottom of the picture frame away from the wall and sure enough the money dropped out, all five hundred quid of it."

Over the many years that Mitch and Heidi lived together they had so many rows, that it would be impossible to list them all. Some were serious, but on the whole most were concerned with trivial matters, such as Heidi's habit of putting best butter on the stale bread before she threw it out into the garden for the birds and insisting that empty milk bottles should be cleaned so thoroughly that they resembled cut diamonds before they were put onto the front step.

"They've got bloody great machines at the dairy that cleans them!" Mitch would point out when he saw her wasting her time polishing the empty milk bottles.

"I don't care what they've got," she would reply stoically, "I'm not having dirty milk bottles on my front step."

But one evening they had a serious row where threats were made and each took a firm unshakeable stance. Eventually Mitch, in a blinding rage, stormed out of the house and made his way to his local pub. With the help of his friends and a few soothing pints, his temper and mood improved and he not only began to enjoy the evening, but also forgot all about his domestic troubles and at about twenty minutes past eleven he returned home and found the house in total darkness.

She's in bed, he thought, but if she's not asleep, what kind of reception am I going to get. Will she continue with the row, or, will it be as had happened on other occasions, a frantic sex session. He opened the front door, switched on the light and for the next two or three minutes he stood transfixed. The whole house was completely empty. All the furniture and ornaments had gone. While he'd been in the pub, Heidi had called for a removal van and crew and had stripped the house bare.

Mitch was to wail in defeated admiration, "There wasn't a tea towel, a knife, a fork or a bleeding spoon; the only thing she'd left was the bloody wallpaper on the walls."

In just three hours, Heidi had cleaned out the furniture from every room in the house and had had it safely locked away in a storage warehouse, while she had booked into a hotel for a few days.

After a few weeks, many grovelling apologies and a couple of passionate sex sessions the pair eventually got back together again and the furniture was restored to its rightful place and a sort of normality was restored into their home for a short while. When discussing the event with his friends, Mitch's lasting comment on the furniture disappearing affair was, "If Heidi had been on Adolf Hitler's staff, the Second World War would have been over in a bleeding fortnight."

Mitch, Gibo and I were sitting at a table in the Bag of Nails pub one evening discussing the troublesome ways of the world and how we would put them right, when somehow the conversation got around to discussing our telephone bills and what we thought was the best way of controlling them. My solution had been to move the telephone out of the comfortable living room and place it in the hallway near the front door where there was no chair to sit on and no way of becoming comfortable. Mitch put his pint down and smugly said, "Well I can go one better than that." He then walked out of the room and when he re-entered he was carrying a cream coloured telephone that he'd just retrieved from the boot of his car. He plonked it onto the table in front of us and simply said, "There then. Beat that!"

"What's that then?" Gibo asked a little puzzled.

"That's the telephone from our house." Mitch replied smugly.

"Come off it." I said while smiling and looking at him suspiciously, "You don't really mean to say that you take the phone out of the house when you come out for the evening do you? That's a spare one isn't it?"

"No," he replied in all seriousness, "That's the real thing. If you had the telephone bills that I've been receiving lately, you'd be doing the same. Once Heidi picks up a telephone she loses all sense of time. She can be on the bloody thing for hours and what gets my goat is that a lot of the calls are to Gale, who only lives two hundred yards away. So the only way to stop her is to bring the bloody thing out with me."

Heidi's legendary telephone calls often involved her best friend Gale and as Mitch often pointed out, as she only lived in the next street, it would have been no great hardship for either of them to visit each other instead of running up such huge telephone bills. Mitch's view was that to visit each other would have been the sensible thing to do, but as Heidi was a compulsive gossip and Gale was a sandwich short of a picnic, logic was never going to come into the equation. We were all aware that age and alcohol abuse had taken its toll and that Gale had gradually become noticeably more and more unpredictable. She once gave a painter and decorator his marching orders for asking her what colour she wanted her living room ceiling painted.

"If he doesn't know that a ceiling should be white, he shouldn't be doing the job." She stated emphatically. The fact that since the nineteen fifties, interior decorating had become an art rather than a tradition cut no ice at all with her. Once when we were celebrating Heidi's birthday in a popular restaurant, Gale slipped into a drunken haze and to everyone's astonishment, began to comb her hair with a table fork.

But the incident that topped the lot was when; during a long telephone conversation, Gale suddenly asked Heidi if she was cooking fish and chips for Mitch's evening meal.

"No," replied Heidi a little puzzled by the question, "I rarely cook fish and chips. If we do have them, we usually have them from the fish and chip shop down the road. Why'd do you ask?"

"Well," Gale replied equally puzzled, "I can distinctly smell fish and chips and I thought the smell might be coming down the telephone line from your house."

Mitch and Heidi finally went their separate ways and Mitch no longer had to worry about Heidi's large telephone bill and within a couple of years they'd both found new partners. Heidi's new partnership, which was based on companionship and financial stability rather than everlasting romantic love, lasted the course, but Mitch's failed miserably and once again he embarked upon a series of romantic liaisons while forever searching for a sole mate.

Eight months after completing his allocated time in prison, Eddie Rogers was ambushed outside one of his night clubs and was badly beaten. He spent several weeks in hospital and from then on he was obliged to use a wheel chair to get about. Eventually he sold his night clubs and moved to Spain where he spent much of his time sitting by his swimming pool getting fatter by the minute. I learned all this through the monkey on my back, Webber, the intrepid sleuth who never gave up asking questions about the missing diamond.

He also informed me that the police knew that Nicos was behind the vicious attack that had put Rogers in a wheel chair, but as they all considered it as an act of poetic justice they were not pursuing their enquiries with much vigour and were planning to get him on a completely different charge. As it turned out, Nicos fooled them all as he suddenly died from a heart attack before they could nail him.

"Pissing about with too many drugs is my guess," was Webbers theory for the sudden heart attack, "Up to his neck in the bloody stuff he was. We had enough evidence to put him away for the next hundred years."

Nicos's son, who hadn't been in touch with his arrogant crooked farther for fifteen years, came over from the USA and disposed of the large house and all its contents and Webber was there in his Sherlock Holmes mode scrutinising every item as it left the house.

I must admit, I was a bit worried for a while as it crossed my mind that Webber might take it into his head to blackmail me by threatening to inform Rogers that I was the one who had tipped Nicos off about who was behind the burglary of his house, but it seems that it never crossed his mind or if it did, he had the good grace not to mention it. Whether he genuinely believed that I didn't know where the missing diamond was or he just didn't want to see me get beaten up again, I don't know, but I was very grateful that he didn't tip Rogers off.

Of all the numerous occupations that my mates and I tackled, the raising of our children was probably the most interesting, educational and exasperating. We'd believed that we knew all that we needed to know and had forgotten what our own attitude to our parents had been when growing up. As our children grew we realised that there was a natural reluctance to being moulded into the child of our dreams and that our well-meaning aspirations were not always what our offspring sort. Although this striving for independence is perfectly natural and has been going on since the jelly fish decided to develop fins and feet to escape life in the primeval swamp back in the murky mists of time, it never the less took each of us by surprise and the only comfort to be found is in realising that each parent has exactly the same problem to contend with, as Shakespeare, who had a quote for every occasion, aptly put it, "Sharper than a serpent's tooth, to have a thankless child."

An early sign of this exasperating behaviour is when your child opens a present and spends more time playing with the cardboard box than the expensive toy and without any help at all your child will gradually turn from a cute cuddly baby into a stubborn awkward, spiteful, angry, irritable monster that constantly moans about anything and everything.

Keeping kids under control becomes a constant battle of willpower, but no matter what you do, they will find a way of embarrassing you. While eating lunch in a small café one-day, young Tom, showing his independent spirit, decided to sit on his own and perched himself on top of a bar stool that was at one end of the room while the rest of Billy's clan sat around a table to eat their meal. When they'd finished eating Billy turned to find that young Tom had, with his small but agile greasy hand, spent much of his time rubbing it all over the chalked menu that had been carefully and artistically written on the café's blackboard. Billy and his family quickly departed before the proprietor discovered what had taken place and they never had the nerve to venture anywhere near that particular cafe again.

One sunny summer's day the toddlers Richard and Debbie liberated an old tin of red paint from grandads garden shed and decided to paint Mrs Bloom's garden fence. It took well over a week to clean up the paint covered kids, the fence and the substantial mess that was left on the pavement after their industrious endeavours. Six year old Shirley presented her mother with a beautiful bunch of daffodils on Mothers Day which she'd brazenly picked from their next door neighbour's garden and Mitch's son decided one day to experiment with Mr Devon's old car and poured a substantial amount of water into the petrol tank.

Billy and his wife were happily resting on a park bench one summer's day whilst their two small children played in the toddlers play area with the other children. Five year old Mary, their youngest suddenly appeared before them holding the hand of a small boy who could just about walk and declared, "I found him on his own over there. Can we take him home with us?" Luckily, they were able to return the toddler to his distraught mother before she had time to call the police.

While standing in a shop, one of mine once asked me loudly, "Why has that women got a big nose? Is she a witch?" and my brothers son stomped angrily into the kitchen one Sunday morning and demanded to know why no one had woke him that morning. "I've been lying there for ages waiting for someone to wake me up!" he declared.

After seeing the film "Home Alone" where a small boy triumphantly takes on a couple of evil burglars and by the clever use of homemade booby traps, makes them both look like idiots, my young sons decided that it would be extremely funny to do the same to me and so one evening I walked into the garage and found that I was expected to step onto a bulbous black bin liner full of blown up balloons and guessing that this was one of the many "Home Alone" booby traps that I'd come across recently, I decided to play along with their little game and stamped my right foot heavily onto the bulbous black plastic bag. I expected to hear a loud bang and made ready to fake a debilitating heart attack. A split second latter, I found to my horror that the black plastic bag wasn't hiding blown up balloons, but a skateboard. Balancing on one leg I shot along the garage at high speed and crashed into the washing machine. My young sons stood doubled up with laughter and Jenny, on hearing this raucous behaviour going on in the garage called from the kitchen, "Will you lot behave yourselves out there, you'll break something?" As I picked myself up off the floor I realised how right she was, "It could have been my bleeding neck," I thought wistfully.

There were times when I had to be as artful as the kids and one year while on holiday in the popular holiday resort of Salou, we visited the large theme park which is situated on the outskirts of the town. The theme park was dominated by a large roller coaster ride that was known as the Dragon and the imposing structure could be seen for miles around and my two young sons were dying to ride it and had been discussing the forthcoming ride with unbridled enthusiasm since the holiday had been booked.

When making our way up the hill towards the Dragon all that began to change and the lad's former enthusiasm noticeably evaporated. As they got closer to the Dragon, its intricate steel structure began to tower above them and they began to have second thoughts about going on it. As they began to dawdle, I overheard one say, "I might not go on it today after all, I'll see how I feel" and the other replied, "That's right, let's go on it next week when we come back again."

I realised that if they did not go on it now, they never would and so I said brightly, "Come on then lads, let's go for it."

"You're not going on it, are you Dad?" they asked, somewhat taken aback by this unexpected discovery.

"Of course I am," I replied cheerily as I clapped my hands and rubbed them together in exited anticipation, "We haven't come all this way just to look at it have we?"

Until that moment I'd had no intention of going on the mighty roller coaster, but I realised that the lads would not allow me to go on the monster on my own as that would put them in a position where they could be seen as cringing wimps instead of me, which they seemed to think was my role in life. And so confidently, I led the way and the three of us boarded the mighty Dragon and were dutifully locked into our seats with the hydraulic mechanism. A few minutes later, having gone up and down and round and round and up and down and round and round again and again at breakneck speed, as there were eight loop-the-loops involved in the frantic ride, we found ourselves back on what seemed to me a jelly like moving terra firma. The two lads were jumping for joy and ran and told Jenny just how exiting the experience had been while I tottered around lurching from side to side like a drunken sop and feeling as sea sick as a novice sailor after rounding Cape Horn. For the next twenty minutes, I lay flat on my back on a nearby grass bank and died a thousand deaths while my spinning brain and churning stomach continued to play havoc.

After regaining my equilibrium, I shuffled gingerly beside Jenny while the two lads excitedly looked forward to the next ride. I noticed that they were wearing T-shirts that Jenny had just purchased for them which declared in large print, "I Survived the Dragon." I asked Jenny if she'd purchased a T-shirt for me. Surprised, she looked at me in disbelief and said, "You actually want to walk about in a T-shirt saying you survived the Dragon?"

"Oh no," I replied shaking my head vigorously, "I was thinking of having one that said "I must keep my big mouth shut in future" and although it was said in jest, I meant every word.

For many years Jenny worked in a residential home that was surrounded by pleasant parkland and was home to forty elderly residents. During her time there, she worked in all its varied departments and was witness to numerous odd incidents.

While many of the elderly residents were finishing their breakfasts, Josey, who was Maltese and spoke with a pronounced Mediterranean accent, decided to lay the unused tables ready for lunch. Although the trolley she was using had been loaded with fresh table clothes, serviettes, glasses and spoons, the knives and forks were missing. On discovering this, she called loudly across the dining room to her helpmate, who was in the kitchen, "There's no fork-an-knives' on the trolley. Can you bring some fork-an-knives' out?" which made many of the well-bred residents sit bolt upright with wide eyed astonishment.

After Ray, the home's maintenance man accidentally bumped into her while entering the kitchen, Josey was heard to shout, "That man is always bonking me, if he does it again I will tat for tit him and give him a bonking he will never forget."

Having been brought up in a strict catholic environment, Josey was ignorant of any form of birth control and had no idea what a contraceptive coil looked like and full of curiosity, she asked if anyone could show her one. The following day Jenny presented her with part of an old alarm clocks mechanism and informed her that it was a birth control coil. Josey, wide-eyed with alarm, shook her head and declared, "My God! That would make me very painful. I don't think I would be able to manage that. Do they make a smaller one?"

Jenny assured her that once fitted; she would soon get used to it, but did admit that it would make her walk like a cowboy for a while.

"Walk like a cowboy!" Wide eyed Josey exclaimed, while shaking her head in disbelief, "With that thing inside me, I would have to walk like a blinkin' crab!"

Arriving for work one frosty winter's morning, Olive, who was one of the care staff, decided to change into her uniform in the comfort of the homes large and pleasantly warm airing cupboard that was situated next to the central heating boiler. She pulled the door to, for a little privacy and after changing, found that the door had jammed and she could not get out. After calling for help and banging on the door, help eventually arrived in the form of Betty the laundress. Now Betty was a very competent laundress, but when it came to opening jammed doors, as she later explained, "it's not something that I'm very good at, I have a problem trying to take the tops off Jam jars."

After several of the staff had pulled and tugged at the door, the manageress was sent for and she took charge of the situation. After a further ten minutes of pulling and tugging at the jammed door, she decided that the fire service would have to be called in. A group of masculine uniformed fire-fighters eventually arrived which caused a little excitement among the female staff and after a few minutes with the help of their specialised equipment they forced the door open and extracted a very grateful Olive. She'd been entombed in the hot airing cupboard for well over an hour and her face resembled a rosy red baked apple. Not only was she glowing brightly, but steam was visibly rising from her head. Betty then declared that Olive looked as though she'd been on a fortnight's holiday, to which Olive's gasping reply was, "I don't know about a bloody holiday, I feel as though I've been cooked for a Christmas dinner."

The painters and decorators, who'd been contracted to redecorate the home, lay white dust sheets over much of the furniture in the lounge. On seeing this, an elderly lady, who'd been a forceful woman in her younger days, marched into the manager's office and demanded to know why she'd not been informed that it was snowing and wished to know what had happened to her Wellington boots as she couldn't find them anywhere. Another resident stopped Jenny in a corridor one day and asked, "Young lady, what time does this aeroplane land in Lisbon?"

Many of the elderly that passed through this particular residential home had been professional people in their younger days and a number had worked overseas in outposts of the British Empire.

"It's quite humbling to see a framed photograph on a bedside table of a fresh faced bright eyed young woman standing side by side with Mahatma Gandhi," Jenny explained, "you realise that this frail old lady has seen and done more in her life than you and I will ever do."

One old gentleman that I got to know while visiting the home was a competent watercolour artist. He was a quiet mild mannered gentle man and spent quite a lot of his time painting delicate pale watery landscapes. After several conversations, I learned that because he was a Quaker and objected to killing his fellow man, he'd served as a stretcher bearer in the First World War and had spent his time rescuing wounded soldiers and picking up dead bodies from no man's land. It must have been a terrifying and daunting experience for a man who was a staunch pacifist and did not believe in the glory of war.

One of the elderly ladies was one of the first women ever to attend a university and for most of her life she'd worked in overseas postings. One day during a conversation concerning law and order she told of an incident that happened after she'd retired. She'd arrived home one day to find that her house had been burgled and many of her treasured artefacts had been stolen.

"The policeman who was investigating the burglary assured me that the culprit would soon be apprehended and he would serve time in prison," she said quite disgusted. "Serve time in prison! I said to him, that's no deterrent young man! You should blow his bollocks off with a twelve bore shot gun."

New handrails were fitted around the home and one was put in front of a large wall mirror in the reception area. When asked by one of the residents what this rail was for, Jenny jokingly informed her that it was for ballet exercises. The following morning after breakfast, three elderly ladies turned up in the reception area, stood in front of the large mirror and with smiles all round they creakily began to exercise their legs by crouching and stretching.

When engrossed in mundane activities, Jenny had a habit of bursting into song and one day she began to sing the Gracie Field song, "Wish me luck as you wave me goodbye." Infectiously, the song spread throughout the home and by the end of the day, all the staff and many of the residents were singing and humming the song. The following day the manageress reprimanded Jenny for introducing the annoying song into the home and declared, "As manager of a respectable residential home, it's not seemly to find myself singing such things as "Wish me luck as you wave me goodbye" and then shouting, "The factories open!"

The following day the song, "I've got a lovely bunch of coconuts" was heard on and off throughout the day and once again the manageress found herself singing it.

After Mr Cain had a fatal heart attack, Turners Building Supplies began to change in attitude and commercial direction. Mr Cain's outmoded business ideas of buying British goods wherever possible and paying outstanding bills on time were quickly dispensed with and a new and more dynamic business policy was introduced into the company. A live wire by the name of Mr Bruce became the managing director of the company and soon proved that he wasn't just a new broom, but a high-powered jet propelled road sweeper. He was confident, forceful and arrogant; the type of man that would overtake another vehicle even though he'd almost reached his destination. He controlled everyone with an eagle eye, a firm hand and a sarcastic tongue and continually harassed his managers and directors. Quick thinking and fast talking, he had an endless supply of boundless energy and as he required little sleep, he arrived early and pushed his work force to the giddy limit.

Although Mr Bruce's constant flow of energy helped him to run the company with powerful leadership, he found it very difficult to relax and as a consequence, he regularly changed hobbies and cars. He changed his car every year and actually changed one, an Armstrong Siddley even quicker when Sam Bane casually suggested that it was an old man's car.

"What do mean an old man's car?" Mr Bruce snapped as he scowled at Sam with obvious annoyance and went on to inform him that, "It's a collector's item; that car is worth a bloody fortune."

"Oh I don't doubt that," Sam replied unperturbed by being chastised, "But I've only ever seen old men driving them."

A week later there was a powerful James Bond Aston Martin parked in place of the collector's item that was deemed to be worth a fortune. It would appear that image was everything.

Being a man that had complete confidence in his own ability, he would not suffer fools gladly and would hold work related conversations on the hoof. While walking briskly around the premises, he would not stop or even slow down, when a member of the staff tried to engage him with a question or two. He had cultivated this annoying tactic so that no one could engage him in long drawn out conversations. This technique forced them to get to the point immediately before he disappeared over the horizon. I learned that the best way of dealing with this cunning ruse was to write a short note explaining my request and drop it onto his desk. Later in the week, while briskly walking past at breakneck speed, he would call out either, "Yes, go ahead" or "No, forget it."

Over time Mr Bruce built himself a reputation for making instant decisions and he was much admired for it by many of his sycophantic cronies and business associates, but what many failed to appreciate was that although many of his instant decisions proved to be successful, there were others that failed miserably and were quietly swept under the carpet. After taking over the company, he surrounded himself with a board of directors that were young, energetic and ambitious, but they were also sycophantic and manipulative. After a while it became obvious to those of us in the lower ranks that because these young directors were ambitious and wished to remain in favour, they were easily bullied and at times, sadistically so.

His ambitious policy was to buy up every ailing company in sight, many of which had nothing to do with the core business of building supplies and during this period, I found myself being introduced to directors and managers from all sorts of companies who were being shown around the company on a guided tour before their own small businesses were swallowed up and once the acquisition had taken place, I never saw them again and by the end of the eighties the company had become a sprawling nationwide conglomerate of miscellaneous companies of all shapes and sizes and on paper it all looked extremely impressive. It was only when one visited some of these run down back street businesses that one got any idea of the reality of the situation. The Windsor Park Printing Company may have been an imposing company title, but as it was housed in dilapidated premises in a Bristol back street and only employed four people, a visit to the place soon changed ones perception.

For a reason that I never quite understood, I was seconded onto a team that was ordered to visit and give judgement on many of these ailing businesses before they were taken over. On this judgemental team, was a down to earth qualified builder who examined the structure of the buildings and a qualified accountant that looked at the daily output of these ailing companies. My role was to give an overview of the management structure and the general operating framework of the business. Together we surveyed many of these run down business sites and when we reported back to Mr Bruce, we were asked for our assessment of the business. The builder would rattle off a list of repairs and alterations that needed doing to the premises to bring it up to scratch. The accountant would give a general view of the state of the order books and possible profit margins and I would give my opinion of the storage layout and how organised the delivery systems were. And invariably we would express the same opinion, "It seems to be run more like a hobby than a business" which often confirmed what Mr Bruce already knew.

The core business of building supplies, which was actually making the bulk of company's profit, was housed in dilapidated buildings and premises that were scattered around the West Midlands and it was decided by Mr Bruce and his board of dynamic directors to bring the whole kit and caboodle together under one roof. This was to be a mammoth task of planning and tight schedules and I was seconded onto, "The new premises planning team."

The place chosen and purchased for the project was a huge site, but as it had not been used for many years the buildings were in a poor state of repair and in need of attention inside and out. The man who was put in charge of regenerating the site was Duncan Green; a bombastic bully who'd joined the company as a salesman and had gradually won the heart and mind of Mr Bruce and was now one of his favourite forceful directors. Duncan had joined the company as a

427

"ruthless go getting" salesman and was extremely good at his job. Although he was brash and loud mouthed, his bullying forceful personality had won many contracts for the company. After a couple of years he'd come up with the idea of forming a tool hire department within the company and had talked Mr Bruce into letting him have the necessary funds to set it up. The department was successful up to a point, but with Duncan being more of a forceful salesman than a planning manager, the department seemed to be forever going two steps forward and one step back. At one point he employed a smart young salesman and set him the task of selling drain cleaning equipment. He put the salesman into a new and fully stocked van and gave him a list of hotels, hospitals and factories to call on and after six months of demonstrating the equipment and cleaning half the drains in Britain, only two drain cleaning machines had been sold. For some extraordinary reason it had never occurred to him that when someone has a blocked drain, they contact a drain cleaning company and do not purchase an expensive machine to store and use once in a lifetime.

As Duncan's tool hire department stuttered along, it became rumoured that there were some shady deals being perpetrated to keep the sales figures looking good, but before any investigation could take place, a mysterious fire broke out one night in the tool hire department's office and much of the department's paperwork was lost forever.

Mr Bruce strongly believed that intimidation was the bedrock of good management and he not only practised it himself, but also encouraged his managers and directors to do likewise. It was a policy that several members of the management disagreed with and I not only openly disagreed with it, but totally ignored and like the others of my ilk, was constantly taunted with the accusation of being too soft.

Duncan was well versed in the art of bullying and he enjoyed throwing his considerable weight about, but that was the main reason why Mr Bruce had put him in charge of the reconstruction programme. The thinking being that Duncan could bully construction workers into working harder than they normally did. Along with the directors and the qualified down to earth builder, I was seconded onto the planning team. We were instructed to draw up plans and a tight timetable for moving five separate companies and the head office into the new premises without losing one day's trade. It was a mammoth task, but one which I truly relished. It was to be our very own "D" Day.

My role in this strategic plan was to be Duncan's right hand man, which meant handling all the paperwork that inevitably accrues on a building site and helping him to organise the timetable for the reconstruction of the site. I also had to help with the planning and the allocation of space for the various companies that were due to move onto the site. The managers of these companies, who were understandably full of their own importance, pushed for more space than they already had in their run down premises. Ignoring these demands, the builder and I, systematically measured the old premises, the bin and storage space that was being used and redesigned it to make the most of the available space that they would have in the new premises. While engaged in these duties, I realised that these companies had for many years been run as individual concerns and had their own management structure and I was sure that the shrewd Mr Bruce knew that once they were all under one roof this system would not work and that ultimately, several of these self-important managers would eventually be dispensed with. I'd been in the world of cut throat commerce long enough to realise that there was no sentiment in the commercial world and I was fully aware that after the move into the new premises had been completed, many heads would inevitably roll and I couldn't help but wonder when my turn would come.

During this period I was extremely busy from morning till night, for not only was I expected to be involved in the hiring of bricklayers, plumbers, plasterers, painters, electricians and ordering supplies, the most important of which was a daily supply of tea, milk and sugar, I was also expected to carry on running the steel tube store which was but a mile away. But for all that, I enjoyed every minute of the experience and I came to the conclusion that the most satisfying occupation would be one that was busy and totally unpredictable as then there would never be time to be idle or bored. It would be a job where numerous and constant problems had to be instantly solved on a daily basis. A comparison in sport would be something like being involved in a fast paced rugby match, rally driving or white water kayak racing. But I was also aware that that kind of employment would be so stressful that after a while, the adrenaline and will power would eventually give out.

Over the Christmas period, after many mishaps, mistakes, blazing rows and petty squabbles, the various companies, finally moved their tonnes of miscellaneous stock into the new premises. Lorry after lorry picked up goods from the outlying premises and delivered them to the new site where they were sorted and put into the new stock bins and the company opened up for business in the first week of January. "D Day" was a complete success and the company now looked forward to being a nationwide major player in the commercial world.

As predicted, the petty squabbles among the different management structures rumbled on as none of them were willing to give up the puny power that they'd enjoyed when operating as satellites and one by one, they were systematically crushed. Eventually and inevitably these autonomous companies lost their independence and became nothing more than departments that were controlled by a main company computer system. The strength of the sales computer is that the operators are not required to have an in depth knowledge of the products that they are selling. They only needed to know the correct description, the stock number and the quantity that is in stock and the computer was quite capable of supplying all that information in seconds. The down side to this system is that the operator, through lack of first-hand knowledge, cannot suggest an alternative when the product they are being asked for is not available. With good stock control this should be avoided, but it was something that those of us that had anything to do with trade counter sales were fully aware of and our answer to the problem was to bring back the independent minded Sam Bane.

After Mr Caine had died, Sam, who'd been Mr Cain's part time chauffeur among other things, had decided to leave the company and try his luck at running his own business which was simply constructing car trailers during the week and selling beef burgers from an old van at various carnivals and fetes at weekends. As well as indulging in these activities, Sam was also an ardent buyer and seller of various items of second hand junk and he visited many car boot sales and auctions. Both Butch and I felt that to make the new setup work effectively, Sam's phenomenal knowledge of building techniques and materials was needed on the new trade counter. If there was a logistical building problem to be solved or a question of which was the best fitting to be used, Sam was the man to solve it. If an item was out of stock he instantly knew what the best alternative would be and its knock on affect to the other items in the line.

The company gradually settled down into the new premises and I had a brand new tube warehouse to run and we were now second to none. With new overhead cranes, we could now load and unload lorries as quickly as any other company in the country. There was a good sense of camaraderie among the storemen and led by Big Guy, I was confident that, if asked, we could have built an Egyptian pyramid within a fortnight.

As is usual in these situations, there had to be a fly in the ointment and in this instance it was the Flying Penguin whose appropriate nick name had now become his title throughout the company. The Penguin, whose sour personality had progressively worsened over the years and who constantly went out of his way to bully and upset drivers, storemen and office staff was now settled into the new premises just like the other managers and as he was a natural born bully, he was considered to be a very good manager by Mr Bruce and therefore safe from the chop.

Exasperated staff members, branch managers from other towns, suppliers and even customers constantly enquired as to why Mr Bruce continued to employ this bombastic bully and although I knew the Penguin and Mr Bruce as well as anyone in the company, I never really discovered the reason why Mr Bruce protected him so much. The general consensus of opinion was that Mr Bruce had murdered someone back in the mists of time and the Penguin knew where the body was buried and after seeing what he got away with over the years, bullying of staff, attempting to rape a young office cleaner, swearing at directors in the presence of other staff and a whole catalogue of other misdemeanours, who could blame them. His record of disruption was appalling and as for customer care; he was at times about as competent and as diplomatic as a raging bull in a china shop.

I eventually came to realise that the Penguin's odd personality was not as complicated as most thought. He seemed to categorised people into three distinct groups, there were those that he disliked, such as his so called friends and members of his family, there were those that he openly hated, these would be work colleagues and then there were foreigners and blacks. If by any chance a person happened to fall into any one of these three categories, they were bound to cross swords with him at one time or another. He was by far the most disliked man that I'd ever met, but the odd thing was, he actually cherished his unpopular reputation, believing that it was the price one had to pay for being a hard and ruthless boss who was always right. The captains of the ancient slave driven galleys probably had the same mind set.

There were many in the company who were far more intelligent and articulate than the Penguin and who time and again tried to combat his hateful bad tempered attacks with sharp cutting jibes that would have reduced a normal man to a whimpering suicidal wreck, but the Penguin possessed little imagination or empathy and this made him impervious to sarcasm. The only chink in his armour was in not taking him and his superior posturing, seriously. I'd stumbled onto this simple fact by accident when I'd laughed at him at a board room confrontation several years earlier and from that day on I realised that by laughing at him instead of arguing, I could wind him up at will, but I also realised that by doing so, I was storing up trouble for the future as I knew that he would inevitably seek revenge.

One day a young friendly bubbly office girl quite innocently, called him "Cuddles" and it cut him to the quick. He was used to being called a little fat arrogant bastard or a flat footed Penguin, but "Cuddles" was totally against his self-made image and he did not rest until he'd hounded the poor girl out of the company.

There were numerous stories that demonstrated his hateful character, in fact every person who ever worked at the company had at least one tale to tell, but those who worked directly under his hateful regime inevitably suffered the most. A storeman that worked in his department accidentally injured his right arm. The first aider's were called and after a quick examination, he was taken to the local hospital for an x-ray and treatment and the accident was duly recorded into the company's accident book. With the injury that he'd sustained, which was a badly gashed arm, no one would have been surprised if he'd stayed off work for a week, but after just three days, with his arm securely bandaged, he returned to work.

At the end of the month, when the injured storeman received his wage slip, he found that the Penguin had stopped him three days' pay for having time off. The aggrieved storeman came to see me and asked if I would look into the matter as having now been lumbered with the duties of safety officer by the directors, I agreed to do. I assumed that the Penguin had not known that the accident had happened on the premises during working hours so I presented the storeman's case to him and to my astonishment, his reaction was surprisingly aggressive.

"I know very well how he hurt his bleeding arm," He said while nodding his head knowingly, "But I'm not paying the idle, lazy, skiving tow-rag to sit at home and watch the bleeding tele all day. As far as I'm concerned the lazy skiving bastard can go and whistle for his money because he's getting fuck all out of me, no matter how much he gripes!"

"If he's such a lazy skiving bastard, why don't you get rid of him?"

Astonished at this suggestion, the Penguin replied, "Get rid of him! Are you mad! He's one of my best workers."

I burst out laughing and shaking my head exclaimed, "Well, if that's how you treat your best workers, God help the other poor buggers."

It was shortly after this incident that I learned on the company grape vine, that the Penguin was moving to a new house that was two mile from his present dwelling. I also learned that the reason why he'd been so secretive about his house move was because he was using a company lorry and driver to move his furniture during working hours. Each day, the Penguins wife would select a few items and put them out for the driver to collect and transport to the new house. At the new house, the Penguin had installed a storeman named Frank, who'd once, worked as a painter and decorator and was now decorating it for him and would help unload the items as they arrived.

That evening, I met Mitch and Billy in the Sailors and over a pint that Billy had just purchased, I began to explain what I had learned concerning the Penguin's move to his new house and was surprised to see both my mates openly laugh and was even more surprised when Billy spluttered, "Actually Jaco, he's just bought you that pint of beer that your drinking."

"Who has?" I asked as I looked at my two mates who were still laughing, "What are you talking about?"

"The flat footed Penguin!" Billy eventually said, laughing fit to burst, "He's paying for all the beer tonight."

"What the bloody hell are you talking about?" I asked once more as I was totally confused by this unexpected answer.

"Well," Said Billy as he began to explain between fits of laughter, "What you were just on about, you know, about the Penguin's new house. Well I already knew about it. Pringle the lorry driver told me all about it yesterday when I bumped into him up at Chances Glass Works. He was moaning like hell about it. He told me that every morning before he could start his deliveries, he had to go up to the Penguin's house and pick up a few items outside his garage and take them round to the new house. Done it for the last three days he reckons. So today, just before nine, I was up there like a shot."

"Up where?" I asked, still not fully understanding.

"Up to the Penguin's house." Billy explained.

"Anyway when I got there, outside his garage, there was some stuff ready to go round to his new house. There was a couple of cardboard boxes and few black plastic bags. So I pick up a couple of the plastic bags, threw them into the van and drove off. When I got to Oldbury where my first drop was and I thought, I'd better have a look at what's in them bags, I mean for all I knew it could have been bags of bloody rubbish. So I pulled up in a quiet street and had a gander. There was all kitchen stuff in the one bag, you know tea towels, table cloths, an electric kettle, a wall clock, a few utensils and a radio and in the other bag some of the Penguin's clothes. Shirts, jumpers, two pairs of jeans, a top coat and a couple of pairs of shoes."

"So what did you do with them?" I asked while shaking my head in disbelief and smiling at Billy's audacious escapade.

"Took them to that shop in Tipton that buys and sells second hand gear and sold the bloody lot. Didn't get much for it, but that worn't the point, after all the things that bastard did on me when I worked there I just wanted to get a little of my own back." Billy replied clapping his hands with satisfaction, "And so tonight Jaco, the drinks are on our mate, the flat footed bastard Penguin."

"Cheers Billy." Mitch said and all three of us lifted our glasses and drank a toast to, "The Penguin."

A couple of years before moving into his new house the Penguin had been involved in an accident at home. While dismantling part of his garage wall, a sizable section had collapsed and fallen on top of him and it was something like ten minutes before his wife heard his cries for help. When a group of the company's senior staff were regurgitating this story a few days later, one of them asked, "I don't quite understand, why did it take so long for his wife to come and help him? She must have heard the bricks crash when they fell on him."

"Well," Quick witted Dawly said, who was one of the company's directors, "when she heard the crash in the garage, she ran upstairs to check that his life insurance was up to date."

Many years later, I happened to bump into the storeman who'd had his pay docked for having the three days off with the gashed arm. We passed a few pleasantries and he informed me that he was now married, had two kids and was working for a local engineering company. We were about to part and go our separate ways when I happened to say, "Oh, and by the way I'm sorry about that three day's pay that you got docked, but at the time, as the Penguin was your manager, I couldn't override his decision."

"Oh don't you worry about that mate," he said smiling brightly, "In the end I got well paid for that."

"Did he pay you then?" I asked in amazement, knowing that if the Penguin had relented and paid him the money, such news would ruin his mean and repugnant reputation.

"Oh no," he replied shaking his head dismissively, "That fat bastard wouldn't give you the steam off his piss. No what happened was, I filled a bag up with brass and copper fittings from the plumbing stores and me and a lorry driver took it down to the scrap yard went half whacks."

At the dawn of 1989, Turners Building Supplies head office along with its accompanying stores, the tube stores and five of the company's satellite businesses were now under one roof and I was promoted to the position of Associate Director. This meant that I had more responsibility, which included the duties of safety officer for the whole site, but had no vote on the board and much to our combined surprise, later that year; Mitch, Billy and I reached our fiftieth birthday.

To celebrate my birthday Jenny told me that she'd organised a small dinner date at a city centre restaurant where we were to meet Mitch, Billy, Gibo and their partners. Just before we set out, Jenny informed me that some friends, who worked at the BBC, would like us to pop into the Pebble Mill club on the way into town and have a quick drink with them.

It was 7.45pm when we arrived at the club and as we opened the door and stepped into the large comfortable lounge, I was surprised to see that the room was full. We were greeted by the friends that I had expected to see and embarrassingly, the disk jockey in the corner of the room began to play a recording of "Happy Birthday" and I noticed that the people sitting at the nearest table were also friends of the family. As I gradually became accustomed to the noisy environment, I began to notice that I knew other people in the room. Slowly, it began to dawn on me that I knew everyone in the room and looking like a startled gold fish I searched for an explanation and it was several seconds before the penny finally dropped. Jenny had cleverly organised a surprise party and I, the dumbbell of the piece, was the only one in the room that did not know. The large clubroom was full of family and friends, many that I'd not seen for some time. After a much needed drink, with back slapping Mitch and Billy, I began to regain my composure and thankfully the disc jockey soon had the dance floor full of happy dancers who were only too glad to strut their stuff.

To have so many people turn up for my fiftieth birthday was a very humbling experience and I felt quite emotional and moved by it, but this mood did not last long as in the wings there was another shock waiting for me, which brought me down to earth with a bump. Other men on their birthdays are surprised by young gorgeous and amply breasted female kiss-a-grams complete with black titillating stockings and suspenders. What I got, courtesy of my mischievous wife was a twenty stone ball breaking Amazon, who was dressed as a Nazi SS Storm Trooper. As soon as I saw her, I knew that there would be no arguing with her. After introducing herself and smirking at the audience that had formed a semi-circle around us, she bounced me on her knee, threw me around and lifted me up and over her shoulder, and at one point with a grip that the Terminator would have been proud of, she grabbed the seat of my trousers and bounced me up and down as though I were a bloody yo-yo. My humiliation was enjoyed by all, including my mother, father, my kids and of course my pleased as Punch wife. What I'd done to deserve this public humiliation I don't know, but whatever it was, I paid for it in full.

After the buffet break, which was fit for a King and a few more drinks, I rolled up my shirtsleeves and had a ball and as far as I could tell, so did everyone else. It turned out to be one of the most memorable nights of my life, but I wouldn't care to meet that domineering Amazon again.

During the nineteen nineties Nelson Mandela was freed after spending twenty-seven years in prison, East and West Germany was reunited, the Soviet Union broke up into semi-independent states and the divisive Thatcher era came to an end, brought about by her own, back stabbing, smiling colleagues. Saddam Hussein invaded Kuwait and began the long Gulf War saga and an attempt to blow up the Twin Tower World Trade Centre in New York with a car park bomb was a sign of things to come and Diana, the Princess of Wales, was tragically killed in a Parisian car crash and was publicly mourned by almost the entire nation.

Webber was In the Sailors one evening doing his usual information gathering pub trawl, which he claimed was much more lucrative than it used to be as this generation of wide boys, as opposed to ours, were much more willing to openly brag about their criminal exploits.

"The brainless twats seem to think that it gives them street cred." Was his surprisingly shrewd observational quote.

He informed me that the fat slob Eddie Rogers had passed away and I was so pleased at hearing the good news I bought him a pint, but I soon found an excuse to move on as he insisted on questioning me about the missing diamond again. He seemed to think that by going over the story time and time again some forgotten clue would eventually emerge, but his problem was and always had been, he couldn't be sure whether I'd been there or not and I certainly wasn't going to tell him was I.

I never quite took to Webber, he was a nice enough bloke and all that, but his occupation always got in the way, I felt uncomfortable in his company as I was always aware that I'd got to be extra careful with what I said, which is not easy when you've had a few drinks. He was normal enough, he had a wife and two kids and all the domestic troubles that we all had and he was always affable, well he would be wouldn't he, I mean that's how he got his information, but it was this obsession with this missing diamond that really got up my nose.

For some reason, I've never been ambitious or driven and I find those that are a bit odd. Obsessions are completely foreign to my way of thinking. As a kid I got involved in all the usual fads, collecting cigarette cards and footballer's autographs and I even went train spotting for a while. I tried stamp collecting until I found that there were millions of the bloody things. So it's not as though I'm not aware of stupid obsessions, but Webber had become a real pain in the arse.

Meeting Webber that evening got me thinking again about the mystery of the missing diamond and I eventually came up with a theory. The diamond was supposed to be in the safe and Mitch swears that when he opened it, it wasn't there and I believe him as not only is he a mate, but the way his transport business has floundered at times, he needed the money more than the rest of us

438

and would certainly have cashed it in. I am quite sure that Billy didn't come across it as Billy is an open book and he couldn't have kept such a secret from us. Bronco never entered the house that night so he's out of the picture, which leaves me and I didn't even know that the bloody thing existed until we were in the van after the job had been done

So that just leaves Nicos, and as he didn't keep it in the safe, where would he safely hide it while he went on holiday with his bit of fluff, and suddenly it came to me, where do you hide a tree? In a forest. So where would you hide a diamond, in a bloody great jar of clear glass marbles that's where. When Billy had suggested taking some of those old toys for his kids, he'd actually lifted up the jar of marbles and had commented on how heavy it was, his very words were, "Bloody hell, this weighs a bleeding ton, there must hundreds of marbles in this jar."

So why keep so many inexpensive marbles? To deter anyone from carrying off such a heavy weight when there were more desirable objects in the house that's why. As far as I can see, it's the only thing that makes sense. So my guess is that somewhere out there tucked away in a corner of a second hand dealers or a charity shop there's a large jar of marbles that no one wants and as kids no longer play with them, well not hundreds of the buggers anyway, that's where it will stay for a very long time.

I didn't mention my theory to Webber, as if he knew that he'd actually seen the house clearance bloke carrying the jar of marbles past him when he put it in his van with all the other junk, it might have sent him over the edge, so I kept my big gob well and truly shut.

There is little doubt that Old Gabby had been a member of the British armed forces at some time or another, but what was in doubt was which branch he'd actually been in and what he'd actually done while serving his time. The problem was, Old Gabby was a habitual liar and it was difficult at times to know when he was telling the truth. On the other hand it was easy to tell when he was not, as that was what he did for most of the time. He claimed that at different times he'd been attached to, the artillery, the tank regiment, the marines, the paratroops and on certain occasions he'd participated in secret missions with the SAS. When disclosing his tales of adventure he never failed to remind those that asked him awkward questions that the details of these missions were covered by the official secrets act. And not only had he had adventures with these units, but somehow he'd found time to serve with the RAF Regiment as an expert dog handler.

He'd not been slack during his civilian life either as he'd tackled most jobs in his time and was a competent sportsman. Whenever anyone at Turners mentioned an activity of one sort or another, Old Gabby would not only claim to have already done the very same thing, but to have done it ten times better. It was said that if ever he appeared on, "This is Your Life," the programme would last at least a week and it would take fifty blokes to carry all the red books that contained his life story.

But for the few years that I knew him, he was nothing more than a crabby old storeman who lived in a dilapidated house along with his elderly mother and a drunken work shy brother and travelled around the city in an old "banger" car that broke down on a regular basis. He was known as Old Gabby because someone said that he reminded them of Gabby Hayes, a crabby old character who'd appeared in many black and white "B" western films alongside Hoppalong Cassidy and Old Gabby lived up to his name by driving me and the other workers to distraction with his habitual gripes. Every day without fail, he would find something or someone to moan about and he would make damn sure that I knew all about it.

At one time, he refused to use the stores canteen for his breaks, because he said, with genuine grievance, "The others are too bloody noisy and they play that loud pop music on the radio all the time."

Now I could fully sympathise with this, as I also found that none stop loud pop music irritating, but when he began building his own substantial canteen, complete with electric kettle, toaster, radio, armchair, carpet, bookcase, mirror, framed photographs and lock up cupboards in one corner of the stores, I was forced to put a stop to it as he was beginning to take up more space in the stores than all the other storemen had for their canteen facilities. The bonus that I received from this acrimonious altercation was that he did not speak to me for three days, but unfortunately, he was a forgiving sort of a chap and on the fourth day, he was back at my office door with his usual catalogue of moans and injustices that needed my immediate attention.

Whether he'd been a fine figure of a man in his youth, no one at Turners knew, but now that he was nearing his sixtieth birthday, he'd developed a natural round shouldered stance, a sunken chest and a beer belly and he was no longer the a six pack Adonis that he claimed he'd once been, but this obvious detail did little to stop him from acting as though he was a body building beach hunk. He would strut confidently around the stores even on the coldest of days, wearing nothing more than a flat cap, a grubby T-shirt and a pair of well-worn jeans while claiming that he was a real man and never felt the cold. He also claimed that he needed no more than three hours sleep and had never had a day's illness in his life. Whenever he did have time off for sickness, he would swear that it was his elderly mother that was ill and that he was forced to have time off to look after her.

The area where he did elicit genuine sympathy was in his dealings with his drunken slob of a brother, who stole money from his pockets when he was asleep and once in desperation, took all the framed pictures off the living room wall and sold them for beer money. Old Gabby was furious and complained bitterly that this act of treachery had not only lost the family heirlooms forever, but had left pale oblong fade marks on the wallpaper where the pictures had hung.

His old battered car was forever breaking down and had to be pushed, pulled and towed on a regular basis. This prompted one stores wit to suggest, "As we have to push Old Gabby's car so often across the car park to get it started, it might be worthwhile welding a set of wheelbarrow handles to the sides to give us a better purchase."

Undaunted by such snide remarks, Old Gabby, with his flat cap wedged on his head and his sharp chin jutting forward in the manner of a warship cutting through a choppy sea, would chug slowly along the busy city roads in his battered old car completely oblivious to the long line of vehicles and their frustrated drivers travelling in his wake while the rear end of his car was enveloped in a cloud of acrid smoke.

"Thank God he doesn't tow a bloody caravan," one storeman said when discussing Gabby's travelling arrangements, "He'd bring the whole of the West Midlands to a halt."

Because he had a short fuse and was easily riled, he often became a target for bored storemen to bait with practical jokes, but one morning when I saw him marching into work in a foul mood, I suspected that someone had gone too far and I got ready to intervene in any altercation that might follow. He confronted a mild mannered storemen named Paul and pointing a warning finger at his surprised face said angrily, "Oi! You! Don't you ever phone me on my mobile phone while I'm in the hospital again. Okay!"

It seems that Paul, had tried to contact Old Gabby during the previous evening, as he wished to know more details about a supposed antique bookcase that Old Gabby was trying to sell.

"What are you talking about you daft old bugger?" Paul replied while frowning as he was completely bewildered by this angry attack.

"You!" stated Old Gabby while continuing to point an accusing finger at him, "Phoning me while I was visiting my old mother in the hospital. That's what I'm on about. I got a right bollocking from the nurses because of you. For your information, you ain't allowed to use mobile phones in a hospital."

Paul shook his head and in wide eyed disbelief as he pointed out the obvious, "How the bleeding hell am I supposed to know that you were in a hospital when I phoned you, you daft old fart. When I phoned you last night, you could have been in Timbuktu for all I knew."

"Well, for your information," Old Gabby replied firmly, "I wornt in no Timbuktu, I was in the bloody hospital and I got a right good bollocking, so don't do it again." And with that he stormed off up the stores to work the rest of the morning on his own while continually muttering to himself.

Being a master of the tall story, so much so that once told, he came to believe that they were true; he was forever being led into conversations by the other storemen that would eventually lead him to invent a new improbable tale. When one day the conversation turned to the training of dogs, it turned out that while serving with the RAF Regiment for a while, he had under his command ten German Shepard dogs while the other handlers had only one and his were not only the best-trained dogs the Regiment had ever possessed, but also, the other handlers begged him to reveal his secret training methods to them. Then while serving in Germany, this time with the army, but which regiment remained a mystery, he became involved in a drunken barroom brawl and to defend himself; he'd used his special unarmed combat techniques. At the subsequent enquiry, it was established that he'd put five men into hospital and was banned from visiting the town for ten years. When asked what the name of the town was, he declared that he could not divulge that kind of information as it was classified and still covered by the official secrets act.

While hiking along a Pembrokeshire coastal path, he and a mate witnessed the sight of an RAF bomber, complete with a payload of atomic bombs, crash into the sea and disappear without trace. "That bomber is still at the bottom of the sea and me and my mate are the only ones who know where it is." he declared with the seriousness of a funeral director.

Hurrying around the stores one day, he accidentally slipped on a patch of spilt oil and fell heavily onto his back. A young storeman, who happened to be working nearby, witnessed the accident and immediately ran over to help him.

"He was obviously dazed and a little shocked," the young lad reported later, "and I said, shall I fetch some help? He shook his head and with my help, he struggled to his feet and as he leaned against a storage rack he gasped, "No it's alright son, I was in the paratroops and I'm trained see, I know how to fall without hurting myself." And with that he staggered off down the stores."

He must have been in great pain as he hid himself away for a whole hour while he slowly recovered and the next day I received a telephone call informing me that he would be absent from work for a few days as his old mother had suddenly taken to her bed with an unknown illness.

Now that I'd been promoted, one of my extra duties was to oversee the company's Health and Safety policy. As the company employed a hundred and twenty people on the site, it needed several first aiders and Old Gabby, because he'd been a first aider in his previous employment, became one of them. I wasn't particularly enamoured with the idea of allowing him to fulfil this role as he wasn't particularly hygienic, but as I could find no other volunteer, I had little choice. To my astonishment, he turned out to be the most successful first aider the company had ever had, for as soon as the injured party knew that Old Gabby was coming to check them over, they made a miraculous recovery and were soon bouncing about like spring lambs.

The stories concerning the antics of Old Gabby are just too numerous to catalogue in this short account and range from the amusingly absurd, to unbelievable blatant lies. For example, he claimed that while in Germany he broke his leg and found himself lying in the next hospital bed to Bobby Charlton after the Munich air disaster in 1958. He was the first to shake Roger Bannister's hand after the runner had broken the four-minute mile, he had spared with Muhammad Ali, sung a duet with Tom Jones and had not only met the Beatles in Hamburg, but had told them where they were going wrong. If he'd claimed to have been the first man on the moon, no one at Turners would have batted an eyelid.

But for all his round shouldered stories, no one could deny that his heart was in the right place and when he announced that he was going to join a charity marathon walk, all the staff rallied round and sponsored him. But he could not do the walk without being completely different from everyone else and he walked and staggered along the dedicated twenty mile course in full Second World War army kit which consisted of a thick serge uniform, heavy black boots, a kaki canvas back pack, a steel helmet and a heavy Lee Enfield rifle and totally exhausted, he was almost dead when he eventually crossed the finishing line and had to be whisked off to hospital in an ambulance. No one knew what famous person was in the next bed to him during his short stay in the hospital, as by this time we had learned that it was better not to ask.

A member of the Working Man's Club that Billy occasionally used now that he lived in Stourport, had been registered blind, but having been a member of the club for many years, he had no trouble in negotiating his way around the place and when he discovered that a man had been having a love affair with his wife, he decided to confront him. He waited for the sneaky lover to visit the gent's toilet and he followed in behind. There he ferociously attacked and beat the lover so badly that a paramedic had to patch up the embarrassed, dazed and battered lover, who'd sustained a broken arm in the attack.

"Anyway," Billy said, "what all the blokes in the club wanted to know, was, as Rowley is almost as blind as a bloody bat and can only see varying shades of light and dark, how did he know, that he'd attacked the right man? Somebody said that a blind man uses his acute hearing skills and the sense of touch to compensate for his lack of sight, but I noticed that none of them ever visited the toilet when Rowley was in there. And if he walked in while they were already in there, there was a quick shake of toggers, a zipping of flies and a scramble for the exit."

During the 1990's the film Titanic was shown all around the world and inevitably it spawned a great deal of interest in the 1912 catastrophe, where the great "unsinkable" Atlantic liner had collided with a massive iceberg and had unbelievably sunk, taking with it most of the passengers and crew. Many books giving details of the disaster were duly published and several documentaries appeared on television and the general population suddenly became experts on the sinking of the Titanic.

It was only when Jenny got talking to a little old lady who was a resident in the home where she was employed that she was to feel a real connection to the event. The little old lady described how she'd sat on her father's shoulder and waved to the happy waving passengers as the ship had set sail from Southampton on its doomed voyage. While talking to this little old lady, who had been six years old at the time and full of exited happiness, Jenny suddenly felt a genuine link with the doomed ship.

The old lady had lived through two World Wars and the many other catastrophes that the twentieth century had thrown up, but she said, "The sinking of the Titanic was the one event that shocked me the most. You see we were so thrilled and so full of pride that when we saw her majestically sail out to sea we thought that it was

445

impossible for such a huge ship to sink. And even when the dreadful news came through we could not believe it and thought there had to be some sort of mistake., it was just inconceivable and even now after all these years, I still find it hard to believe that the tragedy actually took place."

Turners had become a very successful company and with orders pouring in on a daily basis and we were working flat out. As an associate director I was allowed to attend board meetings, but as I had no ambition and no interest in boardroom politics, the lack of voting rights did not bother me in the slightest. This new position gave me an insight into the scheming Machiavellian intrigues that the other company directors got up to and because I was no threat to any of them, they often let slip details of their devious plans as they lobbied me for support. It soon became apparent that each one had ambitions to run the company and saw the other directors as a threat to their future prospects.

Being naïve, I'd always assumed that they would see rival companies as their enemy, but not a bit of it, at boardroom meetings, which were meant to solve and smooth out problems, they did their best to score points off each other without seeming to be vindictive. At times I felt as though I was taking part in a film script, as I knew that they were all keeping their real thoughts and feelings close to their chests. I came to realise that Mr Bruce, who was nobody's fool, was well aware of this situation and I became convinced that he actively encouraged the plotting and the subtle back stabbing to go on for his own sadistic amusement, his policy seemed to be, divide and rule and then quietly laugh up his sleeve.

Mr Bruce expected his directors to be commercially minded men who kept a tight rein on the purse strings as well as on their staff and he encouraged a code of bullying. The one director who had great difficulty with this severe policy was Dawley, who was by nature a thoughtful humanitarian and although he was as ambitious as the others, he lacked the killer instinct. Although he ran his department as efficiently as any of the other directors and was liked by his staff and customers, he was constantly criticised for being far too soft. Unfortunately, when conversing and in full flow, he was quite incapable of finishing off a sentence with a full stop and would ramble on and on. The topic in question would be entirely forgotten as his explanations changed course again and again and this had the effect of driving Mr Bruce, who liked to get straight to the point, to distraction. Exasperated, Mr Bruce would state angrily, "Dawley! Will you get to the point and stop going off on yet another tangent. I've already forgotten why we are here and what we are here to discuss."

Dawley also had another annoying habit to which he, with his usual candid good humour, freely confessed to. Whenever he attended a football match, he became so engrossed that he gave running commentary on the match. "Pass it to the wing, don't take all day, come on pass it. That's it, now skin him, that's it, go, go, now cross it. Come on don't mess about, put a cross in. What's he playing at? Get it over. That's it, now shoot! Oh! What the hell was that? My old granny can shoot better than that."

By half time and this was in the days when supporters stood side by side on the terraces in jam packed crowds, Dawley would find himself standing all alone with ten foot of clear space all around him.

To prevent the staff from drinking too much during the lunch break on the day that we were due to break up for the Christmas holiday, I was given the task of organising a disco and running buffet on the premises. This allowed the staff to leave their posts on a rotor basis, eat, drink and make merry with a small m and keep the company ticking over throughout the afternoon. If there was an order to be had that day, Mr Bruce was determined to have it, even if it was Christmas.

At twelve noon the makeshift disco, which had been set up in a spare office kicked off and all went well with the staff alternating their Merry Christmas breaks. After seeing that everything was running smoothly, I carried on with my normal duties and it wasn't until three in the afternoon that I was able to get back to the disco. I could see at once that it was a complete success, office and stores staff were mixing with each other, the food and drink was being consumed at a steady rate, no one was drunk and none of the office girls had been molested against their will.

Feeling at ease, as the day had gone well, I picked up a can of larger and proceeded to open it, but before I could take a drink, a message came over the loud speaker system asking for all the directors to attend an urgent meeting in the boardroom. Feeling thoroughly pissed off at this interruption, I slowly made my way to the boardroom while wondering what the hell had happened and trying to bring to mind anything that I'd done wrong that called for a reprimand in front of the directors. When I reached the boardroom I found that four company directors were already sitting solemnly around the large highly polished table with faces resembling basset hounds trapped in a dog's home.

"Anyone know what it's all about, are we in for a Christmas bonus?" I asked lightly, while attempting to lift the pervading gloom that filled the room, but all I received was a shake of the head and mumbles of, "I doubt it'll be good news," and "God moves in mysterious ways," which was a direct reference to Mr Bruce's nickname among the directors.

"I can't understand why he's still here?" one of them then said and who seemed to speak for all, "Most of the other branches have already called it a day, Ipswich and Bristol were closing at two and I was hoping to be away by now, I've got a dinner and dance to attend tonight."

After a couple of minutes Mr Bruce marched briskly into the boardroom closely followed by the company's financial director. Mr Bruce stood behind his impressive chair which of course was larger than the others and waited for the financial director to settle. When he had our full attention, he then announced in a very clear and precise manner.

"As you know in the last few years the company has grown considerably and is now a nation-wide concern and I find that I have to give the outlying branches more and more of my time. This of course means that I cannot run this particular branch with the same attention anymore and as none of you are capable of running this branch with the competence that it requires, I have decided to bring in a new managing director. He starts on January the eighth and I expect you to give him your full support and co-operation. Merry Christmas."

With that he walked out of the boardroom and as we sat there in stunned silence, his footsteps could be heard clip-clopping along the long corridor as he marched back to his office.

For several minutes we sat in silence as we let this staggering news seep in. For a while, none of the directors were able to find an appropriate response to the stunning news, each one glad that none of the others had been promoted over and above themselves, but thoroughly pissed off at being considered to be too incompetent to fill the position. After a while the transport director, with undisguised angry venom evident in his voice and who seemed to speak for all, spat out the words, "Well that's well and truly fucked up my Christmas" and one by one we rose from the table and filed out of the room in stunned silence.

The new managing director joined the company and started work on the eighth of January as planned and by the following Christmas, he was gone to pastures new. Far from the directors giving him their full support and co-operation, the back stabbing during that year rivalled anything that the senators of ancient Rome had got up to and it became obvious that this situation would never work. Once more Mr Bruce had made an instant decision that had been totally wrong, the man he'd picked to control a pack of snapping wolves was a super salesman and not a hard-nosed no nonsense disciplinarian that the situation required. After the new managing director had become history, Mr Bruce then decided that one of the original directors was capable of running the branch after all, which pleased that particular director and thoroughly enraged the others, and the back stabbing political intrigues started all over again.

Then, quite out of the blue, an in depth audit, and no one seemed to have any idea why we hadn't had one before, discovered that the company was not as wealthy and as successful as everyone had been led to believe. The company had lost the unbelievable sum of five million pounds. The question that was asked by all, from lowly storeman to company director, was how could a company that was booming on all fronts, possibly loose five million-pound? The answer turned out to be quite simple. It was never there in the first place. Many of the companies and their substantial assets that had been acquired over the previous decade, turned out to be worthless.

The stock that these companies held looked very impressive on paper and evidently the financial director had made sure that it did, but when the stock was physically examined by the auditors, most of it was found to be old, rusty, worn out, broken and un-saleable and only fit for the scrap yard. The fallout from this discovery was dramatic, the bank virtually took over the company and the company shares nose-dived till they were almost worthless and the whiz kid financial director was given his marching orders. As for Mr Bruce, the news hit him hard and during this period he lost a considerable amount of weight, developed a nervous twitch and seemed more than a little embarrassed by the events that had taken place.

"After all," as Dawley succinctly put it, "he was supposed to be the all-seeing God who knew everything that was going on in the company and it now seems, he was as much in the dark as we were."

The man that the bank put in charge of the company's finances was an amiable, but no nonsense disciplinarian and he quickly introduced strict accountancy at every level including the director's considerable expenses which I knew were more than a bit iffy as many years before I'd inadvertently come across a number of invoices that were supposedly for electrical work that had been carried out on the premises and as I was responsible for checking all the maintenance work, these invoices had mistakenly found their way onto my desk. All the invoices were for work that had been carried out on the director's houses. I wasn't surprised by this revelation as I'd known for a long time that this sort of thing was going on, but as yet, I'd not been invited to join the lucrative gravy train and now with the new man from the bank in charge I never would be. But far from being downhearted, I was quite happy with the situation as I had my own bonus scheme in place which none of the directors were aware of.

Over a number of years the banks disciplinarian gradually pulled the company around which was good news for the shareholders, but the staff knew that the writing was on the wall and as soon as the company was a viable concern once more, it was liable to be the subject of a takeover bid and that would inevitably mean that many, as there is no sentiment in business, would be given the elbow no matter how much effort they had put into the company over the previous years. But the dark cloud had a silver lining, the Penguin, who had most of his early retirement plans tied up in company shares, lost the lot and had to postpone his dream of moving his substantial beer belly to Spain where he'd planned to acquire a dream villa. We learned that his wife, a brassy Welsh lass who constantly sang the praises of Wales, but never went there, gave him a real ear bashing for putting all his eggs in one basket.

Big Ron was the best chess player that Turners had ever had and that fact alone was a symptom of his problem; he was far too intelligent for the job that he was employed to do. He was in his late thirties and as yet had not settled down into the humdrum commercial time consuming world that most of us have to exist in. He'd yet to learn that earning a weekly wage to pay for his daily bread was rarely an exciting process and that coming to terms with this fact is all part of growing up.

Although intelligent, he'd been extremely restless from an early age, been disruptive at school and had given up on academic studies far too early and unlike his mates who'd chosen a safe path in life, had gone out into the wide world seeking adventure, fame and fortune. He'd tried his hand at various occupations in numerous countries, but found that adventure and the acquisition of wealth do not necessarily go hand in hand. During his travels he'd worked in hotels, holiday camps, on cruise liners and on a North Sea oil rig where the pay was excellent, but earning it was mind numbingly boring. And now, looking dismally forward to middle age, he'd washed up at Turners like a piece of battered flotsam with a head full of memories, but empty pockets.

His hum-drum daily task was testing steam valves, an occupation that needed no more than two days training and he found life on the bottom rung of the ladder frustrating and would often seek relief by playing practical jokes or flirting with the office girls. His habit of flirting with almost every woman that he met got him into many domestic scrapes and he bounced from one romantic crisis to another and seemed to be under constant threat from either a scorned woman or a jealous husband. To occupy his active mind, he took to buying and selling stolen goods as it not only boosted his meagre income, but appealed to his sense of adventure. One of the products that he was able to obtain for a while was good quality joints of pre-packed meat and many of the staff became willing weekly customers.

George Brown and his thirty-four year old rotund son Roger, who was known to be a "Mommies boy," were both employed as storemen and they became eager to purchase one of Big Ron's cheap joints of meat, but before doing so, they were obliged to discuss the matter with "Mother Brown," who was George's clinging wife and Rogers doting mother. At least four times a day they would telephone home and discuss company business and any tittle-tattle that they'd picked up during the day with "Mother Brown." There were many occasions when I was convinced that "Mother Brown," knew more about what was going on in the company than I did. After a protracted conversation on the telephone, "Mother Brown" agreed to the purchase of a joint of reasonably priced meat for the weekend and having taken the order, Big Ron duly supplied the meat to George and rotund Roger.

On the following Monday morning, George and his son informed Big Ron that not only had they thoroughly enjoyed the meat, but that "Mother Brown" would like to thank him personally for supplying it. Big Ron pointed out that supplying the meat had been a simple business transaction and that any form of "thanks" was completely unnecessary. But Big Ron did not know the Browns and their peculiar ways as well as the rest of us and did not realise that things would not be allowed to rest there. Getting involved with the Brown's domestic life was on a par with becoming entrapped in a lake of treacle as all three would never tire of smothering their victim with sweet sycophantic compliments.

Later in the day, Big Ron happened to be passing the Brown's during one of their informative telephone conversations with "Mother Brown" and was gleefully handed the telephone with the message that "Mother" was on the line and wished to speak with him. Reluctantly Big Ron took the telephone and listened to ten minutes of claptrap designed to help him bond with the Brown family, but before ringing off, "Mother" asked him to say a few words to "Little Peter", as it would "make his day." To oblige, Big Ron reluctantly agreed and found himself saying, "are you alright?

Have you been in the garden playing with your toys?" but was a little bemused as he heard no words of recognition in reply.

After putting the telephone down, George and his son, thanked Big Ron for conversing with "Mother" and said that he could call in at their home anytime that he was passing. It was an invitation that Big Ron later confided, "Scared the shit out of me. I couldn't think of anything more nauseating. That would be my room 101. I'd rather face a room full of rats than that."

As he went to walk away, he suddenly asked, "Oh, by the way, I didn't know that you had a small boy named Peter at home."

"We don't," said George smiling with pride, "Little Peter is our dog. He's a lovely little miniature poodle."

Big Ron was gobsmacked and exclaimed, "Do you mean to tell me, that I've just spent three minutes of my precious life, talking to a bleeding miniature poodle on the telephone?"

"Oh yes," said George as he beamed with pleasure, "Our little Peter loves to listen to people talking on the telephone."

A couple of days later, I heard Big Ron tell the manager of the local pub, "The Brown's have completely ruined my street credibility, If my mates at the Punch Bowl find out that I've been talking to a bleeding poodle on the telephone, I'll have to change my name and leave the country."

Big Ron eventually parted company with Turners, which was no great surprise and he became, with the help of another man's wife, the landlord of a small Black Country pub. Less than a year later, he and his new love had split up and the last that any of us heard of him was that he'd gone back to work on the North Sea oil rigs and as far as anyone knows little Peter, the miniature poodle is still waiting for his call.

Sam Bane, who we'd enticed back to fill the role of, "Trade Counter Expert," was a unique character in many ways. He would automatically take the opposite view to everyone else, was as pessimistic as Eeyore and as bloody minded as a religious fanatic, but on the other hand, if a technical problem cropped up, he was the man to sort it out. Although a rough-hewn man, he took to technical

453

problems with the fervour of a dedicated scientist and would not rest until he'd solved them.

Sam's hobby during the nineteen sixties and seventies was potholing, an activity that held little interest for me as I preferred to be on top of a hill looking at the panoramic view, rather than crawling through the dark damp tunnels that ran beneath it. Sam, accompanied by his brother-in-law, who was just as odd as Sam, would regularly set off at weekends in an old battered Land Rover loaded up with ropes, clamps, lamps, waterproofs and camping gear to some distant wind swept crag and spend the day crawling and slithering through numerous wet potholes and dark caves having a wonderful exhausting time. On one occasion his long-suffering wife, who was five months pregnant, accompanied him and the nutty brother-in-law for a weekend of fun in the damp dark Derbyshire potholes. They'd been crawling through one particular set of tunnels for about an hour, when Sam's wife decided that enough was enough and she needed to rest. It was decided that she should stay and rest in the small gallery that they'd reached, while Sam and his brother-in-law carried on and explored a little further. And so, leaving his wife sitting on a damp rock, with a chocolate biscuit in one hand and a lamp in the other, Sam and his brother-in-law carried on exploring.

The plan to pick her up on the way back seemed to have slipped Sam's mind when they found another way out because it was while they were back at base camp brewing a pot of tea on the old Primus stove that Sam suddenly remembered that his long suffering pregnant wife was still waiting for them underground. Her remarks when rescued are unrecorded, but are thought to have contained quite a number of very basic Anglo-Saxon expletives.

Sam's overriding passion was collecting and hoarding odd objects that one day would become very useful or would appreciate in value. He collected bent nails which could be straightened, bits of string, office clip boards, old box files, nuts bolts and washers, numerous pieces of discarded wood, an assortment of scrap metal, a motor bike engine, rolls of electrical wire, tools of every description, a jumble of car parts from different models, a judge's wig in a leather carry case and a camouflaged Second World War army bicycle. In fact, Sam collected anything that anyone was willing to throw away or sell at a reasonable price. He often went to a car boot sale with the intention of selling a car full of objects and came back with more than he had started out with. To store his huge hoard of useful things, he built himself a shed and every two or three years, he extended it to accommodate the extra useful things that he had acquired.

"His bloody shed is as big as a hangar at RAF Cosford." Was Butch's comment when discussing Sam's shed and he was only half joking.

At one car boot sortie Sam bought an old, bright red, factory fire alarm bell and fitted it to the door of his large shed to act as a burglar alarm. As he lived in the countryside near Hagley, when activated it could be heard quite clearly five mile away. After a couple of months, he reluctantly disconnected the unique burglar alarm and threw it into the shed with all the other useful objects. His reason for dismantling the factory fire bell wasn't because his neighbours had complained about the noise, although they had done just that, but because he kept forgetting that the damn thing was there.

"Every time I opened the door, it frightened the life out of me and I couldn't hear a bleeding thing for twenty minutes," he informed us with a defeated shake of his head.

One winter's evening there was a major electrical power failure in the district where Sam lived and all his neighbours were forced to seek out torches and candles. Much to his sceptical wife surprise; from somewhere in the bowels of his enormous shed, Sam produced a large Calor gas searchlight. He erected the searchlight, complete with its metal tripod legs, in the middle of the back garden and directed the strong beam of light onto the back of the house. This had the desired effect of lighting up the living room, the kitchen and the back bedrooms, but as the bright light was directed horizontally at the house, it also dazzled to distraction anyone that was in its powerful beam. To counteract this slight problem, Sam then unearthed a box of assorted sunglasses and issued a pair to each member of his family. Butch was to point out, when he heard Sam relate this series of events, "You must be the only family in the whole bleeding world that wear sunglasses in a blackout."

Sam had many odd items hidden away in his large shed, but one that intrigued Butch, was a Second World War army bicycle that was painted in camouflage colours. Intrigued, Butch asked Sam that having put a camouflaged bike into a shed full of assorted oddments, how would he ever find it again and how could he ever be sure that it was still there. To which Sam replied with a thoughtful frown on his face, "Come to think of it, I haven't seen that bike for several years. I wonder if the missis has given it away," to which butch replied, "Well, without completely emptying the shed and falling over it, you'll never know will you?"

During one conversation the topic of treasure hunters came up and Butch wondered just how effective the metal detectors that they used were when they went out looking for King Johns lost treasure and only found metal bottle tops. On hearing this Sam declared, "Well I've got one that's bloody efficient. The trouble is, it's so bleeding heavy, I have to put it in a wheel barrow when I take it any distance."

Butch and I looked at each other, shook our heads at hearing this incomprehensible statement and once more, as we often did when conversing with Sam, asked him for a simple and rational explanation.

"Well I was at an auction of ex-army stuff see," Sam explained, as he looked forlornly into the middle distance, "And these metal detectors came up and I bid for them and no other bugger did and so I finished up with them."

"But why is it so heavy?" Butch asked who was still puzzled by Sam's explanation.

"Well it's not just an ordinary metal detector see," Sam answered, "It's a Second World War mine detector. It's for clearing mine fields."

"Hang on," Butch then asked, a puzzled frown on his face, "You said that you bid for "these" metal detectors. How many were there?"

"Four," Sam replied without emotion, "Three are still in their boxes at the back of my shed completely untouched."

I noticed one day that Sam, who rarely looked happy even when he was, appeared to be much more miserable than usual. After enquiring about his health Sam reluctantly disclosed that he was sick to death of pink trifle pudding. Butch and I, who were quite used to his odd ways, were never the less; a little puzzled by this bizarre answer and demanded an explanation. He went on to explain that nine days earlier, a Saturday night fund raising dance and buffet had taken place in the local church hall and his wife, being on the committee, had been heavily involved in organising the event. But because of poor advertising and the fact that it was taking place in a dingy church hall, the event had been a total failure and hardly anyone had turned up, including many who had been persuaded to buy tickets in advance. This left those that had turned up with a large amount of prepared food to dispose of. Sam's wife had left the church hall that night with six large bowls of pink trifle pudding and Sam and his two dogs had been eating it ever since.

"After eight days of eating the bloody stuff, even the dogs have refused to eat anymore and I know just how they feel," He complained mournfully.

Although I was aware that my constant clashes with the Penguin would not be forgotten or forgiven and that I was probably somewhere near the top of his hit list, I found it impossible not to upset him at every opportunity. Time and again the Penguin would try to bully me and I would retaliate by openly laughing at him and belittling his arguments and point of view. On several occasions he'd tried to embarrass me in management meetings by highlighting some company procedure that had gone wrong that I was responsible for, but each time I'd quickly thought of an excuse and wriggled out of it. Although being able to fend off these open attacks made me feel good, I knew that this would only encourage him to seek other ways of bringing me down. My only consolation was that the he was not particularly bright so I was confident that the attacks would not be very sophisticated and that I would be able to cope with them when they came.

Then during one hectic morning while I was overseeing the normal daily procedures and making sure that urgent orders were being completed on time, one of the Penguin's subordinates who was not entirely enamoured with his bosses bullying behaviour, whispered to me as he passed by, "Watch your back this morning Jaco, he's up to something."

Now although the company's enormous stock range was controlled by a computer system, there was a glaring fault that had been introduced into the company's paperwork system that had worried me for some considerable time. It was simply that the delivery drivers used hand written loading lists and did not have to show their official delivery notes to the storemen when loading tube onto their lorries. For someone sitting in an office there would seem to be nothing wrong with this system, the hand written loading notes were checked at both ends of the loading procedure and the procedure helped to keep the official delivery notes clean and presentable when handed to the customer, but to someone like me who was fully aware of how underhand deals worked, the system looked completely different. I realised that when storemen were busy, the checking procedure could become very lax and during some hectic periods, completely none existent. And mistakes could be made, thirty could be scribbled to look like fifty and it didn't take a genius to see that a naught could be added to single figure and a hand written loading list could easily be lost during the course of the day.

On several occasions I'd pointed out this glaring fault in the paperwork system at management meetings, but I always got the same answer, "It's up to you to see that every load is checked," but on a busy morning it was impossible to police every load and those around the table were well aware of it, but to them, that was my problem, not theirs.

With the office lad's warning ringing in my ears, I immediately thought of the hand written loading lists and I hurried round to the tube store and warned Big Guy to make sure that every load was checked that morning and if possible, I would double check. As I was responsible for both the tube store and the general store it was impossible for me to be in both places at the same time, but at every opportunity I raced back into the tube store and checked the driver's loads.

It was Big Guy who found the suspicious loading list. Halfway down there was an item that looked decidedly odd. It was for an unusually large quantity of copper tube and this particular customer rarely purchased large quantities of anything, especially copper tube.

I checked the loading note against the driver's official delivery note and there it was. The figure ten had been altered to one hundred and ten.

"Who wrote this item on your list?" I asked the driver warily.

"The Penguin," The driver answered, without concern, "He said that they'd just phoned up and increased the order."

"So where's the official paperwork to cover it?"

"I don't know. He sees to that, not me. I'm just in a hurry to get loaded and get on my way; it's up to him to sort the paperwork out."

"That's all bollocks," Big Guy stated, "That customer never has that much copper tube."

"I think your right, but one thing's for sure, that amount of copper tube is not going out without the correct paperwork." I said and added, "Just put on the lorry what's on the official delivery note."

"Are you going to tell Mr Bruce what the bastard has been up to?" Big Guy asked when the driver, who was moaning about his morning being disrupted, had walked away.

"I can't," I replied with a shrug, "He's got us by the short and curlies."

"What do you mean, the bastards trying to get us into trouble. He's trying to get me the bleeding sack."

"Look, I know exactly what he's up to, but at the moment I can't do anything about it. If I go and play my face to Mr Bruce, all that the Penguin will say is that it was a genuine mistake and it's our job to check the loads as a safeguard to stop this type of mistake anyway."

"I've a good mind to go round to his office and punch his fucking head." Was Big Guy's predictable reply to what to him sounded like a wishy washy explanation.

Although I felt exactly the same, I just said calmly and hoped that Big Guy would believe me, "Leave it to me, I'll sort it. He won't try that again for a while when I've finished with him."

Although I said it with confidence, I was far from sure that the Penguin would not try the same trick again within days as I knew that he was a bear of very little brain and not much imagination and would find it exceedingly difficult to come up with a different plan.

Big Guy was convinced that the scam had been aimed at him, which was a view that I decided not to challenge as I knew that for the next few weeks he would scrupulously check every delivery note that passed his way. I realised that if the lorry had been loaded with that incorrect amount of copper tube, the list would have gone missing and Penguin would have bounded up to Mr Bruce's office and demanded that I be reprimanded for running a loose ship and would have spread the poison by saying, "It makes you wonder how many times this has happened," and I would have been well and truly black listed.

I confronted the Penguin, but instead of accusing him of duplicity I just commented casually, "I see that your department made another balls up this morning on a loading list."

"Oh the customer got mixed up," was the Penguin's well-rehearsed reply, "He rang back and cancelled it just after."

"It's a bloody good job that some of us know what we're doing." I said while laughing and as I walked away I surreptitiously winked at the lad who had forewarned me and made a mental note to pay for his beer the next time that I saw him in the pub.

I felt elated that I'd foiled the Penguin's plan, but I was under no illusions, I knew that before long his unimaginative doggedness would catch me out and over the next few weeks, the pressure of looking for the next attack began to tell. As I had predicted, a few weeks later the Penguin tried the same trick again, but once again it was easily spotted, but then he changed tack, during management meetings he began to claim that that some item had been wrongly labelled and although my investigations found that these accusations were false, the other managers went away from the meetings believing that the general stores were not being run efficiently. The whole process was very wearing and I began to see plots where there were none and wasted time on checking things that did not need checking and eventually, over a few pints of beer, I confessed all to my two mates, Mitch and Billy.

"I thought I could handle him, but the strain is beginning to tell," I said to them wearily, "I can handle the bastard head on, that's easy, the prat gets flustered as soon as I laugh at him, but this sneak thief

460

sabotage is different, I just don't know where the next attack is going to come from."

"Why don't you go and have a quiet word with old Brucie and explain things, then when it does happen he'll know that you've been set up." Mitch suggested logically.

"No, that's no good," I pointed out, "first off, he'll just say that it's my job to see that company procedures are adhered to and secondly, he enjoys seeing his managers and directors stabbing each other in the back, in fact he encourages it. It's one of his stupid hobbies."

"Yeah, you're probably right; he's always been a queer fish ain't he."

"There's only one answer." Stated no nonsense Billy.

"And what's that?"

"Shoot the bastard!"

The Penguin was an avid drinker and he carried a large amount of excess blubber to prove it. He drank heavily during his lunch break and often popped into a local pub before going home at night. The pub that he used had a large car park and one dark winter's night as he was just about to get into his car, a hooded figure stepped out of the dark shadows and hit him hard across his right shin with a heavy metal bar. There was a sickening crack of bone and an instantaneous scream of pain, but as loud music was emanating from within the pub, only the Penguin and his shadowy assailant heard it. He was eventually found writhing in agony and screaming blue murder and carted off to hospital where they found that he had a broken leg. He was off work for many weeks and when he did return, he needed the aid of a aluminium elbow crutch for some considerable time and every time I saw him hobbling around the place, I smiled pleasantly and enquired as to how his damaged leg felt and gave him the impression that I knew more about the incident than I actually did.

There were many rumours as to who was responsible for the late night attack upon the Penguin, but as the list of suspects was as long as the road to Lichfield, no one other than the Penguin cared who'd done the dreadful deed. The general consensus was that the attack was not only something that he deserved, but that it was a pity that he hadn't had both legs broken. Six months after his unfortunate accident, he left the company and went to work with his brother at a company in Coventry and I never laid eyes on him again and I felt all the better for it.

Many years later, Billy asked me one day if I knew how the Flat Footed Penguin was getting along with his bad leg.

"I've no idea and I don't bloody care either," I answered truthfully, "I haven't seen or heard of the bastard for years and I hope he has to walk with a limp for the rest of his life. Why do you want to know anyway, you thinking of sending him a Christmas card?"

"Oh no particular reason, I was just wondering if the leg was still giving him some jip and whether he needed another reminder" and knowingly, he winked at me.

"Does Mitch know anything about this?" I asked as this wink of Billy's confirmed my long held suspicions.

"Who do you think was driving the getaway car that night?" Billy asked and winked at me once more.

Mitch's transport business gradually became firmly established in the world of cut throat commerce and although by the middle of the nineties the money was rolling into his coffers as never before, a good deal of it was also rolling out due to his carefree and lavish lifestyle. He now lived in a large house, employed a part time gardener and had a brand new Jaguar car sitting on his drive. He possessed more shirts and suits than he needed and was never short of cheerful acquaintances that were willing to help him spend his new found wealth, but as yet he'd not found a soul mate, a woman that would help steady his ship. On the few occasions that Billy and I now saw him, we sensed that deep down; his new found wealth had not brought him the happiness that he'd expected.

As we had slipped quietly into middle age, we found that our differing work and family commitments and the fact that we all lived in different parts of the Midlands, meant that we saw less and less of each other. Not only were we living miles apart, but were moving in different social circles. Billy and his family had moved to Stourport and Mitch, after moving several times since his break-up with Heidi, now lived in affluent Streetly and much of his leisure time was spent playing golf with his business associates and visiting race meetings up and down the country. Gibbo and his wife having tired of city life, moved to rugged Cornwall where ironically he found employment with the probation service and having been involved in criminal activity all his life, there was no one who understood the criminal mind better than he did. It was a case of poacher turning gamekeeper and there was not a young yob in the whole of Cornwall who could pull the wool over his eyes.

When we did occasionally meet, we would exchange our latest news and update each other on family affairs, but it was always Mitch who had the most interesting tales to tell and as usual, his adventures involved passionate women. Although we were much older now and had begun to develop the unmistakable signs of age, Mitch still retained his good looks and mesmerising eyes and was still capable of attracting many bored women, but they tended to have a history of broken marriages and relationships and what often seemed to be a promising partnership, disintegrated into dust after the messy domestic complications were eventually revealed. One woman that he got to know well was an attractive divorcee who had two school aged children and worked in an estate agents office. He met her at a dinner and dance while with some friends and after a few dates he seriously toyed with the idea of settling down once more. Unfortunately he discovered that her ex-husband was not only a jealous man, but an extremely violent one and did not take kindly to the knowledge that Mitch was now sleeping with his ex-wife.

"As far as he was concerned," Mitch explained, while shaking his head in disbelief, "no matter what the court had said, they were still a married couple and the lunatic came after me with a bloody machete."

"A machete?" I questioned, as that was the last thing that I'd expected him to say.

"So what happened?" Billy asked while laughing gleefully at Mitch's unforeseen predicament.

"Well she rang me one evening see and warned me that her ex-husband had found out that she was seeing another man and that he wasn't happy about it and he was in his car outside her house waiting for me to turn up. So I said, "That's okay love, I won't come round tonight, let him cool off and I'll see you on Saturday." Then she says,

"Oh and by the way, he's got a machete in his hand, but I don't think he'd use it." Well this put a completely different complexion on the whole affair and the next time I saw her, which I made sure was in a quiet pub in the back of beyond, she tells me he's been done twice for GBH and the last time it took six coppers to bring him in. So now I'm thinking, do I really need this kind of agro at my time of life?"

"So what did you do?" asked Billy, who was thoroughly enjoying Mitch's tale of discomfort.

"Well, I contacted Big Guy and for the next few weeks I took him with me riding shotgun in the car when I went out to meet her at a quiet pub and I took to carrying a small plastic squeeze bottle filled with washing up liquid in my pocket."

"What the bloody hell for?"

"To squirt in the nutters eyes if he came at me with his bloody machete. Well I wasn't going to carry a bloody big sword and take him on like Errol Flynn was I?"

"I could have sold tickets for something like that."

"Anyway, one night I'm with her in the Bell, that quiet old pub over by your place and Big Guy is in the passageway keeping his eyes open and after a quiet chat and couple of drinks, I go up to the bogs and while I'm in there pointing Percy, this nutter comes in behind me. I recon the woman who was looking after her kids had told him where we were. Anyway he's there with a face like slab of granite and ready to rip me in half and the bottle of Fairy liquid is in my coat pocket which is hanging on the back of a chair in the pub. Luckily, he wants to give me a right good bollocking before beating the crap out of me and while he's poking me in the chest, Big Guy comes up behind him and whacks him over the head with a piece of hard wood that he's been carrying around and the big lummox goes down like a ton of bricks. Anyway, I rushed back into the pub, grab's my coat, tell this bird that I'll be in touch and me and Guy piss off leaving the nutter sprawled out on the lavatory floor."

"Did he have his machete with him?" Billy asked.

"No thank God, I suppose it was still in his car."

"So then what happened?"

"Not a lot. As far as I was concerned that was the end of that romance, I wasn't going to take any more chances on having that prat following me about every night. You never know what somebody like that is going to do and anyway it had cost me a fortune paying for Big Guy to ride around with me at night and after a month of listening to him rabbit on about the breading habits of birds of prey from Kestrels to Golden bloody eagles, I'd had more than enough I can tell you."

As expected, as Turners became a viable concern once more, and as the shareholders craved a better return on their investment, the company was eventually taken over by a larger concern and I, along with several other long serving personnel, like the old grey mare, were deemed surplus to requirements and we were subsequently made redundant.

"Thirty five years with the same company, it's about time you looked for another job. You don't want to become type cast do you?" Was Jenny's comforting comment when I brought home the expected news.

Realising that I was only five years away from the statutory retirement age I set out to find myself a comfortable mundane job to tide me over for the next few years as I could not face the prospect of sitting around all day and after applying for twenty five vacancies and getting nowhere, I began to realise that my age had become a formidable barrier in the jobs market. Although the jobs that I applied for were nothing more enterprising than van driving or store man, I didn't receive an answer from most of the companies. The job that I did eventually find and willingly took was as a receptionist security guard at a large city centre office block.

The duties were very simple and required no mental or physical taxation whatsoever and the situation suited me perfectly. There were four of us and we had to cover the reception desk from six in the morning till eight at night. To do this there were three alternating shifts spread over a three week period. As well as looking after the reception desk we occasionally had to patrol the building looking for doors that should be locked, fire hazards and any water leaks. I found the job was stress free and the alternating shifts allowed me to spend many hours at home during daylight hours. It was a luxury that I'd never experienced before and I took full advantage of it by painting water colour pictures, reading and taking the dog for a walk. From my semi-retirement point of view it was a perfect situation, but of course there were also such things as lawns to be mowed, carpets to be vacuumed, clothes to be ironed, occasional shopping trips, decorating and numerous other odd jobs. It is said that a woman's work is never done and I soon found that being at home during daylight hours, neither was mine.

When I did finally retire from full time employment, far from diminishing, my list of odd jobs actually increased, "Got to keep you active, can't allow you to vegetate," Jenny repeatedly said while smiling as she added more items to my ever growing list of things to do. The familiar cry of, "Can you peel some potatoes? That woollen jumper needs hand washing and those letters need posting and if you've got time...." became the norm. I eventually realised that retirement simply meant exchanging ones boss for another.

My new mundane occupation was a perfect tonic as I was now able to use what little brain power I had at home and could rest my mental faculties while at work. It was a complete reversal of my working life, for many years I'd had to make decisions on a daily basis and now someone else did it for me and while working on the reception desk of this large building, I became aware once more just how odd and unpredictable human nature can be. The first oddity that I had to adjust to was the general public's reaction to the black military style uniform that we guards were obliged to wear. Many saw the uniform and the jobs worth power that went with it, as a direct challenge to their liberty and civil rights. As soon as they saw the uniform, they automatically assumed that we were there to disrupt and interfere with their lives by enforcing stupid rules. Even when they fully agreed with the regulations, for some extraordinary reason, they assumed that the rules applied to others and not to themselves.

"Me show a pass? But I work here! Everyone knows me; I'm the deputy head of my department!" "Can't park there? But I'm attending an important meeting! I'll only be a couple of hours." "Fire drill! What a complete waste of time. We've never had a fire in all the time I've worked here." "Boxes blocking the exit door? But they'll be gone in a day or two."

As a way of taking a little steam out of the situation we referred to these people as "The Celebrities" and in a building that had twenty seven floors and housed seventeen separate companies, there were dozens of them. I began to realise that for most people, a security guards uniform is a sure sign of stupidity, after all, the reasoning goes, "Who would become a security guard other than someone who couldn't hold down a proper job?" And after meeting many of the dumb night guards, I fully understood this point of view. As the building was closed at night, the night guards were not picked for their intelligence or linguistic skills as they did not have to deal with the general public, they were only required to snooze on and off all night which they did admirably. Personally I wouldn't have let them look after my gold fish bowl, never mind a large office block, but insurance companies insist that guards should be on site no matter how incompetent they are.

I arrived at the building at six o' clock one morning to find that a tramp was sitting in the staff rest room drinking a cup of tea and reading a newspaper. The two security guards, who'd been on duty all night, had left the back door wide open and the intrepid gentleman of the road had gratefully taken full advantage of the situation without their knowledge.

On another occasion I arrived to find a wonderful majestic waterfall spewing out of the building and splashing merrily onto the service road below. A pipe had burst on the twenty first floor and the water was and had been, cascading into the road below for several hours. When I enquired as to which emergency telephone number the guards had wrung, I was informed that they hadn't contacted anyone.

"We thought we would wait until you came on duty in case we rang the wrong number."

Another guard who was due to attend a training course one morning in a building that was just a quarter of a mile away from where we were, asked the unbelievable question of, "How do I get back here from over there? I know where it is and how to get there when I get off the bus, but I've never walked back from there before."

Although many of these guards were of limited intelligence, it must also be pointed out that the Building Manager, who employed these men was woefully negligent in training these employees to any worthwhile standard. In fact many of these guards received little or no training whatsoever and were left entirely to their own devises. I met night guards who could hardly speak a word of English and had little knowledge or understanding of how the buildings lifts worked and more importantly, what to do if one broke down with people trapped inside. They had little knowledge of door alarms and how they were activated and many were lacking in even the most basic of fire drill procedures.

The Building Manager was a constant source of amusement and how he'd obtained the position was a mystery to all. He regularly left his lunch at home, went to shops to buy items and found that he had no money on him, issued contradictory orders on a regular basis, mislaid keys and constantly forgot the names of his employees. This caused great confusion as he would be talking about one person while meaning another. "Have you seen Joe?" "No." "There he is." "That's Bill." "That's who I mean."

"I was travelling from London to Birmingham by train and I fell asleep and I ended up in Manchester." he explained during a bizarre conversation that he had with his maintenance staff during a tea break, "I got on a train in Manchester, fell asleep again and found myself back at Euston. I lived near Sutton Coldfield at the time and it took me all day to get home."

For five consecutive years I witnessed this Manager, with the help of his maintenance crew, erect a Christmas tree in the reception area during the first week of December and because the tree was too tall for the room, at least two foot of it had to be lopped off. But instead of cutting two foot off the bottom of the tree, he ordered his men to lop two foot off the top. For five years in a row the big tree ended up looking stumpy and shapeless and not once did he ever think to measure the height of the room before purchasing the tree.

Although I understood the general public's attitude to the guard's uniform and the perceived dumbbell that it covered, it was hard at times to come to terms with. After spending many years in the commercial world, where I'd been dealing with staff problems, customer complaints and chasing various suppliers, it was quite a shock to be suddenly seen as a mindless automaton that lacked a brain. There was one man, who I regularly passed the time of day with, who lived just two hundred yards from my home and not once in the five years that I worked there did he recognised me, he only ever saw the uniform.

For many years in the commercial world, workers had confronted me with numerous problems and I'd been expected to solve them and now I was not only ignored, but considered too thick to even pass the time of day with, but this situation did at times have its compensations. When someone talks down to you in a superior manner and you're able to answer their arrogance with an articulate reply, the look of utter shock on their face is a picture worth seeing. But what was mind boggling about this reception work was the never-ending examples of stupidity that educated people were capable of. We four guards came face to face with unbelievable brainless behaviour, almost every day of the week.

One morning a well-dressed businessman, complete with leather brief case came bounding into the reception area, having just walked passed the buildings prominent name sign and asked with some considerable irritation, "Is this the Burlington Hotel?"

"No sir," I replied and added helpfully while pointing in the general direction of where the hotel was, "The Burlington is in New Street, which is about half a mile away in that direction."

"But I was told it was here!" The man said challengingly as he glanced at his wrist watch, "I have a very important meeting to attend! Are you quite sure that this is not The Burlington?"

"Yes sir, I am quite sure."

"Could you please check with someone else?" The man then said impatiently, "You may have made a mistake."

Delivery drivers regularly arrived at the building with vans full of heavy boxes of stationary that they had to deliver to one of the companies that resided in the tall building and had no trolley with them with which to transport the boxes from their van to their destination. They would complain because we had no trolley to give them and they had to carry the heavy boxes to the relevant offices. Many of them expected us to unload and deliver the boxes for them. For some reason these van drivers seemed to be under the impression that their duties ceased once they had found the right building.

There were numerous visitors who having signed in the visitor's register on the way into the building could not recognise their names on the way out. They would ask in an accusing tone to whoever was on the reception desk where their name was, believing no doubt that someone had stolen it. Now, when the receptionist had no idea what their name was, or, due to a shift change, what time they actually came into the building, this question became rather difficult to answer without becoming very sarcastic.

Surprisingly, many visitors on arriving at the building, had no idea of what time of the day it was, even though they had come for a specific meeting or a job interview, which they were required to attend at a specific time. Visitors came into the building, a building that housed seventeen companies and they had no idea which company they had come to visit. Sometimes we were asked to contact a particular person who worked in the building and was informed that they only knew the persons first name, had no idea which company that the person worked for and had no contact telephone number.

"But everyone knows Jim," one amazed numbskull stated when he was told that a little more information was required.

A woman, who I'd never seen before, came in to collect a package. She looked surprised when I asked her what her name was as there were several packages awaiting collection. She became visibly annoyed and seemed to be under the impression that I should have known who she was and which package she'd come to collect. After checking the five packages that I had in front of me, I informed her that there was no package with her name on it. She tutted, accused me of being an idiot and then suddenly remembered that she was picking the package up for a work colleague and that it had an entirely different name on it.

It was at times like this when we guards had to learn to bite our tongues and resist giving a sarcastic comment.

"Where do I find floor nine?" (Try looking between eight and ten.)

"Do I sign in here?" "Yes please" "And do I have to put _my_ name? (No, idiot will do.)

470

"Is it alright to leave my car outside?" (No, bring it in and I'll put it under the desk.)

"You haven't got a toilet have you?" (No sir, we use a bucket.)

There were times when questions were asked that defied any sarcastic comment.

"Why do I have to sign in? I signed in the last time I visited."

"How do I get my car out of the car park?"

"Excuse me, where did I park my car?"

"Which way did I come in? Was it this door or that one?"

"I'm looking for a woman that works here, but I can't remember her name. She smokes. Do you know her? She's a bit of a loud mouth."

"Take a lift to the twenty third floor? Oh no, I can't do that! I'm terrified of riding in lifts." This statement came from a young woman who'd arrived for an interview for a vacancy with a company that was on the twenty third floor of the building.

"There's some glass on the pavement out there. I think it must have fallen off a helicopter." A visitor reported.

"I didn't hear a helicopter go over sir."

"Well no you wouldn't, it's very cloudy out there today."

And to top them all, a middle aged woman claimed to have stepped into the number one lift at the top of the building and stepped out of number four lift when it reached the ground floor.

"How does it do that?" She asked rather puzzled, "Is it something to do with the funny shape of the building?"

These events were not particularly extraordinary in themselves, but in there frequency. Day after day similar incidents happened on a regular basis, so much so that I began to suspect that there were some sort of mystical lay lines near the entrance to the building and as people stepped through them it affected their brains and they lost whatever common sense they'd recently possessed.

Just as the use of cars and television changed the habits of earlier generations; the mobile cell phone is doing the same to this one. The first mobile phone that I ever used, which was at the end of the nineteen eighties, was as big as a house brick and heavy enough to knock six inch nails into a plank of wood. Now they're so small many women have trouble finding them among the clutter in their hand bags, but for all their technical sophistication, it seems that they only work if they are yelled at. A telephone call used to be a private conversation between two people, now everyone within half a mile is invited to listen to endless drivel and mundane chatter. "I'm just leaving the office." "It's raining here, is it raining there?" "Oh it is, yes well it's raining here as well."

One of the beneficial effects the mobile phone has is how much exercise they can encourage when used in the open. Looking out onto the wide piazza through the plate glass windows that surrounded much of the reception area, we witnessed numerous mobile phone users walk many miles each day and not move more than ten foot from where they started from. Some became quite intense and marched backwards and forwards when they conversed, while others looked as though, while spinning on one leg and waving an expressive hand, they were conducting a Beethoven symphony.

While travelling on the top deck of a crowded bus one day, Jenny overheard a young man who was sitting at the rear of the bus talking on his mobile to his girlfriend who was sitting at the front.

"What made it so bizarre," Jenny said, "was that they were both speaking so loudly, that everyone on the bus could hear every word that they said; the phones were completely superfluous."

"You'll never guess who I bumped into the other night." Mitch said brightly as we settled comfortably at a corner table in the White Swan, our meetings at the Sailors being a thing of the past now that the pub had become a tired and old establishment.

"Go on then, I'll buy it." I replied as I had no idea who Mitch had seen and had no intention of getting into a long drawn out guessing game.

"Do you remember the bouncer who used to be on the door of the Moat House, you know, the night club that was in Bradford Street at the back of the market?" Mitch then asked.

"Vaguely," I replied, "But blimey Mitch, that was years ago, back in the early sixties in the coffee bar days. I don't remember the names of half the people we knew then."

"Well you'd remember this one," He assured me, "He was a body builder named Dave, a friend of that other body builder Tony from the Rum Runner."

"Oh yes I remember him," I replied as the memory of the two muscular bouncers came back to me through the mists of time, "A real hard man. He had a sharp featured face which I thought was a bit deceptive."

"What are you on about, what was deceptive?"

"His face. It wasn't the right face for a bouncer."

"Do bouncers have to have special faces then?" Billy asked while smirking at me.

"Look, if I was drawing a tough guy for a cartoon, I'd make his face flat and pudgy with a big square jaw, a bit like Desperate Dan, but this blokes face wasn't like that was it, it was sharp featured."

"Trust you to think of a thing like that."

"Didn't he go to the same school as Gibbo?" I asked while trying to put meat onto the memory.

"Yeah, that's right; they were in the same class."

"And didn't he have a bust up with Zac and his mates one night?"

"Yeah, there was a whole bunch of them fighting in the street. I can't remember what it was all about, but Dave ended up with a knife wound across the side of his neck. You can still see the scar."

"So how is he? Where did you meet him?"

"Oh he looks fine. In better shape than me that's for sure." Mitch said as he continued with his story, "I saw him in the Bell, I couldn't place him at first and then all of a sudden it came to me, the bloody Moat House night club. That's where I know you from. Anyway I had a chat with him and bought him a drink. Oh and you'll never guess what he told me."

"What?"

"Do you remember that whenever Johnny Prescott the heavyweight boxer walked into the night club he was always surrounded by a bunch of hangers on who bathed in his glory and spent his money for him."

"Yeah, like wasps around a jam jar."

"Well do you remember, there used to be a gorgeous blond girl among them. A real sexy good looker."

"I remember you drooling and fantasizing over one."

"Well Dave recons that it was Mandy Rice-Davies."

"What, her that was involved in the Profumo scandal?"

"Yes, that's the one. He said she used to be in the club a lot before she moved down to London."

"I remember at the time of the court case that they said she came from Birmingham, but I never connected the two. Did Christine Keeler use the place as well?"

"I never thought to ask, but I wouldn't be surprised, they were always gorgeous birds that hung around Johnny."

"So that's another famous person that we've met in the past and never knew it." I pointed out.

"The trouble was," Mitch said philosophically, "we were having such a bloody good time, we had no time for worshipping so called celebrities."

"Did he have anything else to say?" I asked.

"Not much, but he did say that he'd heard that Cato had died in that fire in Spain."

"Did he know any more details, as I've always wondered if it was a scam. A neat way of disappearing."

"You've been reading to many crime novels." Billy suggested.

"No seriously," Mitch replied on my behalf as he also had doubts about the story, "from what I heard, Cato had a lot of enemies at the time. He owed a lot of money to some real big time villains. He was up to his neck in drug smuggling see, so it was the type of thing that he could have thought up and he was certainly capable of it. Zac probably knows the truth, but you'll have to wait until he's on his death bed before he'd tell you what really happened."

"So what were the details then?" Billy asked. "I'd just heard that he was drugged up and had died in a fire."

"Well," Mitch explained, "Cato was dealing in antiques and he was using the business as a cover to smuggle drugs across Europe and he had this old dockyard warehouse in Spain and one night the whole bloody lot burnt down and they found his badly burnt body inside the ruins. But then the rumours started, the police said that it was accidental death, his friends said that he had been murdered and his enemies said it wasn't him at all, but an old tramp who'd been sleeping in there. So you see, no bugger knows for sure whether he's dead or alive."

"Well didn't they check his dental records and all that sort of thing like they do on the tele?" Billy asked.

"I don't know. It was an out of the way place see. A small fishing village, so I don't suppose anyone there was really interested and anyone who was involved in the drug smuggling racket wasn't going to speak out was they?"

"What's Zac up to these days?" I asked as I hadn't seen him for many years, "Has he still got that Greek restaurant?"

"Oh yeah," Mitch replied, who was still a fountain of knowledge concerning the goings on in the towns underworld, "He's still got the restaurant and he's still running prostitutes and drugs on the side, but which makes the most money is anyone's guess, but I'd bet it isn't the restaurant and by the way, did you know that he once rode shotgun for that bastard Eddie Rogers?"

"No I didn't." I said a little shocked, "Why would he do that?"

"Money of course," Mitch replied, "Peter the Greek told me, it seems that not long after Rogers opened his night clubs, the Kray brothers asked him to meet them in London. They were thinking of taking over the Brummagem night club scene see and were thinking of making Rogers an offer he couldn't refuse."

"Have you been watching the Godfather again?" Billy asked, while smiling and shaking his head.

"No, its true Billy," Mitch replied, "anyway nothing came of it, it turns out they had more important things on their mind at the time."

"But where does Zac fit into this?" I asked.

"Well as you can imagine Rogers was shitting himself when the Krays sent for him and he paid Zac to go with him down to London as a bit of insurance." Mitch explained.

Unconvinced Billy said, "Look, we know Zac could handle himself, but even he wouldn't want to take on the Krays mob would he?"

"No you don't understand Billy," Mitch replied, "Zac didn't have to take them on, he just had to be there, you see if they set about him, Zac's London mates would seek revenge wouldn't they and the last thing the Krays wanted was to start a gang war. It was all about business see, not beatings."

"Well it all sounds a bit farfetched to me." Billy said, while smiling, "But saying that, I've got some farfetched news for you."

"Go on then, astound us."

"Last week I had a drink with Trapper and he told me that he'd recently bumped into Bronco and Bronco, wait for it, is now a property millionaire."

"Get away! And you believed him."

"Not at first I didn't. You know what I'm like, there's no one more sceptical than me, but when Trapper had explained, it all made sense."

"So what's the lucky bugger done then, won the lottery or robbed a bloody bank?" Mitch asked.

"Nothing as simple as that." Billy explained, "You know how Bronco has always had more than his fair share of energy. When we were all knackered, he was always ready to run a bloody marathon, well he's still got it; he's still as fit as a bleeding fiddle and running about like a dog with two pricks. Anyway, a few years ago, a mate of his, who was renovating an old property for the council had got behind with the work and he asked Bronco to come and help him out and when the big noise from the council turned up to inspect the work, he sees Bronco working like a man possessed and they got chatting. Anyway, Bronco hits it off with this bloke and he asks him if he could put in a tender for the next property that they want renovating and the bloke says yes. Well when the next property comes up, Bronco puts in a very low tender gets the job, rounds up all his mates in the building trade and he completes the job in record time and he's been doing it ever since and in the last ten years, with all the money he's made, he's invested it into a string of houses and an old folks home and he's now worth millions."

"Bloody hell! Good for him," Exclaimed Mitch with genuine delight, "I haven't seen the bugger for years and I tell you what, that news would shake a few of the old buggers from the Forty Club wouldn't it? James for one, he was always running Bronco down behind his back and calling him a Neanderthal. He'd be green with envy he would. I'll invite him for a game of golf and tell him the good news just before he's about to drive off the first tee."

"Anyway talking about Neanderthals and all that," Billy then said, quite seriously, "Do you two ever wonder about how the apes developed into men? You know, evolution and all that."

"Not very often," Mitch answered a little puzzled, "I can't say that it's ever been at the top of my list of priorities Billy, why?"

"Well it's just that I've come up with a theory. I've been thinking about it for some time." Billy then said and added, "See what you think."

"Go on then Professor Darwin," Mitch quipped, "Astound us with your evolutionary theory."

Ignoring Mitch's sarcastic comment, which he'd fully expected, Billy began to explain. "Well in all the books on the subject it's assumed that millions of years ago as the climate altered and part of the African landscape changed from dense jungle to open grass lands, a bunch of enterprising apes began to stand up and eat the berries off the bushes and eventually got used to running around on two legs and that's how the human evolution tree began."

"And what's wrong with that?" I asked, genuinely puzzled "How else could it have happened?"

"Well I don't think that it makes much sense," Billy answered while shaking his head, "If you look at a chimpanzee, it can run much faster when its running on all fours and using the knuckles of its hands to balance on than it can standing up on two legs, so why would it want to change? I mean, if a bloody great lion is chasing you, you're going to use the quickest way to out run it aint you? You're not going to hang about prating about on two bloody legs are you?"

"So what's your theory then?" I asked, fully intrigued.

"Water." Billy answered while smiling.

"What do you mean? Water."

"Well think about it this way," Billy then said as he now had our full attention, "If you were shipwrecked on a tropical island like Robinson Crusoe, how would you survive? Where would you find a sustainable supply of food? You could pick berries and fruit and trap the odd small animal or a bird now and again, but your best chance of finding food every day would be out of the sea. There you can catch fish and crabs and pick up mussels and clams and things like that can't you?"

"But there is no bloody sea in the middle of Africa Billy. Even I know that." Mitch pointed out.

Undeterred Billy said, "That was just an example you prat, it could have been the sea or it could have been a huge lake. Perhaps the Rift Valley in East Africa was a lake full of fish. Look there's something else to bear in mind."

"And what's that?"

"Defence. Think of it this way, one bunch of apes are out foraging on the grass lands picking berries and nuts off bushes and another bunch of apes are settled next to a lake or by the sea. Who's got the best chance of surviving? The ones in the open can band together and throw sticks and stones when they are attacked by lions or whatnot, but there's still no reason for them to walk about on two legs is there, whereas the ones that live by the lake, when they're attacked they can still throw stones, but they can also retreat into the water right up to their necks and by doing that, it would force them to stand on two legs. So the ones living by the lake end up having a safer environment in which to protect their young, plenty of food to eat and don't forget its food that's rich in omega 3 which is good for an expanding brain and they not only have a reason to stand on two legs, but also a reason to shed body hair and it must have been easier to eat raw fish than raw mammoth."

"Be easier to put on a dinner plate as well I should think." Added Mitch while smiling at his own joke, "And you recon all this happened before they invented fire?"

"Oh long before that, these changes didn't happen overnight you know, it took thousands of years for anything to happen."

For a few seconds Mitch and I sat absolutely dumbfounded as we had never expected Billy to come up with such a well worked out augment. Whether he was right or not we had no idea, but his analysis certainly made us think.

Eventually Mitch asked," When did you become interested in all this evolution stuff, you've never mentioned it before."

"Oh, it was that bloody Jack Rushton that got me started on it. Do you remember all the things he used to talk about and explain to us in the tea breaks? Well once, he got going on about why there were sea shells half way up a mountain and evolution and the dinosaurs and I just got fascinated by it and now whenever I see something about it on the tele or in a book I just get sucked in."

"So what are you going to do with this theory of yours Billy," I asked, "Send it off to some expert in palaeontology at the British Museum?"

"Don't be silly," Billy replied while shaking his head, "They wouldn't take any notice of me would they? I'm just a lorry driver, who the hell is going to listen to me? Anyway drink up it's my round."

About eight months after that meeting in the White Swan, Bronco got in touch with Mitch who in turn got in touch with me and Billy. Bronco had news that Webber, the ace detective, who'd retired from the force and gone to live in Bournemouth, was back in Brum and had sort Bronco out and had been pumping him for information about the missing diamond again. It seemed that although retired, instead of pottering about in the garden, or writing his exciting memoirs, the daft sod was still determined to find the bloody diamond and now that he'd got nothing better to do, he intended to call on us once more and drive us all batty with his repetitious questions. I suppose he believed that if he found the bloody thing, it would boost his retirement fund considerably and he could bugger off to Spain.

After the tip off, I thought long and hard about my glass marble theory and whether I should disclose it to the others or not? Eventually I decided to say nothing, as I still thought that it might upset them knowing that they'd been so close to a fortune.

George Cadbury was a Quaker, a philanthropist and a successful manufacturer of chocolate. As his business became successful it outgrew its premises and he decided to build a new factory for the manufacture of his chocolate and surround it with a model village and being a shrewd business man, he decided to call the whole area

Bournville. He reasoned that as his main rival was French chocolate, the name Bournville would give his products a certain continental air.

As well as a factory that created the wealth, Bournville would have churches, educational facilities for all ages, arms house for the elderly, recreational areas, shops, small businesses and a mixture of dwellings suitable for a whole range of incomes. What it would not have was any public houses that sold the demon drink and to this day there are still no public houses in Bournville, but members and visitors can drink alcohol at the Cadbury Club any day of the week. What George Cadbury would make of this situation can only be guessed at.

Jenny and I attended many functions at the Cadbury club, but the one that stood out in my mind, but not in hers, was the night we went to see a hypnotist. With a group of friends, we were in the large concert room, consuming the demon drink, when the hypnotist called for volunteers and he invited Jenny to join him on the stage. After some simple vetting, he eventually settled on his chosen victims and the show got under way. He put each one into a hypnotic trance and gave them a key word or sound. He then got them to say daft things and act out silly actions.

Jenny's hypnotic trigger was a piece of taped music that was played on a portable radio/cassette player. Every time she heard this particular piece music, she would go under the hypnotic spell and do whatever he asked, no matter how stupid it was. The show was extremely funny and entertaining and everyone enjoyed it, all that is except the hypnotised victims, they were completely oblivious to what they had done while on stage. Jenny returned to our table and swore that she could not remember a single thing that she'd done and had to be told what silly antics she'd got up to.

It was the end of the evening, the bar was closed and many were finishing off their drinks, or on the way out and saying their fond farewells and, almost unnoticed, the hypnotist's assistant was busy clearing the stage of the paraphernalia that had been used in the show. As he picked up the radio/cassette player, he switched it on and off just to check that the tape was in place. For a few seconds the music played and Jenny was once more put into a hypnotic trance. I jumped up and looked around in a blind panic, the concert room was emptying fast and the hypnotist was nowhere to be seen.

The thought flashed through my mind that if I couldn't find him, Jenny would be a zombie for the rest of the weekend and I wasn't quite sure whether that would be a good thing or not. But not wishing to take the chance, I dashed over to the dressing room and found the hypnotist packing away his gear.

"Excuse me!" I said, in a voice full of menace, "Your assistant has just played the music on that tape out there and my wife as just gone back into a hypnotic trance again."

"Oh I am sorry," the hypnotist replied all apologetic, "But I assure you, it will be alright, it will wear of straight away. You will find that she will already be back to normal, it doesn't last."

"But what happens if we switch the radio on in the morning and the same music starts to play?" I asked a little worried.

"Nothing," he assured me, "It will wear off long before that." but I was far from convinced.

When I got back to the table, Jenny asked, "Where have you been, were ready to go" and to this day she doesn't believe that she went under the hypnotic spell for a second time and as for enjoying the night, she only remembers going to the show and coming home again.

"I might just as well have gone on my own and saved the cost of her ticket." I thought, but I had the good sense not to say it.

Throughout our married life, Jenny and I lived happily together and we had very few disagreements, but there have been times when I wished that I could remember what that bloody tune was so that I could find out if it still worked.

"It's not the kind of thing you expect in middle of the afternoon is it?" Billy said as he explained his latest experience, "But as soon as I turned the corner, I knew something was up. I'd finished work early and Linda was at her sister's see, her sister's still getting over her divorce, so the Missis goes over once a week to cheer her up. Anyway as I say, I'm driving home without a care in the world and thinking I can get the grass cut before the weekend and I see this young yob in a hoodie standing on the pavement outside my house and looking furtive. He's got that twitchy look about him, glancing up and down the street and pacing backwards and forward like he's got a bus ticket stuck up his arse. So I drive past and park round the corner and walk back quickly and I keep looking at my watch as I approached the skinny squirt so he thinks I'm in a hurry to catch a bus or something. I can see that he's worried to death and he keeps looking at my house, so I've got the picture now, he's the lookout and his mate is inside filling his bleeding pockets with my stuff, so when I get level with him, I whack him in the guts with my fist and as he doubles up I cop him in the face and leave him coughing a sputtering while I stride up to my front door which is slightly open. Now I think, shall I burst in or wait for the creep to come out, anyway I hear him coming towards the front door see, so I crouch down and just as I see his fingers grab the side of the door to pull it open, I kicked the door with all my might, the door smashed into him and he went crashing up the hallway. He was flat on his back and screaming like a tart and I was on him like lightning and punching and stamping on him until I was exhausted. I tell you straight, if I hadn't run out of steam, I'd have killed the slimy bastard."

"So what did you do with him?"

"Well, when I'd got my breath back, I dragged him into the street and left him lying in the gutter, I phoned for an ambulance and told them that there'd been a hit a run accident and they come and took him away."

"What happened to the other bloke, the lookout?"

"Fuck knows, he must have run off and I never did get round to cutting my grass."

After many years of searching, Mitch finally found his soul mate. She was attractive and had a pleasant disposition and had been a nurse for many years. Her marriage had disintegrated and ended in divorce and now that her children had grown up and flown the nest, she was free to do whatever she pleased, but had no real idea what that might be.

They met by chance at the Queen Elizabeth Hospital. Mitch had just been for another series of intensive tests for his puzzling debilitating illness and she'd been visiting a friend and while sorting out their small change at the ticket machine they got into conversation and Mitch feeling the need for company after what had been a stressful morning, offered to buy her lunch at the White Swan and she thinking, "Well why not, I'm only going home to an empty house" accepted his invitation.

Over lunch they got on like a house on fire as she found him witty, charming and entertaining and to his delight he found that she was not only completely open and friendly, but showed no sign of pretence. He realised that she was an intelligent well-read warm homely woman and the fact that he had his own business and drove around in a big car did not seem to impress her in the slightest and at the end of their lunch, which had flown by, she not only agreed to meet him again, but offered to bake him a fruit cake, it was something that no woman had ever offered before and which touched him deeply.

"It's not the kind of thing that you expect is it?" He said as he tried to put his feelings into words, "it knocked me bandy. In most of the relationships I've had, they've spent at least six months pretending to be someone they're not and she was an open book. She had no thought of trying to impress anyone, never mind me"

Mitch's mystery illness, which had developed so slowly that it was many months before he'd sort medical advice, had the effect of slowing him down considerably. As it took hold he was forced to cut down drastically on his alcohol intake and as he found running his transport business was causing him considerable stress, he decided to sell up. The illness, which after many months and extensive tests was eventually diagnosed as a small brain tumour that could only be controlled by a daily dose of medication, gave him no option but to change his wild lifestyle and he slowed down to walking pace.

He continued to see his new found guardian angel on a regular basis and after selling his business he eventually asked her to marry him and she willingly accepted. They found an isolated bungalow near Ross-on-Wye and there they surrounded themselves with three stray dogs, a pen full of chickens, several ducks, fruit trees and a vegetable plot and settled down to a quiet and contented life. All of which was a complete reversal of Mitch's former life and many of his friends found it hard to believe that he could have changed so much in such a short span of time. Because of the illness, he lost much of his former zip and tired quickly and without substantial periods of rest, he became very irritable or as Billy put it, "A right pain in the arse."

Mitch had always had a strong liking for classical music, poetry and Mother Nature. At times he'd been quite content to sit and strum a guitar or settle down with a book of poetry and he'd always enjoyed a countryside hike. And now, just by chance, after many years of philandering, he'd found a woman that was not only willing to pander to his domestic needs and put up with his mood swings, but was also happy to share in his uplifting pursuits. And bar from his regular hospital appointments and the fact that his Jack Russell dog was apt to worry the nearby farmer's sheep; he was able to live a stress free life in an environment that was a million miles from the slums of Maxstoke Street.

Now that we lived a considerable distance from each other, we only met when there was a special reason to do so, such as a former friend's funeral. Charlie's being one of them.

Charlie was shot dead one night while in Handsworth when a group of drug dealers decided to settle a turf war by shooting each other. It was said that Charlie's death was a tragic accident and that he'd been in the wrong place at the wrong time, but knowing Charlie as well as we did, we suspected that a more likely explanation was that he was probably up to his neck in a drugs deal that had gone horribly wrong. But having survived a devastating car crash on the M 6, being thrown from a horse while on holiday in Colorado, gored by a small bull at a novice bull fighting ranch in Spain and stabbed by an irate cuckolded husband, Charlie's nine lives were probably well and truly up by the time the fateful bullet hit him anyway.

At the funeral, Billy forgave Charlie for hiring his holiday caravan for a paltry sum and then re-renting it to an acquaintance for a larger sum. No one would have known if the acquaintance hadn't got drunk and accidently set fire to the bed and the site manager had been forced to intervene with his fire extinguisher.

Annette was an extraordinary person and her funeral was also extraordinary. Among the mourners there were high ranking policemen who stood alongside hard bitten criminals, market traders, wealthy businessmen, factory workers, housewives, office workers, shopkeepers and a whole mixture of nationalities, including Chinese, Asians, West Indians and even a Peruvian, the first that I'd ever knowingly met

Over the years, Annette had many partners and had lived with several, but she'd never married any of them, but the two that she'd spent most time with were there and they both considered her to be the best friend that they'd ever had. The church was packed to the gunwales for the service and a large crowd of mourners who could not get in stood outside on the pavement and when the hearse began its slow journey up to the cemetery, there were thirty seven cars in its wake. Many a celebrity would have had a problem attracting so many people.

Back in the Sailors, after the funeral, a young Asian asked me if I was a relative of Annette's. When I informed him that I was, he shook my hand warmly and said that he was extremely proud to have known her.

"When I first came to Brum looking for work," he explained, "I knew no one and I came into this pub purely by chance and Annette, saw straight away that I was a stranger. I told her I was looking for a job and she said, "I'll see what I can do mate." Anyway three days later she said, "Oi! Sabu. Come over here mate, I've got you an interview at the factory down the road," I went to the interview and now I'm working in the office there. The gaffer of the place has his lunch in here and she'd told him about me. She was like that with everyone. She'd lend money to anyone who asked, even though there was little chance of getting it back, she'd help anyone who was in trouble.

She spent her final days in a hospice in Selly Park and there she treated her continual flow of visitors to her own brand of gallows humour.

"Oh, look what the bloody cat's brought in. I suppose you've come to see me kick the bucket. Well your to bloody early mate, I aint bleeding ready to go yet so you'll have to come back another day."

Whenever I visited her, either at the hospital or in the hospice, there was always someone already there beside her bed and when I

485

was leaving there was always someone arriving. I was there one day when in walked Trapper and Annette's response to his visit was typical.

"Oh God blimey, now look who they've let in. I tell you Jaco, they let any bugger into this place, the pubs must be shut or else he's run out of money. I suppose you've come to eat my bleeding grapes. Well your too late mate, Mitch was in this morning and he's bloodywell eaten the lot."

"Well I aint come to eat your bleeding grapes see, smart arse, I've brought my own, so you can watch me eat these buggers."

"I can remember when it was my tits you was after not my bleeding grapes. Anyway, have you brought me any "weed" to smoke?"

"No I aint. Anyway, you can't smoke that stuff in here."

"Who can't, young Billy's been bringing me some in for weeks. He's more thoughtful than you, you tight arsed bleeder."

"What do the nurses say about you smoking bloody "weed" in their scented garden?"

"Bugger them; they can bloodywell buy their own."

The truth was, she would offer to share her "weed" with nurses and doctors alike and when she was told by one doctor that she should not be smoking it, she just said, "Now look Doc, I know it's your job, but you're not daft enough to tell me that it could kill me are you? Because for your information, I'm already knocking on the Devils door."

Annette had been a dunce at school, common as muck and as blunt as a builder's brick and had sort to be nothing more enterprising in life than being a barmaid and yet during her short existence she'd managed to touch the heart of a whole community. The secret of her phenomenal popularity was that she was naturally gregarious and made friends in an instant and she treated everyone, tinker, tailor, soldier, sailor, Prince or pauper, in exactly the same manner. To put it perspective, I'd met an awful lot of people in my life and yet I know that if it was me that had died instead of Annette, not a fifth of the number of people who turned up for her funeral would have turned up for mine.

486

Many years before her death, Nan, having become a widow, had gone to live with Annette in a block of flats and just a few weeks before one Christmas, they arrived home together to find a Christmas hamper sitting on their doorstep. Now although Annette knew for certain that the hamper was not hers, she was never one to look a gift horse in the mouth and she swiftly bundled Nan and the heavy hamper into the flat and slammed the door shut behind her.

"Anyway, I put it on the kitchen table," she said when telling me the tale, "Looked at the label and although it had our flat number, it didn't have our name on it. So I say's to Nan, do you know anyone around here named Harman? And after she's gone through a whole list of neighbour's names, some of whom had kicked the bloody bucket years ago, she says no. So I opens the hamper and bloody hell, it's full of booze. Whiskey, gin, vodka and cans of beer. "Oh!" Nan says, all worried, "we'd better find out who it belongs to, they'll have ordered that for Christmas." So I say's, alright, let's put it away until we find out who it belongs to. So in the pub that night I ask if anyone knows somebody named Harmen and Nan does the same in the Emily Arms, but nobody does. So that night when I got in from work I says to Nan, do you fancy a little nightcap and she says, "Ar, I bloodywell do", so we got the hamper out and fixed ourselves a little drink. Anyway this went on for a couple of weeks and then bugger me, you won't believe this, but another bloody hamper turned up on the door step with the same label on it, so we had that one away as well. Then after Christmas Nan's sitting in the Emily Arms one night with her mates and she hears this woman going on about how she'd ordered a hamper of booze from the catalogue and it had never turned up and how they wanted to charge her for it and then she said the cheeky buggers said they'd sent two, but she recons the delivery driver has had them for himself. Well when I heard this from Nan, I went and found this woman and I took her along to the citizen's advice bureau in town and they sorted it out for her and she didn't have to pay in the end."

"And did you tell her that you and Nan had been drinking her booze?"

"Did I buggery, we were already halfway through the second hamper by then. I wornt going to tell her then was I? Besides, her trip to the citizen's advice bureau had cheered her up no end. It was the most exciting thing that had happened to the poor old cow since her lodger had buggered off and took her ormolu clock with him."

As old age crept up on us and we began to call things thingy-mi-jigs and do-dar-days, along came a whole catalogue of ailments. Joints stiffened up and putting on a pair of socks became more of an Olympic challenge than a simple daily task. The tele had to be turned up a notch as our hearing became impaired, a magnifying glass was required for reading small print and at odd times, our concentration seems to slip a gear or two.

One Saturday night Gibbo put his clocks forward one hour and two days later he found that he'd been a week to early and had to turn them all back again. After arriving back from a holiday in Italy, Billy accidentally fell onto the airports luggage carousel while trying to retrieve his heavy suitcase and was whisked away lying on his back and gesticulating wildly while his wife Linda, stood helplessly doubled up with laughter. As for Mitch, he had a small problem whilst travelling on a bus.

"I was visiting my sister in Smethwick for a few days." He explained, "Anyway I decided to hop on the bus that runs past her place and go up to West Brom. I got on the bus with all the others and I could see at a glance that it was standing room only so I decided to go upstairs. I grabbed the pole, stepped onto the first step and found that I was standing on a luggage rack. There were no stairs; the bloody bus was a single decker."

Over in Leicester, Danny Page's masochistic life time hobby of sitting on river banks and fishing in all weathers paid off at last. During a very cold winter spell, he took his small dog up the garden for its evening run out and he was struck down with a stroke. He collapsed onto the frozen ground and found that he could not move properly. He was unable to stand or even crawl and throughout the night, he drifted in and out of consciousness. He was found twenty three hours later by his younger sister Wendy.

"The dog was still with him and barking like mad which is what made me look for him up the garden," She said when explaining what had happened, "and when I found him, he was covered in a layer of snow and literally frozen to the ground. I rang 999 on my mobile, ran inside the house, grabbed some blankets and covered him as quickly as possible and the paramedics had to put a tent around him and thaw him out slowly before they could move him and take him off to hospital."

A week later, Jenny and I visited him in the Leicester Infirmary and found him sitting up in bed and but for a little paralysis in one hand, slow speech and an unreliable memory, he was as bright and affable as ever. A month later he was making plans for what he was going to plant in his garden and pencilling in a number of fishing trips and all done as though nothing extraordinary had happened to him. He was seventy five years old and saw no reason why he should be expected to sit around in an armchair all day. "There's enough fat lazy buggers in this world without me joining them." He declared.

After arriving at a hired holiday caravan on the South Coast I discovered that I'd left one of our suitcases at home. Unfortunately, it was the one that was full of Jenny's clothes. I offered to lend her some of mine, but my kind offer was rejected out of hand and I spent most of the holiday traipsing around numerous shops buying her new clothes and being reminded of what a bloody idiot I was.

I built a bonfire in the back garden and not only managed to burn down my own garden shed, but also my neighbours along with his garden fence and his prized rose bushes. Jenny's comment on these and other minor incidents was quite philosophical, "Other men grow old gracefully, you however seem determined to go out with a bang."

But my mates and I were all comforted in knowing that we were not the only idiots on the planet. A man living in Mobile, Alabama became convinced that the next hurricane to pass his way would bring down the large tree that was growing in his back yard. He took a chain saw to the mighty menace and felled it. Unfortunately, it fell onto his house.

As the end of nineties approached, the whole world, with the help of the sensation seeking media, became obsessed with the forthcoming Millennium night. New Year's Eve would be a night that everyone would remember and in years to come people would ask, "Where were you on Millennium night?" and with this in mind, many went a little bonkers. Some booked into private parties while others took expensive holidays at exotic locations as they felt the need to be somewhere special when the clock struck twelve. We were encouraged stockpile food, beer and crates of expensive sparkling champagne and to put a little worry into everyone's minds, the ever caring media informed us, that because so much champagne was being ordered there would be a worldwide shortage, which caused panic buying. The outcome was that for several years after, many were still drinking Millennium night champagne.

We were then informed by technical experts, who knew all about electronics, computer pixels, mega bites and voodoo magic, that on the stroke of midnight, all the computers in the world would go bananas and there would be complete chaos. And so, for the developed world, Millennium night, far from being the beginning of a bright new future, would be a technical form of Armageddon. Nothing much came of these scare stories, but quite a lot of people made a packet out of selling champagne at extortionate prices and reprogramming millions of computers that didn't need any attention.

After a short discussion, lasting all of two minutes, Jenny and I and a few of our friends decided not to fly off to the Bahamas for the Millennium celebrations, but to go to a simple barn dance at a church hall on the Bournville village green. We took along cans of beer, bottles of wine, party hats and a merry party mood.

The church hall, which was used throughout the year as a venue for Girl Guide meetings, children's dance classes and jumble sales, had been decked out with bunting and coloured fairy lights. The tables were covered with bright gingham table cloths and on each table was a lighted candle stuck in the neck of a wine bottle which gave the room the require subdued lighting and with a chequered shirted fiddle band at the ready, the scene was set for a warm friendly New Year's Eve party.

As the fiddle band played the lively barn dance music, we danced about, kicking our legs and does-e-doed as best we could, but as most of us knew very little about the complexities of barn dancing our efforts were often clumsy and somewhat eccentric. But no one seemed to mind and a good time was had by all. I saw quite clearly what others were doing and it all looked so simple, but my limbs seemed to react completely differently to theirs and at times, I was not only dancing the wrong steps, but because of the constant crossing over, with the wrong group of people.

We all had a great night dancing, singing, drinking, eating and laughing and a few minutes before midnight we assembled, along with other partygoers from nearby venues, on the Bournville Village Green to hear the Millennium played in on the forty-eight bell Carillon. As we stood chatting in friendly groups on the gently sloping pathways that run across the Green and around the Rest House, the rows of coloured lights that had been strung up were swinging in the winter breeze above our heads and the fiddler from the band began playing a lively tune.

"It's just like standing on the Titanic." Val pointed out, which was an accurate description of our lopsided stance under the swinging lights with the fiddle music playing in the background and brought laughter from all around. Across the road, the fingers on the large brass clock reached midnight and from miles around, distant bells began to chime and fireworks rent the dark sky and sent cascades of pretty bright particles raining down. We all kissed, hugged and shook hands with each other and wished each other a happy New Year, danced about and sang Auld Lang Syne, but no Carillon bells had chimed as expected. Five minutes past, but not a ding nor a single dong had been heard emanating from the Carillon bells.

Eventually, fed up with waiting around in the cold night air, people began singing and entertaining themselves while still waiting for the promised concert to begin. At fifteen minutes past midnight, we decided to go back inside the church hall to finish off our drinks. Singing and dancing as we went, we attempted to enter the hall and found our path blocked by a group of sympathetic people who were surrounding a woman who was clearly in great distress.

"He's mislaid the keys," the wife of the carillon keyboard player was saying, "And he was so looking forward to tonight, he's been practising for months."

It transpired that the Carillon player had somehow mislaid the keys to the building and at the vital moment he'd been unable to reach the keyboard and play the proposed midnight concert. Val had been right after all, it was indeed a tragic Titanic moment. On hearing this explanation, an inebriated wit was heard to call out, "Never mind love,

I'm sure they'll let him play at the next one. After all, it's only a thousand years away. It'll soon roll round."

What the next thousand years will bring is anyone's guess, but what is certain is that the people of the future will be just as pompous, unpredictable and as daft as we were. As Polly Garter, a warm and cuddlesome woman who has been loved by many a man in the long grass, says in Dylan Thomas's play for voices, "Under Milk Wood."

"Oh, isn't life a terrible thing, thank God."

A short while after I'd been discharged from the hospital and been declared fit enough to fall off a ladder and bounce once more, Mitch, Billy, Bronco and I met up for a little get to getter. There was no real reason for a celebration other than to congratulate each other on having all lived longer than any of us had expected and of course we always enjoyed reminiscing about the good old days, when beer was a penny a pint and the sun shone every day, but during our diverse conversation the mystery of the missing diamond inevitably raised its ugly head once more and I finally disclosed my glass marble theory. Well, I thought, at our age there's always the chance that we might never see each other again, so let's get it out into the open and bugger the consequences.

After I'd finished my detailed explanation, Mitch shook his head in disbelief and asked, "And just how long have you been holding that nugget of wisdom in your head?"

"About twenty years or more I suppose, why?" I replied.

"Because you prat, I had the very same idea."

"So why didn't you say something?"

"Why didn't you?"

"Because I didn't want to upset Billy, you know how sensitive he is."

"Me sensitive?" Billy said, surprised at the accusation, "Why would it upset me?"

"Well if it's true and the diamond is in that bloody great jar of marbles," Mitch explained, "it means that when we were in that house, you had your grubby hands on it and if you'd taken it home, you could have lived the rest of your life in luxury, instead of scrounging off me all the time."

"You cheeky bleeder," Billy said while chuckling, "When have I ever scrounged off you, you tight fisted sod? Look you pair of prats, I've had a bostin life, the only thing that would have upset me is if I'd found out that one of you two crafty cows had found it and not told me."

"Well I wish someone had told me about it," Bronco said, with genuine feeling, "I'd have found the bloody thing you can be sure of that, I'd have turned every antique shop in the country upside down."

"You greedy bastard," Billy said while smiling at him, "Aint you rich enough, you can't even spend what you've got, why do you want more?"

"I wasn't always rich was I? I've been through some bloody rough times Billy." Bronco pointed out, "I can remember when I couldn't pay the bleeding rent and had to steal milk off next doors step. Besides, I'd love to wave that diamond in front of Webber's face wouldn't you?"

"And talking of Webber," I said, "Do we tell him of our glass marble theory or let him wonder about in the dark forever."

"Bugger him," Mitch stated defiantly, "If he was any good as a detective, he'd have figured it out years ago, I bet that pompous Belgium prat Porirot, would have solved the case without any bother."

"I agree," said Billy nodding, "Besides, if you think about it, we're doing him a favour, if he found the diamond now, he'd have nothing left to live for would he?"

"Let's drink to that then," Mitch said while raising his glass," May ace detective Webber search for ever and die happy but frustrated, not knowing that he was so near and yet so far."

So that's it then, as you can see, none of us old buggers are really interested in looking for the missing diamond so the field is wide open for any of you to try your luck if you fancy a lifelong quest, but I warn you, it could be a hard slog and it could be all for nothing, as it's possible that its already been found and that there is a child out there playing with it right now who is completely oblivious to what the pretty glittering item is or of its enormous life changing value.

The End.

Lightning Source UK Ltd.
Milton Keynes UK
UKHW020626310322
400889UK00008B/271

9 781326 637958